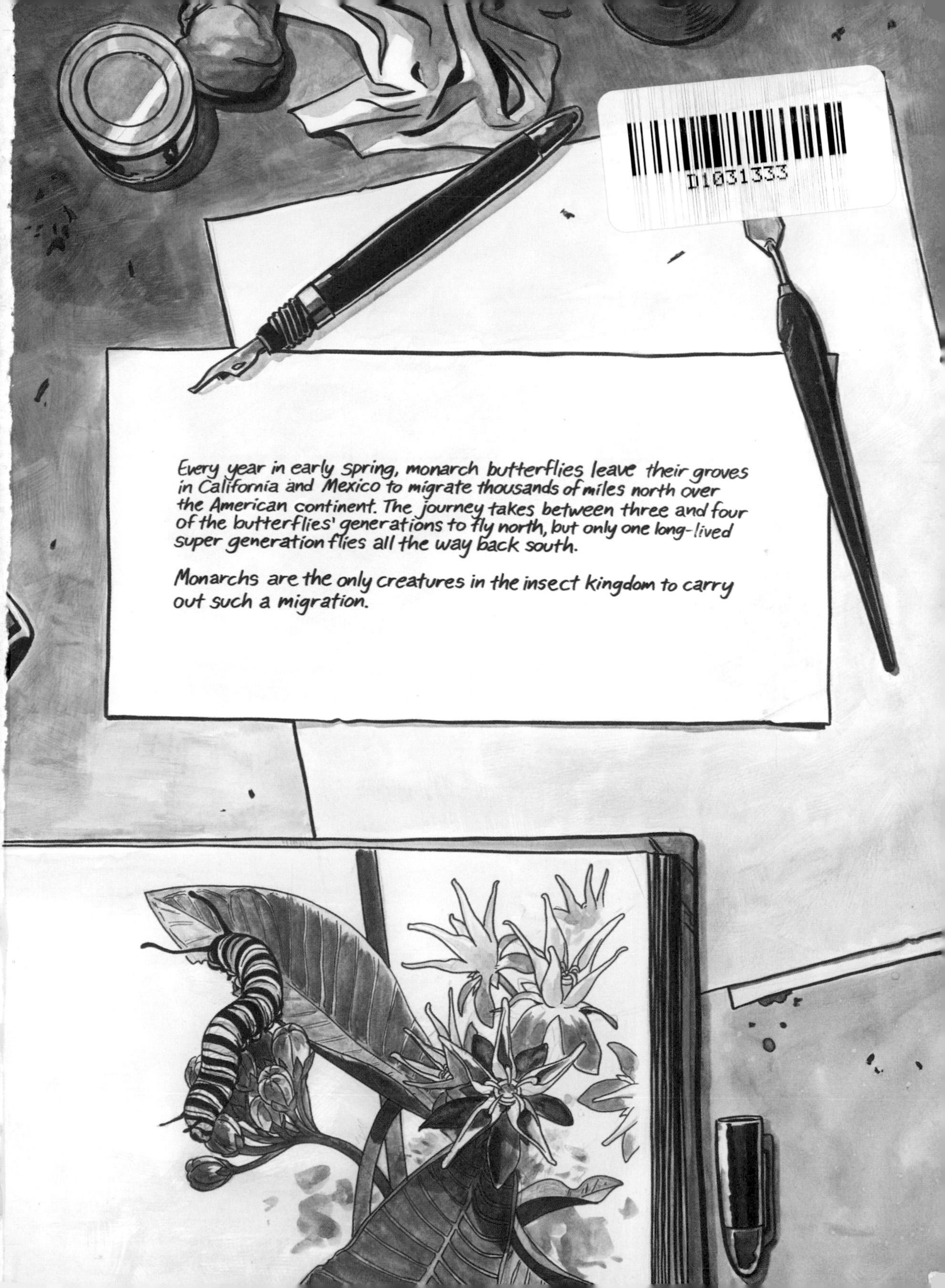
Every year in early spring, monarch butterflies leave their groves in California and Mexico to migrate thousands of miles north over the American continent. The journey takes between three and four of the butterflies' generations to fly north, but only one long-lived super generation flies all the way back south.
Monarchs are the only creatures in the insect kingdom to carry out such a migration.

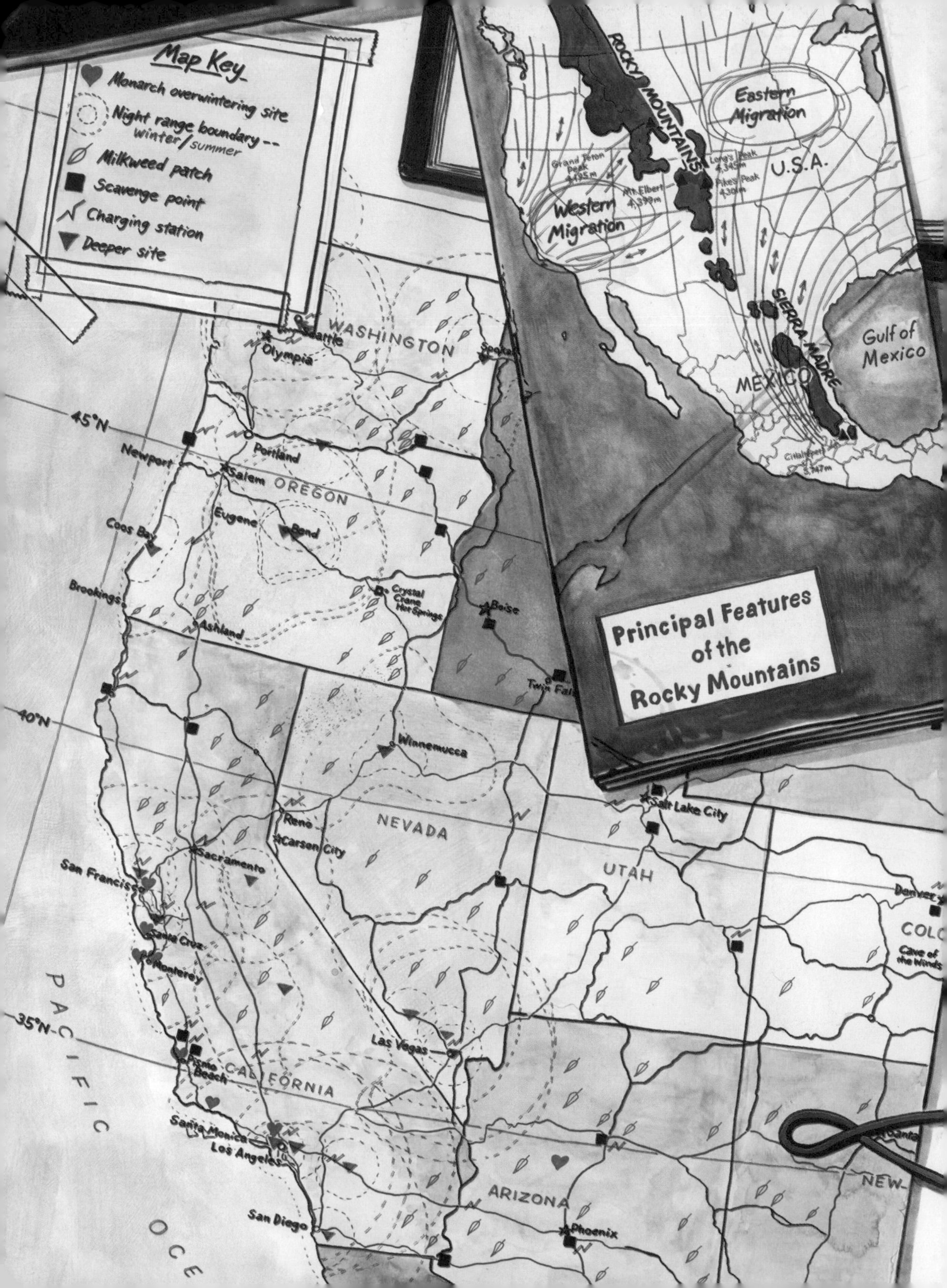
Map Key
Monarch overwintering site
Night range boundary -- winter/summer
Milkweed patch
Scavenge point
Charging station
Deeper site
ROCKY MOUNTAINS
Eastern Migration
Western Migration
U.S.A.
Grand Teton Peak 4,195m
Long's Peak 4,345m
Pike's Peak 4,301m
Mt. Elbert 4,399m
SIERRA MADRE
MEXICO
Gulf of Mexico
Principal Features of the Rocky Mountains
WASHINGTON
Seattle
Olympia
Spokane
45°N
Newport
Portland
Salem
OREGON
Eugene
Bend
Coos Bay
Brookings
Crystal Crane Hot Springs
Boise
Ashland
Twin Falls
40°N
Winnemucca
Salt Lake City
Reno
NEVADA
Carson City
Sacramento
San Francisco
UTAH
Santa Cruz
Monterey
Cave of the Winds
PACIFIC OCE
35°N
Las Vegas
Pismo Beach
CALIFORNIA
Santa Monica
Los Angeles
ARIZONA
San Diego
Phoenix
NEW

WITHDRAWN

Jonathan Case
Little Monarchs

Margaret Ferguson Books
Holiday House
New York

For Dorothy, Otis, and Miriam

Margaret Ferguson Books

Text and illustrations copyright © 2022 by Jonathan Case

All Rights Reserved

HOLIDAY HOUSE is registered in the U.S. Patent and Trademark Office.

Printed and bound in December 2021 at Toppan Leefung, DongGuan, China.

The art and lettering was created with pencil, pen, brush, ink, and watercolor on mixed media paper.

www.holidayhouse.com

First Edition

1 3 5 7 9 10 8 6 4 2

Library of Congress Cataloging-in Publication Data

Names: Case, Jonathan, author, illustrator.

Title: Little monarchs / Jonathan Case.

Description: First edition. | New York : Margaret Ferguson Books/Holiday House, [2022] | Audience: Ages 10 to 12.
Audience: Grades 4–6. | Summary: In the twenty-second century, a sun shift has made it impossible for mammals to
survive in the daylight, and ten-year-old Elvie and her caretaker, Flora, are studying the migration route of monarch
butterflies along what used to be the western coast of the United States, hoping that something in the butterfly's wing
scales can be used to protect people from the sun and save humanity from extinction.

Identifiers: LCCN 2021010212 | ISBN 9780823442607 (hardcover)

Subjects: LCSH: Monarch butterfly—Comic books, strips, etc. | Monarch butterfly—Juvenile fiction.
Monarch butterfly—Migration—Comic books, strips, etc. | Monarch butterfly—Migration—Juvenile fiction.
Global environmental change—Comic books, strips, etc. | Global environmental change—Juvenile fiction.
Environmental disasters—Comic books, strips, etc. | Environmental disasters—Juvenile fiction. | Graphic novels.
Pacific Coast (America)—Comic books, strips, etc. | Pacific Coast (America)—Juvenile fiction. | CYAC: Graphic novels.
Monarch butterfly—Migration—Fiction. | Butterflies—Fiction. | Environmental disasters—Fiction. | Science fiction.
Pacific Coast (America)—Fiction. | LCGFT: Graphic novels. | Dystopian fiction.

Classification: LCC PZ7.7.C373 Li 2022 | DDC 741.5/973—dc23

LC record available at https://lccn.loc.gov/2021010212

ISBN: 978-0-8234-4260-7 (hardcover)

ISBN: 978-0-8234-5139-5 (paperback)

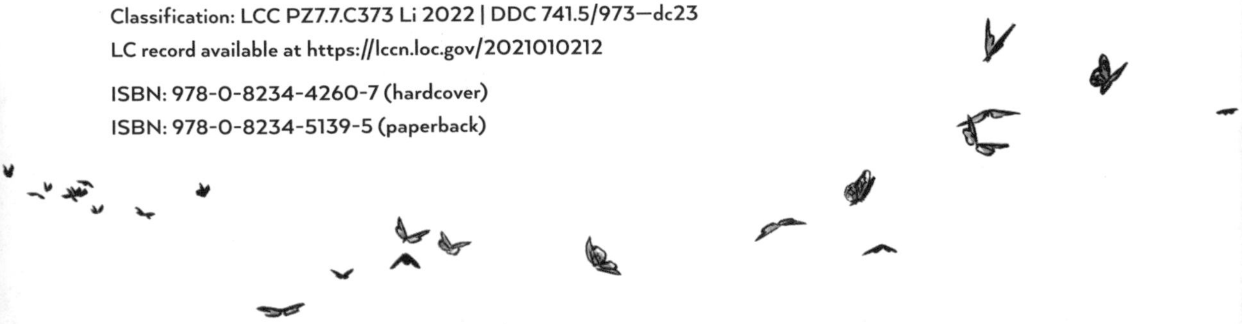

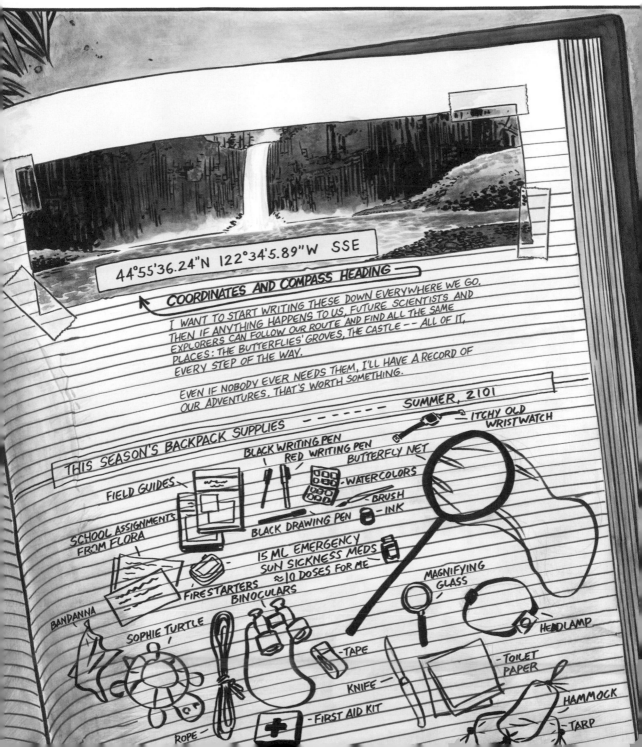

44°55'36.24"N 122°34'5.89"W SSE

COORDINATES AND COMPASS HEADING

I WANT TO START WRITING THESE DOWN EVERYWHERE WE GO. THEN IF ANYTHING HAPPENS TO US, FUTURE SCIENTISTS AND EXPLORERS CAN FOLLOW OUR ROUTE AND FIND ALL THE SAME PLACES: THE BUTTERFLIES' GROVES, THE CASTLE -- ALL OF IT, EVERY STEP OF THE WAY.

EVEN IF NOBODY EVER NEEDS THEM, I'LL HAVE A RECORD OF OUR ADVENTURES. THAT'S WORTH SOMETHING.

SUMMER, 2101

THIS SEASON'S BACKPACK SUPPLIES

- ITCHY OLD WRISTWATCH
- FIELD GUIDES
- BLACK WRITING PEN
- RED WRITING PEN
- BUTTERFLY NET
- WATERCOLORS
- BRUSH
- BLACK DRAWING PEN
- INK
- SCHOOL ASSIGNMENTS FROM FLORA
- 15 ML EMERGENCY SUN SICKNESS MEDS ≈10 DOSES FOR ME
- MAGNIFYING GLASS
- FIRESTARTERS
- BINOCULARS
- BANDANNA
- SOPHIE TURTLE
- HEADLAMP
- TAPE
- TOILET PAPER
- KNIFE
- HAMMOCK
- ROPE
- FIRST AID KIT
- TARP

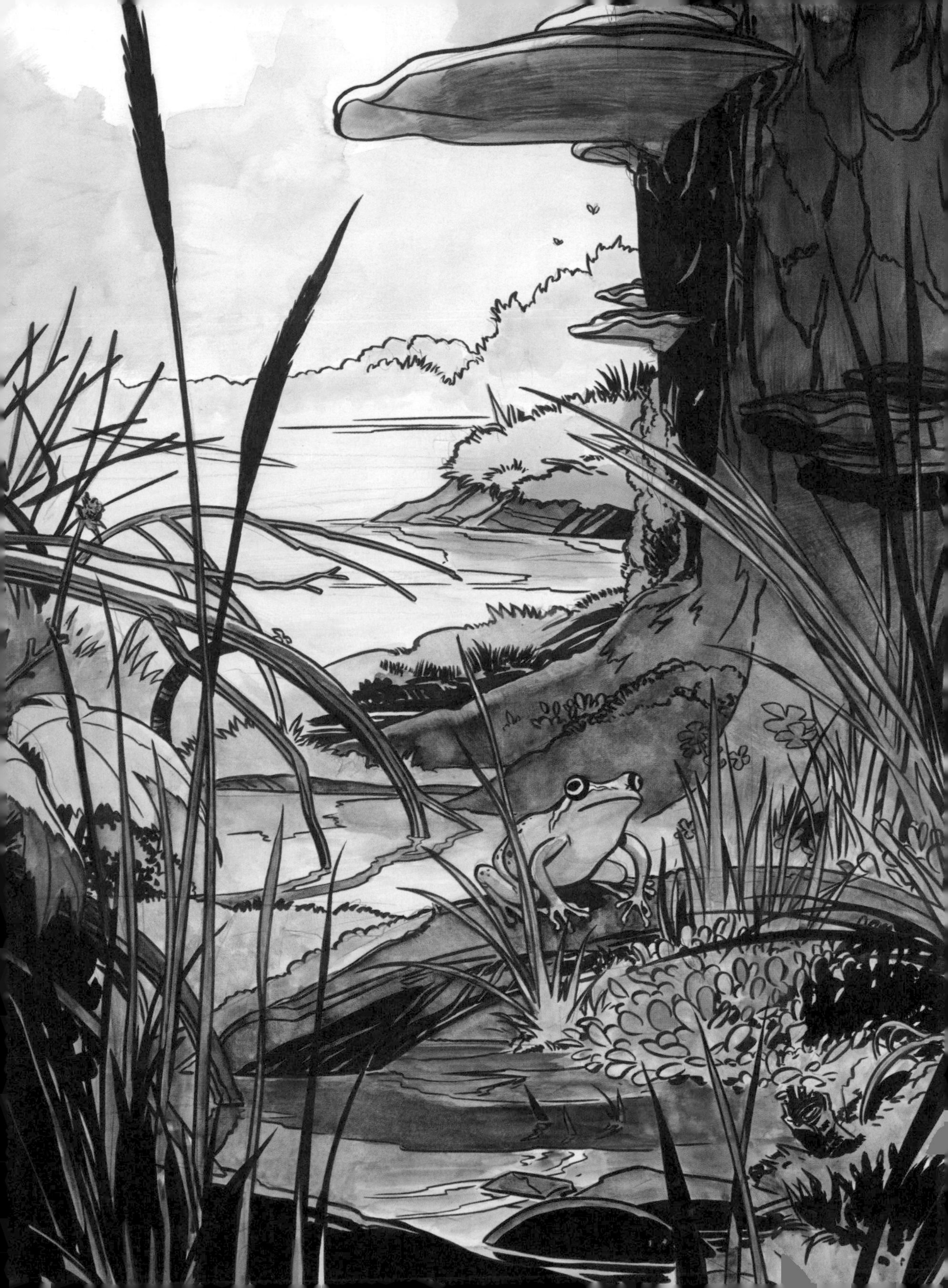

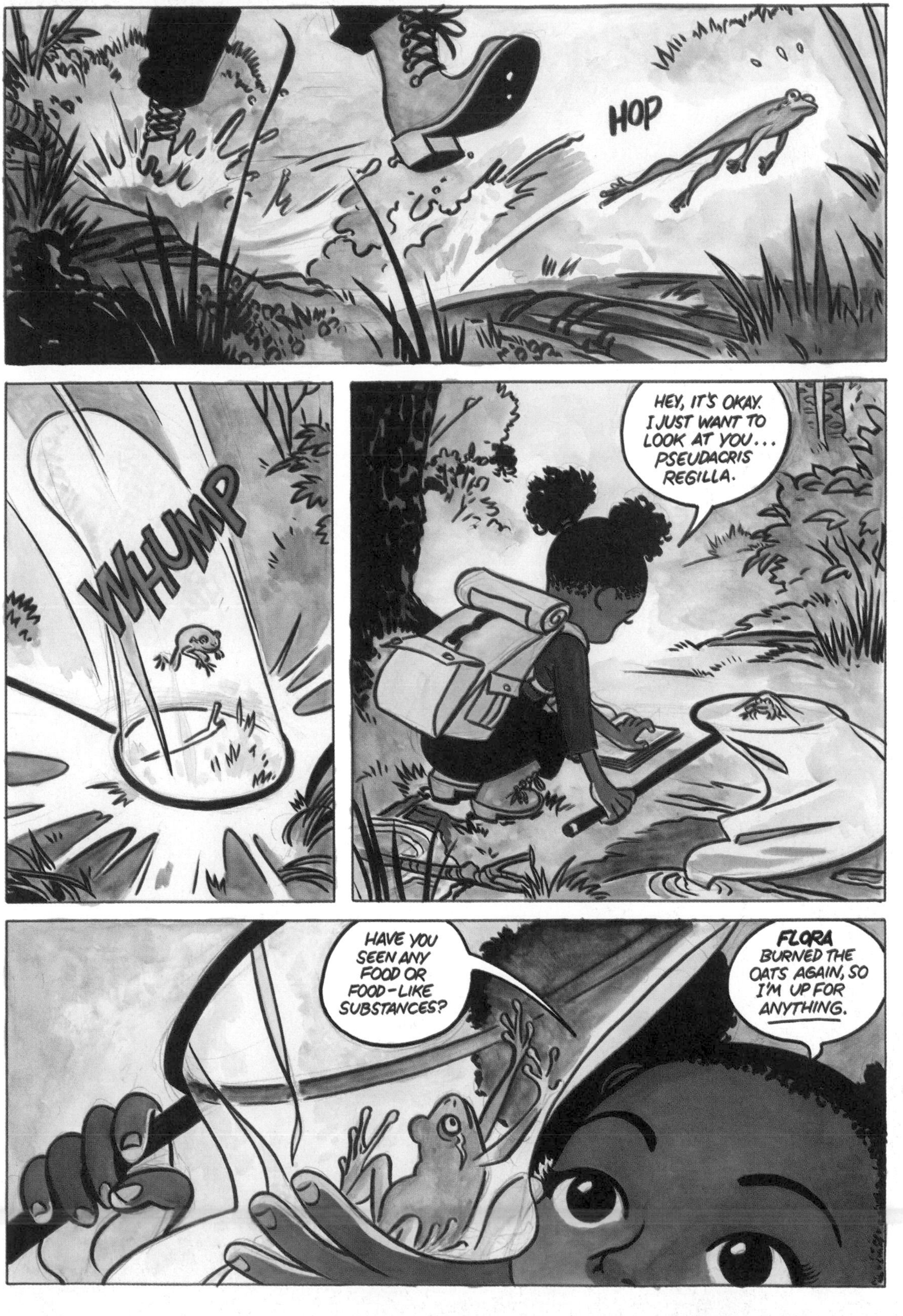
HOP
WHUMP
HEY, IT'S OKAY. I JUST WANT TO LOOK AT YOU... PSEUDACRIS REGILLA.
HAVE YOU SEEN ANY FOOD OR FOOD-LIKE SUBSTANCES?
FLORA BURNED THE OATS AGAIN, SO I'M UP FOR ANYTHING.

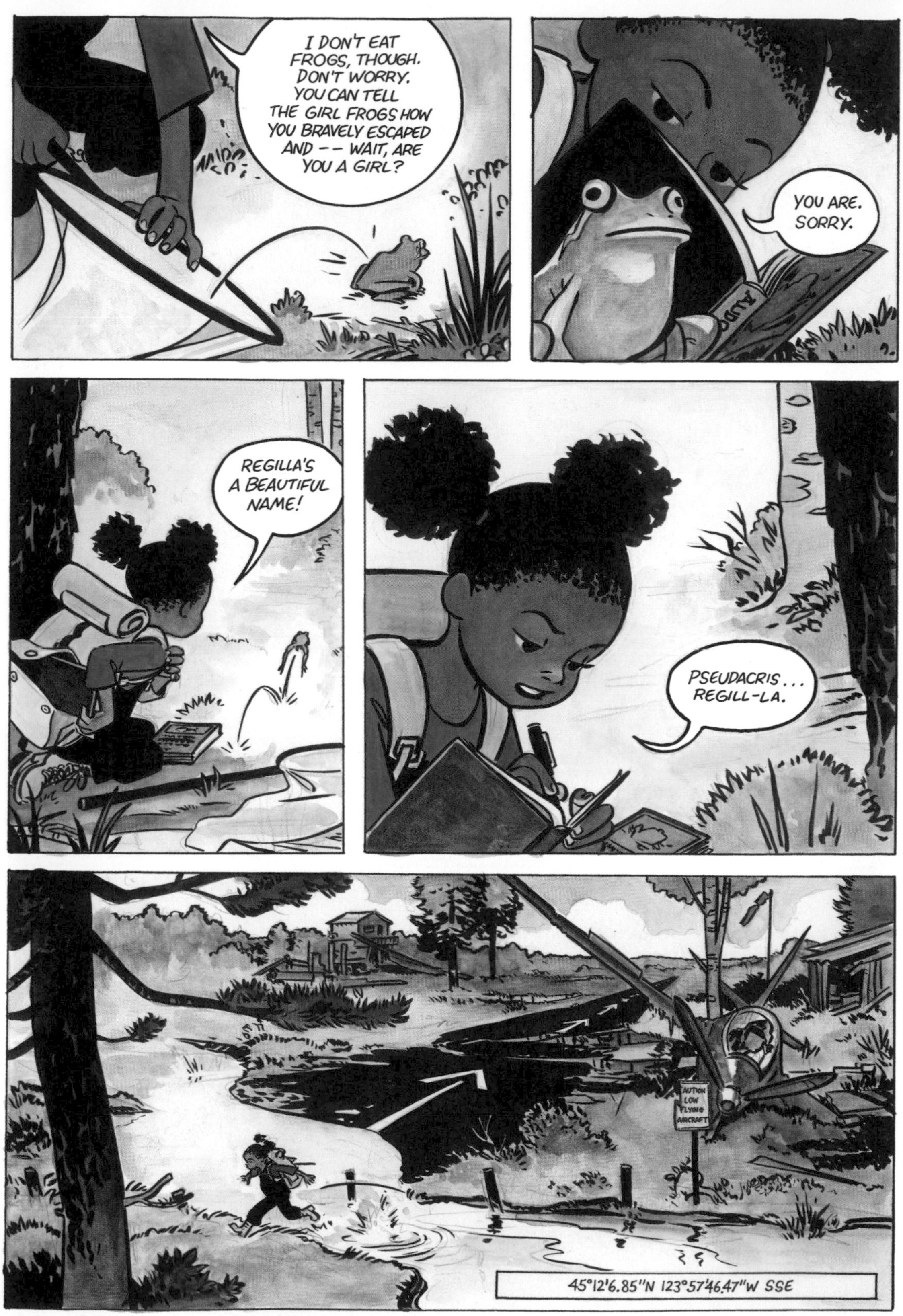
I DON'T EAT FROGS, THOUGH. DON'T WORRY. YOU CAN TELL THE GIRL FROGS HOW YOU BRAVELY ESCAPED AND -- WAIT, ARE YOU A GIRL?
YOU ARE. SORRY.
REGILLA'S A BEAUTIFUL NAME!
PSEUDACRIS... REGILL-LA.
AUTION LOW FLYING AIRCRAFT
45°12'6.85"N 123°57'46.47"W SSE

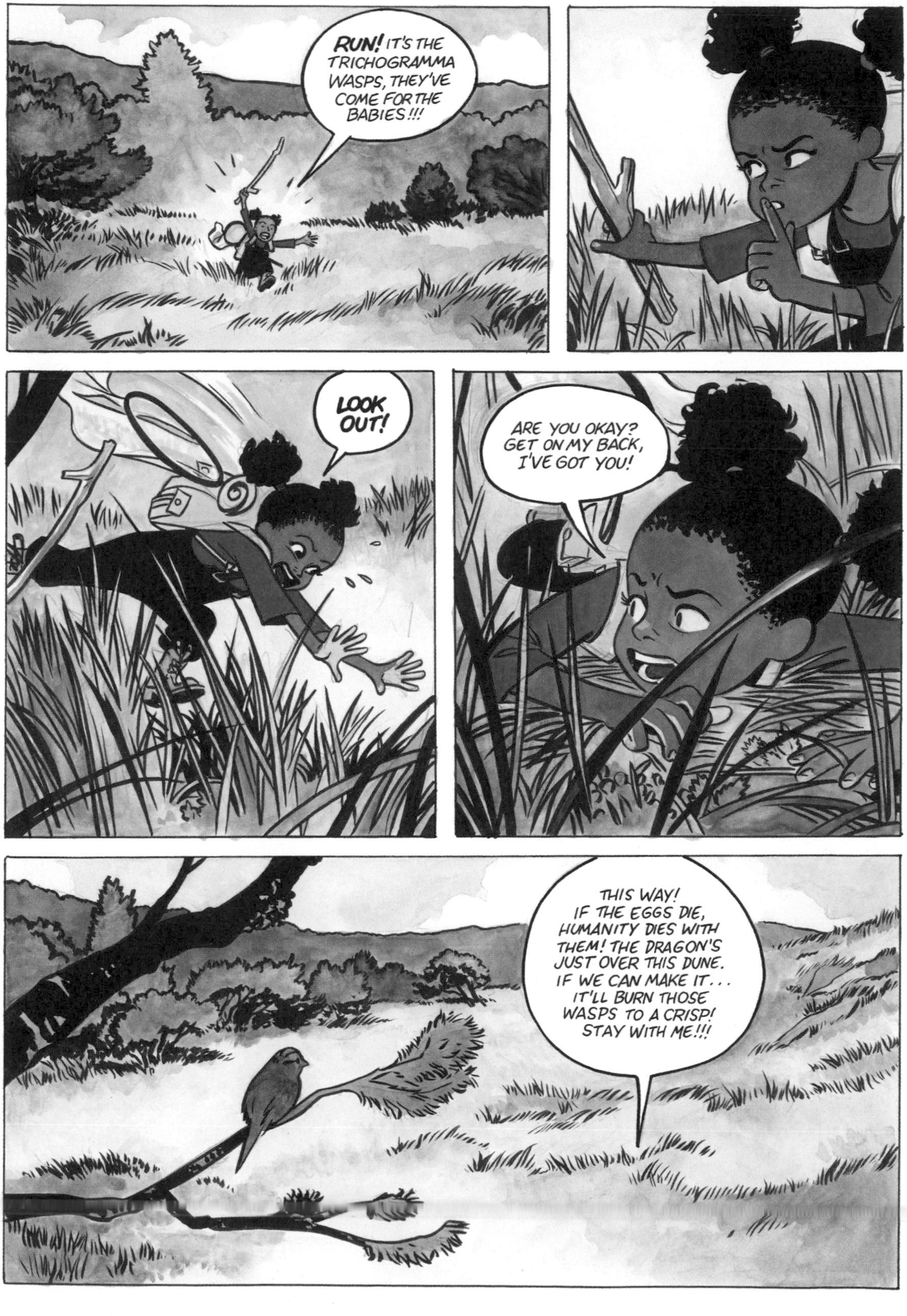
RUN! IT'S THE TRICHOGRAMMA WASPS, THEY'VE COME FOR THE BABIES!!!
LOOK OUT!
ARE YOU OKAY? GET ON MY BACK, I'VE GOT YOU!
THIS WAY! IF THE EGGS DIE, HUMANITY DIES WITH THEM! THE DRAGON'S JUST OVER THIS DUNE. IF WE CAN MAKE IT... IT'LL BURN THOSE WASPS TO A CRISP! STAY WITH ME!!!

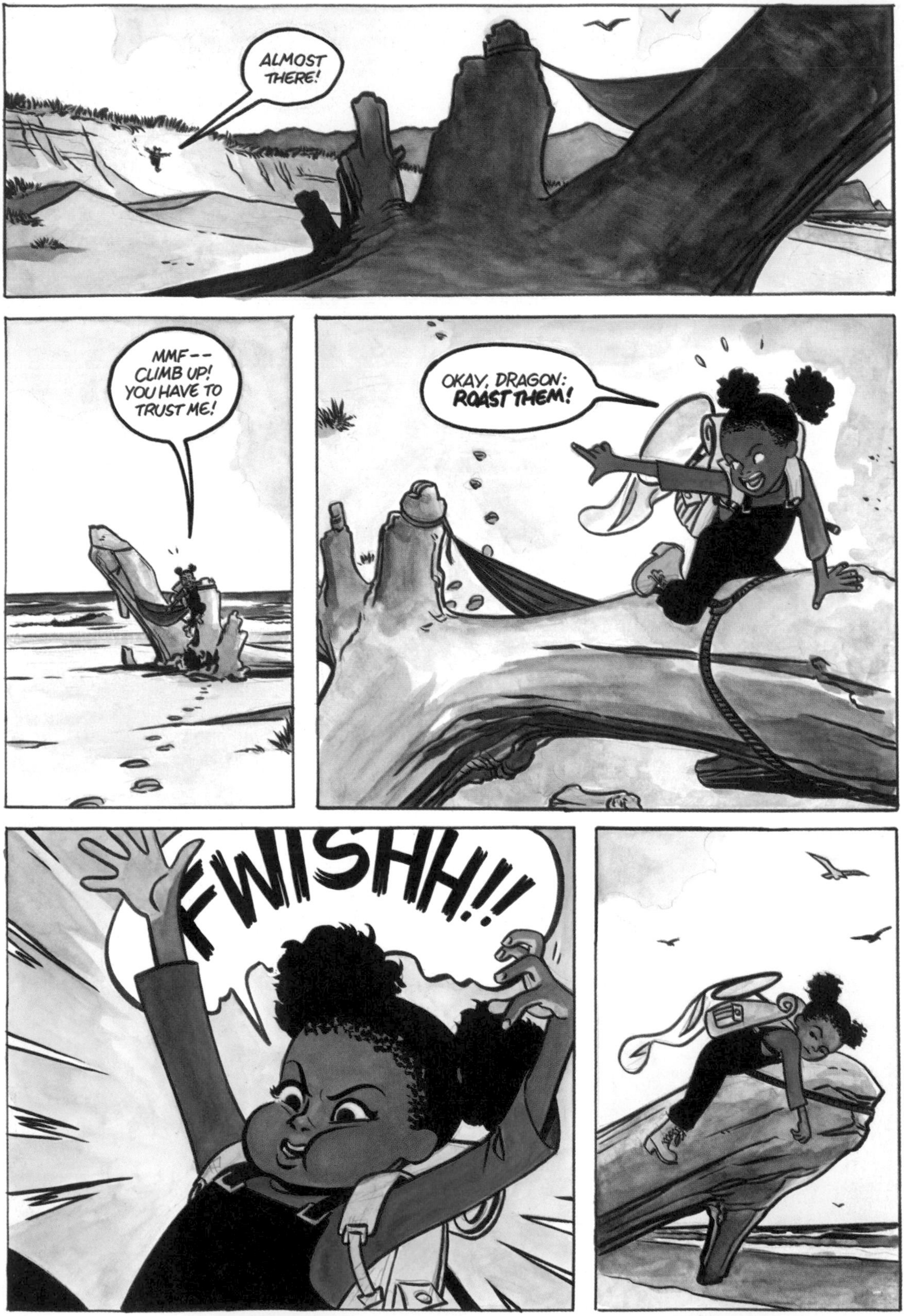
ALMOST THERE!
MMF-- CLIMB UP! YOU HAVE TO TRUST ME!
OKAY, DRAGON: ROAST THEM!
FWISHH!!

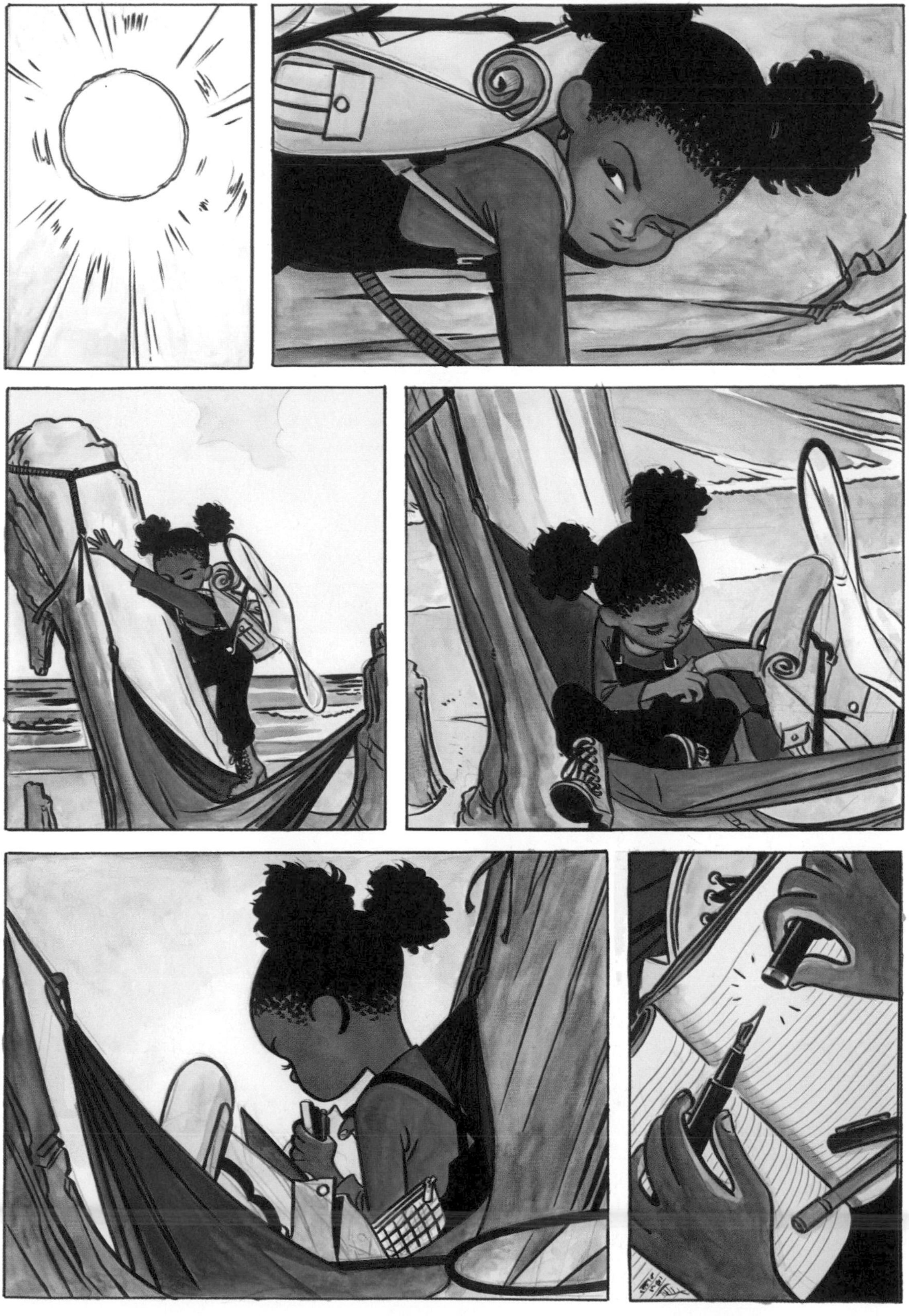

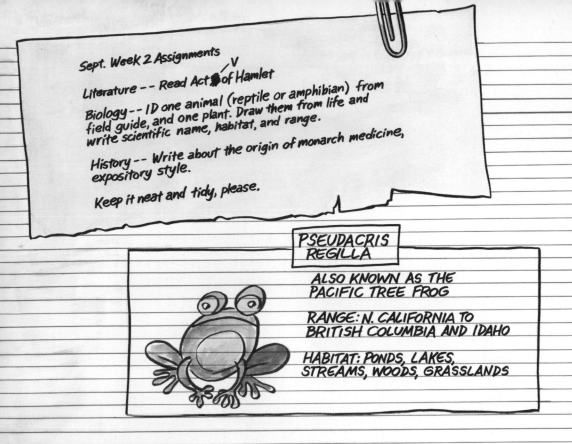

Sept. Week 2 Assignments

Literature -- Read Act V of Hamlet

Biology -- ID one animal (reptile or amphibian) from field guide, and one plant. Draw them from life and write scientific name, habitat, and range.

History -- Write about the origin of monarch medicine, expository style.

Keep it neat and tidy, please.

PSEUDACRIS REGILLA

ALSO KNOWN AS THE PACIFIC TREE FROG

RANGE: N. CALIFORNIA TO BRITISH COLUMBIA AND IDAHO

HABITAT: PONDS, LAKES, STREAMS, WOODS, GRASSLANDS

ELVIRE'S NATURALIST JOURNAL -- VOLUME FIVE, 2101

PACIFIC CITY, OREGON. SEPTEMBER 10. WE HAVE NINETEEN DAYS UNTIL OUR MONARCH MEDICINE EXPIRES. WE'RE HEADED SOUTH NOW. THIS'LL BE OUR SEVENTH YEAR FOLLOWING THE BUTTERFLIES' MIGRATION. SEVEN YEARS, AND **FLORA** STILL HASN'T FIGURED OUT HER SUN SICKNESS **VACCINE**. IF SHE DOESN'T FIND SOMETHING THAT WORKS SOON, I'M STAGING A MUTINY WITH OUR **PIGEONS**.

ARRR!

WHAT IF WE'RE ALONE UP HERE FOR **ANOTHER** SEVEN YEARS? I'D BE SEVENTEEN! YOU'RE SUPPOSED TO HAVE A BOYFRIEND WHEN YOU'RE SEVENTEEN. I'VE NEVER EVEN SEEN A B HOLY DUNGBALLS, MY BLACK PEN IS DEAD AND I HAD TO SWITCH. WRITING IS HARD. THIS RED PEN WAS SUPPOSED TO BE ONLY FOR FACTS. NOW THIS IS ALL MESSED UP! I'LL TRY AGAIN.

THIS IS MY BLACK DRAWING PEN, BUT IT'LL HAVE TO DO:

$2+2 = 94,208!$
$2-2 = 0$ ... THINGS THAT I KNOW TO BE FACTS SHOULD ALWAYS BE IN RED.

I BETTER START OVER ON THE NEXT PAGE, OR THIS WON'T BE UP TO HER MAJESTY'S NEAT AND TIDY STANDARDS. IF I WERE IN CHARGE, MY JOURNALS WOULD JUST BE JOURNALS: NOT SCHOOL-WORK, TOO. HOW CAN YOU WRITE ANYTHING GOOD WHEN YOU'RE TRYING NOT TO MAKE MISTAKES? IT'S IMPOSSIBLE!

ELVIRE'S NATURALIST JOURNAL-- VOLUME FIVE

PACIFIC CITY, OREGON. SEPTEMBER 10. WE HAVE NINETEEN DAYS UNTIL OUR MONARCH MEDICINE EXPIRES... AGAIN. OUR LAST BATCH OF MEDS CAME FROM THIRTY MONARCHS UP IN WALLA WALLA, WASHINGTON. WE MADE 240 ML FOR DAILY USE AND 150 ML FOR EMERGENCIES. ABOUT 70 DOSES. I DON'T KNOW WHY SHE THINKS WE NEED SO MUCH EXTRA MEDICINE. IT'LL JUST GO BAD AND BE WASTED. AND IT LEAVES BARELY ANY BASE FLUID FOR VACCINE TESTS. IT'S NO WONDER SHE'S SO SLOW WITH HER RESEARCH.

MAYBE THE TRICK TO STAYING POSITIVE IS TO JUST KEEP SAYING WALLA WALLA, WASHINGTON. I BET THE PEOPLE WHO LIVED THERE ALWAYS HAD THESE GOOFY SMILES, LIKE, "WELCOME TO WALLA WALLA, WASHINGTON! WE HOPE YOU WIKE IT!" IT'S TOO MUCH FUN TO SAY.

I THINK I WON'T REDO MY FROG DRAWING ON THIS PAGE. SHE'S ABOUT AS GOOD AS SHE'S GONNA GET. SHE'LL DEFINITELY NEVER LOOK AS GOOD AS FLORA'S DRAWINGS. SORRY, FROGGY. I CANNOT COMPARE TO HER LEVEL OF OBSESSION -- YOU'LL BE REMEMBERED HERE AS A VAGUELY FROGGISH BLOB.

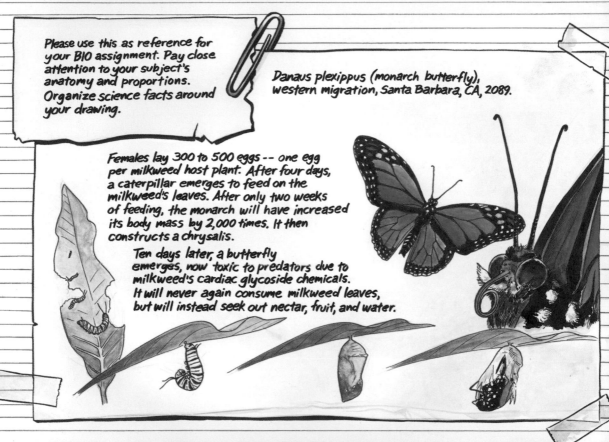

Please use this as reference for your BIO assignment. Pay close attention to your subject's anatomy and proportions. Organize science facts around your drawing.
Danaus plexippus (monarch butterfly), western migration, Santa Barbara, CA, 2089.
Females lay 300 to 500 eggs -- one egg per milkweed host plant. After four days, a caterpillar emerges to feed on the milkweed's leaves. After only two weeks of feeding, the monarch will have increased its body mass by 2,000 times. It then constructs a chrysalis.
Ten days later, a butterfly emerges, now toxic to predators due to milkweed's cardiac glycoside chemicals. It will never again consume milkweed leaves, but will instead seek out nectar, fruit, and water.

SPEAKING OF SCIENCE FACTS: DID YOU KNOW THAT EVEN IN LATE SUMMER, IF YOU SIT IN A HAMMOCK ON THE OREGON COAST WITHOUT INSULATION UNDER YOUR BUTT, SAID BUTT GETS SO COLD THAT IT FREEZES, FALLS OFF, AND WADDLES SOUTH TO A WARMER CLIMATE? IT'S TRUE. BUT I DIDN'T USE MY RED PEN, DID I? SO MAYBE IT'S NOT TRUE. I'M STILL GETTING A BLANKET.

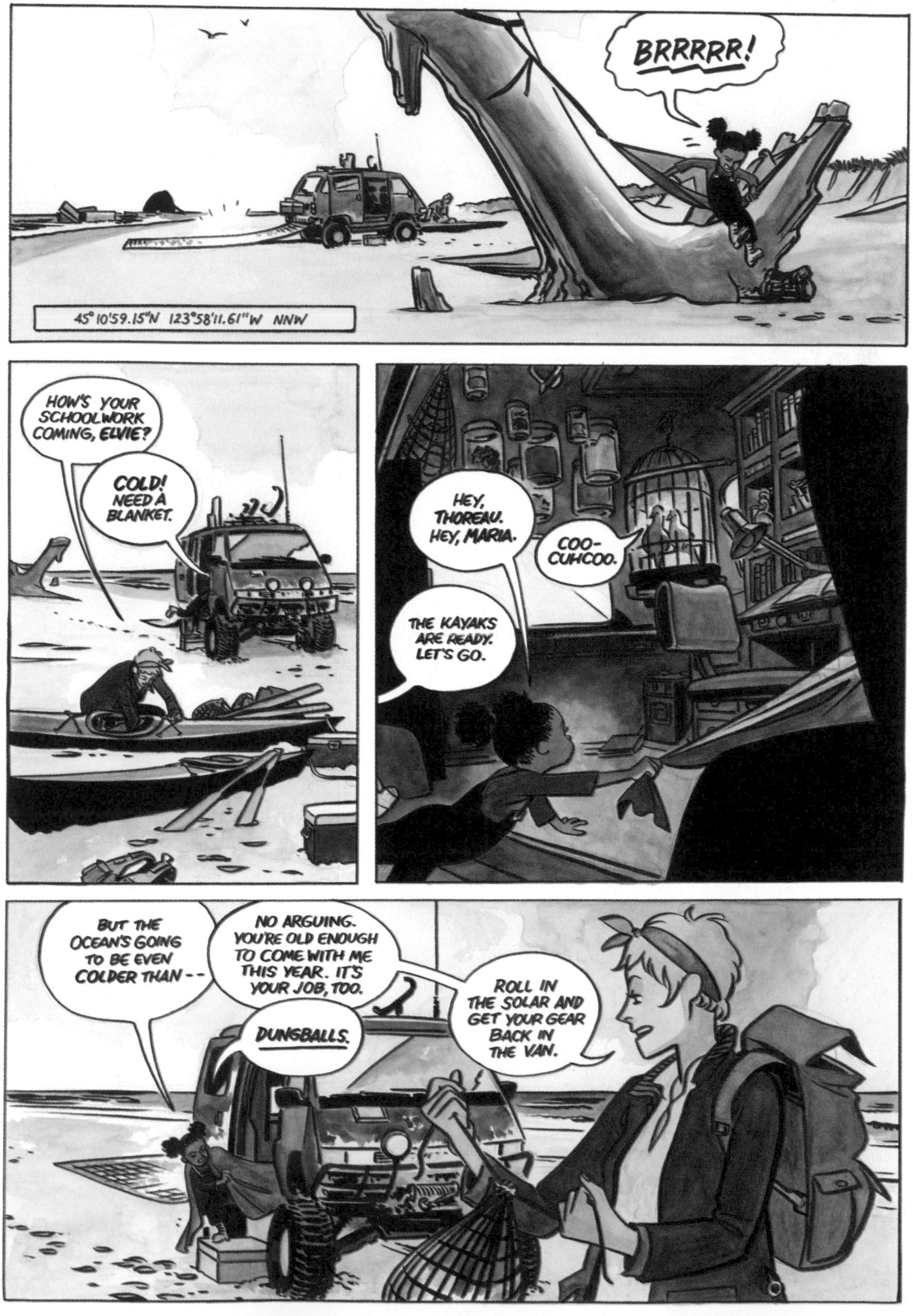
BRRRRR!
45° 10'59.15"N 123°58'11.61"W NNW
HOW'S YOUR SCHOOLWORK COMING, ELVIE?
COLD! NEED A BLANKET.
HEY, THOREAU. HEY, MARIA.
COO-CUHCOO.
THE KAYAKS ARE READY. LET'S GO.
BUT THE OCEAN'S GOING TO BE EVEN COLDER THAN--
NO ARGUING. YOU'RE OLD ENOUGH TO COME WITH ME THIS YEAR. IT'S YOUR JOB, TOO.
DUNGBALLS.
ROLL IN THE SOLAR AND GET YOUR GEAR BACK IN THE VAN.

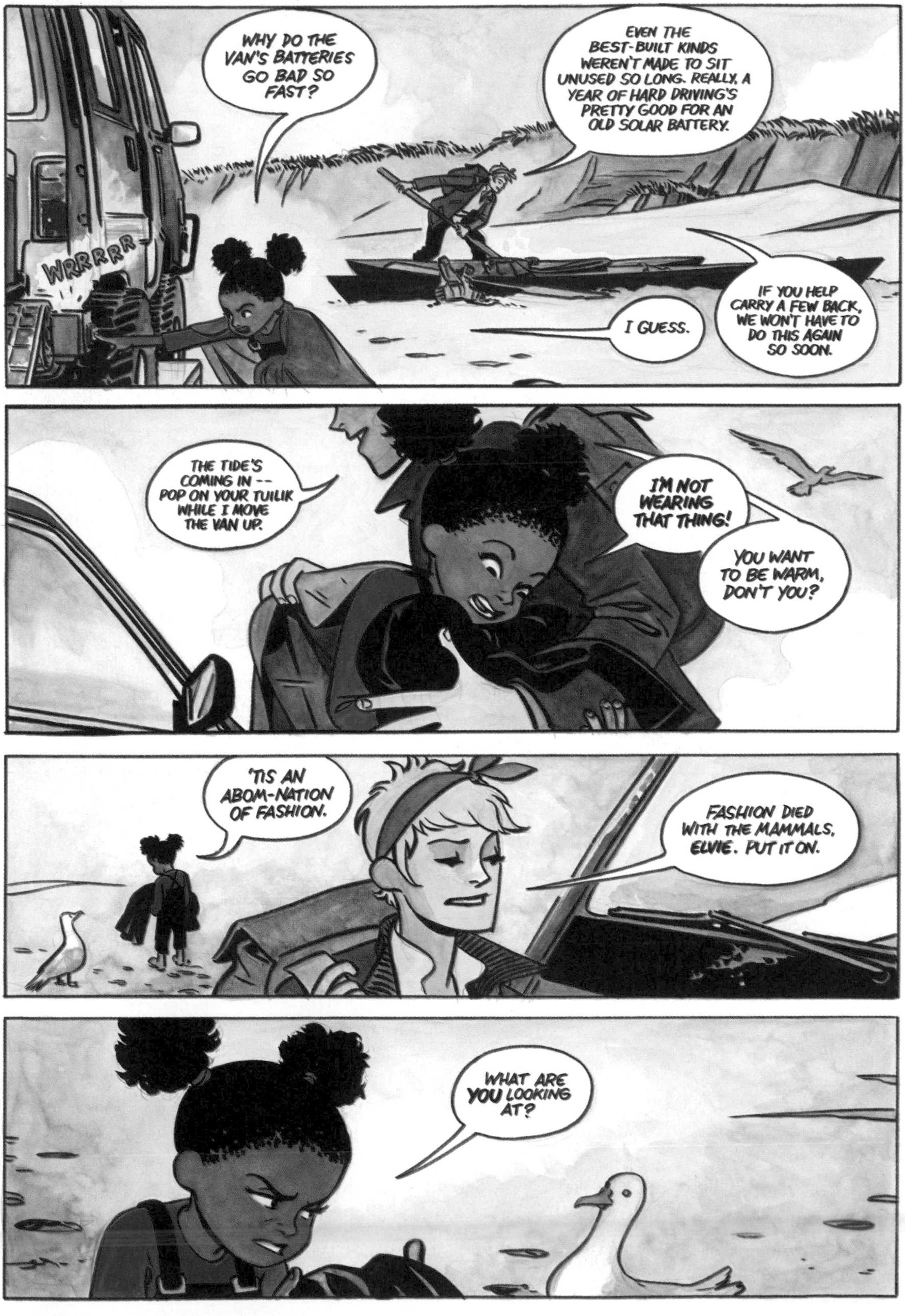
WHY DO THE VAN'S BATTERIES GO BAD SO FAST?
EVEN THE BEST-BUILT KINDS WEREN'T MADE TO SIT UNUSED SO LONG. REALLY, A YEAR OF HARD DRIVING'S PRETTY GOOD FOR AN OLD SOLAR BATTERY.
WRRRRR
I GUESS.
IF YOU HELP CARRY A FEW BACK, WE WON'T HAVE TO DO THIS AGAIN SO SOON.
THE TIDE'S COMING IN -- POP ON YOUR TUILIK WHILE I MOVE THE VAN UP.
I'M NOT WEARING THAT THING!
YOU WANT TO BE WARM, DON'T YOU?
'TIS AN ABOM-NATION OF FASHION.
FASHION DIED WITH THE MAMMALS, ELVIE. PUT IT ON.
WHAT ARE YOU LOOKING AT?

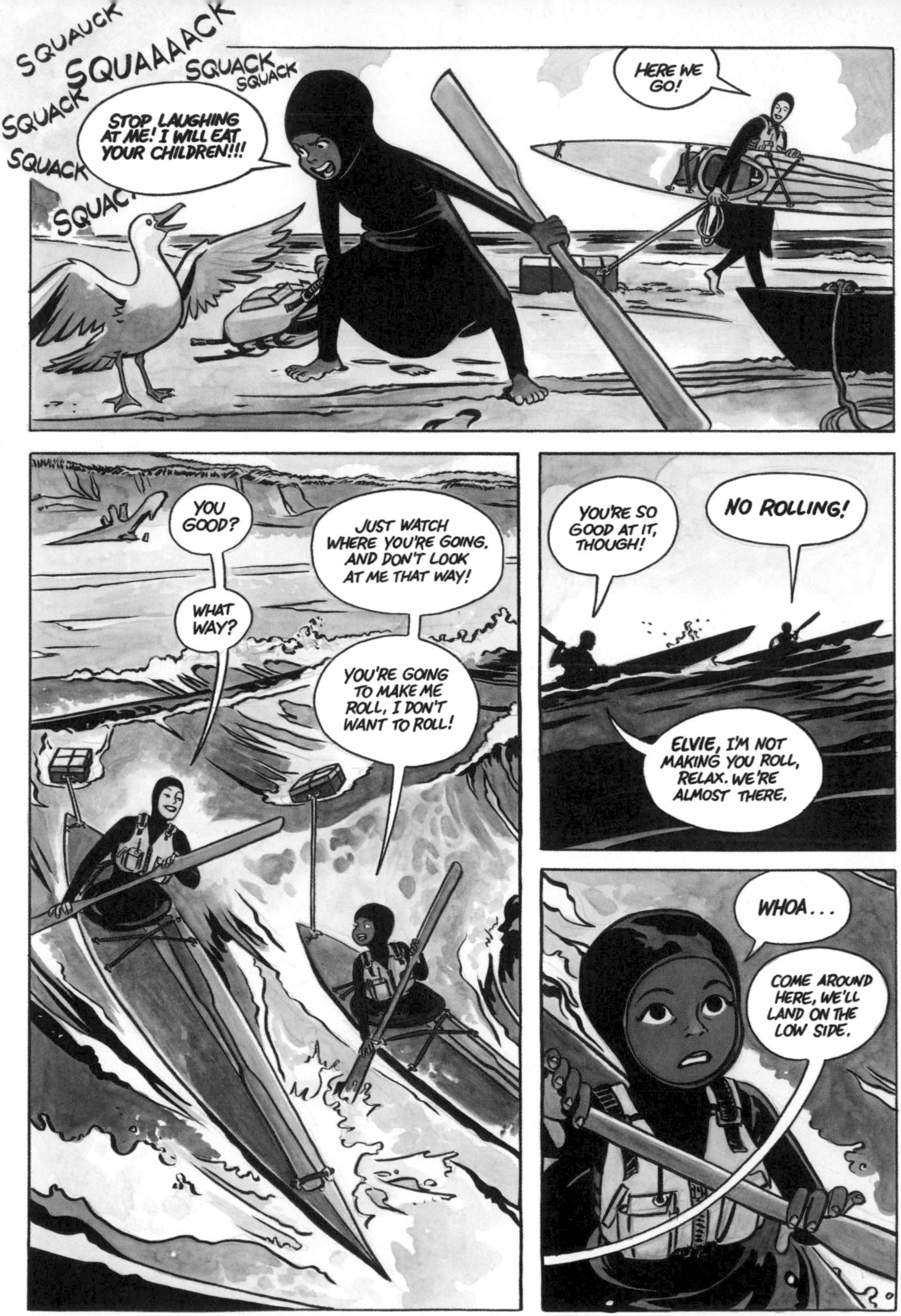
SQUAUCK
SQUAAAACK
SQUACK
SQUACK
SQUACK
SQUACK
SQUACK
SQUAC
STOP LAUGHING AT ME! I WILL EAT YOUR CHILDREN!!!
HERE WE GO!
YOU GOOD?
WHAT WAY?
JUST WATCH WHERE YOU'RE GOING. AND DON'T LOOK AT ME THAT WAY!
YOU'RE GOING TO MAKE ME ROLL, I DON'T WANT TO ROLL!
YOU'RE SO GOOD AT IT, THOUGH!
NO ROLLING!
ELVIE, I'M NOT MAKING YOU ROLL, RELAX. WE'RE ALMOST THERE.
WHOA...
COME AROUND HERE, WE'LL LAND ON THE LOW SIDE.

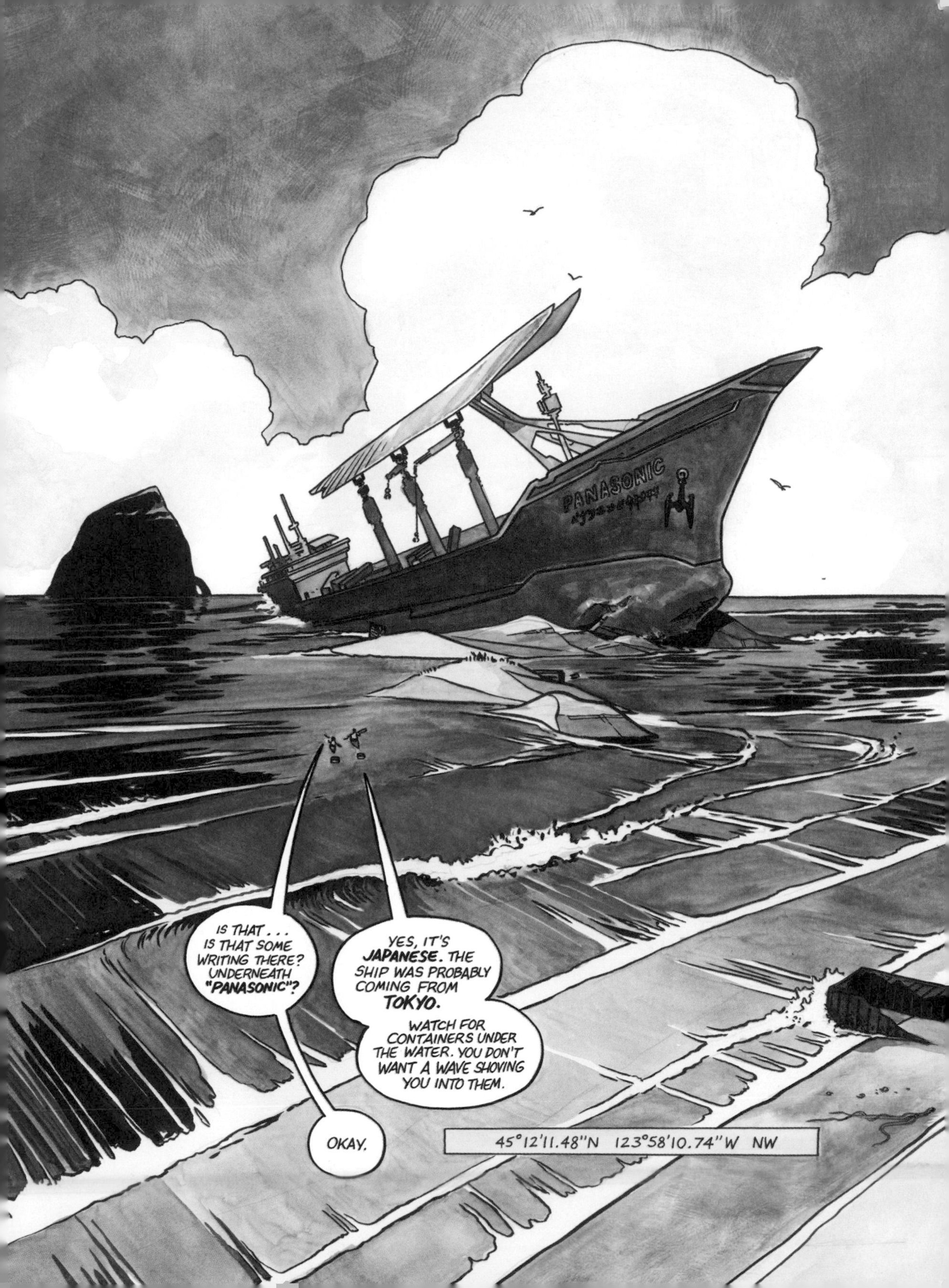
PANASONIC
IS THAT . . . IS THAT SOME WRITING THERE? UNDERNEATH "PANASONIC"?
YES, IT'S JAPANESE. THE SHIP WAS PROBABLY COMING FROM TOKYO.
WATCH FOR CONTAINERS UNDER THE WATER. YOU DON'T WANT A WAVE SHOVING YOU INTO THEM.
OKAY.
45°12'11.48"N 123°58'10.74"W NW

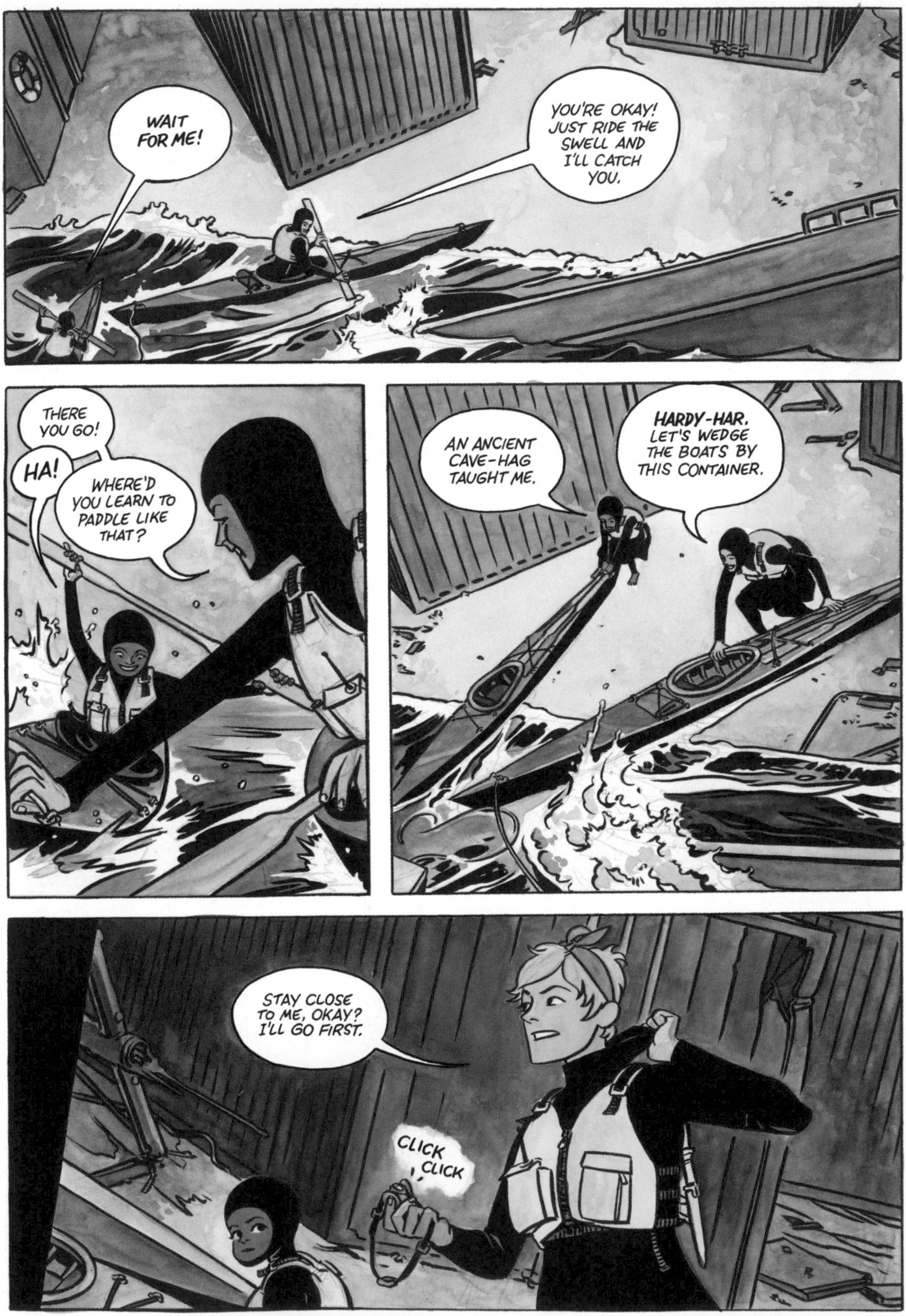
WAIT FOR ME!
YOU'RE OKAY! JUST RIDE THE SWELL AND I'LL CATCH YOU.
THERE YOU GO!
HA!
WHERE'D YOU LEARN TO PADDLE LIKE THAT?
AN ANCIENT CAVE-HAG TAUGHT ME.
HARDY-HAR. LET'S WEDGE THE BOATS BY THIS CONTAINER.
STAY CLOSE TO ME, OKAY? I'LL GO FIRST.
CLICK CLICK

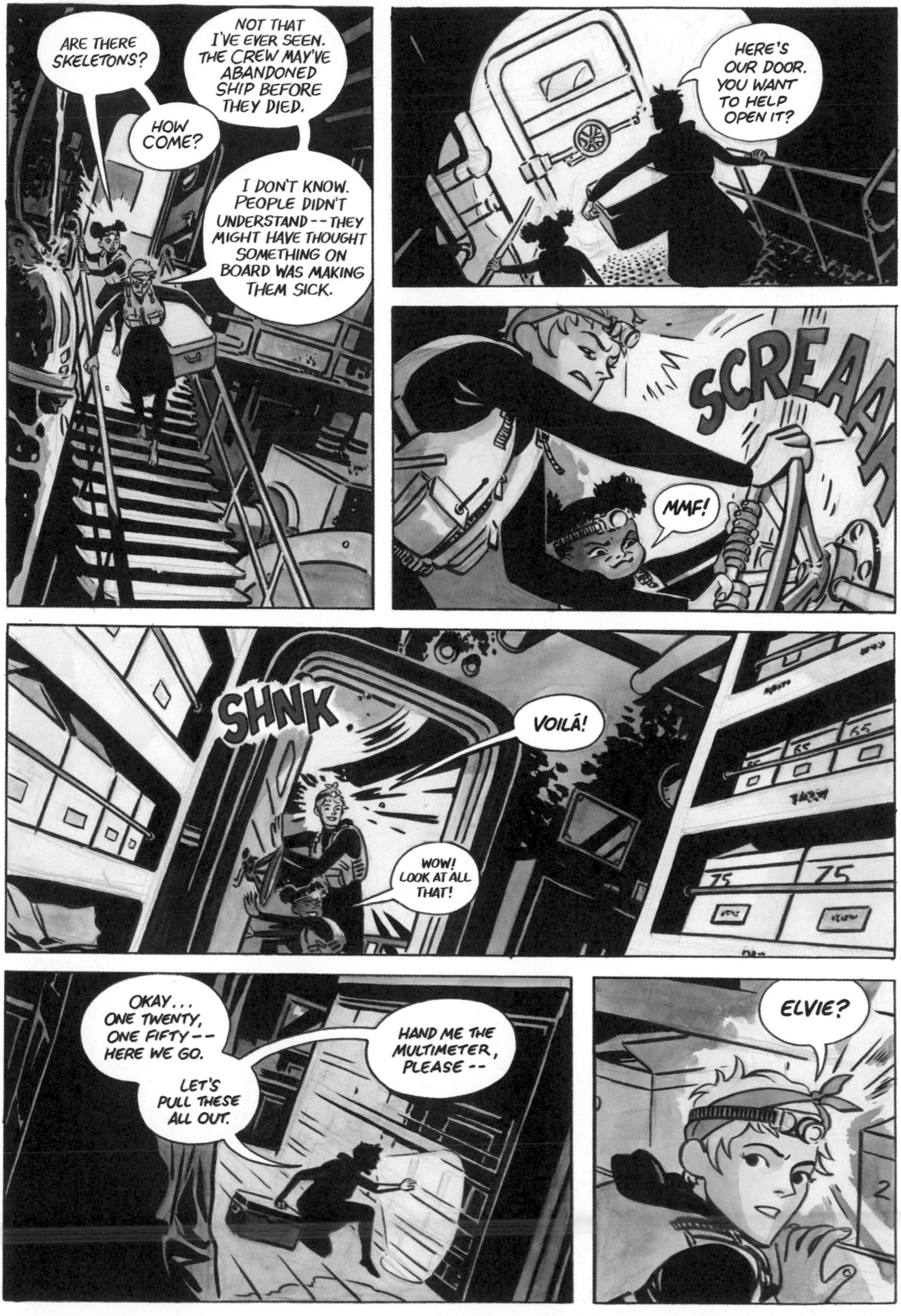
ARE THERE SKELETONS?
NOT THAT I'VE EVER SEEN. THE CREW MAY'VE ABANDONED SHIP BEFORE THEY DIED.
HOW COME?
I DON'T KNOW. PEOPLE DIDN'T UNDERSTAND -- THEY MIGHT HAVE THOUGHT SOMETHING ON BOARD WAS MAKING THEM SICK.
HERE'S OUR DOOR. YOU WANT TO HELP OPEN IT?
SCREAAK
MMF!
SHNK
VOILÁ!
WOW! LOOK AT ALL THAT!
65
75
75
OKAY... ONE TWENTY, ONE FIFTY -- HERE WE GO.
HAND ME THE MULTIMETER, PLEASE --
LET'S PULL THESE ALL OUT.
ELVIE?

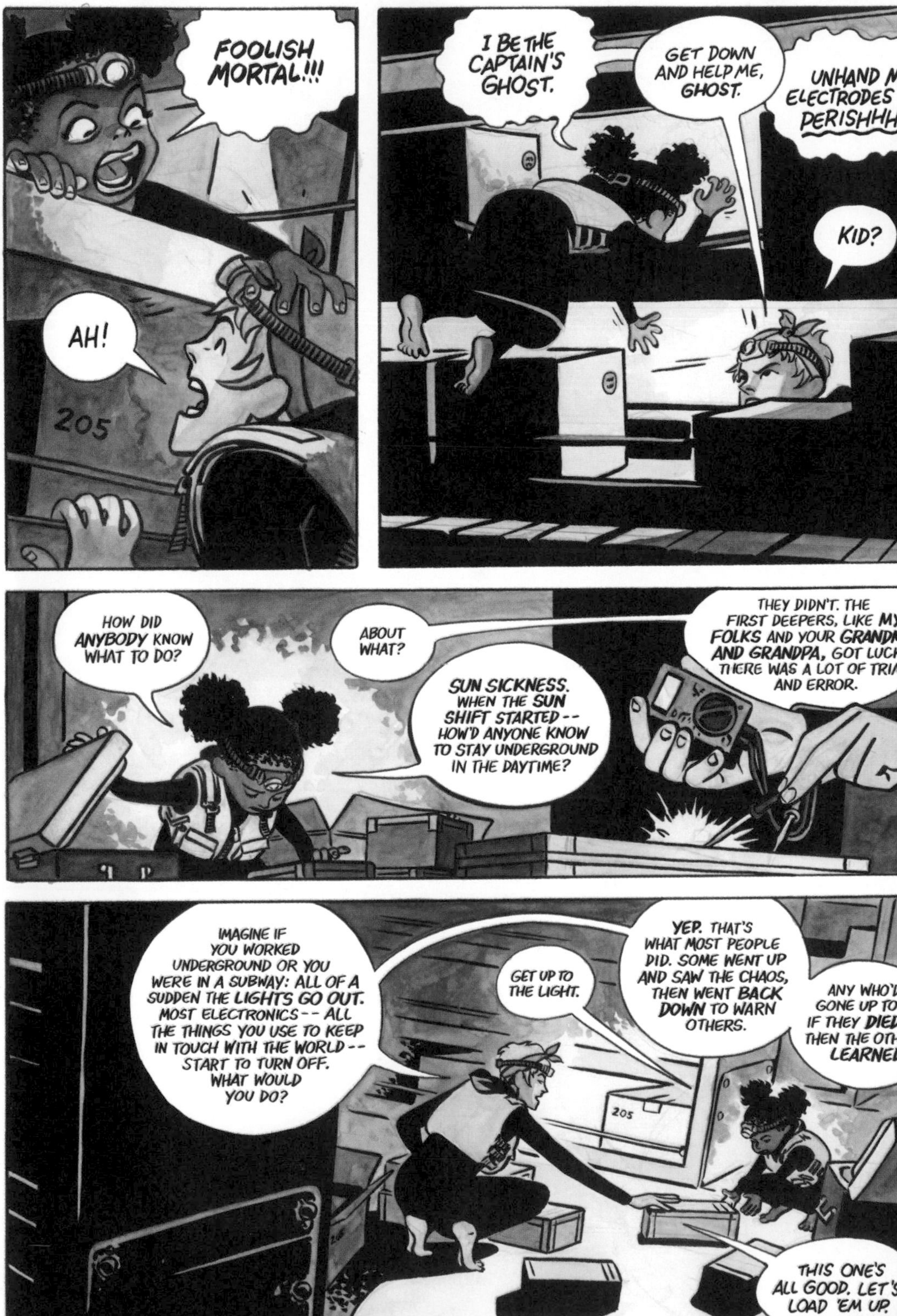
FOOLISH MORTAL!!!
AH!
205
I BE THE CAPTAIN'S GHOST.
GET DOWN AND HELP ME, GHOST.
UNHAND MY ELECTRODES OR PERISHHHH!
KID?
HOW DID ANYBODY KNOW WHAT TO DO?
ABOUT WHAT?
SUN SICKNESS. WHEN THE SUN SHIFT STARTED -- HOW'D ANYONE KNOW TO STAY UNDERGROUND IN THE DAYTIME?
THEY DIDN'T. THE FIRST DEEPERS, LIKE MY FOLKS AND YOUR GRANDMA AND GRANDPA, GOT LUCKY. THERE WAS A LOT OF TRIAL AND ERROR.
IMAGINE IF YOU WORKED UNDERGROUND OR YOU WERE IN A SUBWAY: ALL OF A SUDDEN THE LIGHTS GO OUT. MOST ELECTRONICS -- ALL THE THINGS YOU USE TO KEEP IN TOUCH WITH THE WORLD -- START TO TURN OFF. WHAT WOULD YOU DO?
GET UP TO THE LIGHT.
YEP. THAT'S WHAT MOST PEOPLE DID. SOME WENT UP AND SAW THE CHAOS, THEN WENT BACK DOWN TO WARN OTHERS.
ANY WHO'D GONE UP TOP, IF THEY DIED -- THEN THE OTHERS LEARNED.
205
THIS ONE'S ALL GOOD. LET'S LOAD 'EM UP.

WATER BOWLINE KNOT

FSHEW! THOSE WERE HEAVY. I NEED A STRAWBERRY REWARD, STAT!

YOUR ICE CHEST IS TIED OFF, ALL RIGHT? I'LL PUSH YOU OUT.

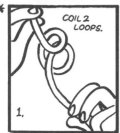

1. COIL 2 LOOPS.

2. BRING THE "WORKING" END UP THROUGH THOSE.

THIS BIG LOOP IS FOR ATTACHING TO STUFF.

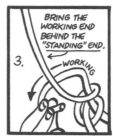

3. BRING THE WORKING END BEHIND THE "STANDING" END.

WORKING

4. NOW PLUNGE BACK DOWN THROUGH THE COILS.

5. TIGHTEN! WON'T EASILY SLIP OR BIND, EASY TO UNTIE EVEN WHEN WET!

HEAVE AWAY, ME JOHNNY!

HEY, WAIT A MINUTE, I DON'T HAVE MY HOOD TIGHT!

SORRY!

YOU OKAY?

JEEZ!!

YOU HAVE TO WAIT TILL I'M READY!

I'LL BE RIGHT WITH YOU!

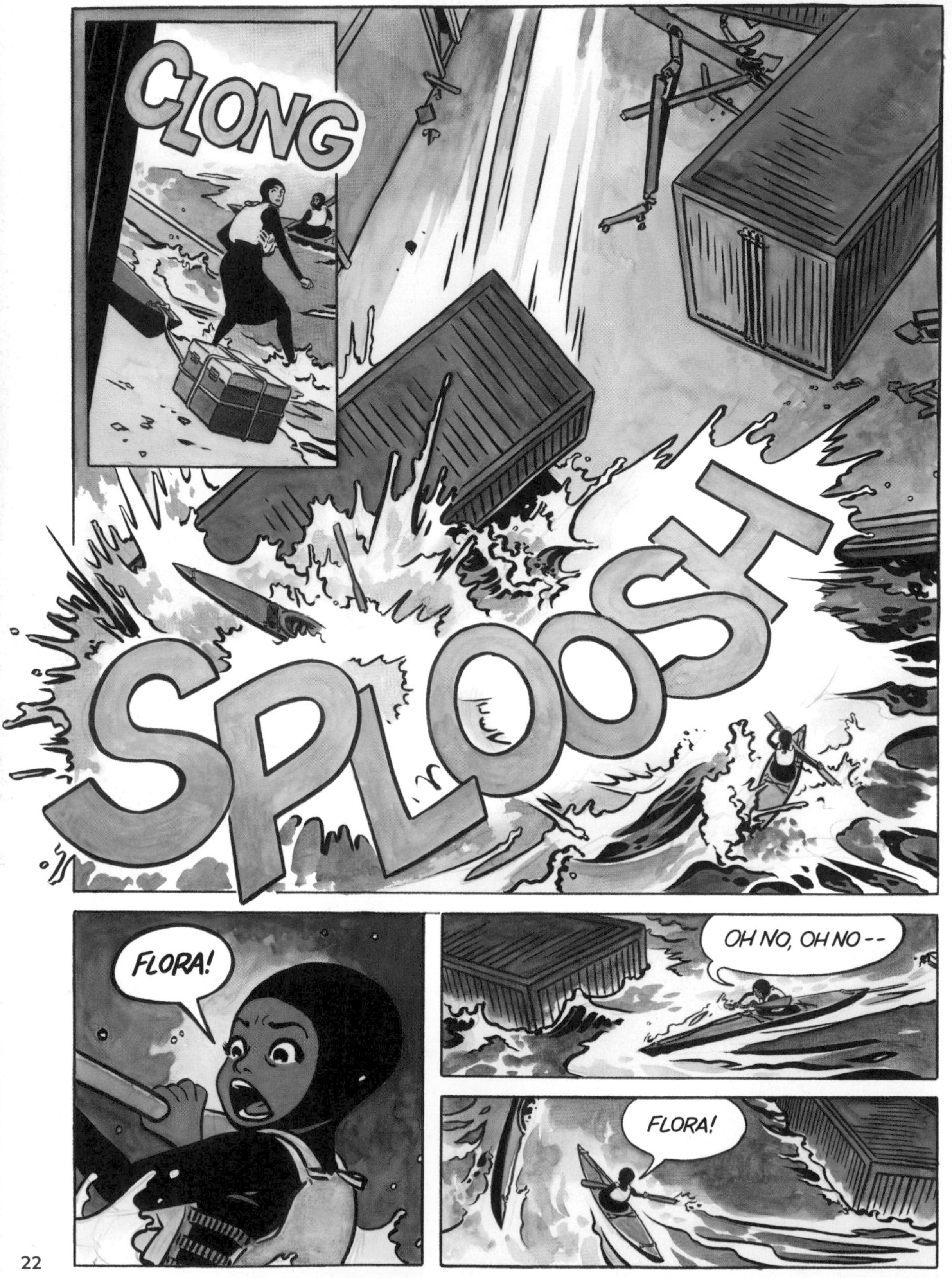
CLONG
SPLOOSH
FLORA!
OH NO, OH NO --
FLORA!

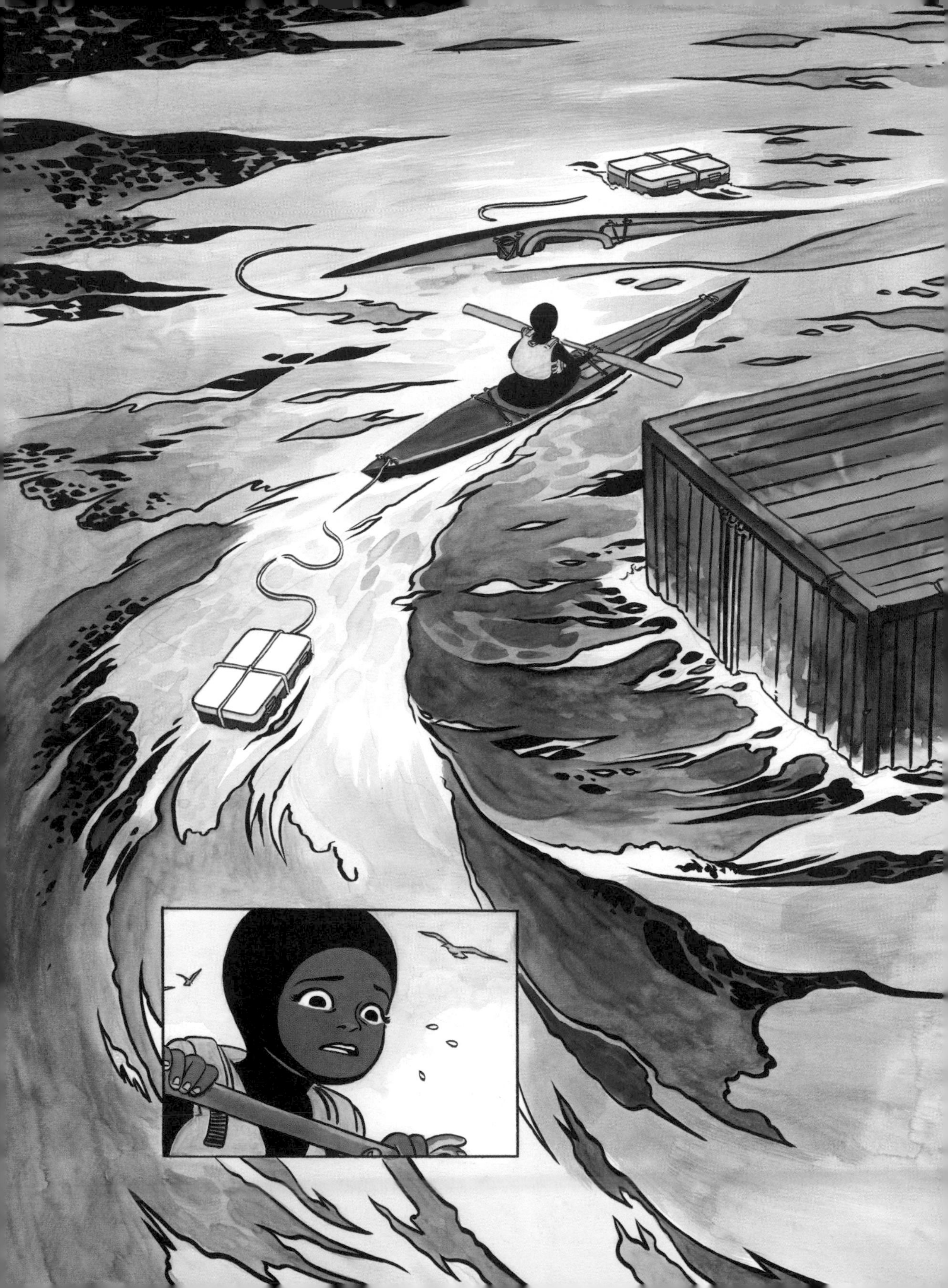

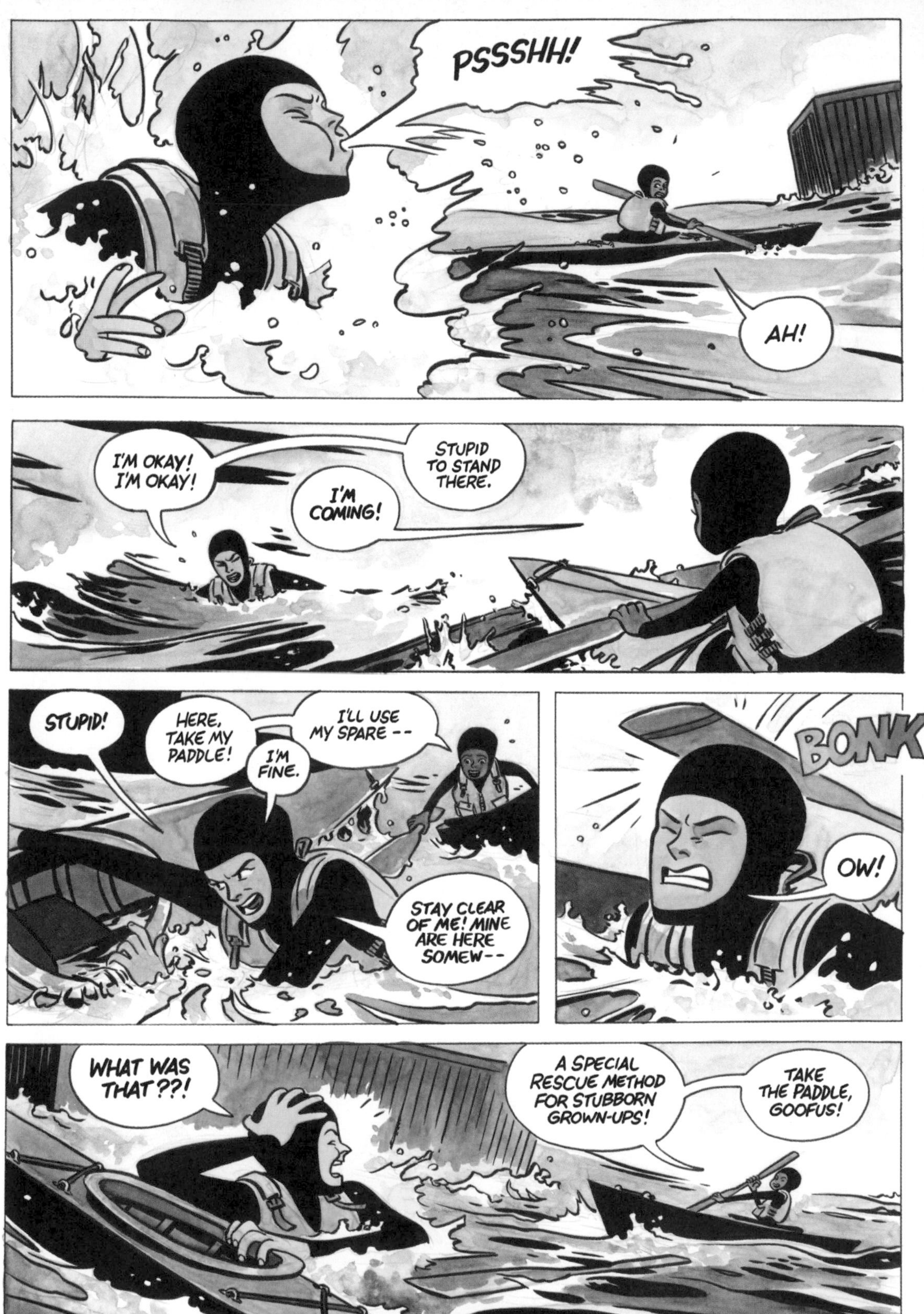
PSSSHH!
AH!
I'M OKAY! I'M OKAY!
STUPID TO STAND THERE.
I'M COMING!
STUPID!
HERE, TAKE MY PADDLE!
I'LL USE MY SPARE --
I'M FINE.
STAY CLEAR OF ME! MINE ARE HERE SOMEW--
BONK
OW!
WHAT WAS THAT??!
A SPECIAL RESCUE METHOD FOR STUBBORN GROWN-UPS!
TAKE THE PADDLE, GOOFUS!

CHAPTER TWO
SUPPLIES

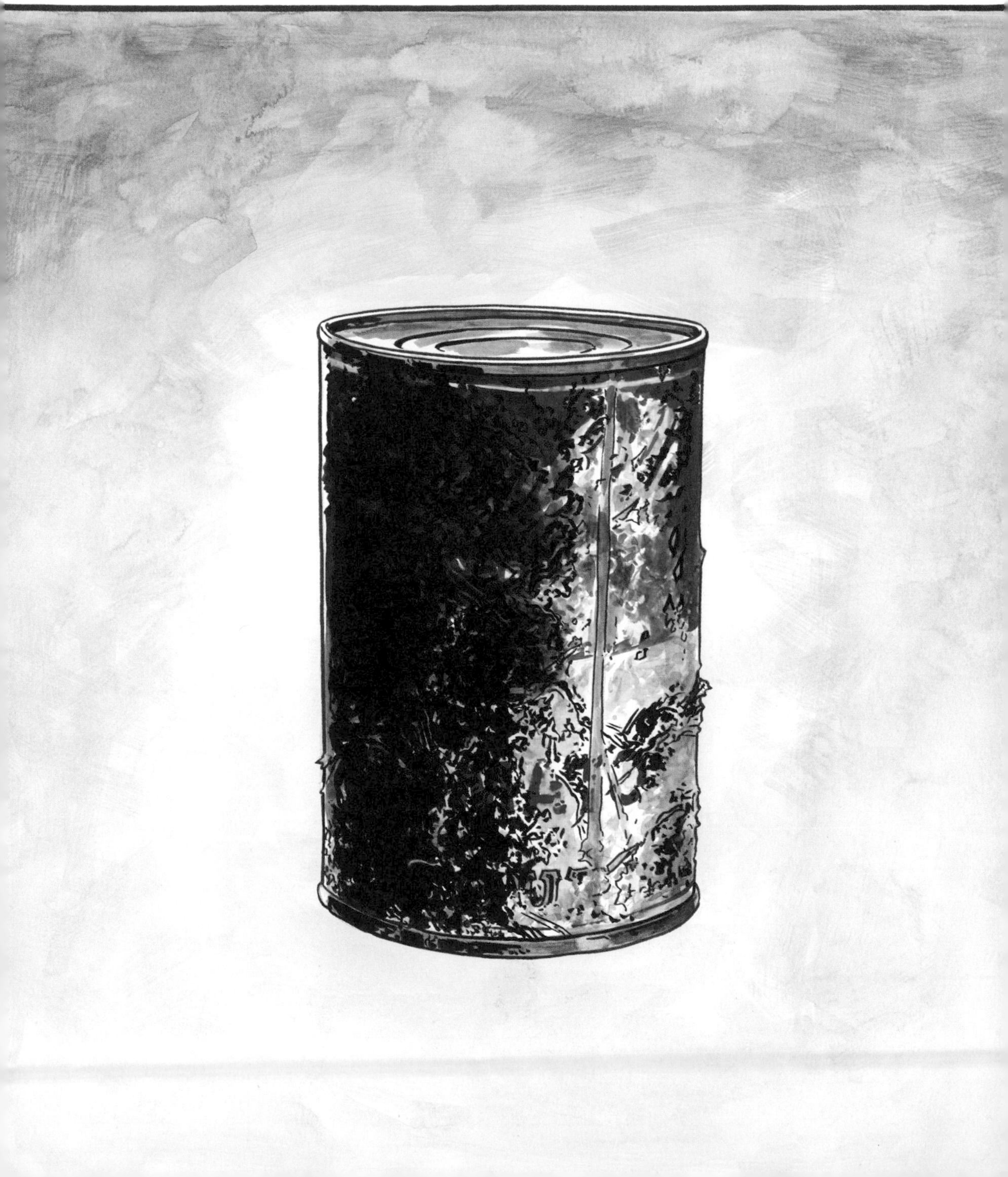

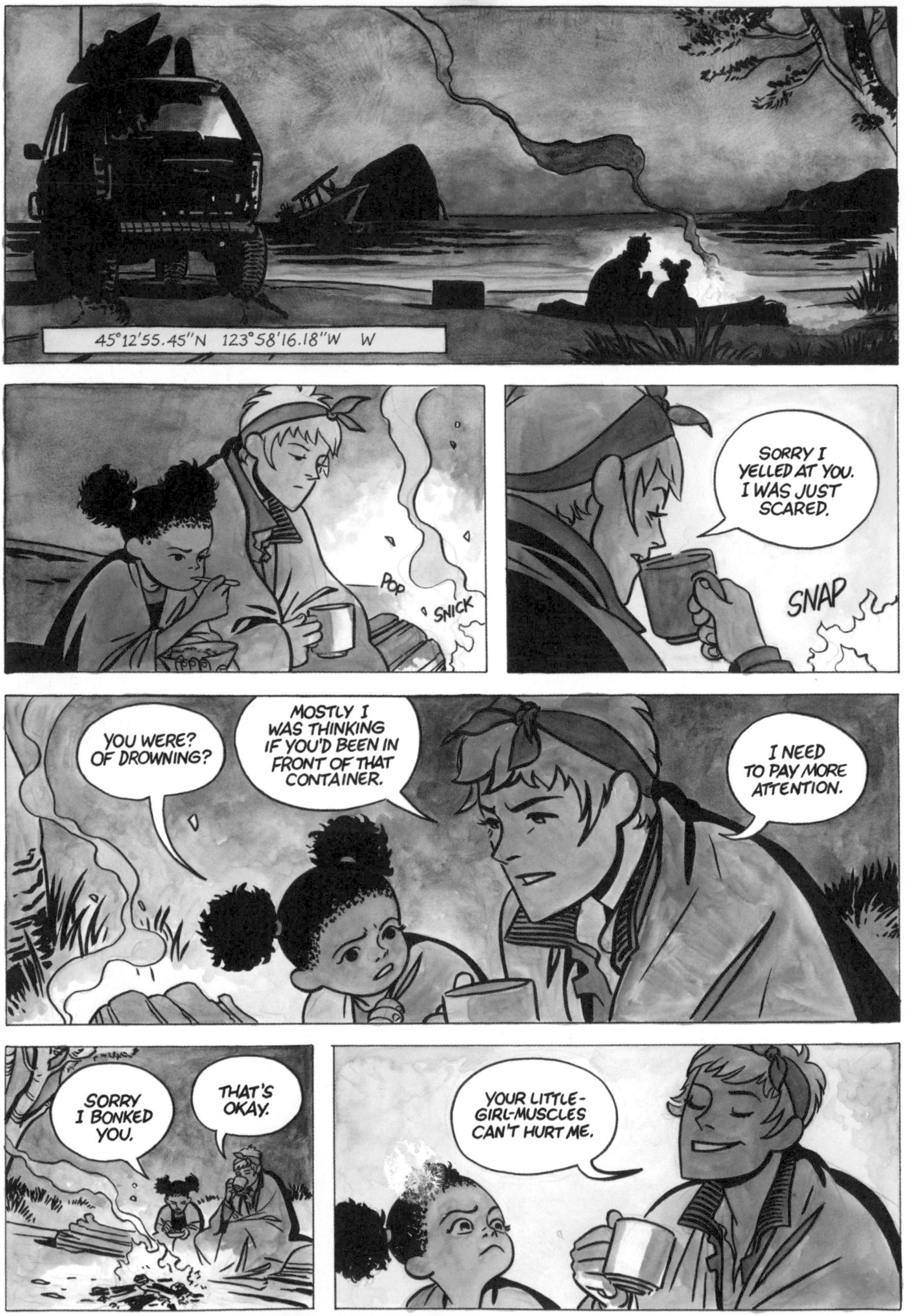
45°12'55.45"N 123°58'16.18"W W
POP
SNICK
SORRY I YELLED AT YOU. I WAS JUST SCARED.
SNAP
YOU WERE? OF DROWNING?
MOSTLY I WAS THINKING IF YOU'D BEEN IN FRONT OF THAT CONTAINER.
I NEED TO PAY MORE ATTENTION.
SORRY I BONKED YOU.
THAT'S OKAY.
YOUR LITTLE-GIRL-MUSCLES CAN'T HURT ME.

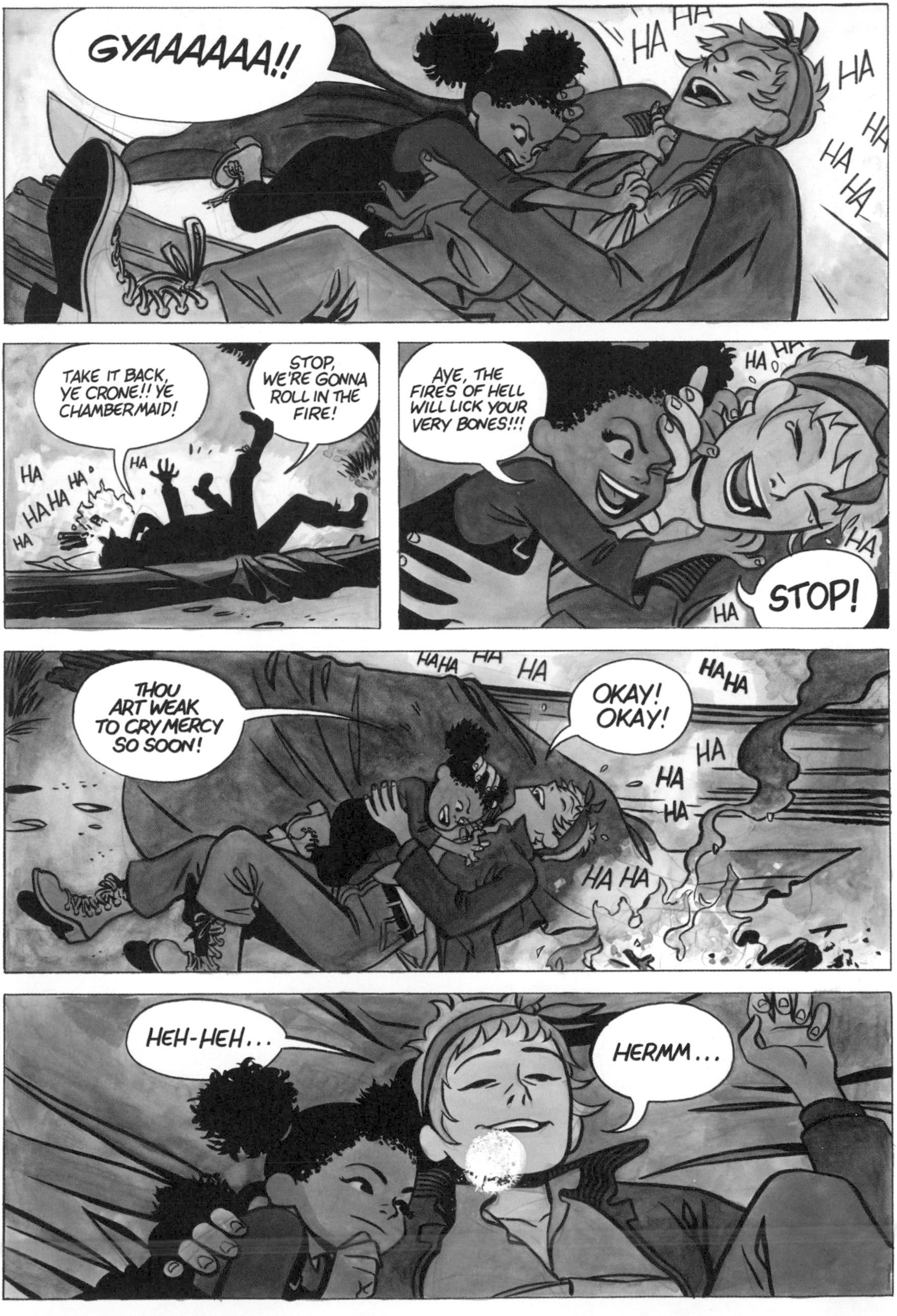
GYAAAAAA!!
HA HA
HA
HA
HA HA
HA
TAKE IT BACK, YE CRONE!! YE CHAMBERMAID!
STOP, WE'RE GONNA ROLL IN THE FIRE!
HA
HA
HA HA
HA
HA
AYE, THE FIRES OF HELL WILL LICK YOUR VERY BONES!!!
HA HA
HA
HA
STOP!
THOU ART WEAK TO CRY MERCY SO SOON!
HAHA HA HA
HA HA
OKAY! OKAY!
HA
HA
HA
HA HA
HEH-HEH...
HERMM...

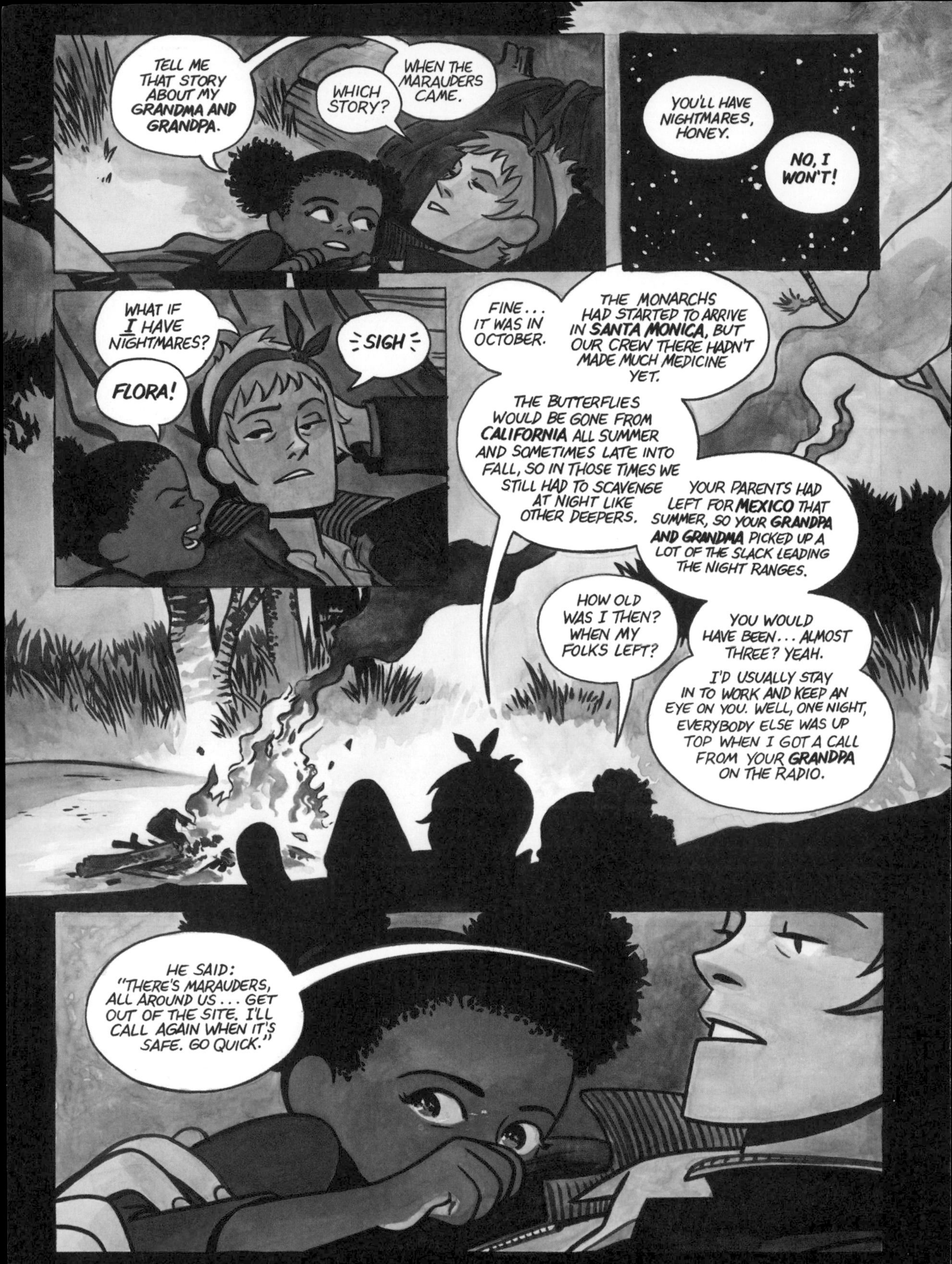

TELL ME THAT STORY ABOUT MY GRANDMA AND GRANDPA.
WHICH STORY?
WHEN THE MARAUDERS CAME.
YOU'LL HAVE NIGHTMARES, HONEY.
NO, I WON'T!
WHAT IF I HAVE NIGHTMARES?
FLORA!
SIGH
FINE . . . IT WAS IN OCTOBER.
THE MONARCHS HAD STARTED TO ARRIVE IN SANTA MONICA, BUT OUR CREW THERE HADN'T MADE MUCH MEDICINE YET.
THE BUTTERFLIES WOULD BE GONE FROM CALIFORNIA ALL SUMMER AND SOMETIMES LATE INTO FALL, SO IN THOSE TIMES WE STILL HAD TO SCAVENGE AT NIGHT LIKE OTHER DEEPERS.
YOUR PARENTS HAD LEFT FOR MEXICO THAT SUMMER, SO YOUR GRANDPA AND GRANDMA PICKED UP A LOT OF THE SLACK LEADING THE NIGHT RANGES.
HOW OLD WAS I THEN? WHEN MY FOLKS LEFT?
YOU WOULD HAVE BEEN . . . ALMOST THREE? YEAH.
I'D USUALLY STAY IN TO WORK AND KEEP AN EYE ON YOU. WELL, ONE NIGHT, EVERYBODY ELSE WAS UP TOP WHEN I GOT A CALL FROM YOUR GRANDPA ON THE RADIO.
HE SAID: "THERE'S MARAUDERS, ALL AROUND US . . . GET OUT OF THE SITE. I'LL CALL AGAIN WHEN IT'S SAFE. GO QUICK."

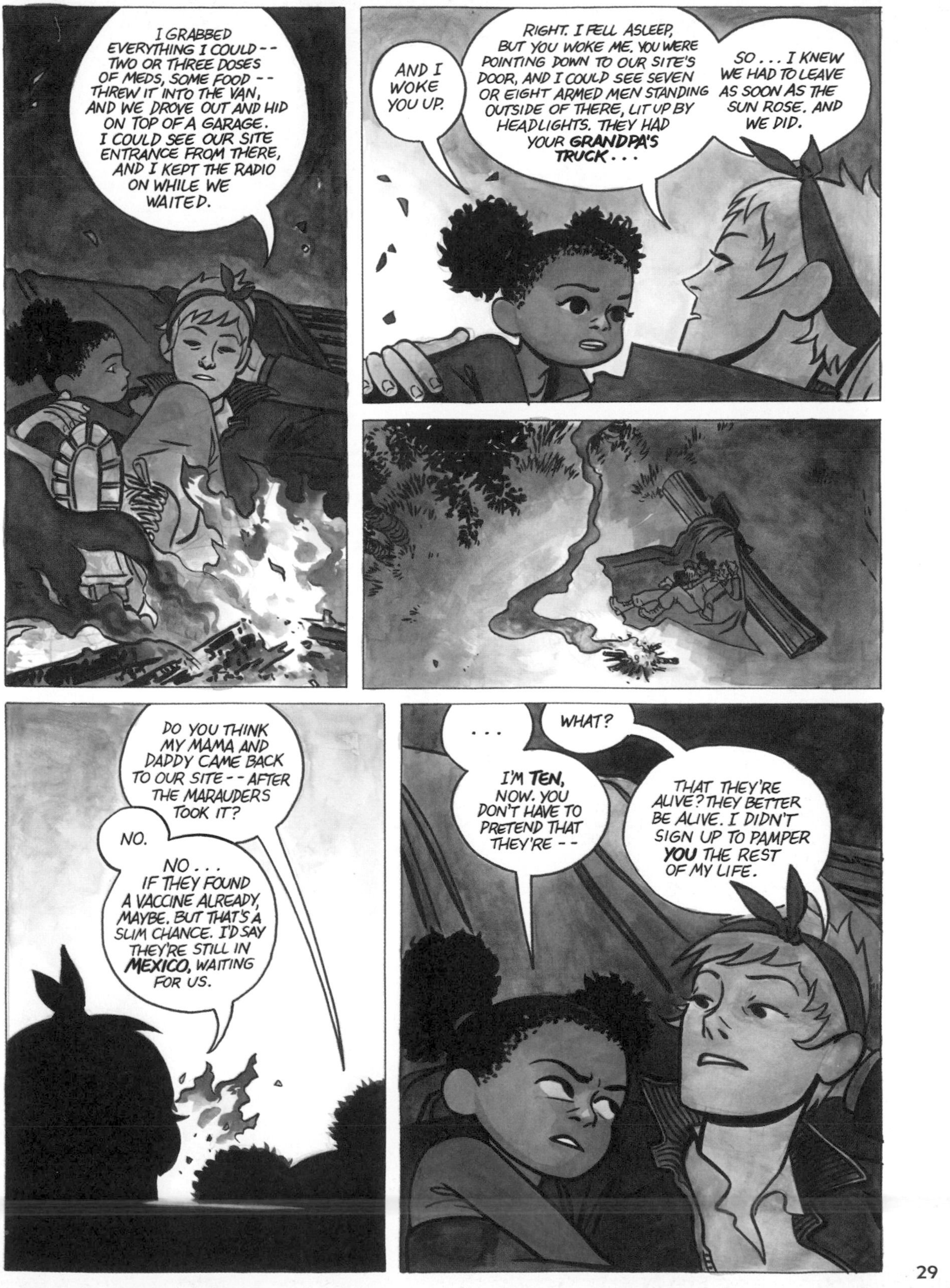
I GRABBED EVERYTHING I COULD - - TWO OR THREE DOSES OF MEDS, SOME FOOD - - THREW IT INTO THE VAN, AND WE DROVE OUT AND HID ON TOP OF A GARAGE. I COULD SEE OUR SITE ENTRANCE FROM THERE, AND I KEPT THE RADIO ON WHILE WE WAITED.
AND I WOKE YOU UP.
RIGHT. I FELL ASLEEP, BUT YOU WOKE ME. YOU WERE POINTING DOWN TO OUR SITE'S DOOR, AND I COULD SEE SEVEN OR EIGHT ARMED MEN STANDING OUTSIDE OF THERE, LIT UP BY HEADLIGHTS. THEY HAD YOUR **GRANDPA'S TRUCK** . . .
SO . . . I KNEW WE HAD TO LEAVE AS SOON AS THE SUN ROSE. AND WE DID.
DO YOU THINK MY MAMA AND DADDY CAME BACK TO OUR SITE - - AFTER THE MARAUDERS TOOK IT?
NO.
NO . . . IF THEY FOUND A VACCINE ALREADY, MAYBE. BUT THAT'S A SLIM CHANCE. I'D SAY THEY'RE STILL IN **MEXICO,** WAITING FOR US.
. . .
WHAT?
I'M **TEN,** NOW. YOU DON'T HAVE TO PRETEND THAT THEY'RE - -
THAT THEY'RE ALIVE? THEY BETTER BE ALIVE. I DIDN'T SIGN UP TO PAMPER **YOU** THE REST OF MY LIFE.

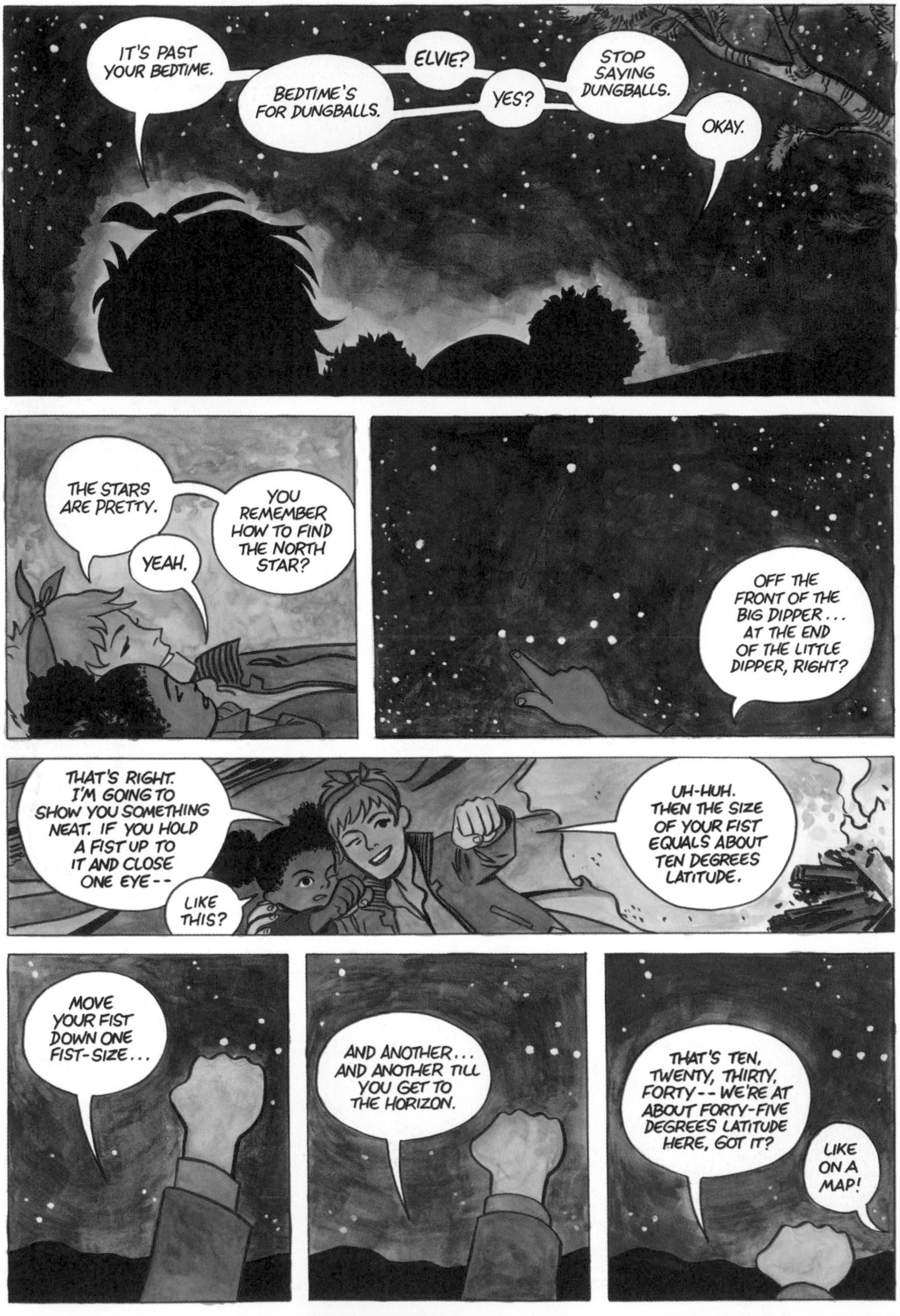
IT'S PAST YOUR BEDTIME.
BEDTIME'S FOR DUNGBALLS.
ELVIE?
YES?
STOP SAYING DUNGBALLS.
OKAY.
THE STARS ARE PRETTY.
YOU REMEMBER HOW TO FIND THE NORTH STAR?
YEAH.
OFF THE FRONT OF THE BIG DIPPER . . . AT THE END OF THE LITTLE DIPPER, RIGHT?
THAT'S RIGHT. I'M GOING TO SHOW YOU SOMETHING NEAT. IF YOU HOLD A FIST UP TO IT AND CLOSE ONE EYE - -
LIKE THIS?
UH-HUH. THEN THE SIZE OF YOUR FIST EQUALS ABOUT TEN DEGREES LATITUDE.
MOVE YOUR FIST DOWN ONE FIST-SIZE . . .
AND ANOTHER . . . AND ANOTHER TILL YOU GET TO THE HORIZON.
THAT'S TEN, TWENTY, THIRTY, FORTY - - WE'RE AT ABOUT FORTY-FIVE DEGREES LATITUDE HERE, GOT IT?
LIKE ON A MAP!

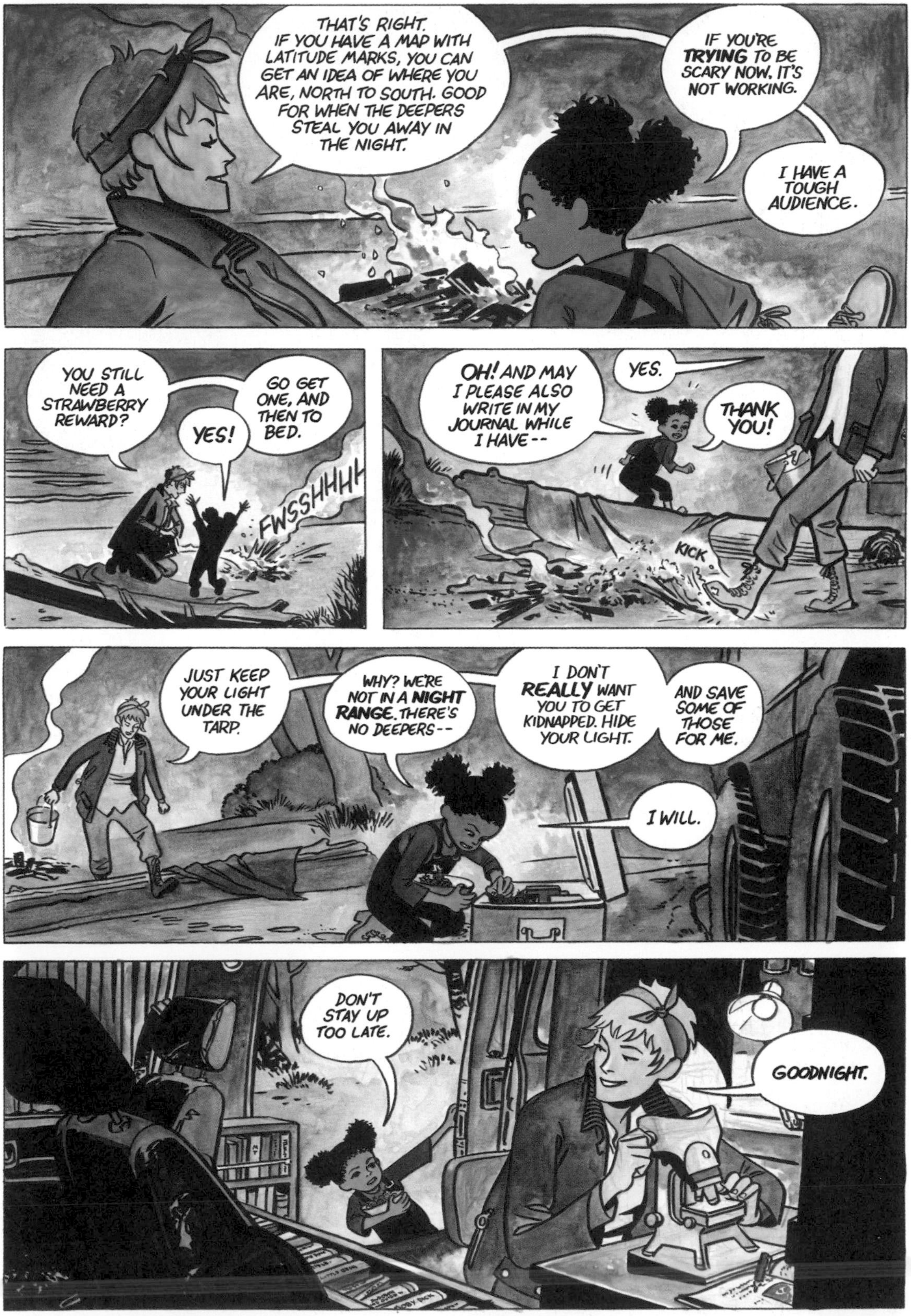
THAT'S RIGHT. IF YOU HAVE A MAP WITH LATITUDE MARKS, YOU CAN GET AN IDEA OF WHERE YOU ARE, NORTH TO SOUTH. GOOD FOR WHEN THE DEEPERS STEAL YOU AWAY IN THE NIGHT.
IF YOU'RE TRYING TO BE SCARY NOW, IT'S NOT WORKING.
I HAVE A TOUGH AUDIENCE.
YOU STILL NEED A STRAWBERRY REWARD?
YES!
GO GET ONE, AND THEN TO BED.
FWSSHHHH
OH! AND MAY I PLEASE ALSO WRITE IN MY JOURNAL WHILE I HAVE--
YES.
THANK YOU!
KICK
JUST KEEP YOUR LIGHT UNDER THE TARP.
WHY? WE'RE NOT IN A NIGHT RANGE. THERE'S NO DEEPERS--
I DON'T REALLY WANT YOU TO GET KIDNAPPED. HIDE YOUR LIGHT.
AND SAVE SOME OF THOSE FOR ME.
I WILL.
DON'T STAY UP TOO LATE.
GOODNIGHT.

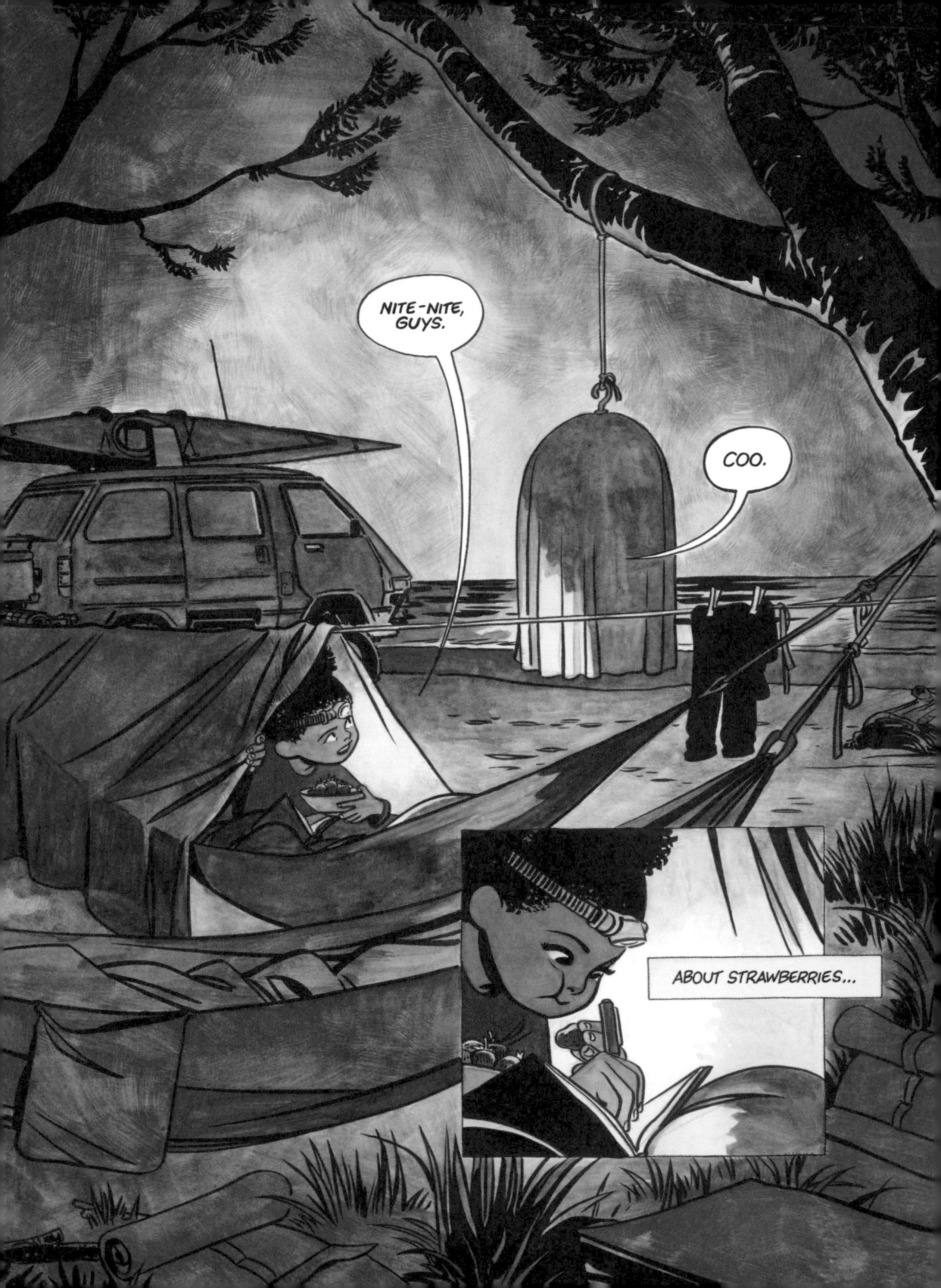
NITE-NITE, GUYS.
COO.
ABOUT STRAWBERRIES...

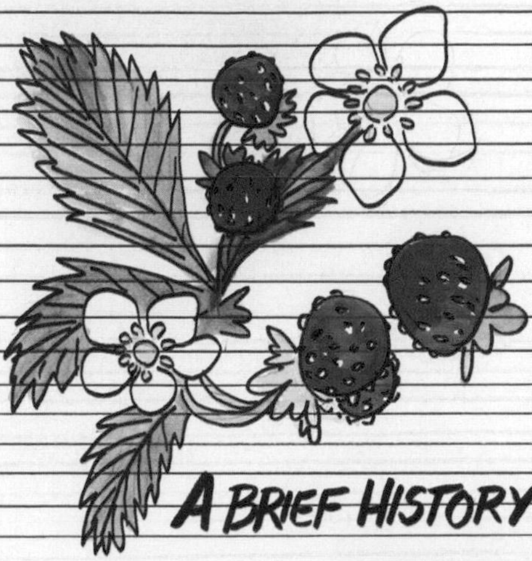

WILD STRAWBERRIES (FRAGARIA VESCA). THESE ARE ACTUALLY A MEMBER OF THE ROSE FAMILY. THEY'RE RIPE MAY-SEPTEMBER AFTER THEY BLOOM WITH LITTLE WHITE-AND-YELLOW FLOWERS. IF YOU SEE THOSE, BERRIES WILL ARRIVE IN A COUPLE WEEKS. THEY DON'T GET BIG, BUT THEY TASTE GOOD.

HABITAT: BY TRAILS, ROADS, HILLSIDES, PATHS, MEADOWS, WOODS, AND CLEARINGS.
RANGE: MOST OF U.S., EXCEPT NEVADA AND SOUTHEAST STATES.

A BRIEF HISTORY OF MONARCH MEDICINE

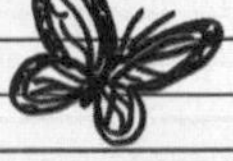

AN EXPOSITORY-STYLE PAPER BY YOU-KNOW-WHO

EVERY ANIMAL HAS A UNIQUE HEARTBEAT, SORT OF LIKE A FINGERPRINT. IF YOU COULD LISTEN CLOSE ENOUGH, YOU COULD TELL ONE PERSON'S HEARTBEAT FROM ANOTHER, AND THAT PERSON FROM ANOTHER MAMMAL, AND MAMMALS FROM EVERYTHING ELSE. IT'S NOT ONLY THE SOUND OF A HEARTBEAT THAT MAKES IT UNIQUE; IT'S THE ELECTRICITY. EVERY HEART IS A UNIQUE ELECTRICAL-POWERED SYSTEM.

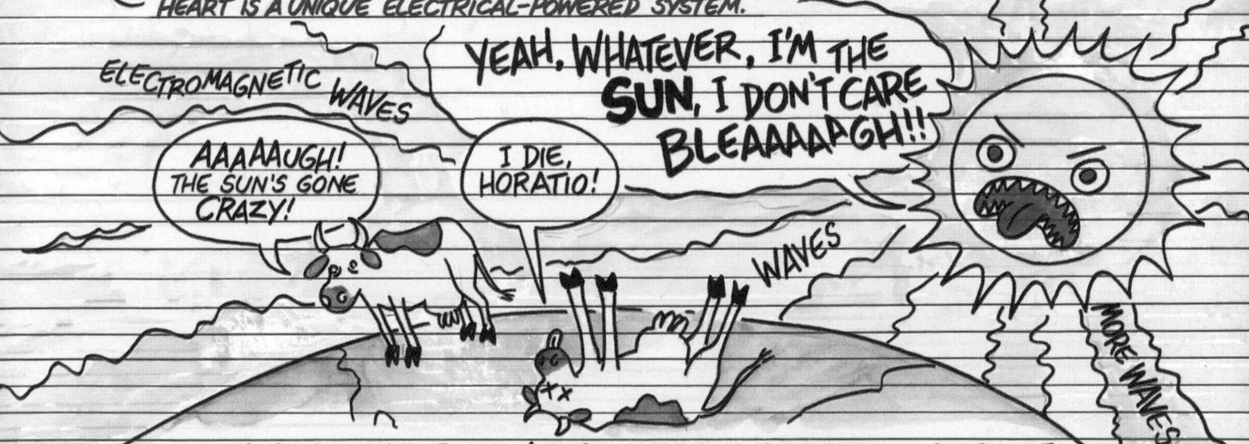
ELECTROMAGNETIC WAVES
YEAH, WHATEVER, I'M THE SUN, I DON'T CARE BLEAAAAAGH!!
AAAAAUGH! THE SUN'S GONE CRAZY!
I DIE, HORATIO!
WAVES
MORE WAVES

IN 2049 THE SUN SHIFT BEGAN, AND THAT MESSED UP THE ELECTRICAL SYSTEM OF EVERY MAMMAL ON THE PLANET. NOT OTHER ANIMALS -- ONLY MAMMALS. UNLESS THEY WERE DEEP UNDERGROUND (30 FT OR MORE), THE SUN'S ALTERED RADIATION KILLED THEM WITHIN A FEW HOURS. THAT'S WHAT YOU CALL **SUN SICKNESS.**

SOME SMALL CRITTERS LIKE BATS CAN HANDLE TWILIGHT, BUT OTHER THAN THAT, MAMMALS ARE ALMOST ALL EXTINCT. A VERY, VERY SMALL NUMBER OF PEOPLE (LIKE **FLORA'S** PARENTS AND MY GRANDPA AND GRANDMA) WERE IN DEEP PLACES WHEN THE SUN SHIFT STARTED. THEY SURVIVED LONG ENOUGH TO LEARN WHAT WAS HAPPENING AND STAY UNDERGROUND DURING THE DAY. THEY BECAME THE FIRST **"DEEPERS."**

AND BECAUSE I'M ALREADY BORED WITH WRITING AN EXPOSITORY PAPER, HERE'S THE REST, BUT TOLD IN **COMICS** . . .

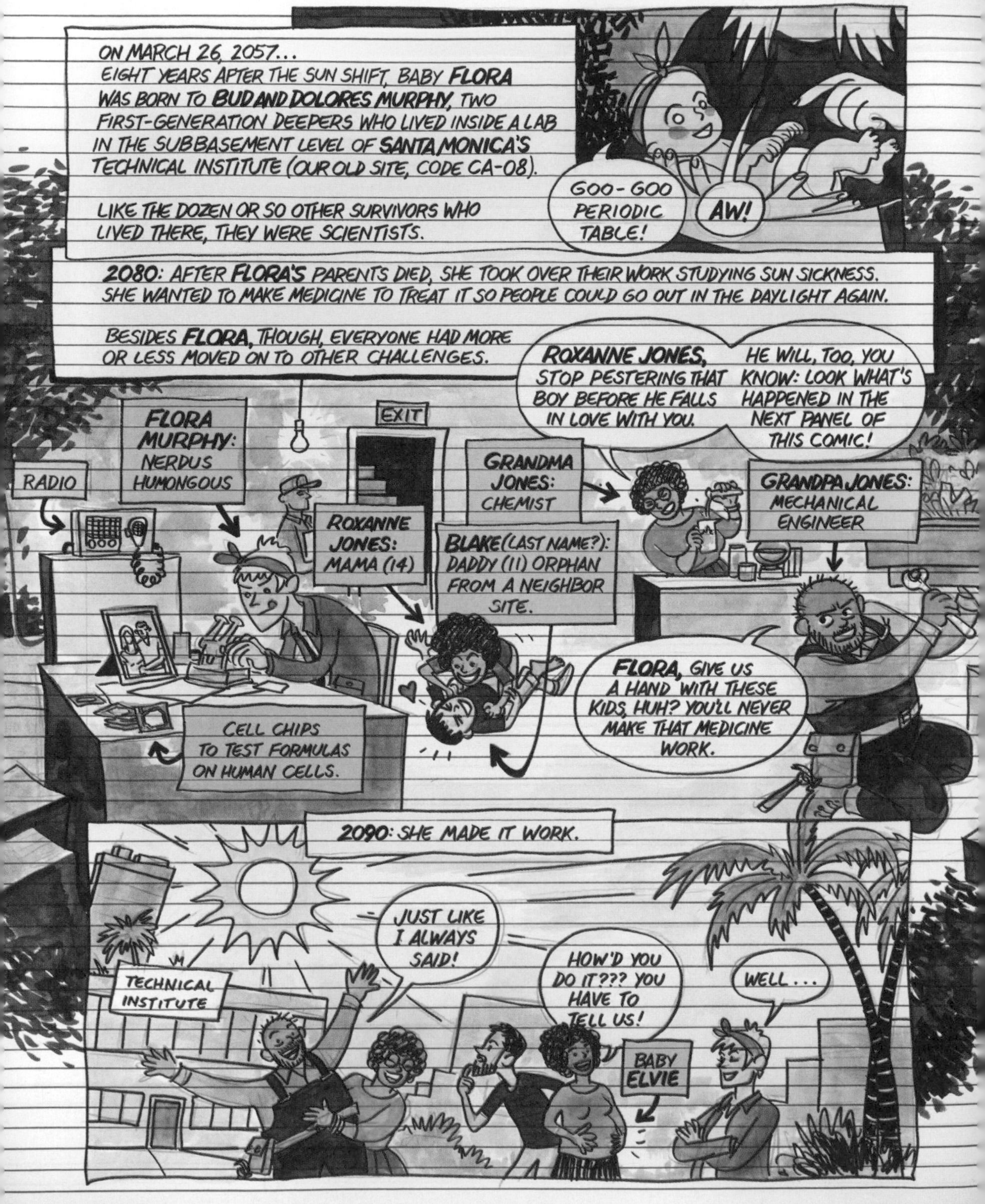

ON MARCH 26, 2057...
EIGHT YEARS AFTER THE SUN SHIFT, BABY FLORA WAS BORN TO BUD AND DOLORES MURPHY, TWO FIRST-GENERATION DEEPERS WHO LIVED INSIDE A LAB IN THE SUBBASEMENT LEVEL OF SANTA MONICA'S TECHNICAL INSTITUTE (OUR OLD SITE, CODE CA-08).
LIKE THE DOZEN OR SO OTHER SURVIVORS WHO LIVED THERE, THEY WERE SCIENTISTS.
GOO-GOO PERIODIC TABLE!
AW!
2080: AFTER FLORA'S PARENTS DIED, SHE TOOK OVER THEIR WORK STUDYING SUN SICKNESS. SHE WANTED TO MAKE MEDICINE TO TREAT IT SO PEOPLE COULD GO OUT IN THE DAYLIGHT AGAIN.
BESIDES FLORA, THOUGH, EVERYONE HAD MORE OR LESS MOVED ON TO OTHER CHALLENGES.
ROXANNE JONES, STOP PESTERING THAT BOY BEFORE HE FALLS IN LOVE WITH YOU.
HE WILL, TOO, YOU KNOW: LOOK WHAT'S HAPPENED IN THE NEXT PANEL OF THIS COMIC!
EXIT
FLORA MURPHY: NERDUS HUMONGOUS
RADIO
GRANDMA JONES: CHEMIST
GRANDPA JONES: MECHANICAL ENGINEER
ROXANNE JONES: MAMA (14)
BLAKE (LAST NAME?): DADDY (11) ORPHAN FROM A NEIGHBOR SITE.
FLORA, GIVE US A HAND WITH THESE KIDS, HUH? YOU'LL NEVER MAKE THAT MEDICINE WORK.
CELL CHIPS TO TEST FORMULAS ON HUMAN CELLS.
2090: SHE MADE IT WORK.
JUST LIKE I ALWAYS SAID!
HOW'D YOU DO IT??? YOU HAVE TO TELL US!
WELL...
TECHNICAL INSTITUTE
BABY ELVIE

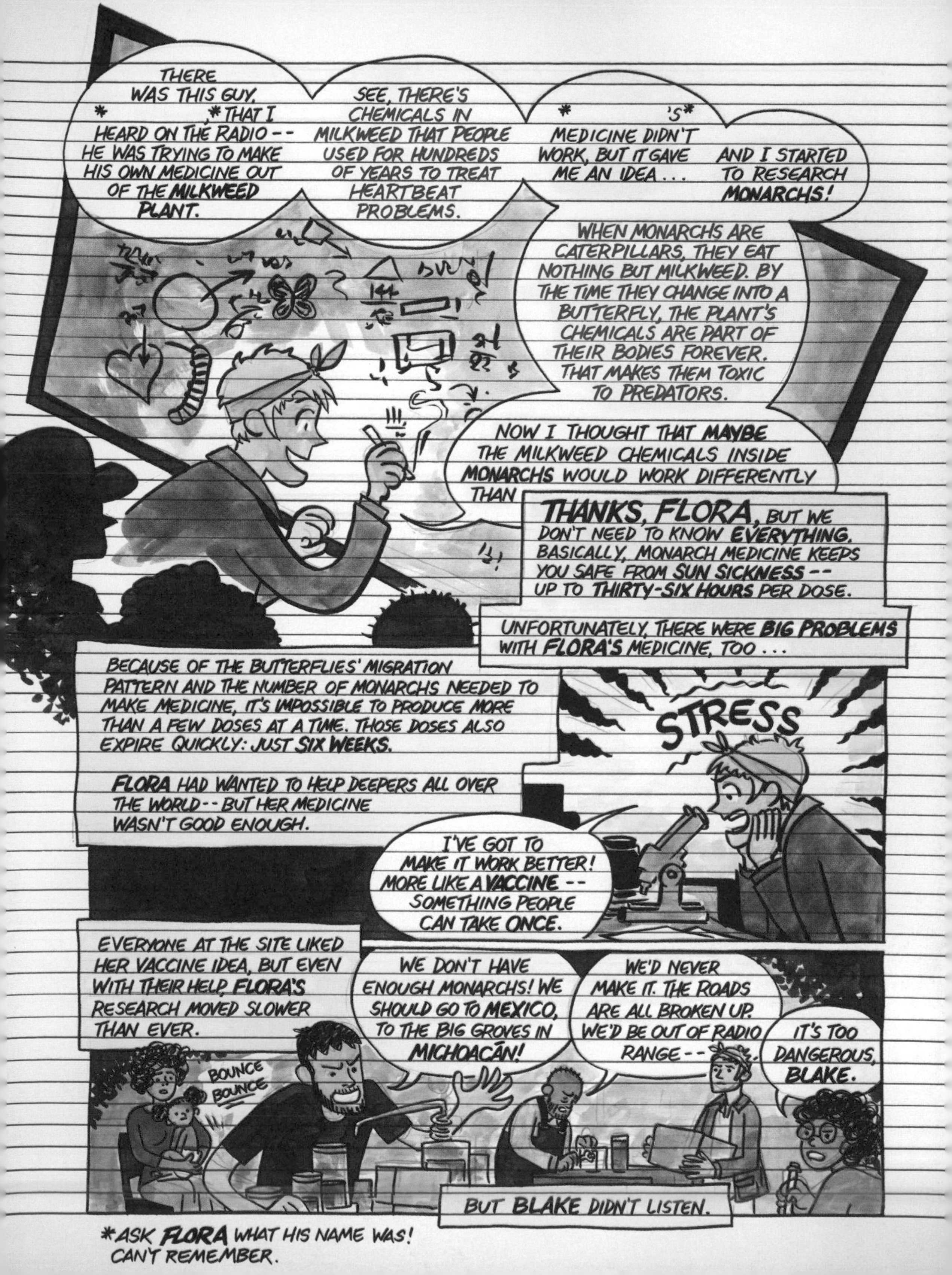

THERE WAS THIS GUY, * ,* THAT I HEARD ON THE RADIO -- HE WAS TRYING TO MAKE HIS OWN MEDICINE OUT OF THE MILKWEED PLANT.
SEE, THERE'S CHEMICALS IN MILKWEED THAT PEOPLE USED FOR HUNDREDS OF YEARS TO TREAT HEARTBEAT PROBLEMS.
* 'S* MEDICINE DIDN'T WORK, BUT IT GAVE ME AN IDEA . . .
AND I STARTED TO RESEARCH MONARCHS!
WHEN MONARCHS ARE CATERPILLARS, THEY EAT NOTHING BUT MILKWEED. BY THE TIME THEY CHANGE INTO A BUTTERFLY, THE PLANT'S CHEMICALS ARE PART OF THEIR BODIES FOREVER. THAT MAKES THEM TOXIC TO PREDATORS.
NOW I THOUGHT THAT MAYBE THE MILKWEED CHEMICALS INSIDE MONARCHS WOULD WORK DIFFERENTLY THAN
THANKS, FLORA, BUT WE DON'T NEED TO KNOW EVERYTHING. BASICALLY, MONARCH MEDICINE KEEPS YOU SAFE FROM SUN SICKNESS -- UP TO THIRTY-SIX HOURS PER DOSE.
UNFORTUNATELY, THERE WERE BIG PROBLEMS WITH FLORA'S MEDICINE, TOO . . .
BECAUSE OF THE BUTTERFLIES' MIGRATION PATTERN AND THE NUMBER OF MONARCHS NEEDED TO MAKE MEDICINE, IT'S IMPOSSIBLE TO PRODUCE MORE THAN A FEW DOSES AT A TIME. THOSE DOSES ALSO EXPIRE QUICKLY: JUST SIX WEEKS.
FLORA HAD WANTED TO HELP DEEPERS ALL OVER THE WORLD -- BUT HER MEDICINE WASN'T GOOD ENOUGH.
STRESS
I'VE GOT TO MAKE IT WORK BETTER! MORE LIKE A VACCINE -- SOMETHING PEOPLE CAN TAKE ONCE.
EVERYONE AT THE SITE LIKED HER VACCINE IDEA, BUT EVEN WITH THEIR HELP, FLORA'S RESEARCH MOVED SLOWER THAN EVER.
BOUNCE BOUNCE
WE DON'T HAVE ENOUGH MONARCHS! WE SHOULD GO TO MEXICO, TO THE BIG GROVES IN MICHOACÁN!
WE'D NEVER MAKE IT. THE ROADS ARE ALL BROKEN UP. WE'D BE OUT OF RADIO RANGE --
IT'S TOO DANGEROUS, BLAKE.
BUT BLAKE DIDN'T LISTEN.

*ASK FLORA WHAT HIS NAME WAS! CAN'T REMEMBER.

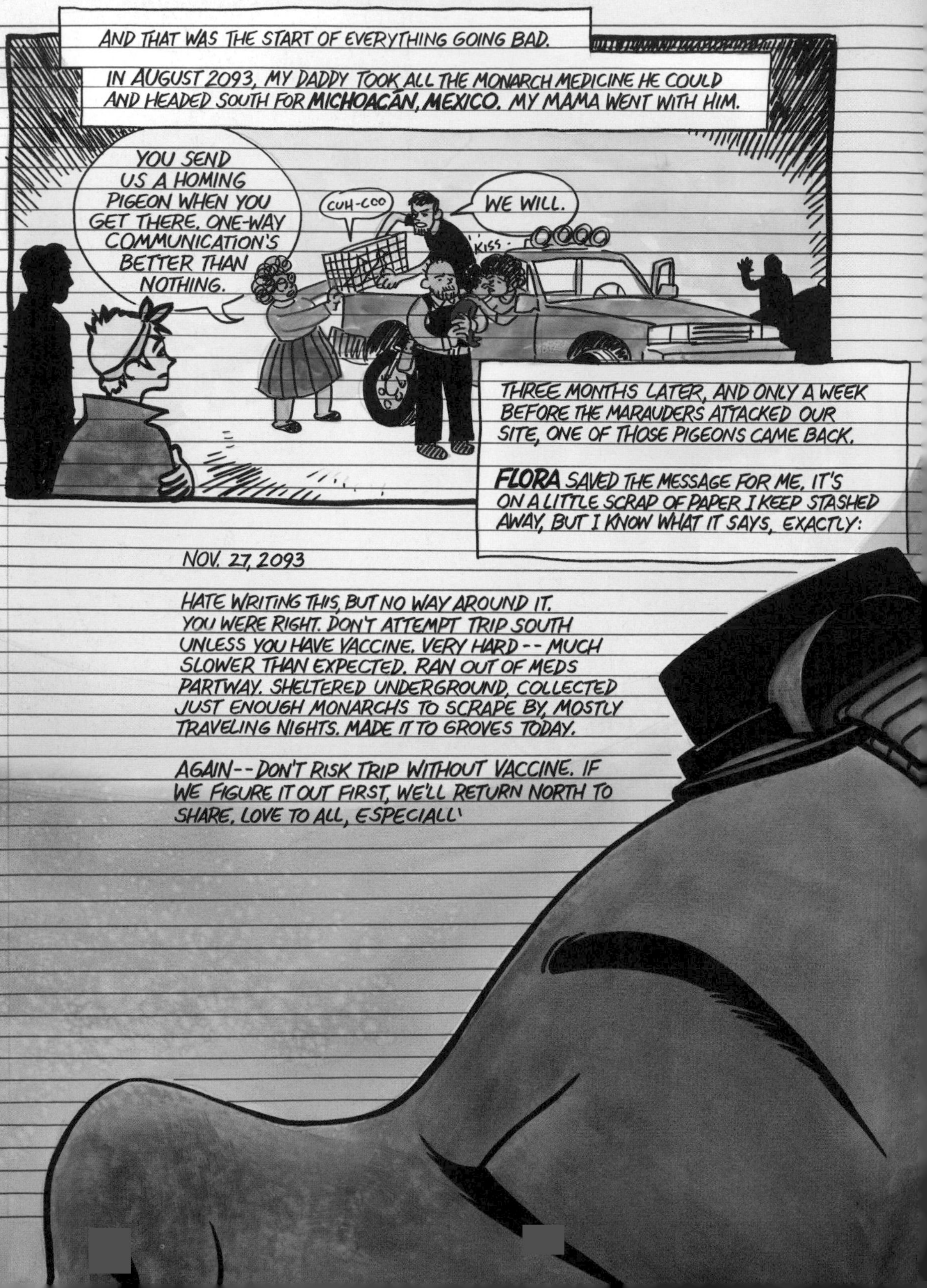
AND THAT WAS THE START OF EVERYTHING GOING BAD.
IN AUGUST 2093, MY DADDY TOOK ALL THE MONARCH MEDICINE HE COULD AND HEADED SOUTH FOR MICHOACÁN, MEXICO. MY MAMA WENT WITH HIM.
YOU SEND US A HOMING PIGEON WHEN YOU GET THERE. ONE-WAY COMMUNICATION'S BETTER THAN NOTHING.
CUH-COO
WE WILL.
KISS
THREE MONTHS LATER, AND ONLY A WEEK BEFORE THE MARAUDERS ATTACKED OUR SITE, ONE OF THOSE PIGEONS CAME BACK.
FLORA SAVED THE MESSAGE FOR ME. IT'S ON A LITTLE SCRAP OF PAPER I KEEP STASHED AWAY, BUT I KNOW WHAT IT SAYS, EXACTLY:
NOV. 27, 2093
HATE WRITING THIS, BUT NO WAY AROUND IT. YOU WERE RIGHT. DON'T ATTEMPT TRIP SOUTH UNLESS YOU HAVE VACCINE. VERY HARD -- MUCH SLOWER THAN EXPECTED. RAN OUT OF MEDS PARTWAY. SHELTERED UNDERGROUND, COLLECTED JUST ENOUGH MONARCHS TO SCRAPE BY, MOSTLY TRAVELING NIGHTS. MADE IT TO GROVES TODAY.
AGAIN -- DON'T RISK TRIP WITHOUT VACCINE. IF WE FIGURE IT OUT FIRST, WE'LL RETURN NORTH TO SHARE. LOVE TO ALL, ESPECIALL

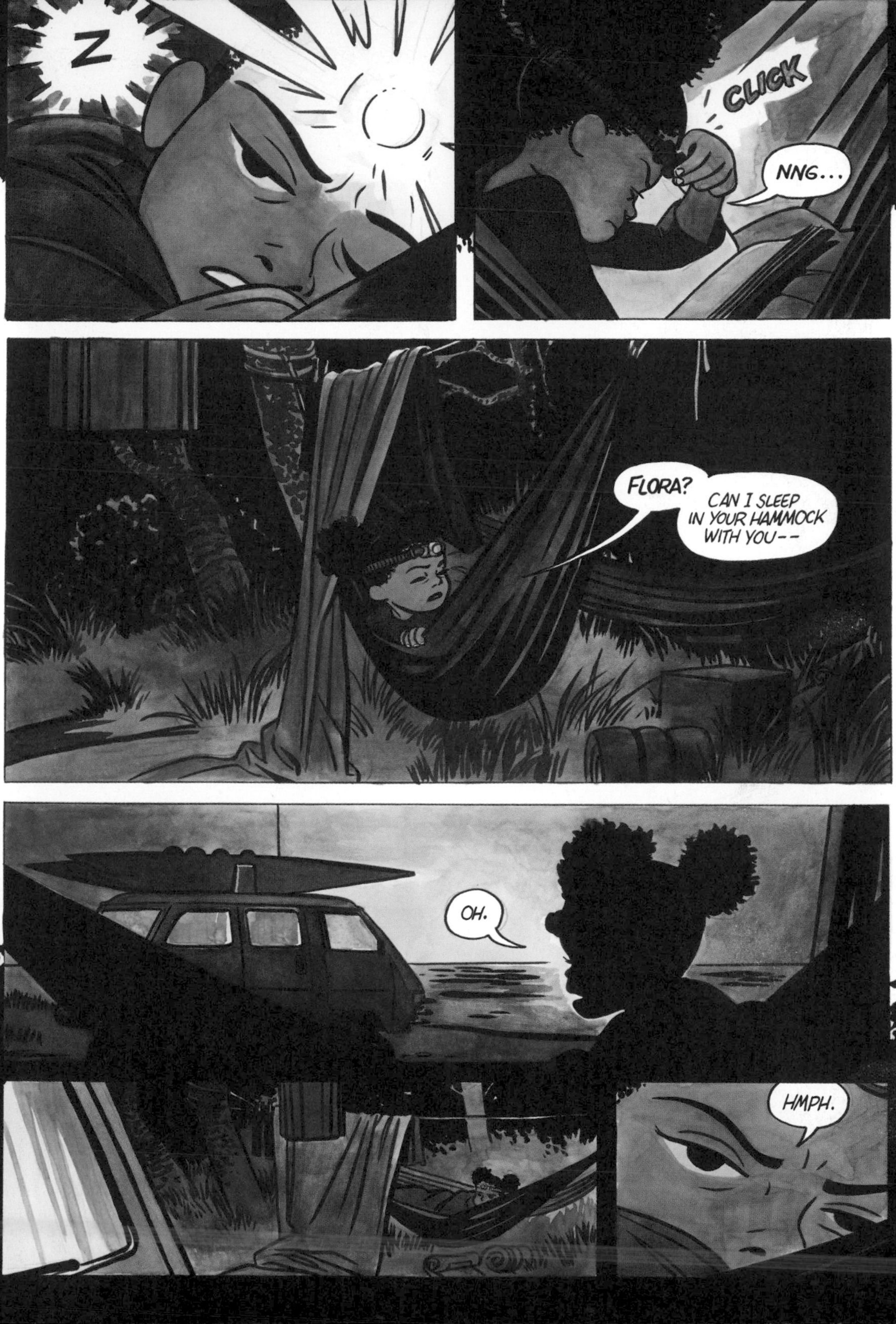
Z
CLICK
NNG...
FLORA?
CAN I SLEEP IN YOUR HAMMOCK WITH YOU--
OH.
HMPH.

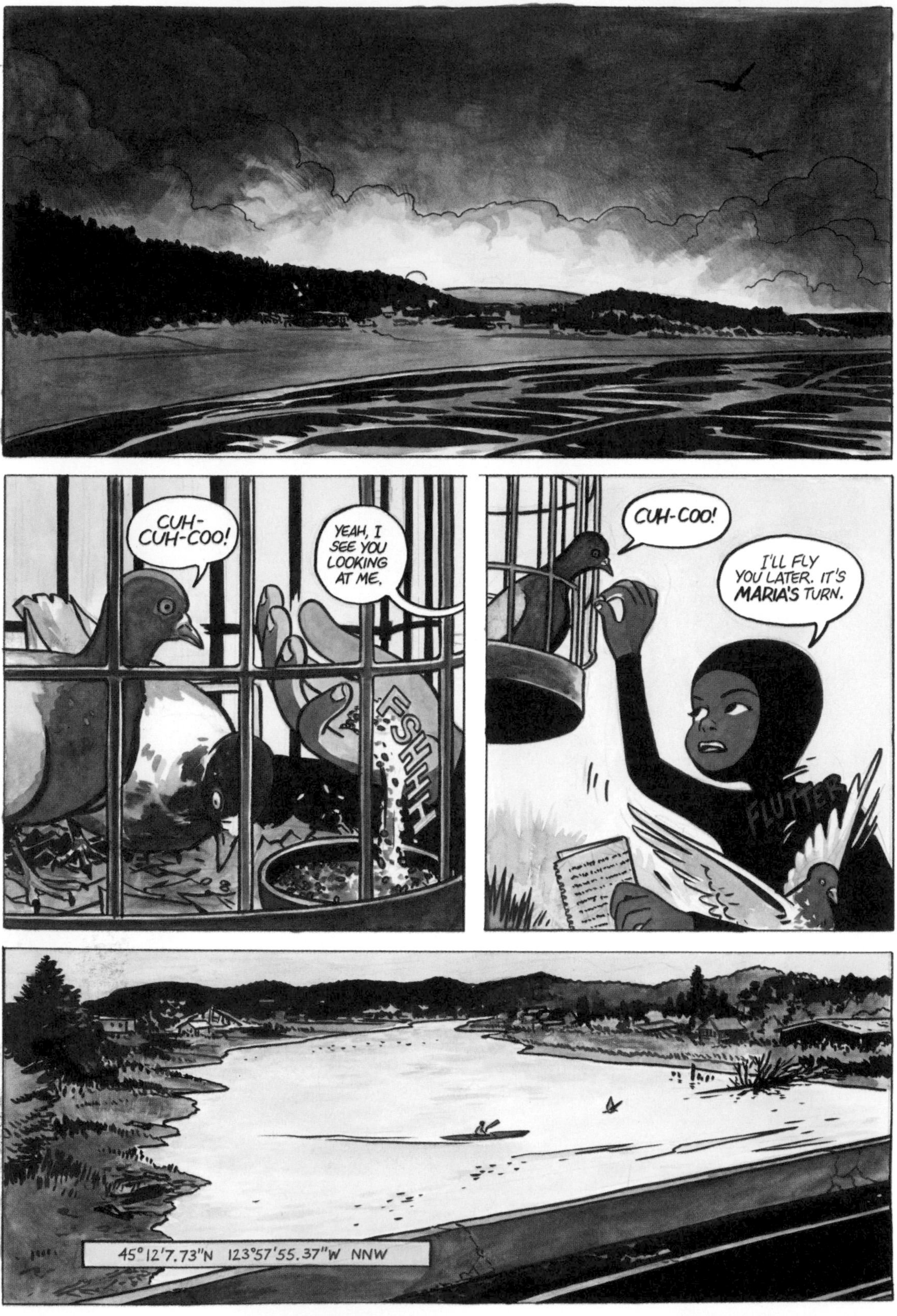
CUH-CUH-COO!
YEAH, I SEE YOU LOOKING AT ME.
FSHHH
CUH-COO!
I'LL FLY YOU LATER. IT'S **MARIA'S** TURN.
FLUTTER
45° 12'7.73"N 123°57'55.37"W NNW

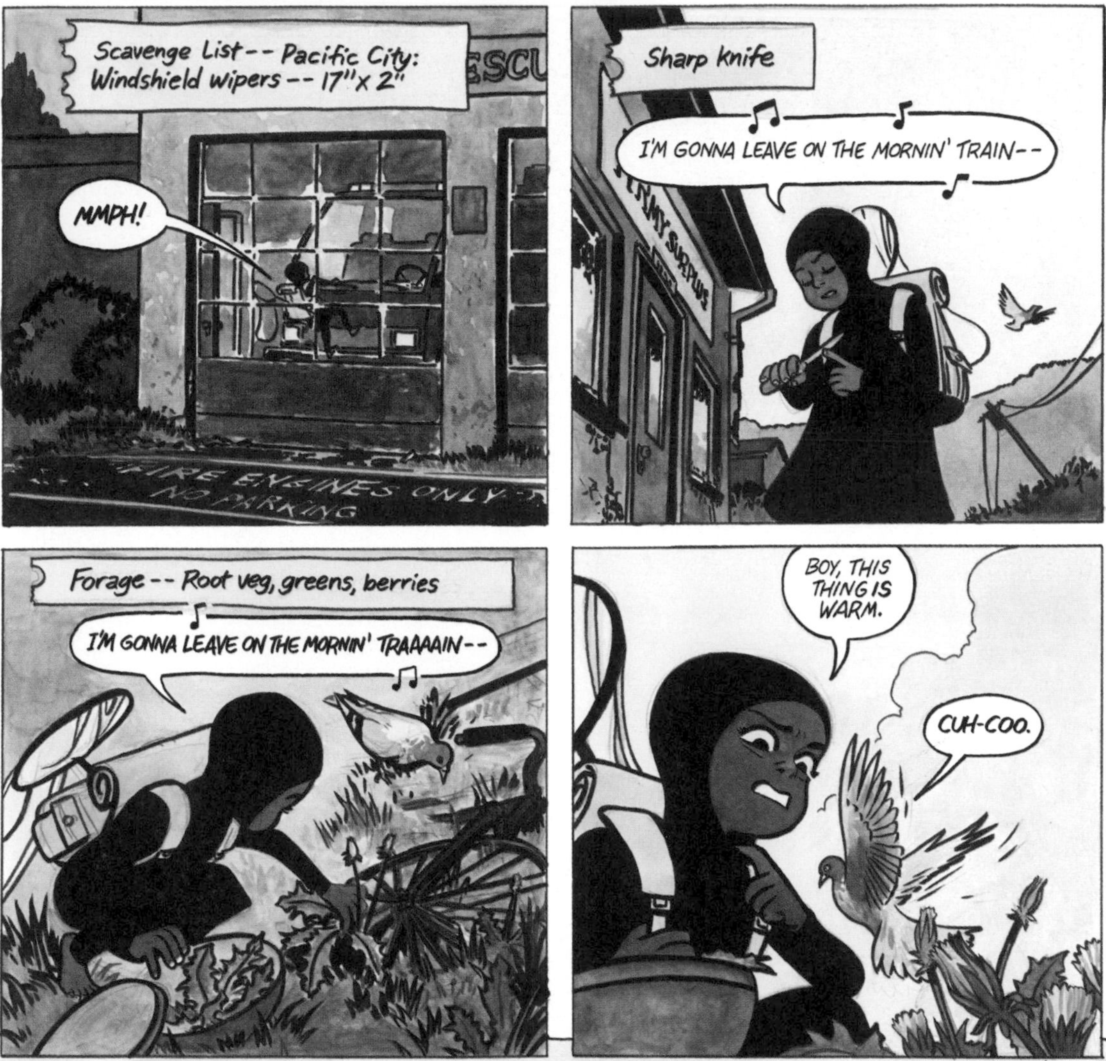
Scavenge List -- Pacific City: Windshield wipers -- 17" x 2"
ESCU
MMPH!
FIRE ENGINES ONLY
NO PARKING
Sharp knife
I'M GONNA LEAVE ON THE MORNIN' TRAIN--
ARMY SURPLUS
Forage -- Root veg, greens, berries
I'M GONNA LEAVE ON THE MORNIN' TRAAAAIN--
BOY, THIS THING IS WARM.
CUH-COO.

When foraging, if you can't remember a plant exactly, or are unsure in any way, PLEASE ask me before you put something in your mouth/on your body. Remember: Go SLOW, study CLOSELY, and be CERTAIN.

Cattail: One of the best. Many uses. Harvest pollen in midsummer and add to bread, soups, etc. Dry the roots and pound to flour (high in carbs and protein). Young shoots -- boil/steam/stir-fry. Use "jelly" between young leaves as a topical antiseptic, or take by mouth to relieve pain and inflammation. "Cigar heads" excellent as fire starter, even after rain. The wool inside can also be used for insulation (alternative to duck/goose down).

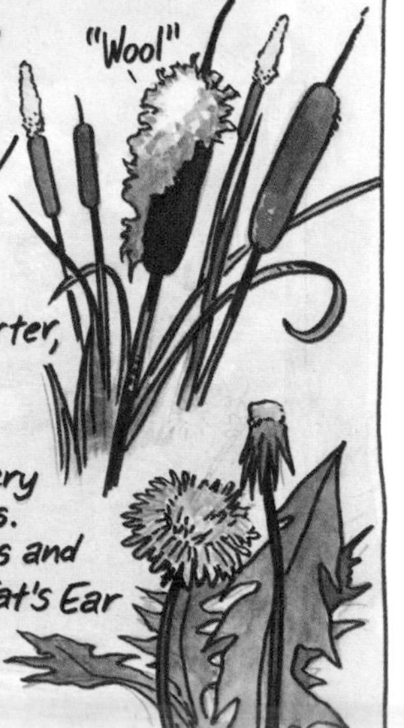
"Wool"
Pollen

Dandelion: Entire plant -- stems, flowers, roots, leaves -- edible and very nutritious. Younger leaves better. Blanche/sauté to reduce bitterness. Less bitter before it flowers. True dandelion has nonbranching stems and pointed, smooth, serrated leaves. Many lookalike plants including Cat's Ear species (Hypochoeri spp) and Hawkweed species (Hieracium spp). Lookalikes are also safe for edible/medicinal use.

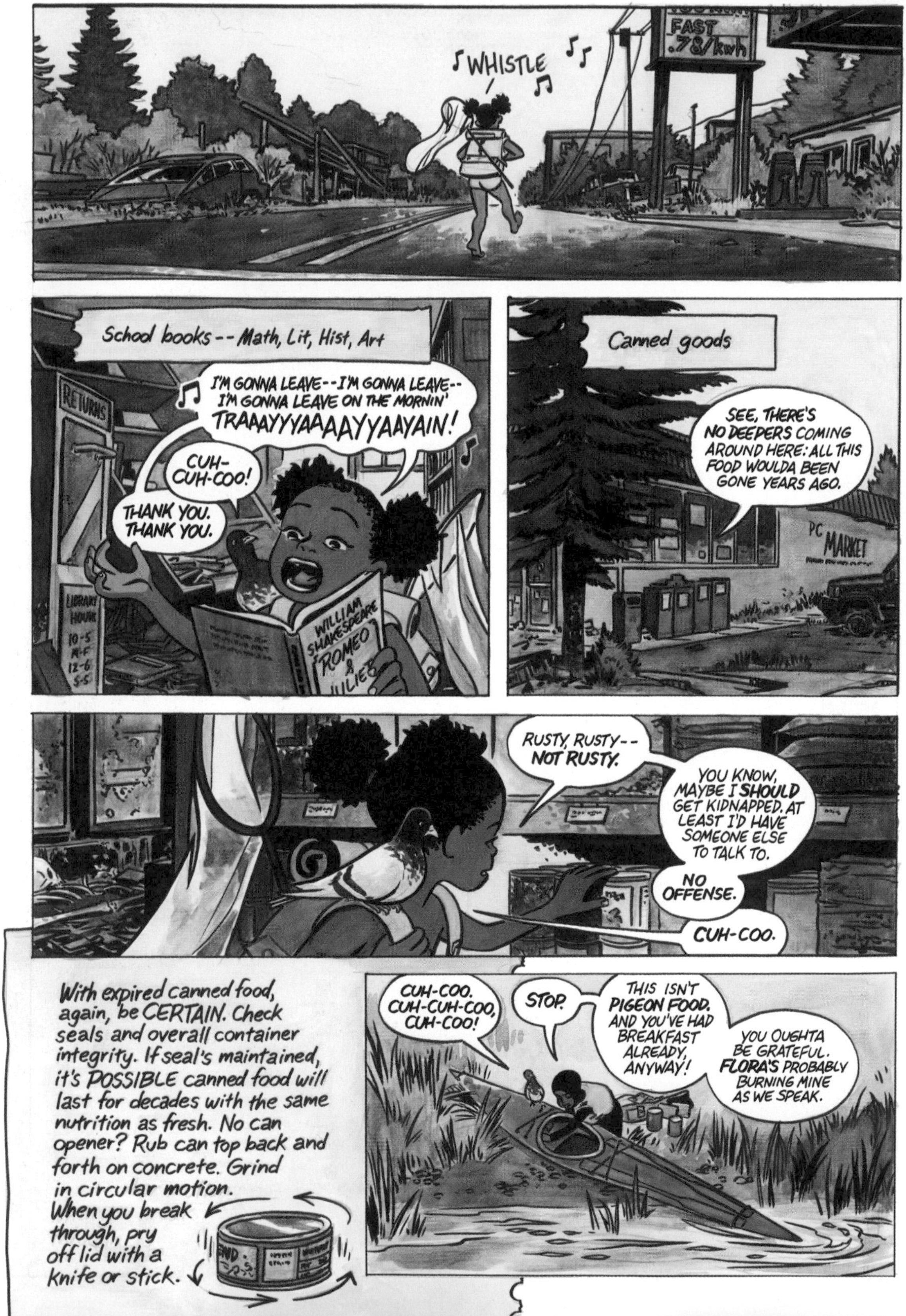
FAST
.78/kwh
WHISTLE
School books -- Math, Lit, Hist, Art
RETURNS
LIBRARY HOURS 10-5 M-F 12-6 S-S
I'M GONNA LEAVE--I'M GONNA LEAVE--I'M GONNA LEAVE ON THE MORNIN' TRAAAYYYAAAAYYAAYAIN!
CUH-CUH-COO!
THANK YOU. THANK YOU.
WILLIAM SHAKESPEARE ROMEO &
Canned goods
SEE, THERE'S NO DEEPERS COMING AROUND HERE: ALL THIS FOOD WOULDA BEEN GONE YEARS AGO.
PC MARKET
RUSTY, RUSTY-- NOT RUSTY.
YOU KNOW, MAYBE I SHOULD GET KIDNAPPED. AT LEAST I'D HAVE SOMEONE ELSE TO TALK TO.
NO OFFENSE.
CUH-COO.
With expired canned food, again, be CERTAIN. Check seals and overall container integrity. If seal's maintained, it's POSSIBLE canned food will last for decades with the same nutrition as fresh. No can opener? Rub can top back and forth on concrete. Grind in circular motion. When you break through, pry off lid with a knife or stick.
CUH-COO. CUH-CUH-COO, CUH-COO!
STOP.
THIS ISN'T PIGEON FOOD. AND YOU'VE HAD BREAKFAST ALREADY, ANYWAY!
YOU OUGHTA BE GRATEFUL. FLORA'S PROBABLY BURNING MINE AS WE SPEAK.

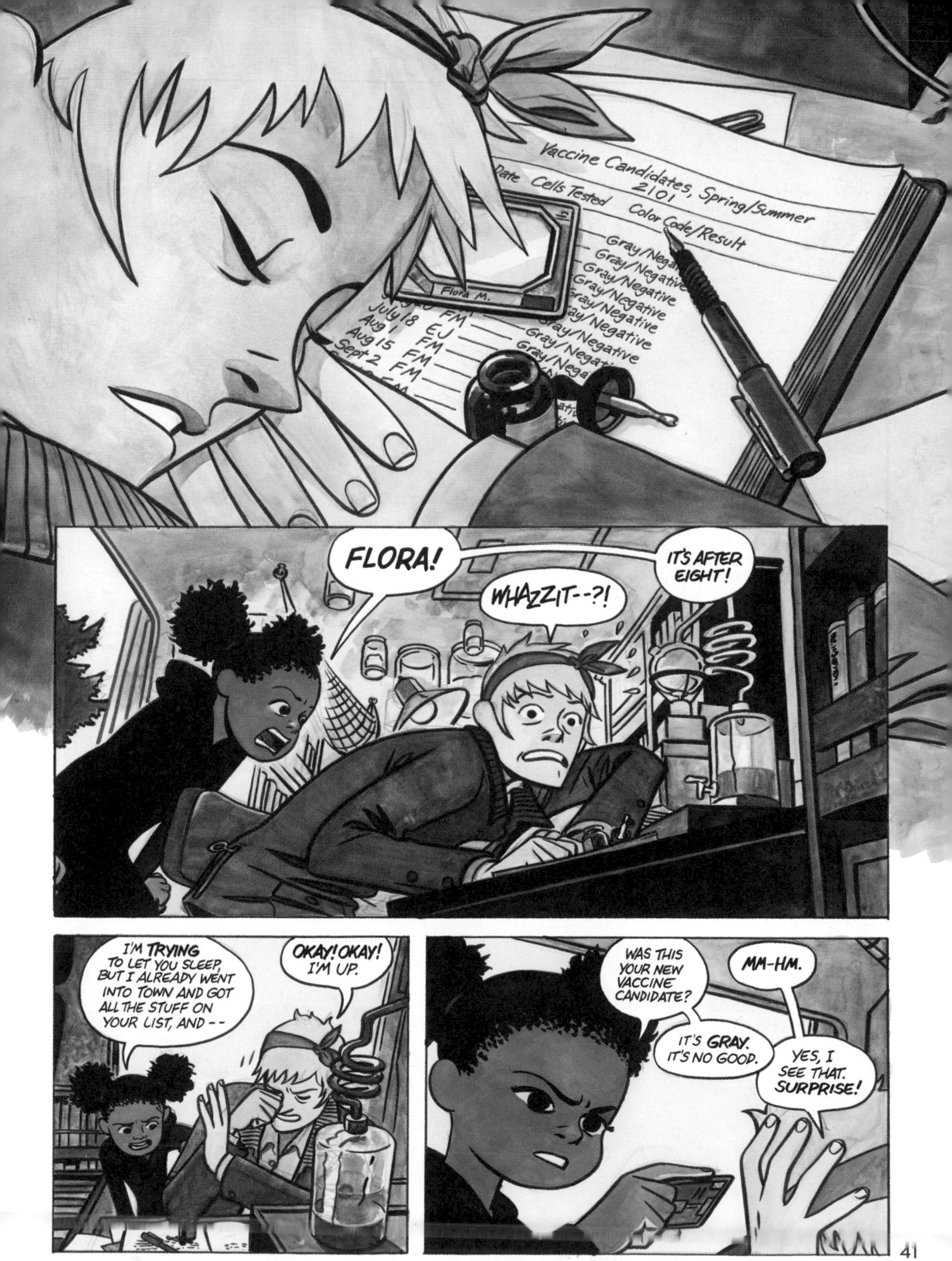
Vaccine Candidates, Spring/Summer 2101
Date Cells Tested Color Code/Result
July 18 FM Gray/Negative
Aug 1 EJ Gray/Negative
Aug 15 FM Gray/Negative
Sept 2 FM Gray/Negative
Flora M.
FLORA!
IT'S AFTER EIGHT!
WHAZZIT--?!
I'M TRYING TO LET YOU SLEEP, BUT I ALREADY WENT INTO TOWN AND GOT ALL THE STUFF ON YOUR LIST, AND --
OKAY! OKAY! I'M UP.
WAS THIS YOUR NEW VACCINE CANDIDATE?
MM-HM.
IT'S GRAY. IT'S NO GOOD.
YES, I SEE THAT. SURPRISE!

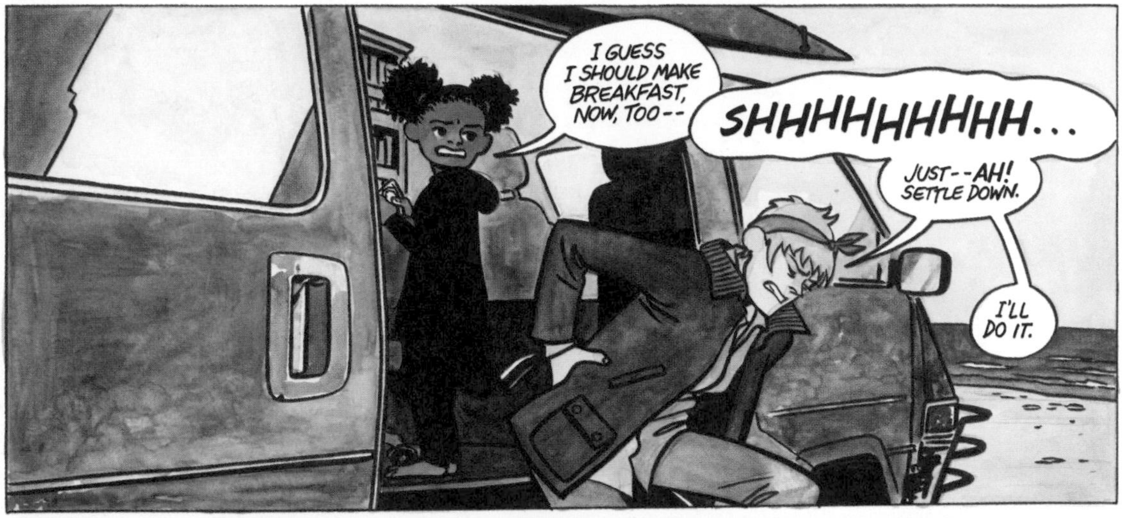
I GUESS I SHOULD MAKE BREAKFAST, NOW, TOO--
SHHHHHHHHH...
JUST--AH! SETTLE DOWN.
I'LL DO IT.

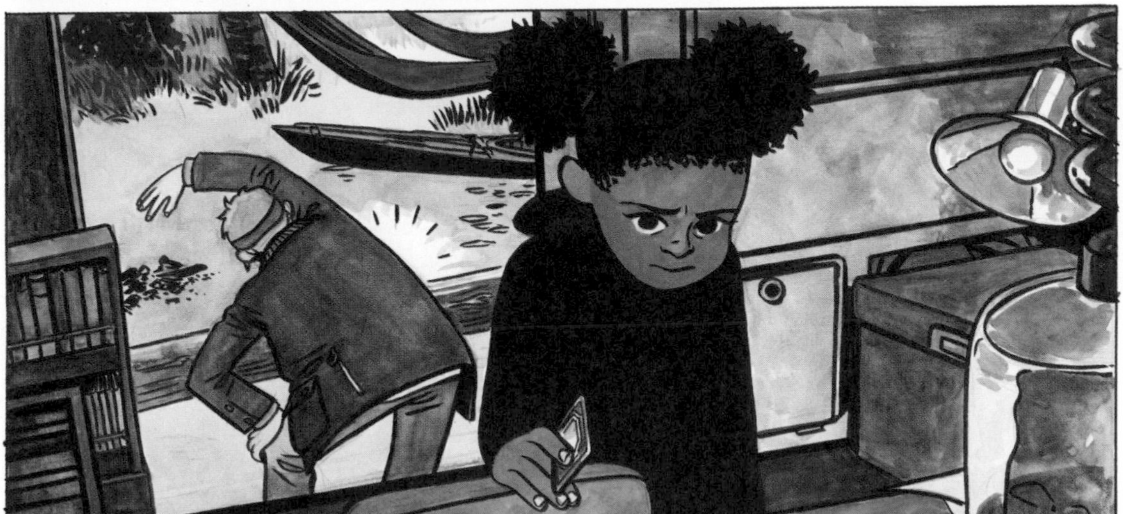

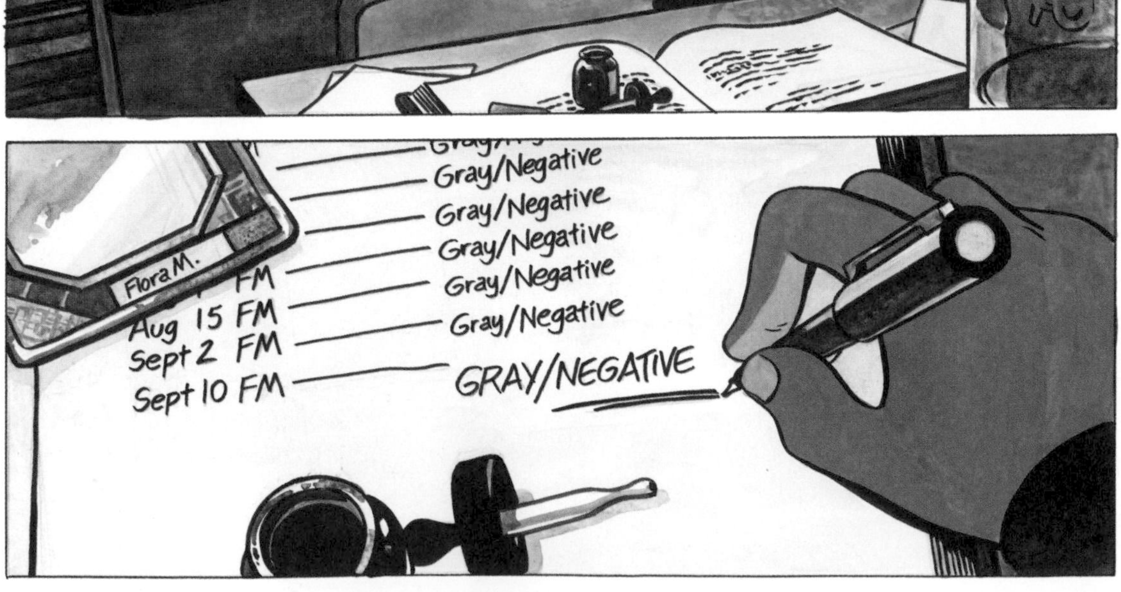
Gray/Negative
Gray/Negative
Gray/Negative
Flora M.
FM
Gray/Negative
Aug 15 FM
Gray/Negative
Sept 2 FM
Sept 10 FM
GRAY/NEGATIVE

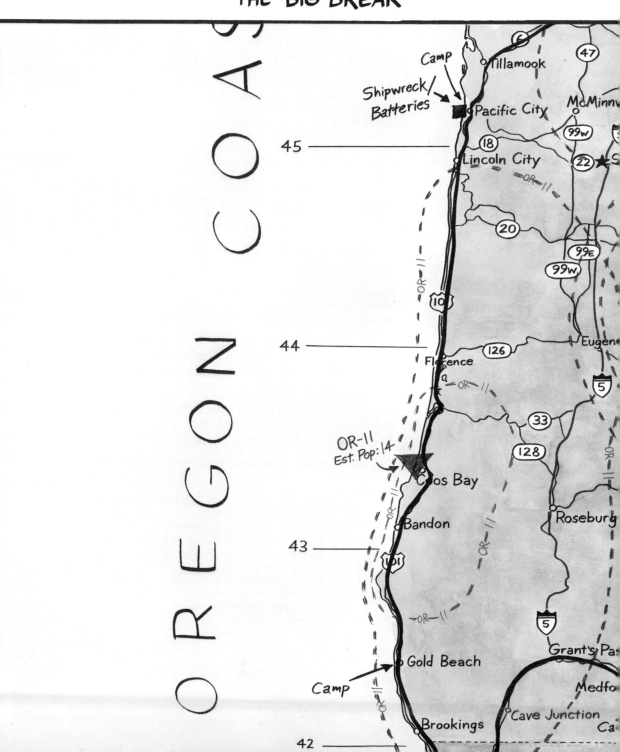

OREGON COAST

Tillamook

47

Camp

Shipwreck/
Batteries

Pacific City

McMinnv

99w

45

18

Lincoln City

22

OR-11

20

OR-11

10

44

126

Eugen

Florence

OR-11

5

33

OR-11

128

OR-11 Est. Pop: 14

Coos Bay

Bandon

Roseburg

43

101

OR-11

5

OR-11

Gold Beach

Grant's Pa

Camp

OR-11

Medfo

Brookings

Cave Junction

Ca

42

45° 1'9.69"N 123°56'58.93"W E

WHAT?

THIS IS A NEW LOW FOR BREAKFAST.

GREEN BEANS ARE GOOD FOR YOU! HERE, DRINK YOUR MEDS.

PLINK

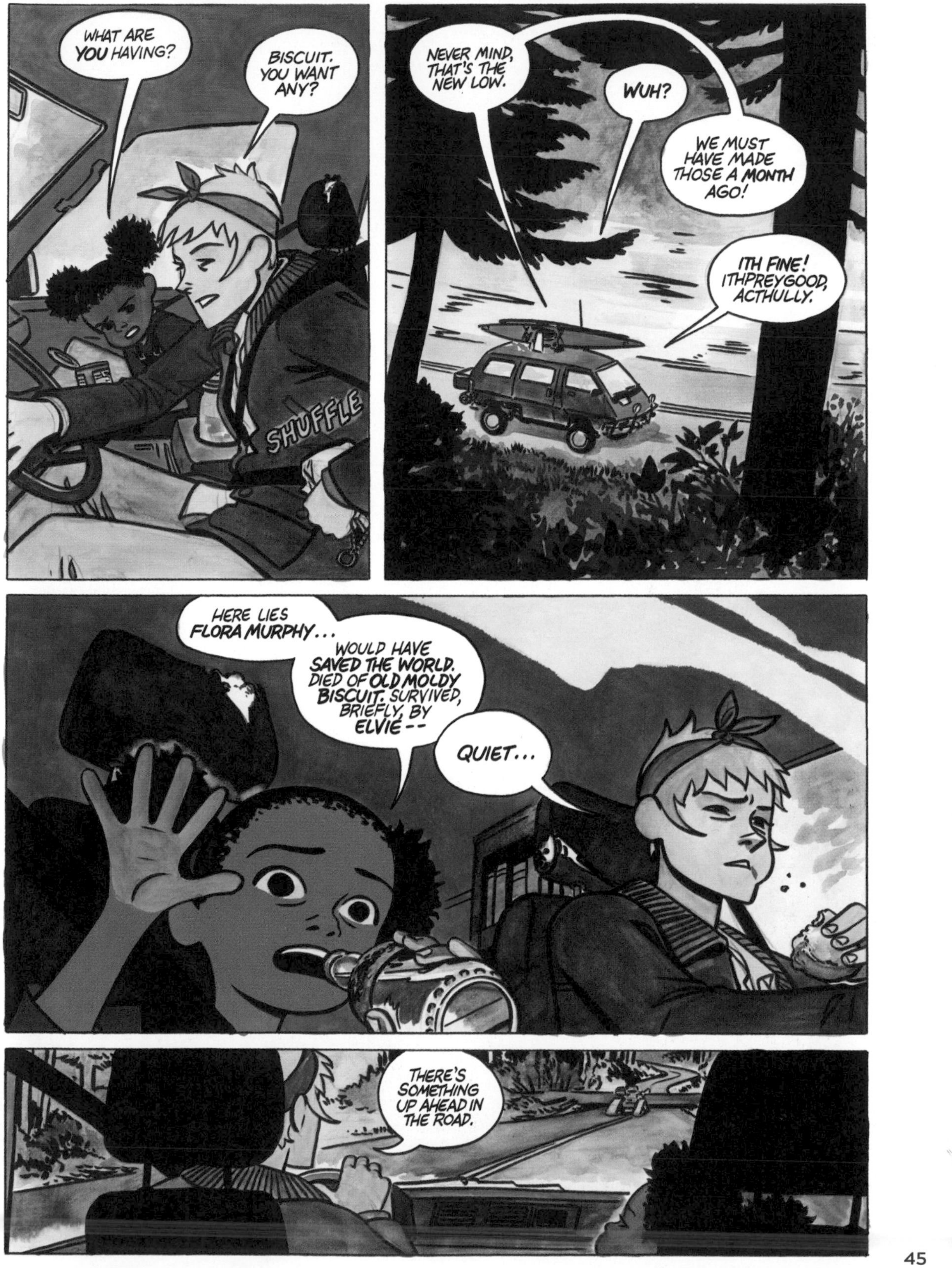
WHAT ARE YOU HAVING?
BISCUIT. YOU WANT ANY?
SHUFFLE
NEVER MIND, THAT'S THE NEW LOW.
WUH?
WE MUST HAVE MADE THOSE A MONTH AGO!
ITH FINE! ITHPREYGOOD, ACTHULLY.
HERE LIES FLORA MURPHY...
WOULD HAVE SAVED THE WORLD. DIED OF OLD MOLDY BISCUIT. SURVIVED, BRIEFLY, BY ELVIE--
QUIET...
THERE'S SOMETHING UP AHEAD IN THE ROAD.

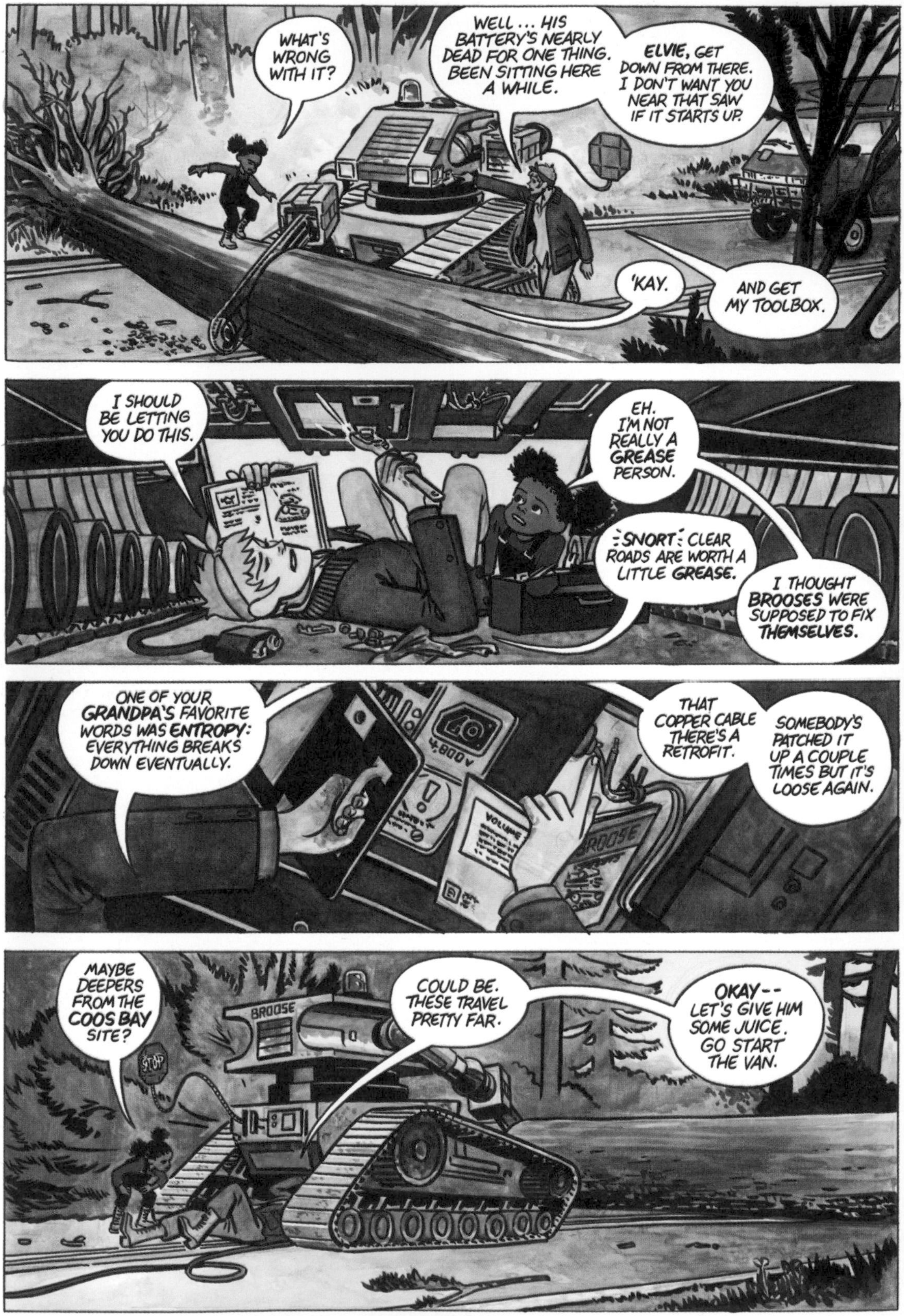
WHAT'S WRONG WITH IT?
WELL ... HIS BATTERY'S NEARLY DEAD FOR ONE THING. BEEN SITTING HERE A WHILE.
ELVIE, GET DOWN FROM THERE. I DON'T WANT YOU NEAR THAT SAW IF IT STARTS UP.
'KAY.
AND GET MY TOOLBOX.
I SHOULD BE LETTING YOU DO THIS.
EH. I'M NOT REALLY A GREASE PERSON.
SNORT CLEAR ROADS ARE WORTH A LITTLE GREASE.
I THOUGHT BROOSES WERE SUPPOSED TO FIX THEMSELVES.
ONE OF YOUR GRANDPA'S FAVORITE WORDS WAS ENTROPY: EVERYTHING BREAKS DOWN EVENTUALLY.
40
4,800V
VOLUME
BROOSE
THAT COPPER CABLE THERE'S A RETROFIT.
SOMEBODY'S PATCHED IT UP A COUPLE TIMES BUT IT'S LOOSE AGAIN.
MAYBE DEEPERS FROM THE COOS BAY SITE?
STOP
BROOSE
COULD BE. THESE TRAVEL PRETTY FAR.
OKAY -- LET'S GIVE HIM SOME JUICE. GO START THE VAN.

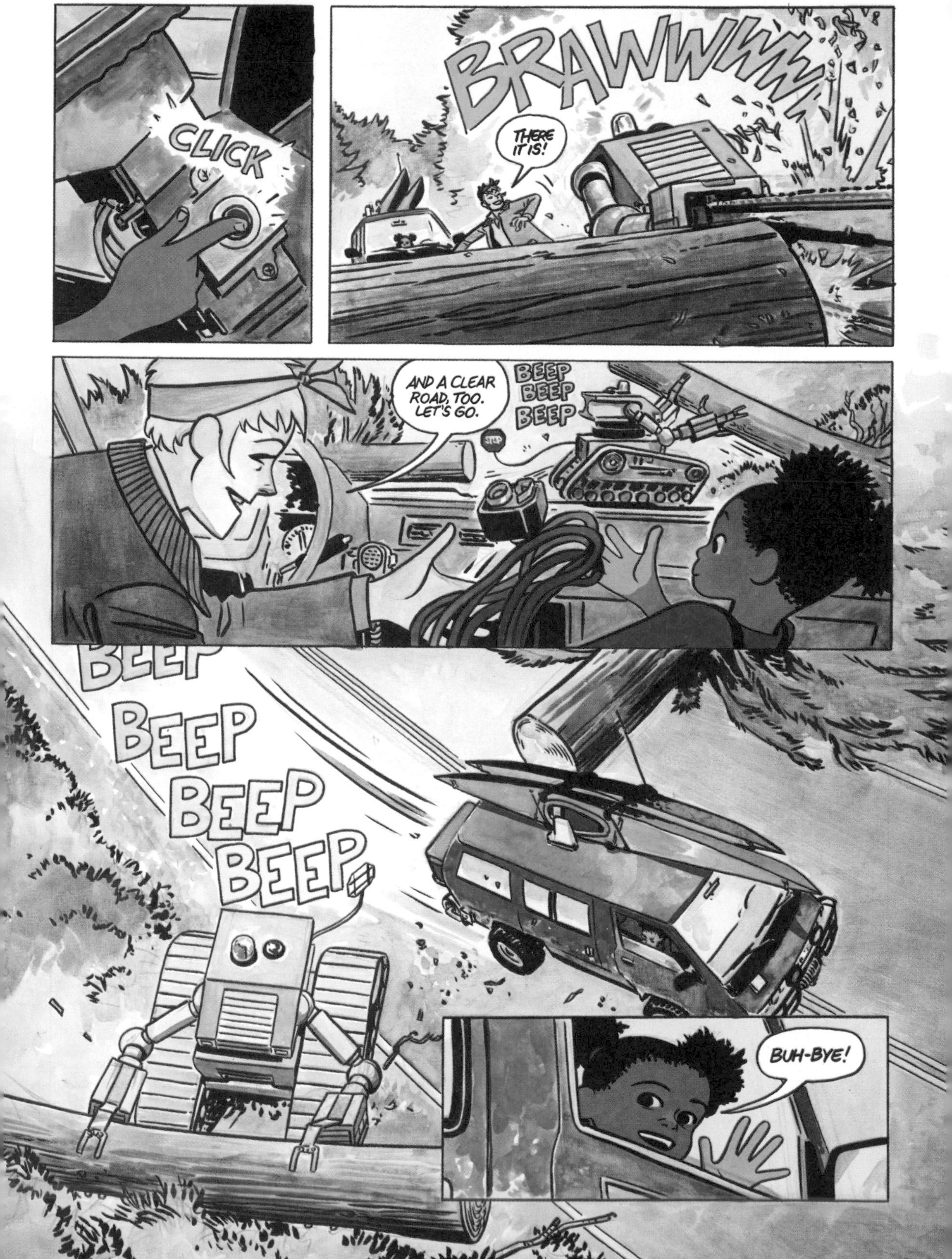
CLICK
BRAWWWW
THERE IT IS!
AND A CLEAR ROAD, TOO. LET'S GO.
BEEP BEEP BEEP
STOP
BEEP
BEEP
BEEP
BEEP
BUH-BYE!

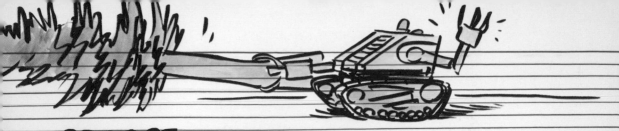

BROOSE: BRIDGE AND ROAD OPERATIONAL OVERLAND · SELF-SUFFICIENT ELECTRONICS (SHEESH!)

SOME INTERESTING TIDBITS -- **BROOSES** WERE BUILT TO **RGD** (RUGGEDIZED) STANDARDS LIKE ALL THE GOVERNMENT AND MILITARY ELECTRONICS THAT SURVIVED THE **SUN SHIFT**. THAT MEANS THEIR PARTS AND ANY SOLAR STATIONS WHERE THEY CHARGE UP ARE SHIELDED FROM RADIATION, DUST, WATER, ETC. JUST LIKE OUR **RGD RADIO, WALKIE-TALKIES, BATTERIES,** AND **SOLAR CHARGERS.**

WHAT ELSE IS THERE TO KNOW ABOUT **BROOSES?** THEIR "BRAINS" CARRY ALL THEIR OPERATING INFO, SO THEY CAN DO THEIR STUFF WITHOUT ANY BIGGER NETWORK. THEY DO HAVE RADIOS TO CONNECT AND COORDINATE WITH EACH OTHER (UP TO SEVERAL HUNDRED MILES AWAY) FOR BIG REPAIR JOBS, BUT ASIDE FROM THAT THEY OPERATE ON THEIR OWN WITHOUT HUMAN SUPERVISION.

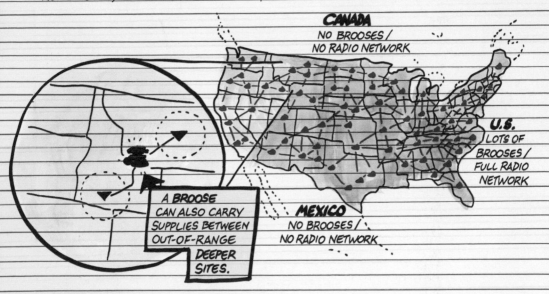

CANADA
NO BROOSES / NO RADIO NETWORK

U.S.
LOTS OF BROOSES / FULL RADIO NETWORK

A **BROOSE** CAN ALSO CARRY SUPPLIES BETWEEN OUT-OF-RANGE DEEPER SITES.

MEXICO
NO BROOSES / NO RADIO NETWORK

A FEW YEARS AFTER THE **SUN SHIFT**, A DEEPER FIGURED OUT HOW TO PATCH INTO A **BROOSE** AND EXTEND HIS OWN RADIO RANGE. HE EVEN LOADED A BUNCH OF **RGD RADIOS** INSIDE THE **BROOSES'** LOCKERS WITH A BIG **TAKE ONE** SIGN. PRETTY SOON OTHER PEOPLE COPIED HIS IDEA, PUT **MORE RADIOS** IN **MORE BROOSES**, AND SET UP A RADIO NETWORK TO COVER MOST OF THE **UNITED STATES**. THEY EVEN MADE A LIST OF KNOWN DEEPER SITES BY **STATE AND NUMBER**, LIKE OURS IN **SANTA MONICA: CA-08**. AFTER A CENSUS, THEY ESTIMATED THE **AMERICAN** POPULATION TO BE ABOUT 7,500 PEOPLE. **FLORA** SAID THAT WAS A SAD NUMBER FOR HER PARENTS TO HEAR. IT'S SURE MORE HUMANS THAN I CAN IMAGINE.

THESE DAYS, MOST PEOPLE TRY TO STAY OFF THE PUBLIC RADIO CHANNELS. THE FACT IS, WHEN EVERYONE KNOWS WHERE MOST OF THE SITES ARE (AND WHO LIVES IN THEM), THEY BECOME EASY TARGETS FOR **MARAUDERS**. AND SO, WE REALLY DON'T KNOW ANYMORE WHO LIVES WHERE... OR WHETHER THEY'RE FRIENDLY.

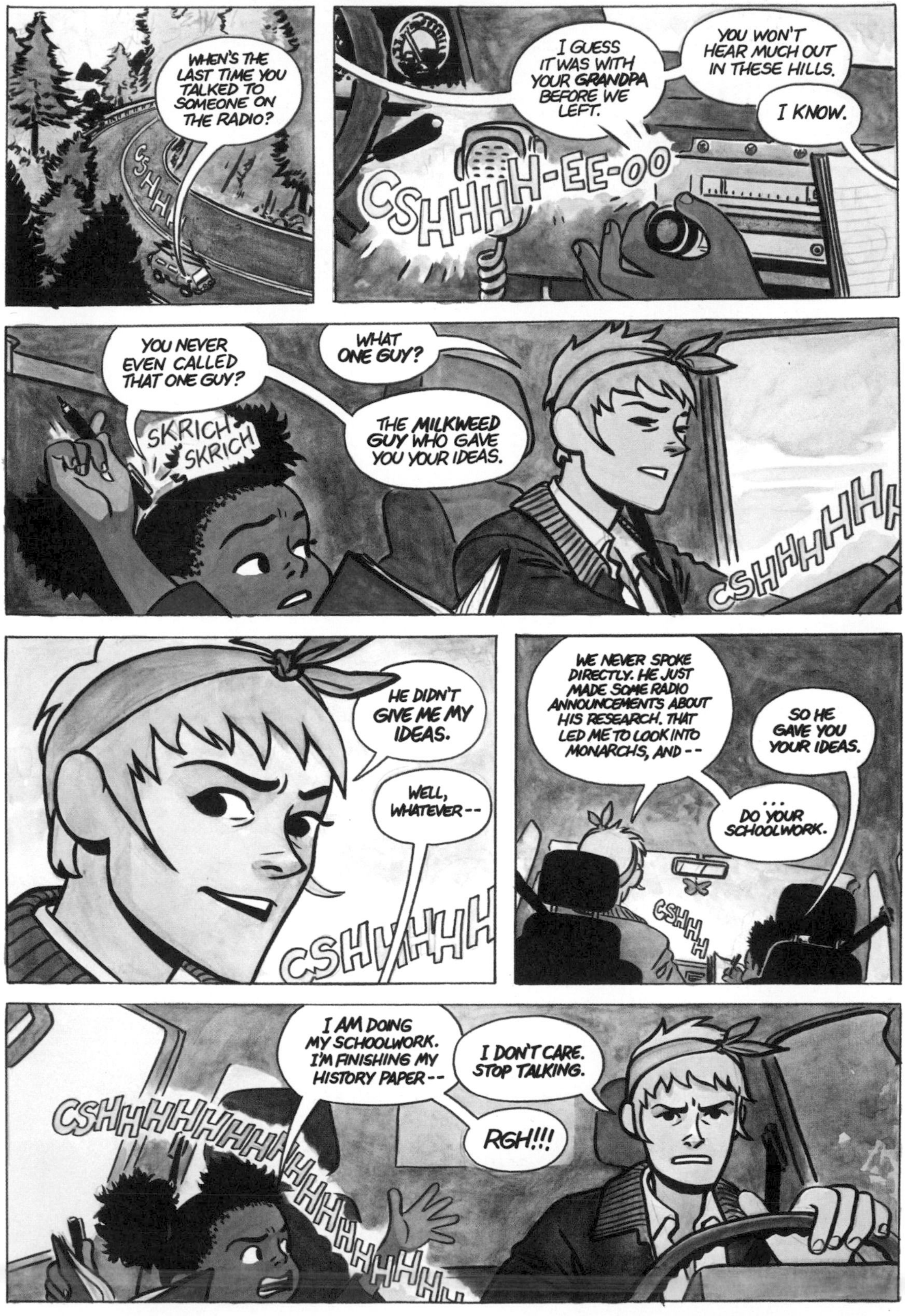
WHEN'S THE LAST TIME YOU TALKED TO SOMEONE ON THE RADIO?
CSHH
I GUESS IT WAS WITH YOUR GRANDPA BEFORE WE LEFT.
YOU WON'T HEAR MUCH OUT IN THESE HILLS.
I KNOW.
CSHHHH-EE-OO
YOU NEVER EVEN CALLED THAT ONE GUY?
WHAT ONE GUY?
THE MILKWEED GUY WHO GAVE YOU YOUR IDEAS.
SKRICH SKRICH
CSHHHHHH
HE DIDN'T GIVE ME MY IDEAS.
WELL, WHATEVER--
CSHHHHH
WE NEVER SPOKE DIRECTLY. HE JUST MADE SOME RADIO ANNOUNCEMENTS ABOUT HIS RESEARCH. THAT LED ME TO LOOK INTO MONARCHS, AND--
SO HE GAVE YOU YOUR IDEAS.
... DO YOUR SCHOOLWORK.
CSHHH
I AM DOING MY SCHOOLWORK. I'M FINISHING MY HISTORY PAPER--
I DON'T CARE. STOP TALKING.
RGH!!!
CSHHHHHHHHHHHHHHHHHH

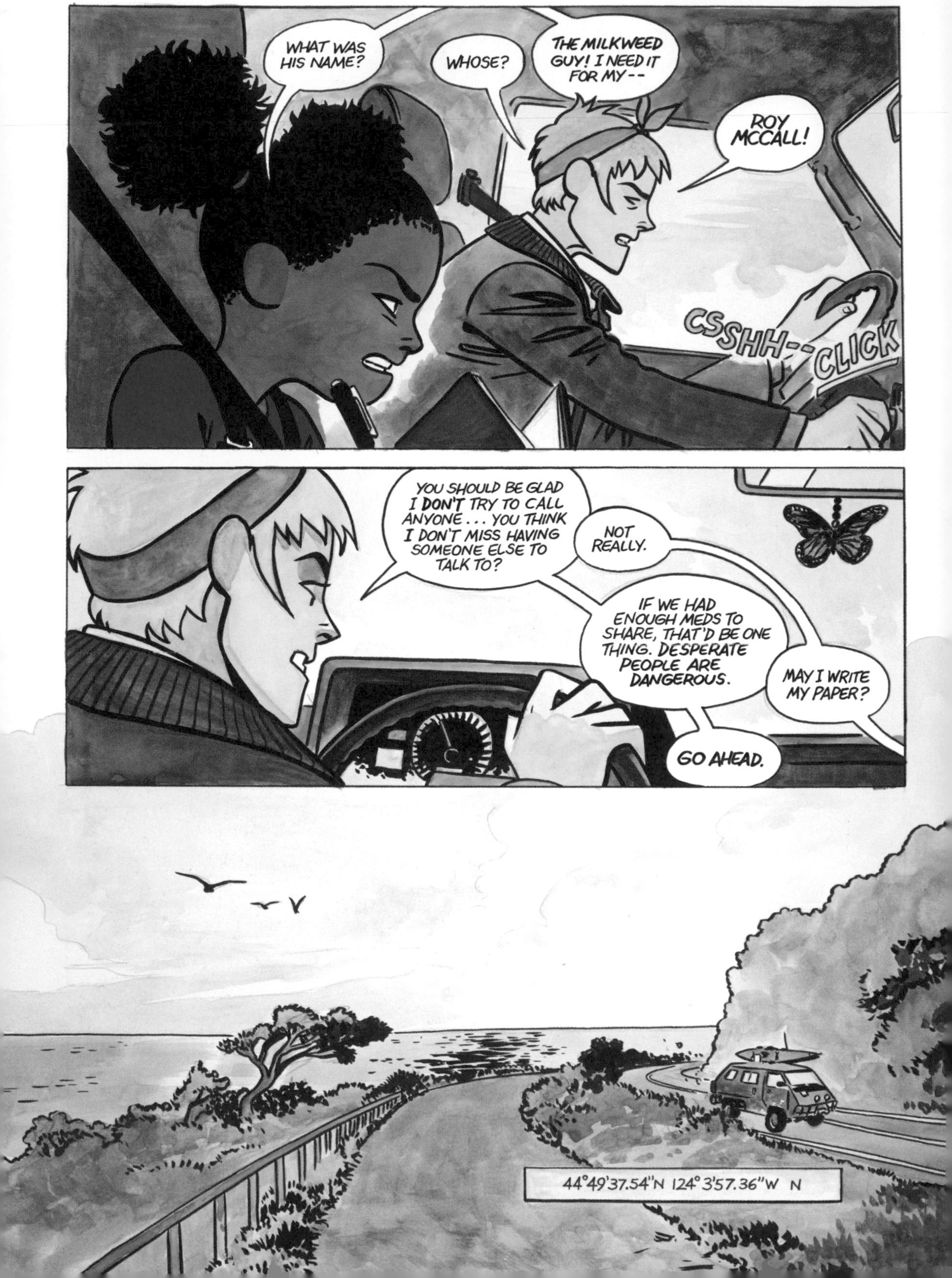
WHAT WAS HIS NAME?
WHOSE?
THE MILKWEED GUY! I NEED IT FOR MY --
ROY MCCALL!
CSSHH--CLICK
YOU SHOULD BE GLAD I DON'T TRY TO CALL ANYONE . . . YOU THINK I DON'T MISS HAVING SOMEONE ELSE TO TALK TO?
NOT REALLY.
IF WE HAD ENOUGH MEDS TO SHARE, THAT'D BE ONE THING. DESPERATE PEOPLE ARE DANGEROUS.
MAY I WRITE MY PAPER?
GO AHEAD.
44°49'37.54"N 124° 3'57.36"W N

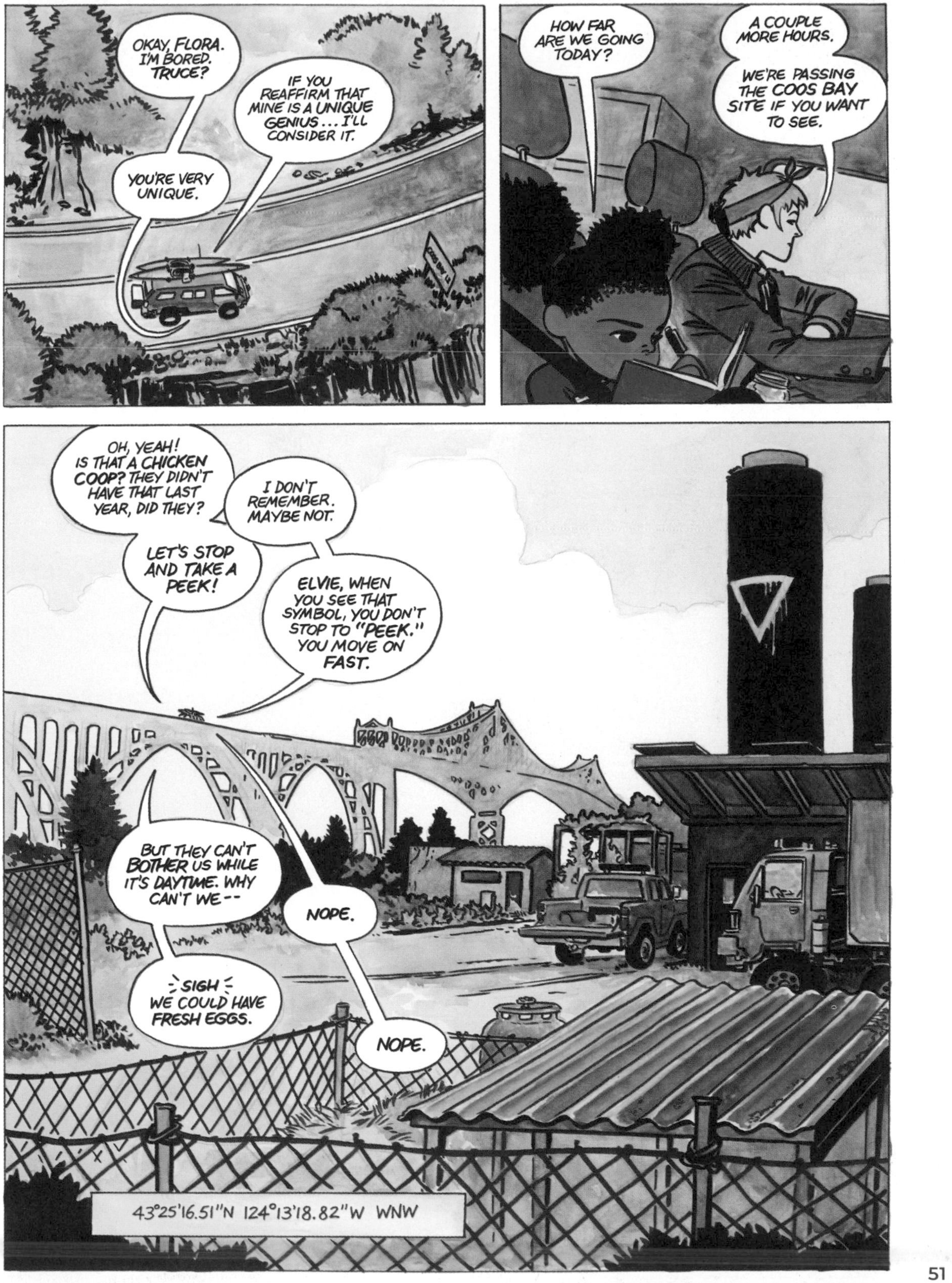
OKAY, FLORA. I'M BORED. TRUCE?
IF YOU REAFFIRM THAT MINE IS A UNIQUE GENIUS . . . I'LL CONSIDER IT.
YOU'RE VERY UNIQUE.
HOW FAR ARE WE GOING TODAY?
A COUPLE MORE HOURS.
WE'RE PASSING THE COOS BAY SITE IF YOU WANT TO SEE.
OH, YEAH! IS THAT A CHICKEN COOP? THEY DIDN'T HAVE THAT LAST YEAR, DID THEY?
I DON'T REMEMBER. MAYBE NOT.
LET'S STOP AND TAKE A PEEK!
ELVIE, WHEN YOU SEE THAT SYMBOL, YOU DON'T STOP TO "PEEK." YOU MOVE ON FAST.
BUT THEY CAN'T BOTHER US WHILE IT'S DAYTIME. WHY CAN'T WE --
NOPE.
SIGH
WE COULD HAVE FRESH EGGS.
NOPE.
43°25'16.51"N 124°13'18.82"W WNW

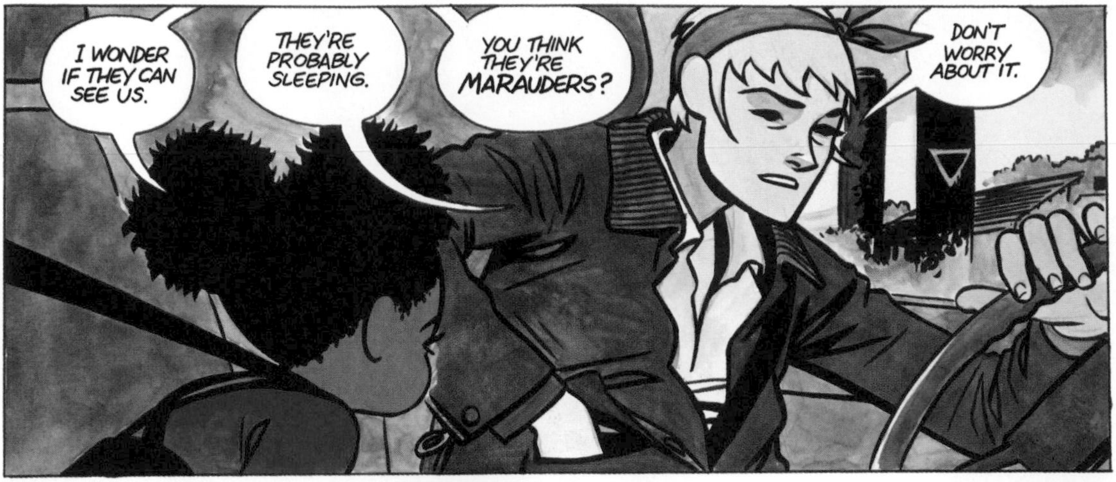
I WONDER IF THEY CAN SEE US.
THEY'RE PROBABLY SLEEPING.
YOU THINK THEY'RE MARAUDERS?
DON'T WORRY ABOUT IT.

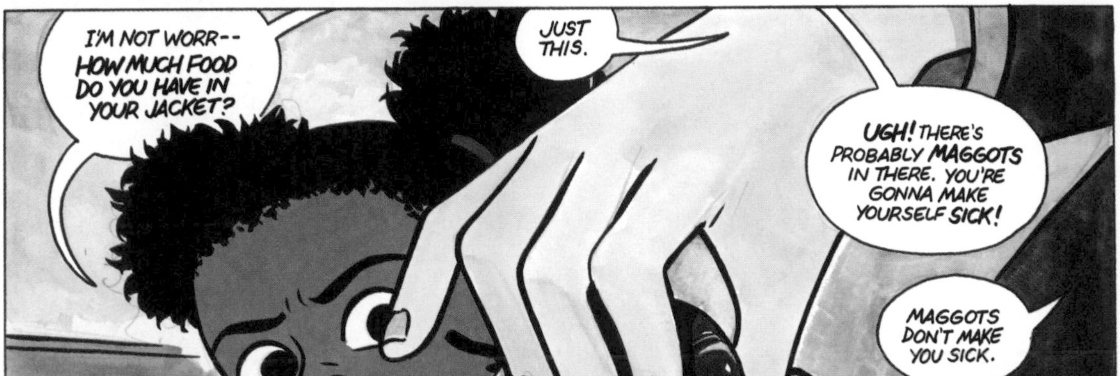
I'M NOT WORR-- HOW MUCH FOOD DO YOU HAVE IN YOUR JACKET?
JUST THIS.
UGH! THERE'S PROBABLY MAGGOTS IN THERE. YOU'RE GONNA MAKE YOURSELF SICK!
MAGGOTS DON'T MAKE YOU SICK.

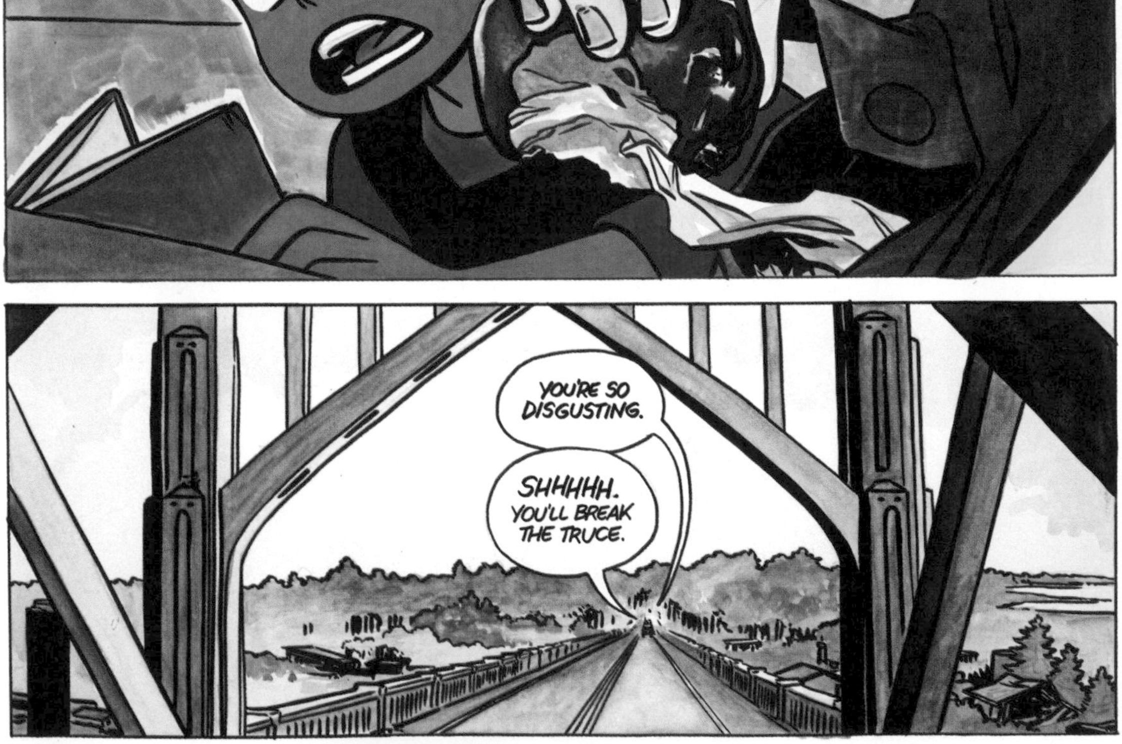
YOU'RE SO DISGUSTING.
SHHHHH. YOU'LL BREAK THE TRUCE.

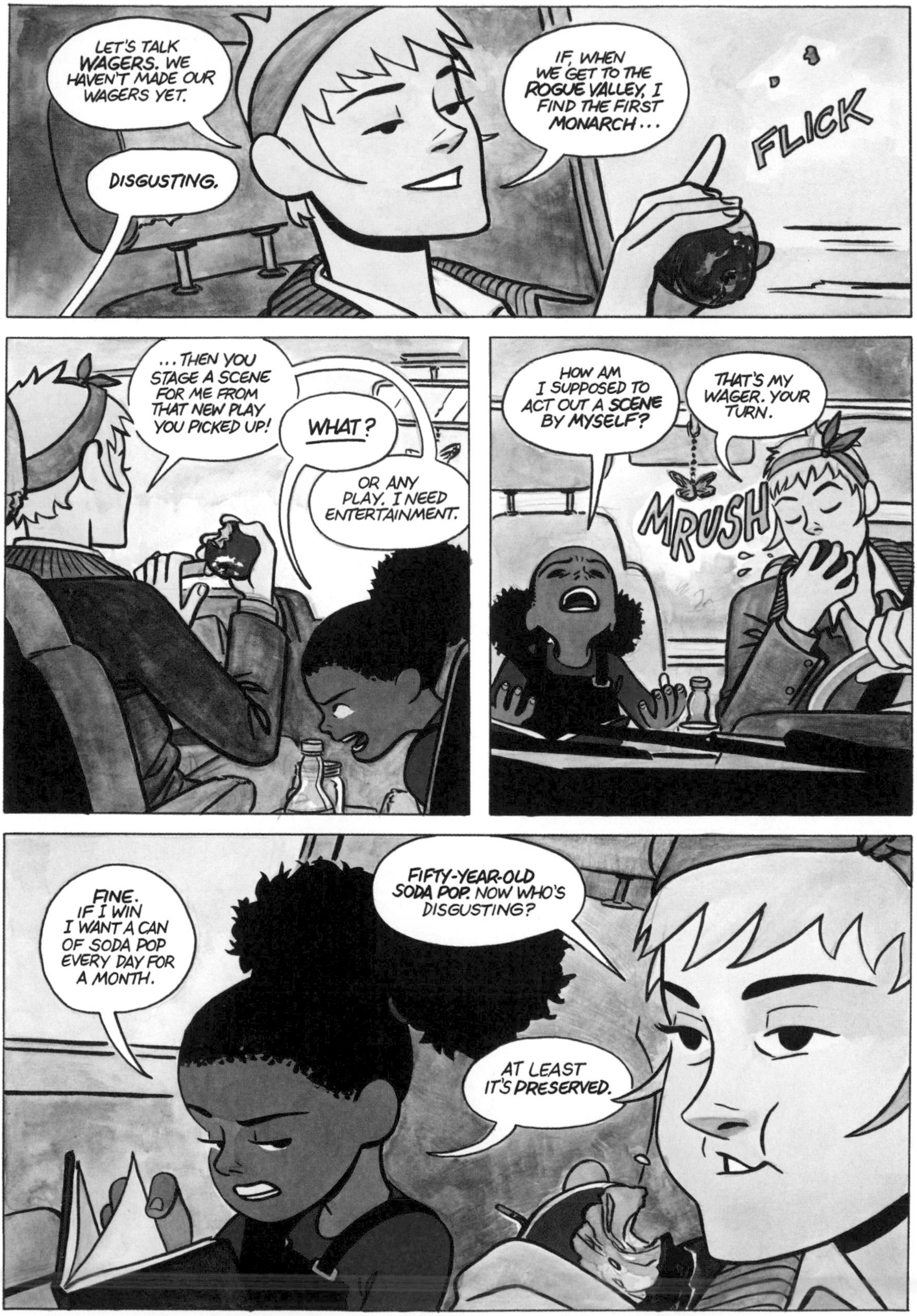
LET'S TALK WAGERS. WE HAVEN'T MADE OUR WAGERS YET.
DISGUSTING.
IF, WHEN WE GET TO THE ROGUE VALLEY, I FIND THE FIRST MONARCH...
FLICK
...THEN YOU STAGE A SCENE FOR ME FROM THAT NEW PLAY YOU PICKED UP!
WHAT?
OR ANY PLAY. I NEED ENTERTAINMENT.
HOW AM I SUPPOSED TO ACT OUT A SCENE BY MYSELF?
THAT'S MY WAGER. YOUR TURN.
MRUSH
FINE. IF I WIN I WANT A CAN OF SODA POP EVERY DAY FOR A MONTH.
FIFTY-YEAR-OLD SODA POP. NOW WHO'S DISGUSTING?
AT LEAST IT'S PRESERVED.

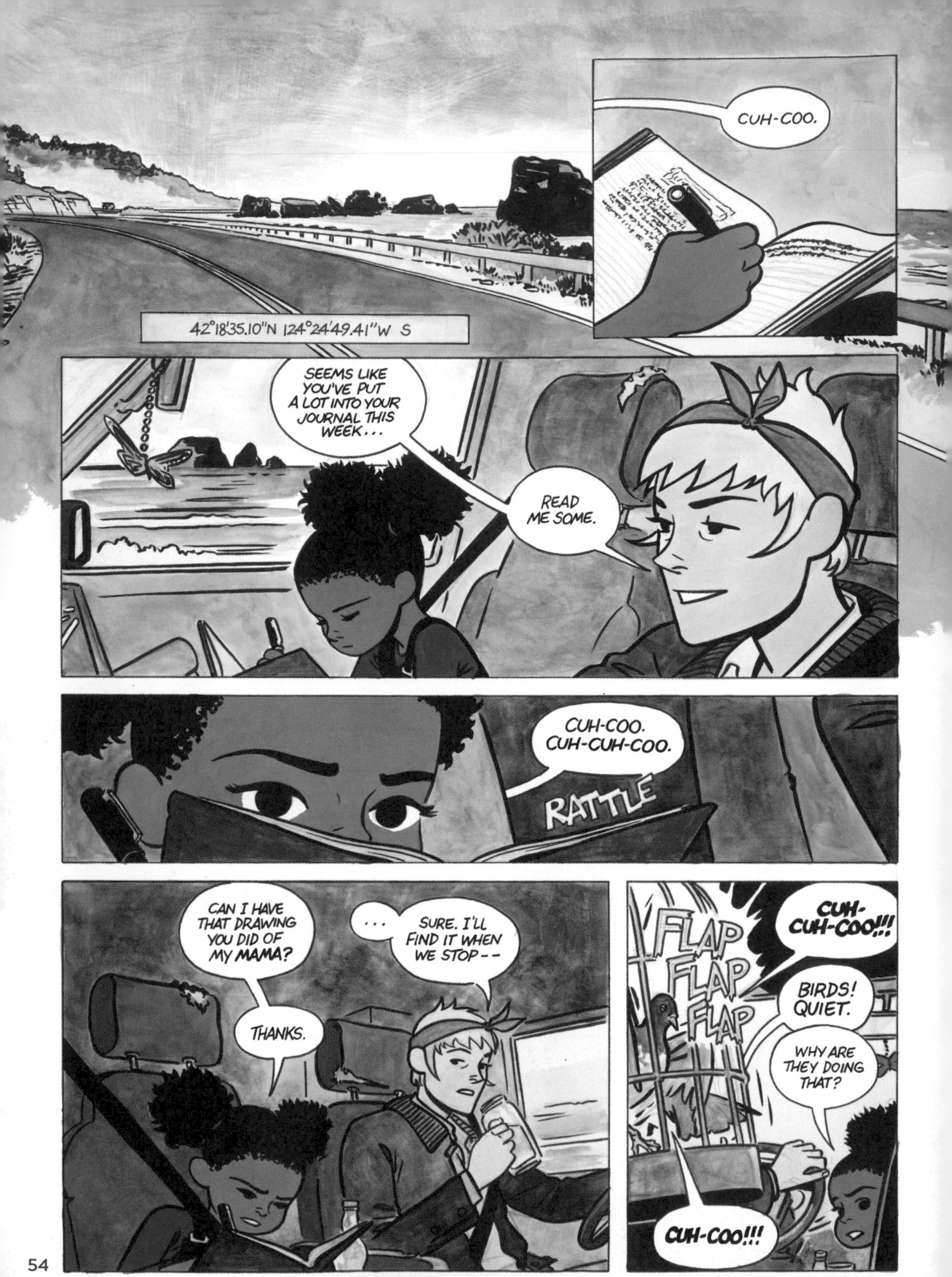

42°18'35.10"N 124°24'49.41"W S
CUH-COO.
SEEMS LIKE YOU'VE PUT A LOT INTO YOUR JOURNAL THIS WEEK...
READ ME SOME.
CUH-COO. CUH-CUH-COO.
RATTLE
CAN I HAVE THAT DRAWING YOU DID OF MY **MAMA**?
...
SURE. I'LL FIND IT WHEN WE STOP--
THANKS.
FLAP FLAP FLAP
CUH-CUH-COO!!!
BIRDS! QUIET.
WHY ARE THEY DOING THAT?
CUH-COO!!!

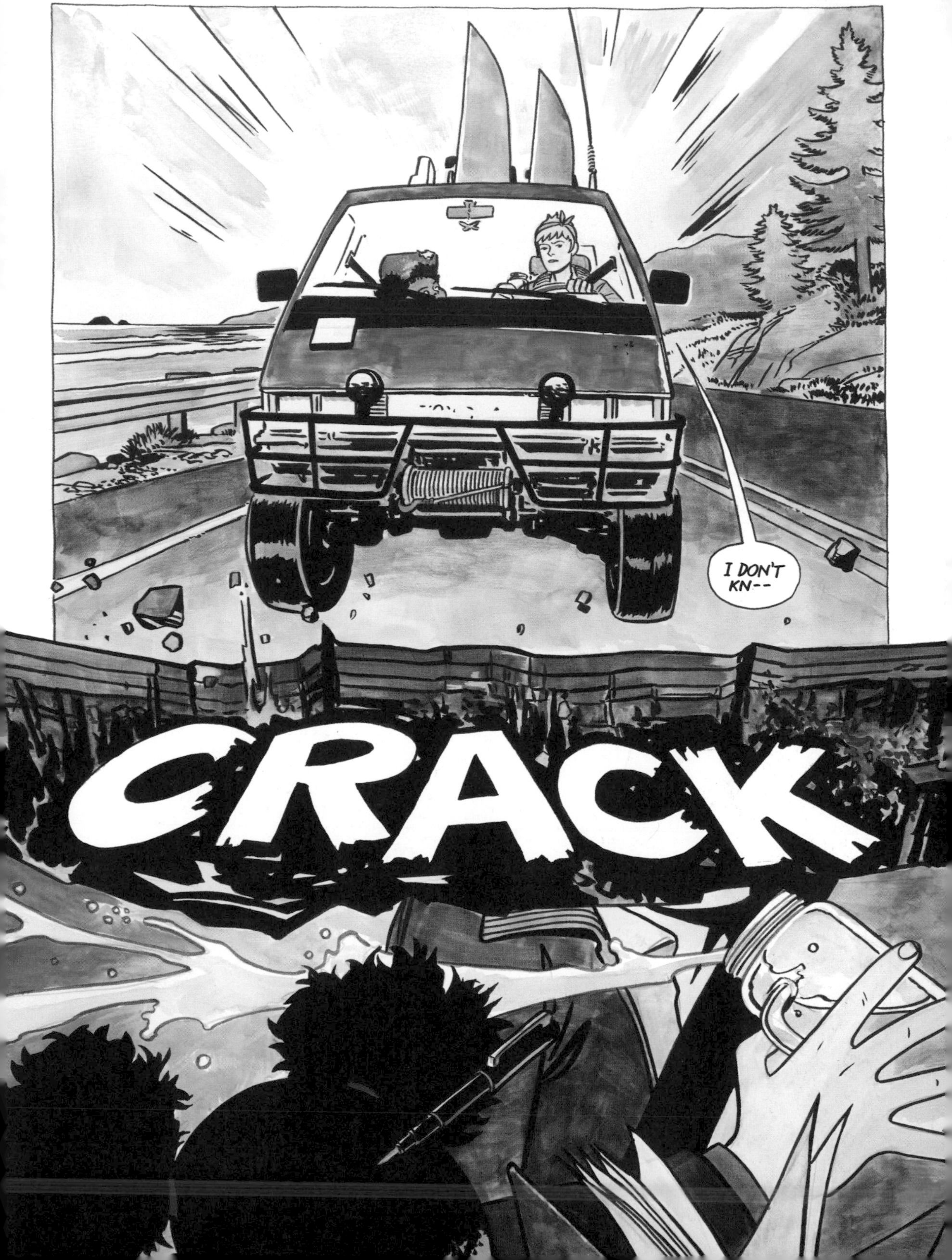
I DON'T KN--
CRACK

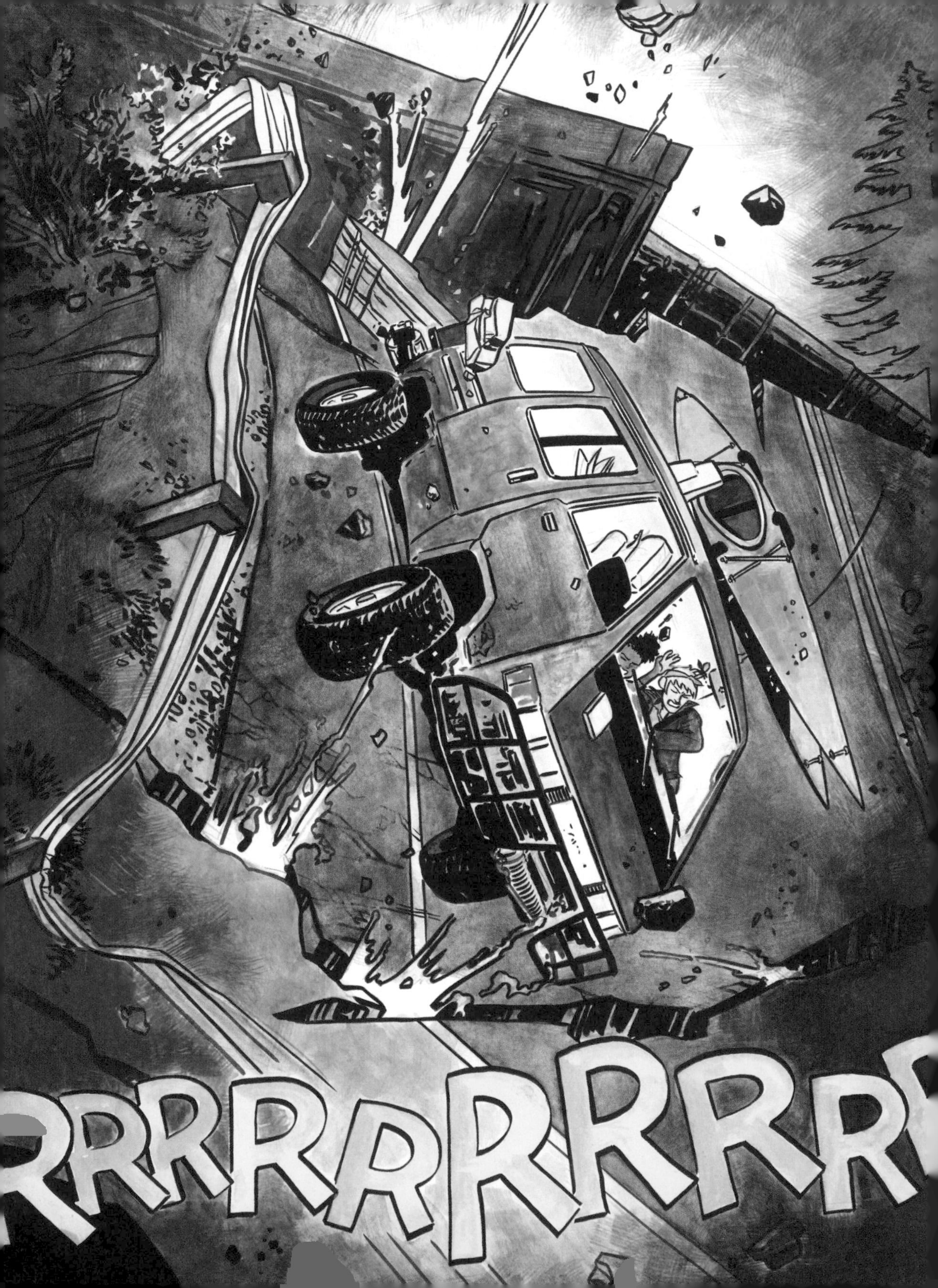
RRRRRRRRRR

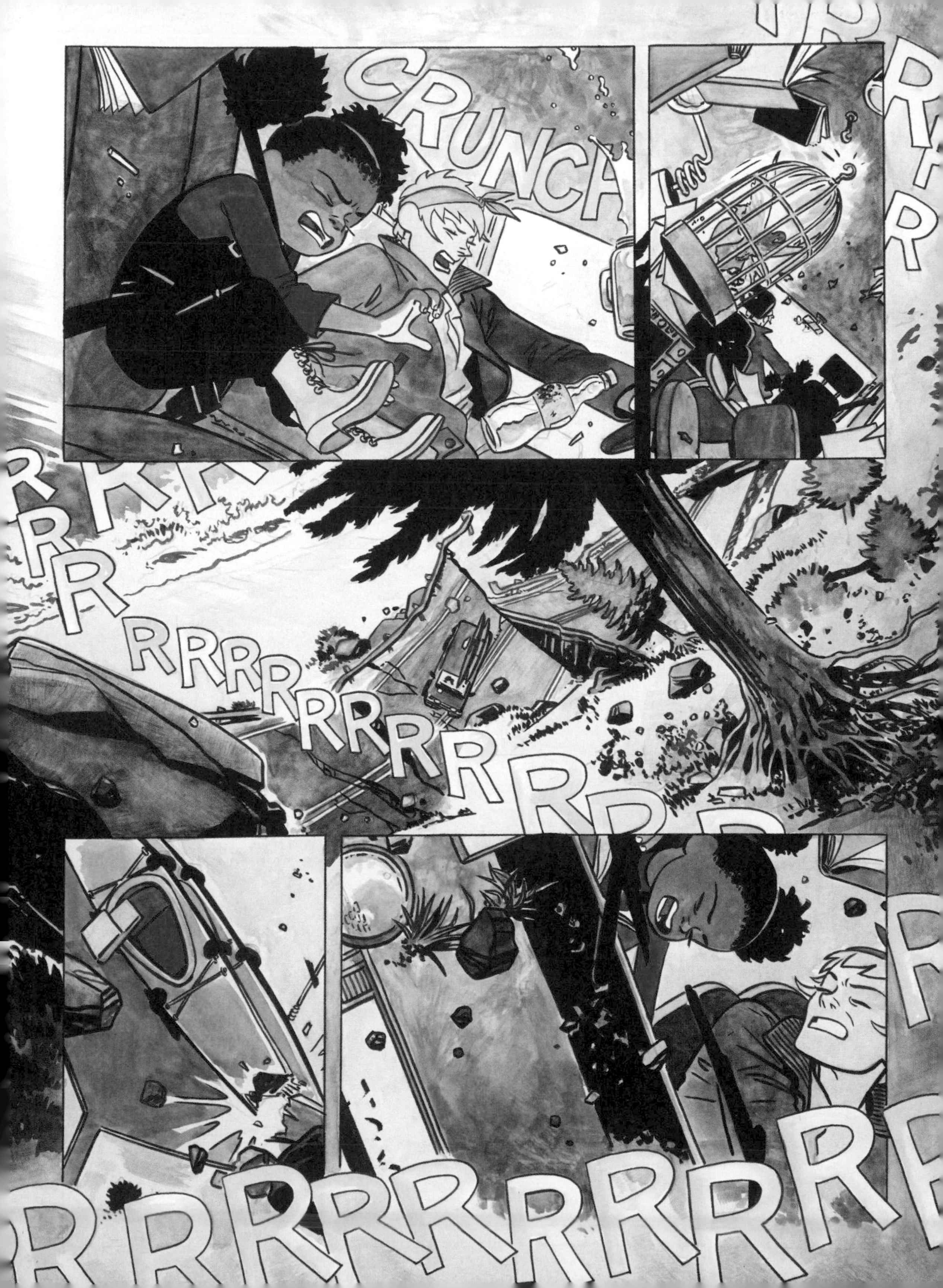
CRUNCA
RRRR
RRRRRRRRRRRRRRRRR
RRRRRRRRRRRR

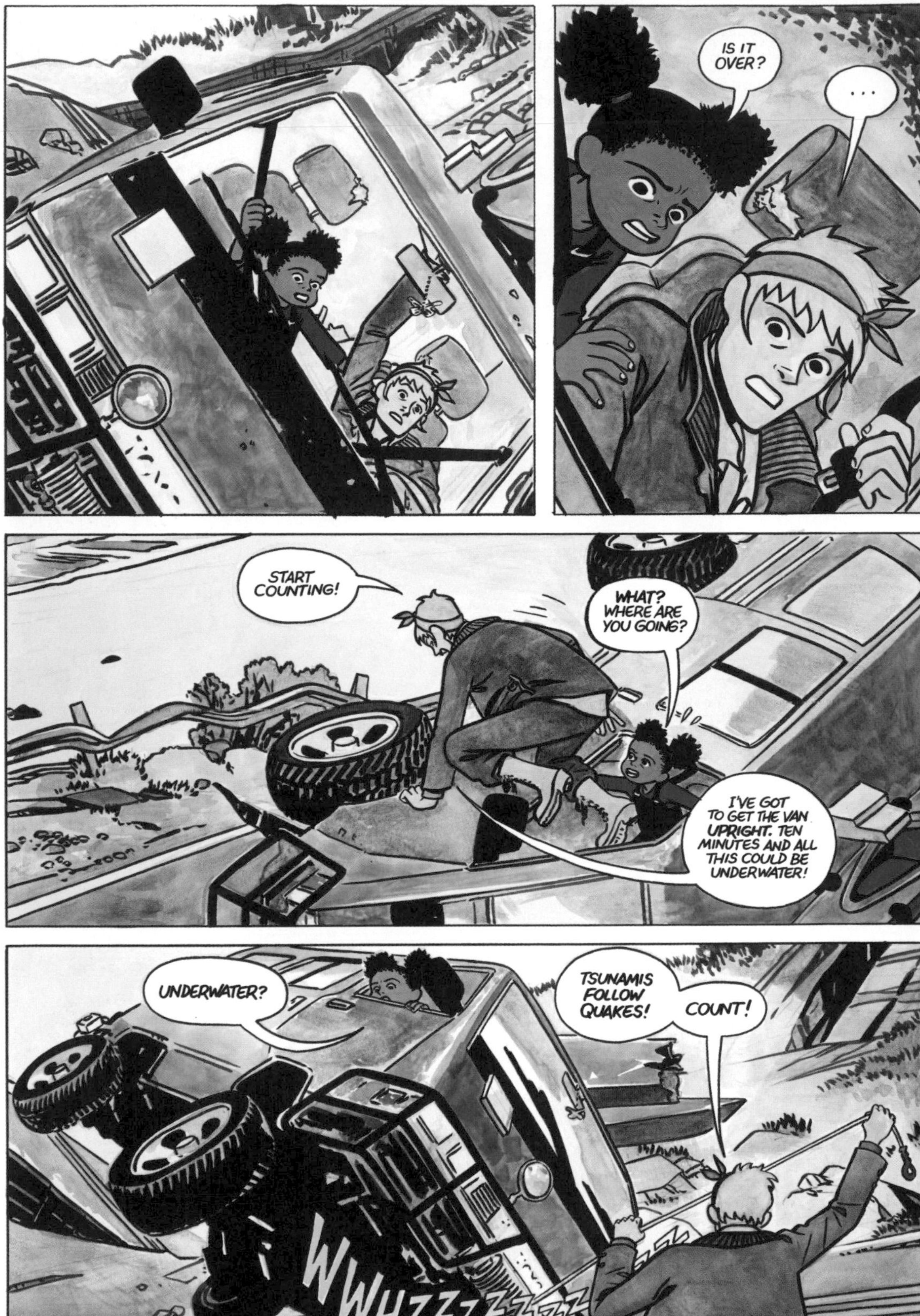
IS IT OVER?
. . .
START COUNTING!
WHAT? WHERE ARE YOU GOING?
I'VE GOT TO GET THE VAN UPRIGHT. TEN MINUTES AND ALL THIS COULD BE UNDERWATER!
UNDERWATER?
TSUNAMIS FOLLOW QUAKES!
COUNT!
WWHZZZZZZZZZ

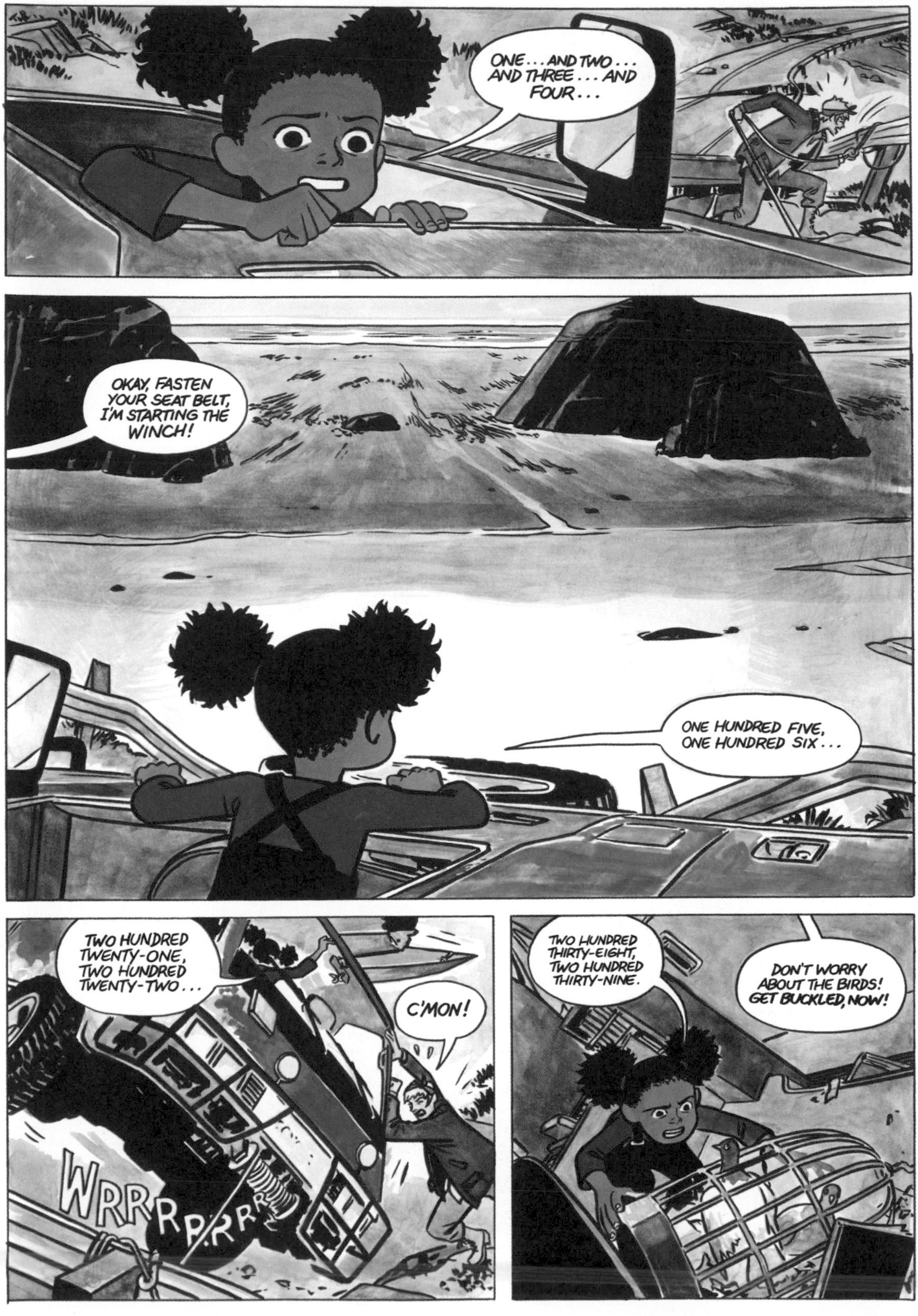
ONE . . . AND TWO . . . AND THREE . . . AND FOUR . . .
OKAY, FASTEN YOUR SEAT BELT, I'M STARTING THE WINCH!
ONE HUNDRED FIVE, ONE HUNDRED SIX . . .
TWO HUNDRED TWENTY-ONE, TWO HUNDRED TWENTY-TWO . . .
C'MON!
WRRRRRRR
TWO HUNDRED THIRTY-EIGHT, TWO HUNDRED THIRTY-NINE.
DON'T WORRY ABOUT THE BIRDS! GET BUCKLED, NOW!

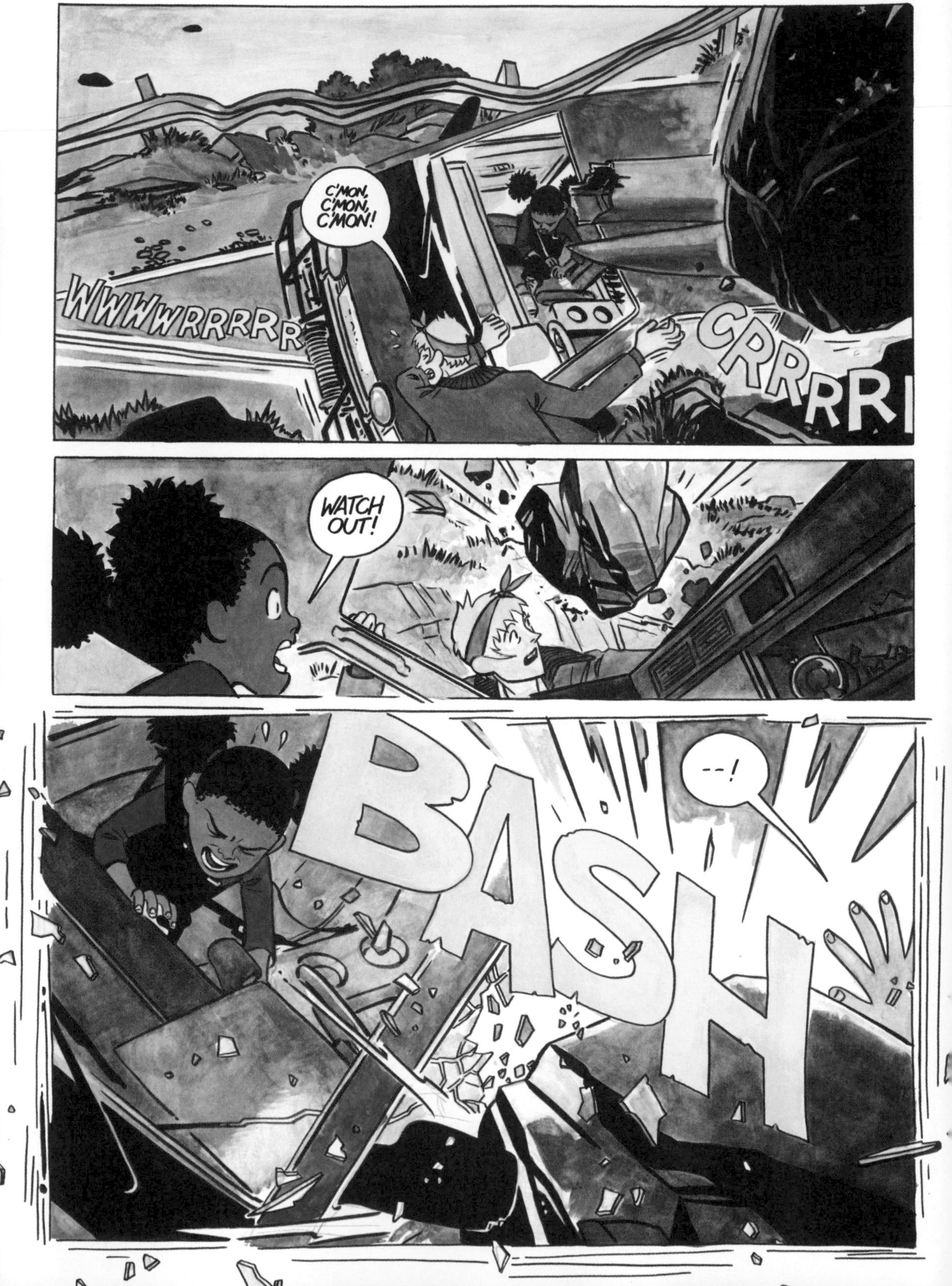
C'MON, C'MON, C'MON!
WWWWRRRRRR
CRRRRI
WATCH OUT!
BASH
--!

CRINCHA
CRUNCHA
ARE YOU OKAY?
YEAH. ARE YOU?
YEAH. BUT I LOST TRACK. WHERE WAS I?
DOESN'T MATTER NOW--
--HHH!
HOLD ON.
CHNK

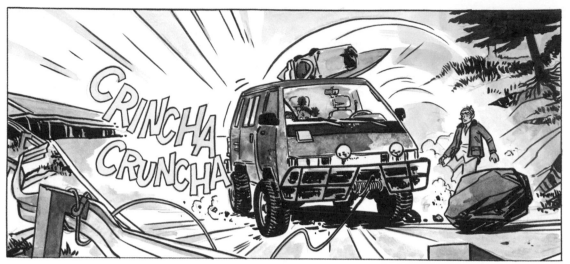

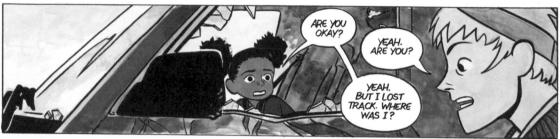

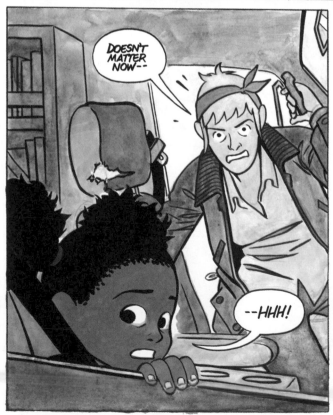

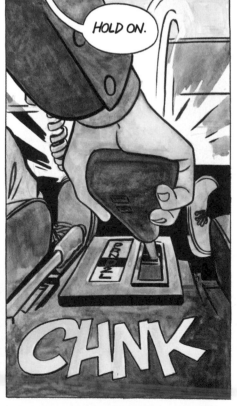

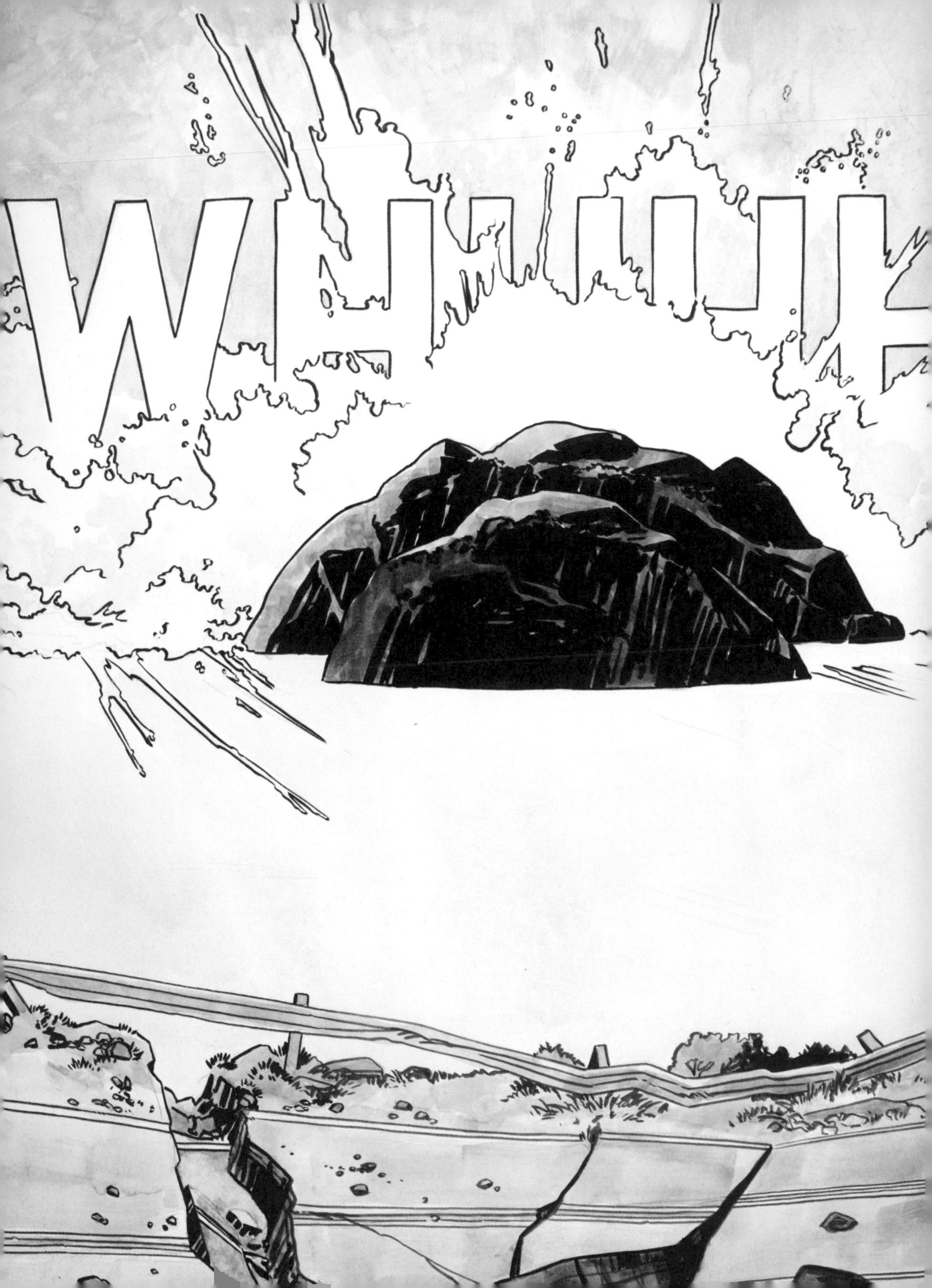

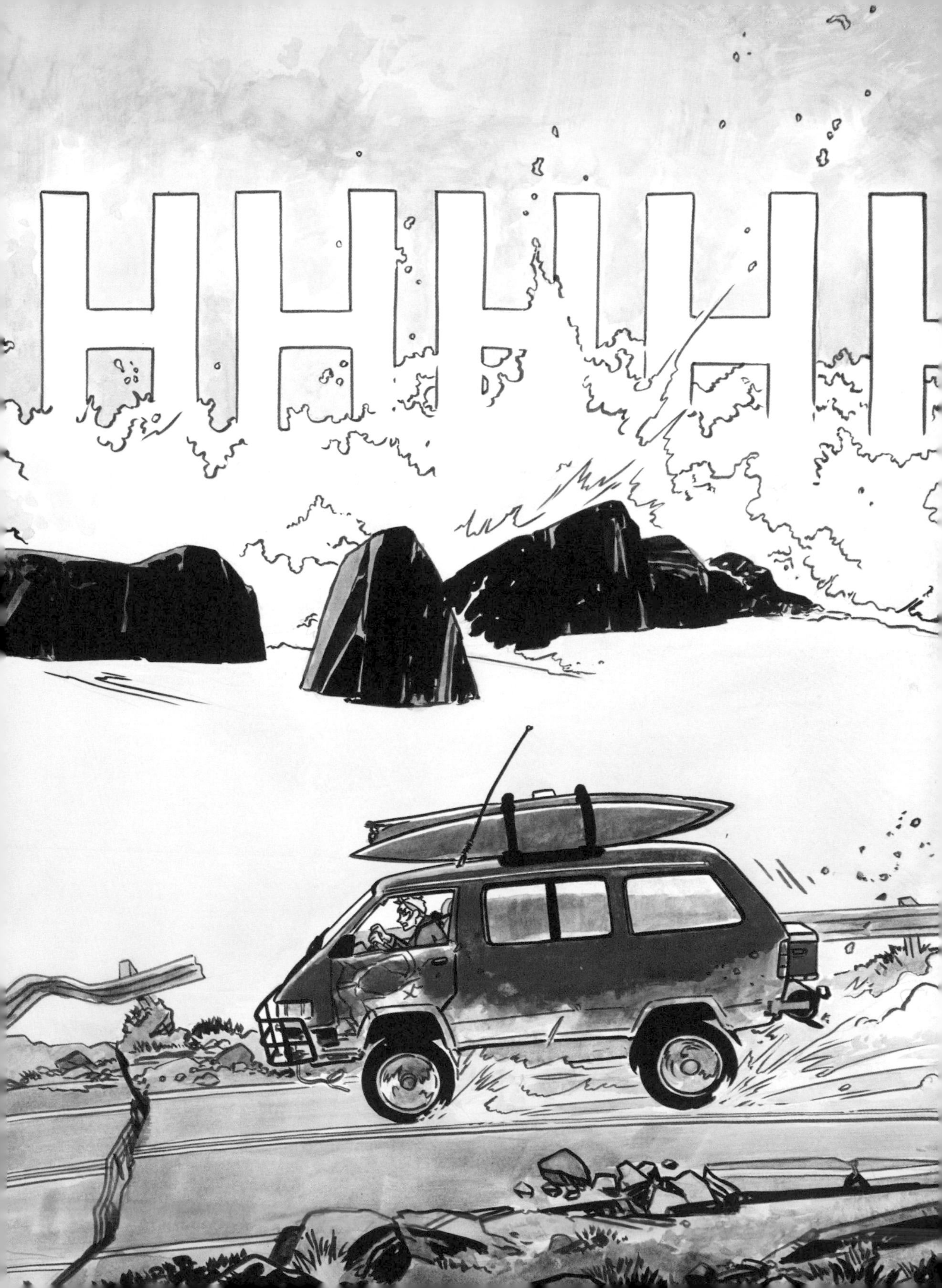

HHHHH

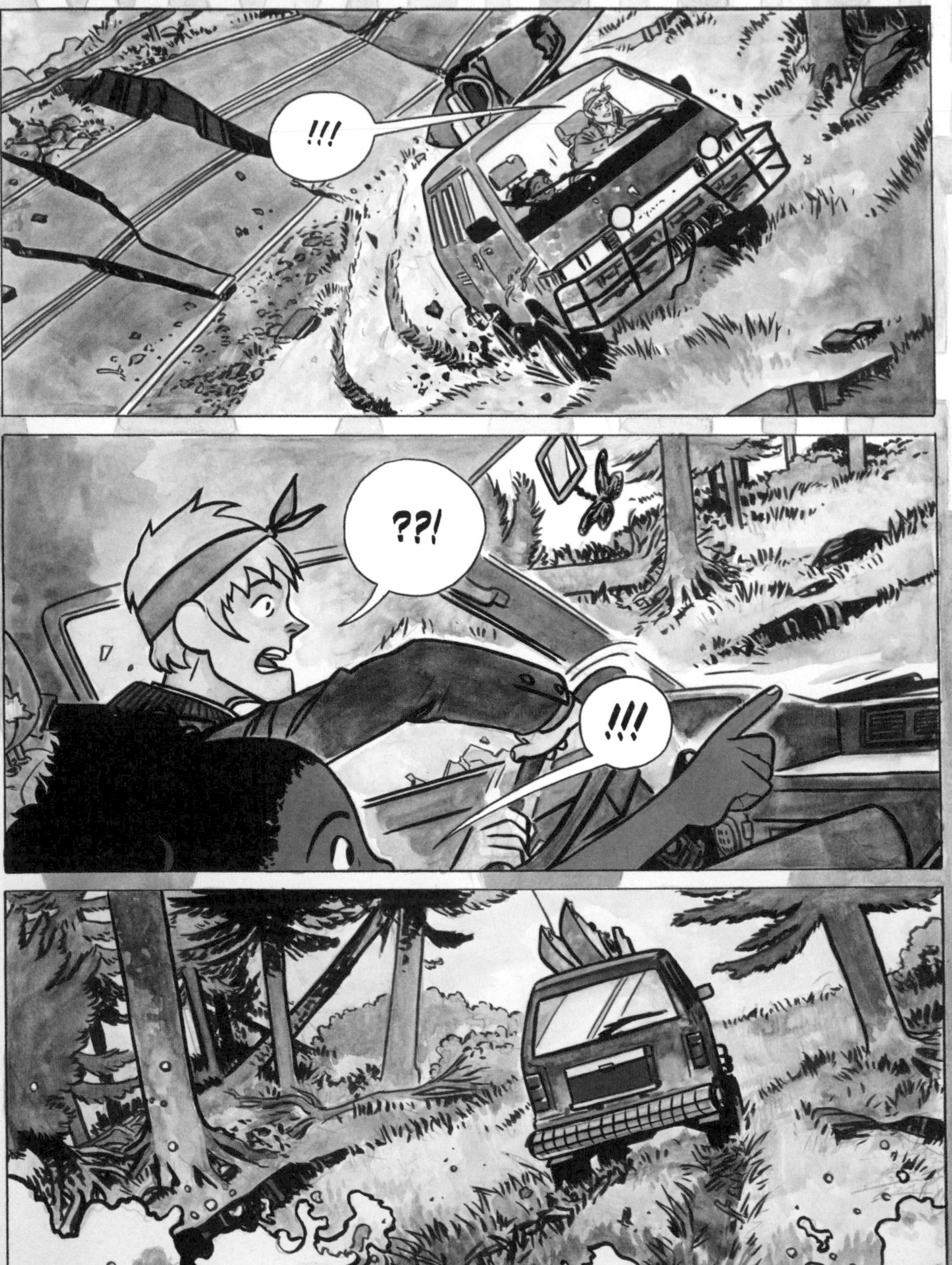
!!!
??!
!!!

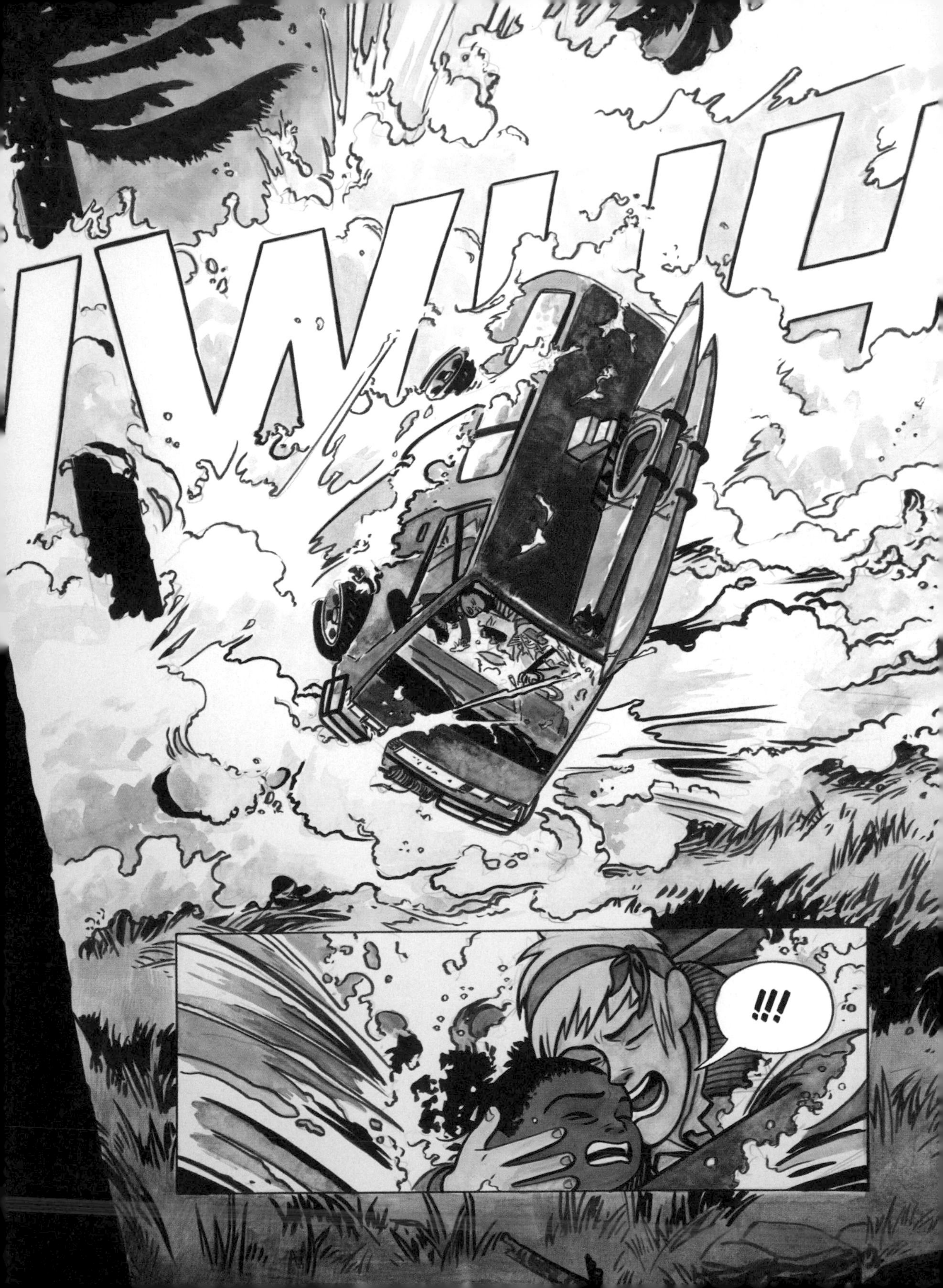
!!!

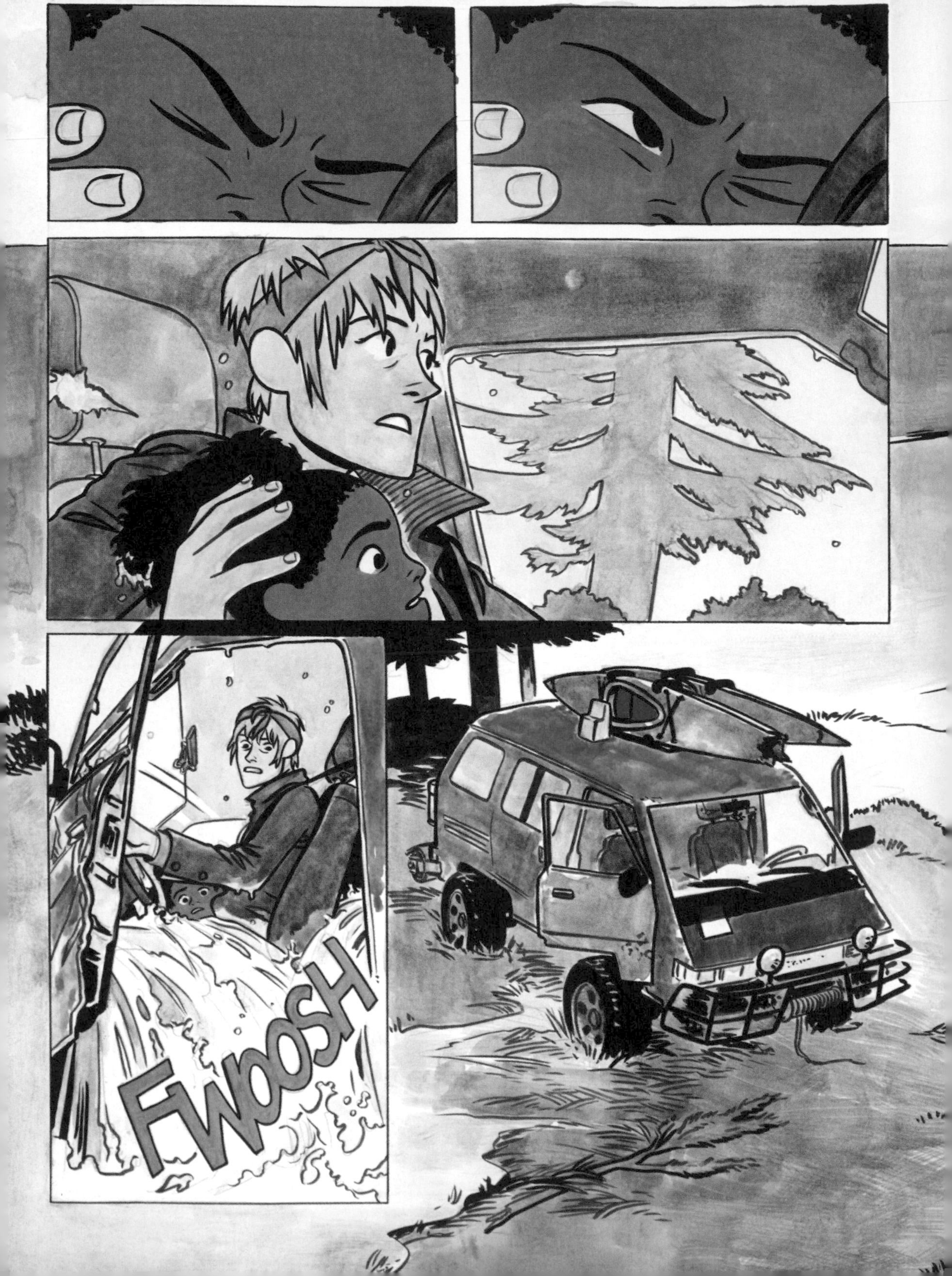
FWOOSH

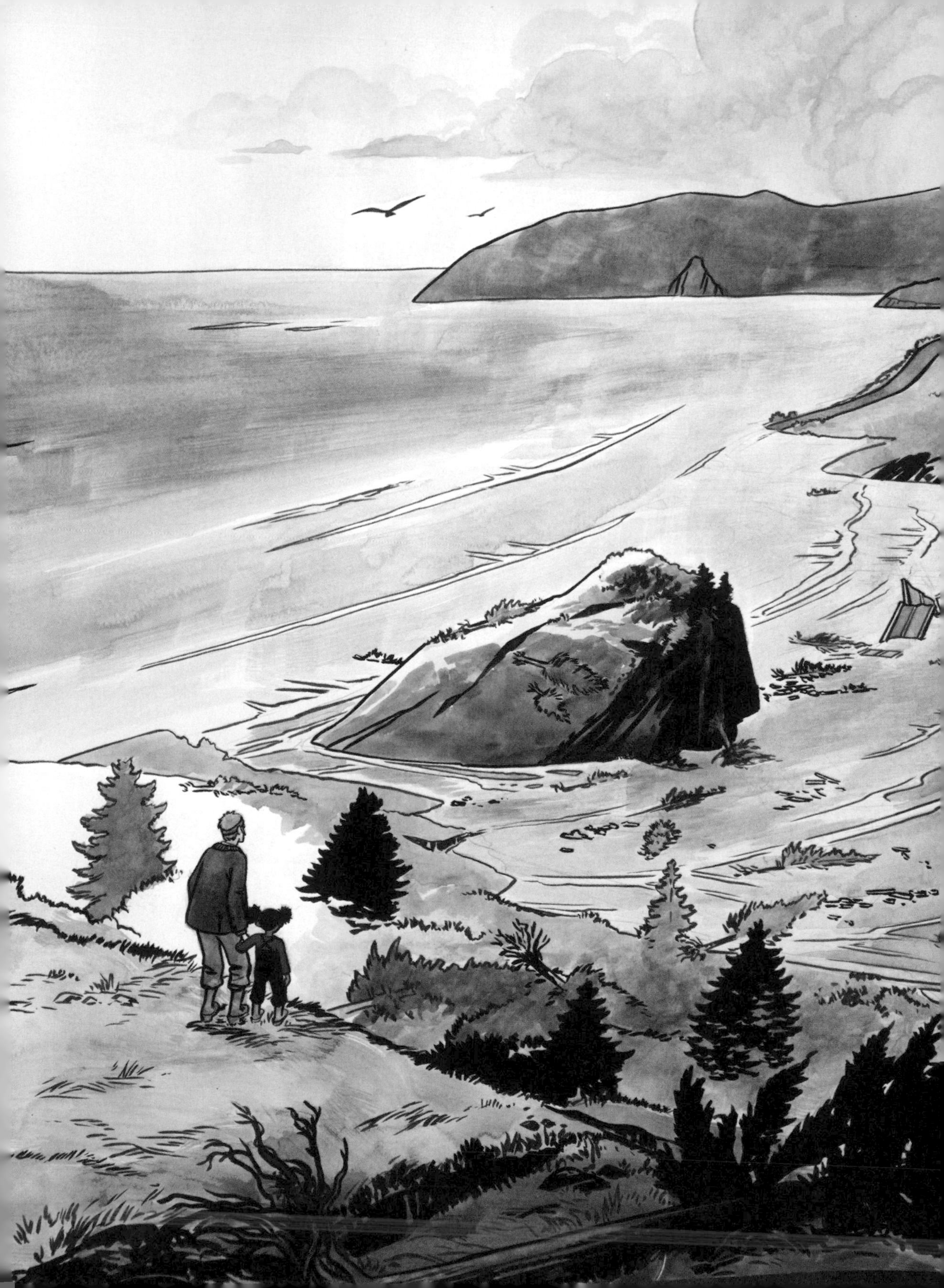

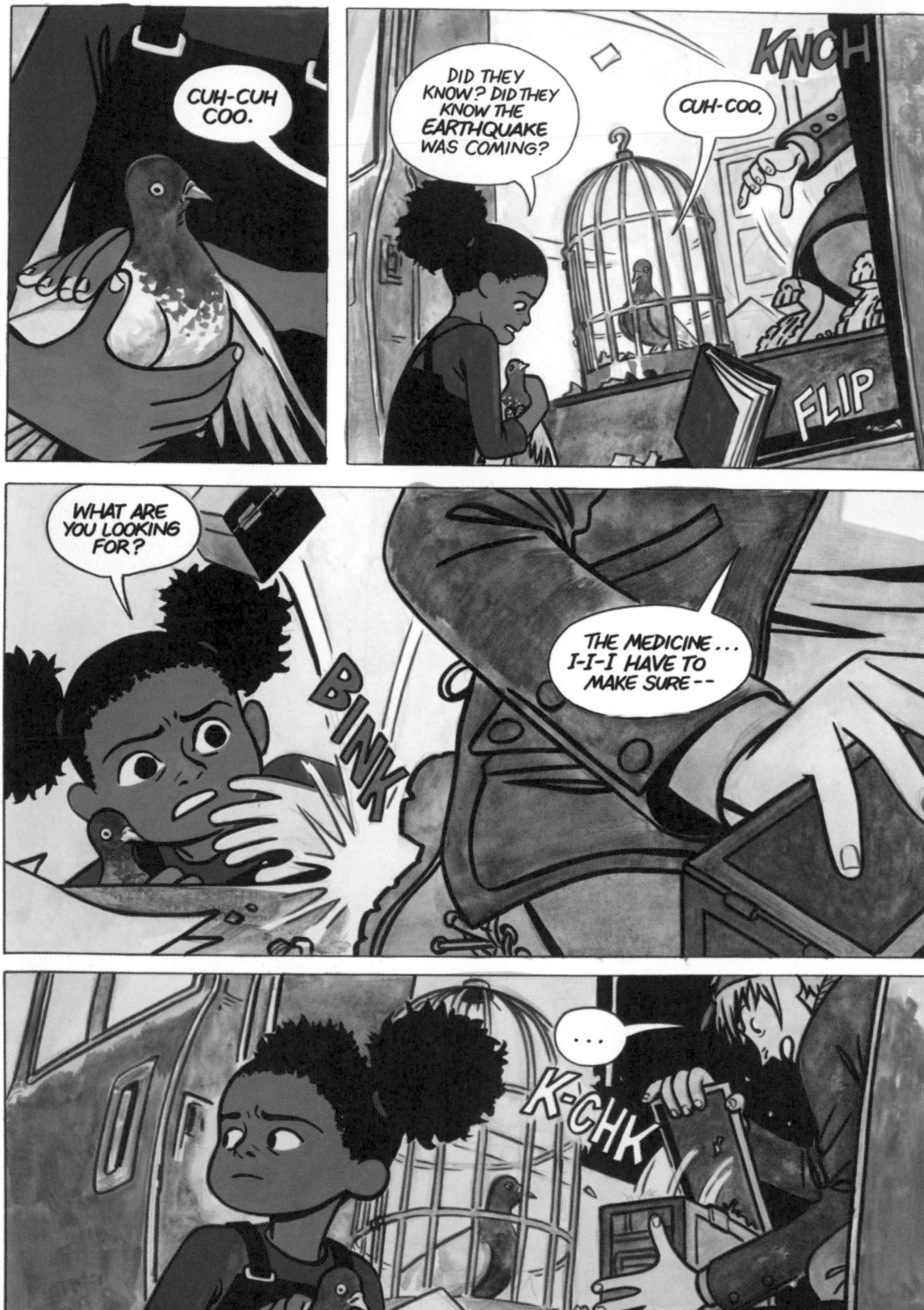
CUH-CUH COO.
DID THEY KNOW? DID THEY KNOW THE EARTHQUAKE WAS COMING?
KNCH
CUH-COO.
FLIP
WHAT ARE YOU LOOKING FOR?
THE MEDICINE . . . I-I-I HAVE TO MAKE SURE --
BINK
. . .
K-CHK

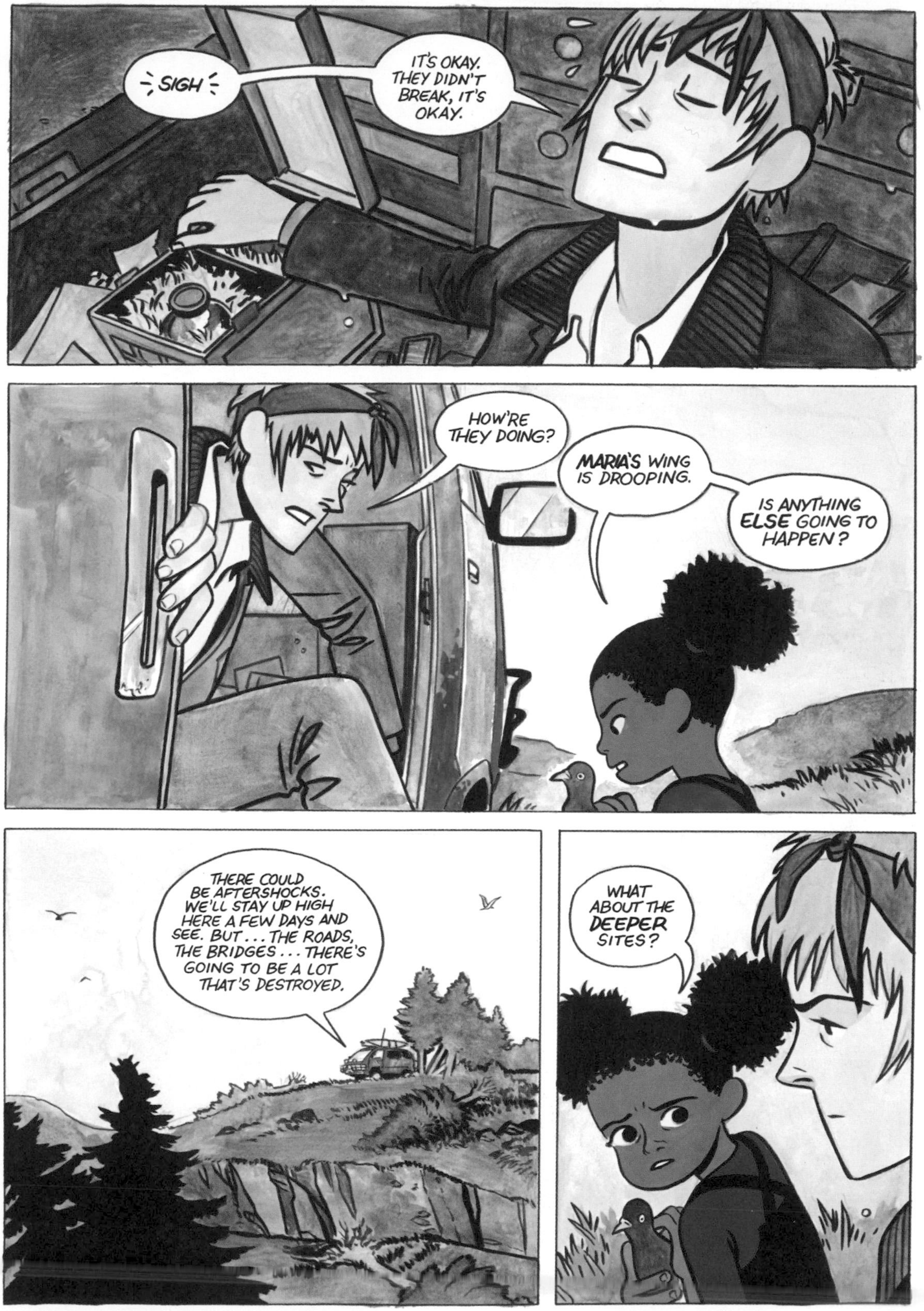
SIGH
IT'S OKAY. THEY DIDN'T BREAK, IT'S OKAY.
HOW'RE THEY DOING?
MARIA'S WING IS DROOPING.
IS ANYTHING ELSE GOING TO HAPPEN?
THERE COULD BE AFTERSHOCKS. WE'LL STAY UP HIGH HERE A FEW DAYS AND SEE. BUT . . . THE ROADS, THE BRIDGES . . . THERE'S GOING TO BE A LOT THAT'S DESTROYED.
WHAT ABOUT THE DEEPER SITES?

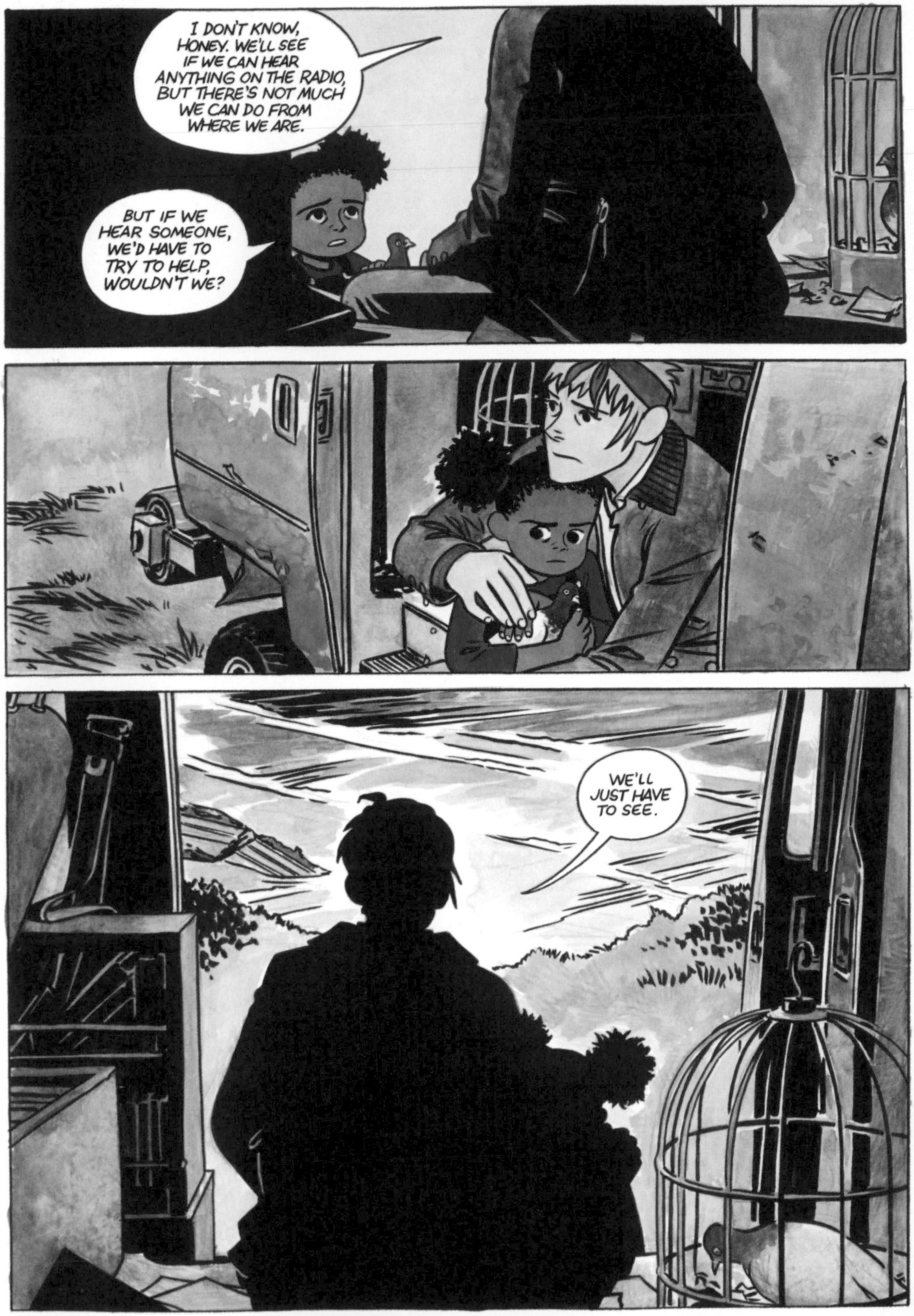
I DON'T KNOW, HONEY. WE'LL SEE IF WE CAN HEAR ANYTHING ON THE RADIO, BUT THERE'S NOT MUCH WE CAN DO FROM WHERE WE ARE.
BUT IF WE HEAR SOMEONE, WE'D HAVE TO TRY TO HELP, WOULDN'T WE?
WE'LL JUST HAVE TO SEE.

CHAPTER FOUR
I CATCH ONE

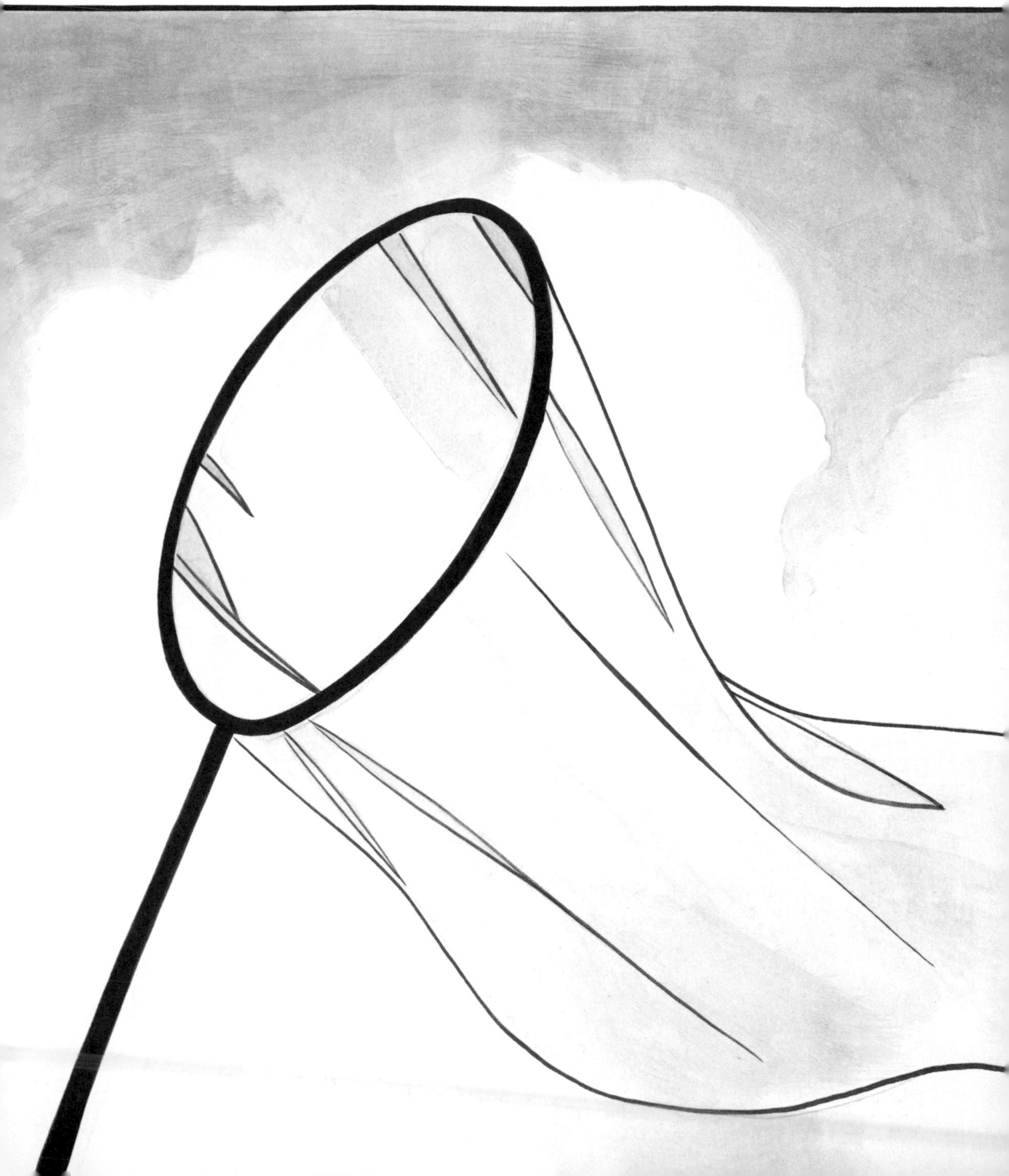

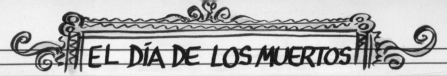

EL DÍA DE LOS MUERTOS

THERE USED TO BE A HOLIDAY CALLED THE **DAY OF THE DEAD** (IT'S ACTUALLY SEVERAL DAYS LONG) WHERE PEOPLE WOULD "WELCOME" THEIR DEARLY DEPARTED BACK HOME FOR A LITTLE VISIT. THE FESTIVAL WENT ON AT THE SAME TIME OF YEAR THAT MONARCHS RETURN SOUTH FOR THE WINTER: AROUND **LATE OCTOBER AND EARLY NOVEMBER.** PEOPLE CELEBRATING SAID THE BUTTERFLIES WERE THE SPIRITS COMING BACK.

I DON'T KNOW IF ANYONE REALLY BELIEVED THAT, OR IF IT WAS JUST A STORY -- BUT THERE IS A MYSTERY ABOUT MONARCHS THAT EVEN **FLORA** CAN'T EXPLAIN...

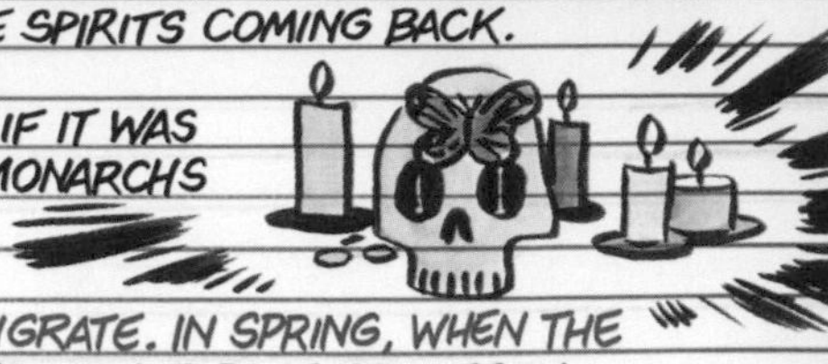

IT TAKES THE BUTTERFLIES FOUR GENERATIONS TO MIGRATE. IN SPRING, WHEN THE OVERWINTERING MONARCHS LEAVE THEIR EUCALYPTUS AND PINE GROVES IN CALIFORNIA AND MEXICO, THEY START LAYING EGGS IMMEDIATELY. THE FIRST GENERATION HATCHES, FLIES FARTHER NORTH, MATES, AND LAYS MORE EGGS. THIS CONTINUES THROUGH THE SUMMER WITH THE SECOND AND THIRD GENERATIONS, UNTIL MOST OF THE MIGRATION MAKES IT INTO THE UPPER HALF OF THE UNITED STATES.

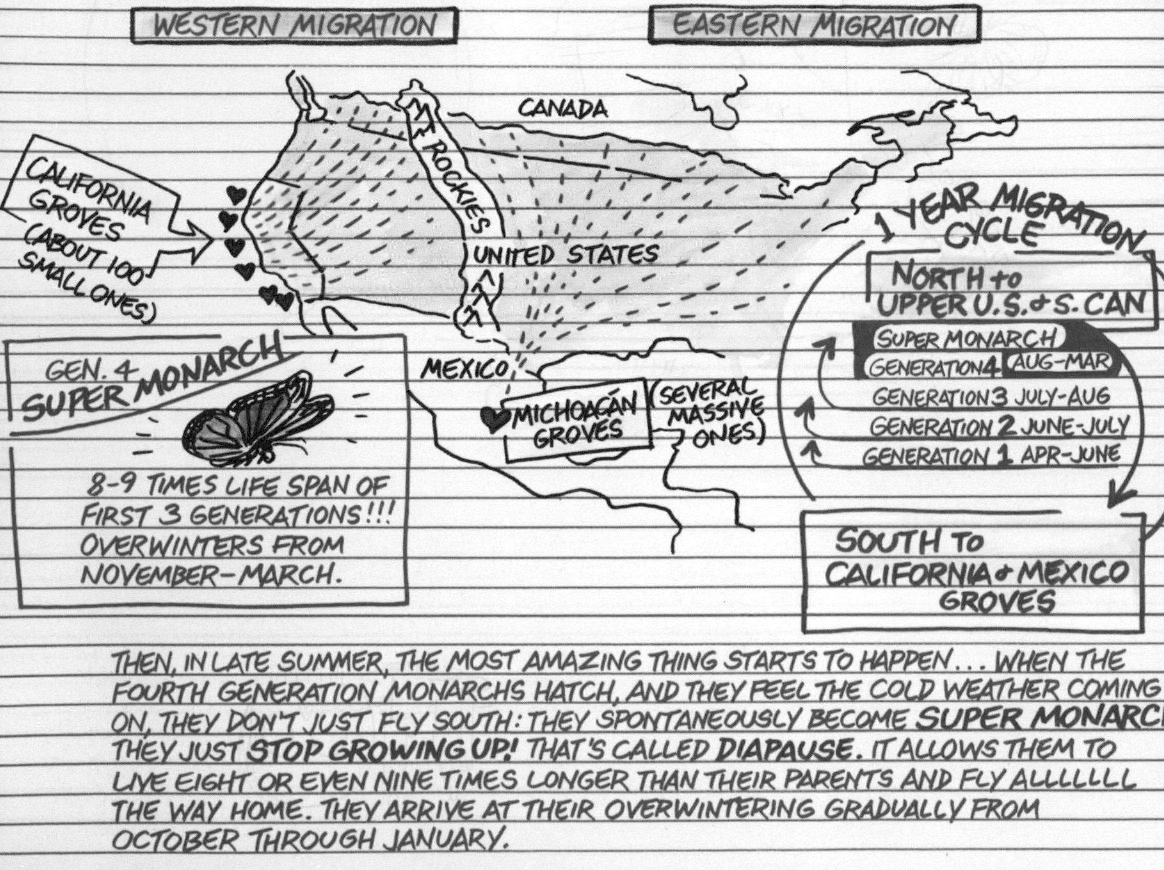
WESTERN MIGRATION
EASTERN MIGRATION
CANADA
MT ROCKIES
UNITED STATES
MEXICO
CALIFORNIA GROVES (ABOUT 100 SMALL ONES)
MICHOACÁN GROVES
(SEVERAL MASSIVE ONES)
GEN. 4
SUPER MONARCH
8-9 TIMES LIFE SPAN OF FIRST 3 GENERATIONS!!!
OVERWINTERS FROM NOVEMBER-MARCH.
1 YEAR MIGRATION CYCLE
NORTH to UPPER U.S. & S. CAN
SUPER MONARCH
GENERATION 4 AUG-MAR
GENERATION 3 JULY-AUG
GENERATION 2 JUNE-JULY
GENERATION 1 APR-JUNE
SOUTH TO CALIFORNIA & MEXICO GROVES

THEN, IN LATE SUMMER, THE MOST AMAZING THING STARTS TO HAPPEN... WHEN THE FOURTH GENERATION MONARCHS HATCH, AND THEY FEEL THE COLD WEATHER COMING ON, THEY DON'T JUST FLY SOUTH: THEY SPONTANEOUSLY BECOME **SUPER MONARCHS.** THEY JUST **STOP GROWING UP!** THAT'S CALLED **DIAPAUSE.** IT ALLOWS THEM TO LIVE EIGHT OR EVEN NINE TIMES LONGER THAN THEIR PARENTS AND FLY ALLLLLLL THE WAY HOME. THEY ARRIVE AT THEIR OVERWINTERING GRADUALLY FROM OCTOBER THROUGH JANUARY.

NO MONARCHS SINCE THEIR GREAT-GRANDPARENTS HAVE SEEN THOSE GROVES, BUT SOMEHOW, EVERY GENERATION CARRIES THE COORDINATES INSIDE THEM. IT'S NOT LIKE THE MAMA MONARCHS WHISPER DIRECTIONS TO THEIR BABIES, EITHER -- THEY FLY AWAY AND DIE BEFORE THE EGGS HATCH.

I WONDER SOMETIMES WHAT IT'D BE LIKE TO KNOW SOMETHING MY MAMA KNEW. EVEN IF I STILL COULDN'T REMEMBER HER VOICE OR ANY WORDS SHE SAID BEFORE SHE LEFT, WHAT IF I COULD KNOW **SOMETHING** -- LIKE THE MONARCHS DO.

THE CLOSEST I COME TO THAT IS THIS **OLD RECORD** OF HERS. MY **GRANDPA** FOUND IT ON A NIGHT RANGE AND GAVE IT TO HER WHEN SHE WAS A GIRL. **FLORA** SAID THEY DIDN'T HAVE A WAY TO PLAY IT FOR YEARS. MAMA JUST LIKED THE PHOTO ON THE ALBUM COVER. **GRANDPA JONES** WAS A REALLY GOOD ENGINEER, THOUGH, AND EVENTUALLY HE MADE HER THIS LITTLE ROLLING GADGET THAT RUNS A NEEDLE AROUND AND AROUND AND PLAYS THE MUSIC FROM A SPEAKER ON TOP. I STILL HAVE IT. I'M NOT SURE HOW HE GOT IT TO WORK. **FLORA** SAID HE USED SOME PARTS FROM AN RGD WALKIE-TALKIE. PRETTY SMART! ANYWAY, I LIKE TO LISTEN TO THE MUSIC AND WONDER WHAT SHE THOUGHT ABOUT IT.

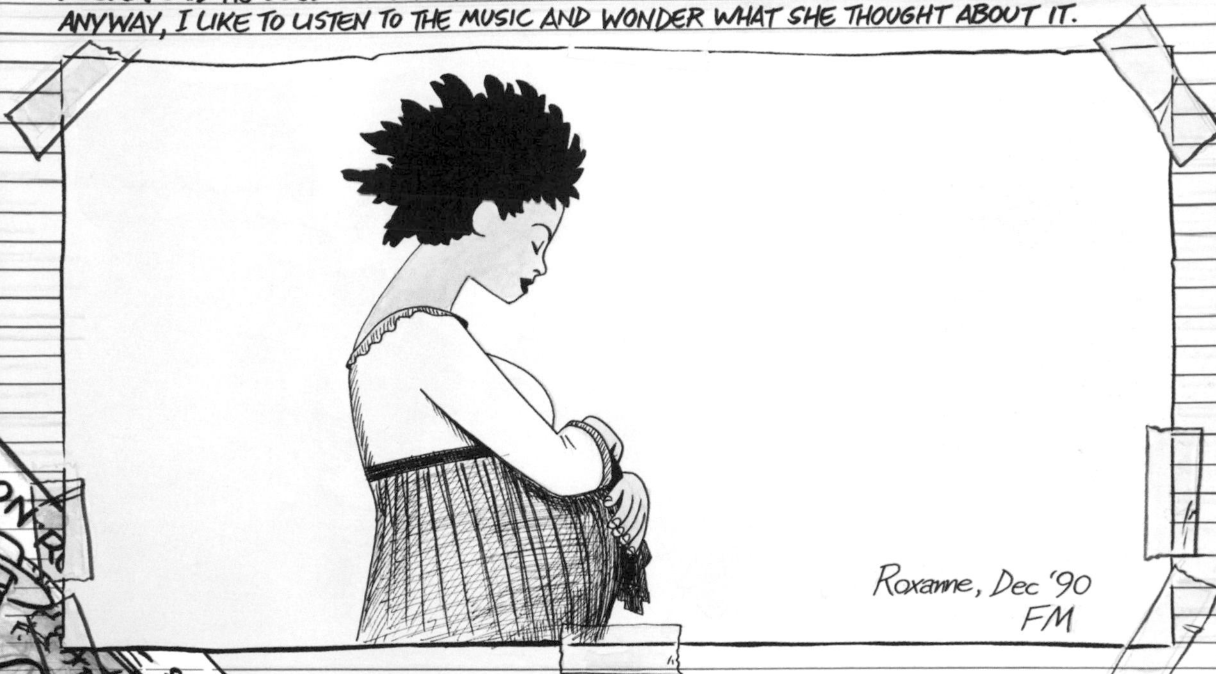
Roxanne, Dec '90
FM

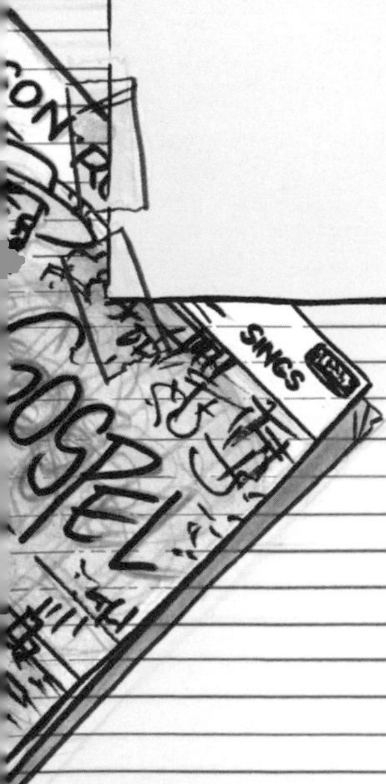
SINGS

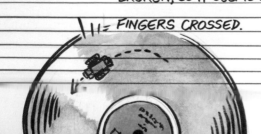

SEPTEMBER 14. WE HAVE FIFTEEN DAYS UNTIL OUR MONARCH MEDICINE EXPIRES, AND IT'S BEEN THREE DAYS SINCE THE **CASCADIA QUAKE.** THAT'S WHAT **FLORA** THINKS IT WAS, ~~AT~~ AT LEAST. SUPPOSEDLY IT HAPPENS ABOUT EVERY 250 YEARS AND WRECKS EVERYTHING ON THE WEST COAST FROM CANADA TO NORTHERN CALIFORNIA. TODAY WE SAW A **BROOSE** DRIVING AROUND IN CIRCLES LIKE IT COULDN'T FIGURE OUT WHAT TO FIX FIRST. IT WAS KIND OF FUNNY UNTIL I THOUGHT AGAIN OF ALL THE PEOPLE WHO MIGHT BE STUCK UNDERGROUND. WE'RE STILL ON THE COAST NOW, IN **BROOKINGS,** BUT TOMORROW WE'LL TURN EAST, AWAY FROM THE OCEAN. THE HIGHWAY'S ALREADY A LITTLE LESS BROKEN, SO IT SEEMS LIKE WE'LL GET TO THE **ROGUE VALLEY** OKAY.

FINGERS CROSSED.

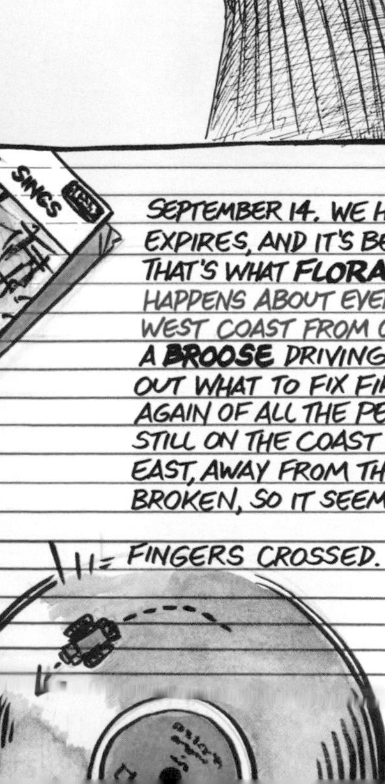

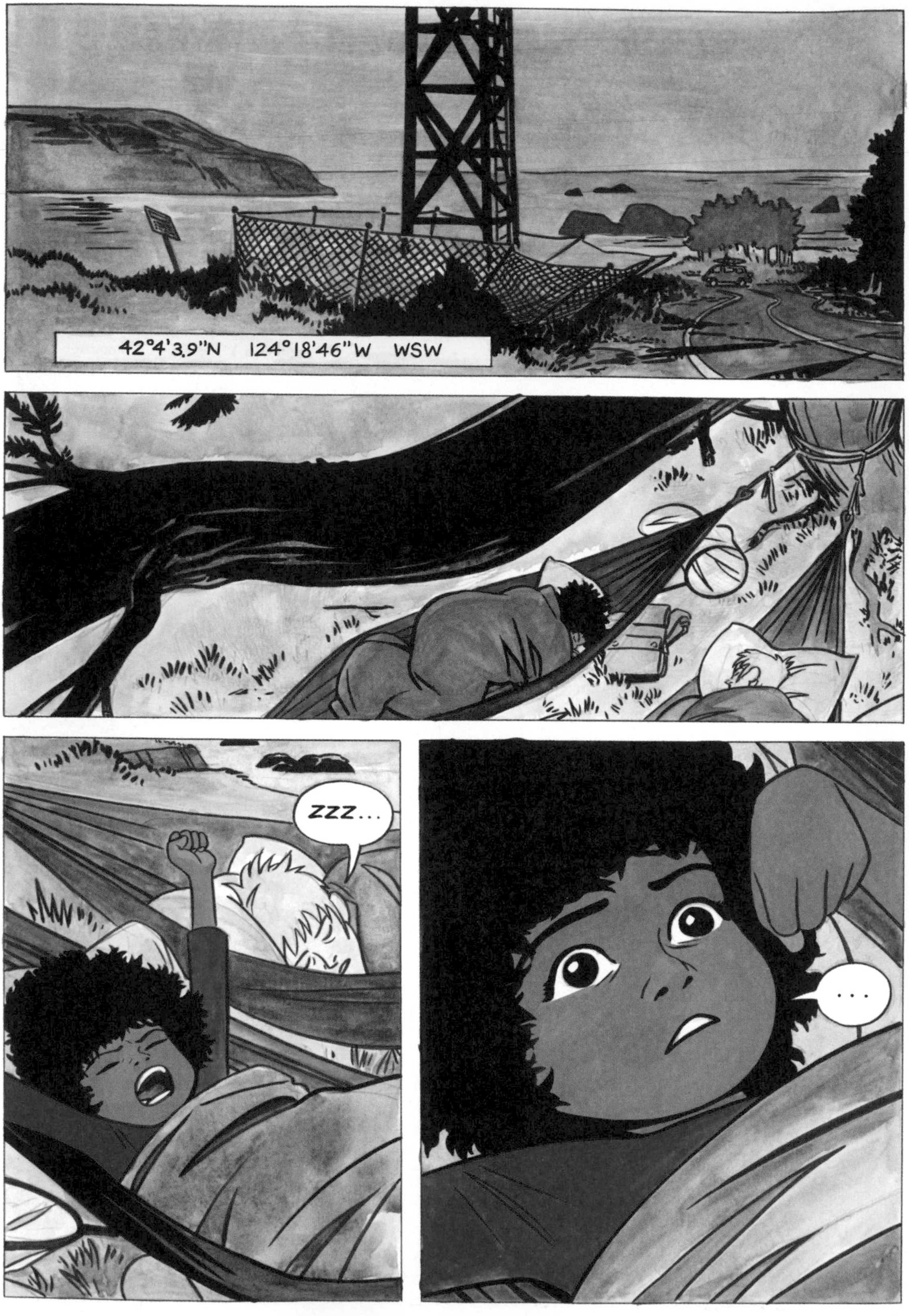
42°4'3.9"N 124°18'46"W WSW
ZZZ...
...

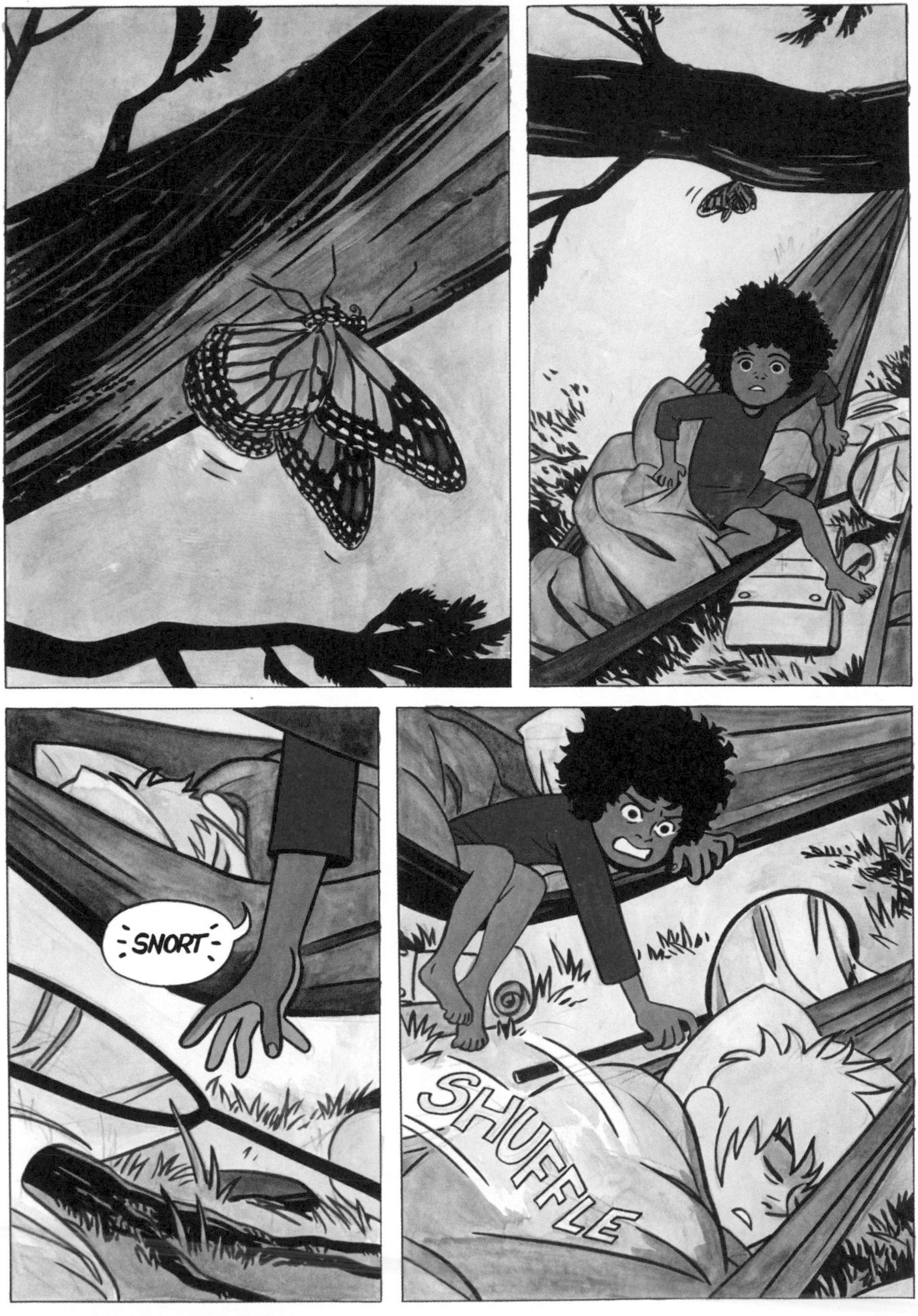
SNORT
SHUFFLE

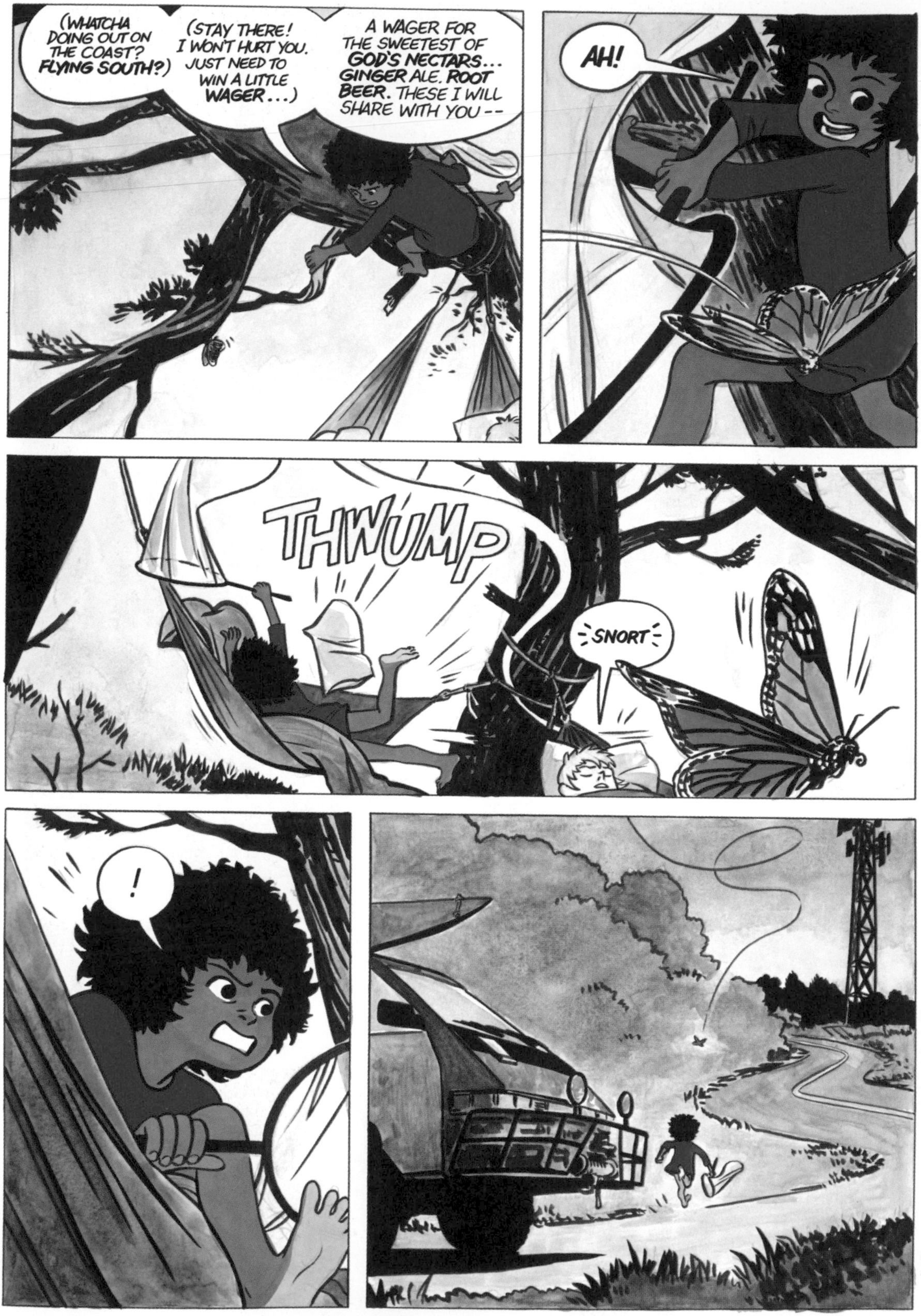
(WHATCHA DOING OUT ON THE COAST? FLYING SOUTH?)
(STAY THERE! I WON'T HURT YOU. JUST NEED TO WIN A LITTLE WAGER...)
A WAGER FOR THE SWEETEST OF GOD'S NECTARS... GINGER ALE. ROOT BEER. THESE I WILL SHARE WITH YOU --
AH!
THWUMP
SNORT
!

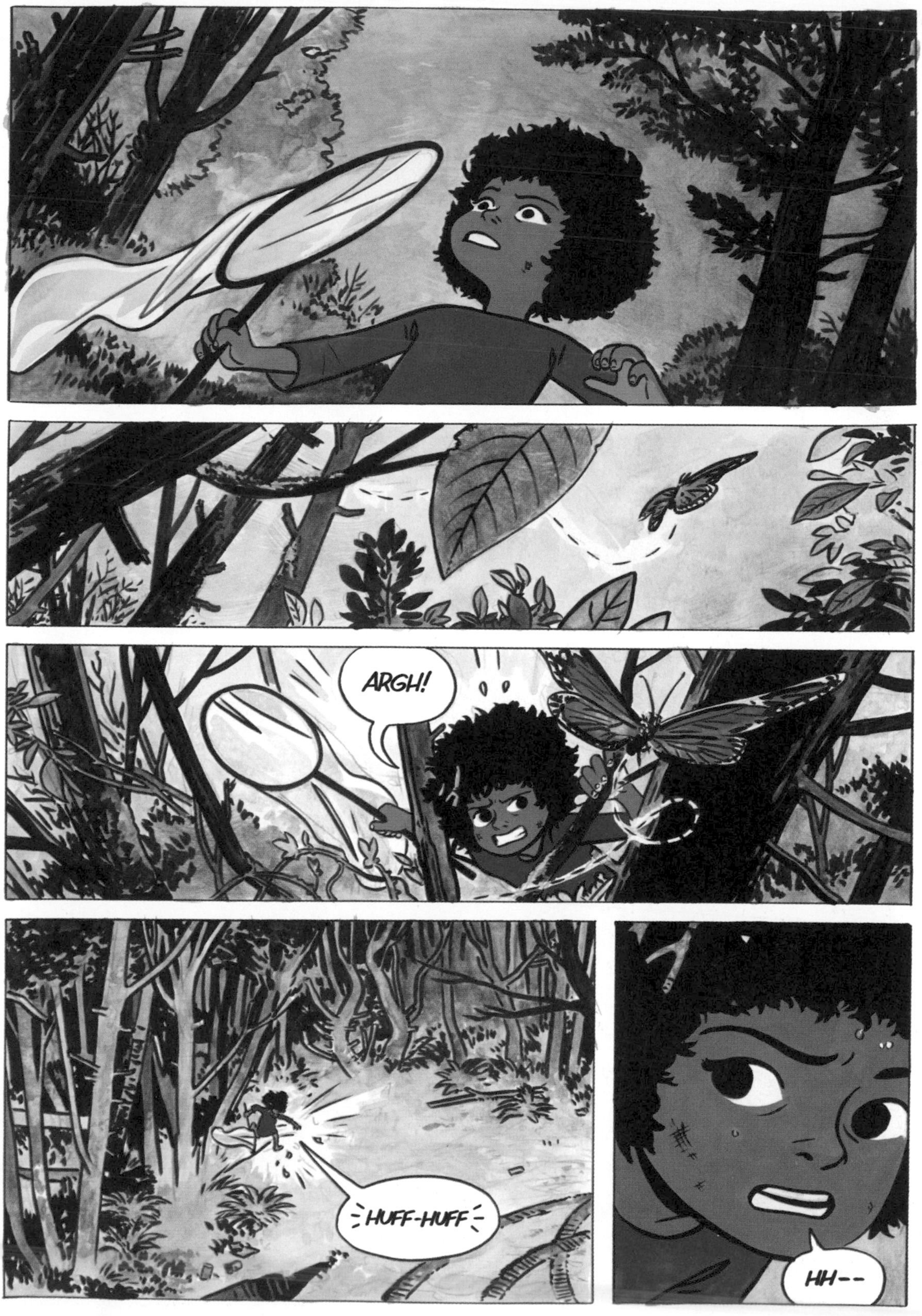
ARGH!
HUFF-HUFF
HH--

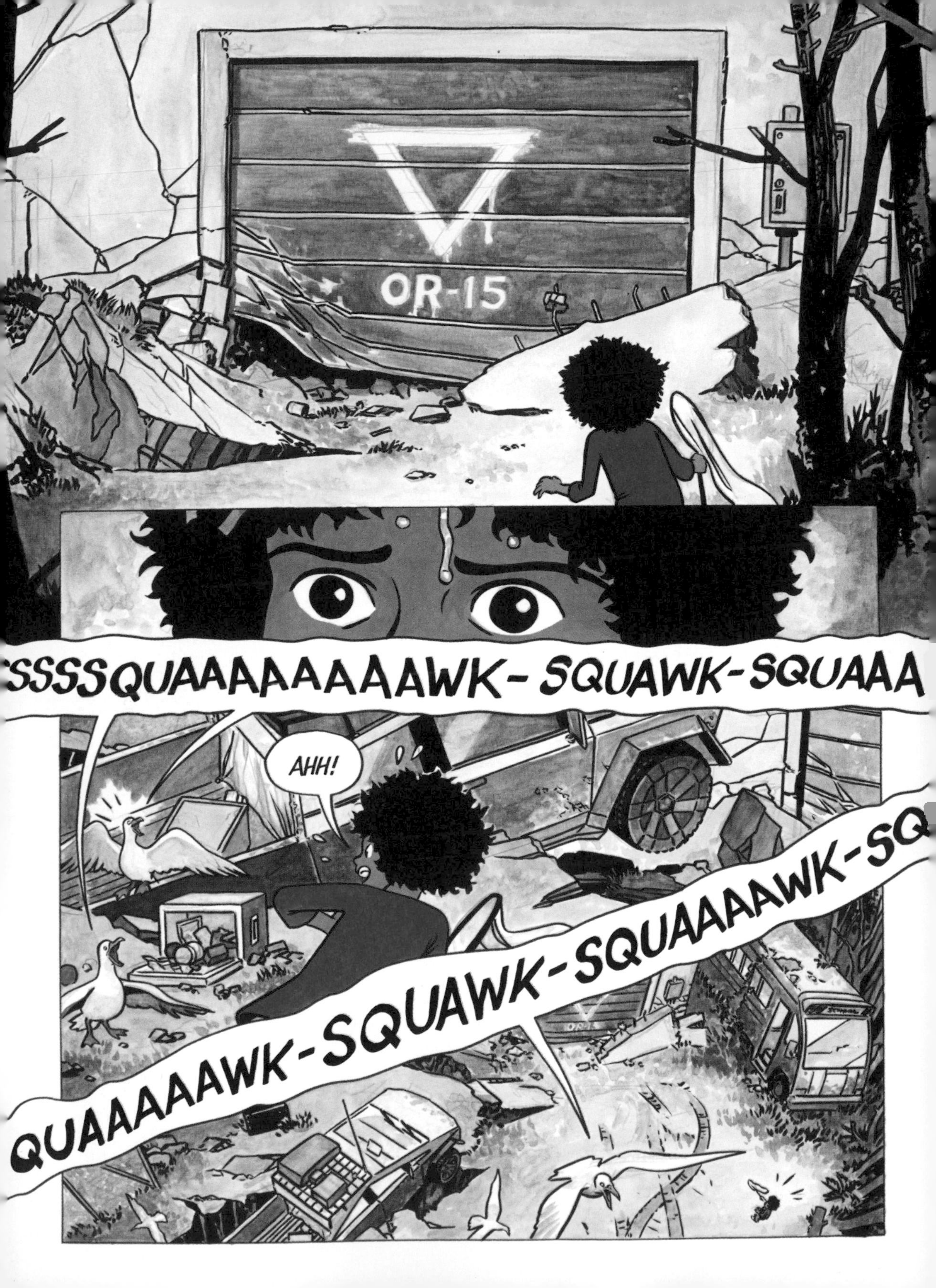
OR-15
SSSSQUAAAAAAAAAWK- SQUAWK-SQUAAA
AHH!
QUAAAAAAWK-SQUAWK-SQUAAAAAWK-SQ
OR-15

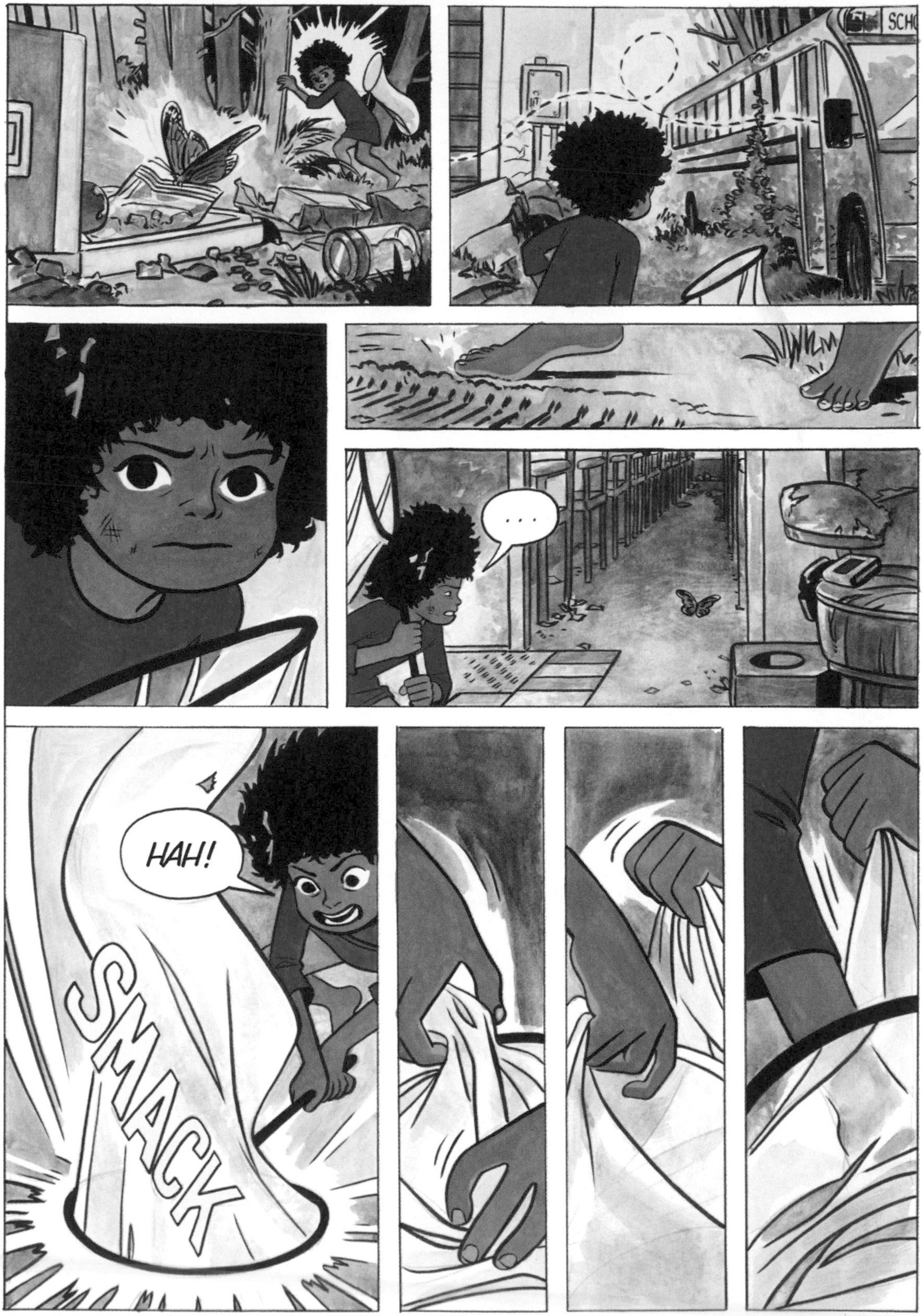
SCHO
...
HAH!
SMACK

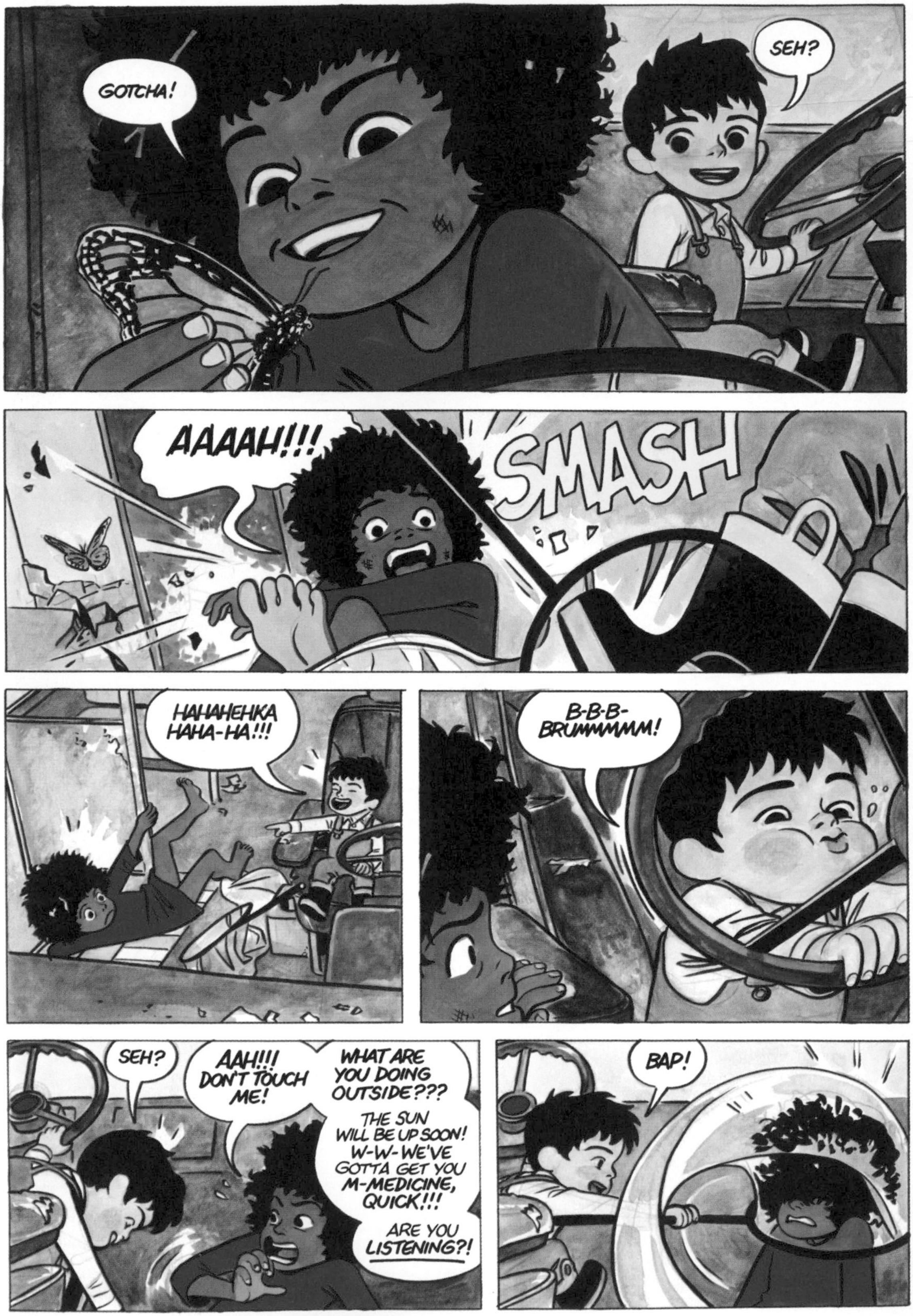
GOTCHA!
SEH?
AAAAH!!!
SMASH
HAHAHEHKA HAHA-HA!!!
B-B-B-BRUMMMMM!
SEH?
AAH!!! DON'T TOUCH ME!
WHAT ARE YOU DOING OUTSIDE???
THE SUN WILL BE UP SOON! W-W-WE'VE GOTTA GET YOU M-MEDICINE, QUICK!!!
ARE YOU LISTENING?!
BAP!

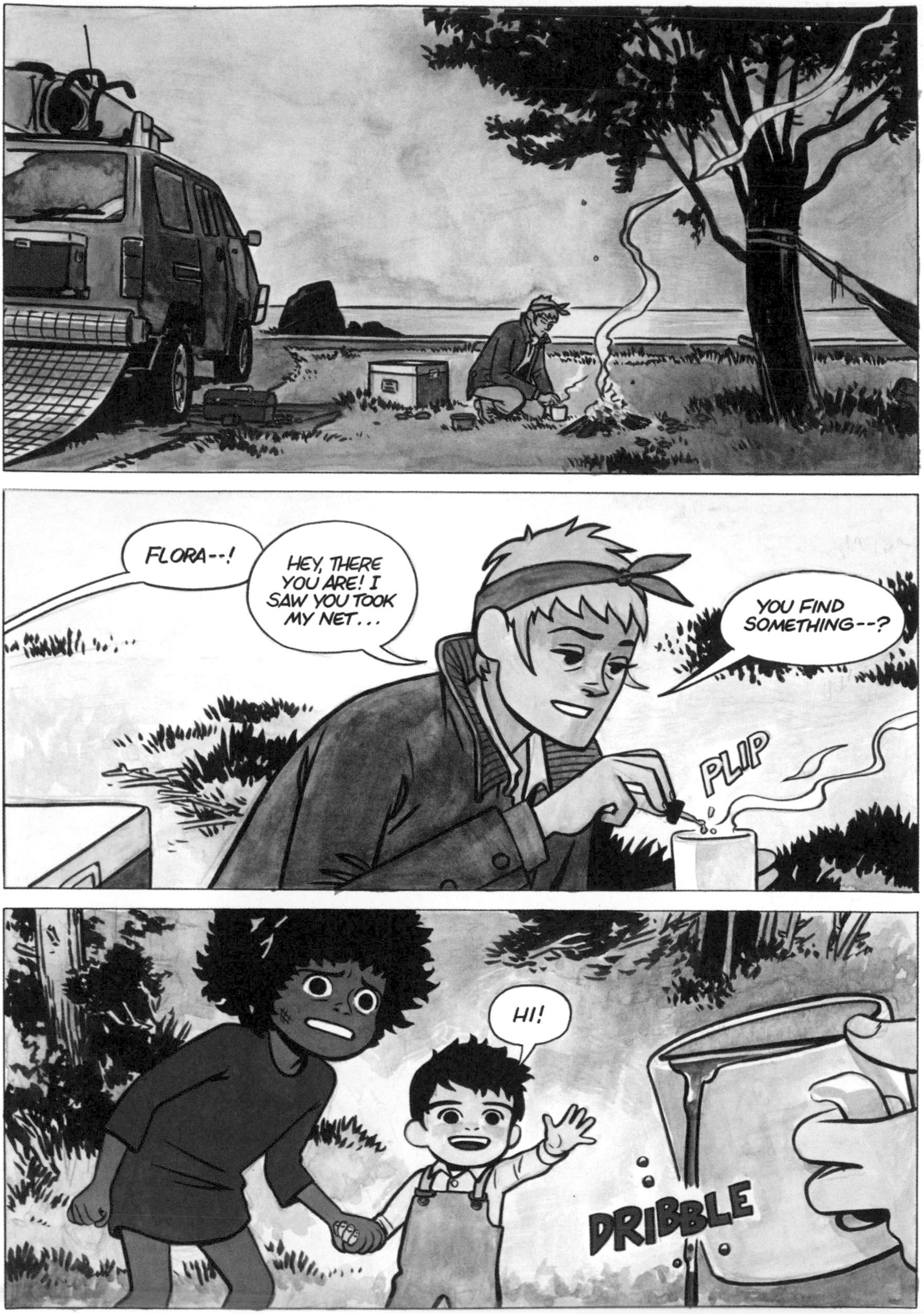
FLORA--!
HEY, THERE YOU ARE! I SAW YOU TOOK MY NET...
YOU FIND SOMETHING--?
PLIP
HI!
DRIBBLE

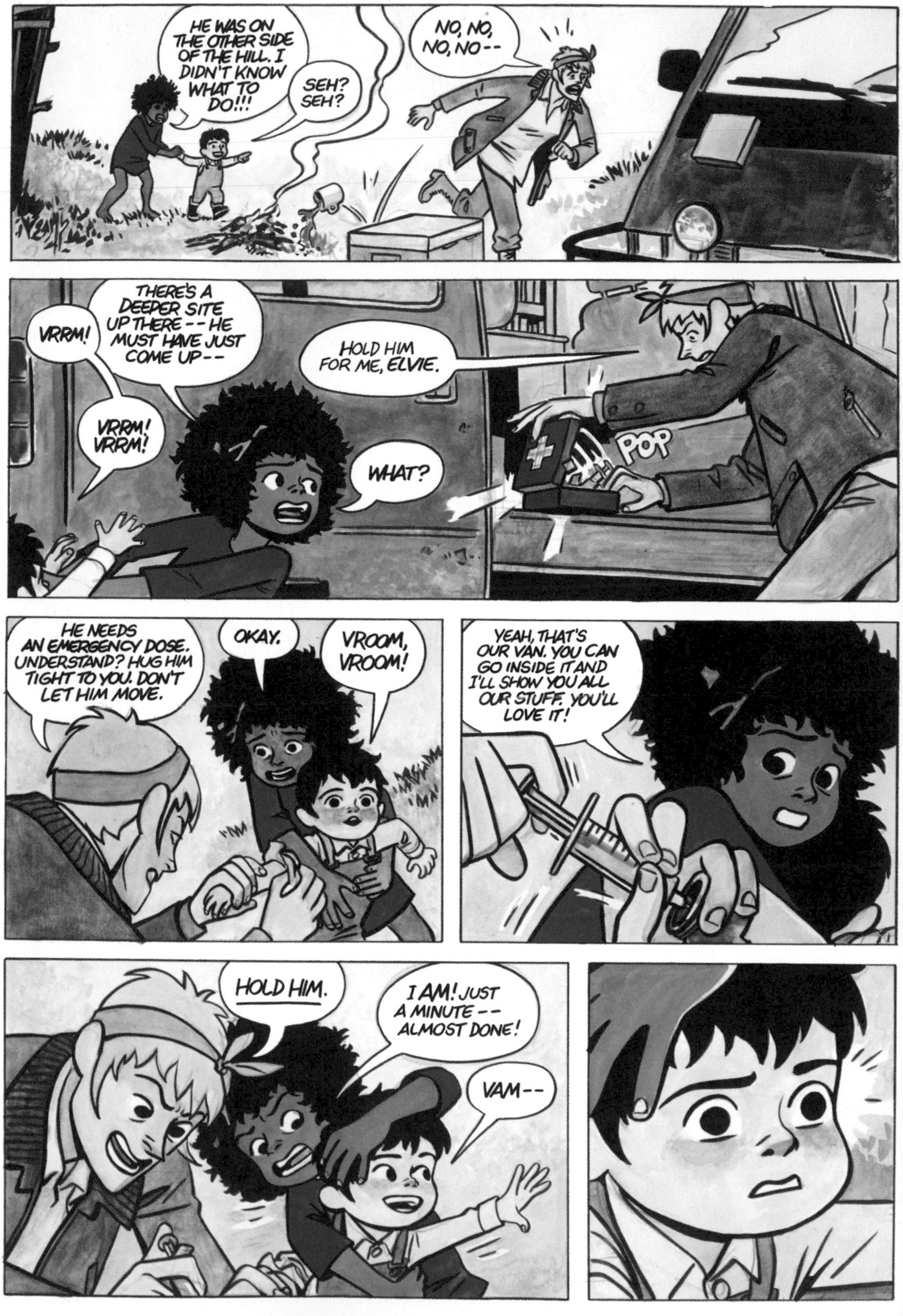
HE WAS ON THE OTHER SIDE OF THE HILL. I DIDN'T KNOW WHAT TO DO!!!
SEH? SEH?
NO, NO, NO, NO--
VRRM!
THERE'S A DEEPER SITE UP THERE--HE MUST HAVE JUST COME UP--
HOLD HIM FOR ME, ELVIE.
VRRM! VRRM!
WHAT?
POP
HE NEEDS AN EMERGENCY DOSE. UNDERSTAND? HUG HIM TIGHT TO YOU. DON'T LET HIM MOVE.
OKAY.
VROOM, VROOM!
YEAH, THAT'S OUR VAN. YOU CAN GO INSIDE IT AND I'LL SHOW YOU ALL OUR STUFF. YOU'LL LOVE IT!
HOLD HIM.
I AM! JUST A MINUTE--ALMOST DONE!
VAM--

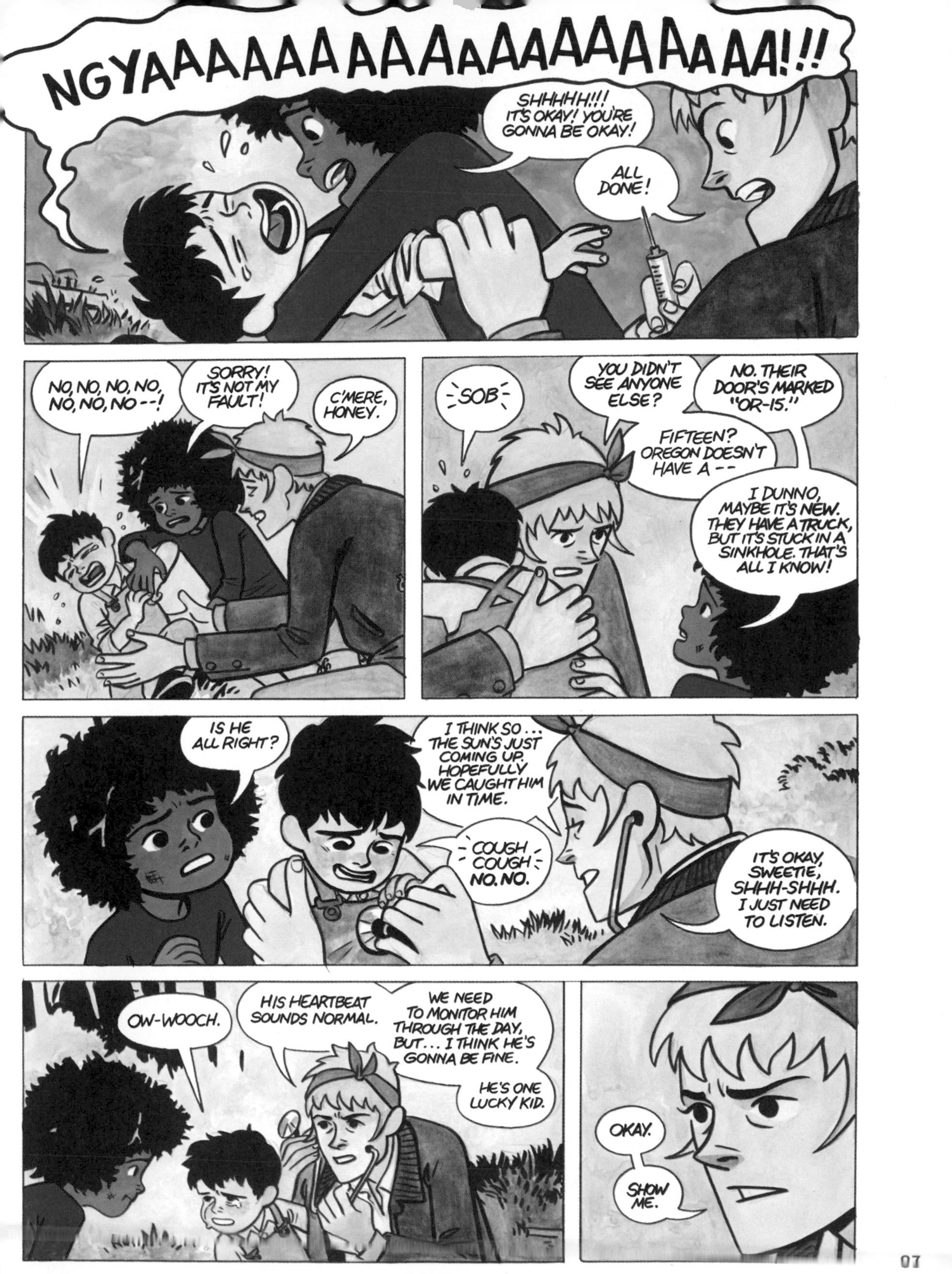
NGYAAAAAAAAAAAAAAAAAAAA!!!
SHHHHH!!! IT'S OKAY! YOU'RE GONNA BE OKAY!
ALL DONE!
NO, NO, NO, NO, NO, NO, NO--!
SORRY! IT'S NOT MY FAULT!
C'MERE, HONEY.
SOB
YOU DIDN'T SEE ANYONE ELSE?
NO. THEIR DOOR'S MARKED "OR-15."
FIFTEEN? OREGON DOESN'T HAVE A --
I DUNNO, MAYBE IT'S NEW. THEY HAVE A TRUCK, BUT IT'S STUCK IN A SINKHOLE. THAT'S ALL I KNOW!
IS HE ALL RIGHT?
I THINK SO... THE SUN'S JUST COMING UP. HOPEFULLY WE CAUGHT HIM IN TIME.
COUGH COUGH NO. NO.
IT'S OKAY, SWEETIE, SHHH-SHHH. I JUST NEED TO LISTEN.
OW-WOOCH.
HIS HEARTBEAT SOUNDS NORMAL.
WE NEED TO MONITOR HIM THROUGH THE DAY, BUT... I THINK HE'S GONNA BE FINE.
HE'S ONE LUCKY KID.
OKAY.
SHOW ME.

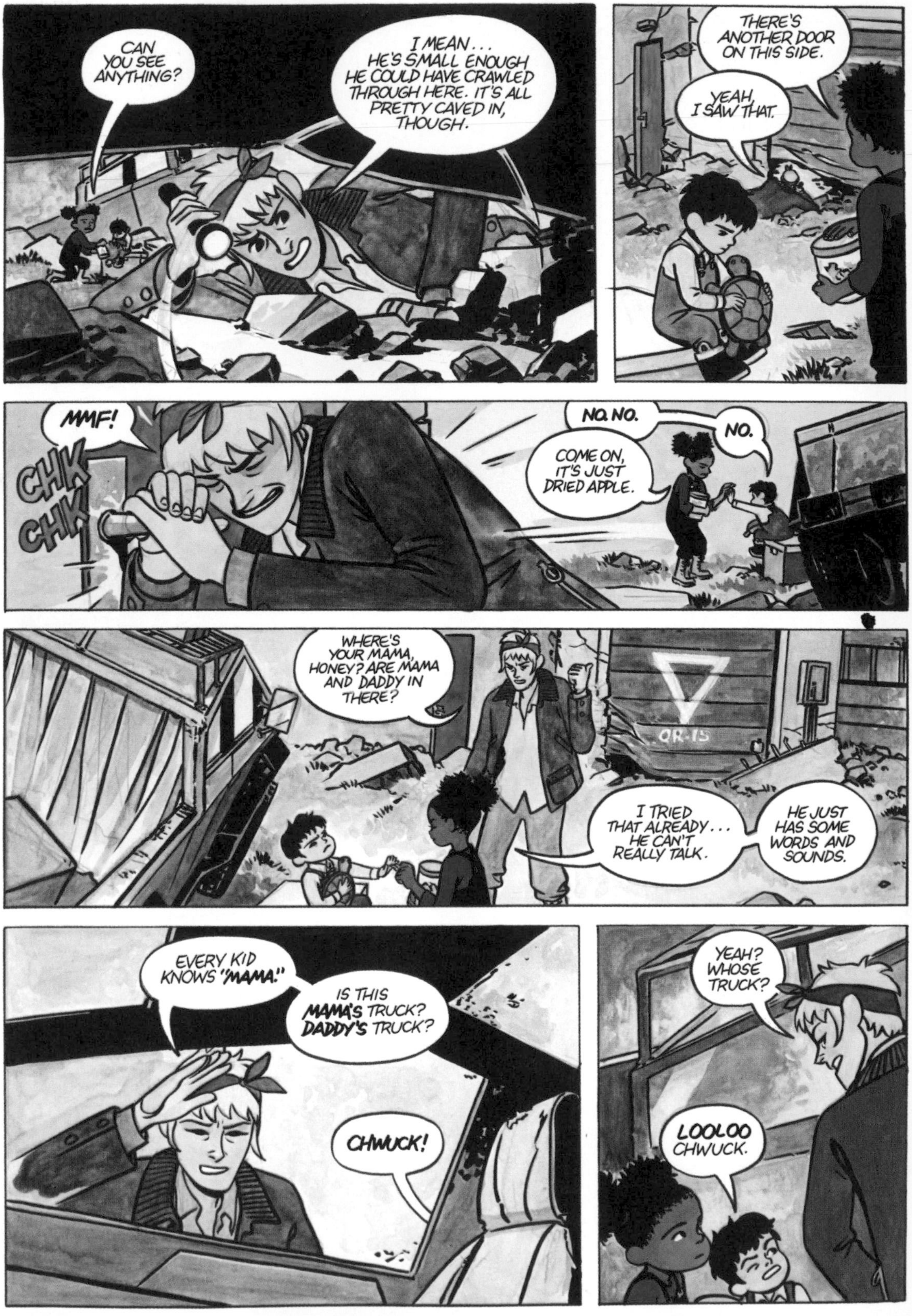
CAN YOU SEE ANYTHING?
I MEAN... HE'S SMALL ENOUGH HE COULD HAVE CRAWLED THROUGH HERE. IT'S ALL PRETTY CAVED IN, THOUGH.
THERE'S ANOTHER DOOR ON THIS SIDE.
YEAH, I SAW THAT.
MMF!
CHK CHK
NO. NO.
NO.
COME ON, IT'S JUST DRIED APPLE.
WHERE'S YOUR MAMA, HONEY? ARE MAMA AND DADDY IN THERE?
QR-15
I TRIED THAT ALREADY... HE CAN'T REALLY TALK.
HE JUST HAS SOME WORDS AND SOUNDS.
EVERY KID KNOWS "MAMA."
IS THIS MAMA'S TRUCK? DADDY'S TRUCK?
CHWUCK!
YEAH? WHOSE TRUCK?
LOOLOO CHWUCK.

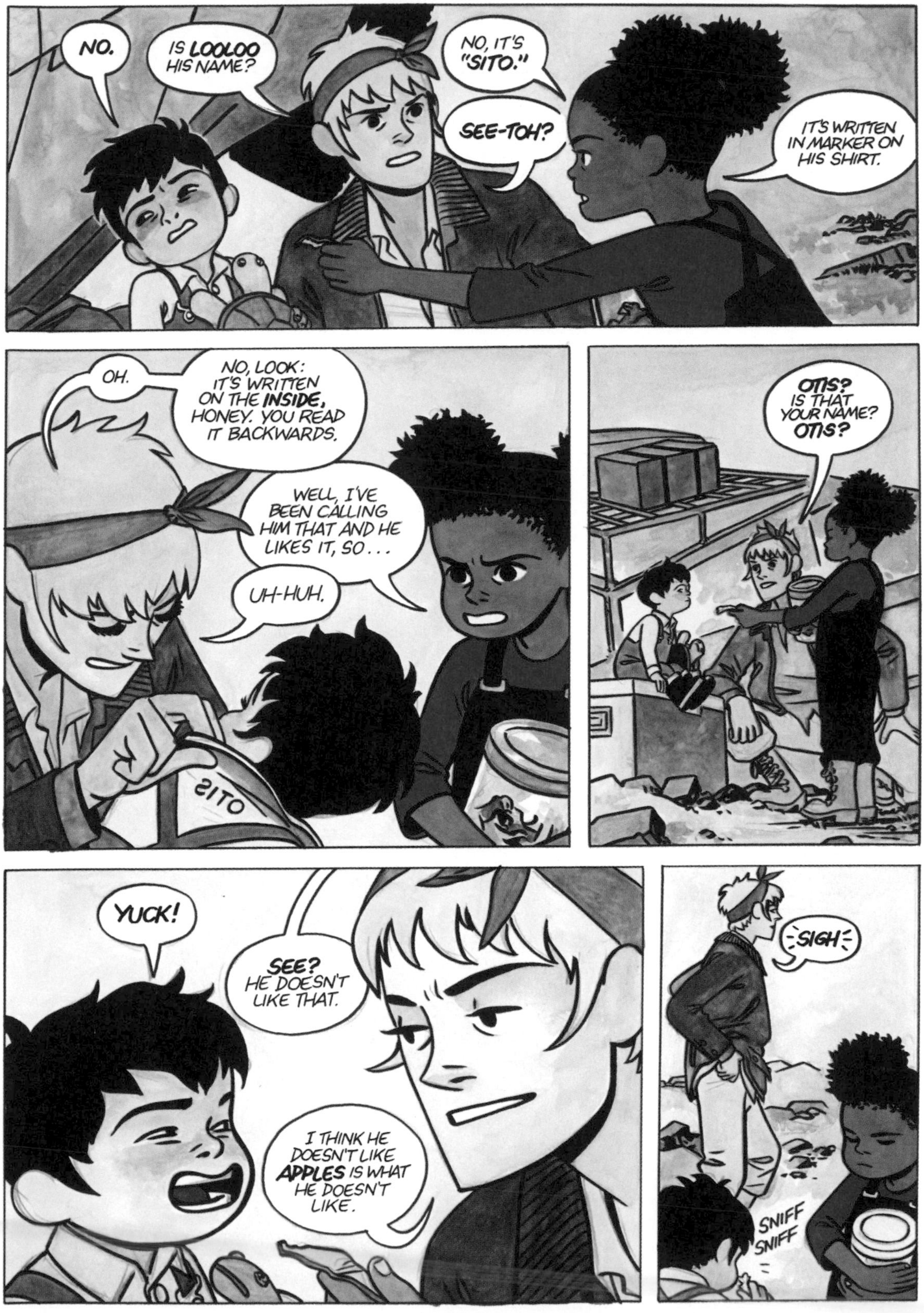

NO.
IS LOOLOO HIS NAME?
NO, IT'S "SITO."
SEE-TOH?
IT'S WRITTEN IN MARKER ON HIS SHIRT.
OH.
NO, LOOK: IT'S WRITTEN ON THE INSIDE, HONEY. YOU READ IT BACKWARDS.
WELL, I'VE BEEN CALLING HIM THAT AND HE LIKES IT, SO . . .
UH-HUH.
OTIS
OTIS? IS THAT YOUR NAME? OTIS?
YUCK!
SEE? HE DOESN'T LIKE THAT.
I THINK HE DOESN'T LIKE APPLES IS WHAT HE DOESN'T LIKE.
SIGH
SNIFF SNIFF

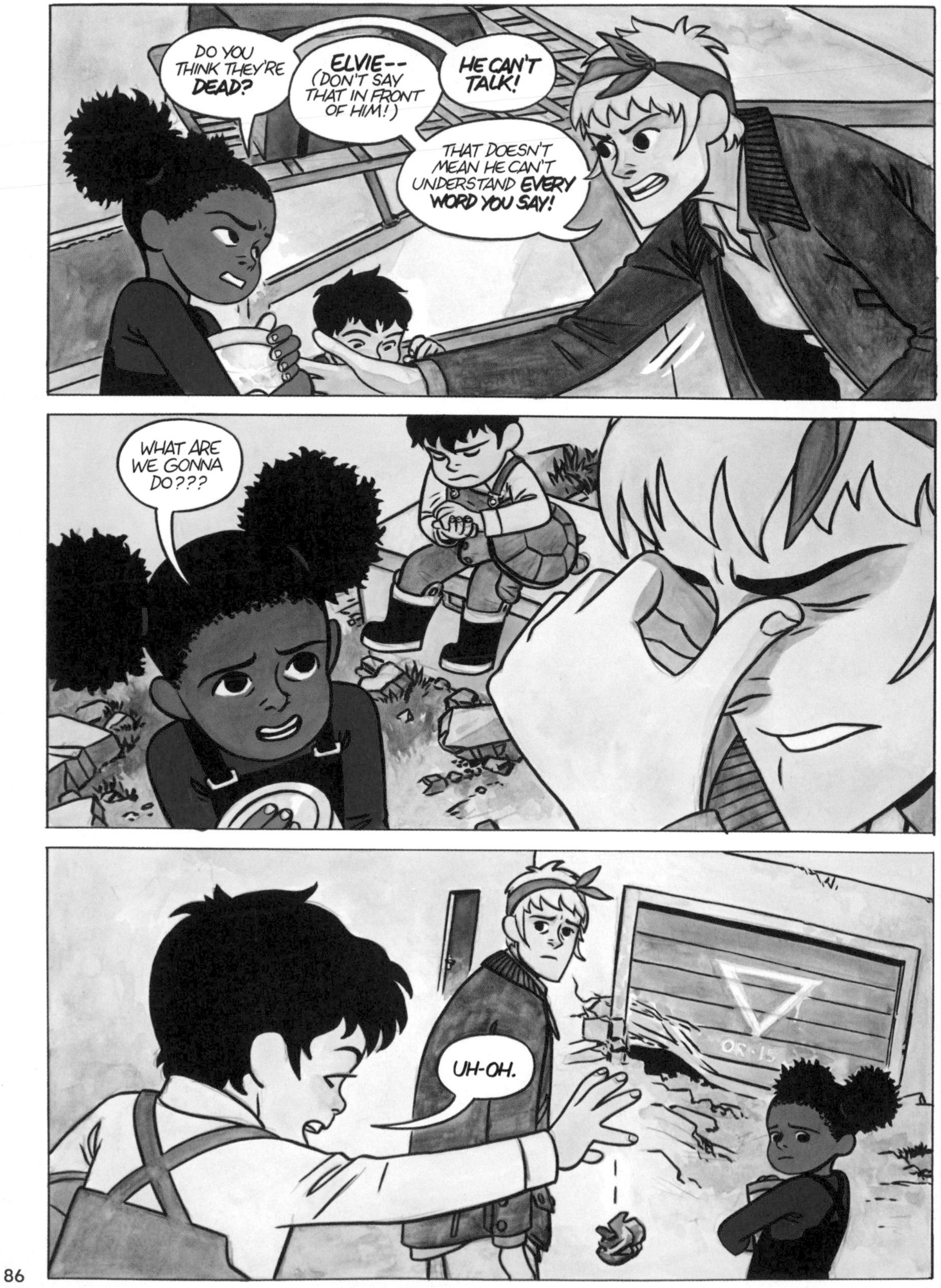
DO YOU THINK THEY'RE DEAD?
ELVIE-- (DON'T SAY THAT IN FRONT OF HIM!)
HE CAN'T TALK!
THAT DOESN'T MEAN HE CAN'T UNDERSTAND EVERY WORD YOU SAY!
WHAT ARE WE GONNA DO???
UH-OH.

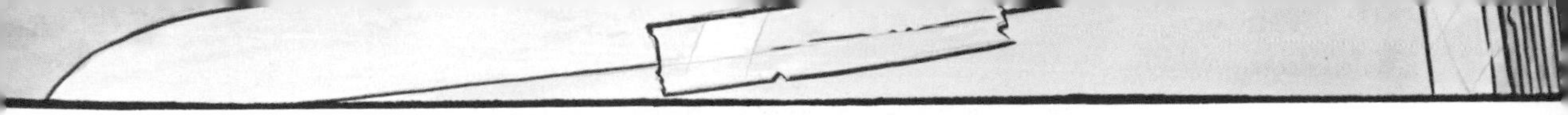

CHAPTER FIVE
(UN)EDUCATED RISKS

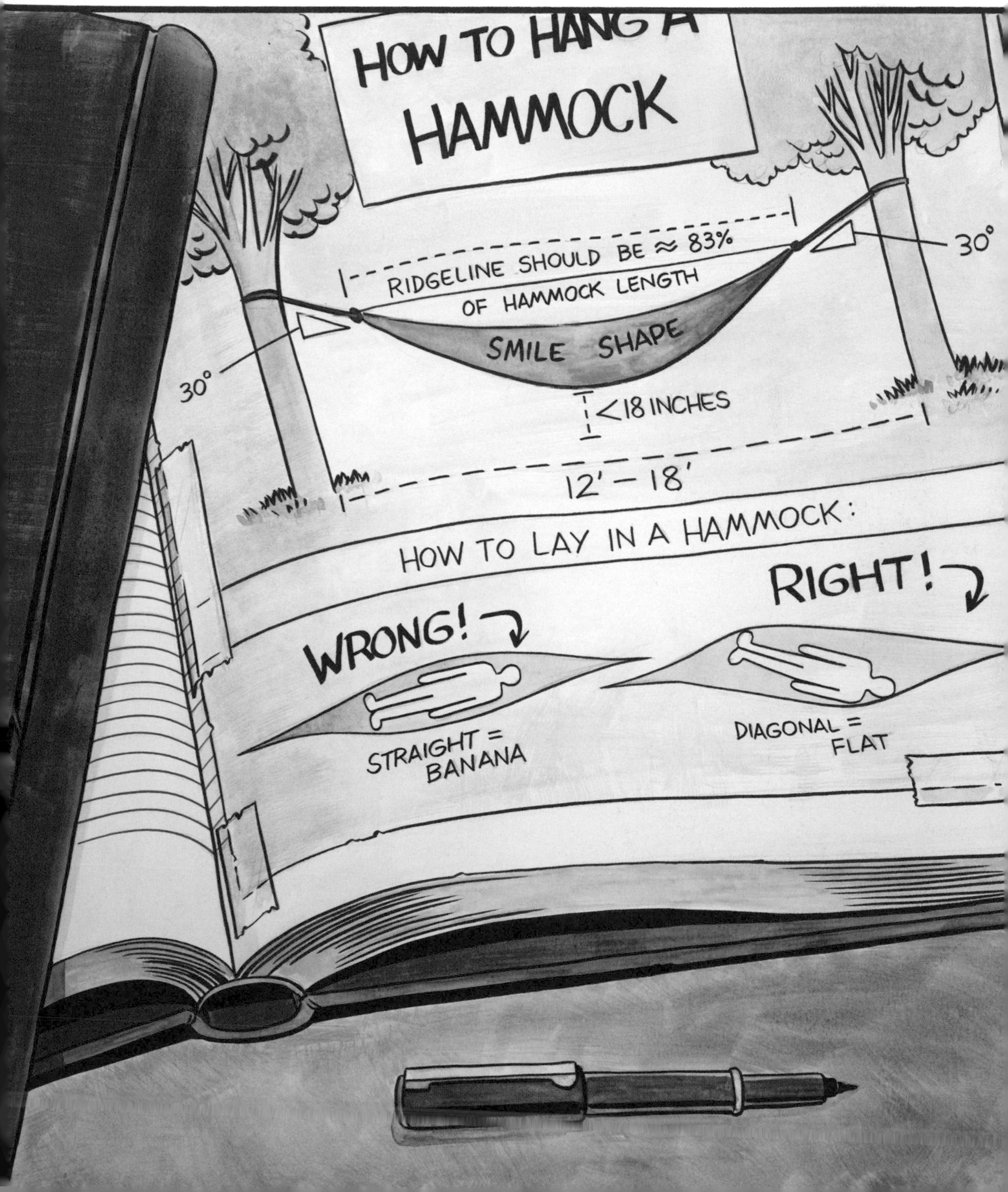

HOW TO HANG A HAMMOCK
RIDGELINE SHOULD BE ≈ 83% OF HAMMOCK LENGTH
30°
30°
SMILE SHAPE
<18 INCHES
12′ – 18′
HOW TO LAY IN A HAMMOCK:
WRONG!
RIGHT!
STRAIGHT = BANANA
DIAGONAL = FLAT

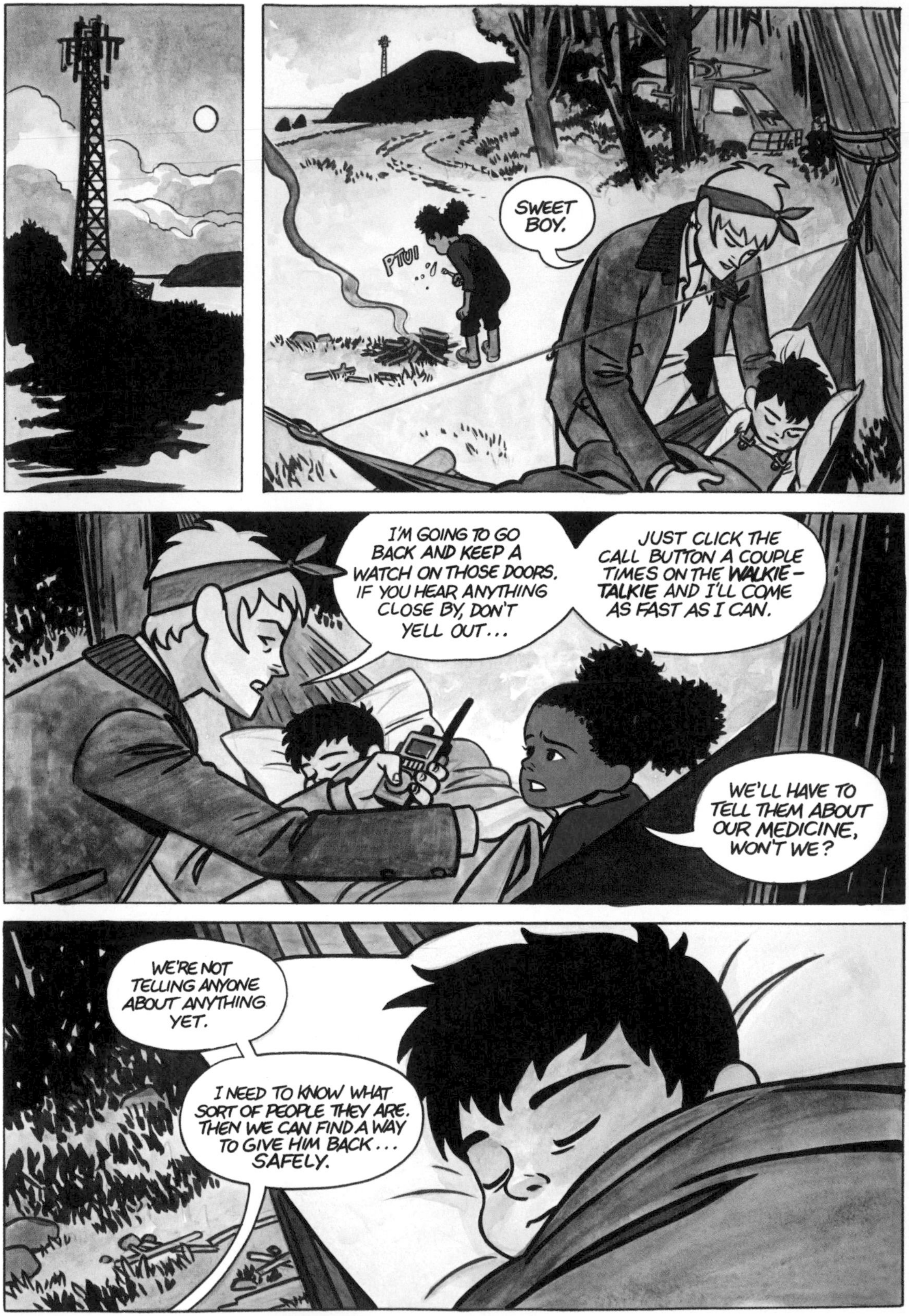
PTUI
SWEET BOY.
I'M GOING TO GO BACK AND KEEP A WATCH ON THOSE DOORS. IF YOU HEAR ANYTHING CLOSE BY, DON'T YELL OUT...
JUST CLICK THE CALL BUTTON A COUPLE TIMES ON THE WALKIE-TALKIE AND I'LL COME AS FAST AS I CAN.
WE'LL HAVE TO TELL THEM ABOUT OUR MEDICINE, WON'T WE?
WE'RE NOT TELLING ANYONE ABOUT ANYTHING YET.
I NEED TO KNOW WHAT SORT OF PEOPLE THEY ARE. THEN WE CAN FIND A WAY TO GIVE HIM BACK... SAFELY.

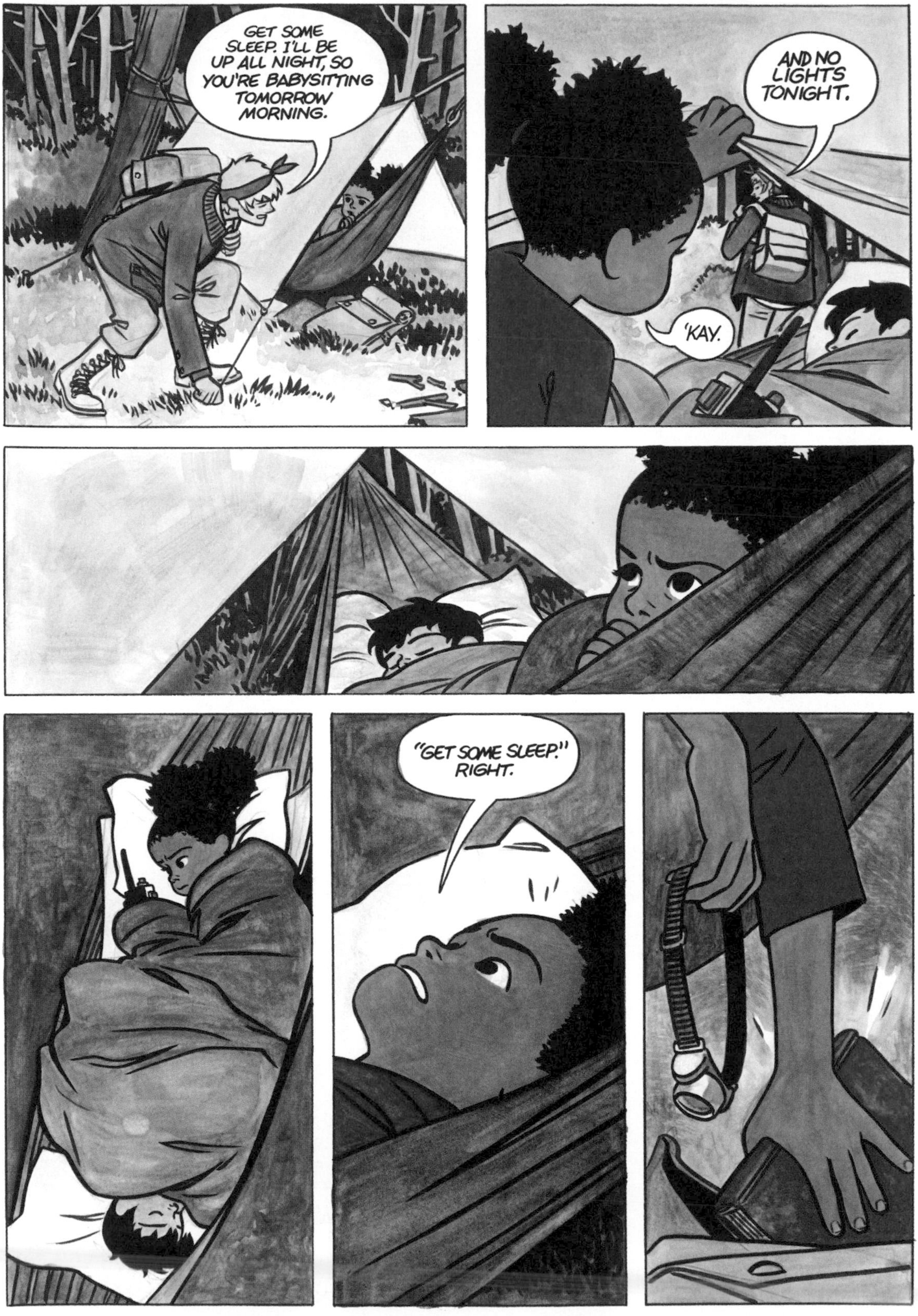
GET SOME SLEEP. I'LL BE UP ALL NIGHT, SO YOU'RE BABYSITTING TOMORROW MORNING.
AND NO LIGHTS TONIGHT.
'KAY.
"GET SOME SLEEP." RIGHT.

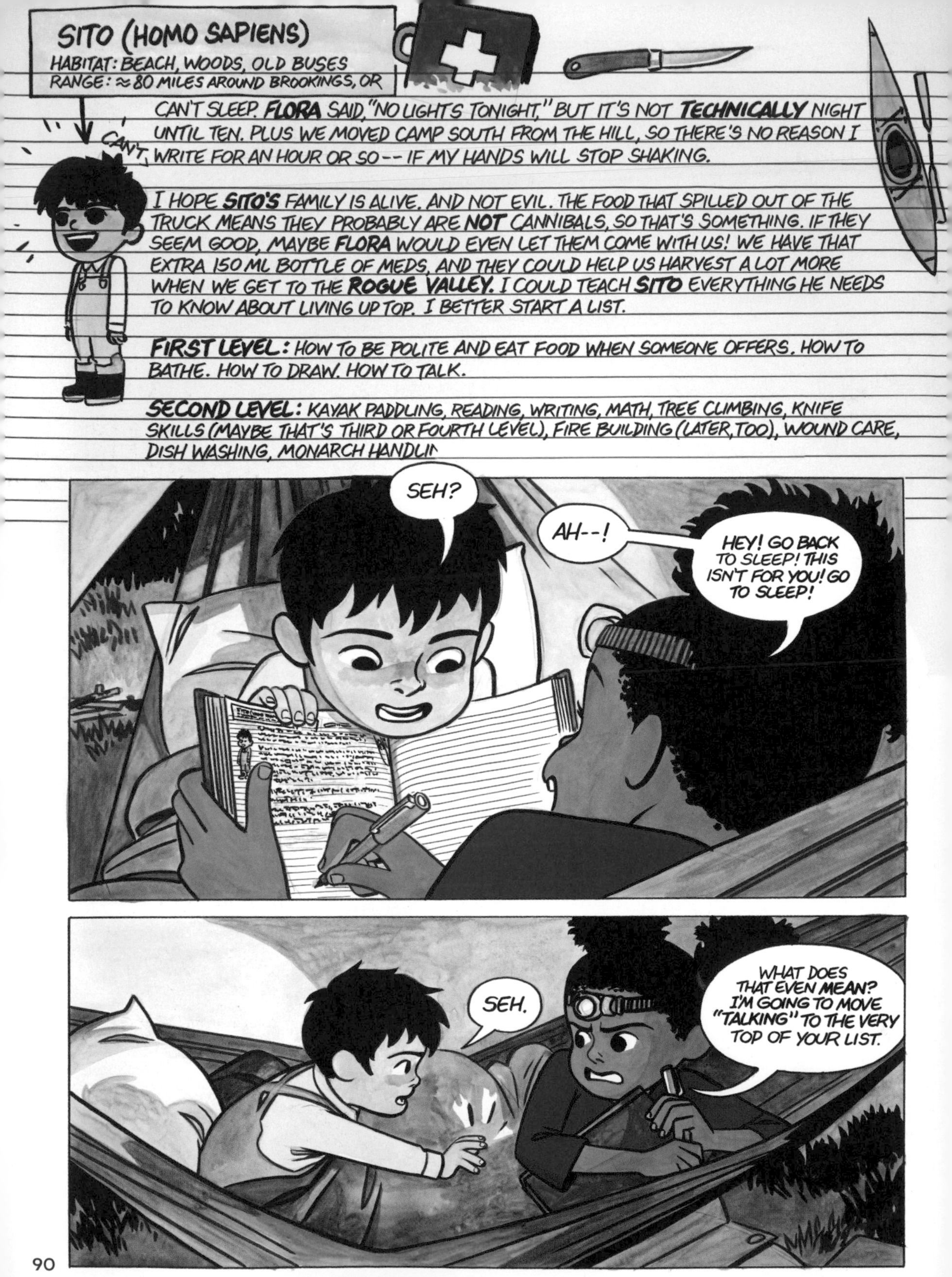
SITO (HOMO SAPIENS)
HABITAT: BEACH, WOODS, OLD BUSES
RANGE: ≈ 80 MILES AROUND BROOKINGS, OR
CAN'T
CAN'T SLEEP. FLORA SAID, "NO LIGHTS TONIGHT," BUT IT'S NOT TECHNICALLY NIGHT UNTIL TEN. PLUS WE MOVED CAMP SOUTH FROM THE HILL, SO THERE'S NO REASON I WRITE FOR AN HOUR OR SO -- IF MY HANDS WILL STOP SHAKING.
I HOPE SITO'S FAMILY IS ALIVE. AND NOT EVIL. THE FOOD THAT SPILLED OUT OF THE TRUCK MEANS THEY PROBABLY ARE NOT CANNIBALS, SO THAT'S SOMETHING. IF THEY SEEM GOOD, MAYBE FLORA WOULD EVEN LET THEM COME WITH US! WE HAVE THAT EXTRA 150 ML BOTTLE OF MEDS, AND THEY COULD HELP US HARVEST A LOT MORE WHEN WE GET TO THE ROGUE VALLEY. I COULD TEACH SITO EVERYTHING HE NEEDS TO KNOW ABOUT LIVING UP TOP. I BETTER START A LIST.
FIRST LEVEL: HOW TO BE POLITE AND EAT FOOD WHEN SOMEONE OFFERS. HOW TO BATHE. HOW TO DRAW. HOW TO TALK.
SECOND LEVEL: KAYAK PADDLING, READING, WRITING, MATH, TREE CLIMBING, KNIFE SKILLS (MAYBE THAT'S THIRD OR FOURTH LEVEL), FIRE BUILDING (LATER, TOO), WOUND CARE, DISH WASHING, MONARCH HANDLIN
SEH?
AH--!
HEY! GO BACK TO SLEEP! THIS ISN'T FOR YOU! GO TO SLEEP!
SEH.
WHAT DOES THAT EVEN MEAN? I'M GOING TO MOVE "TALKING" TO THE VERY TOP OF YOUR LIST.

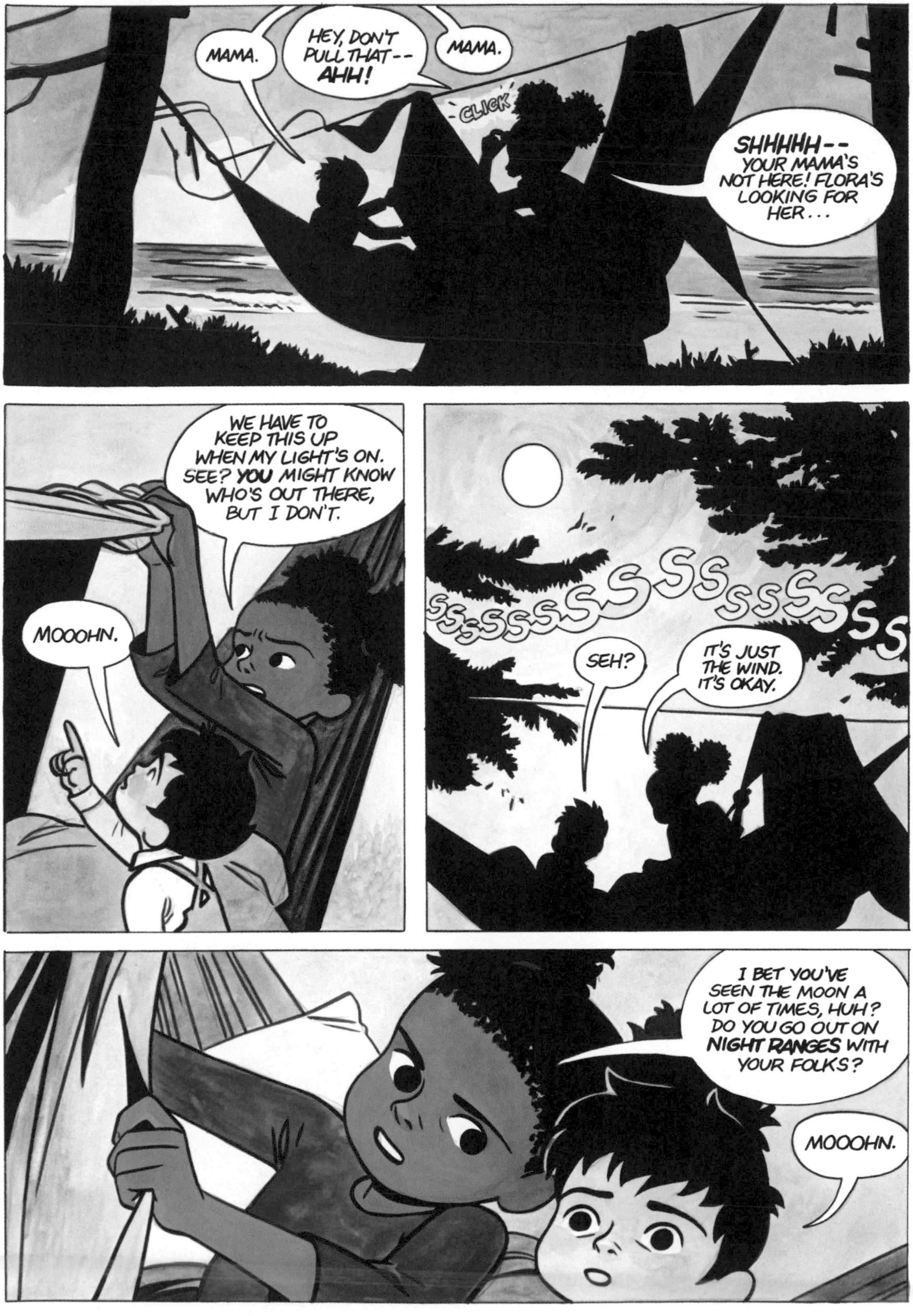
MAMA.
HEY, DON'T PULL THAT-- AHH!
MAMA.
CLICK
SHHHHH-- YOUR MAMA'S NOT HERE! FLORA'S LOOKING FOR HER...
WE HAVE TO KEEP THIS UP WHEN MY LIGHT'S ON. SEE? YOU MIGHT KNOW WHO'S OUT THERE, BUT I DON'T.
MOOOHN.
SSSSSSSSSSSSSSSSSSS
SEH?
IT'S JUST THE WIND. IT'S OKAY.
I BET YOU'VE SEEN THE MOON A LOT OF TIMES, HUH? DO YOU GO OUT ON NIGHT RANGES WITH YOUR FOLKS?
MOOOHN.

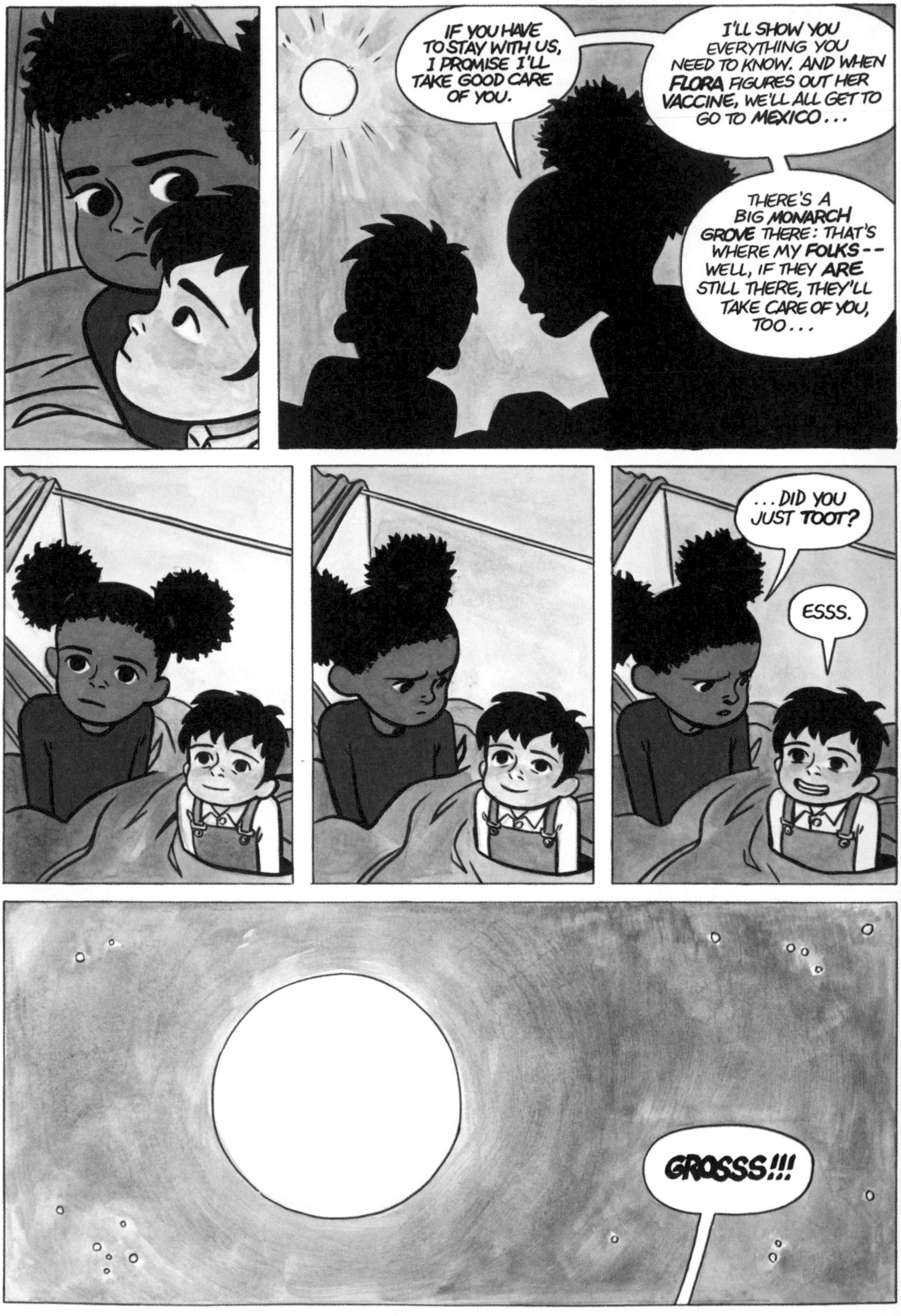
IF YOU HAVE TO STAY WITH US, I PROMISE I'LL TAKE GOOD CARE OF YOU.
I'LL SHOW YOU EVERYTHING YOU NEED TO KNOW. AND WHEN FLORA FIGURES OUT HER VACCINE, WE'LL ALL GET TO GO TO MEXICO...
THERE'S A BIG MONARCH GROVE THERE: THAT'S WHERE MY FOLKS-- WELL, IF THEY ARE STILL THERE, THEY'LL TAKE CARE OF YOU, TOO...
...DID YOU JUST TOOT?
ESSS.
GROSSS!!!

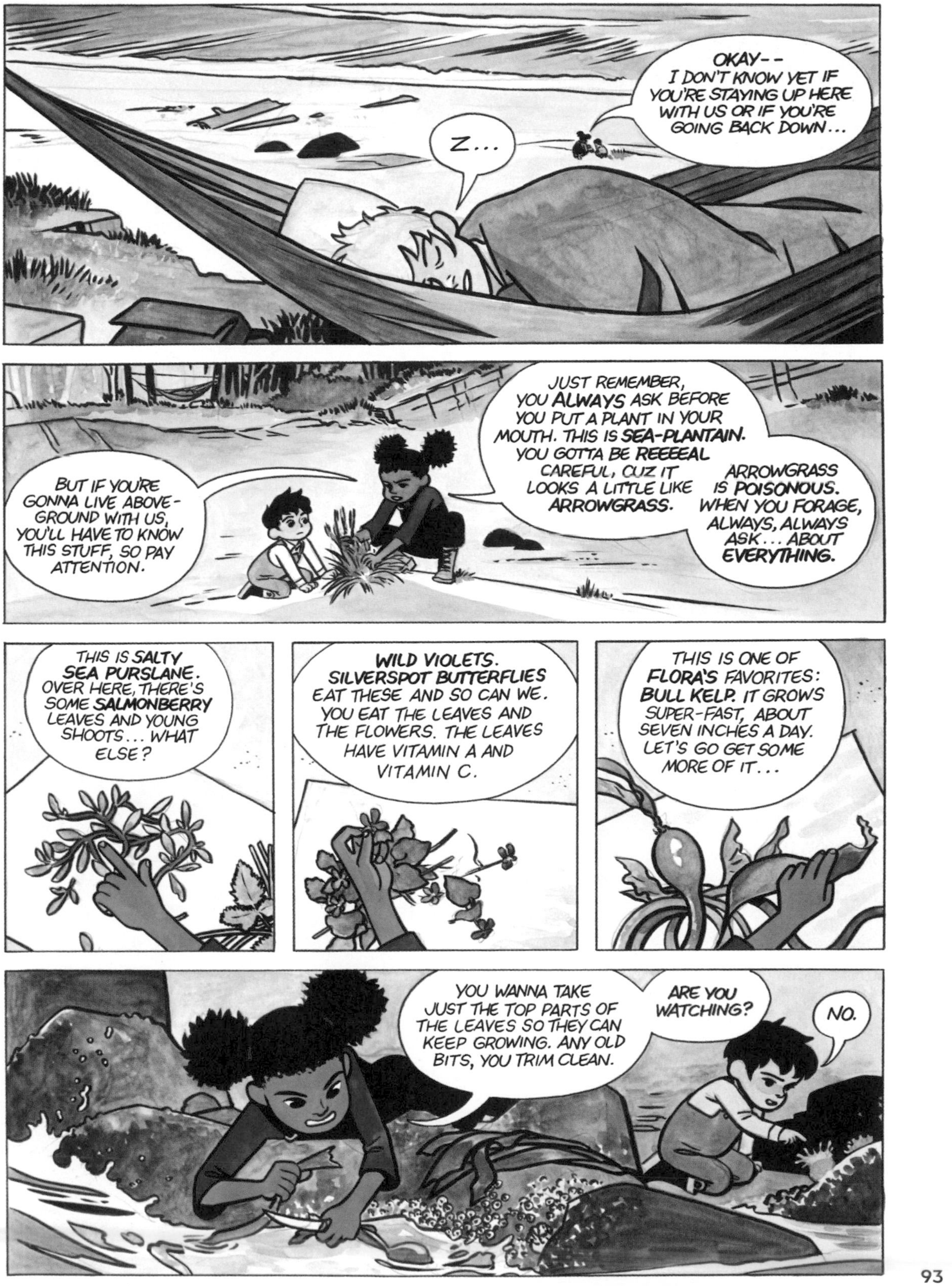

OKAY-- I DON'T KNOW YET IF YOU'RE STAYING UP HERE WITH US OR IF YOU'RE GOING BACK DOWN...
Z...
BUT IF YOU'RE GONNA LIVE ABOVE-GROUND WITH US, YOU'LL HAVE TO KNOW THIS STUFF, SO PAY ATTENTION.
JUST REMEMBER, YOU ALWAYS ASK BEFORE YOU PUT A PLANT IN YOUR MOUTH. THIS IS SEA-PLANTAIN. YOU GOTTA BE REEEEAL CAREFUL, CUZ IT LOOKS A LITTLE LIKE ARROWGRASS.
ARROWGRASS IS POISONOUS. WHEN YOU FORAGE, ALWAYS, ALWAYS ASK... ABOUT EVERYTHING.
THIS IS SALTY SEA PURSLANE. OVER HERE, THERE'S SOME SALMONBERRY LEAVES AND YOUNG SHOOTS... WHAT ELSE?
WILD VIOLETS. SILVERSPOT BUTTERFLIES EAT THESE AND SO CAN WE. YOU EAT THE LEAVES AND THE FLOWERS. THE LEAVES HAVE VITAMIN A AND VITAMIN C.
THIS IS ONE OF FLORA'S FAVORITES: BULL KELP. IT GROWS SUPER-FAST, ABOUT SEVEN INCHES A DAY. LET'S GO GET SOME MORE OF IT...
YOU WANNA TAKE JUST THE TOP PARTS OF THE LEAVES SO THEY CAN KEEP GROWING. ANY OLD BITS, YOU TRIM CLEAN.
ARE YOU WATCHING?
NO.

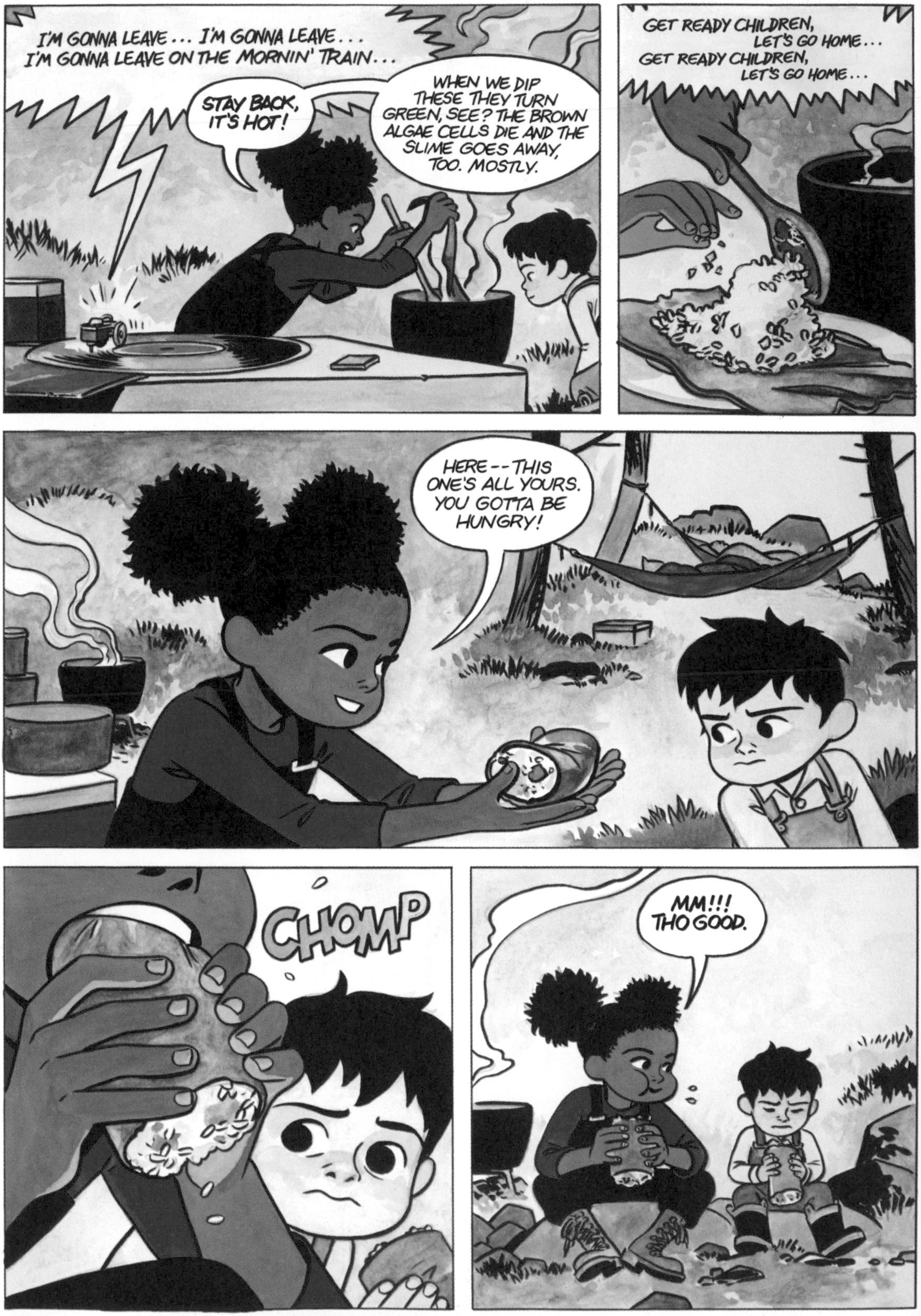
I'M GONNA LEAVE... I'M GONNA LEAVE...
I'M GONNA LEAVE ON THE MORNIN' TRAIN...
STAY BACK, IT'S HOT!
WHEN WE DIP THESE THEY TURN GREEN, SEE? THE BROWN ALGAE CELLS DIE AND THE SLIME GOES AWAY, TOO. MOSTLY.
GET READY CHILDREN, LET'S GO HOME... GET READY CHILDREN, LET'S GO HOME...
HERE--THIS ONE'S ALL YOURS. YOU GOTTA BE HUNGRY!
CHOMP
MM!!! THO GOOD.

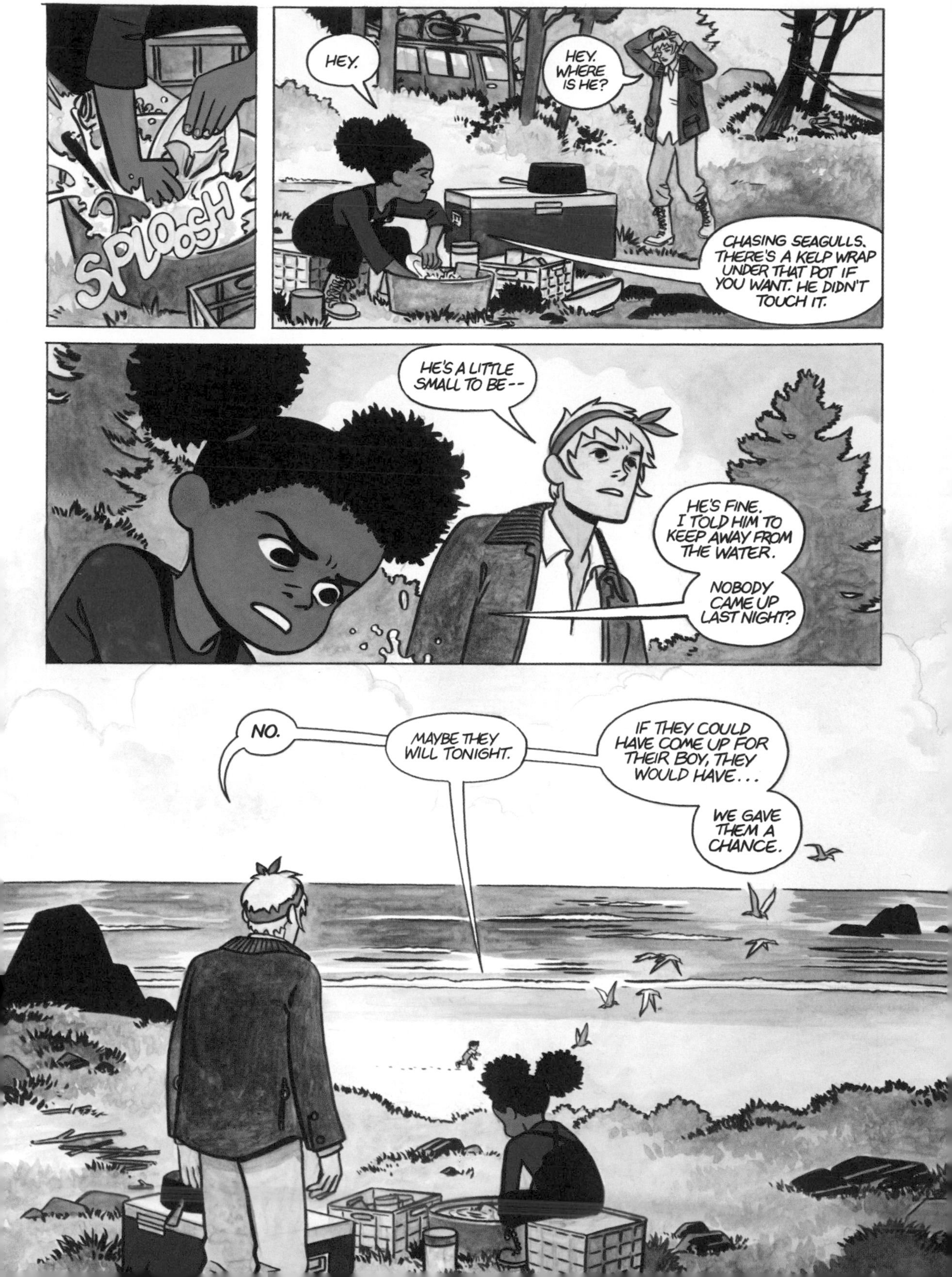
SPLOOSH
HEY.
HEY. WHERE IS HE?
CHASING SEAGULLS. THERE'S A KELP WRAP UNDER THAT POT IF YOU WANT. HE DIDN'T TOUCH IT.
HE'S A LITTLE SMALL TO BE--
HE'S FINE. I TOLD HIM TO KEEP AWAY FROM THE WATER.
NOBODY CAME UP LAST NIGHT?
NO.
MAYBE THEY WILL TONIGHT.
IF THEY COULD HAVE COME UP FOR THEIR BOY, THEY WOULD HAVE...
WE GAVE THEM A CHANCE.

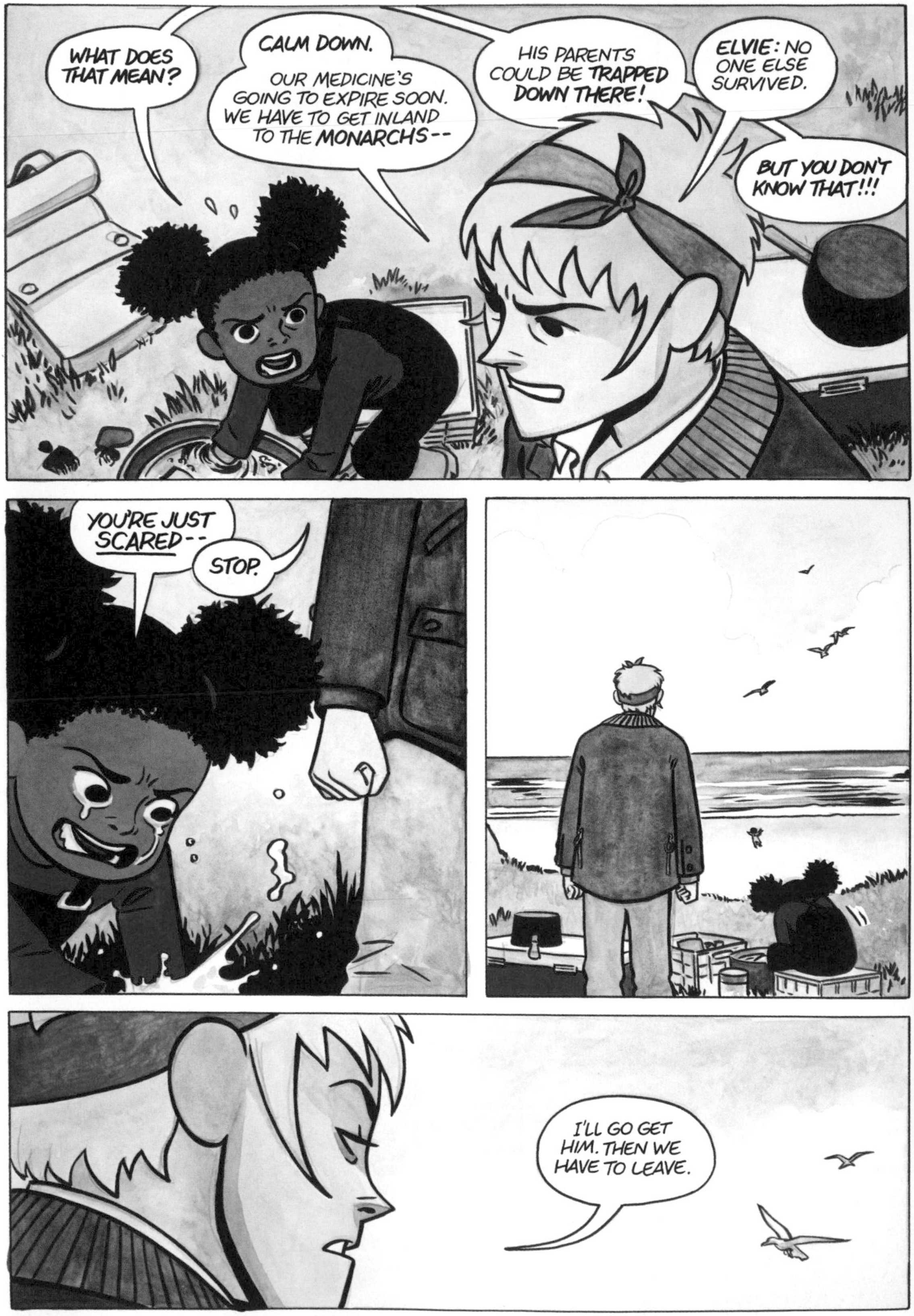
WHAT DOES THAT MEAN?
CALM DOWN.
OUR MEDICINE'S GOING TO EXPIRE SOON. WE HAVE TO GET INLAND TO THE MONARCHS--
HIS PARENTS COULD BE TRAPPED DOWN THERE!
ELVIE: NO ONE ELSE SURVIVED.
BUT YOU DON'T KNOW THAT!!!
YOU'RE JUST SCARED--
STOP.
I'LL GO GET HIM. THEN WE HAVE TO LEAVE.

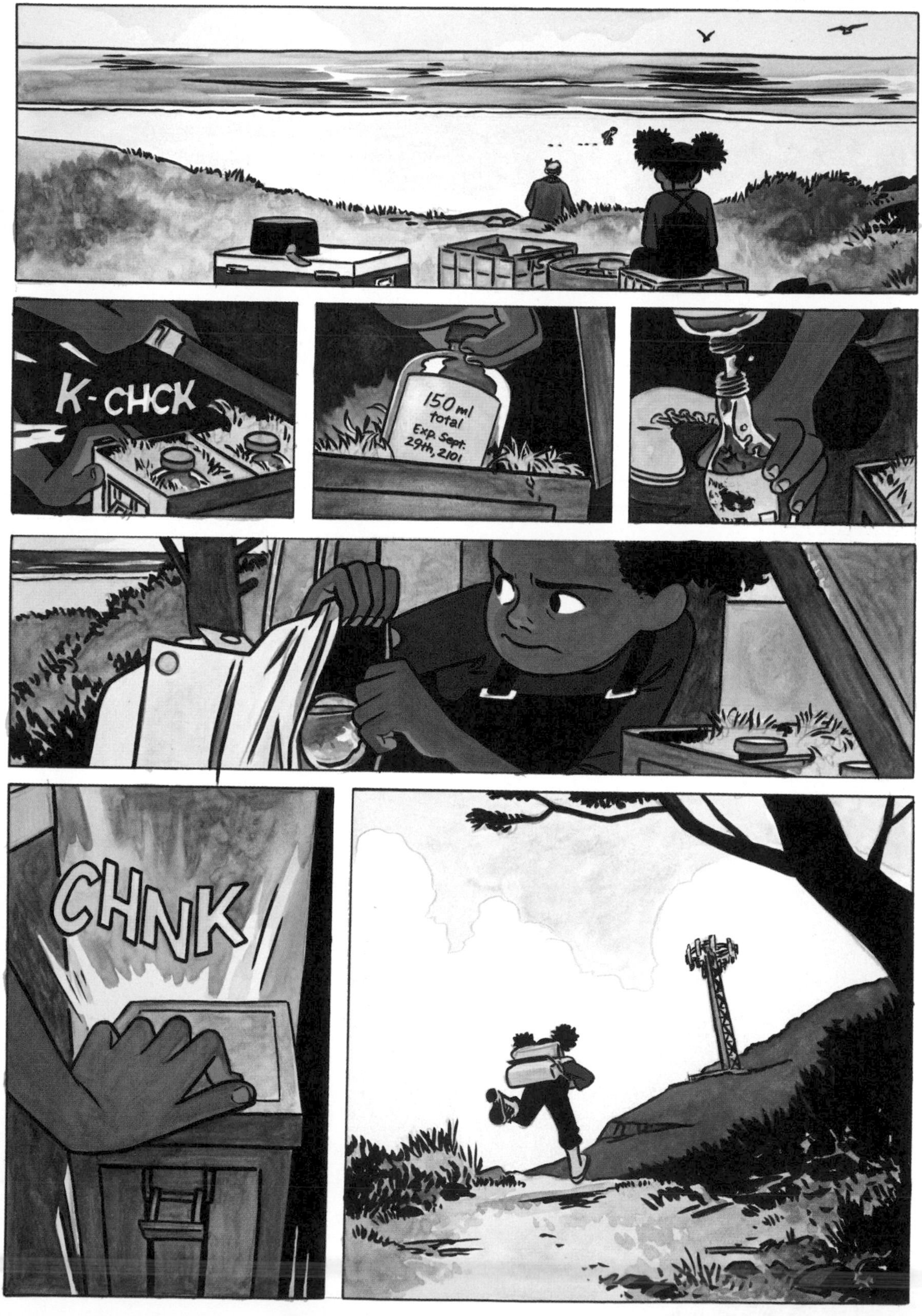
K-CHCK
150 ml total Exp. Sept. 29th, 2101
CHNK

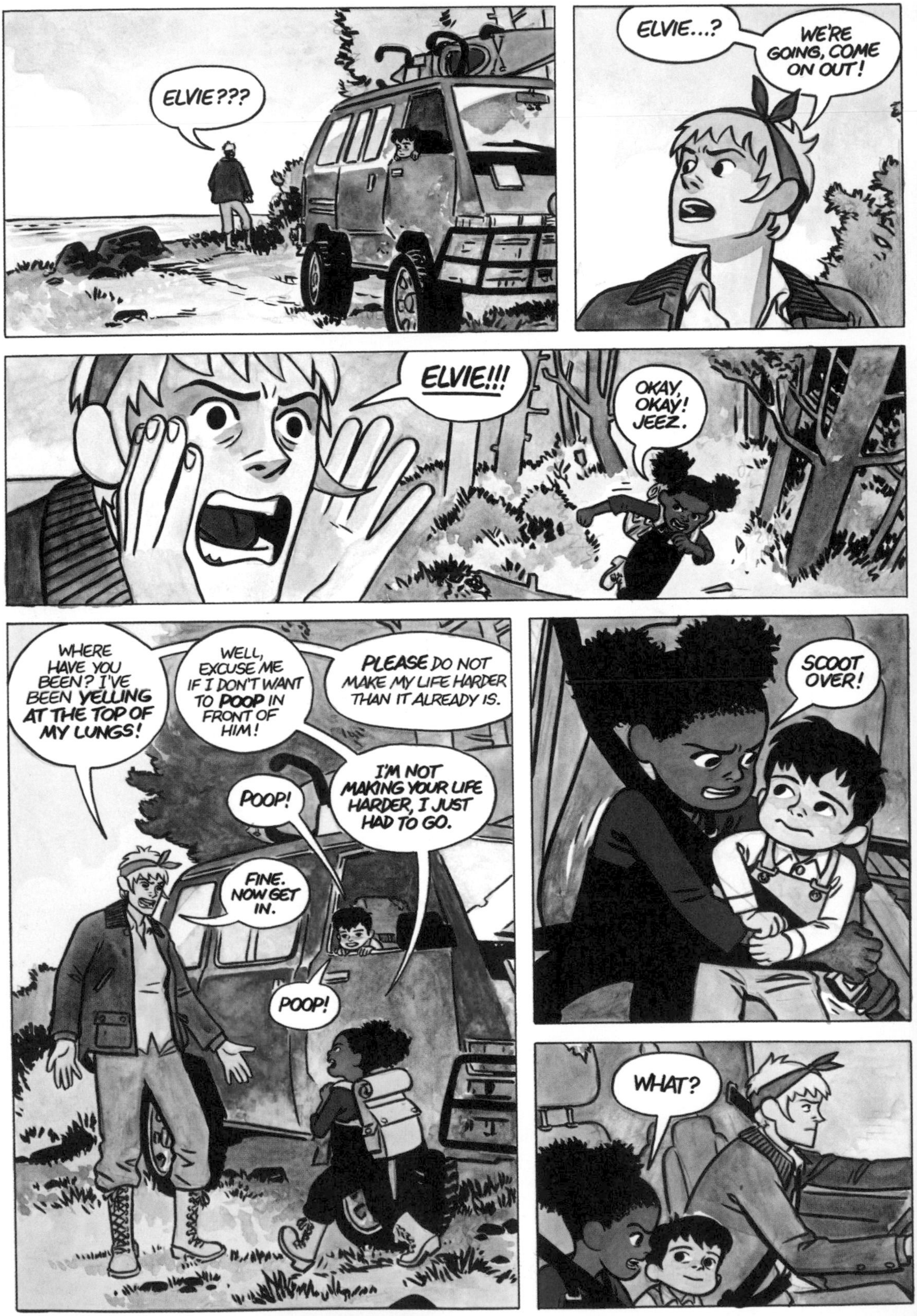

ELVIE???
ELVIE...?
WE'RE GOING, COME ON OUT!
ELVIE!!!
OKAY, OKAY! JEEZ.
WHERE HAVE YOU BEEN? I'VE BEEN YELLING AT THE TOP OF MY LUNGS!
WELL, EXCUSE ME IF I DON'T WANT TO POOP IN FRONT OF HIM!
PLEASE DO NOT MAKE MY LIFE HARDER THAN IT ALREADY IS.
POOP!
I'M NOT MAKING YOUR LIFE HARDER, I JUST HAD TO GO.
FINE. NOW GET IN.
POOP!
SCOOT OVER!
WHAT?

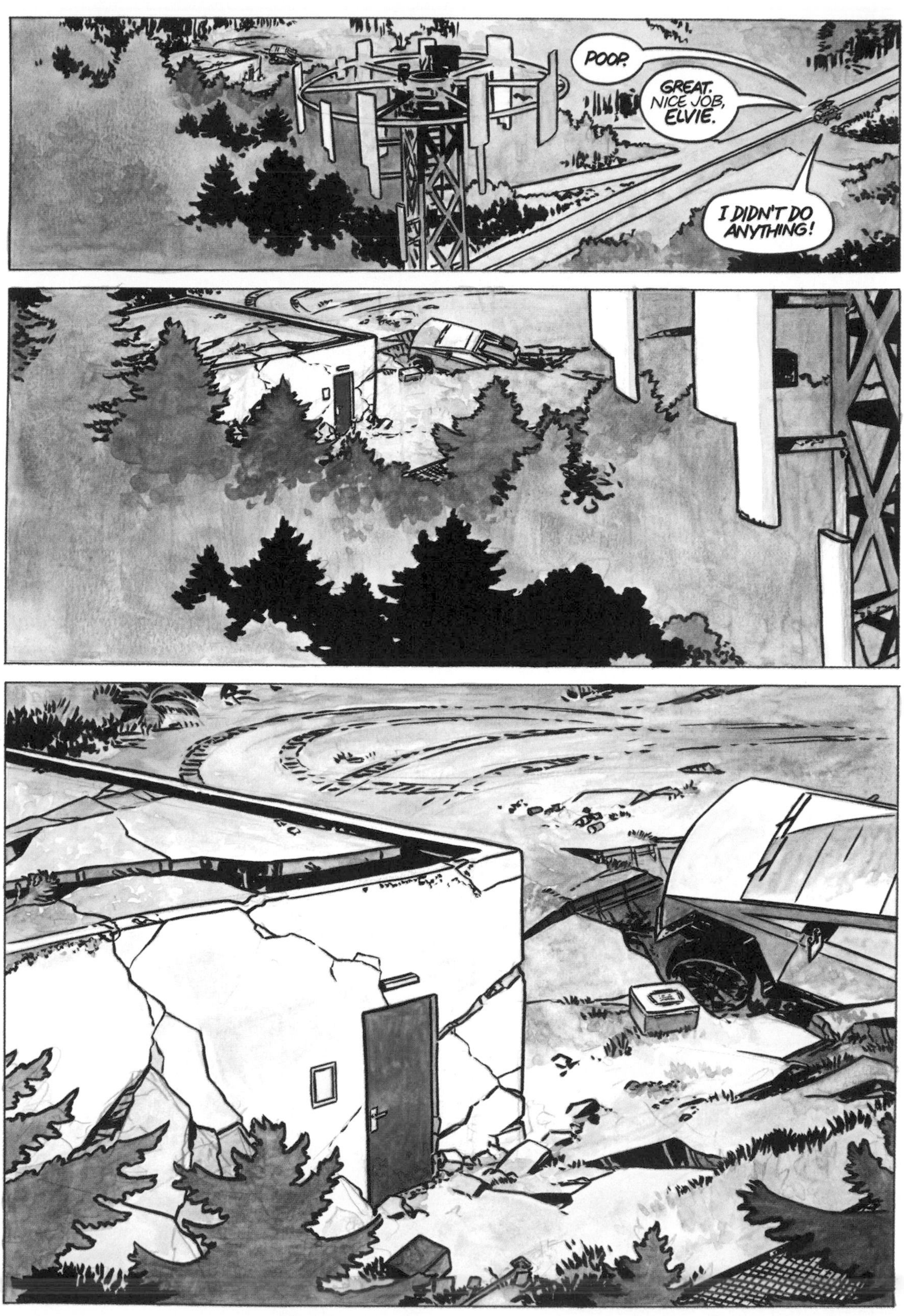
POOP.
GREAT. NICE JOB, ELVIE.
I DIDN'T DO ANYTHING!

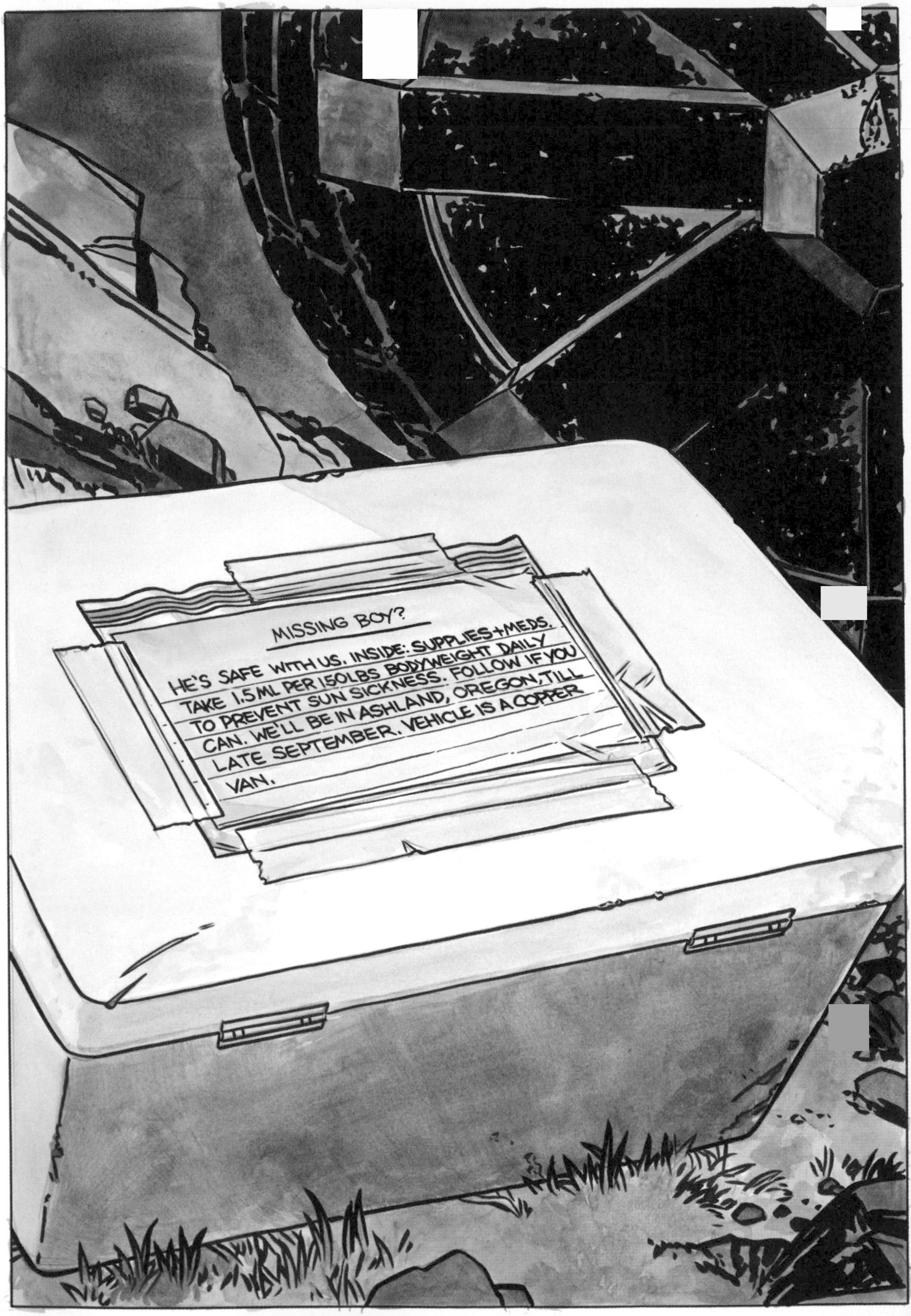
MISSING BOY?
HE'S SAFE WITH US. INSIDE: SUPPLIES+MEDS.
TAKE 1.5ML PER 150LBS BODYWEIGHT DAILY
TO PREVENT SUN SICKNESS. FOLLOW IF YOU
CAN. WE'LL BE IN ASHLAND, OREGON, TILL
LATE SEPTEMBER. VEHICLE IS A COPPER
VAN.

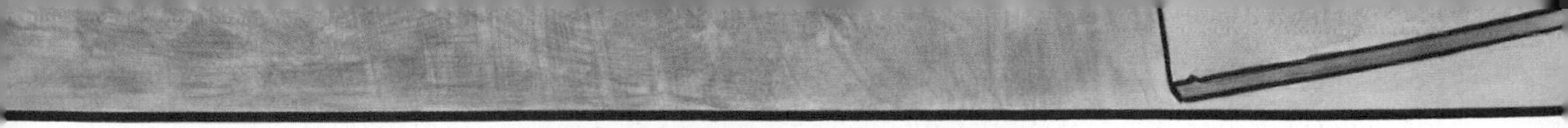

CHAPTER SIX

MORE MONARCHS

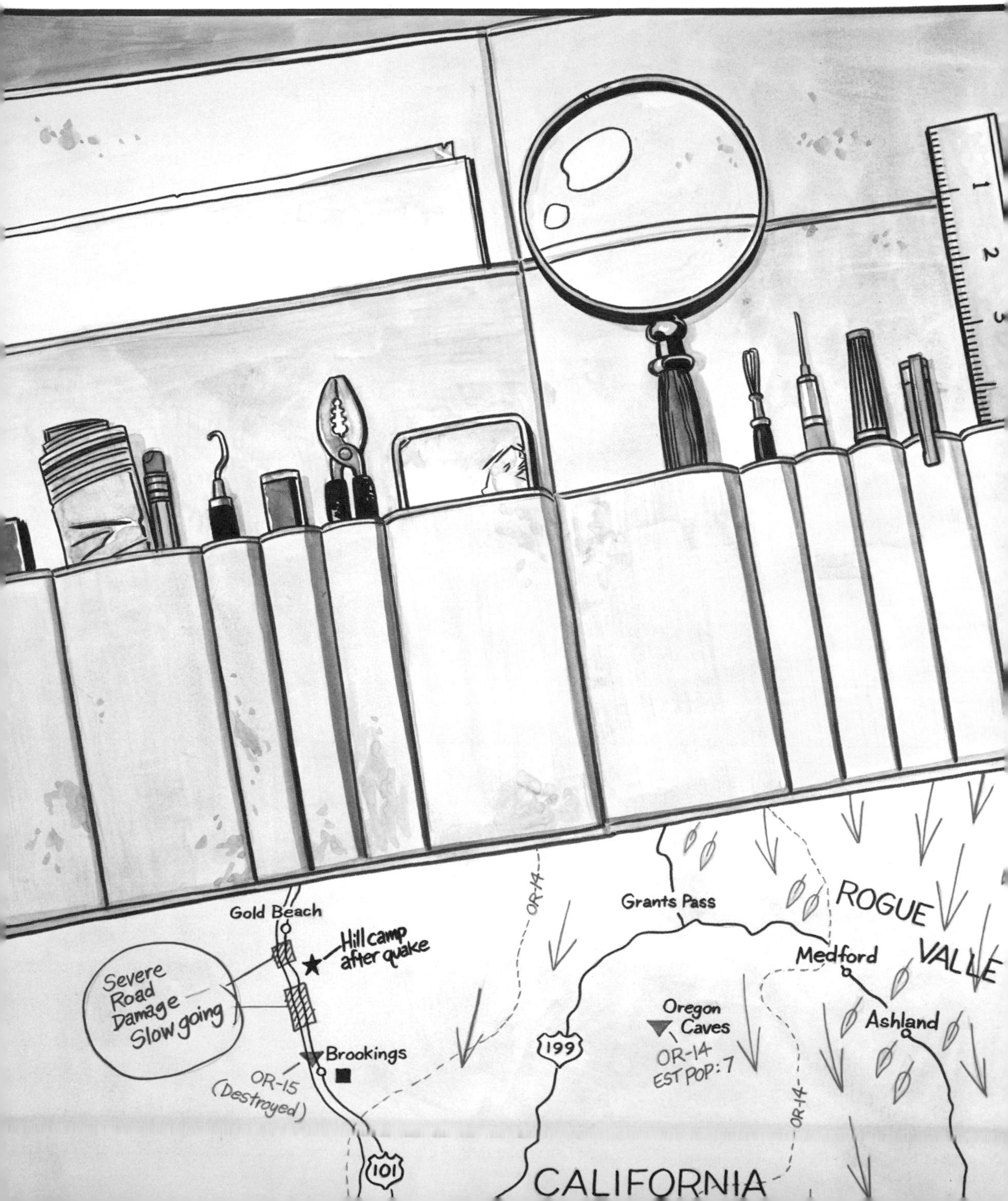

Gold Beach
Hill camp after quake
Severe Road Damage Slow going
Brookings
OR-15 (Destroyed)
101
OR-14
Grants Pass
ROGUE
VALLE
Medford
Oregon Caves
199
OR-14
EST POP: 7
Ashland
OR-14
CALIFORNIA

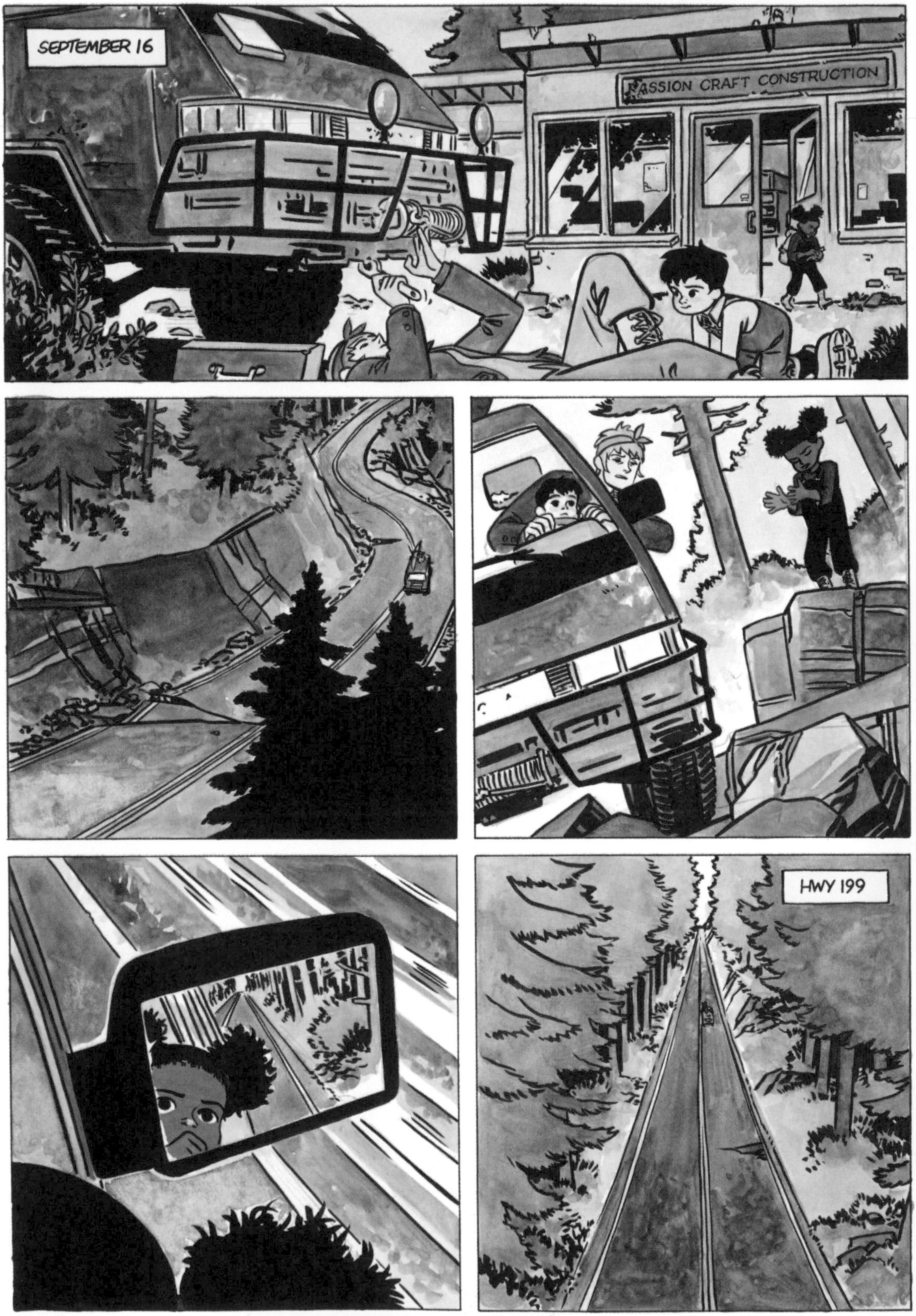
SEPTEMBER 16
ASSION CRAFT CONSTRUCTION
HWY 199

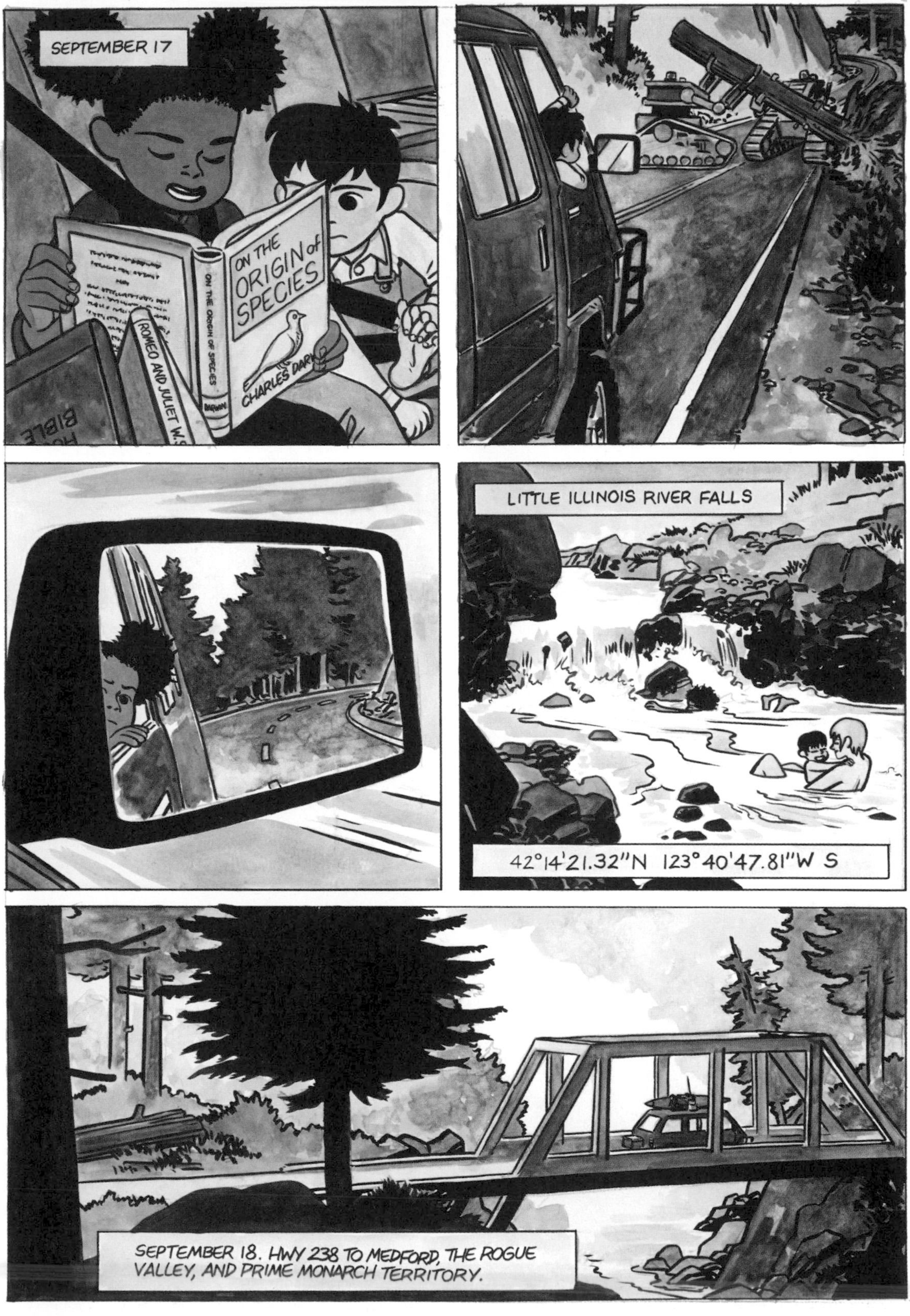
SEPTEMBER 17
ON THE ORIGIN of SPECIES
CHARLES DAR
ON THE ORIGIN OF SPECIES
DARWIN
ROMEO AND JULIET W.S.
BIBLE
LITTLE ILLINOIS RIVER FALLS
42°14'21.32"N 123°40'47.81"W S
SEPTEMBER 18. HWY 238 TO MEDFORD, THE ROGUE VALLEY, AND PRIME MONARCH TERRITORY.

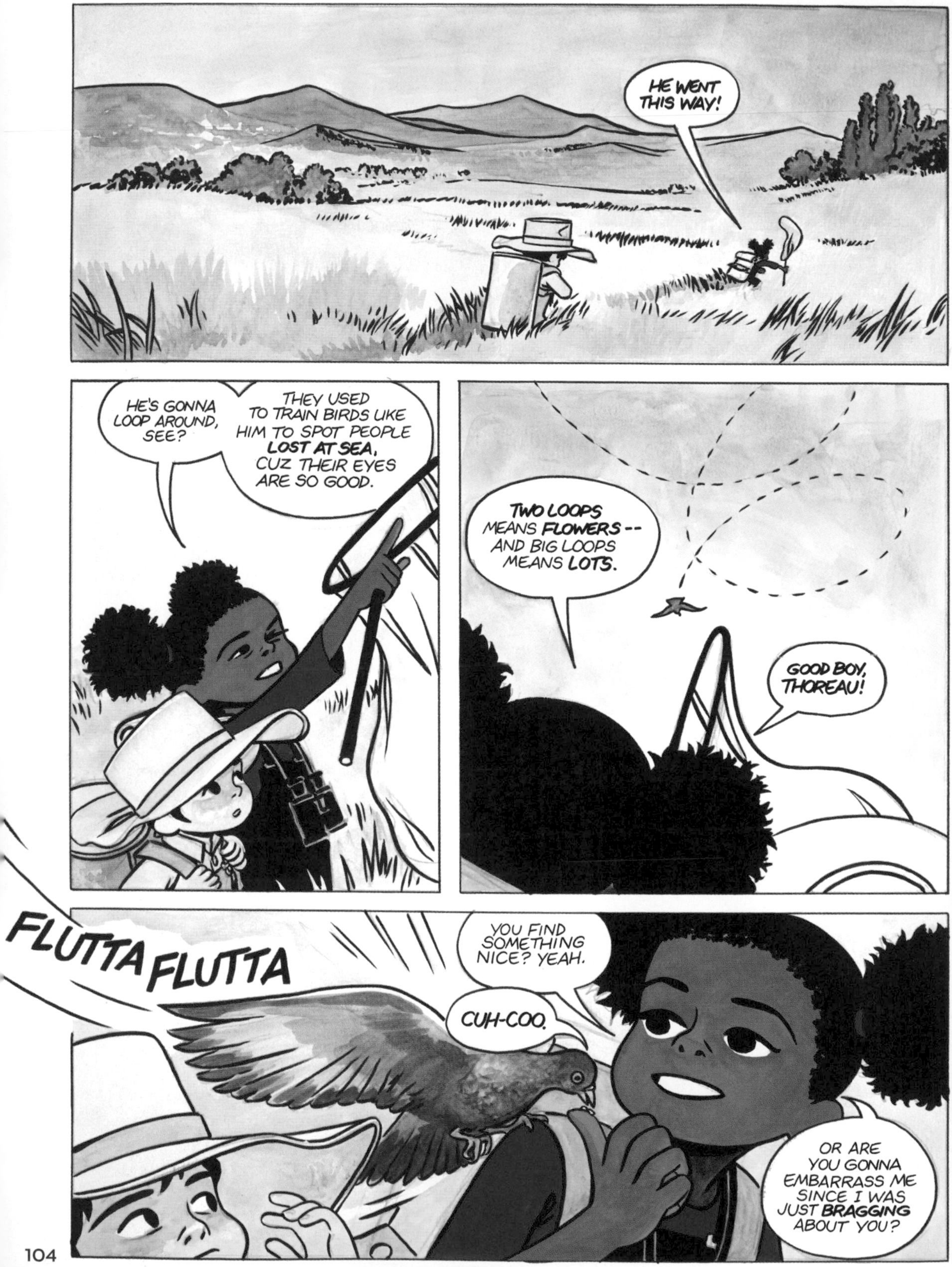
HE WENT THIS WAY!
HE'S GONNA LOOP AROUND, SEE?
THEY USED TO TRAIN BIRDS LIKE HIM TO SPOT PEOPLE **LOST AT SEA**, CUZ THEIR EYES ARE SO GOOD.
TWO LOOPS MEANS **FLOWERS** -- AND BIG LOOPS MEANS **LOTS**.
GOOD BOY, THOREAU!
FLUTTA FLUTTA
YOU FIND SOMETHING NICE? YEAH.
CUH-COO.
OR ARE YOU GONNA EMBARRASS ME SINCE I WAS JUST **BRAGGING** ABOUT YOU?

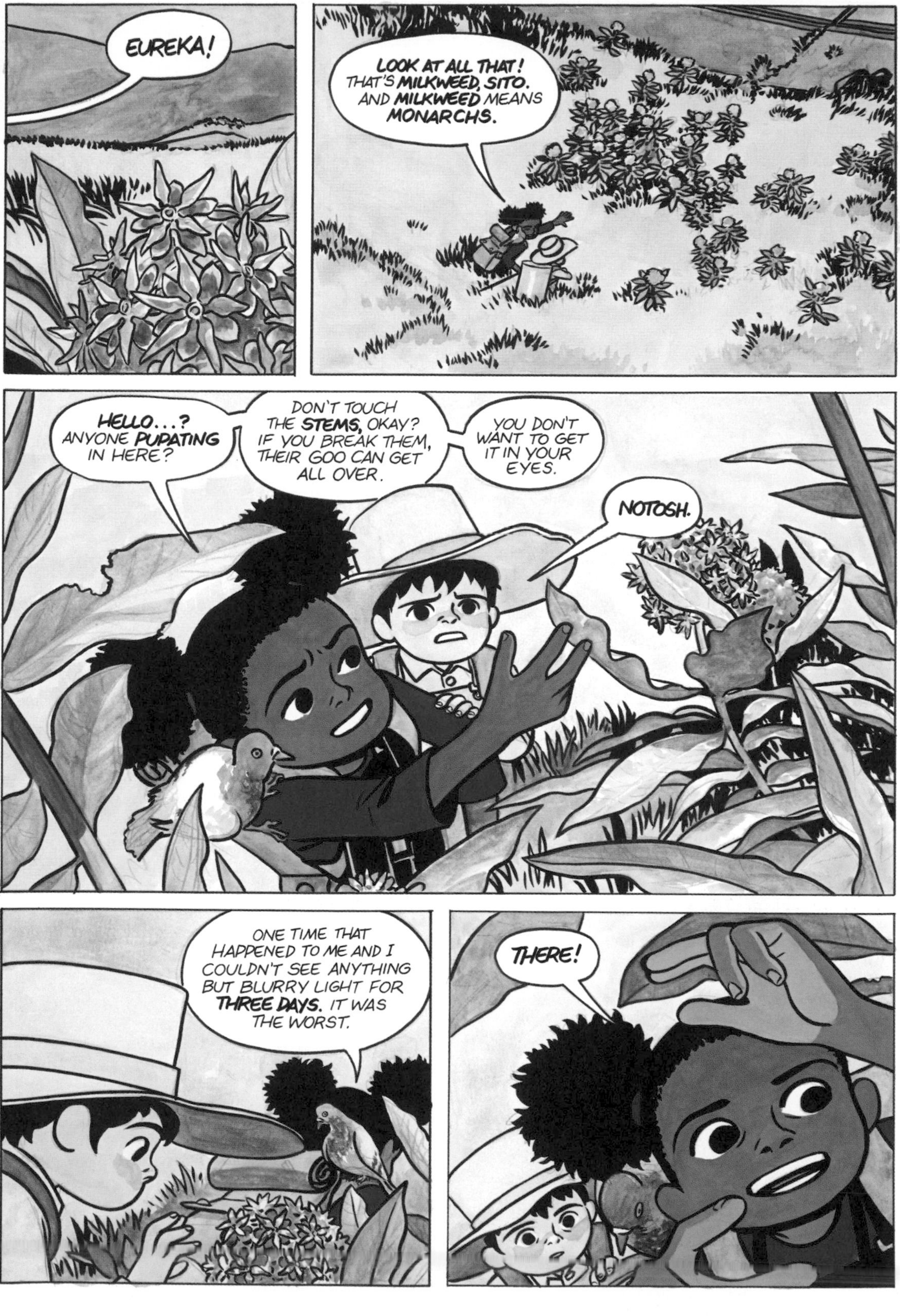
EUREKA!
LOOK AT ALL THAT! THAT'S MILKWEED, SITO. AND MILKWEED MEANS MONARCHS.
HELLO...? ANYONE PUPATING IN HERE?
DON'T TOUCH THE STEMS, OKAY? IF YOU BREAK THEM, THEIR GOO CAN GET ALL OVER.
YOU DON'T WANT TO GET IT IN YOUR EYES.
NOTOSH.
ONE TIME THAT HAPPENED TO ME AND I COULDN'T SEE ANYTHING BUT BLURRY LIGHT FOR THREE DAYS. IT WAS THE WORST.
THERE!

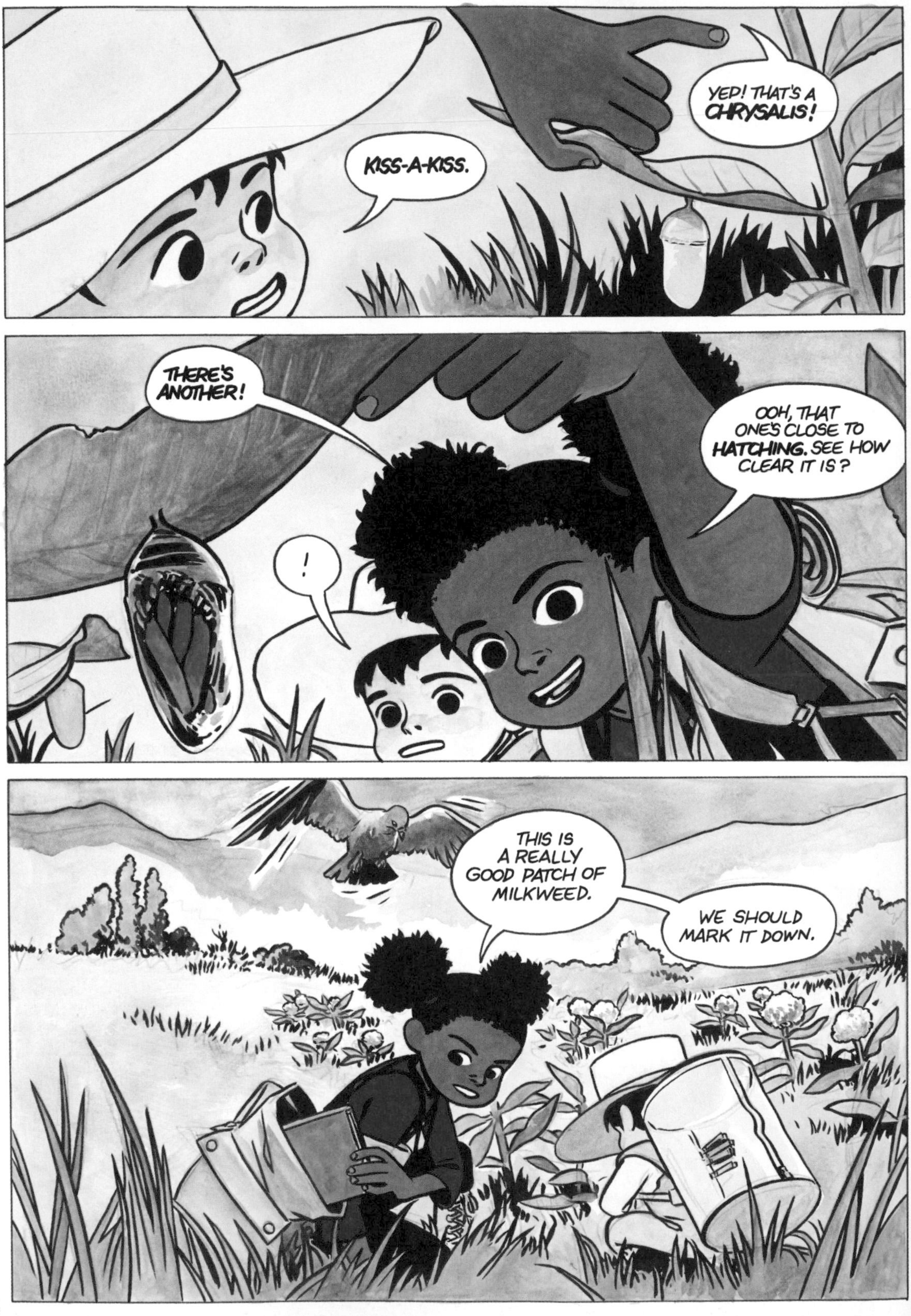
KISS-A-KISS.
YEP! THAT'S A CHRYSALIS!
THERE'S ANOTHER!
!
OOH, THAT ONE'S CLOSE TO HATCHING. SEE HOW CLEAR IT IS?
THIS IS A REALLY GOOD PATCH OF MILKWEED.
WE SHOULD MARK IT DOWN.

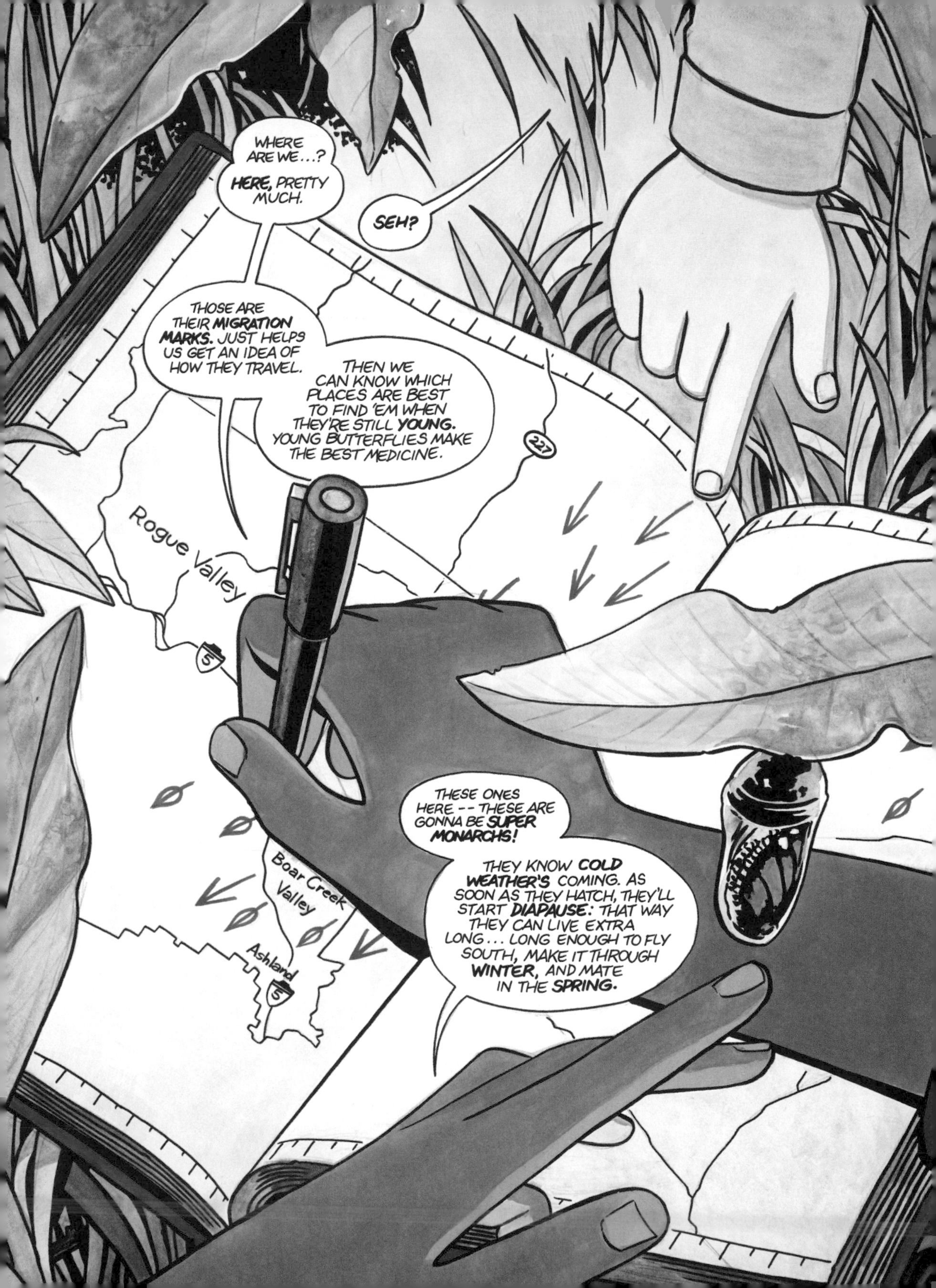
WHERE ARE WE...?
HERE, PRETTY MUCH.
SEH?
THOSE ARE THEIR MIGRATION MARKS. JUST HELPS US GET AN IDEA OF HOW THEY TRAVEL.
THEN WE CAN KNOW WHICH PLACES ARE BEST TO FIND 'EM WHEN THEY'RE STILL YOUNG. YOUNG BUTTERFLIES MAKE THE BEST MEDICINE.
227
Rogue Valley
5
THESE ONES HERE -- THESE ARE GONNA BE SUPER MONARCHS!
THEY KNOW COLD WEATHER'S COMING. AS SOON AS THEY HATCH, THEY'LL START DIAPAUSE: THAT WAY THEY CAN LIVE EXTRA LONG... LONG ENOUGH TO FLY SOUTH, MAKE IT THROUGH WINTER, AND MATE IN THE SPRING.
Boar Creek Valley
Ashland
5

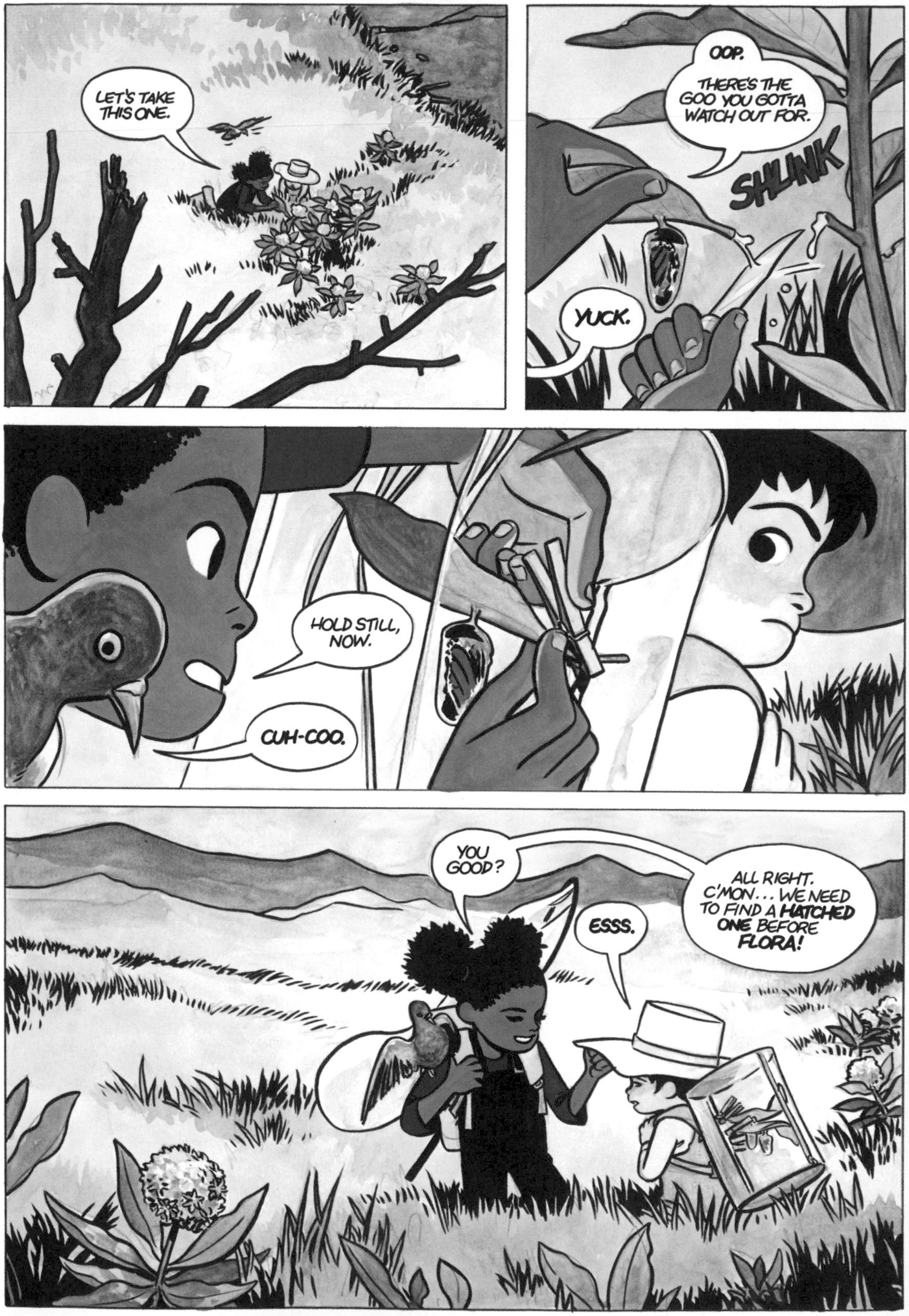
LET'S TAKE THIS ONE.
OOP.
THERE'S THE GOO YOU GOTTA WATCH OUT FOR.
SHLINK
YUCK.
HOLD STILL, NOW.
CUH-COO.
YOU GOOD?
ESSS.
ALL RIGHT. C'MON... WE NEED TO FIND A **HATCHED ONE** BEFORE **FLORA!**

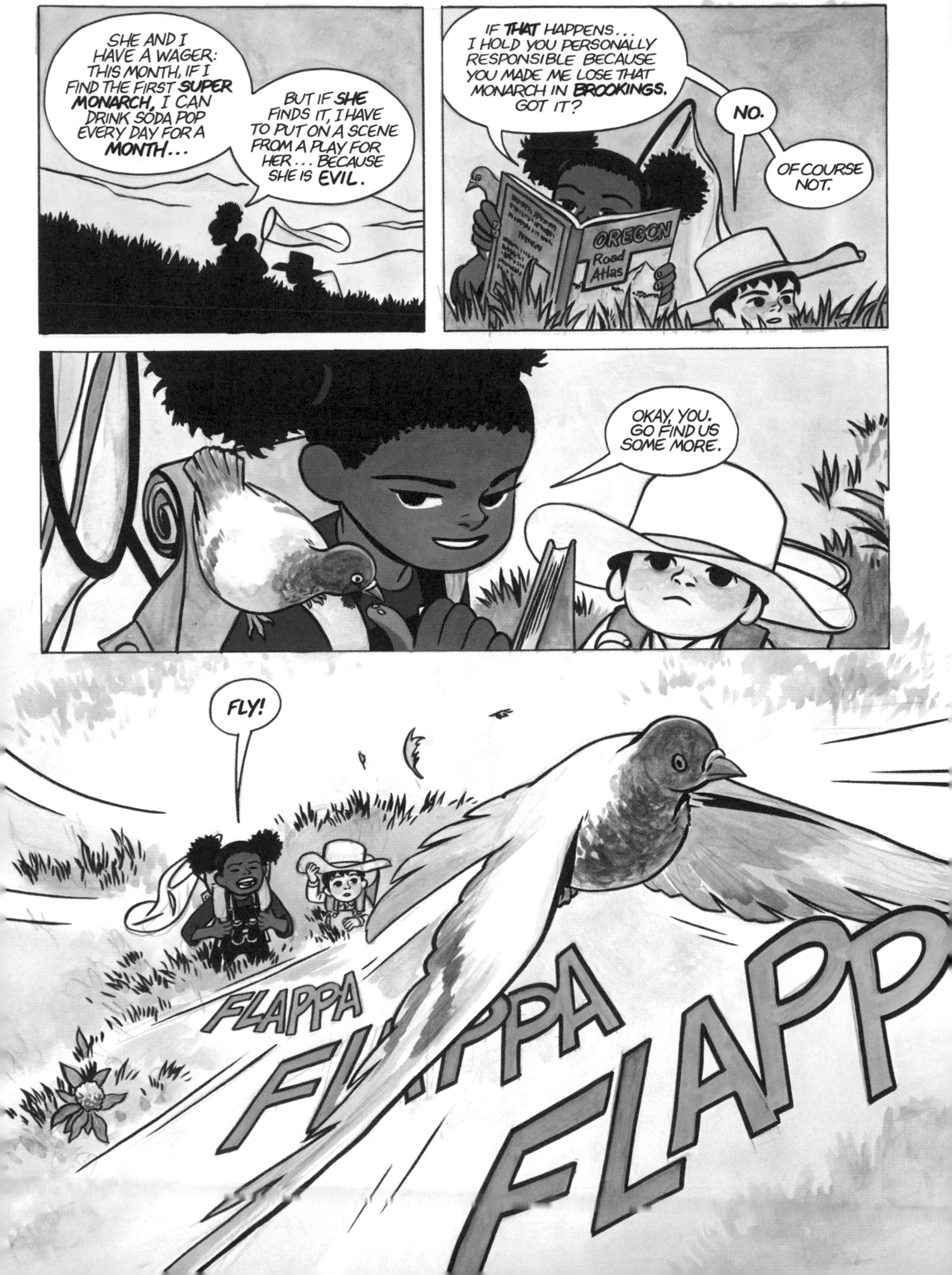
SHE AND I HAVE A WAGER: THIS MONTH, IF I FIND THE FIRST SUPER MONARCH, I CAN DRINK SODA POP EVERY DAY FOR A MONTH...
BUT IF SHE FINDS IT, I HAVE TO PUT ON A SCENE FROM A PLAY FOR HER... BECAUSE SHE IS EVIL.
IF THAT HAPPENS... I HOLD YOU PERSONALLY RESPONSIBLE BECAUSE YOU MADE ME LOSE THAT MONARCH IN BROOKINGS. GOT IT?
NO.
OF COURSE NOT.
OREGON Road Atlas
OKAY, YOU. GO FIND US SOME MORE.
FLY!
FLAPPA
FLAPPA
FLAPP

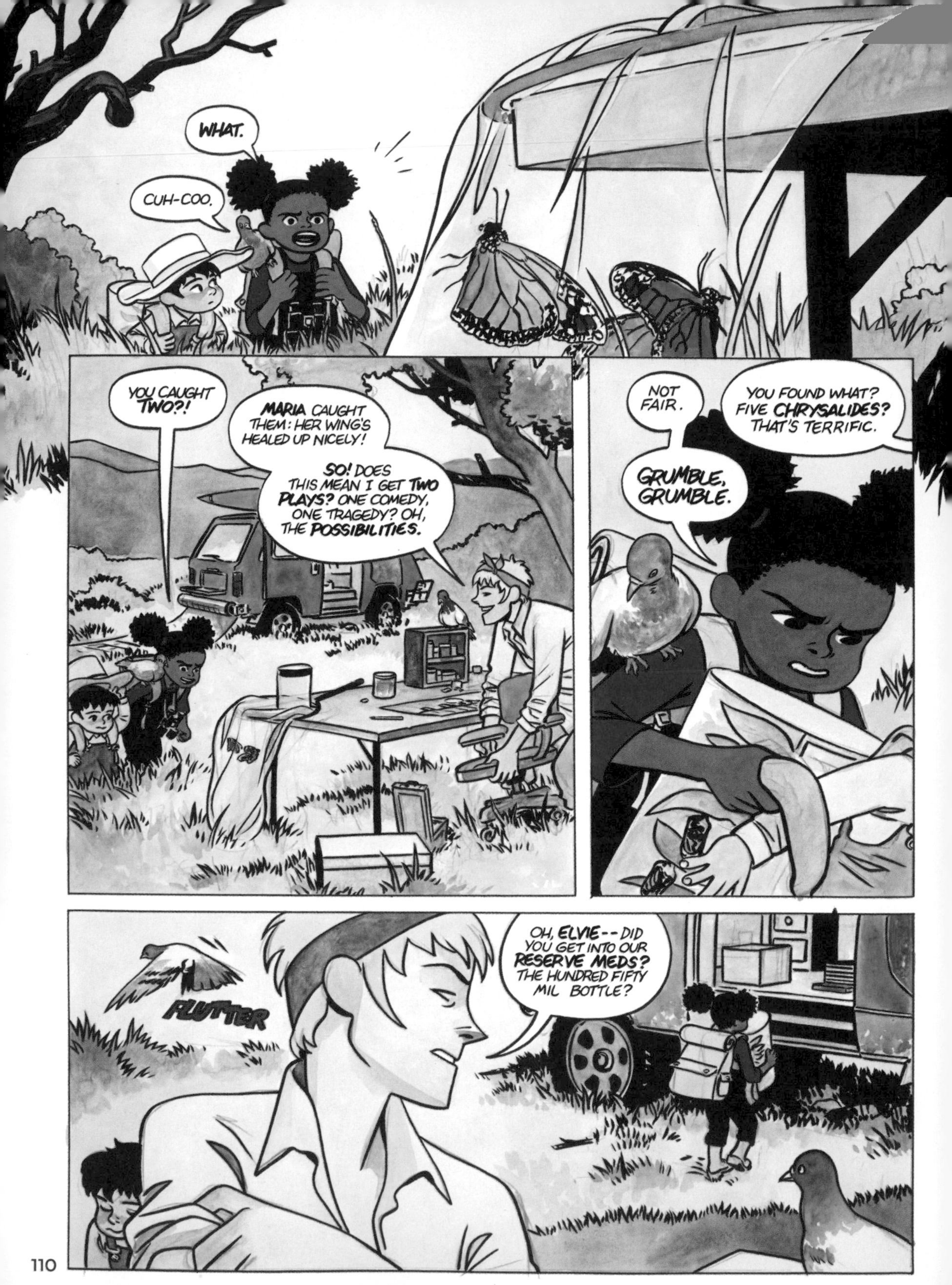
WHAT.
CUH-COO.
YOU CAUGHT TWO?!
MARIA CAUGHT THEM: HER WING'S HEALED UP NICELY!
SO! DOES THIS MEAN I GET TWO PLAYS? ONE COMEDY, ONE TRAGEDY? OH, THE POSSIBILITIES.
NOT FAIR.
YOU FOUND WHAT? FIVE CHRYSALIDES? THAT'S TERRIFIC.
GRUMBLE, GRUMBLE.
FLUTTER
OH, ELVIE-- DID YOU GET INTO OUR RESERVE MEDS? THE HUNDRED FIFTY MIL BOTTLE?

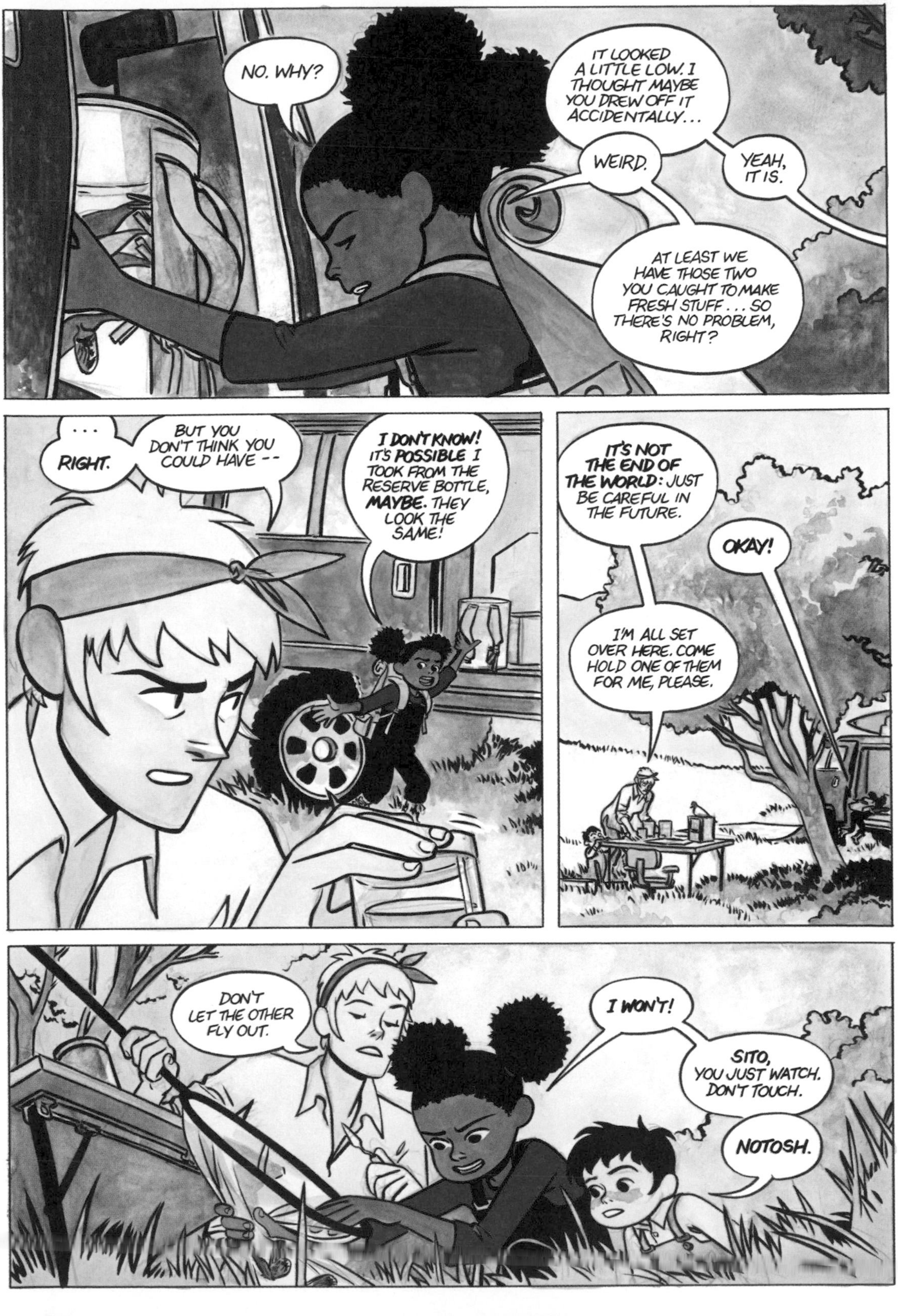
NO. WHY?
IT LOOKED A LITTLE LOW. I THOUGHT MAYBE YOU DREW OFF IT ACCIDENTALLY . . .
WEIRD.
YEAH, IT IS.
AT LEAST WE HAVE THOSE TWO YOU CAUGHT TO MAKE FRESH STUFF . . . SO THERE'S NO PROBLEM, RIGHT?
. . . RIGHT.
BUT YOU DON'T THINK YOU COULD HAVE --
I DON'T KNOW! IT'S POSSIBLE I TOOK FROM THE RESERVE BOTTLE, MAYBE. THEY LOOK THE SAME!
IT'S NOT THE END OF THE WORLD: JUST BE CAREFUL IN THE FUTURE.
OKAY!
I'M ALL SET OVER HERE. COME HOLD ONE OF THEM FOR ME, PLEASE.
DON'T LET THE OTHER FLY OUT.
I WON'T!
SITO, YOU JUST WATCH. DON'T TOUCH.
NOTOSH.

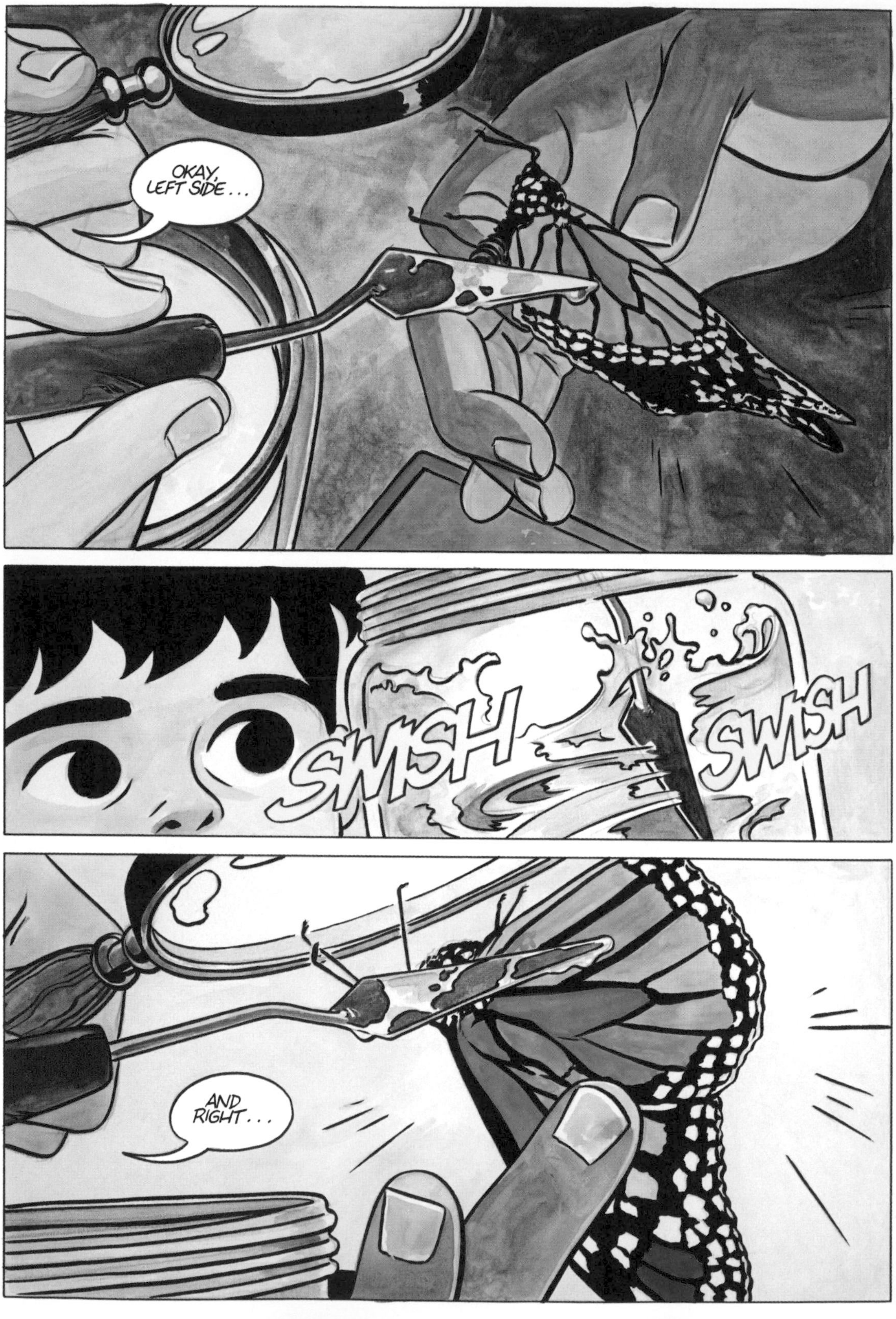

OKAY, LEFT SIDE . . .
SWISH
SWISH
AND RIGHT . . .

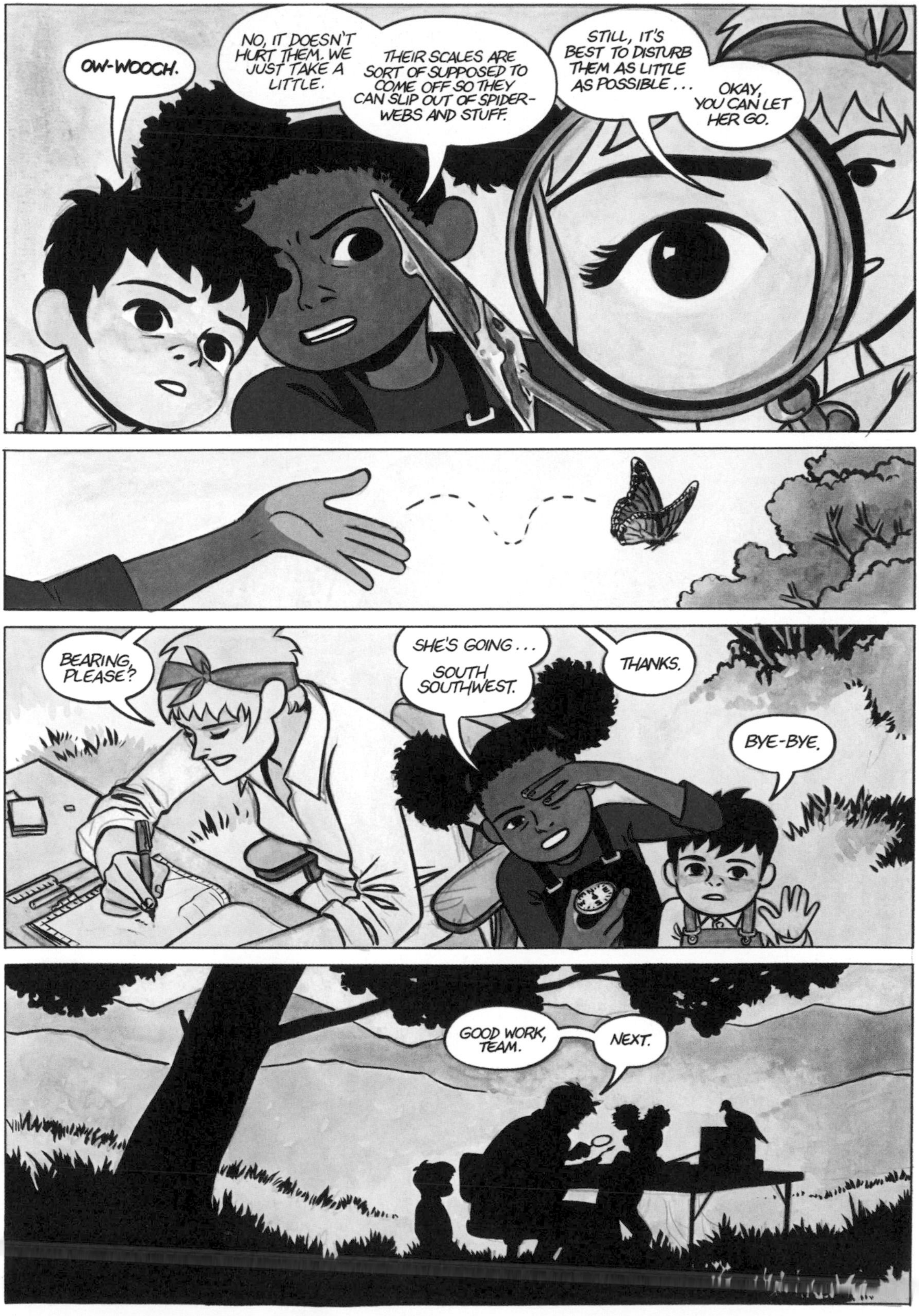
OW-WOOCH.
NO, IT DOESN'T HURT THEM. WE JUST TAKE A LITTLE.
THEIR SCALES ARE SORT OF SUPPOSED TO COME OFF SO THEY CAN SLIP OUT OF SPIDER-WEBS AND STUFF.
STILL, IT'S BEST TO DISTURB THEM AS LITTLE AS POSSIBLE . . .
OKAY, YOU CAN LET HER GO.
BEARING, PLEASE?
SHE'S GOING . . .
SOUTH SOUTHWEST.
THANKS.
BYE-BYE.
GOOD WORK, TEAM.
NEXT.

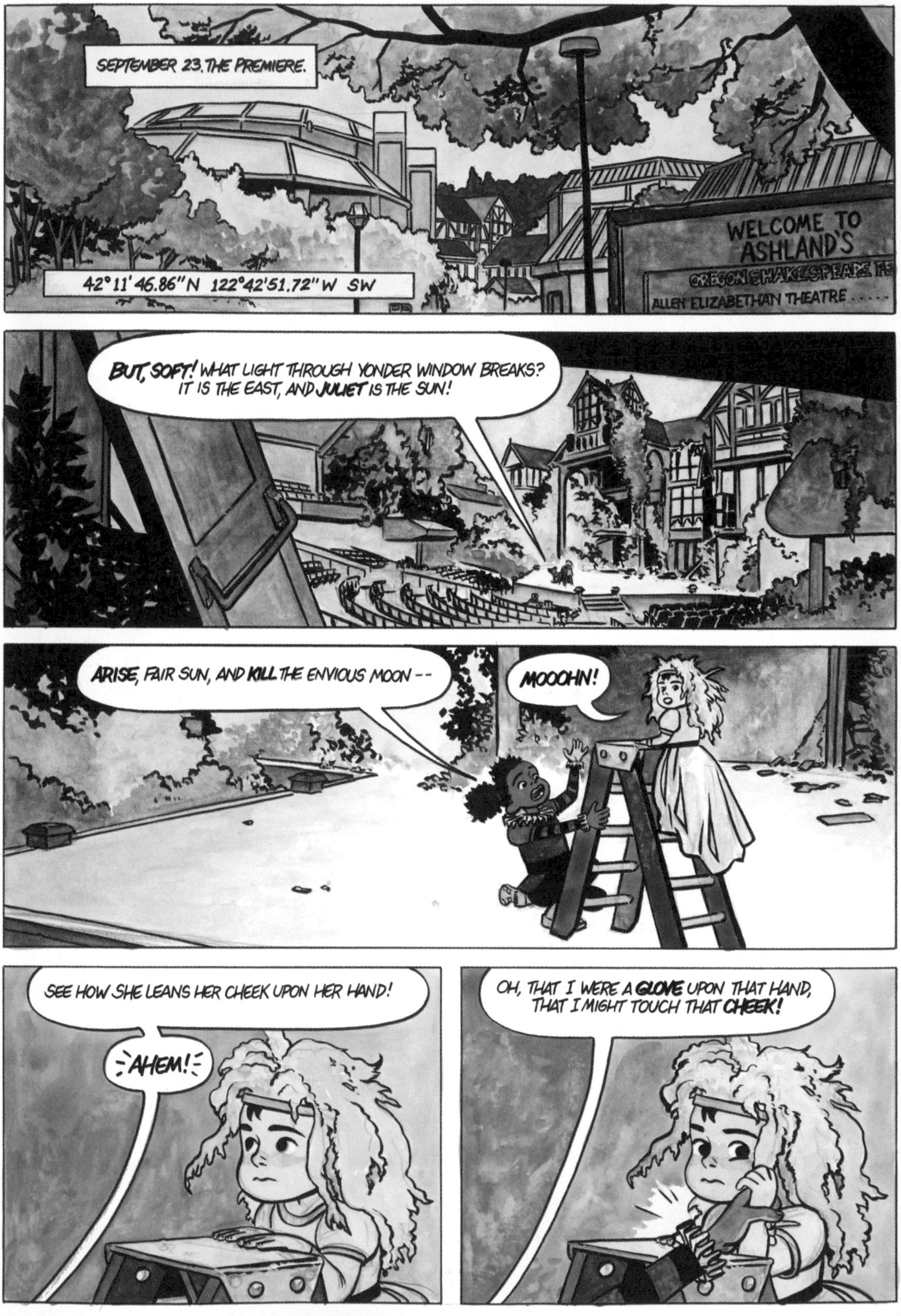
SEPTEMBER 23. THE PREMIERE.
42° 11' 46.86" N 122°42'51.72" W SW
WELCOME TO ASHLAND'S
OREGON SHAKESPEARE FE
ALLEN ELIZABETHAN THEATRE
BUT, SOFT! WHAT LIGHT THROUGH YONDER WINDOW BREAKS? IT IS THE EAST, AND JULIET IS THE SUN!
ARISE, FAIR SUN, AND KILL THE ENVIOUS MOON --
MOOOHN!
SEE HOW SHE LEANS HER CHEEK UPON HER HAND!
AHEM!
OH, THAT I WERE A GLOVE UPON THAT HAND, THAT I MIGHT TOUCH THAT CHEEK!

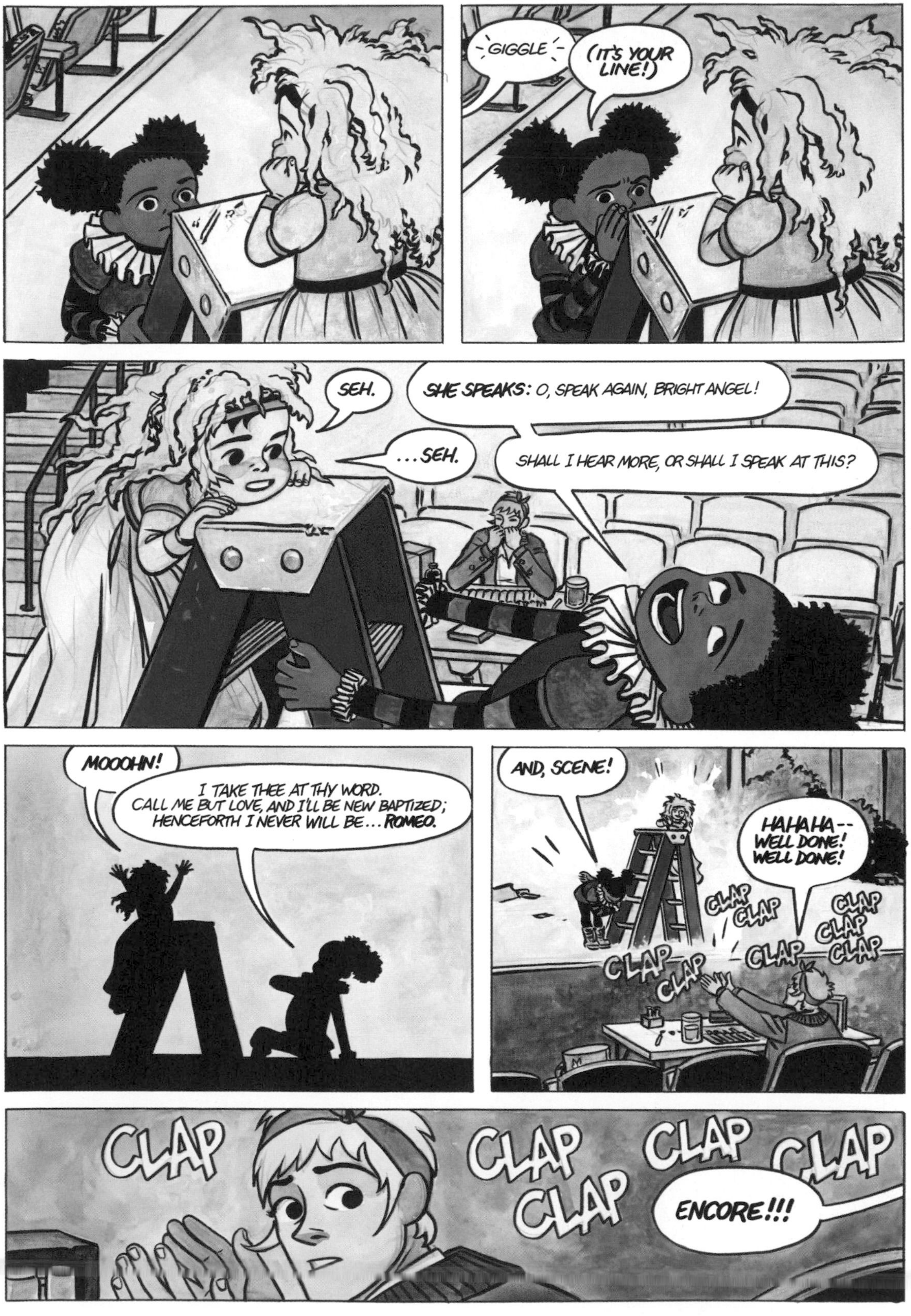
GIGGLE
(IT'S YOUR LINE!)
SEH.
...SEH.
SHE SPEAKS: O, SPEAK AGAIN, BRIGHT ANGEL!
SHALL I HEAR MORE, OR SHALL I SPEAK AT THIS?
MOOOHN!
I TAKE THEE AT THY WORD. CALL ME BUT LOVE, AND I'LL BE NEW BAPTIZED; HENCEFORTH I NEVER WILL BE... ROMEO.
AND, SCENE!
HAHAHA-- WELL DONE! WELL DONE!
CLAP CLAP
CLAP CLAP
CLAP CLAP CLAP
CLAP CLAP
CLAP
CLAP CLAP
CLAP CLAP
ENCORE!!!

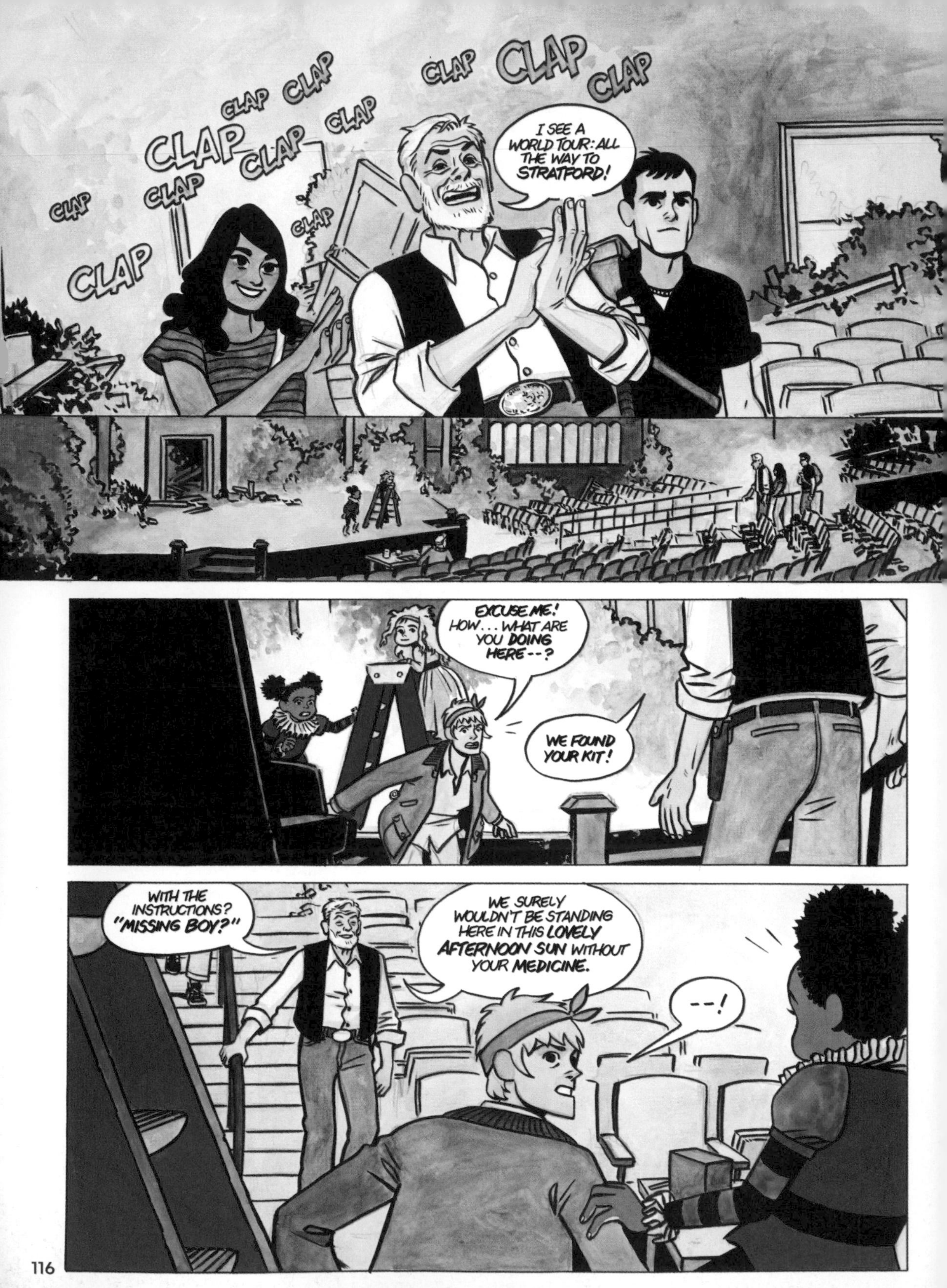
CLAP CLAP CLAP CLAP CLAP CLAP CLAP CLAP CLAP CLAP CLAP CLAP
I SEE A WORLD TOUR: ALL THE WAY TO STRATFORD!
EXCUSE ME! HOW... WHAT ARE YOU DOING HERE--?
WE FOUND YOUR KIT!
WITH THE INSTRUCTIONS? "MISSING BOY?"
WE SURELY WOULDN'T BE STANDING HERE IN THIS LOVELY AFTERNOON SUN WITHOUT YOUR MEDICINE.
--!

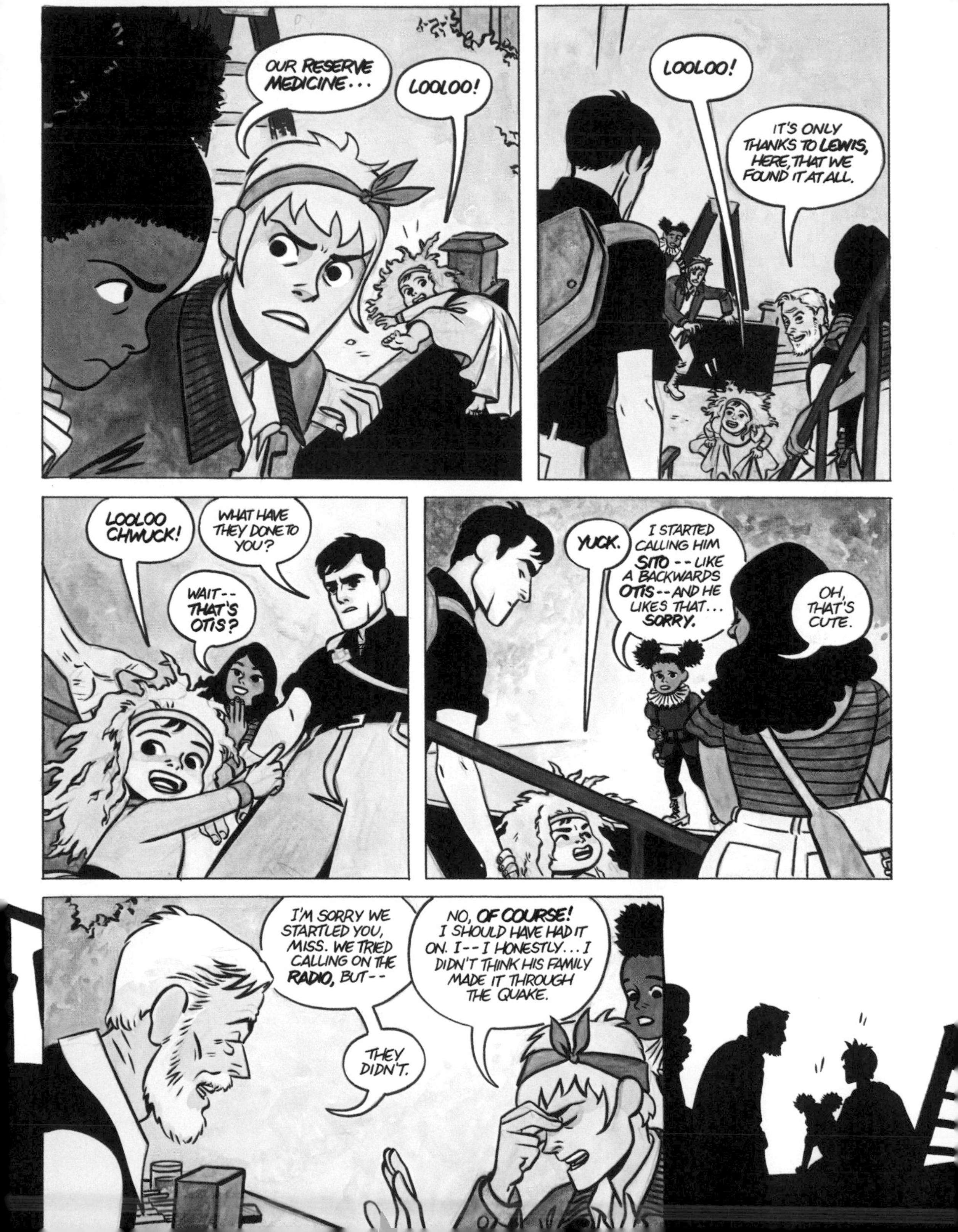
OUR RESERVE MEDICINE...
LOOLOO!
LOOLOO!
IT'S ONLY THANKS TO LEWIS, HERE, THAT WE FOUND IT AT ALL.
LOOLOO CHWUCK!
WHAT HAVE THEY DONE TO YOU?
WAIT-- THAT'S OTIS?
YUCK.
I STARTED CALLING HIM SITO -- LIKE A BACKWARDS OTIS -- AND HE LIKES THAT... SORRY.
OH, THAT'S CUTE.
I'M SORRY WE STARTLED YOU, MISS. WE TRIED CALLING ON THE RADIO, BUT--
NO, OF COURSE! I SHOULD HAVE HAD IT ON. I-- I HONESTLY... I DIDN'T THINK HIS FAMILY MADE IT THROUGH THE QUAKE.
THEY DIDN'T.

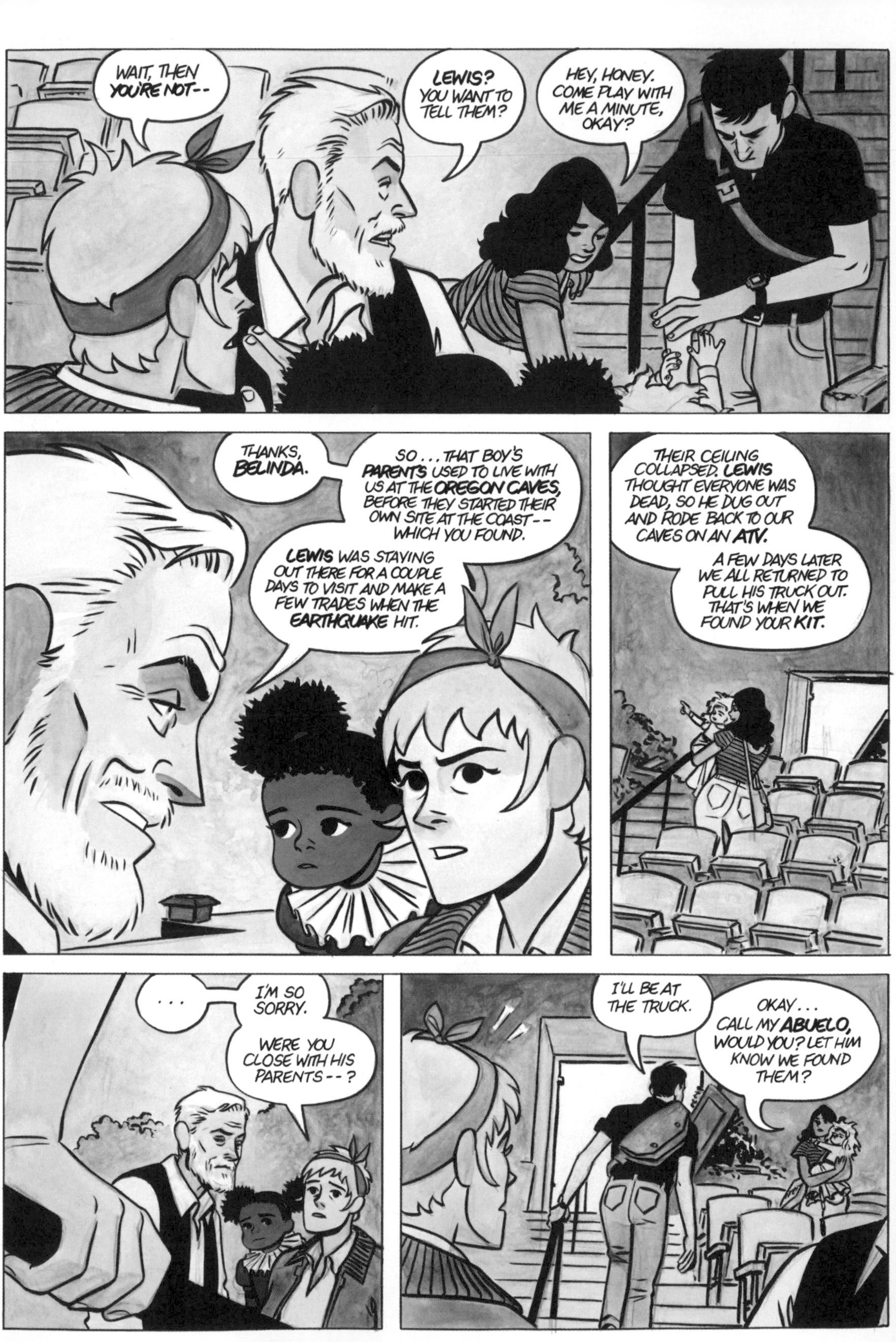
WAIT, THEN YOU'RE NOT--
LEWIS? YOU WANT TO TELL THEM?
HEY, HONEY. COME PLAY WITH ME A MINUTE, OKAY?
THANKS, BELINDA.
SO... THAT BOY'S PARENTS USED TO LIVE WITH US AT THE OREGON CAVES, BEFORE THEY STARTED THEIR OWN SITE AT THE COAST-- WHICH YOU FOUND.
LEWIS WAS STAYING OUT THERE FOR A COUPLE DAYS TO VISIT AND MAKE A FEW TRADES WHEN THE EARTHQUAKE HIT.
THEIR CEILING COLLAPSED. LEWIS THOUGHT EVERYONE WAS DEAD, SO HE DUG OUT AND RODE BACK TO OUR CAVES ON AN ATV.
A FEW DAYS LATER WE ALL RETURNED TO PULL HIS TRUCK OUT. THAT'S WHEN WE FOUND YOUR KIT.
...
I'M SO SORRY.
WERE YOU CLOSE WITH HIS PARENTS--?
I'LL BE AT THE TRUCK.
OKAY... CALL MY ABUELO, WOULD YOU? LET HIM KNOW WE FOUND THEM?

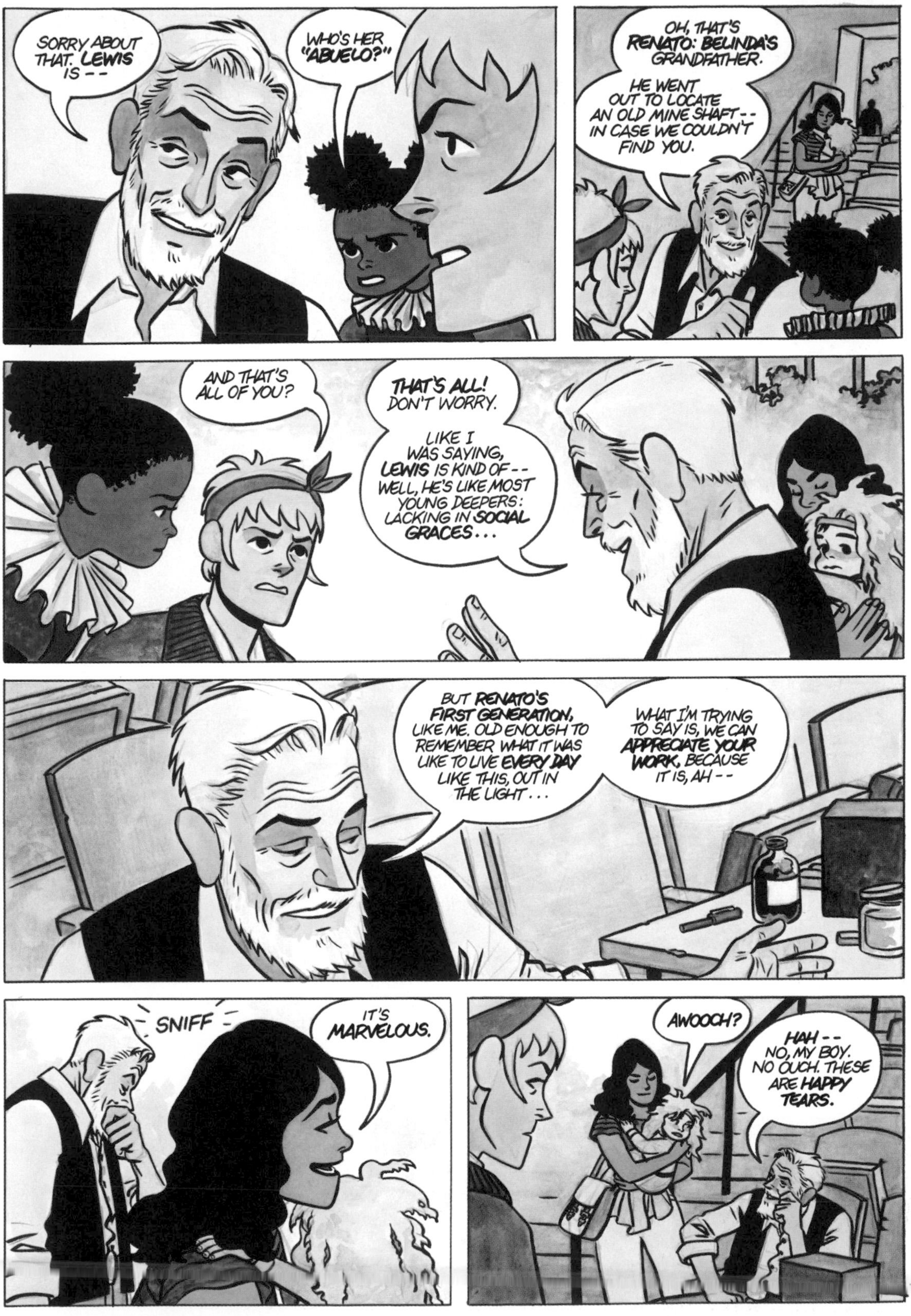
SORRY ABOUT THAT. LEWIS IS --
WHO'S HER "ABUELO?"
OH, THAT'S RENATO: BELINDA'S GRANDFATHER.
HE WENT OUT TO LOCATE AN OLD MINE SHAFT -- IN CASE WE COULDN'T FIND YOU.
AND THAT'S ALL OF YOU?
THAT'S ALL! DON'T WORRY.
LIKE I WAS SAYING, LEWIS IS KIND OF -- WELL, HE'S LIKE MOST YOUNG DEEPERS: LACKING IN SOCIAL GRACES...
BUT RENATO'S FIRST GENERATION, LIKE ME. OLD ENOUGH TO REMEMBER WHAT IT WAS LIKE TO LIVE EVERY DAY LIKE THIS, OUT IN THE LIGHT...
WHAT I'M TRYING TO SAY IS, WE CAN APPRECIATE YOUR WORK, BECAUSE IT IS, AH --
SNIFF
IT'S MARVELOUS.
AWOOCH?
HAH -- NO, MY BOY. NO OUCH. THESE ARE HAPPY TEARS.

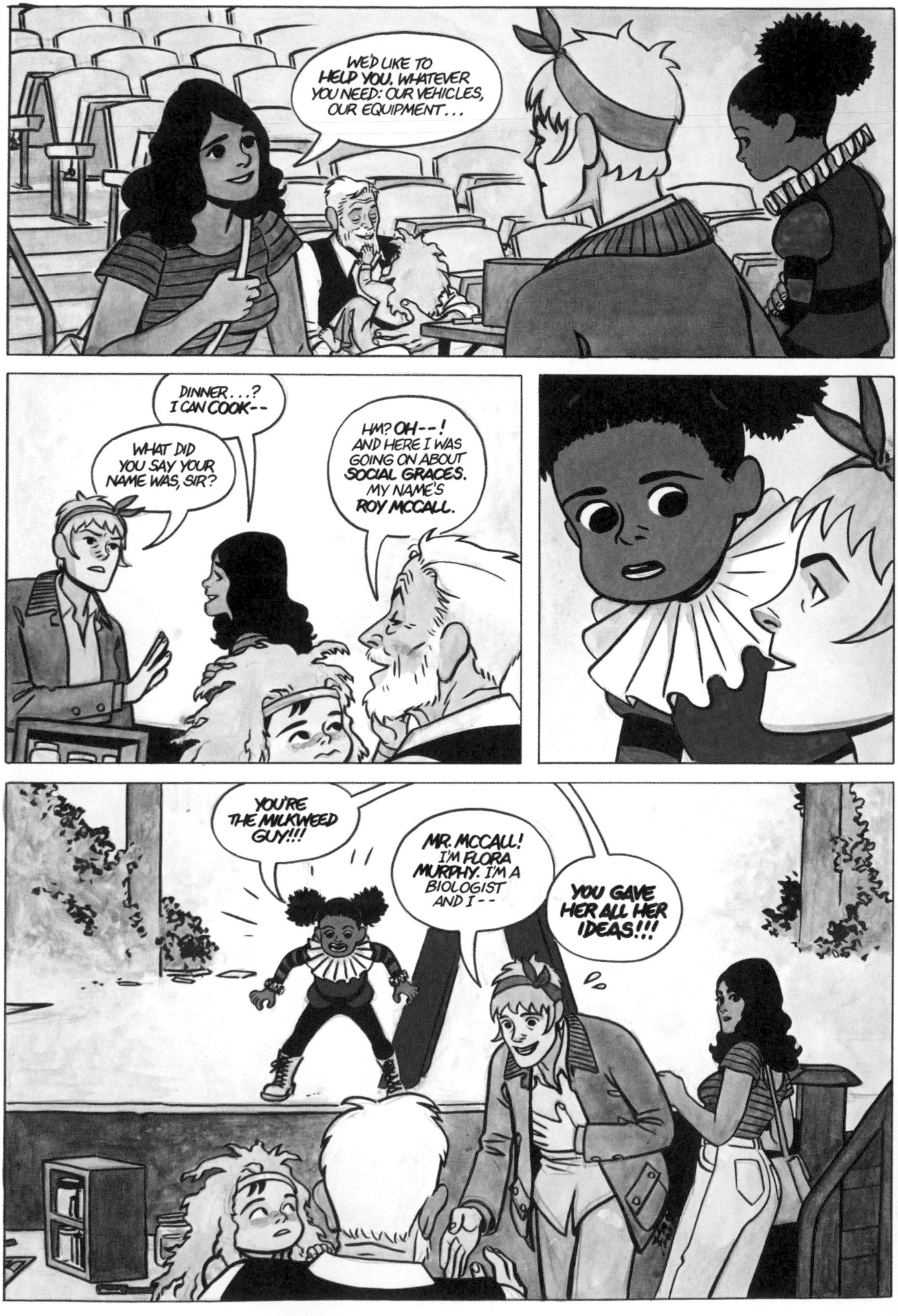
WE'D LIKE TO HELP YOU. WHATEVER YOU NEED: OUR VEHICLES, OUR EQUIPMENT . . .
WHAT DID YOU SAY YOUR NAME WAS, SIR?
DINNER . . .? I CAN COOK--
HM? OH--! AND HERE I WAS GOING ON ABOUT SOCIAL GRACES. MY NAME'S ROY MCCALL.
YOU'RE THE MILKWEED GUY!!!
MR. MCCALL! I'M FLORA MURPHY. I'M A BIOLOGIST AND I--
YOU GAVE HER ALL HER IDEAS!!!

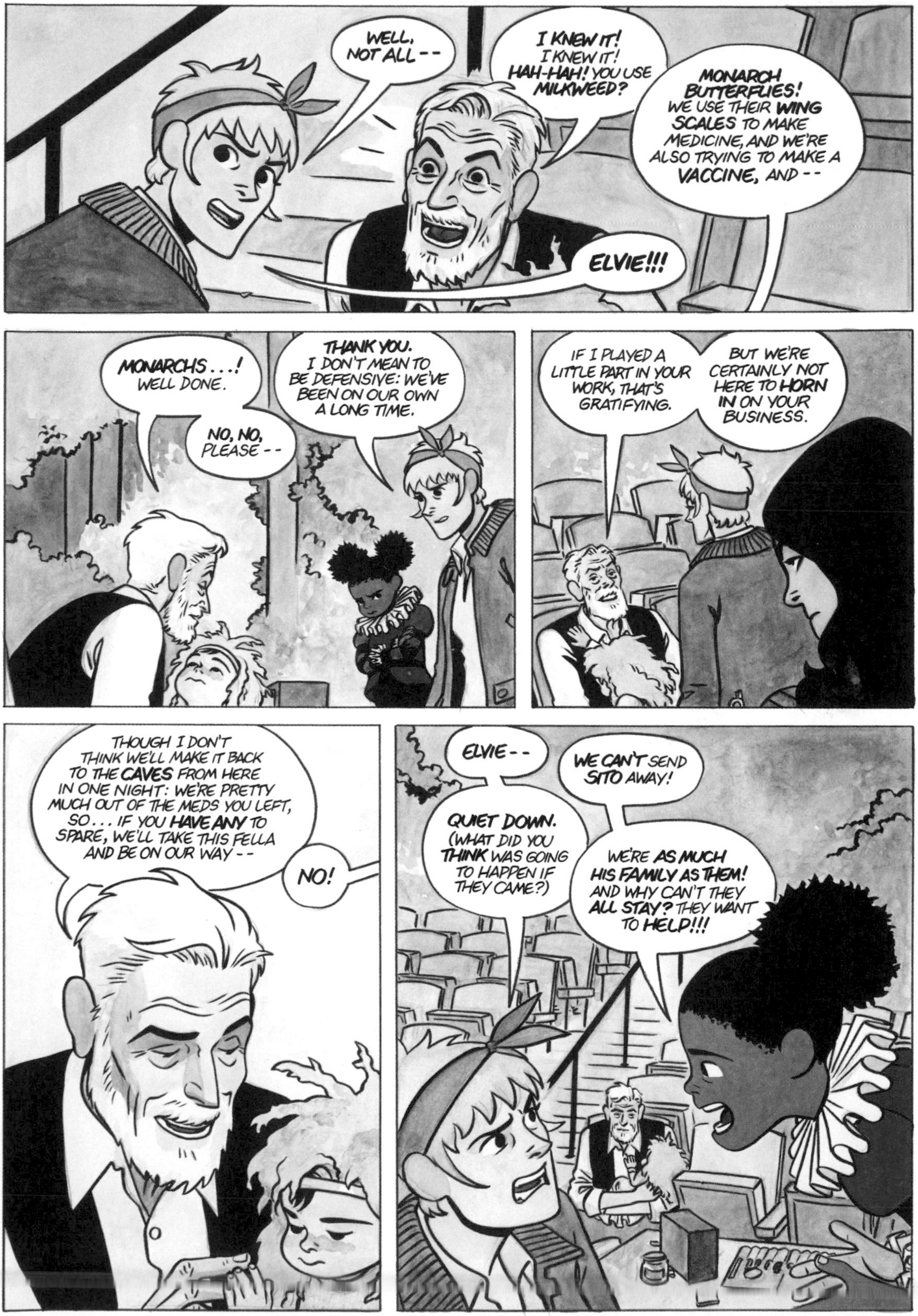
WELL, NOT ALL --
I KNEW IT! I KNEW IT! HAH-HAH! YOU USE MILKWEED?
MONARCH BUTTERFLIES! WE USE THEIR WING SCALES TO MAKE MEDICINE, AND WE'RE ALSO TRYING TO MAKE A VACCINE, AND --
ELVIE!!!
MONARCHS . . .! WELL DONE.
NO, NO, PLEASE --
THANK YOU. I DON'T MEAN TO BE DEFENSIVE: WE'VE BEEN ON OUR OWN A LONG TIME.
IF I PLAYED A LITTLE PART IN YOUR WORK, THAT'S GRATIFYING.
BUT WE'RE CERTAINLY NOT HERE TO HORN IN ON YOUR BUSINESS.
THOUGH I DON'T THINK WE'LL MAKE IT BACK TO THE CAVES FROM HERE IN ONE NIGHT: WE'RE PRETTY MUCH OUT OF THE MEDS YOU LEFT, SO . . . IF YOU HAVE ANY TO SPARE, WE'LL TAKE THIS FELLA AND BE ON OUR WAY --
NO!
ELVIE --
WE CAN'T SEND SITO AWAY!
QUIET DOWN. (WHAT DID YOU THINK WAS GOING TO HAPPEN IF THEY CAME?)
WE'RE AS MUCH HIS FAMILY AS THEM! AND WHY CAN'T THEY ALL STAY? THEY WANT TO HELP!!!

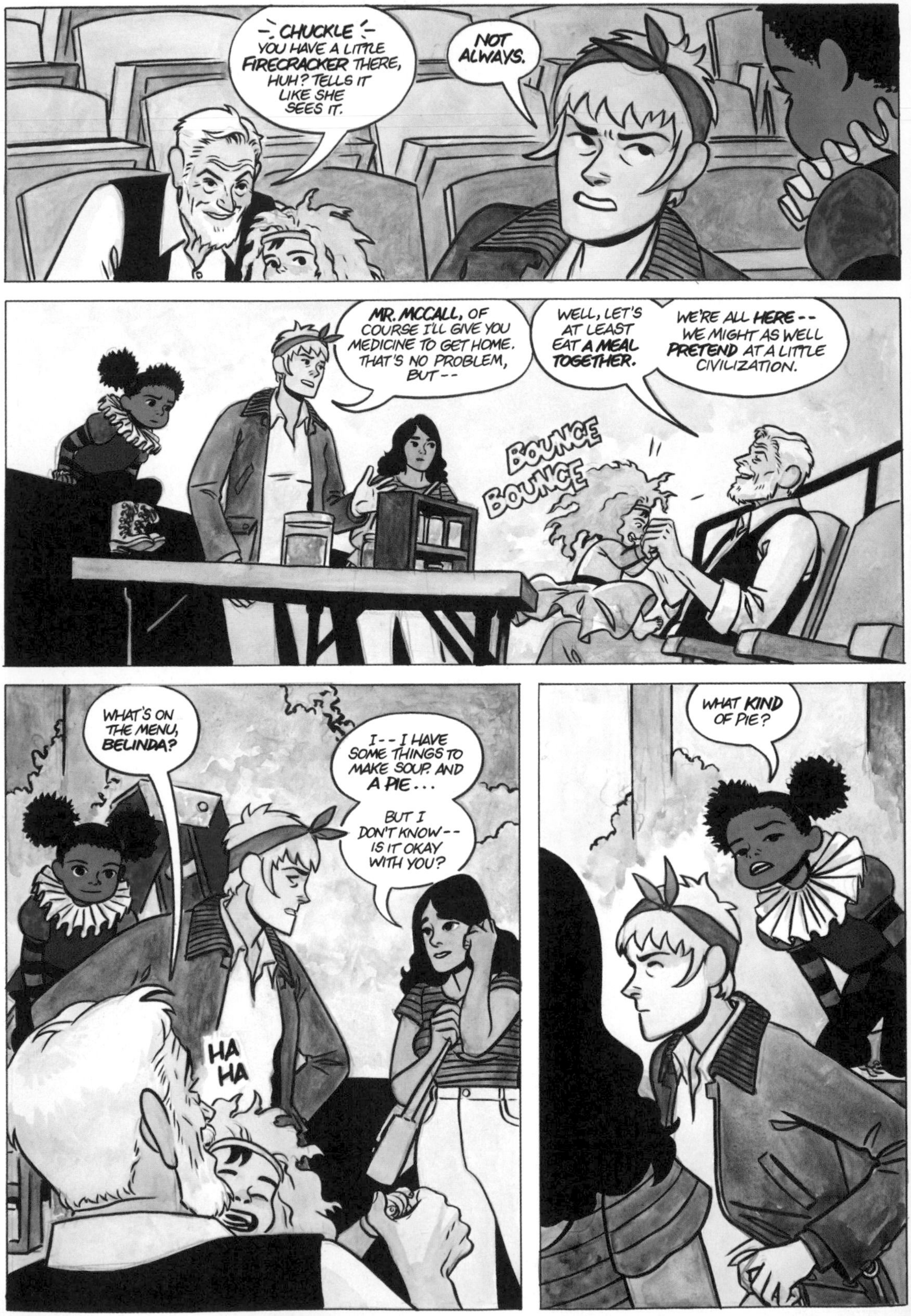
CHUCKLE
YOU HAVE A LITTLE FIRECRACKER THERE, HUH? TELLS IT LIKE SHE SEES IT.
NOT ALWAYS.
MR. MCCALL, OF COURSE I'LL GIVE YOU MEDICINE TO GET HOME. THAT'S NO PROBLEM, BUT--
WELL, LET'S AT LEAST EAT A MEAL TOGETHER.
WE'RE ALL HERE-- WE MIGHT AS WELL PRETEND AT A LITTLE CIVILIZATION.
BOUNCE
BOUNCE
WHAT'S ON THE MENU, BELINDA?
I-- I HAVE SOME THINGS TO MAKE SOUP. AND A PIE...
BUT I DON'T KNOW-- IS IT OKAY WITH YOU?
HA HA
WHAT KIND OF PIE?

CHAPTER SEVEN
DESSERT

BLACKBERRY PIE RECIPE

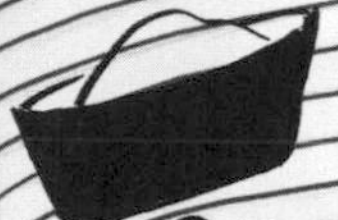

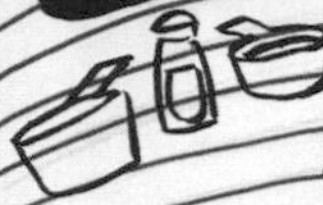

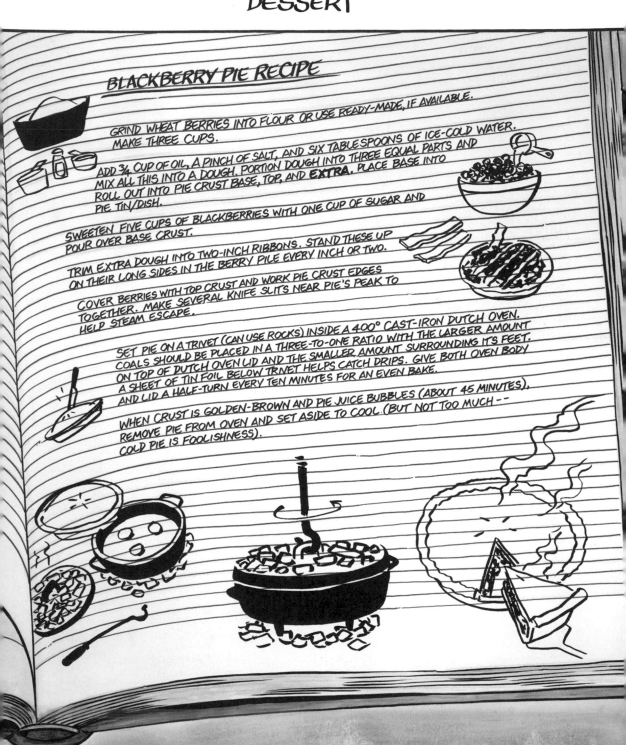

GRIND WHEAT BERRIES INTO FLOUR OR USE READY-MADE, IF AVAILABLE. MAKE THREE CUPS.

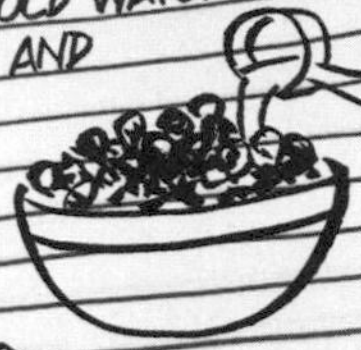

ADD 3/4 CUP OF OIL, A PINCH OF SALT, AND SIX TABLESPOONS OF ICE-COLD WATER. MIX ALL THIS INTO A DOUGH. PORTION DOUGH INTO THREE EQUAL PARTS AND ROLL OUT INTO PIE CRUST BASE, TOP, AND **EXTRA**. PLACE BASE INTO PIE TIN/DISH.

SWEETEN FIVE CUPS OF BLACKBERRIES WITH ONE CUP OF SUGAR AND POUR OVER BASE CRUST.

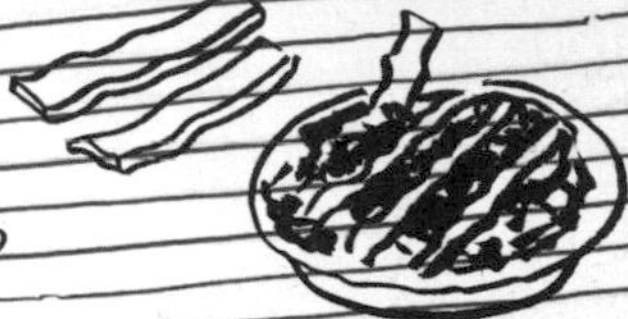

TRIM EXTRA DOUGH INTO TWO-INCH RIBBONS. STAND THESE UP ON THEIR LONG SIDES IN THE BERRY PILE EVERY INCH OR TWO.

COVER BERRIES WITH TOP CRUST AND WORK PIE CRUST EDGES TOGETHER. MAKE SEVERAL KNIFE SLITS NEAR PIE'S PEAK TO HELP STEAM ESCAPE.

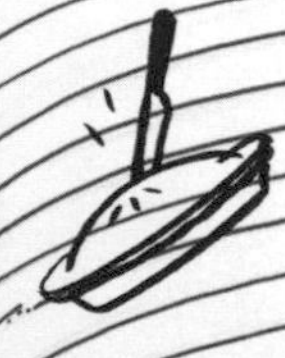

SET PIE ON A TRIVET (CAN USE ROCKS) INSIDE A 400° CAST-IRON DUTCH OVEN. COALS SHOULD BE PLACED IN A THREE-TO-ONE RATIO WITH THE LARGER AMOUNT ON TOP OF DUTCH OVEN LID AND THE SMALLER AMOUNT SURROUNDING IT'S FEET. A SHEET OF TIN FOIL BELOW TRIVET HELPS CATCH DRIPS. GIVE BOTH OVEN BODY AND LID A HALF-TURN EVERY TEN MINUTES FOR AN EVEN BAKE.

WHEN CRUST IS GOLDEN-BROWN AND PIE JUICE BUBBLES (ABOUT 45 MINUTES), REMOVE PIE FROM OVEN AND SET ASIDE TO COOL. (BUT NOT TOO MUCH -- COLD PIE IS FOOLISHNESS).

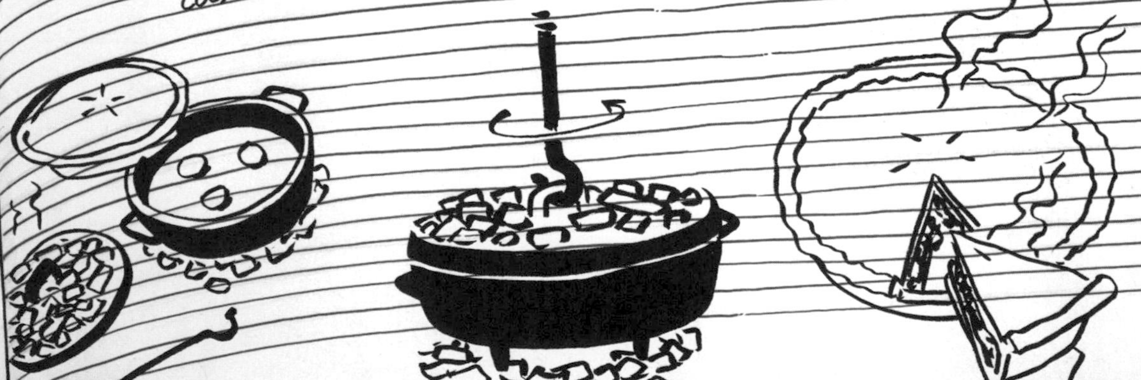

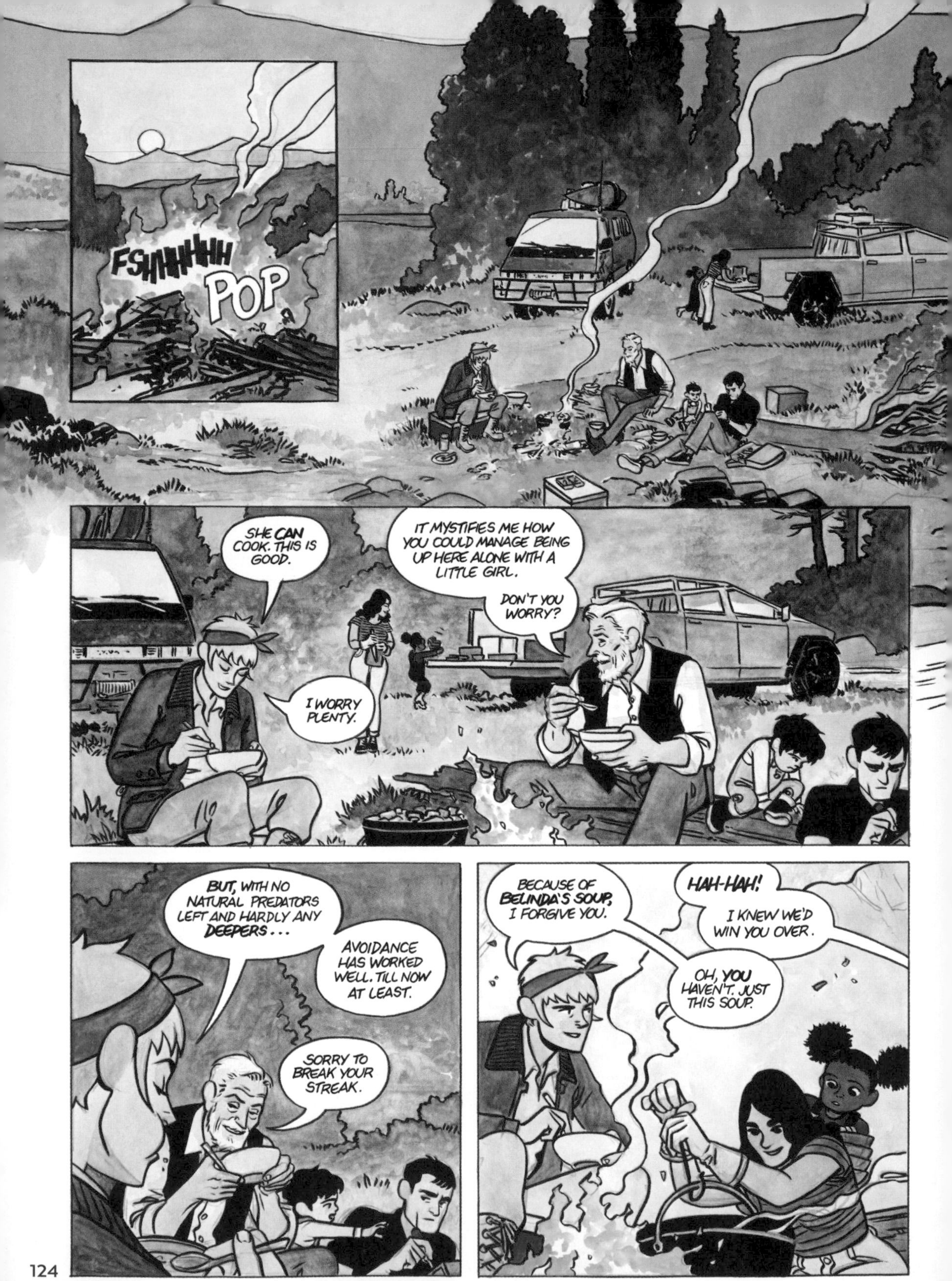
FSHHHHHH
POP
SHE CAN COOK. THIS IS GOOD.
IT MYSTIFIES ME HOW YOU COULD MANAGE BEING UP HERE ALONE WITH A LITTLE GIRL.
DON'T YOU WORRY?
I WORRY PLENTY.
BUT, WITH NO NATURAL PREDATORS LEFT AND HARDLY ANY DEEPERS...
AVOIDANCE HAS WORKED WELL. TILL NOW AT LEAST.
SORRY TO BREAK YOUR STREAK.
BECAUSE OF BELINDA'S SOUP, I FORGIVE YOU.
HAH-HAH!
I KNEW WE'D WIN YOU OVER.
OH, YOU HAVEN'T. JUST THIS SOUP.

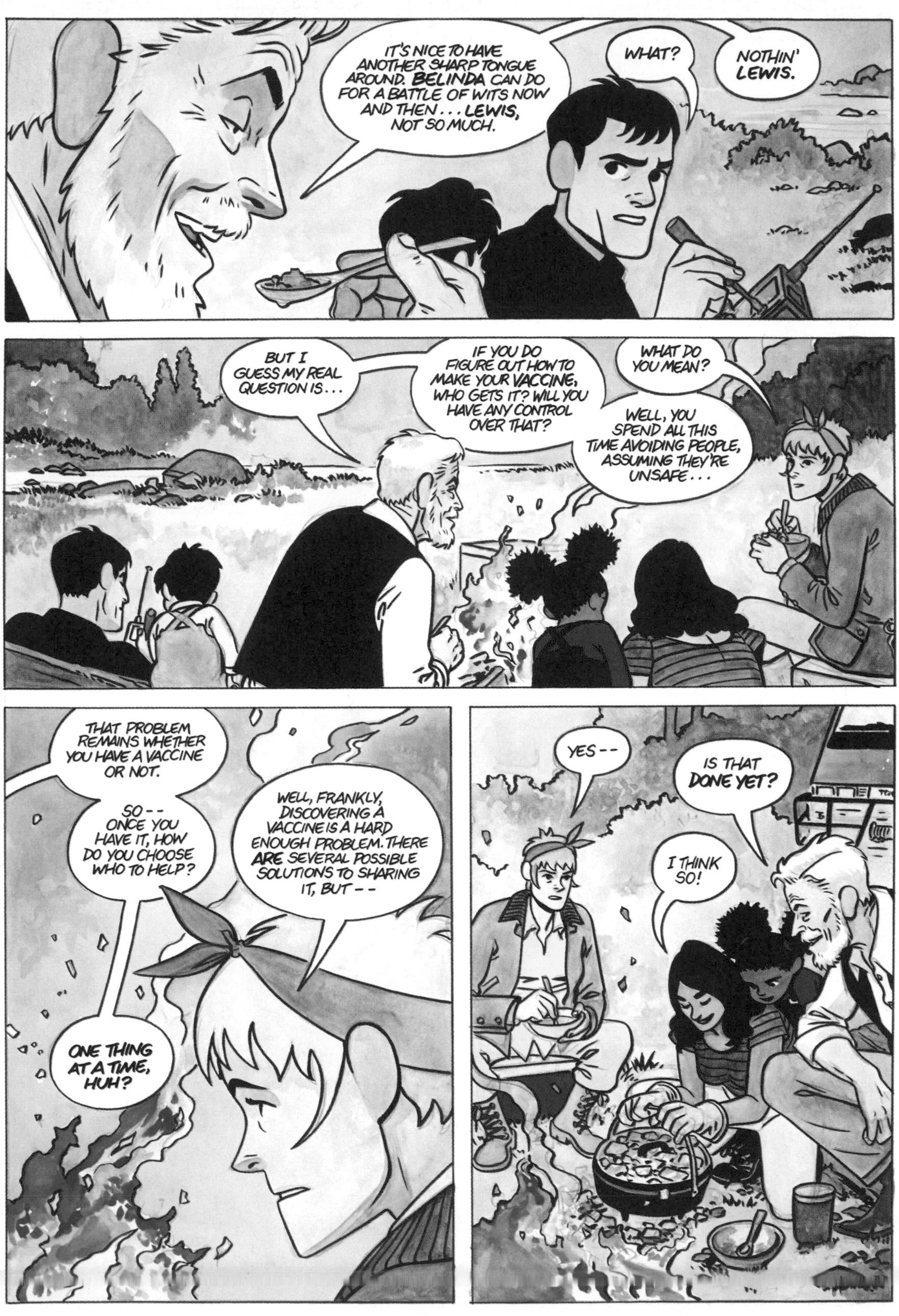
IT'S NICE TO HAVE ANOTHER SHARP TONGUE AROUND. BELINDA CAN DO FOR A BATTLE OF WITS NOW AND THEN . . . LEWIS, NOT SO MUCH.
WHAT?
NOTHIN' LEWIS.
BUT I GUESS MY REAL QUESTION IS . . .
IF YOU DO FIGURE OUT HOW TO MAKE YOUR VACCINE, WHO GETS IT? WILL YOU HAVE ANY CONTROL OVER THAT?
WHAT DO YOU MEAN?
WELL, YOU SPEND ALL THIS TIME AVOIDING PEOPLE, ASSUMING THEY'RE UNSAFE . . .
THAT PROBLEM REMAINS WHETHER YOU HAVE A VACCINE OR NOT.
SO - - ONCE YOU HAVE IT, HOW DO YOU CHOOSE WHO TO HELP?
WELL, FRANKLY, DISCOVERING A VACCINE IS A HARD ENOUGH PROBLEM. THERE ARE SEVERAL POSSIBLE SOLUTIONS TO SHARING IT, BUT - -
ONE THING AT A TIME, HUH?
YES - -
IS THAT DONE YET?
I THINK SO!

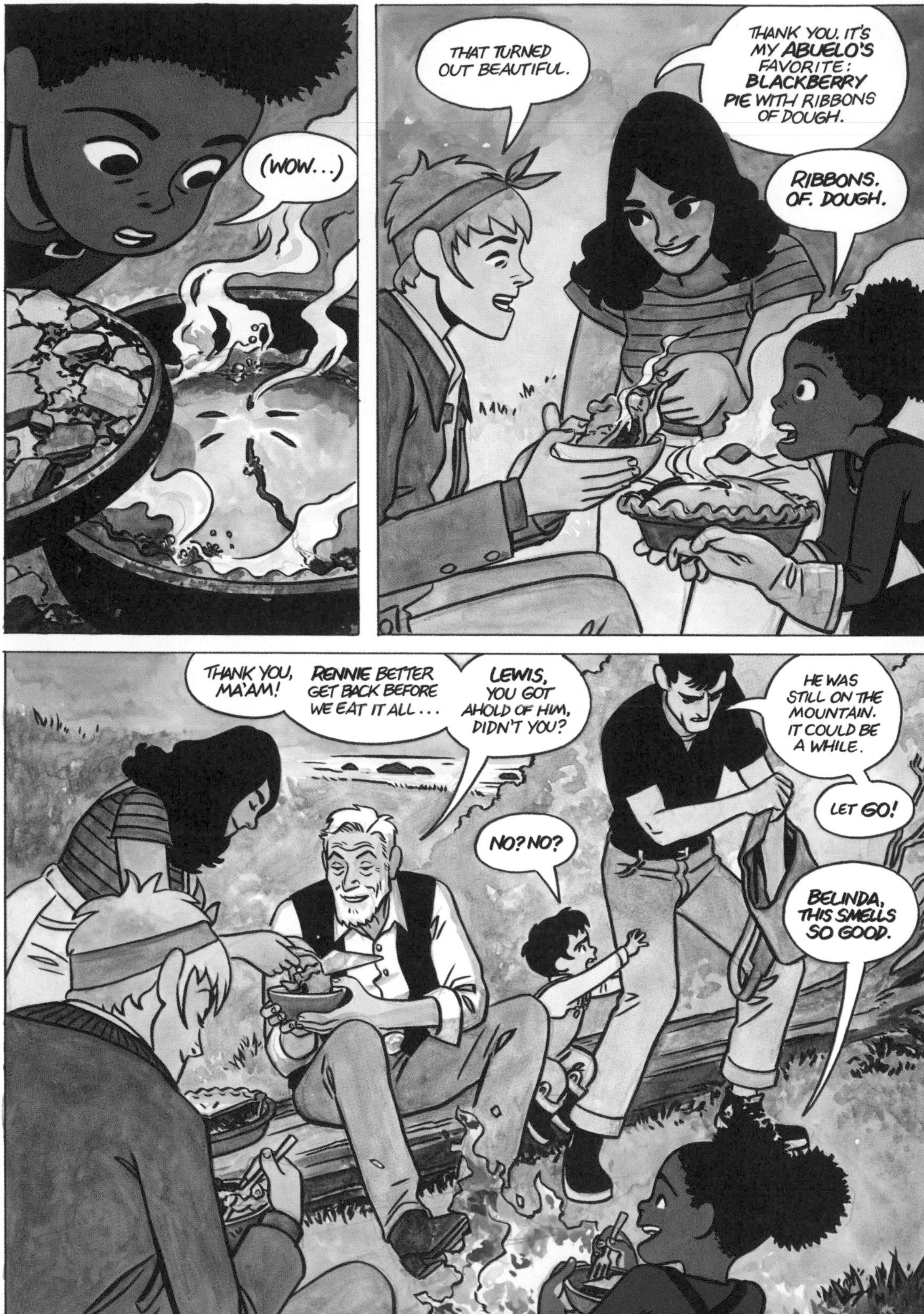
(WOW...)
THAT TURNED OUT BEAUTIFUL.
THANK YOU. IT'S MY ABUELO'S FAVORITE: BLACKBERRY PIE WITH RIBBONS OF DOUGH.
RIBBONS. OF. DOUGH.
THANK YOU, MA'AM!
RENNIE BETTER GET BACK BEFORE WE EAT IT ALL...
LEWIS, YOU GOT AHOLD OF HIM, DIDN'T YOU?
HE WAS STILL ON THE MOUNTAIN. IT COULD BE A WHILE.
NO? NO?
LET GO!
BELINDA, THIS SMELLS SO GOOD.

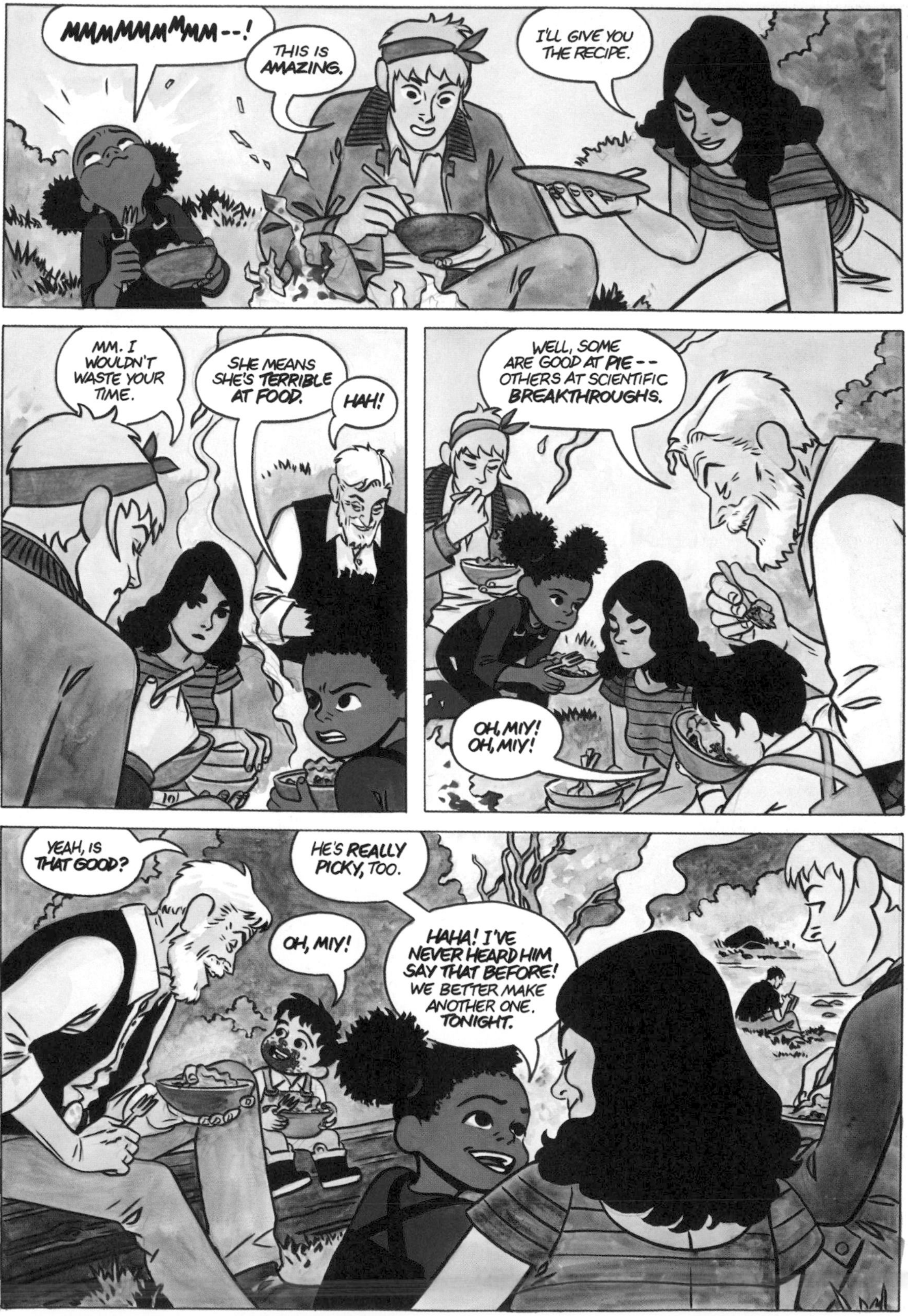
MMMMMMMMM--!
THIS IS AMAZING.
I'LL GIVE YOU THE RECIPE.
MM. I WOULDN'T WASTE YOUR TIME.
SHE MEANS SHE'S TERRIBLE AT FOOD.
HAH!
WELL, SOME ARE GOOD AT PIE-- OTHERS AT SCIENTIFIC BREAKTHROUGHS.
OH, MIY! OH, MIY!
YEAH, IS THAT GOOD?
HE'S REALLY PICKY, TOO.
OH, MIY!
HAHA! I'VE NEVER HEARD HIM SAY THAT BEFORE! WE BETTER MAKE ANOTHER ONE. TONIGHT.

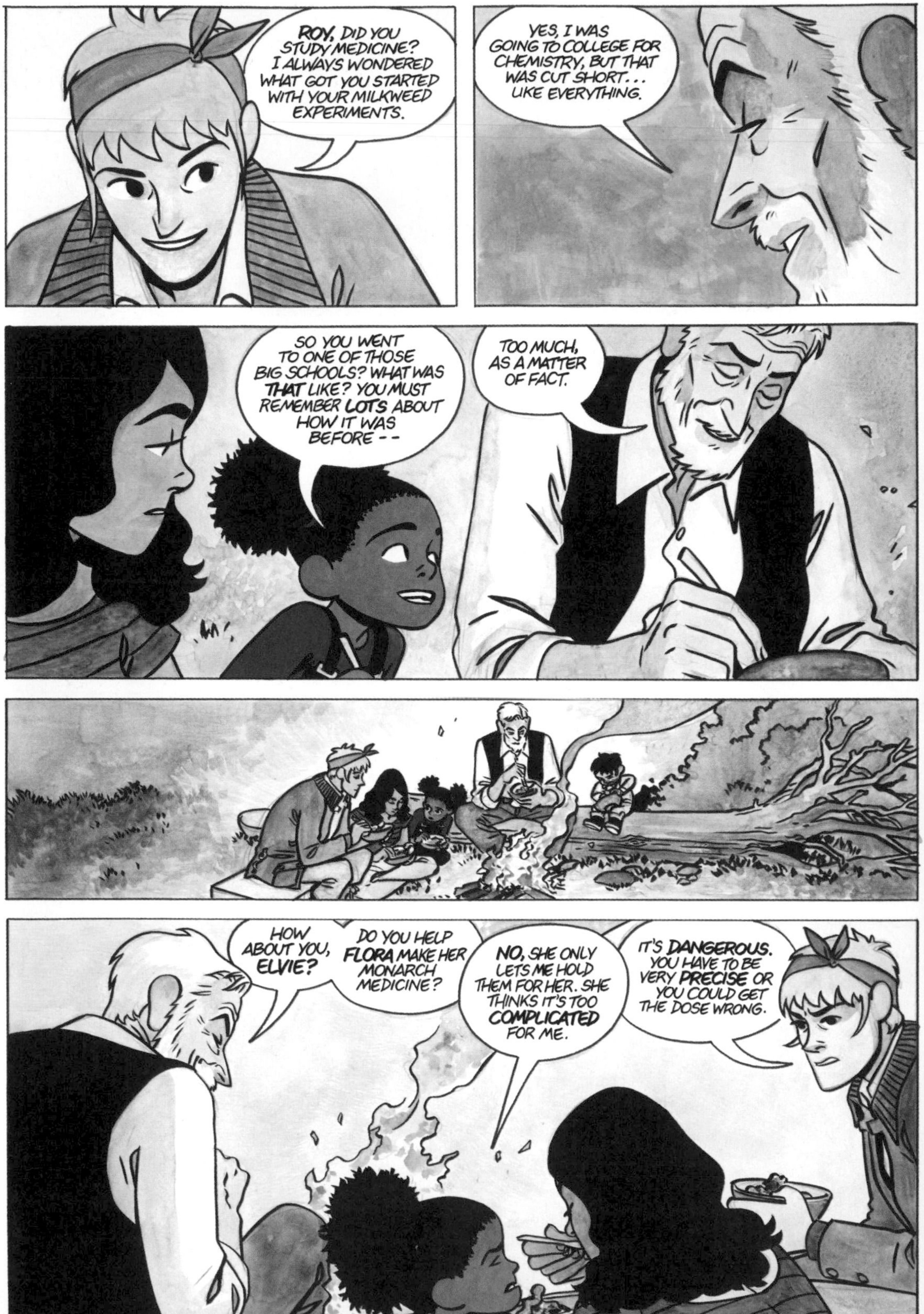
ROY, DID YOU STUDY MEDICINE? I ALWAYS WONDERED WHAT GOT YOU STARTED WITH YOUR MILKWEED EXPERIMENTS.
YES, I WAS GOING TO COLLEGE FOR CHEMISTRY, BUT THAT WAS CUT SHORT . . . LIKE EVERYTHING.
SO YOU WENT TO ONE OF THOSE BIG SCHOOLS? WHAT WAS THAT LIKE? YOU MUST REMEMBER LOTS ABOUT HOW IT WAS BEFORE --
TOO MUCH, AS A MATTER OF FACT.
HOW ABOUT YOU, ELVIE?
DO YOU HELP FLORA MAKE HER MONARCH MEDICINE?
NO, SHE ONLY LETS ME HOLD THEM FOR HER. SHE THINKS IT'S TOO COMPLICATED FOR ME.
IT'S DANGEROUS. YOU HAVE TO BE VERY PRECISE OR YOU COULD GET THE DOSE WRONG.

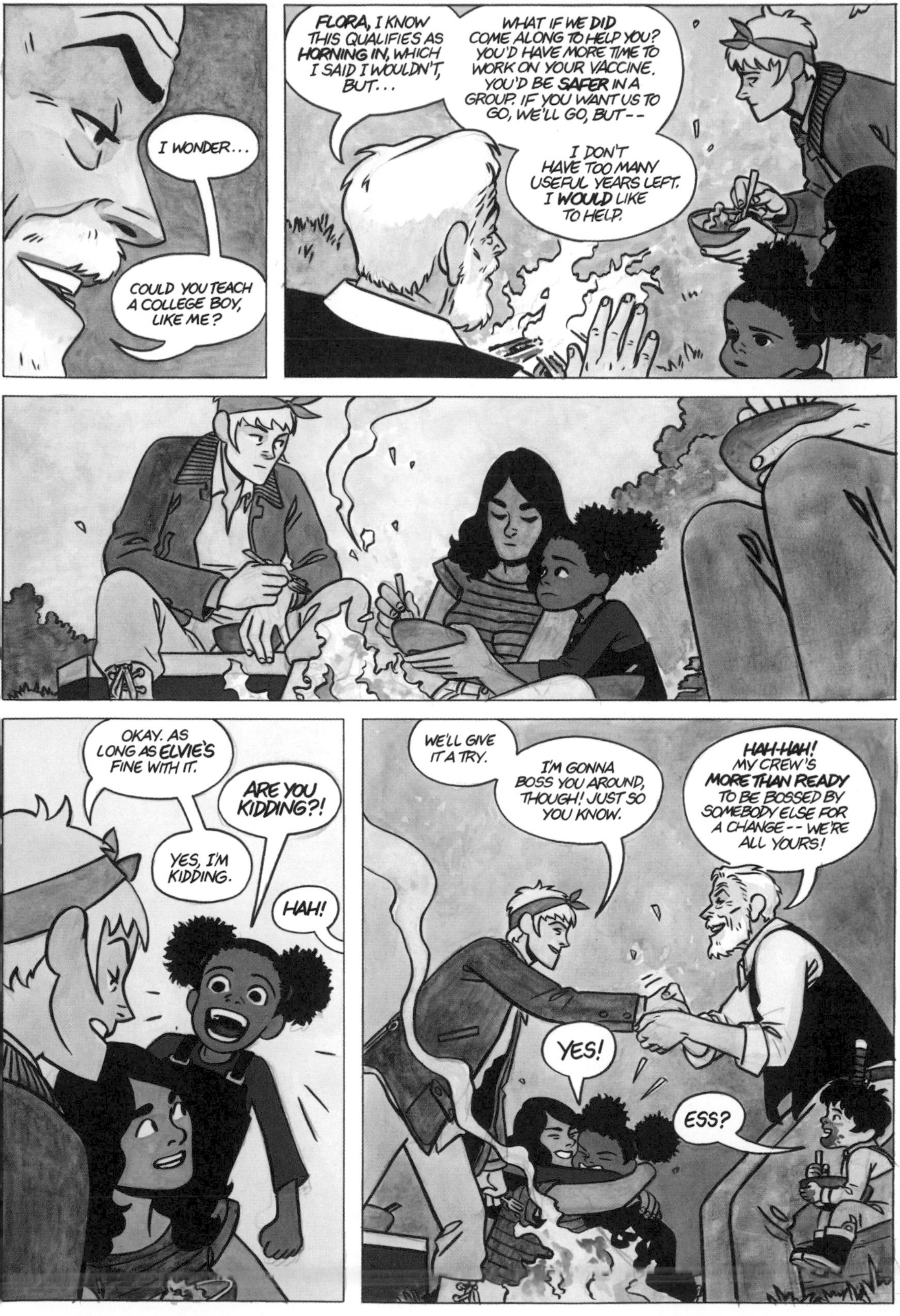
I WONDER...
COULD YOU TEACH A COLLEGE BOY, LIKE ME?
FLORA, I KNOW THIS QUALIFIES AS HORNING IN, WHICH I SAID I WOULDN'T, BUT...
WHAT IF WE DID COME ALONG TO HELP YOU? YOU'D HAVE MORE TIME TO WORK ON YOUR VACCINE. YOU'D BE SAFER IN A GROUP. IF YOU WANT US TO GO, WE'LL GO, BUT--
I DON'T HAVE TOO MANY USEFUL YEARS LEFT. I WOULD LIKE TO HELP.
OKAY. AS LONG AS ELVIE'S FINE WITH IT.
ARE YOU KIDDING?!
YES, I'M KIDDING.
HAH!
WE'LL GIVE IT A TRY.
I'M GONNA BOSS YOU AROUND, THOUGH! JUST SO YOU KNOW.
HAH-HAH! MY CREW'S MORE THAN READY TO BE BOSSED BY SOMEBODY ELSE FOR A CHANGE-- WE'RE ALL YOURS!
YES!
ESS?

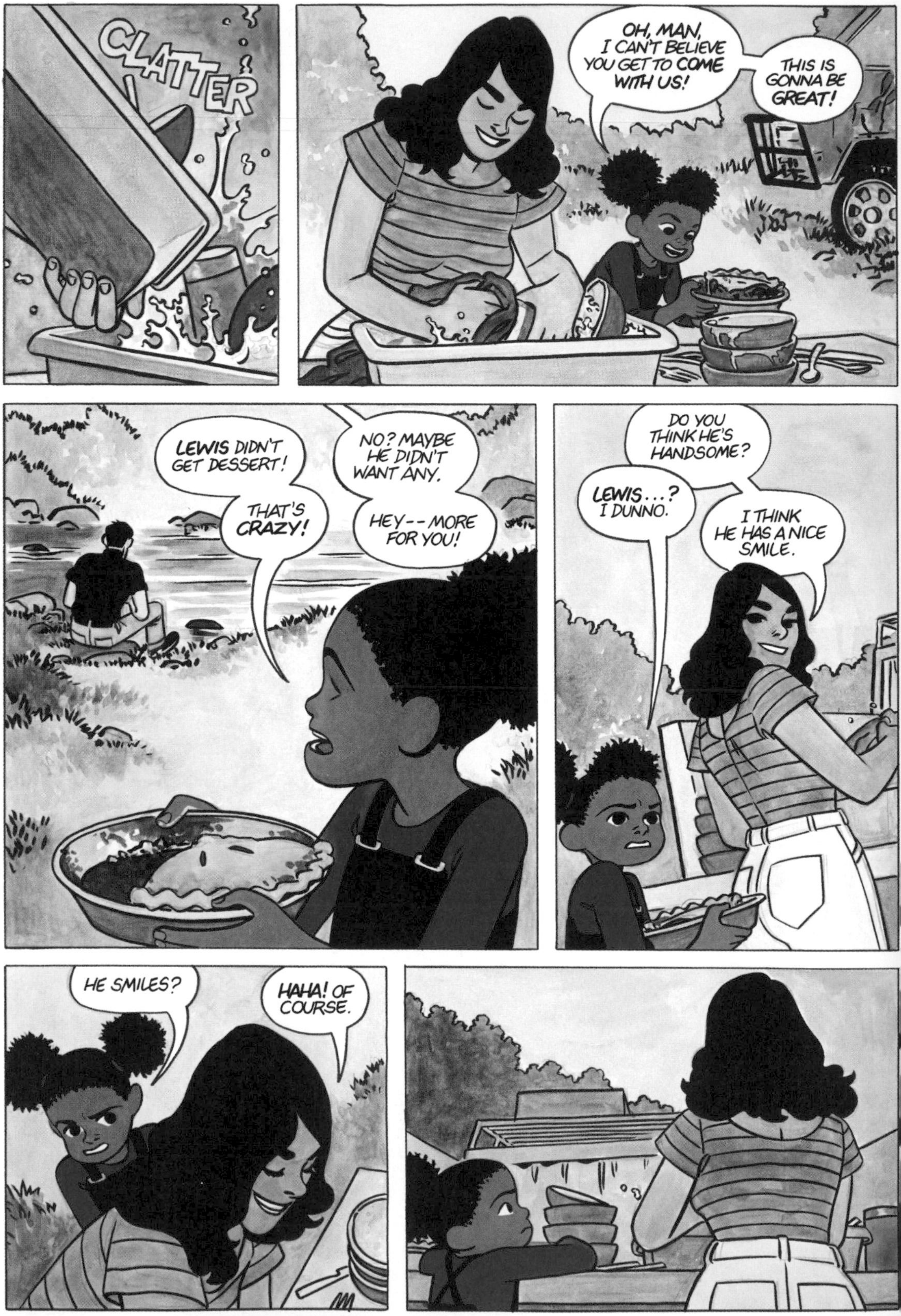
CLATTER
OH, MAN, I CAN'T BELIEVE YOU GET TO COME WITH US!
THIS IS GONNA BE GREAT!
LEWIS DIDN'T GET DESSERT!
THAT'S CRAZY!
NO? MAYBE HE DIDN'T WANT ANY.
HEY--MORE FOR YOU!
DO YOU THINK HE'S HANDSOME?
LEWIS...? I DUNNO.
I THINK HE HAS A NICE SMILE.
HE SMILES?
HAHA! OF COURSE.

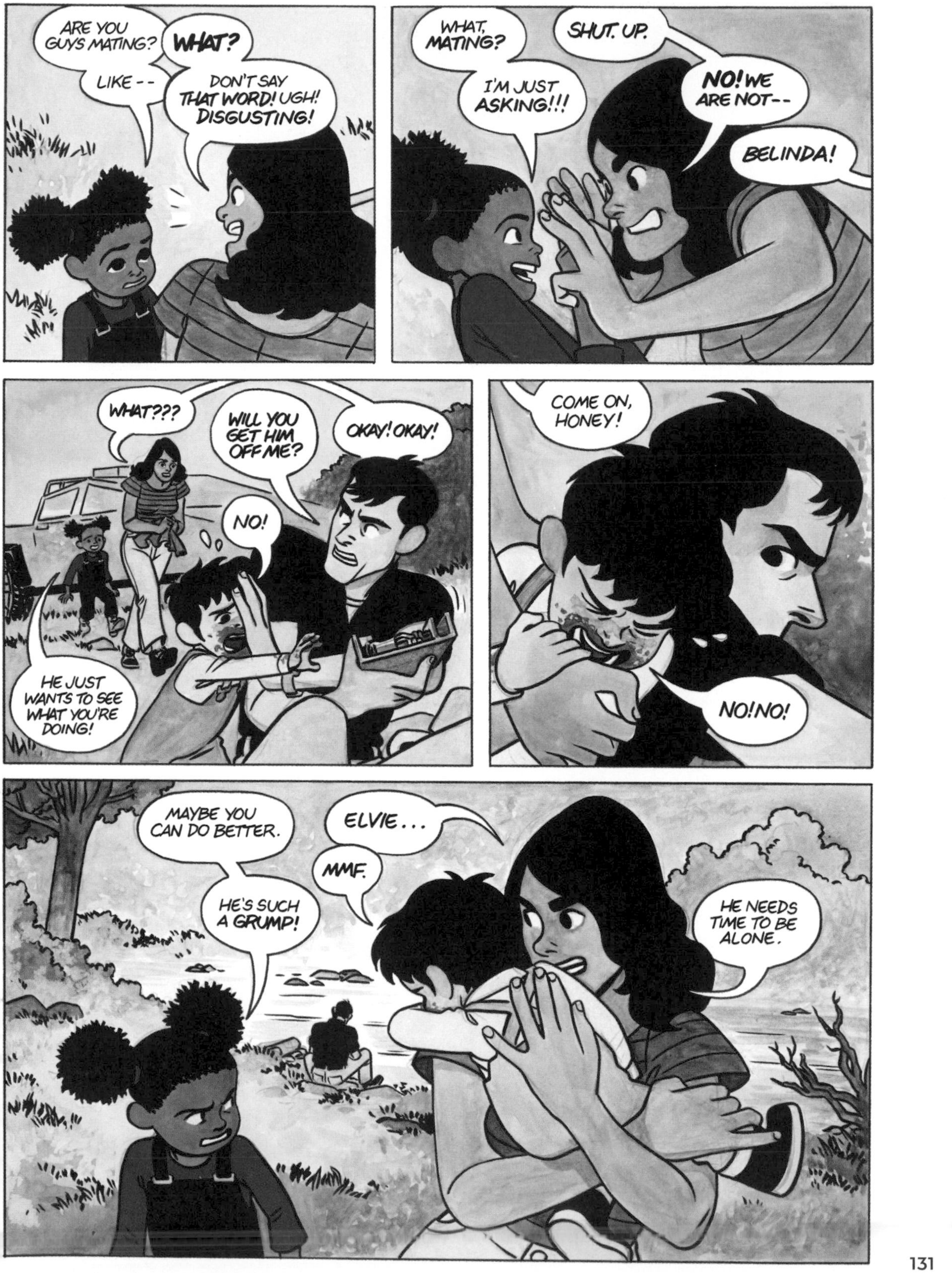
ARE YOU GUYS MATING?
LIKE --
WHAT?
DON'T SAY THAT WORD! UGH! DISGUSTING!
WHAT, MATING?
I'M JUST ASKING!!!
SHUT. UP.
NO! WE ARE NOT--
BELINDA!
WHAT???
WILL YOU GET HIM OFF ME?
OKAY! OKAY!
NO!
HE JUST WANTS TO SEE WHAT YOU'RE DOING!
COME ON, HONEY!
NO! NO!
MAYBE YOU CAN DO BETTER.
HE'S SUCH A GRUMP!
ELVIE...
MMF.
HE NEEDS TIME TO BE ALONE.

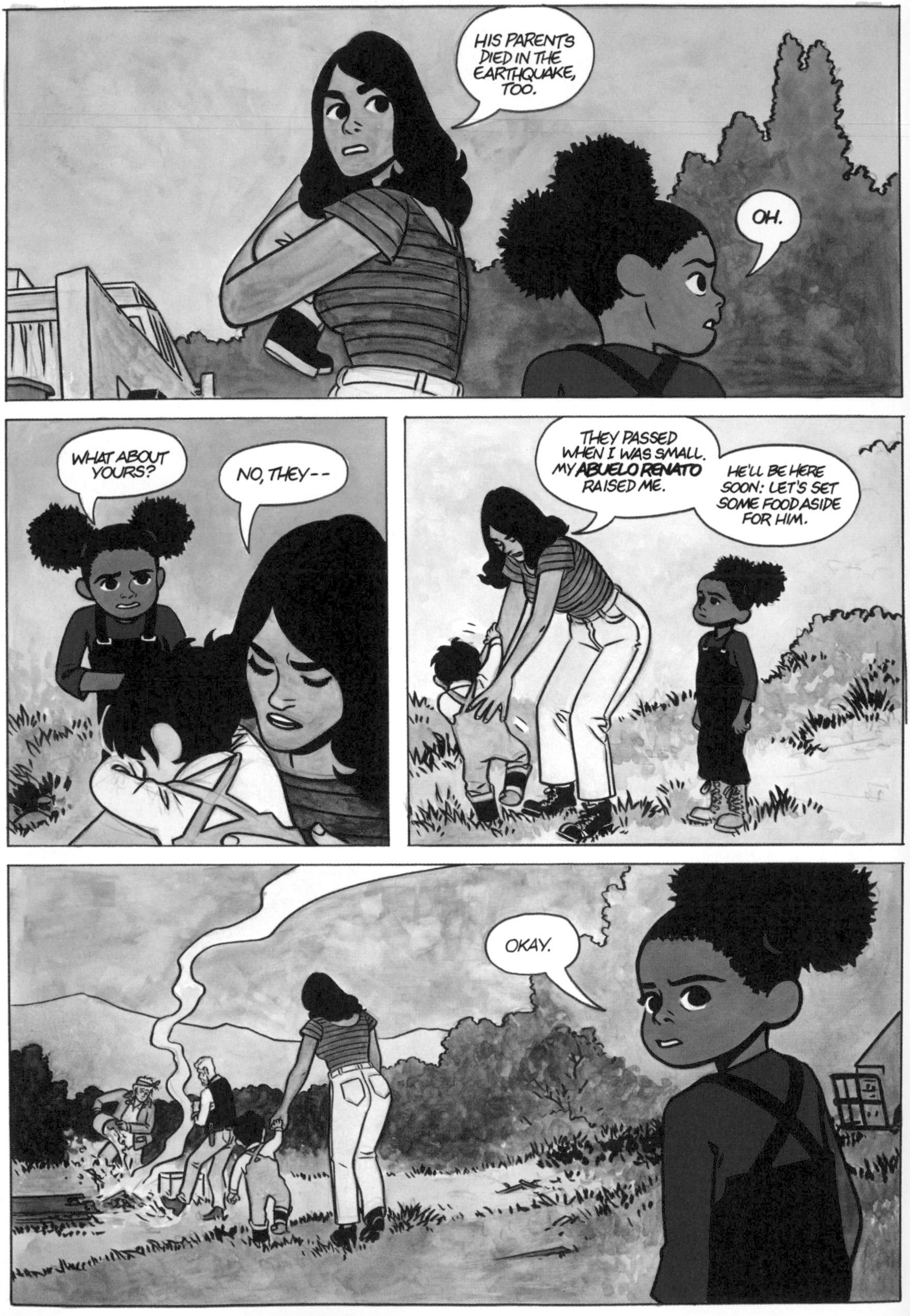
HIS PARENTS DIED IN THE EARTHQUAKE, TOO.
OH.
WHAT ABOUT YOURS?
NO, THEY--
THEY PASSED WHEN I WAS SMALL. MY **ABUELO RENATO** RAISED ME.
HE'LL BE HERE SOON: LET'S SET SOME FOOD ASIDE FOR HIM.
OKAY.

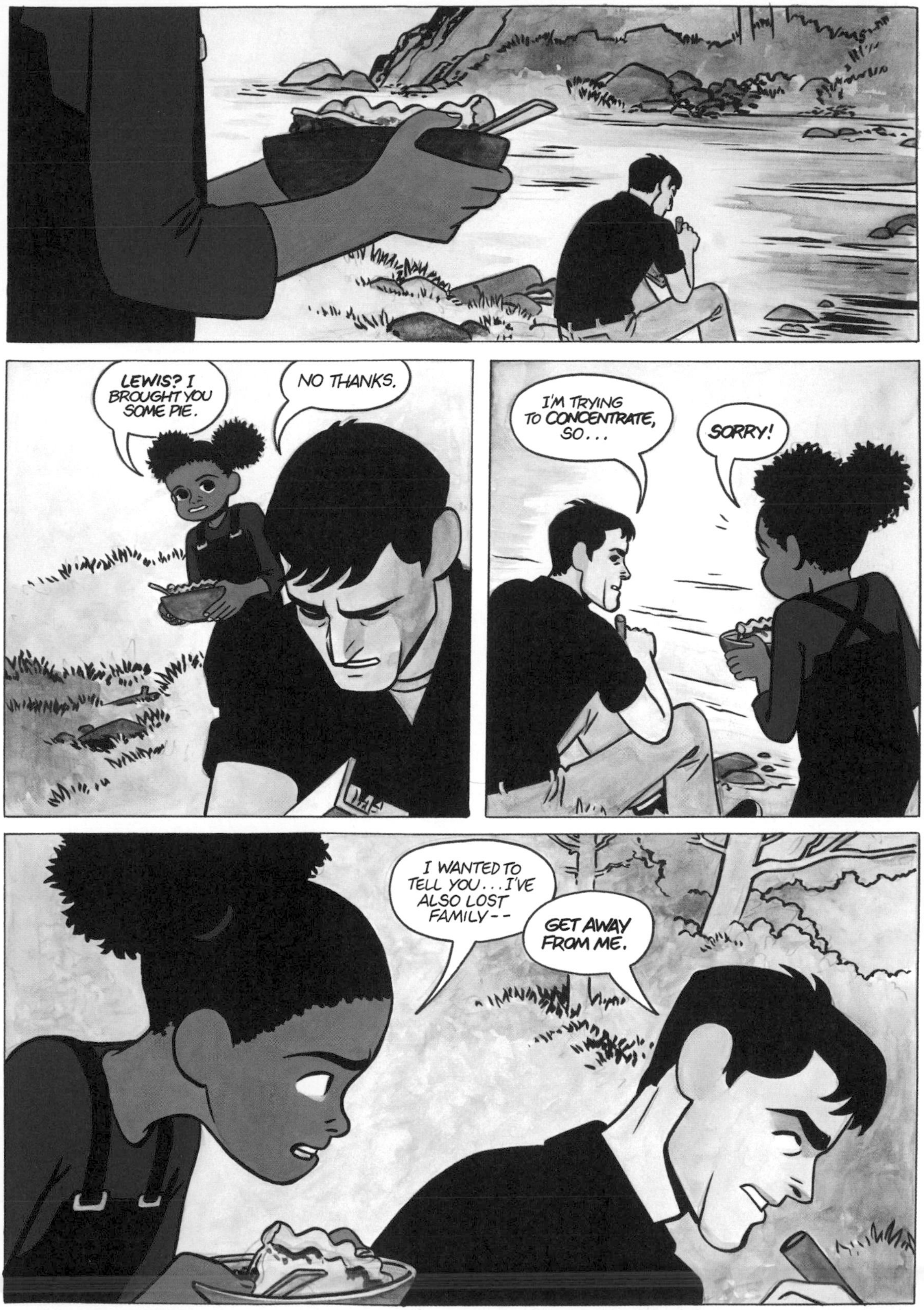
LEWIS? I BROUGHT YOU SOME PIE.
NO THANKS.
I'M TRYING TO CONCENTRATE, SO...
SORRY!
I WANTED TO TELL YOU... I'VE ALSO LOST FAMILY--
GET AWAY FROM ME.

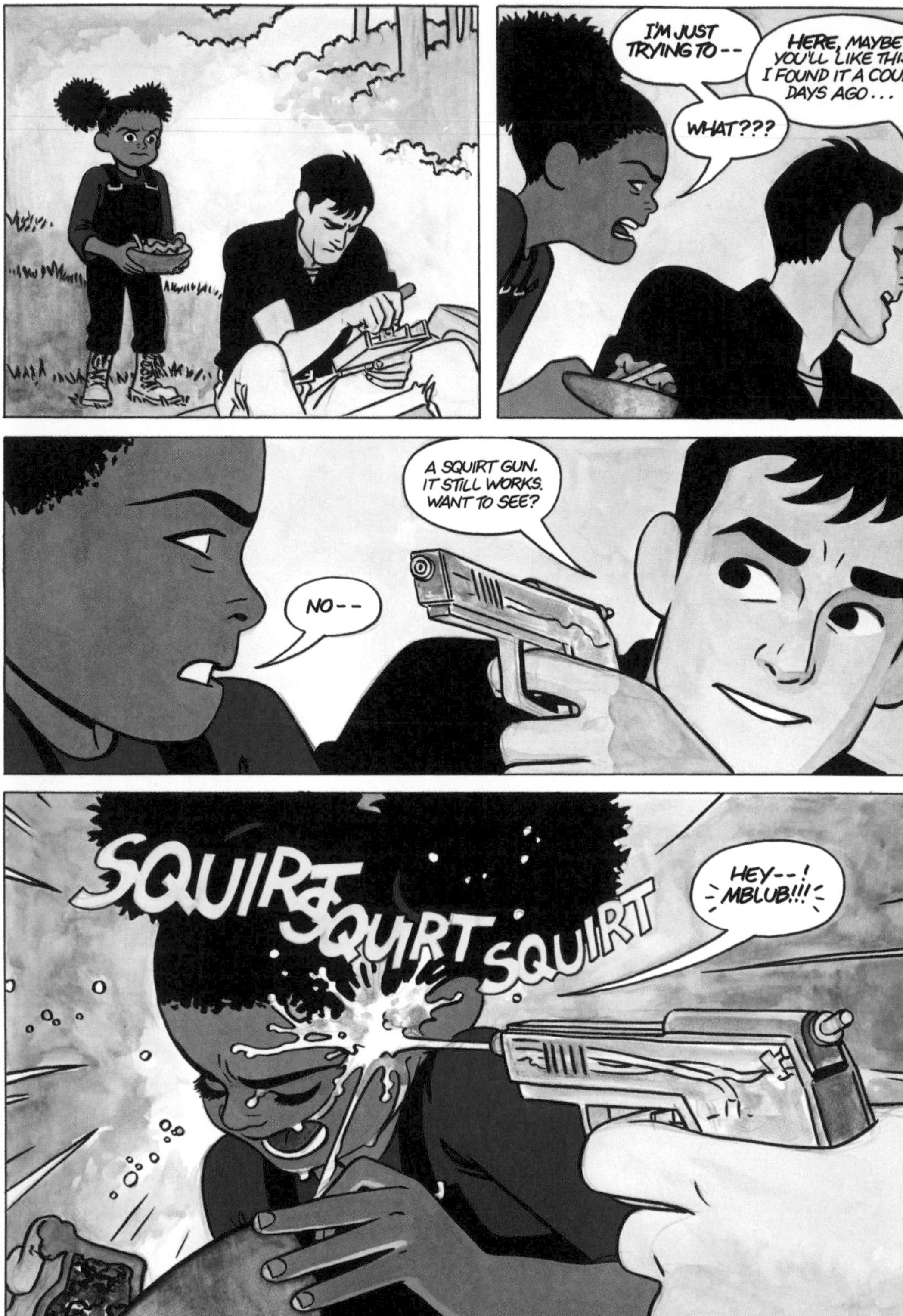
I'M JUST TRYING TO --
WHAT???
HERE, MAYBE YOU'LL LIKE THIS: I FOUND IT A COUPLE DAYS AGO...
A SQUIRT GUN. IT STILL WORKS. WANT TO SEE?
NO--
SQUIRT SQUIRT SQUIRT
HEY--! MBLUB!!!

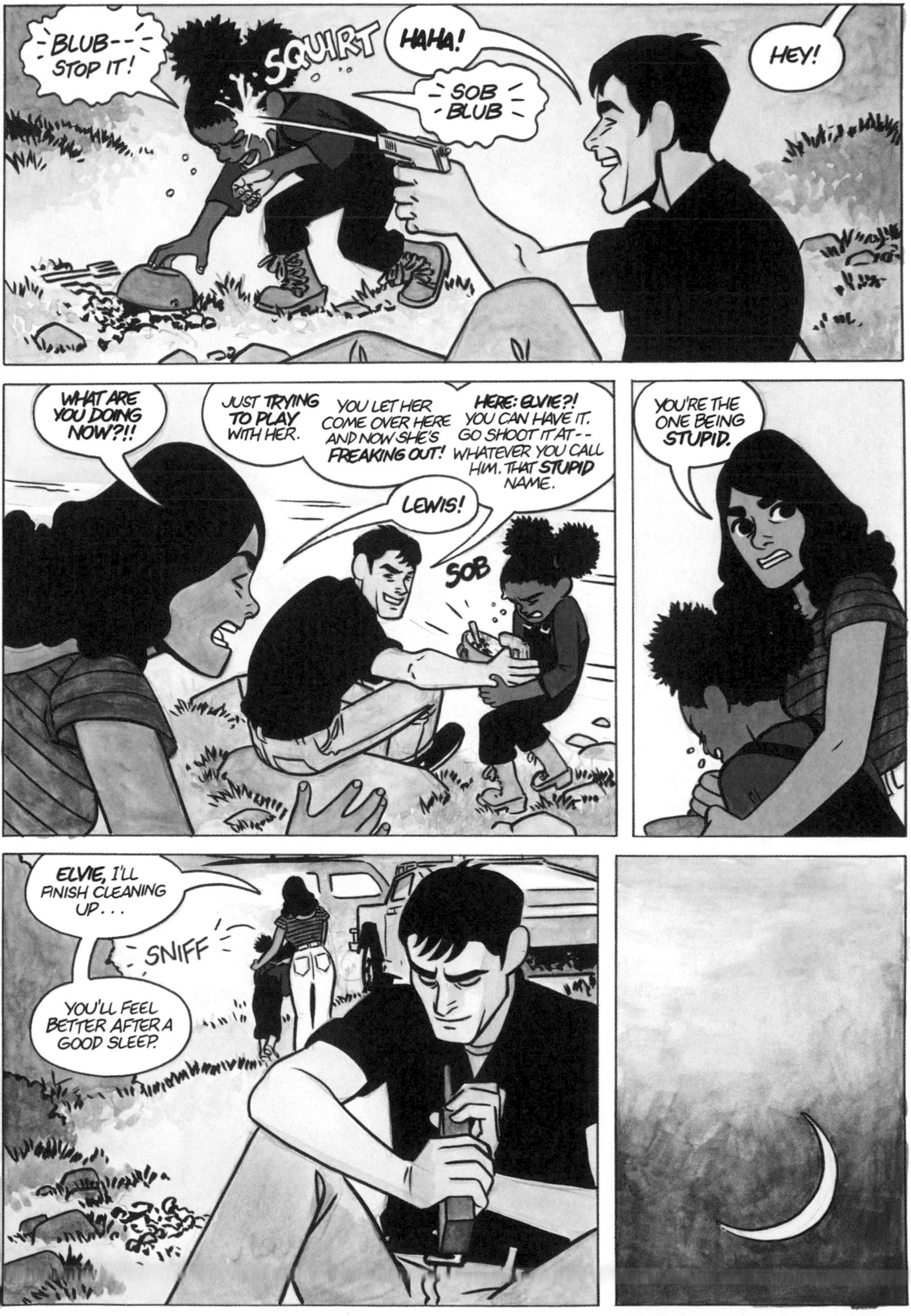

BLUB-- STOP IT!
SQUIRT
HAHA!
SOB BLUB
HEY!
WHAT ARE YOU DOING NOW?!!
JUST TRYING TO PLAY WITH HER.
YOU LET HER COME OVER HERE AND NOW SHE'S FREAKING OUT!
HERE: ELVIE?! YOU CAN HAVE IT. GO SHOOT IT AT-- WHATEVER YOU CALL HIM. THAT STUPID NAME.
LEWIS!
SOB
YOU'RE THE ONE BEING STUPID.
ELVIE, I'LL FINISH CLEANING UP...
SNIFF
YOU'LL FEEL BETTER AFTER A GOOD SLEEP.

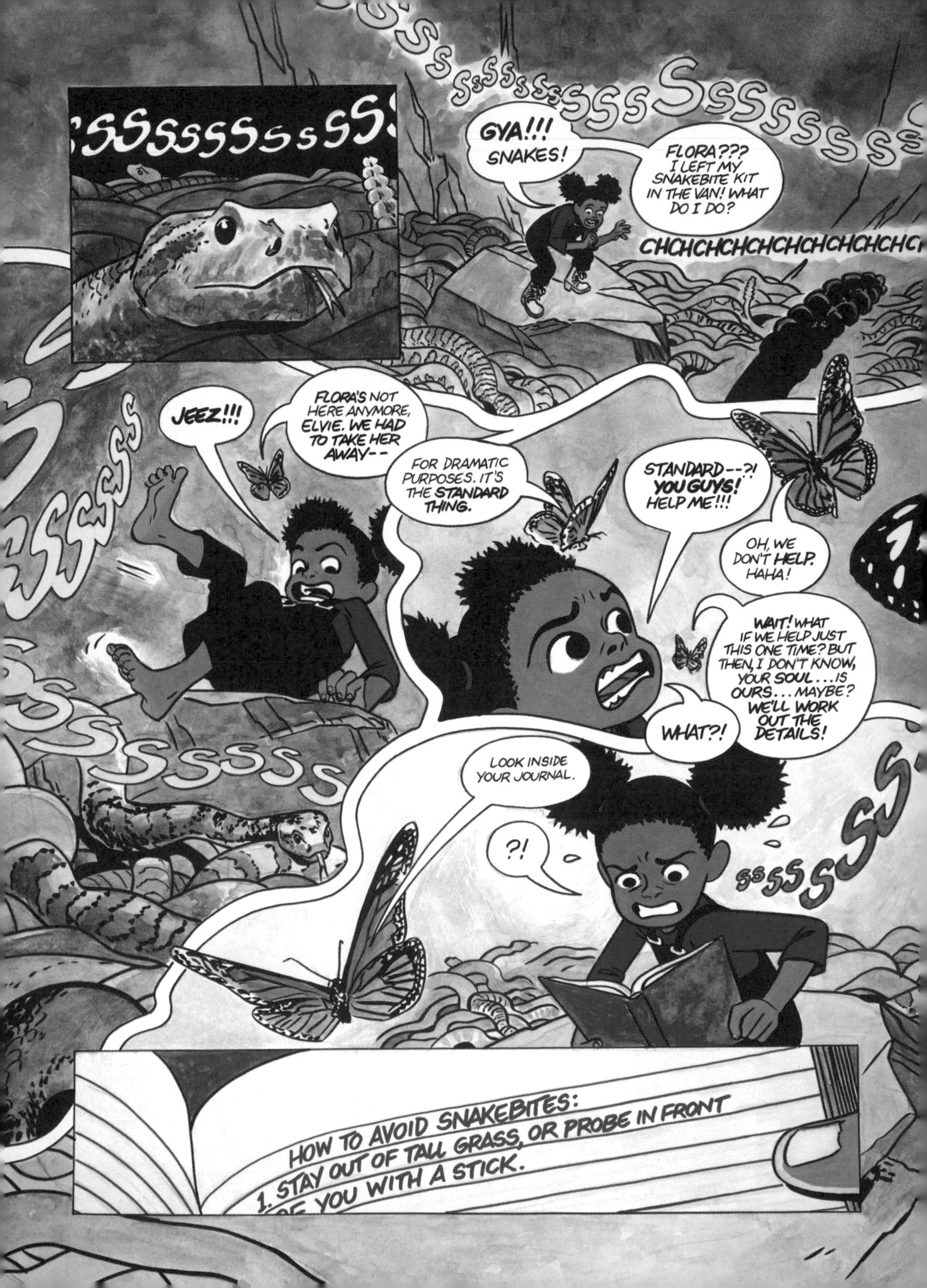
SSSSSSSSSSS
GYA!!! SNAKES!
FLORA??? I LEFT MY SNAKEBITE KIT IN THE VAN! WHAT DO I DO?
CHCHCHCHCHCHCHCHCHCHCHCH
JEEZ!!!
FLORA'S NOT HERE ANYMORE, ELVIE. WE HAD TO TAKE HER AWAY--
FOR DRAMATIC PURPOSES. IT'S THE STANDARD THING.
STANDARD--?! YOU GUYS! HELP ME!!!
OH, WE DON'T HELP. HAHA!
WAIT! WHAT IF WE HELP JUST THIS ONE TIME? BUT THEN, I DON'T KNOW, YOUR SOUL... IS OURS... MAYBE? WE'LL WORK OUT THE DETAILS!
WHAT?!
LOOK INSIDE YOUR JOURNAL.
?!
HOW TO AVOID SNAKEBITES:
1. STAY OUT OF TALL GRASS, OR PROBE IN FRONT OF YOU WITH A STICK.

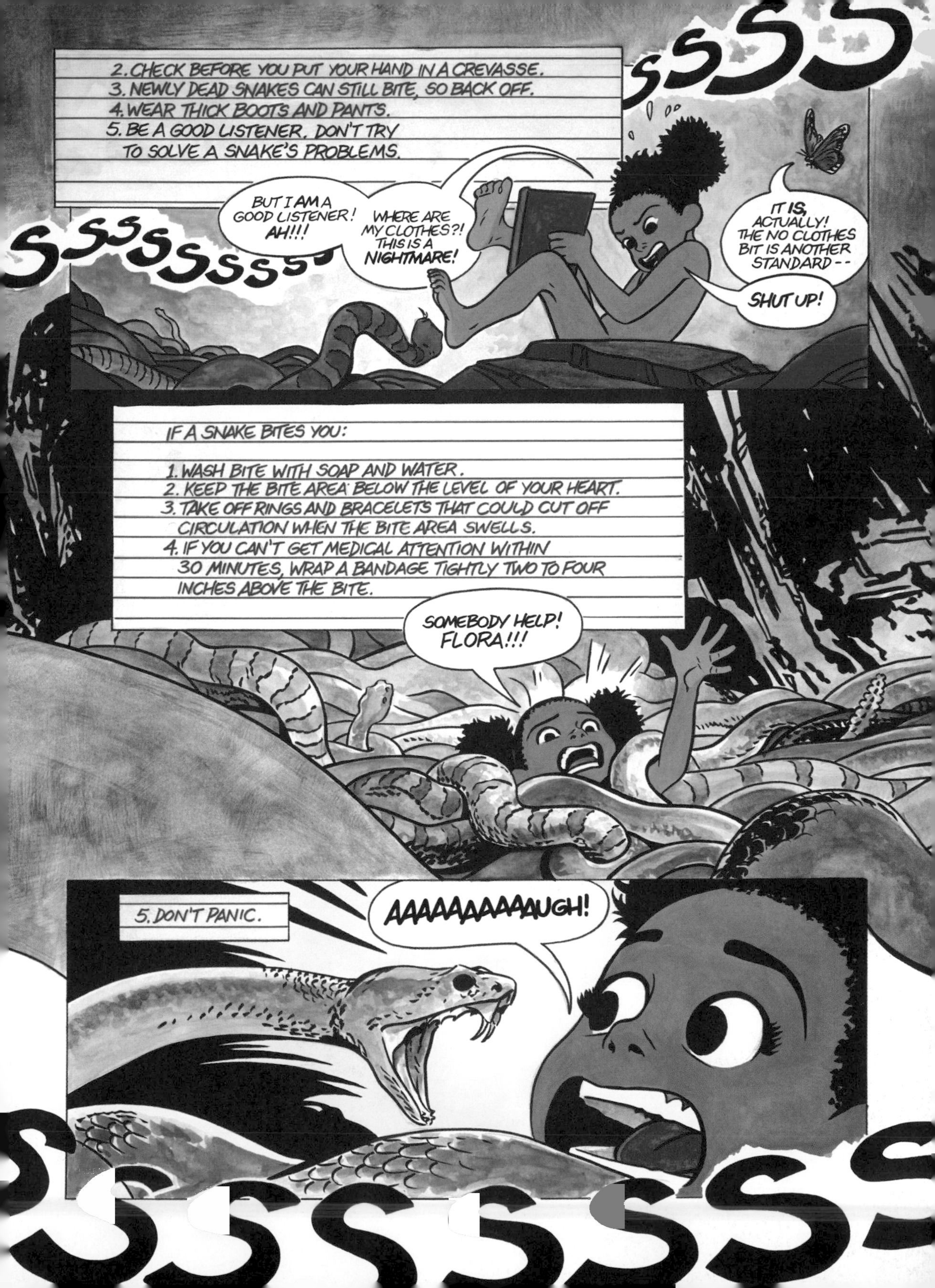
2. CHECK BEFORE YOU PUT YOUR HAND IN A CREVASSE.
3. NEWLY DEAD SNAKES CAN STILL BITE, SO BACK OFF.
4. WEAR THICK BOOTS AND PANTS.
5. BE A GOOD LISTENER. DON'T TRY TO SOLVE A SNAKE'S PROBLEMS.
SSSSS
SSSSSSSSS
BUT I AM A GOOD LISTENER! AH!!!
WHERE ARE MY CLOTHES?! THIS IS A NIGHTMARE!
IT IS, ACTUALLY! THE NO CLOTHES BIT IS ANOTHER STANDARD --
SHUT UP!
IF A SNAKE BITES YOU:
1. WASH BITE WITH SOAP AND WATER.
2. KEEP THE BITE AREA BELOW THE LEVEL OF YOUR HEART.
3. TAKE OFF RINGS AND BRACELETS THAT COULD CUT OFF CIRCULATION WHEN THE BITE AREA SWELLS.
4. IF YOU CAN'T GET MEDICAL ATTENTION WITHIN 30 MINUTES, WRAP A BANDAGE TIGHTLY TWO TO FOUR INCHES ABOVE THE BITE.
SOMEBODY HELP! FLORA!!!
5. DON'T PANIC.
AAAAAAAAAAUGH!
SSSSSSSSS

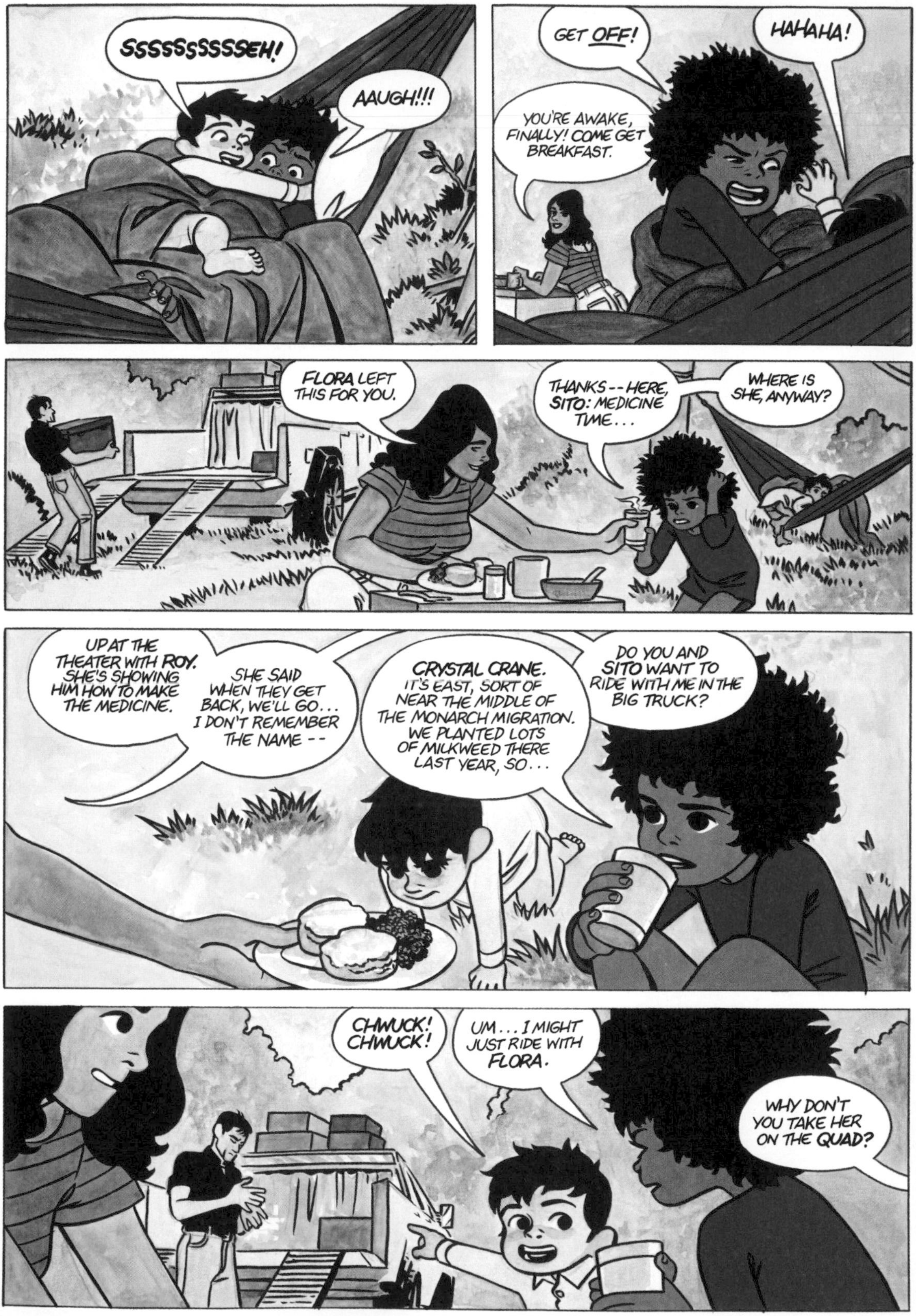
SSSSSSSSSSSEH!
AAUGH!!!
GET OFF!
HAHAHA!
YOU'RE AWAKE, FINALLY! COME GET BREAKFAST.
FLORA LEFT THIS FOR YOU.
THANKS -- HERE, SITO: MEDICINE TIME...
WHERE IS SHE, ANYWAY?
UP AT THE THEATER WITH ROY. SHE'S SHOWING HIM HOW TO MAKE THE MEDICINE.
SHE SAID WHEN THEY GET BACK, WE'LL GO... I DON'T REMEMBER THE NAME --
CRYSTAL CRANE. IT'S EAST, SORT OF NEAR THE MIDDLE OF THE MONARCH MIGRATION. WE PLANTED LOTS OF MILKWEED THERE LAST YEAR, SO...
DO YOU AND SITO WANT TO RIDE WITH ME IN THE BIG TRUCK?
CHWUCK! CHWUCK!
UM... I MIGHT JUST RIDE WITH FLORA.
WHY DON'T YOU TAKE HER ON THE QUAD?

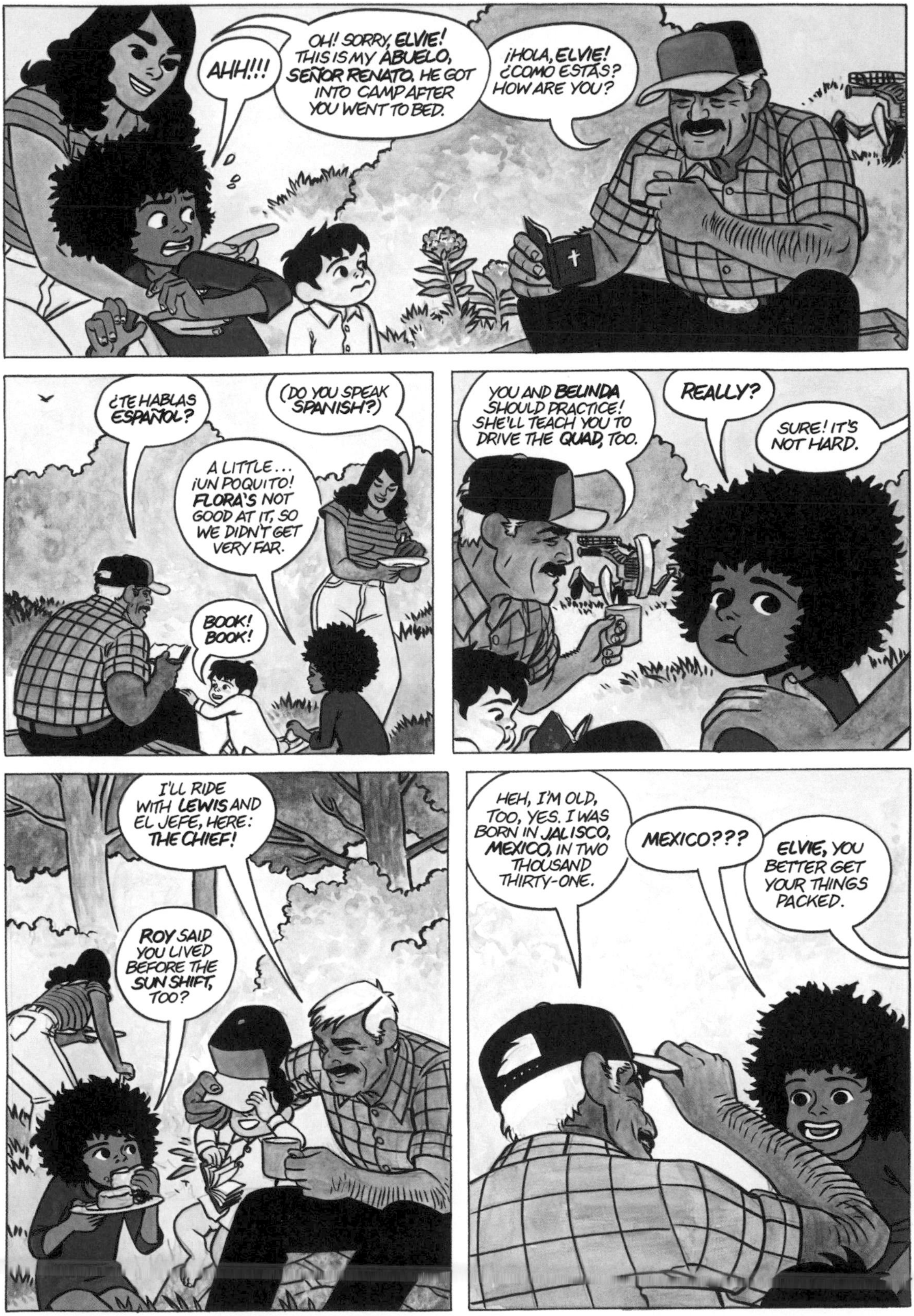
AHH!!!
OH! SORRY, ELVIE! THIS IS MY ABUELO, SEÑOR RENATO. HE GOT INTO CAMP AFTER YOU WENT TO BED.
¡HOLA, ELVIE! ¿COMO ESTÁS? HOW ARE YOU?
¿TE HABLAS ESPAÑOL?
(DO YOU SPEAK SPANISH?)
A LITTLE... ¡UN POQUITO! FLORA'S NOT GOOD AT IT, SO WE DIDN'T GET VERY FAR.
BOOK! BOOK!
YOU AND BELINDA SHOULD PRACTICE! SHE'LL TEACH YOU TO DRIVE THE QUAD, TOO.
REALLY?
SURE! IT'S NOT HARD.
I'LL RIDE WITH LEWIS AND EL JEFE, HERE: THE CHIEF!
ROY SAID YOU LIVED BEFORE THE SUN SHIFT, TOO?
HEH, I'M OLD, TOO, YES. I WAS BORN IN JALISCO, MEXICO, IN TWO THOUSAND THIRTY-ONE.
MEXICO???
ELVIE, YOU BETTER GET YOUR THINGS PACKED.

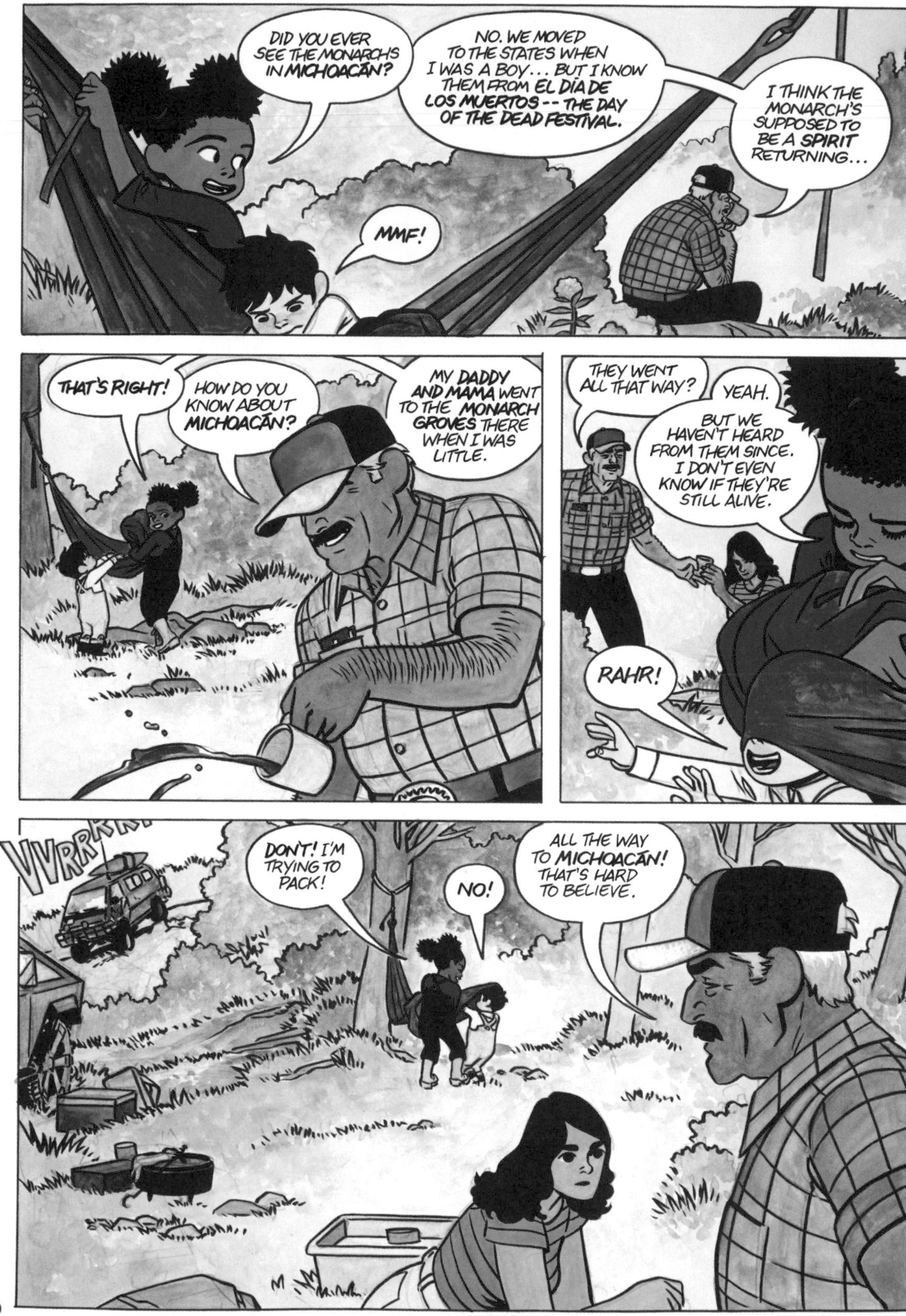
DID YOU EVER SEE THE MONARCHS IN MICHOACÁN?
NO. WE MOVED TO THE STATES WHEN I WAS A BOY... BUT I KNOW THEM FROM EL DÍA DE LOS MUERTOS -- THE DAY OF THE DEAD FESTIVAL.
I THINK THE MONARCH'S SUPPOSED TO BE A SPIRIT RETURNING...
MMF!
THAT'S RIGHT!
HOW DO YOU KNOW ABOUT MICHOACÁN?
MY DADDY AND MAMA WENT TO THE MONARCH GROVES THERE WHEN I WAS LITTLE.
THEY WENT ALL THAT WAY?
YEAH.
BUT WE HAVEN'T HEARD FROM THEM SINCE. I DON'T EVEN KNOW IF THEY'RE STILL ALIVE.
RAHR!
VVRRRRR
DON'T! I'M TRYING TO PACK!
NO!
ALL THE WAY TO MICHOACÁN! THAT'S HARD TO BELIEVE.

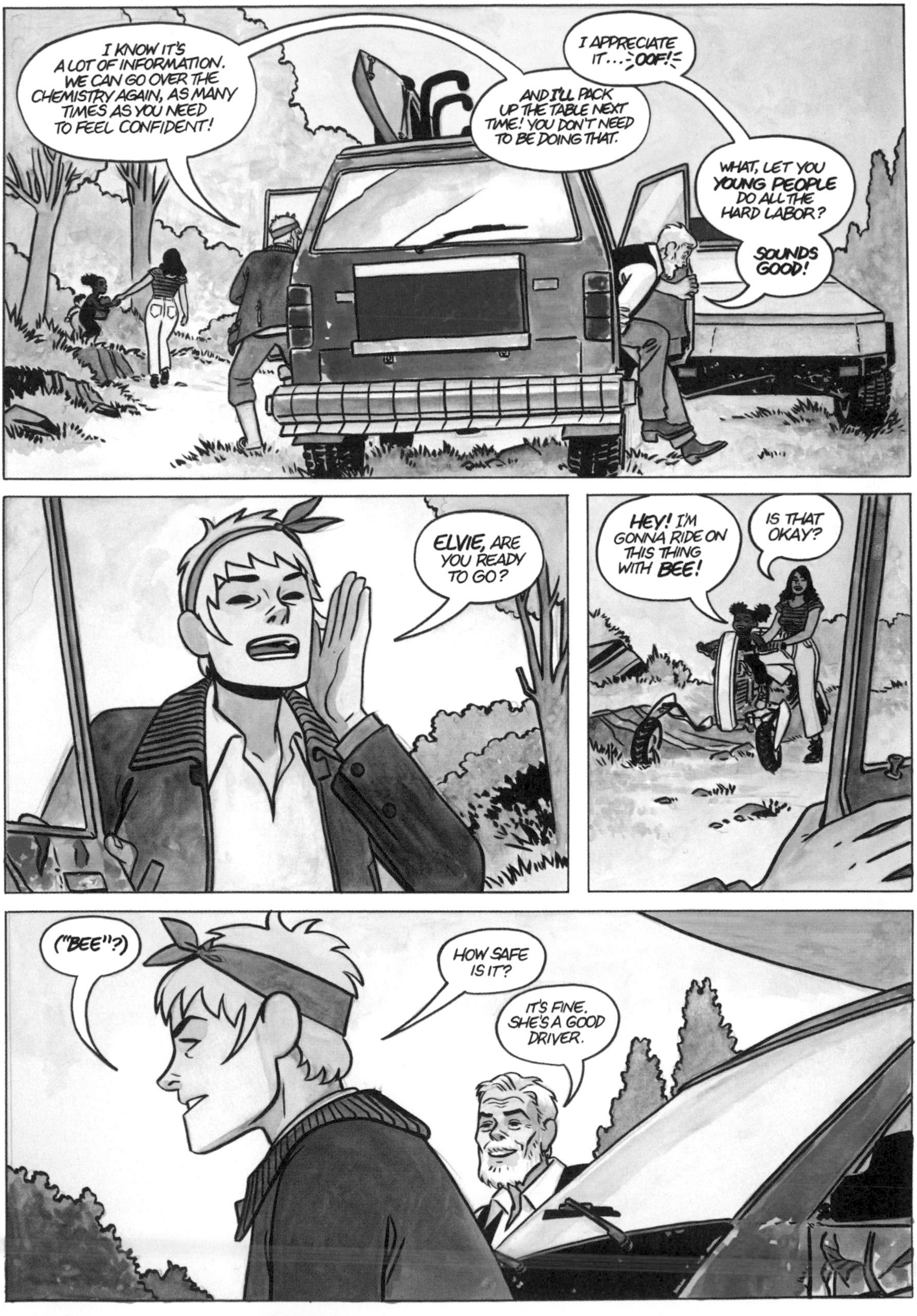

I KNOW IT'S A LOT OF INFORMATION. WE CAN GO OVER THE CHEMISTRY AGAIN, AS MANY TIMES AS YOU NEED TO FEEL CONFIDENT!
AND I'LL PACK UP THE TABLE NEXT TIME! YOU DON'T NEED TO BE DOING THAT.
I APPRECIATE IT... OOF!
WHAT, LET YOU YOUNG PEOPLE DO ALL THE HARD LABOR?
SOUNDS GOOD!
ELVIE, ARE YOU READY TO GO?
HEY! I'M GONNA RIDE ON THIS THING WITH BEE!
IS THAT OKAY?
("BEE"?)
HOW SAFE IS IT?
IT'S FINE. SHE'S A GOOD DRIVER.

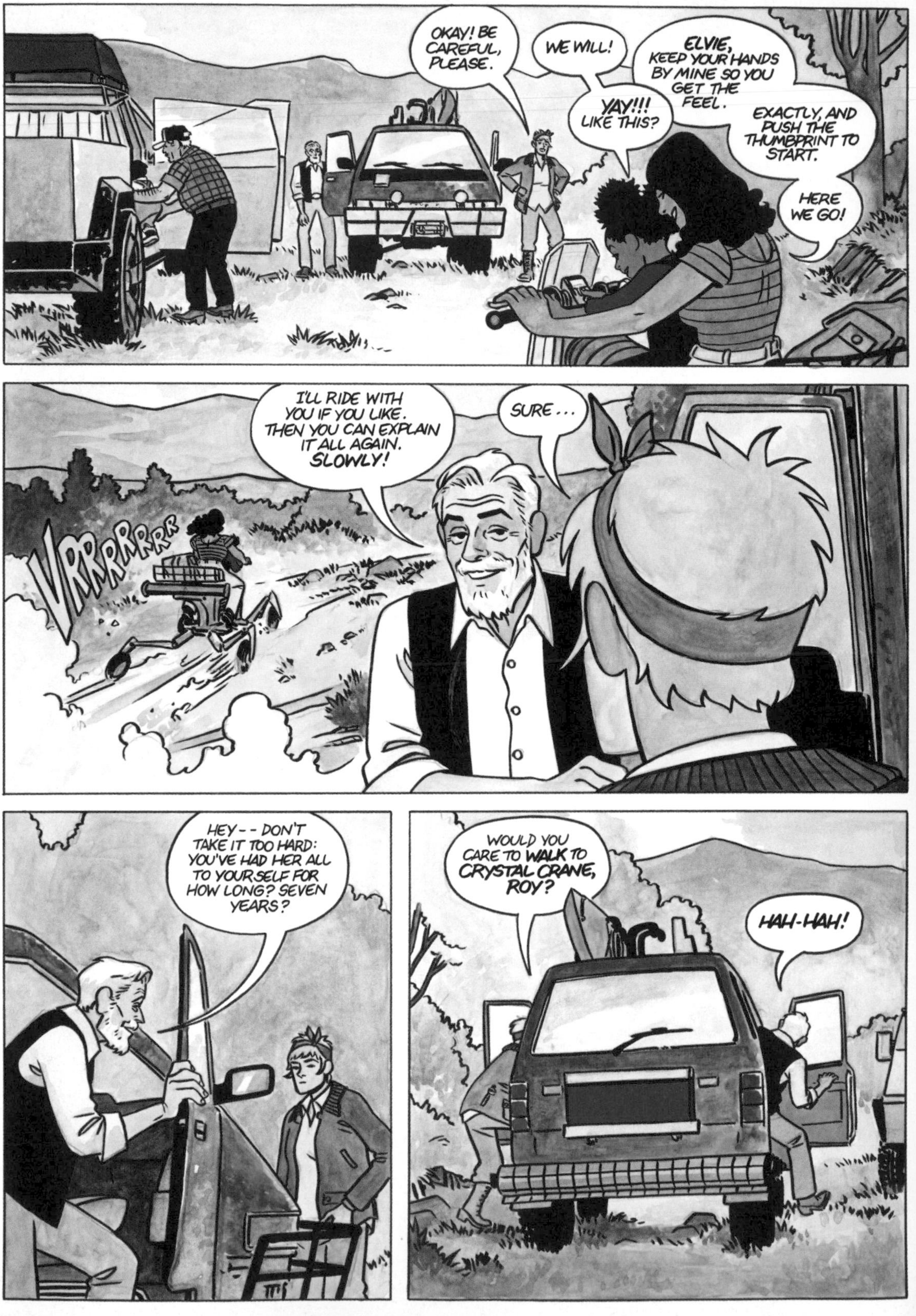
OKAY! BE CAREFUL, PLEASE.
WE WILL!
ELVIE, KEEP YOUR HANDS BY MINE SO YOU GET THE FEEL.
YAY!!! LIKE THIS?
EXACTLY, AND PUSH THE THUMBPRINT TO START.
HERE WE GO!
I'LL RIDE WITH YOU IF YOU LIKE. THEN YOU CAN EXPLAIN IT ALL AGAIN. SLOWLY!
SURE...
VRRRRRRR
HEY-- DON'T TAKE IT TOO HARD: YOU'VE HAD HER ALL TO YOURSELF FOR HOW LONG? SEVEN YEARS?
WOULD YOU CARE TO WALK TO CRYSTAL CRANE, ROY?
HAH-HAH!

CHAPTER EIGHT
DESERT

[redacted]

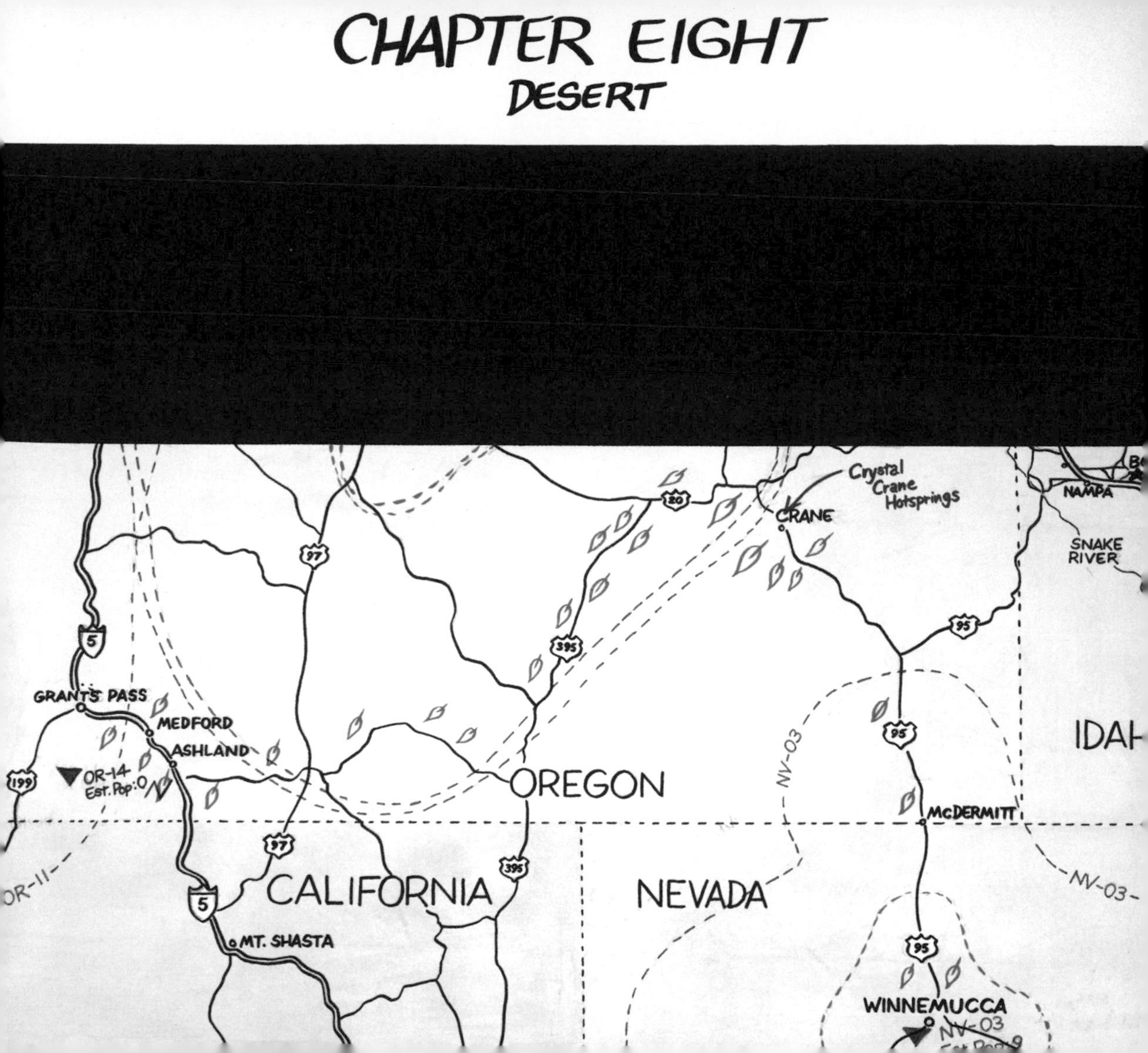
Crystal Crane Hotsprings
NAMPA
CRANE
SNAKE RIVER
20
97
395
95
5
199
GRANTS PASS
MEDFORD
ASHLAND
OR-14
Est. Pop: 0
OREGON
IDAH
NV-03
McDERMITT
CALIFORNIA
NEVADA
OR-11
MT. SHASTA
WINNEMUCCA
NV-03

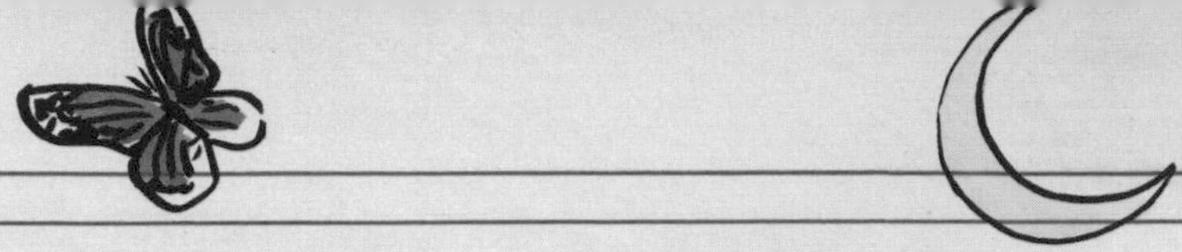

CRYSTAL CRANE, OREGON. SEPTEMBER 30. 34 DAYS UNTIL OUR NEW MONARCH MEDICINE EXPIRES.

I LOVE BELINDA ("BEE" FOR SHORT). SHE'S REALLY GOOD AT EVERYTHING **FLORA'S** TERRIBLE AT: COOKING, SINGING, MAKEUP... SHE SHOWED ME HOW TO PUT ON EYELINER TODAY! **FLORA** SAID I LOOKED LIKE A **GHOUL,** BUT SHE'S JUST JEALOUS.

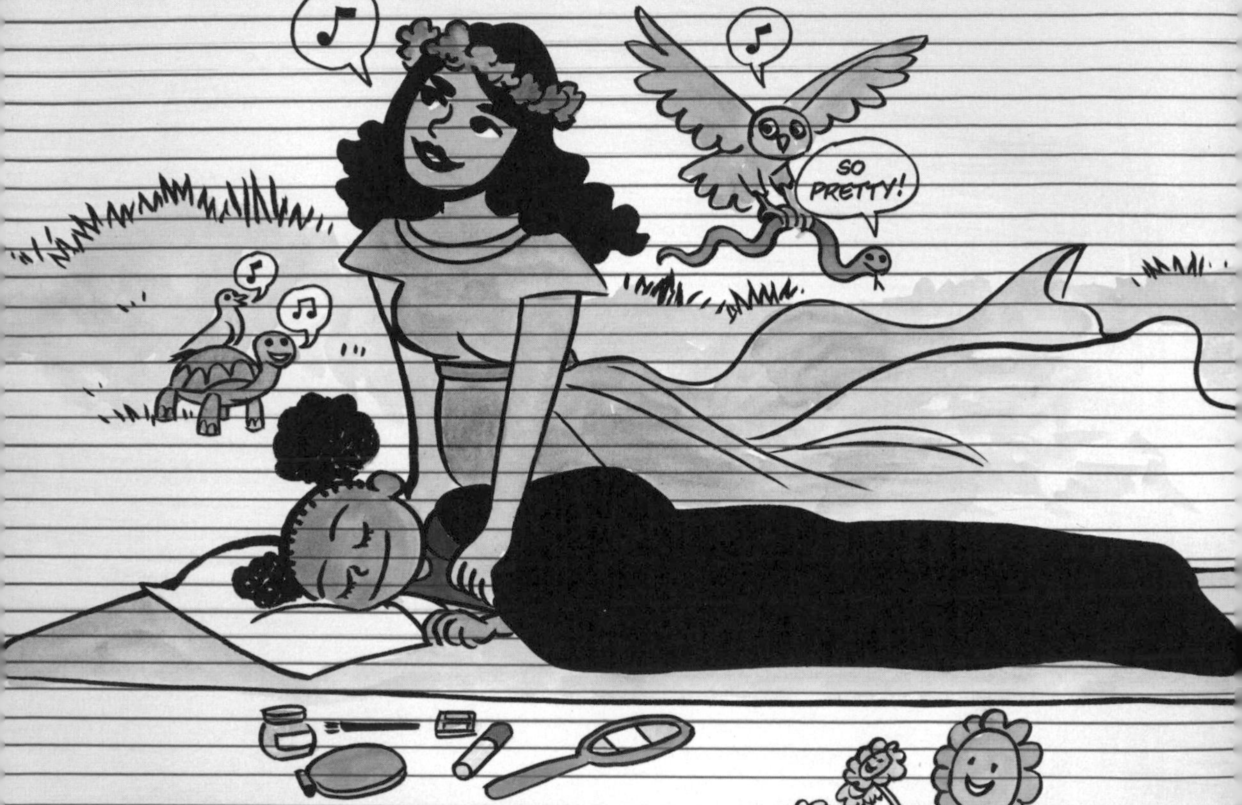
SO PRETTY!

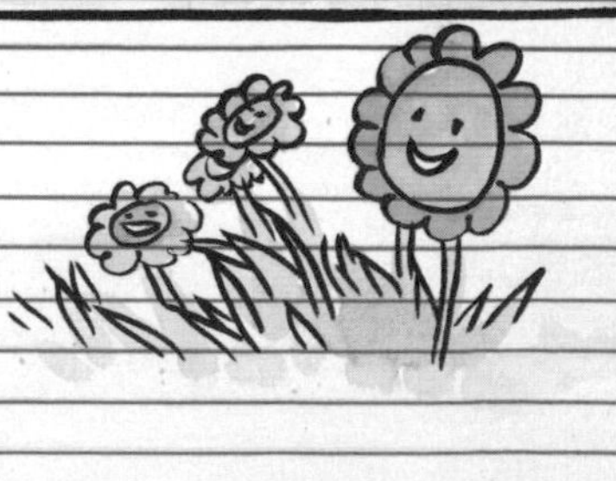

BEE DOESN'T USE A HAMMOCK TO SLEEP. SHE SLEEPS ON THE **GROUND** WITH A MAT! THEY ALL DO THAT. I TRIED IT -- IT'S A LITTLE LESS COZY, BUT I GUESS I COULD GET USED TO IT.

WE'RE IN SOUTHEAST OREGON AT **CRYSTAL CRANE HOT SPRINGS** TONIGHT AFTER TWO LONG DAYS OF HARVEST BY HWY 395. THE MILKWEED **FLORA** AND I PLANTED HERE IN PAST SEASONS GREW WELL, AND WE FOUND LOTS AND LOTS OF MONARCHS. THERE'S MORE THAN ENOUGH MEDS FOR ALL OF US NOW, AND GREAT GOBS OF BASE FLUID FOR **FLORA'S** VACCINE RESEARCH.

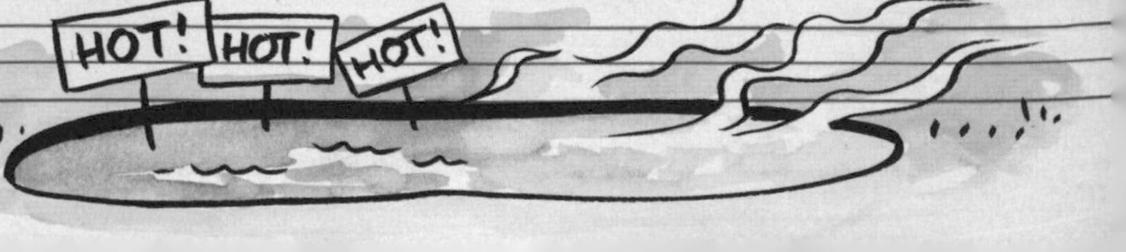
HOT!
HOT!
HOT!

ON THE WAY OVER WE FOUND ANOTHER **BROOSE** STALLED OUT ON THE
ROAD, BUT **FLORA** AND **LEWIS** GOT IT RUNNING AGAIN. HE'S PRETTY GOOD
WITH MACHINES. **LEWIS** GETS SO QUIET AND FOCUSED WHILE HE WORKS
THAT I CAN FORGET THAT HE'S EVEN AROUND AT ALL. WHICH IS NICE.

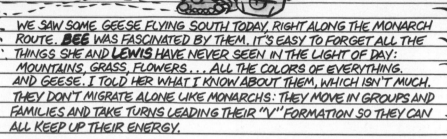

BEEP BEEP BEEP

WE SAW SOME GEESE FLYING SOUTH TODAY, RIGHT ALONG THE MONARCH
ROUTE. **BEE** WAS FASCINATED BY THEM. IT'S EASY TO FORGET ALL THE
THINGS SHE AND **LEWIS** HAVE NEVER SEEN IN THE LIGHT OF DAY:
MOUNTAINS, GRASS, FLOWERS . . . ALL THE COLORS OF EVERYTHING.
AND GEESE. I TOLD HER WHAT I KNOW ABOUT THEM, WHICH ISN'T MUCH.
THEY DON'T MIGRATE ALONE LIKE MONARCHS: THEY MOVE IN GROUPS AND
FAMILIES AND TAKE TURNS LEADING THEIR "V" FORMATION SO THEY CAN
ALL KEEP UP THEIR ENERGY.

THAT'S A LOT LIKE US NOW THAT **ROY** AND HIS CREW SHOWED UP. HAVING
HELP MAKES **SUCH** A DIFFERENCE. **FLORA'S** EVEN SOUND ASLEEP IN HER
HAMMOCK AT THIS VERY MOMENT, NOT THREE FEET AWAY FROM MY HEAD!

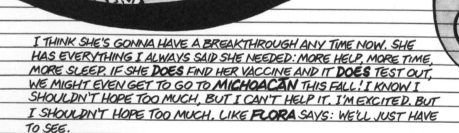

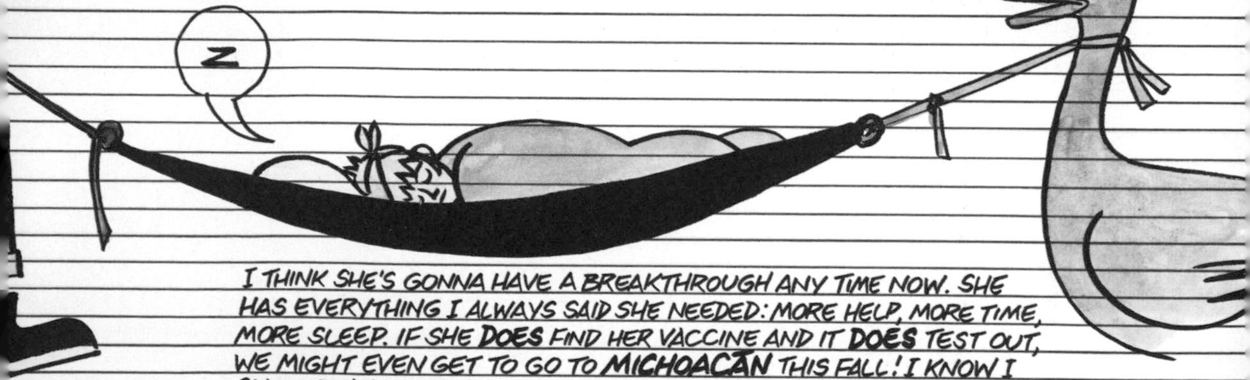

I THINK SHE'S GONNA HAVE A BREAKTHROUGH ANY TIME NOW. SHE
HAS EVERYTHING I ALWAYS SAID SHE NEEDED: MORE HELP, MORE TIME,
MORE SLEEP. IF SHE **DOES** FIND HER VACCINE AND IT **DOES** TEST OUT,
WE MIGHT EVEN GET TO GO TO **MICHOACÁN** THIS FALL! I KNOW I
SHOULDN'T HOPE TOO MUCH, BUT I CAN'T HELP IT. I'M EXCITED. BUT
I SHOULDN'T HOPE TOO MUCH. LIKE **FLORA** SAYS: WE'LL JUST HAVE
TO SEE.

I WISH WE COULD STAY AT THE HOT SPRINGS A LITTLE LONGER, BUT WE HAVE
TO HEAD OUT TOMORROW. WE'RE GONNA TRY TO CROSS THROUGH NEVADA AND
INTO CALIFORNIA IN ONE DAY SO WE DON'T HAVE TO CAMP INSIDE THE **WINNEMUCCA**
DEEPER RANGE. IT'LL BE ANOTHER LONG DRIVE.

MAYBE I'LL HAVE ONE LAST MORNING SOAK BEFORE EVERYONE GETS UP.

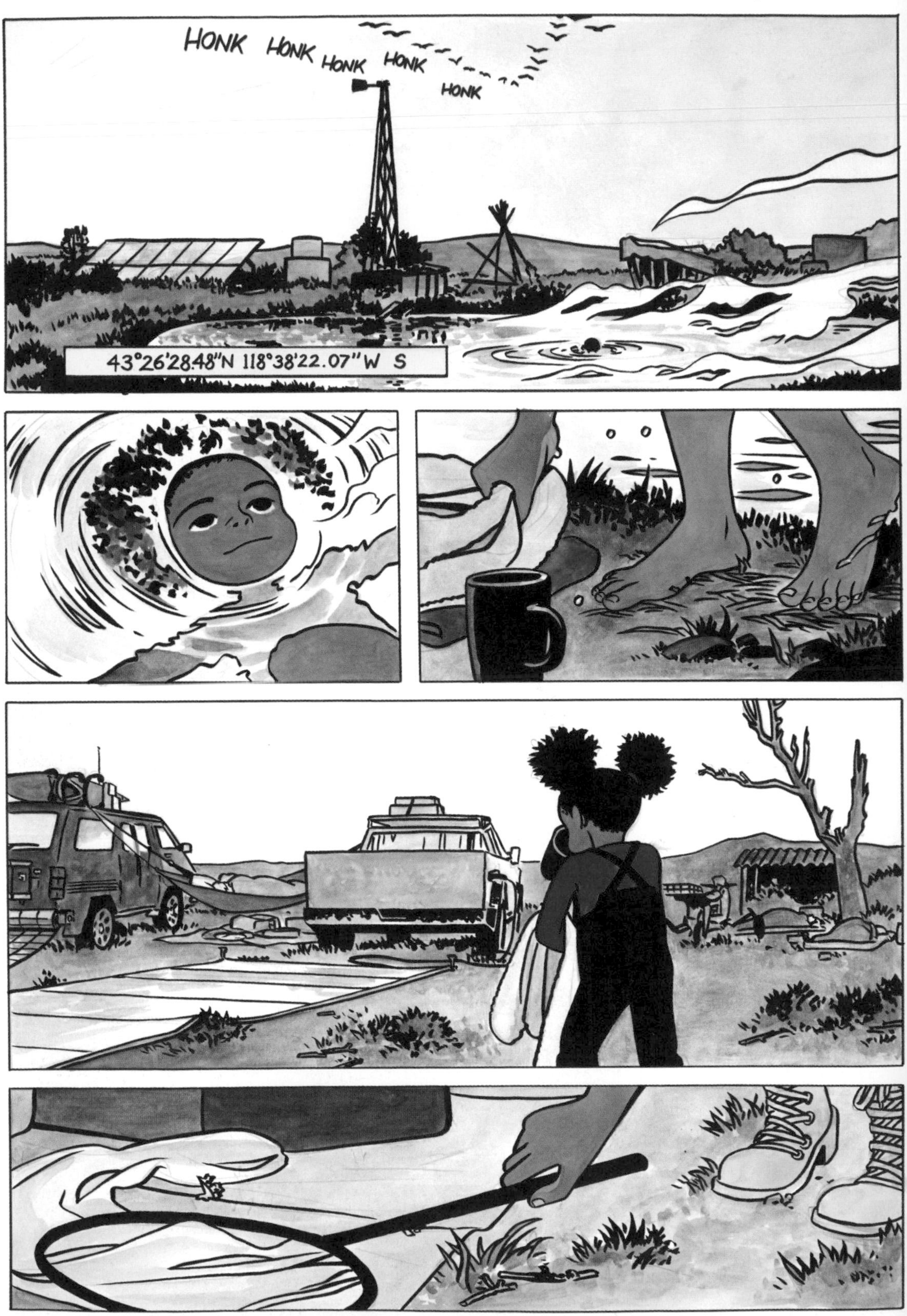
HONK HONK HONK HONK
HONK
43°26'28.48"N 118°38'22.07"W S

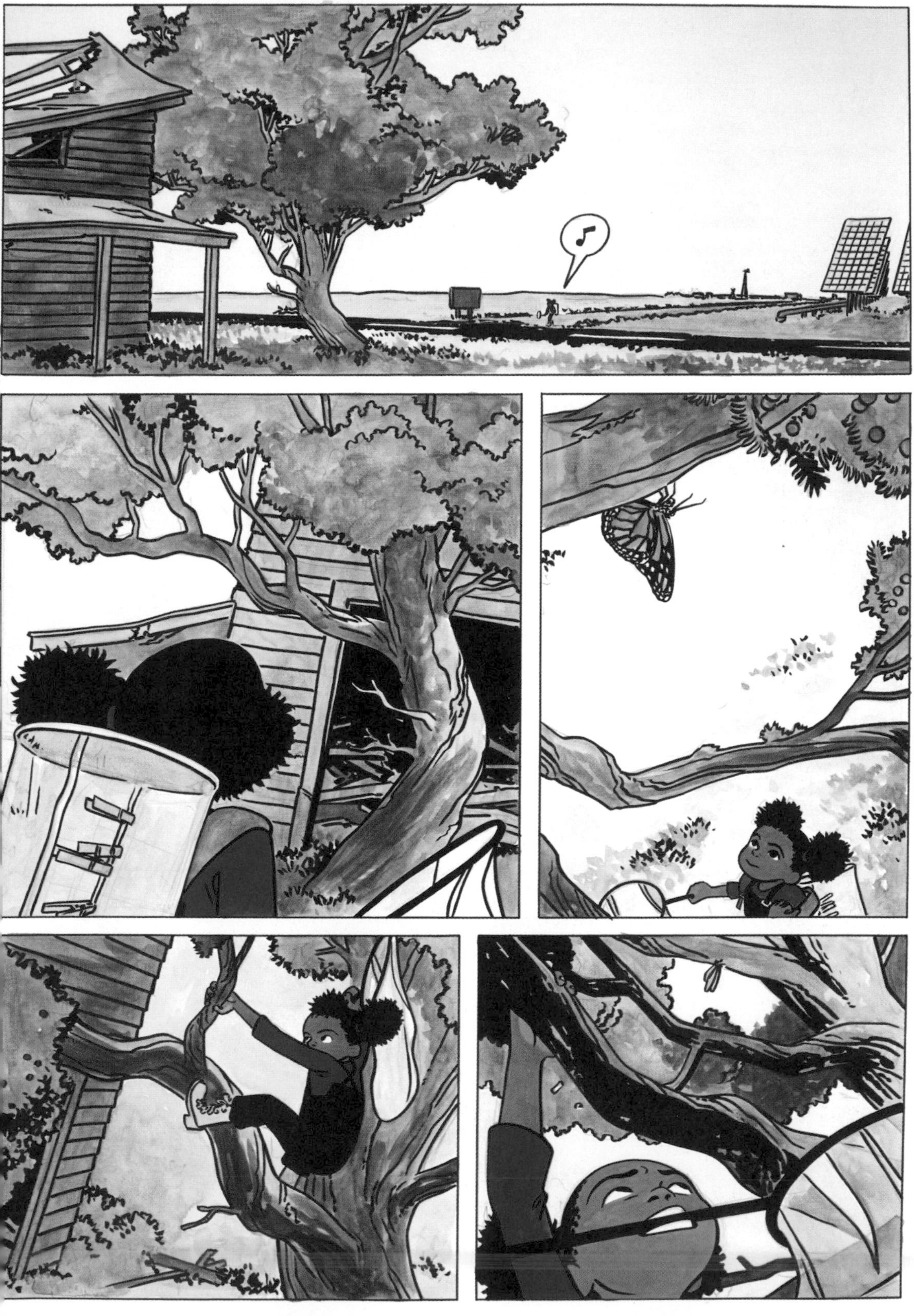

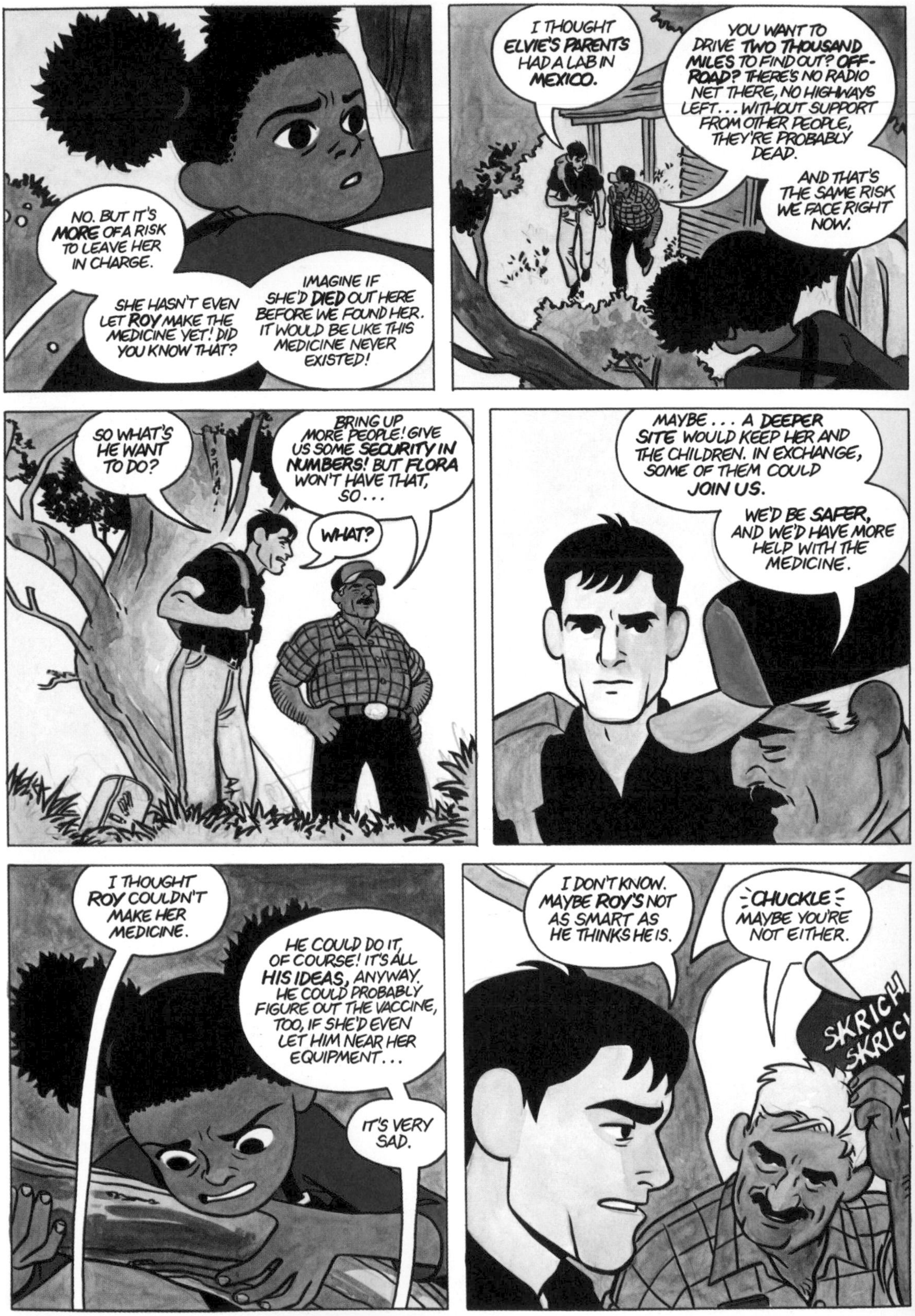
NO. BUT IT'S MORE OF A RISK TO LEAVE HER IN CHARGE.
SHE HASN'T EVEN LET ROY MAKE THE MEDICINE YET! DID YOU KNOW THAT?
IMAGINE IF SHE'D DIED OUT HERE BEFORE WE FOUND HER. IT WOULD BE LIKE THIS MEDICINE NEVER EXISTED!
I THOUGHT ELVIE'S PARENTS HAD A LAB IN MEXICO.
YOU WANT TO DRIVE TWO THOUSAND MILES TO FIND OUT? OFF-ROAD? THERE'S NO RADIO NET THERE, NO HIGHWAYS LEFT... WITHOUT SUPPORT FROM OTHER PEOPLE, THEY'RE PROBABLY DEAD.
AND THAT'S THE SAME RISK WE FACE RIGHT NOW.
SO WHAT'S HE WANT TO DO?
BRING UP MORE PEOPLE! GIVE US SOME SECURITY IN NUMBERS! BUT FLORA WON'T HAVE THAT, SO...
WHAT?
MAYBE... A DEEPER SITE WOULD KEEP HER AND THE CHILDREN. IN EXCHANGE, SOME OF THEM COULD JOIN US.
WE'D BE SAFER, AND WE'D HAVE MORE HELP WITH THE MEDICINE.
I THOUGHT ROY COULDN'T MAKE HER MEDICINE.
HE COULD DO IT, OF COURSE! IT'S ALL HIS IDEAS, ANYWAY. HE COULD PROBABLY FIGURE OUT THE VACCINE, TOO, IF SHE'D EVEN LET HIM NEAR HER EQUIPMENT...
IT'S VERY SAD.
I DON'T KNOW. MAYBE ROY'S NOT AS SMART AS HE THINKS HE IS.
CHUCKLE
MAYBE YOU'RE NOT EITHER.
SKRICH
SKRICH

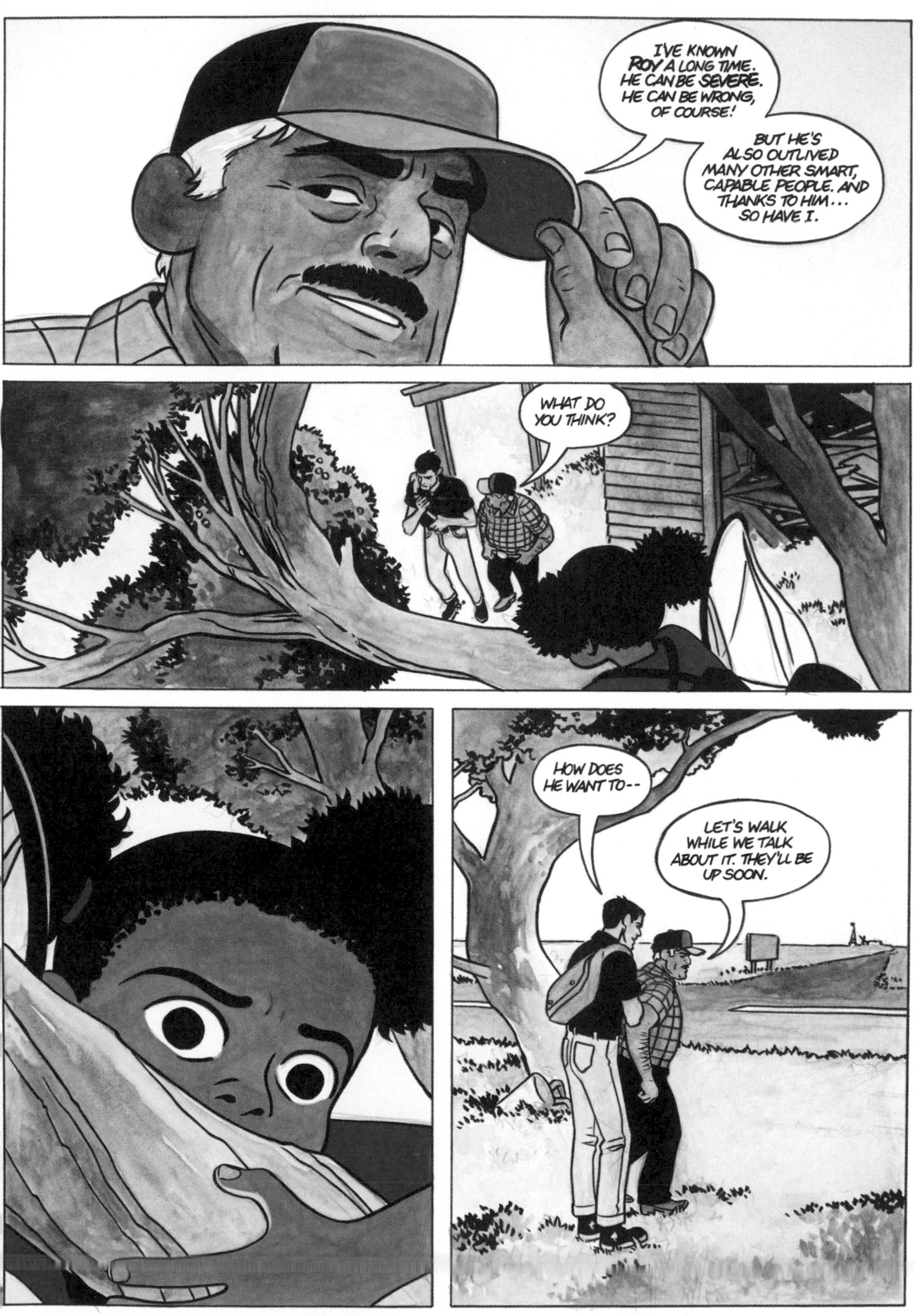
I'VE KNOWN ROY A LONG TIME. HE CAN BE SEVERE. HE CAN BE WRONG, OF COURSE!
BUT HE'S ALSO OUTLIVED MANY OTHER SMART, CAPABLE PEOPLE. AND THANKS TO HIM... SO HAVE I.
WHAT DO YOU THINK?
HOW DOES HE WANT TO--
LET'S WALK WHILE WE TALK ABOUT IT. THEY'LL BE UP SOON.

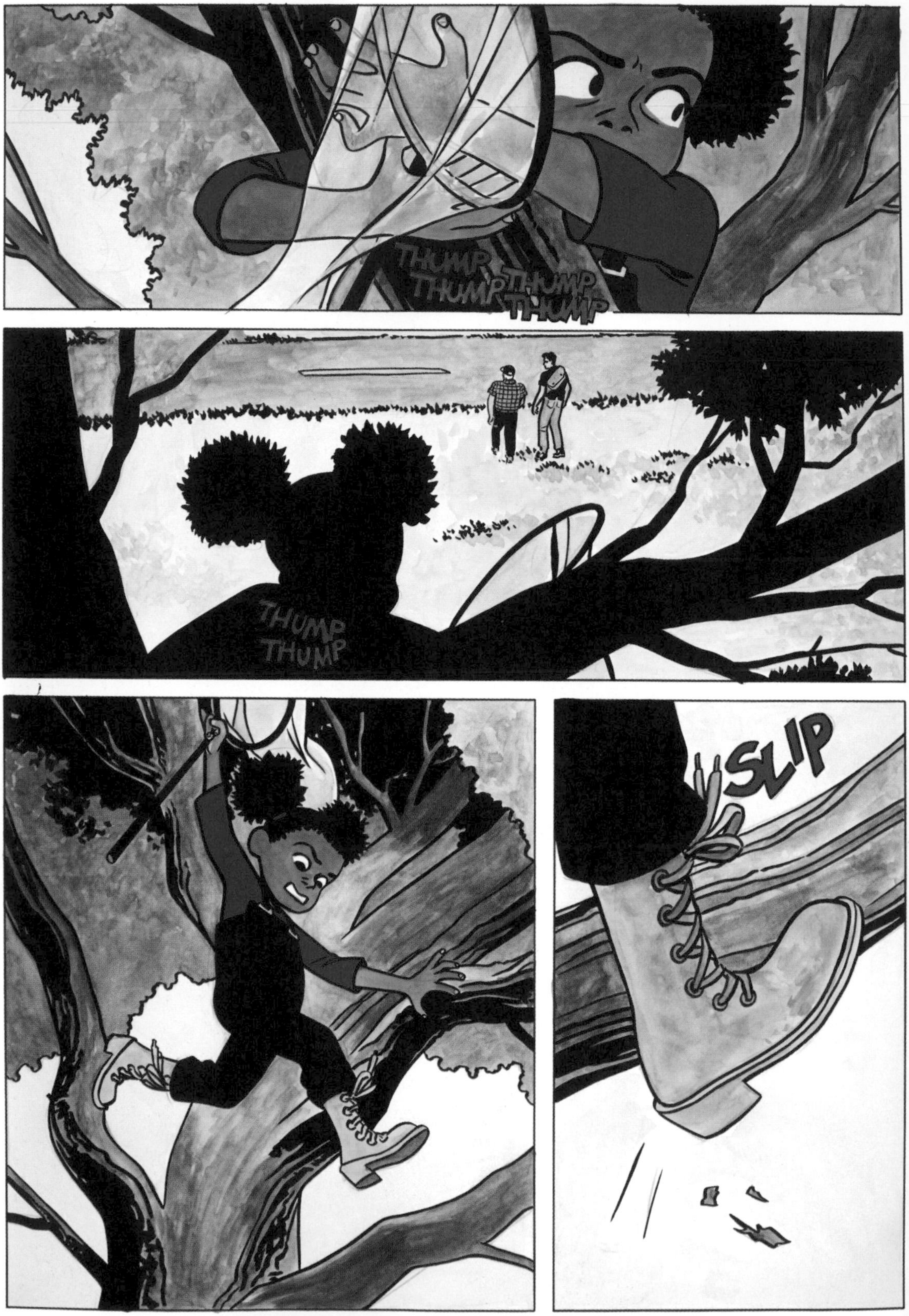
THUMP
THUMP
THUMP
THUMP
THUMP
THUMP
SLIP

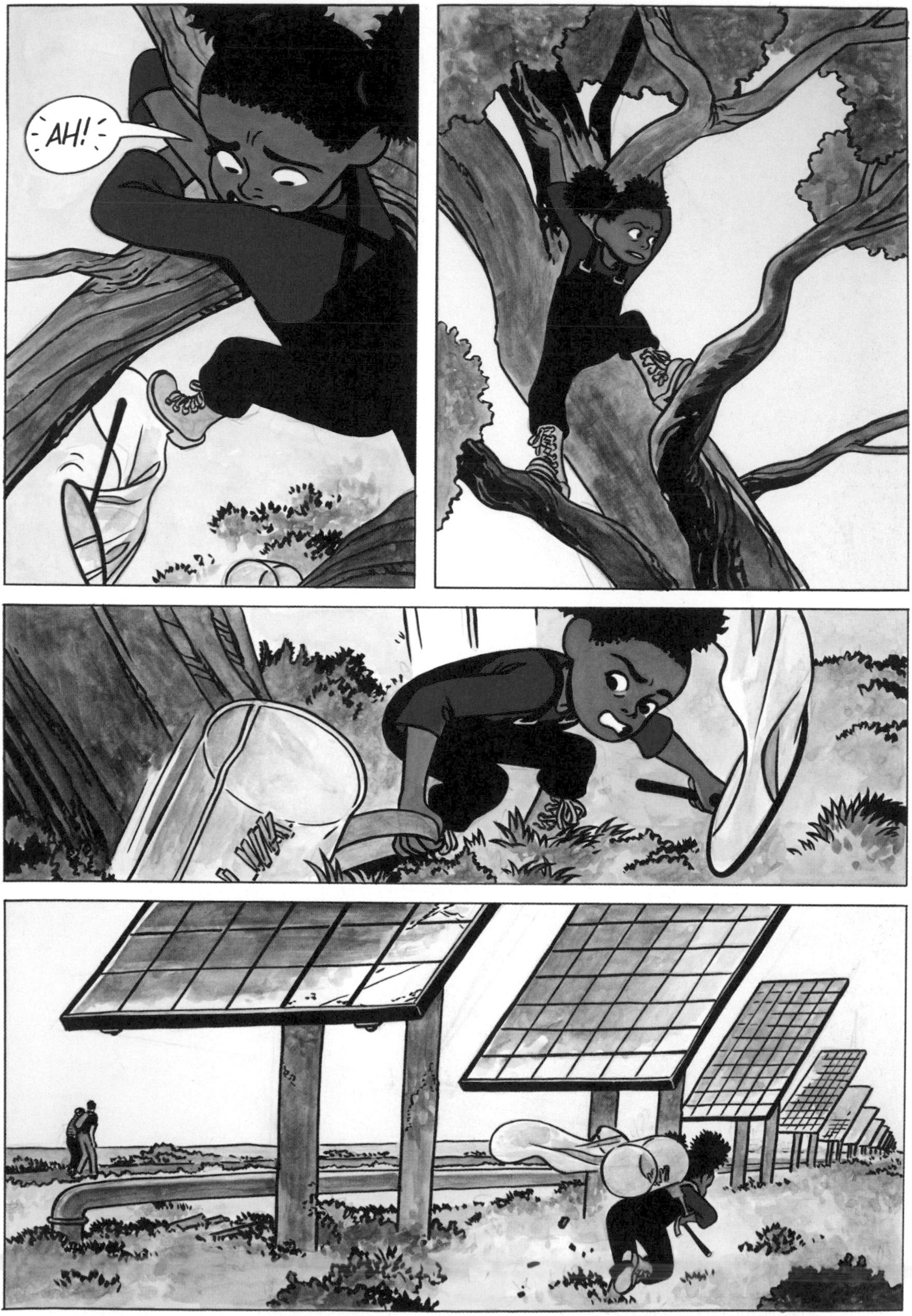
AH!

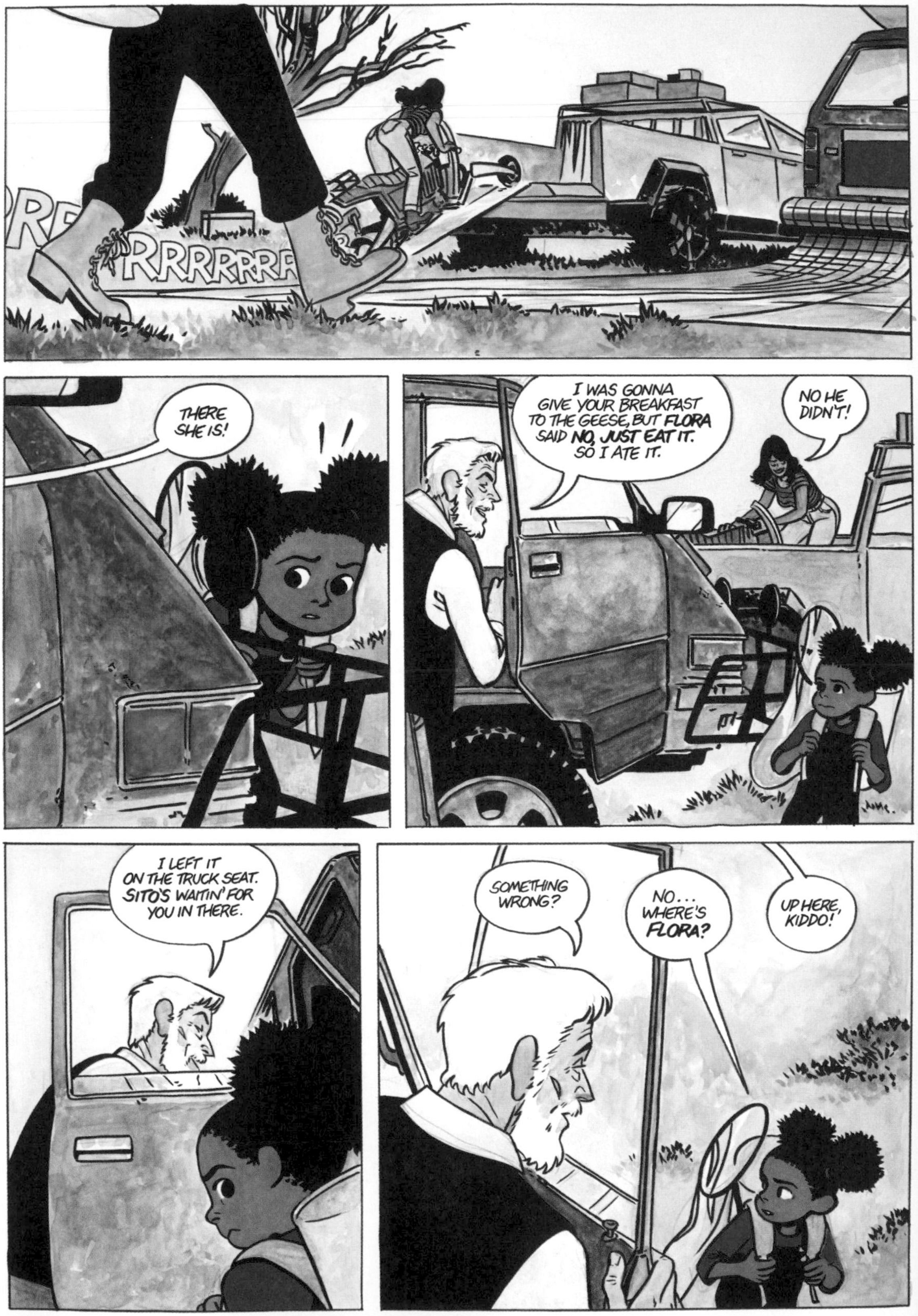
RRRRRRRR
THERE SHE IS!
I WAS GONNA GIVE YOUR BREAKFAST TO THE GEESE, BUT FLORA SAID NO, JUST EAT IT. SO I ATE IT.
NO HE DIDN'T!
I LEFT IT ON THE TRUCK SEAT. SITO'S WAITIN' FOR YOU IN THERE.
SOMETHING WRONG?
NO... WHERE'S FLORA?
UP HERE, KIDDO!

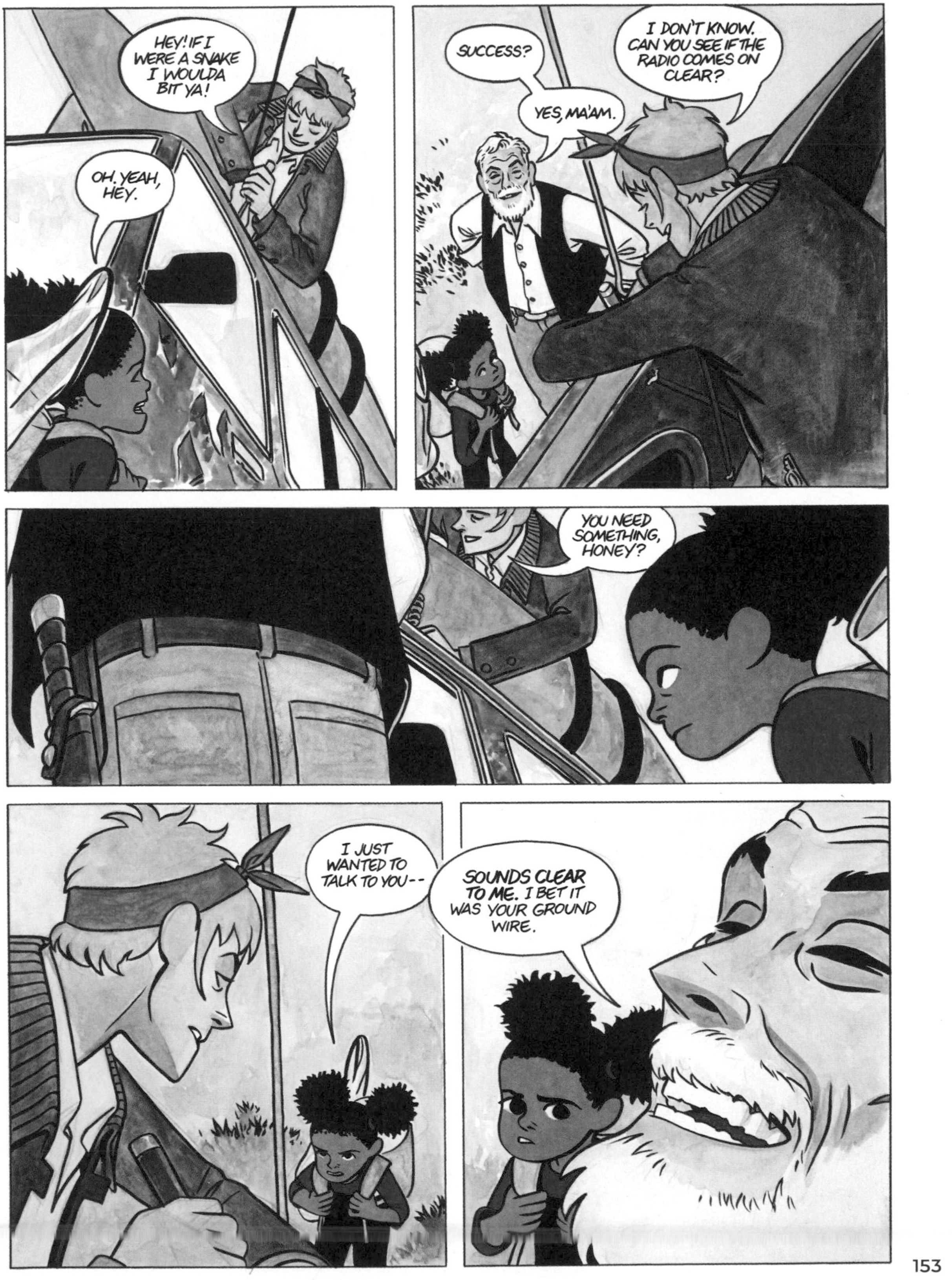
HEY! IF I WERE A SNAKE I WOULDA BIT YA!
OH. YEAH, HEY.
SUCCESS?
I DON'T KNOW. CAN YOU SEE IF THE RADIO COMES ON CLEAR?
YES, MA'AM.
YOU NEED SOMETHING, HONEY?
I JUST WANTED TO TALK TO YOU--
SOUNDS CLEAR TO ME. I BET IT WAS YOUR GROUND WIRE.

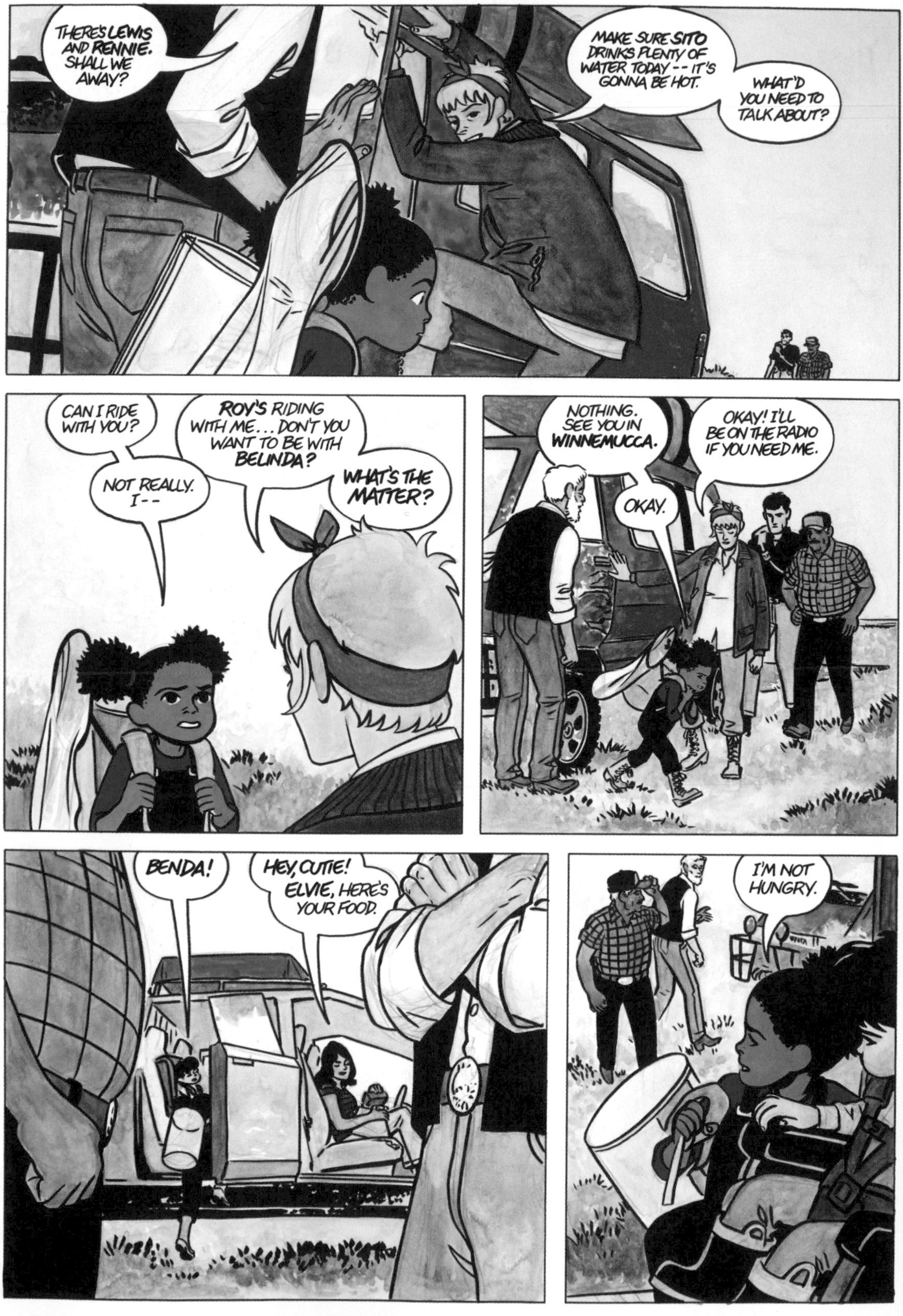
THERE'S LEWIS AND RENNIE. SHALL WE AWAY?
MAKE SURE SITO DRINKS PLENTY OF WATER TODAY -- IT'S GONNA BE HOT.
WHAT'D YOU NEED TO TALK ABOUT?
CAN I RIDE WITH YOU?
ROY'S RIDING WITH ME... DON'T YOU WANT TO BE WITH BELINDA?
NOT REALLY. I--
WHAT'S THE MATTER?
NOTHING. SEE YOU IN WINNEMUCCA.
OKAY! I'LL BE ON THE RADIO IF YOU NEED ME.
OKAY.
BENDA!
HEY, CUTIE! ELVIE, HERE'S YOUR FOOD.
I'M NOT HUNGRY.

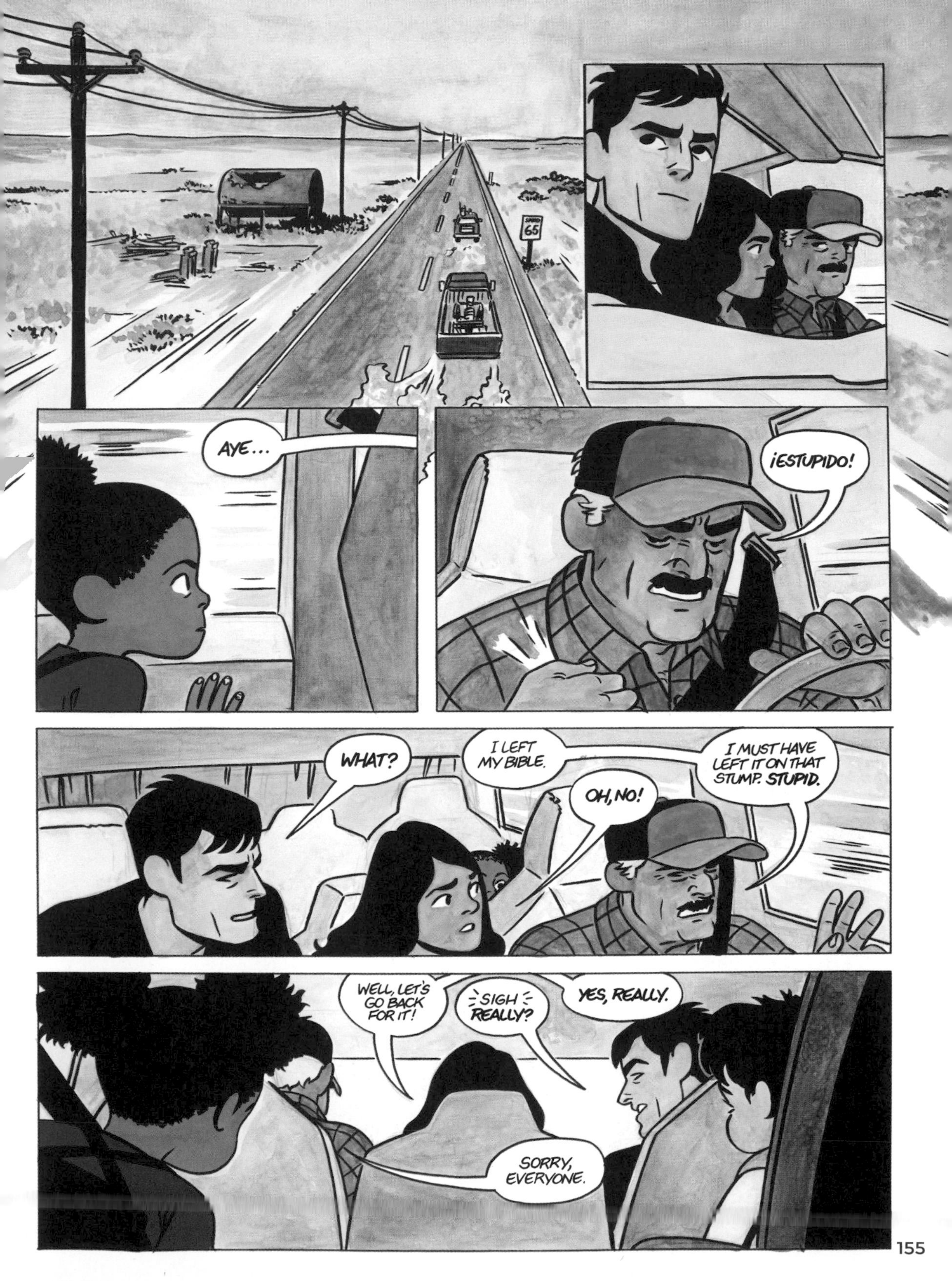
AYE...
¡ESTUPIDO!
WHAT?
I LEFT MY BIBLE.
I MUST HAVE LEFT IT ON THAT STUMP. STUPID.
OH, NO!
WELL, LET'S GO BACK FOR IT!
SIGH REALLY?
YES, REALLY.
SORRY, EVERYONE.

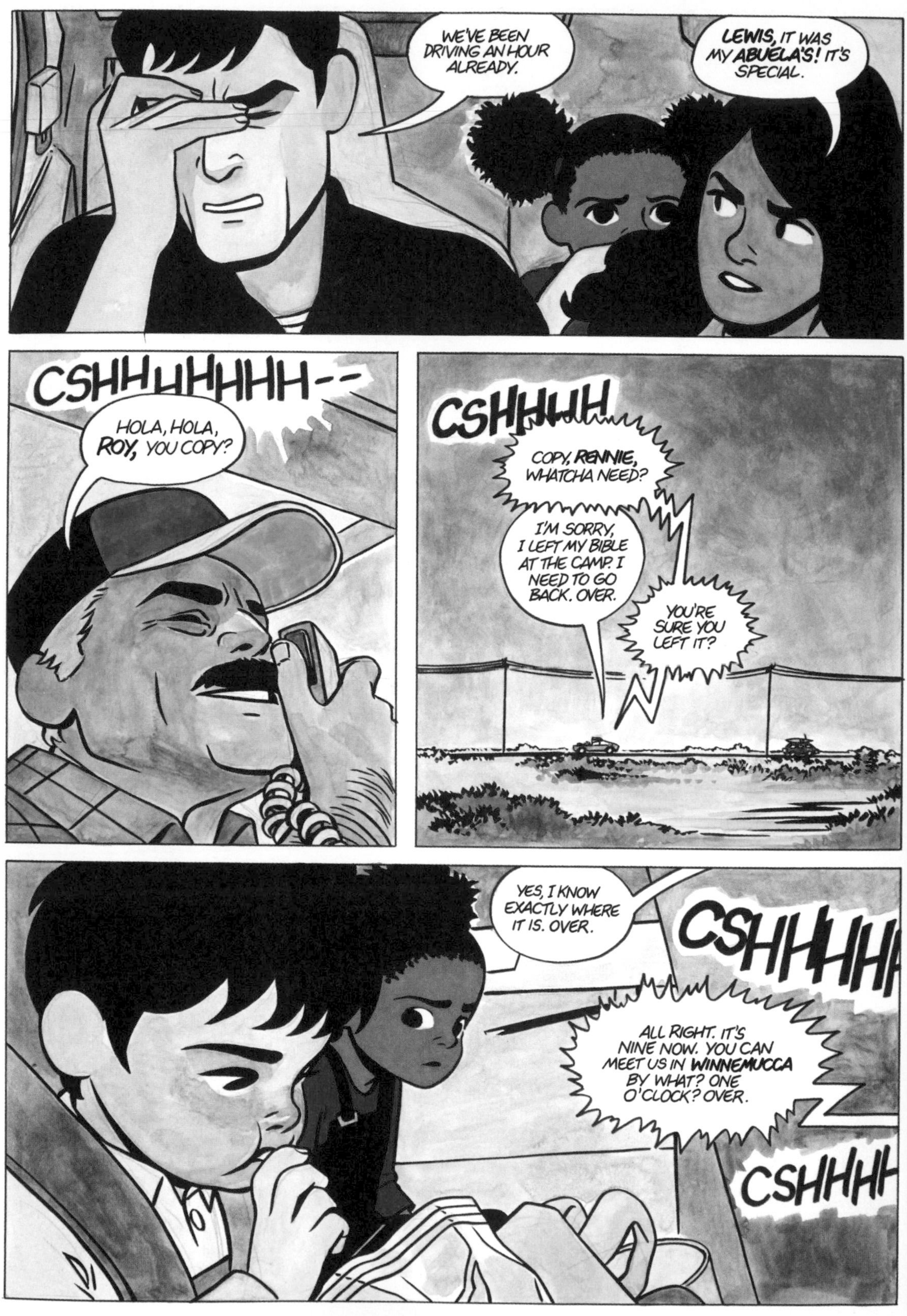
WE'VE BEEN DRIVING AN HOUR ALREADY.
LEWIS, IT WAS MY ABUELA'S! IT'S SPECIAL.
CSHHHHHHH--
HOLA, HOLA, ROY, YOU COPY?
CSHHHH
COPY, RENNIE, WHATCHA NEED?
I'M SORRY, I LEFT MY BIBLE AT THE CAMP. I NEED TO GO BACK. OVER.
YOU'RE SURE YOU LEFT IT?
YES, I KNOW EXACTLY WHERE IT IS. OVER.
CSHHHHH
ALL RIGHT. IT'S NINE NOW. YOU CAN MEET US IN WINNEMUCCA BY WHAT? ONE O'CLOCK? OVER.
CSHHH

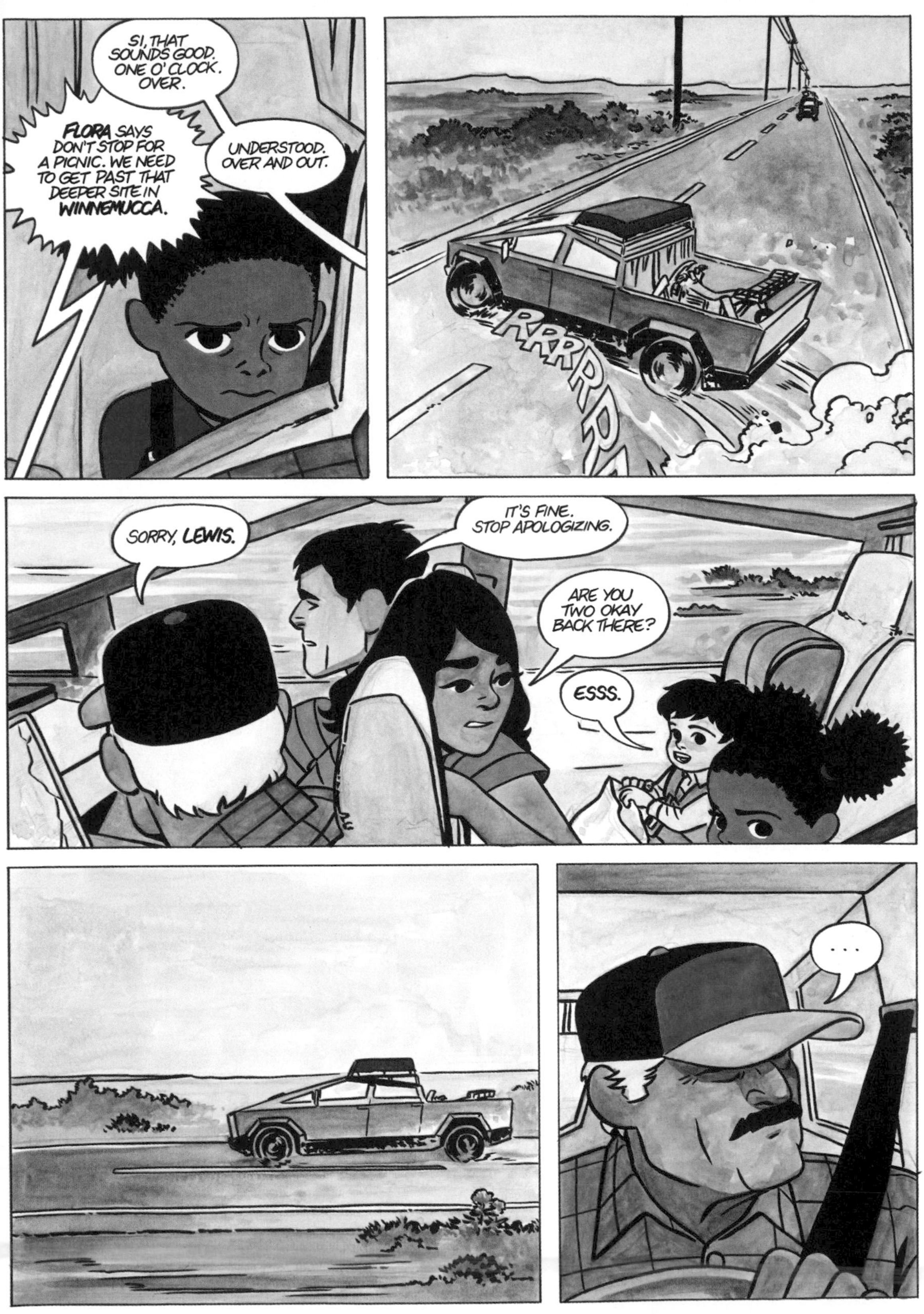
SI, THAT SOUNDS GOOD. ONE O' CLOCK. OVER.
FLORA SAYS DON'T STOP FOR A PICNIC. WE NEED TO GET PAST THAT DEEPER SITE IN WINNEMUCCA.
UNDERSTOOD. OVER AND OUT.
RRRRRR
SORRY, LEWIS.
IT'S FINE. STOP APOLOGIZING.
ARE YOU TWO OKAY BACK THERE?
ESSS.
. . .

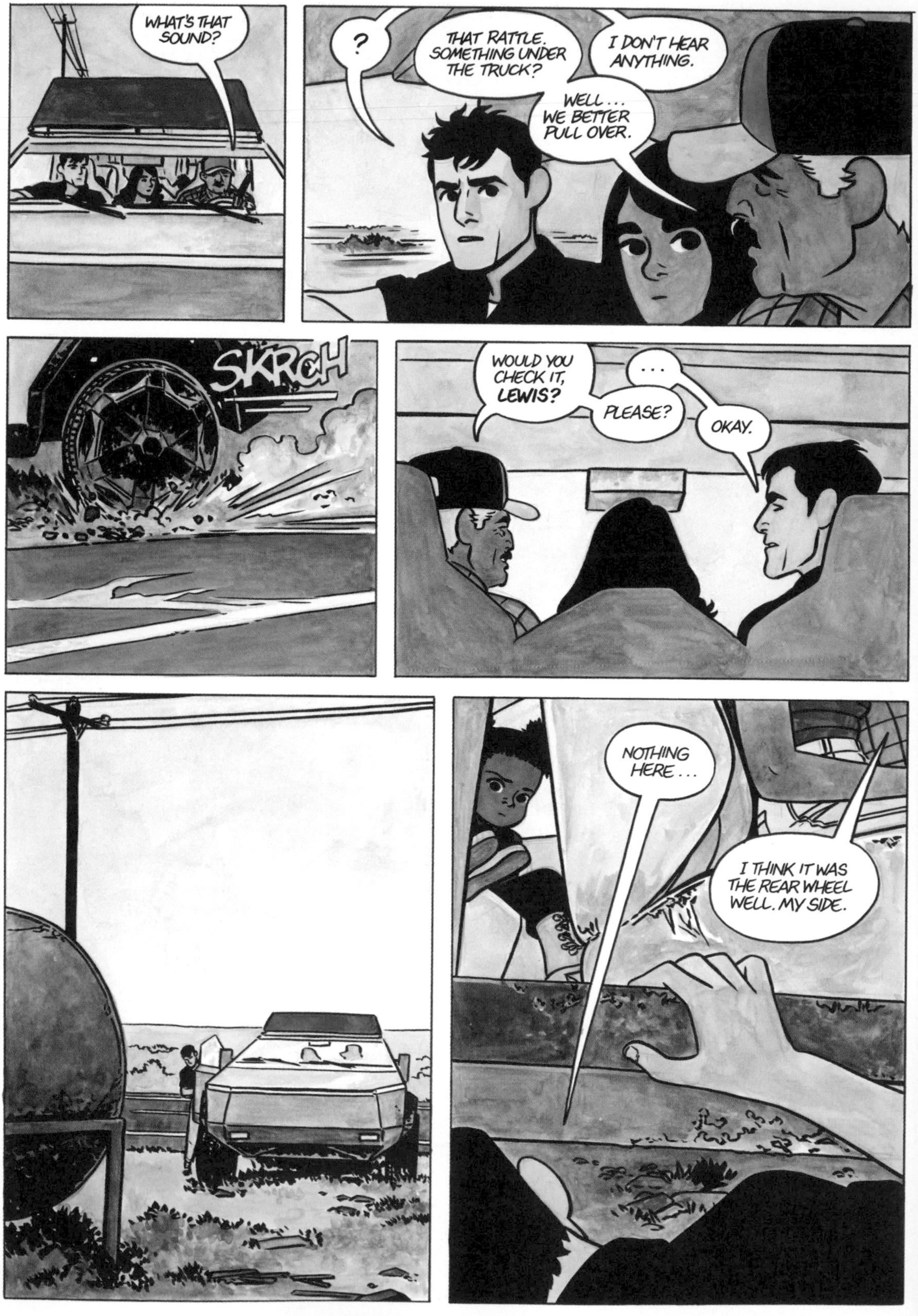
WHAT'S THAT SOUND?
?
THAT RATTLE. SOMETHING UNDER THE TRUCK?
I DON'T HEAR ANYTHING.
WELL... WE BETTER PULL OVER.
SKRCH
WOULD YOU CHECK IT, LEWIS?
...
PLEASE?
OKAY.
NOTHING HERE...
I THINK IT WAS THE REAR WHEEL WELL. MY SIDE.

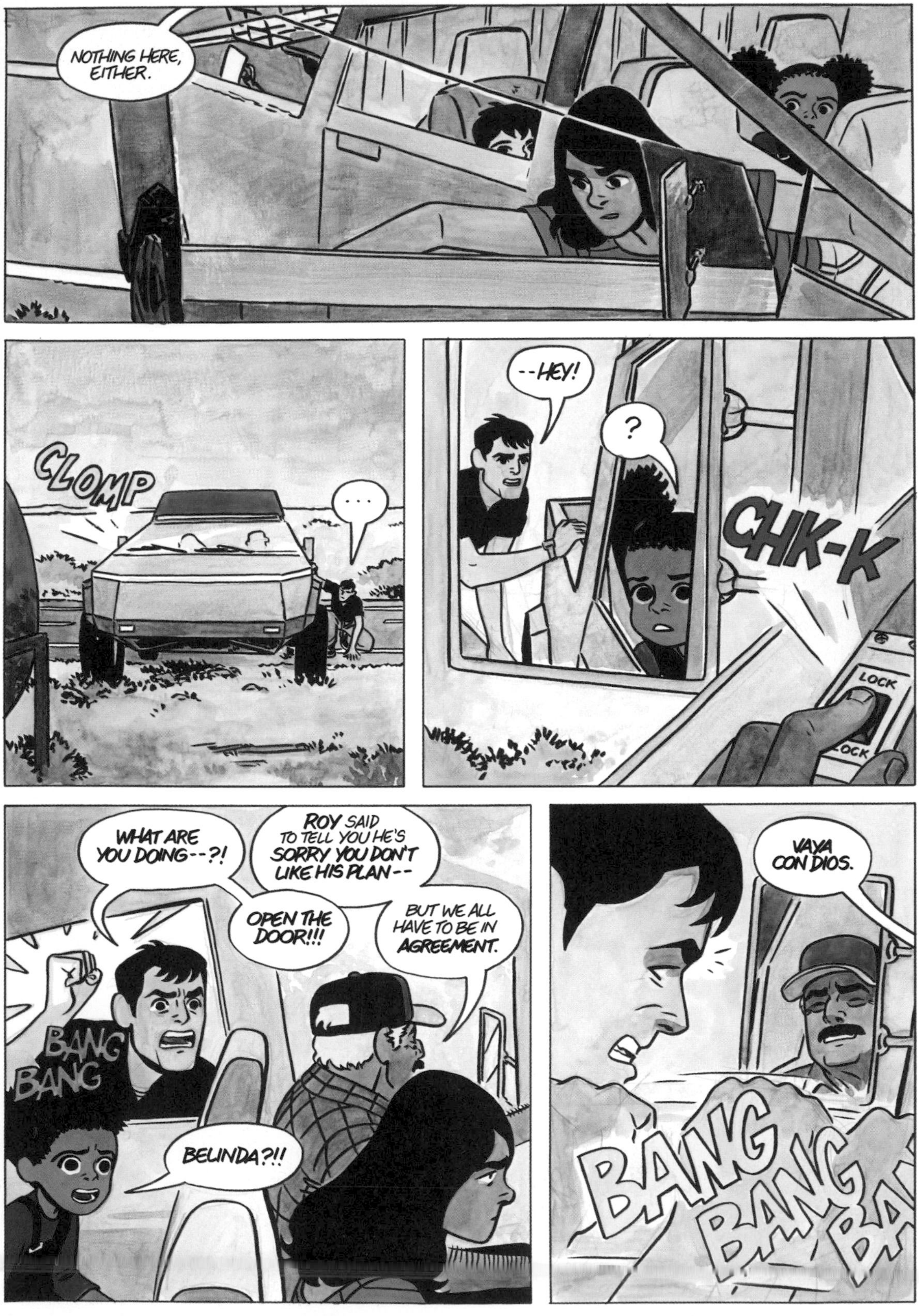
NOTHING HERE, EITHER.
CLOMP
. . .
--HEY!
?
CHK-K
LOCK
LOCK
WHAT ARE YOU DOING--?!
ROY SAID TO TELL YOU HE'S SORRY YOU DON'T LIKE HIS PLAN--
OPEN THE DOOR!!!
BUT WE ALL HAVE TO BE IN AGREEMENT.
BANG BANG
BELINDA?!!
VAYA CON DIOS.
BANG BANG

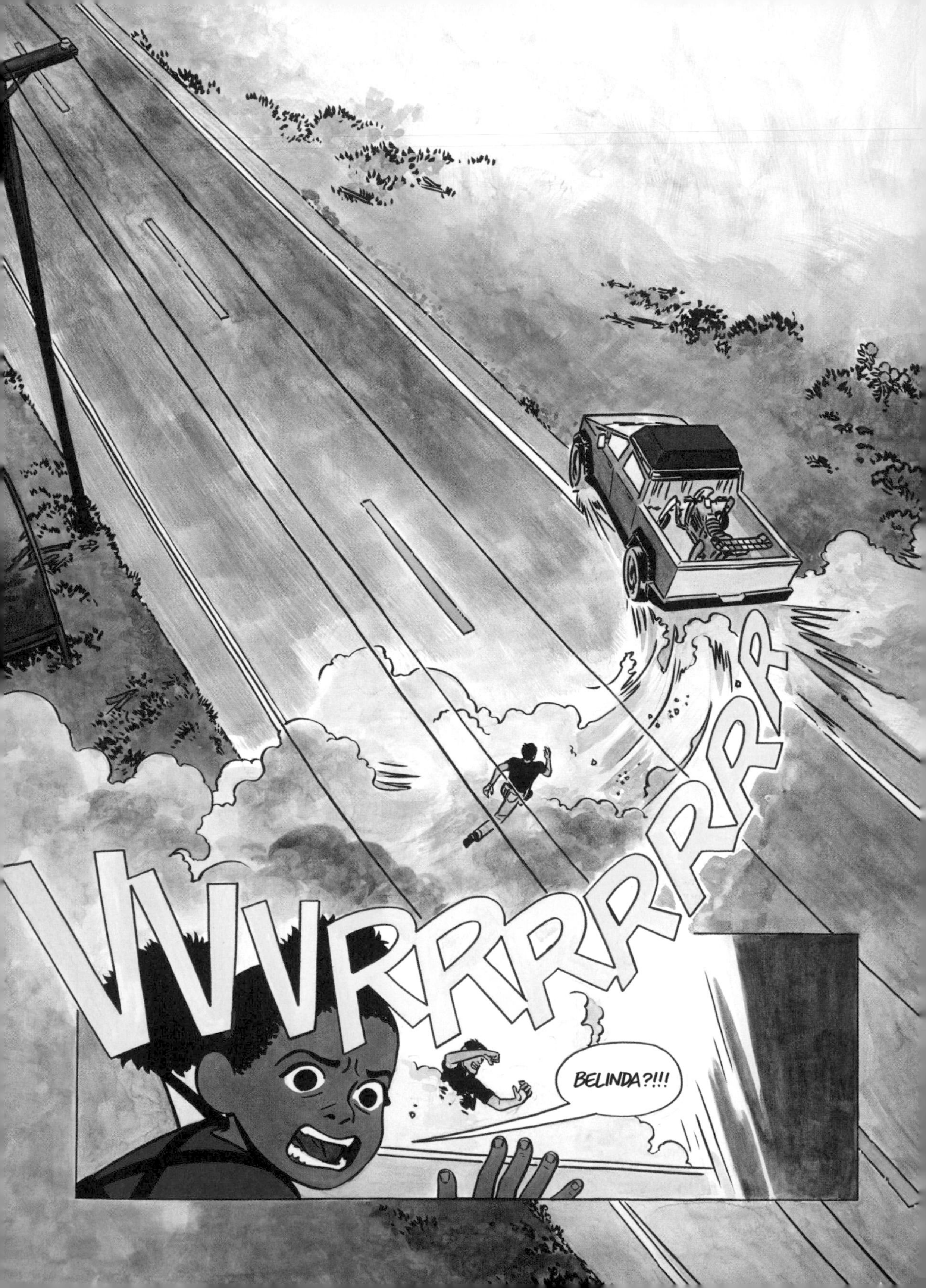
VVVRRRRRRRRR
BELINDA?!!!

CHAPTER NINE
BAD BABYSITTERS

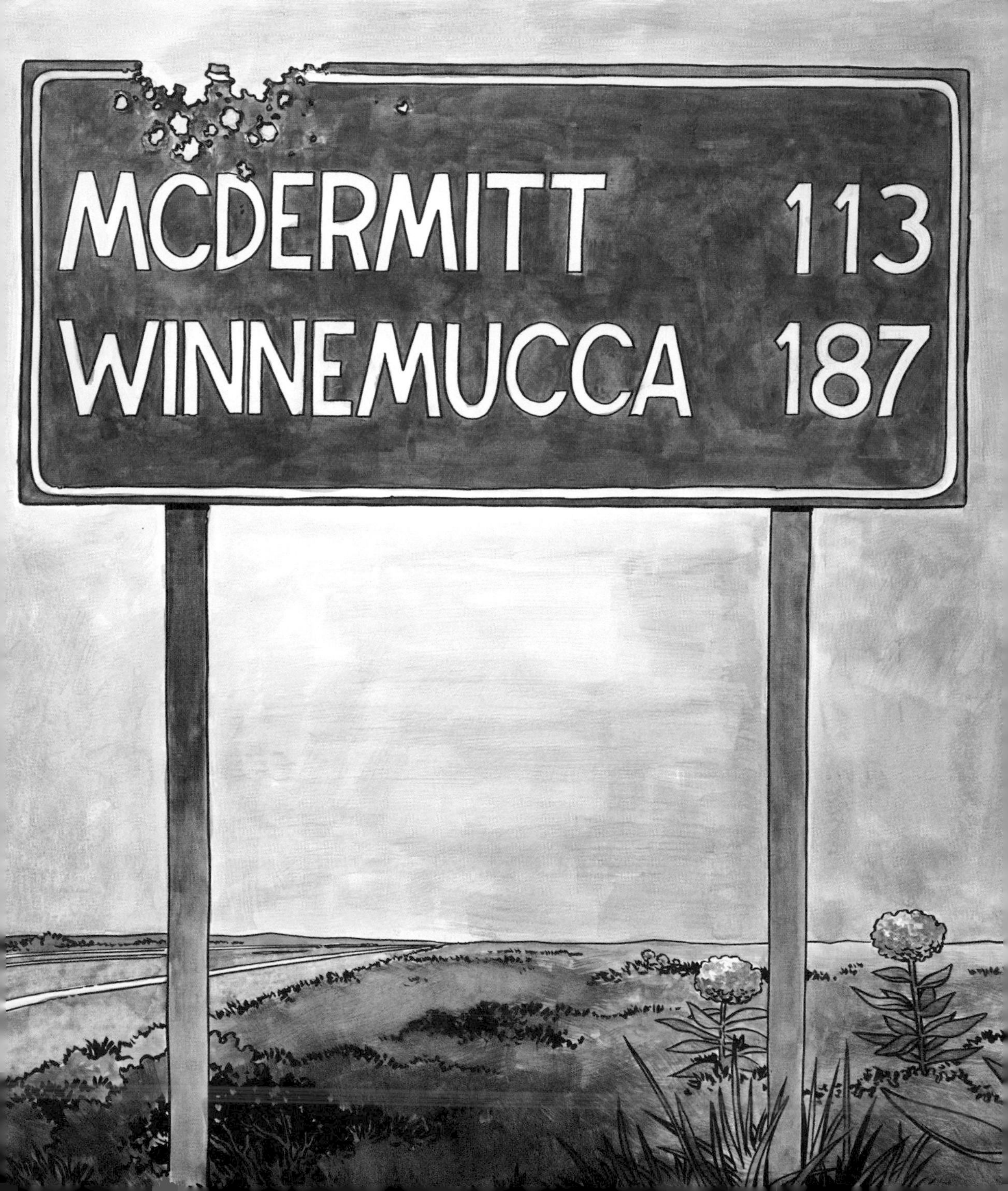
MCDERMITT 113
WINNEMUCCA 187

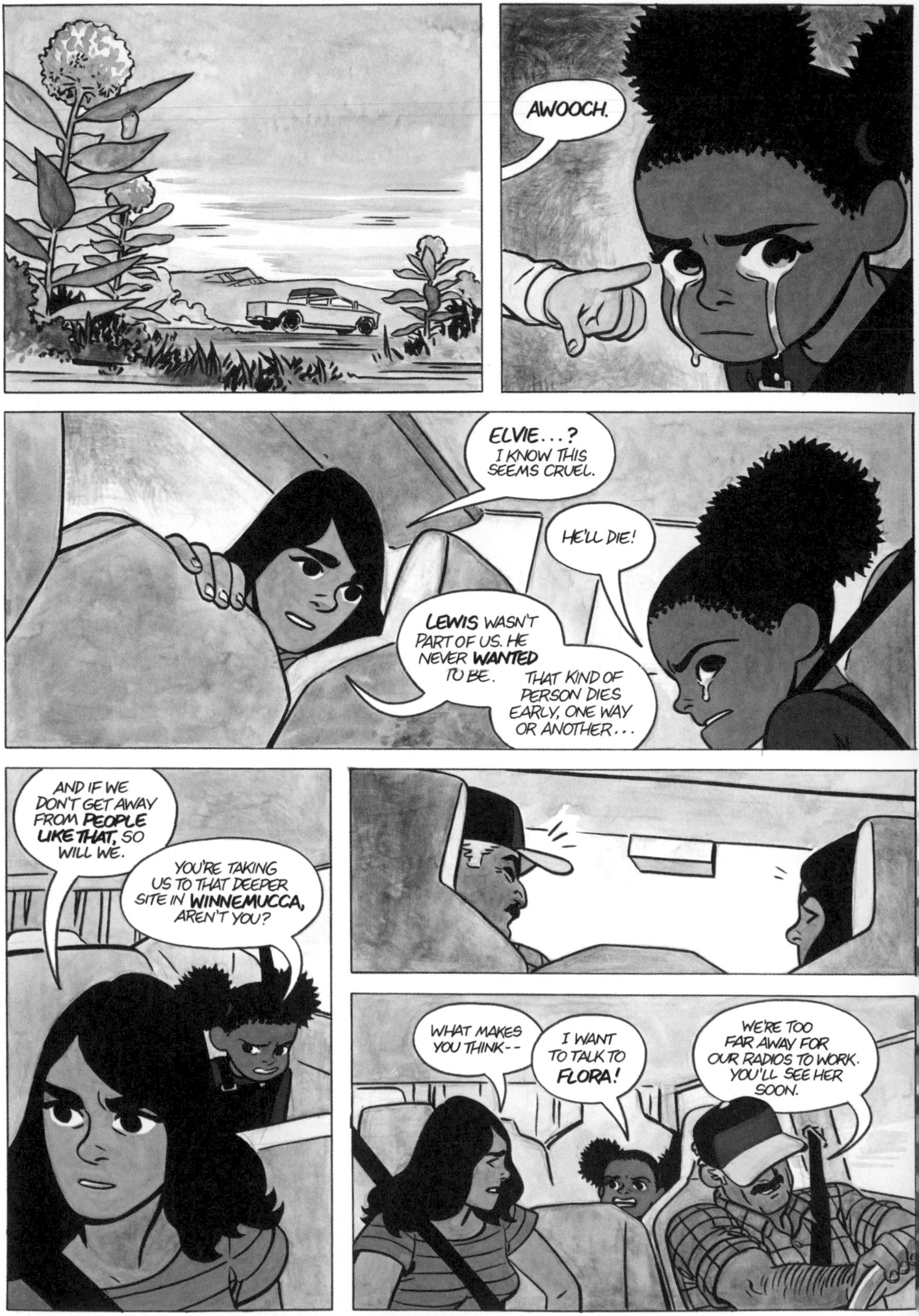
AWOOCH.
ELVIE...? I KNOW THIS SEEMS CRUEL.
HE'LL DIE!
LEWIS WASN'T PART OF US. HE NEVER WANTED TO BE.
THAT KIND OF PERSON DIES EARLY, ONE WAY OR ANOTHER...
AND IF WE DON'T GET AWAY FROM PEOPLE LIKE THAT, SO WILL WE.
YOU'RE TAKING US TO THAT DEEPER SITE IN WINNEMUCCA, AREN'T YOU?
WHAT MAKES YOU THINK--
I WANT TO TALK TO FLORA!
WE'RE TOO FAR AWAY FOR OUR RADIOS TO WORK. YOU'LL SEE HER SOON.

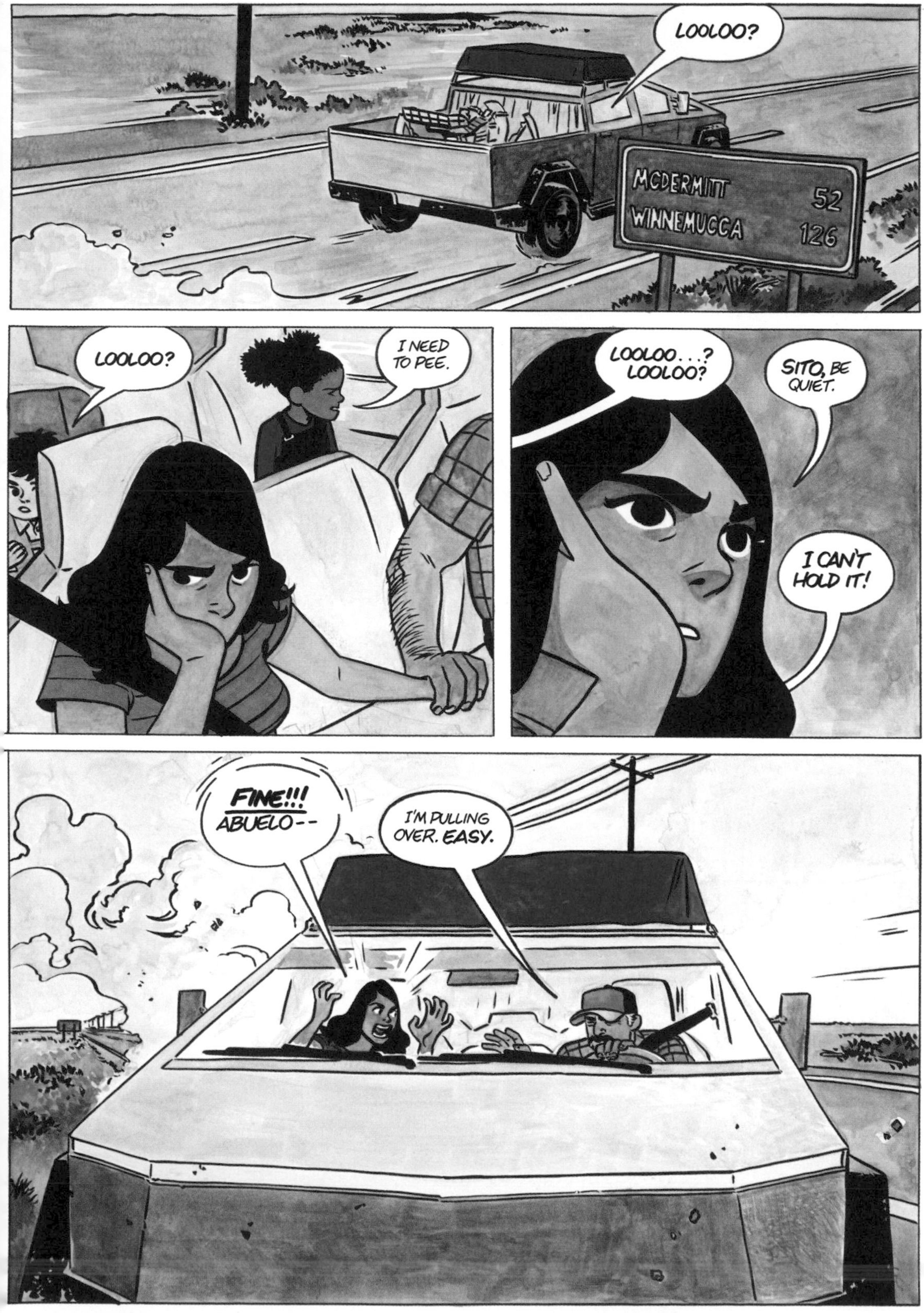

LOOLOO?
MCDERMITT 52
WINNEMUCCA 126
LOOLOO?
I NEED TO PEE.
LOOLOO...? LOOLOO?
SITO, BE QUIET.
I CAN'T HOLD IT!
FINE!!! ABUELO--
I'M PULLING OVER. EASY.

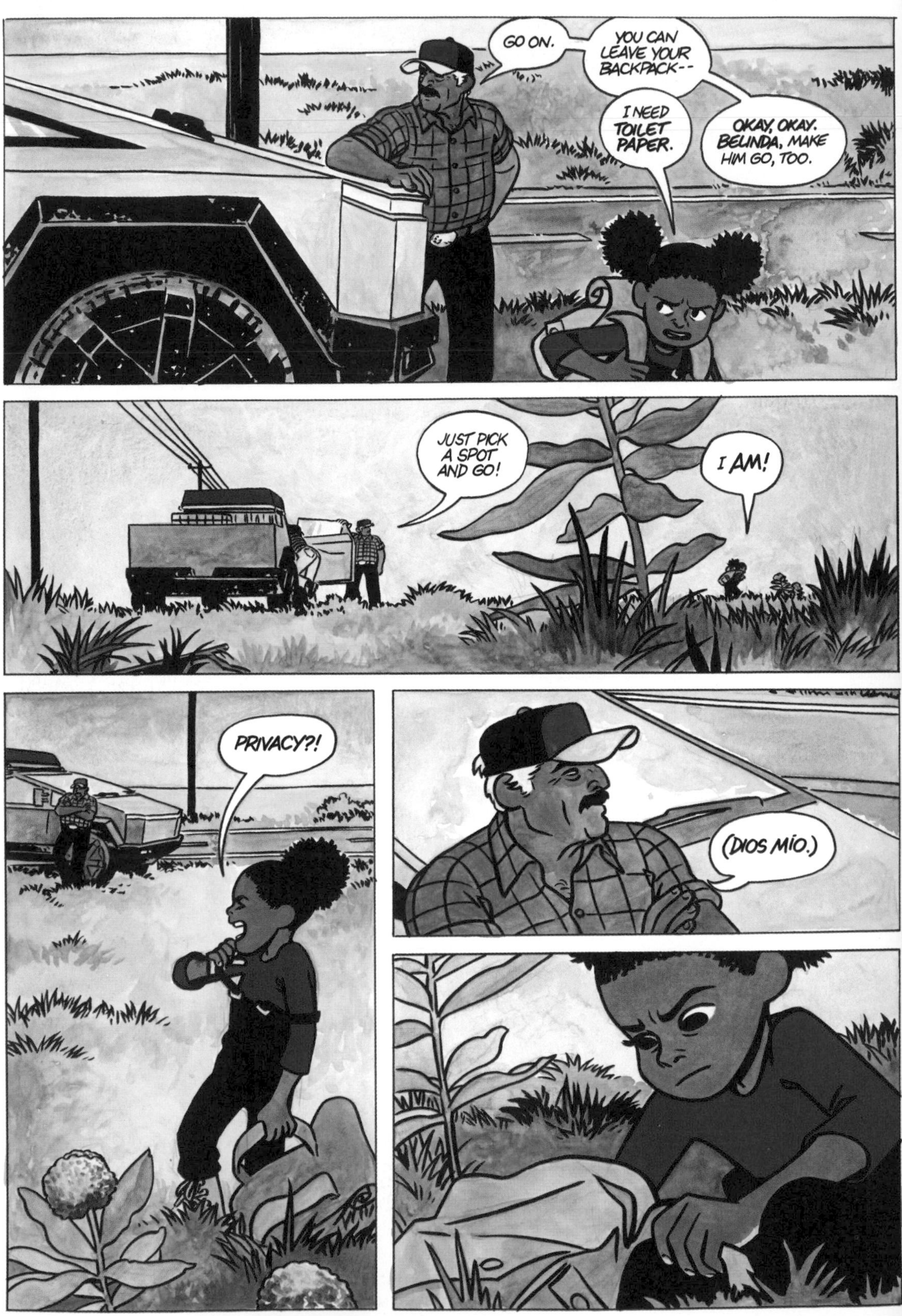
GO ON.
YOU CAN LEAVE YOUR BACKPACK--
I NEED TOILET PAPER.
OKAY, OKAY. BELINDA, MAKE HIM GO, TOO.
JUST PICK A SPOT AND GO!
I AM!
PRIVACY?!
(DIOS MÍO.)

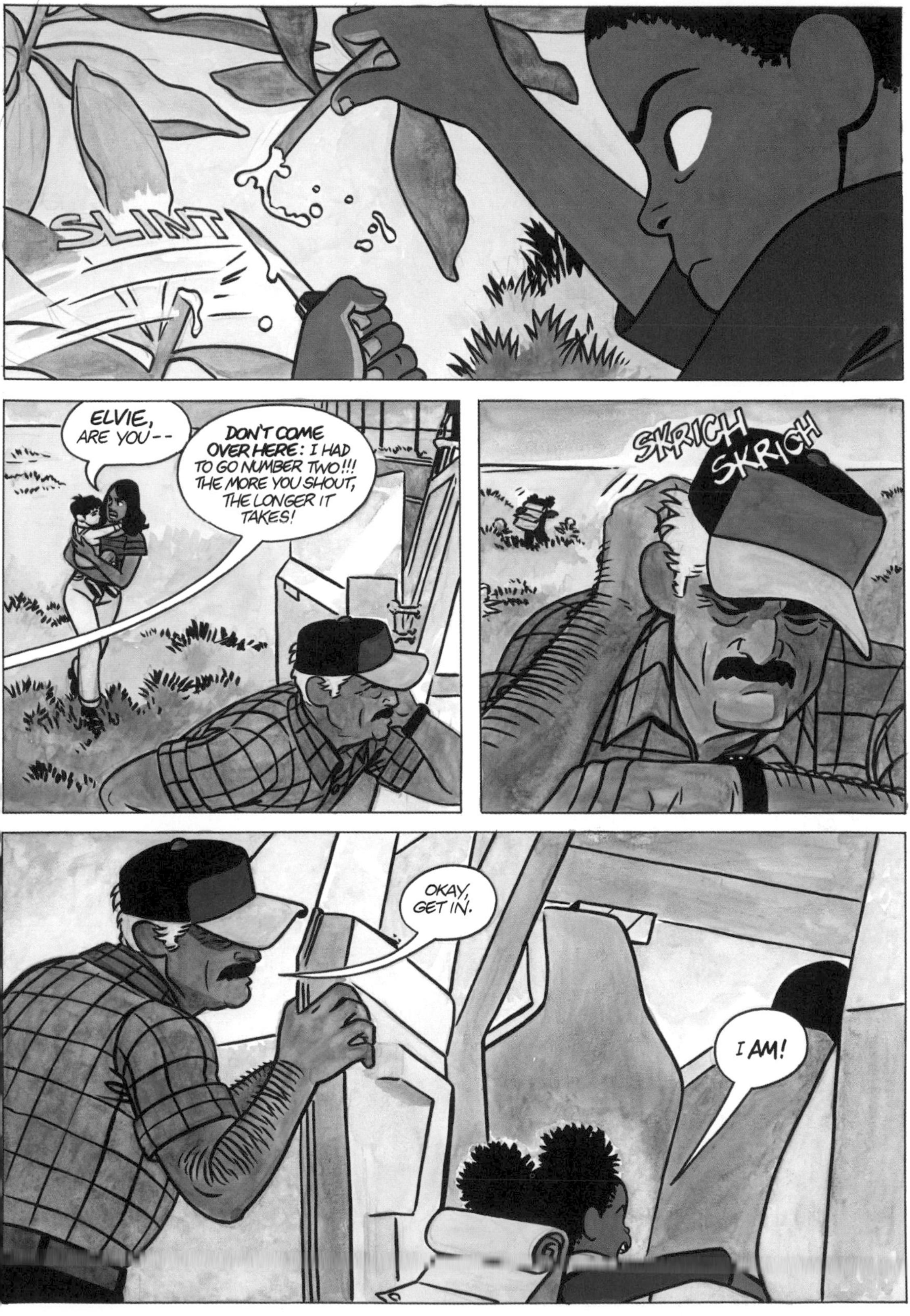
SLINT
ELVIE, ARE YOU--
DON'T COME OVER HERE: I HAD TO GO NUMBER TWO!!! THE MORE YOU SHOUT, THE LONGER IT TAKES!
SKRICH SKRICH
OKAY, GET IN.
I AM!

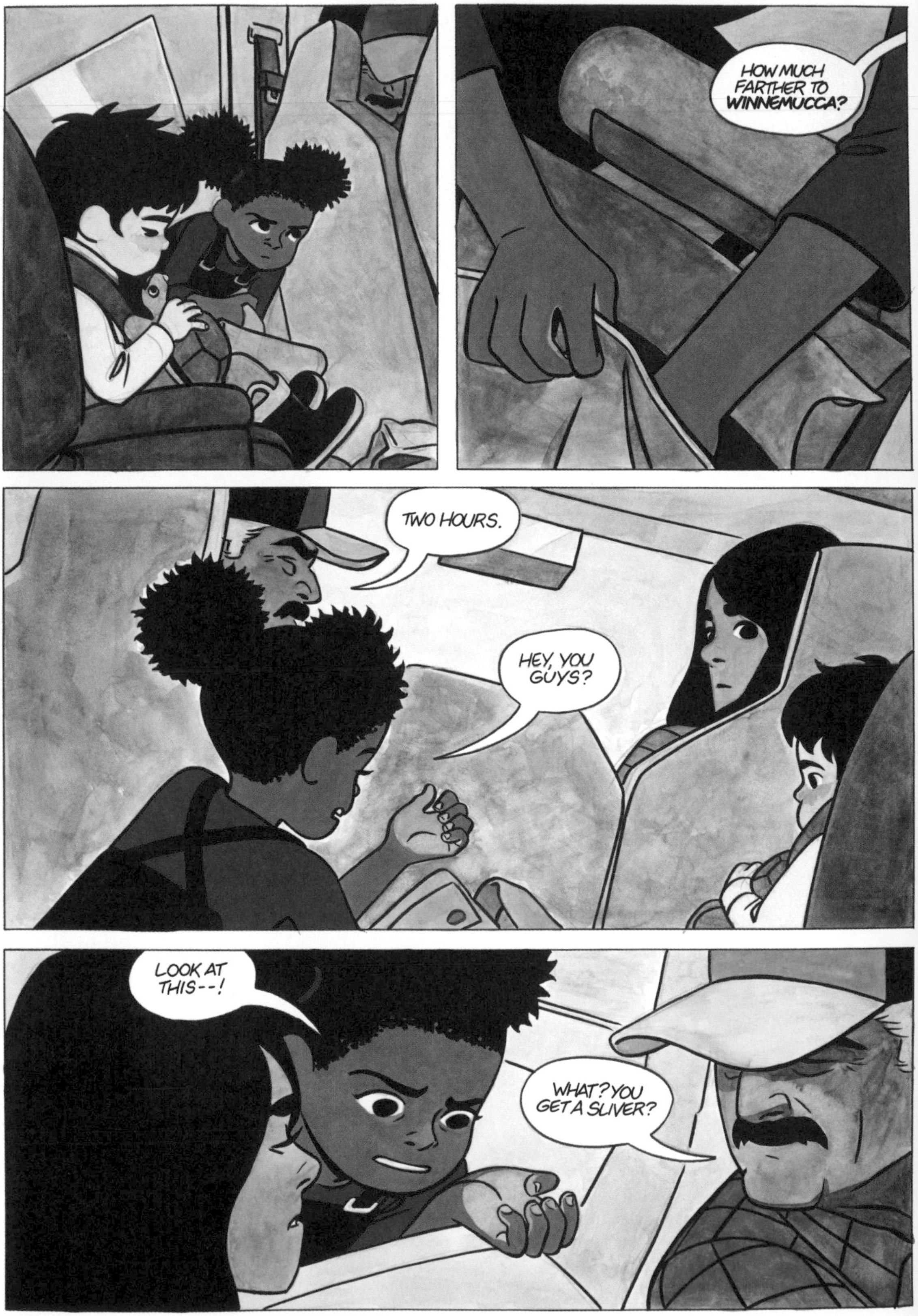
HOW MUCH FARTHER TO WINNEMUCCA?
TWO HOURS.
HEY, YOU GUYS?
LOOK AT THIS--!
WHAT? YOU GET A SLIVER?

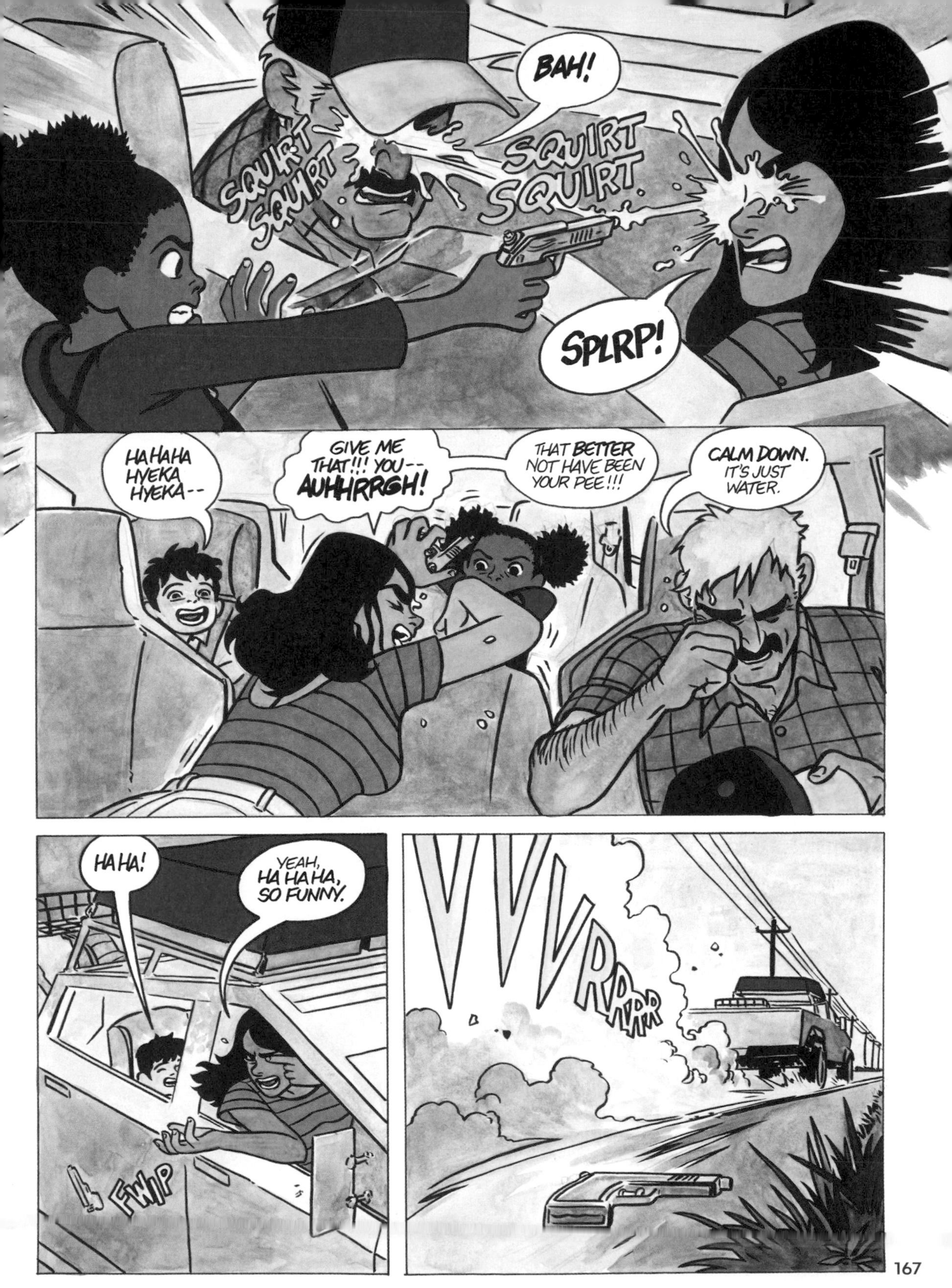
BAH!
SQUIRT SQUIRT
SQUIRT SQUIRT
SPLRP!
HA HA HA HYEKA HYEKA--
GIVE ME THAT!!! YOU-- AUHHRRGH!
THAT BETTER NOT HAVE BEEN YOUR PEE!!!
CALM DOWN. IT'S JUST WATER.
HA HA!
YEAH, HA HA HA, SO FUNNY.
FWIP
VVVRRRRRR

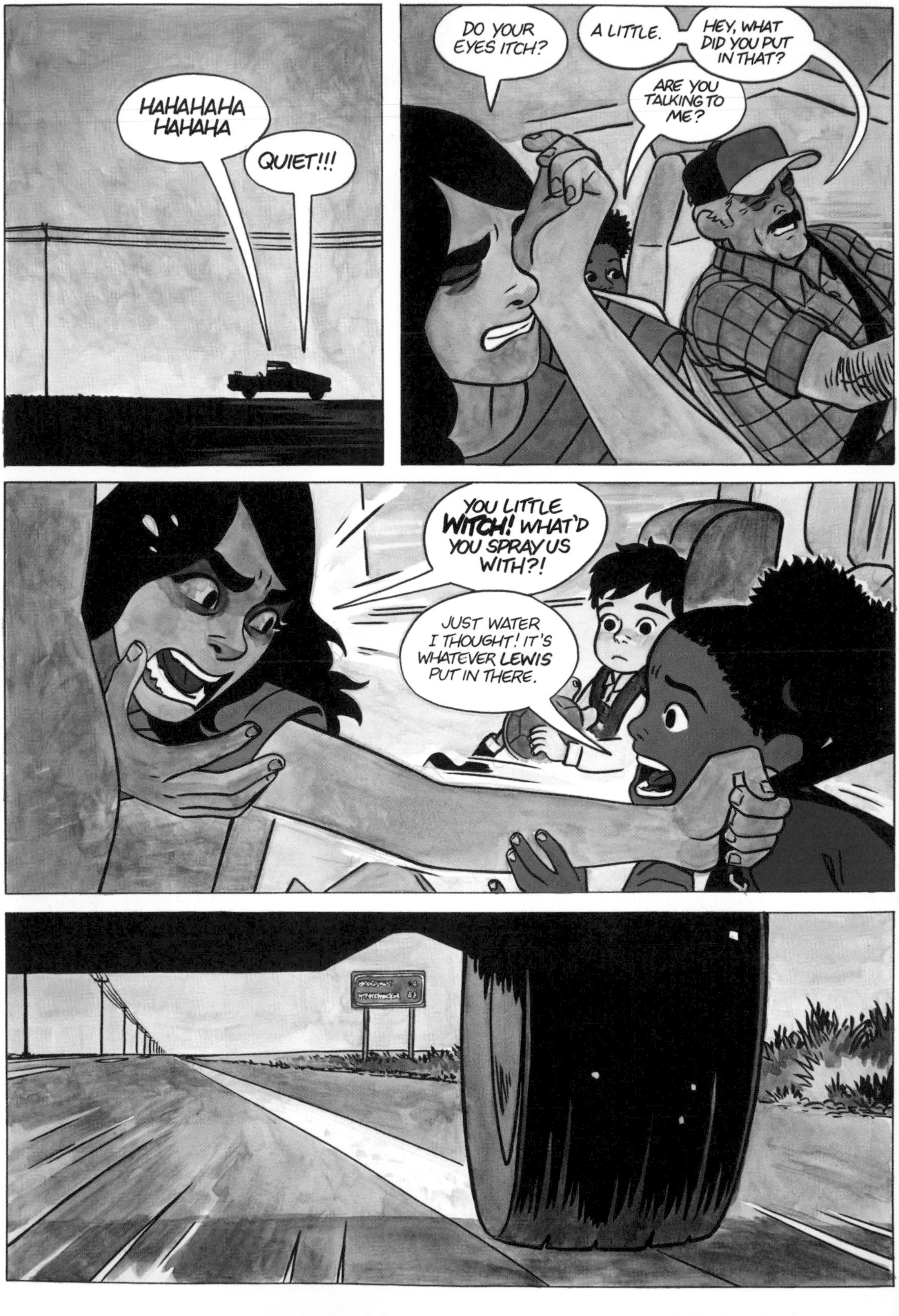
HAHAHAHA HAHAHA
QUIET!!!
DO YOUR EYES ITCH?
A LITTLE.
HEY, WHAT DID YOU PUT IN THAT?
ARE YOU TALKING TO ME?
YOU LITTLE WITCH! WHAT'D YOU SPRAY US WITH?!
JUST WATER I THOUGHT! IT'S WHATEVER LEWIS PUT IN THERE.

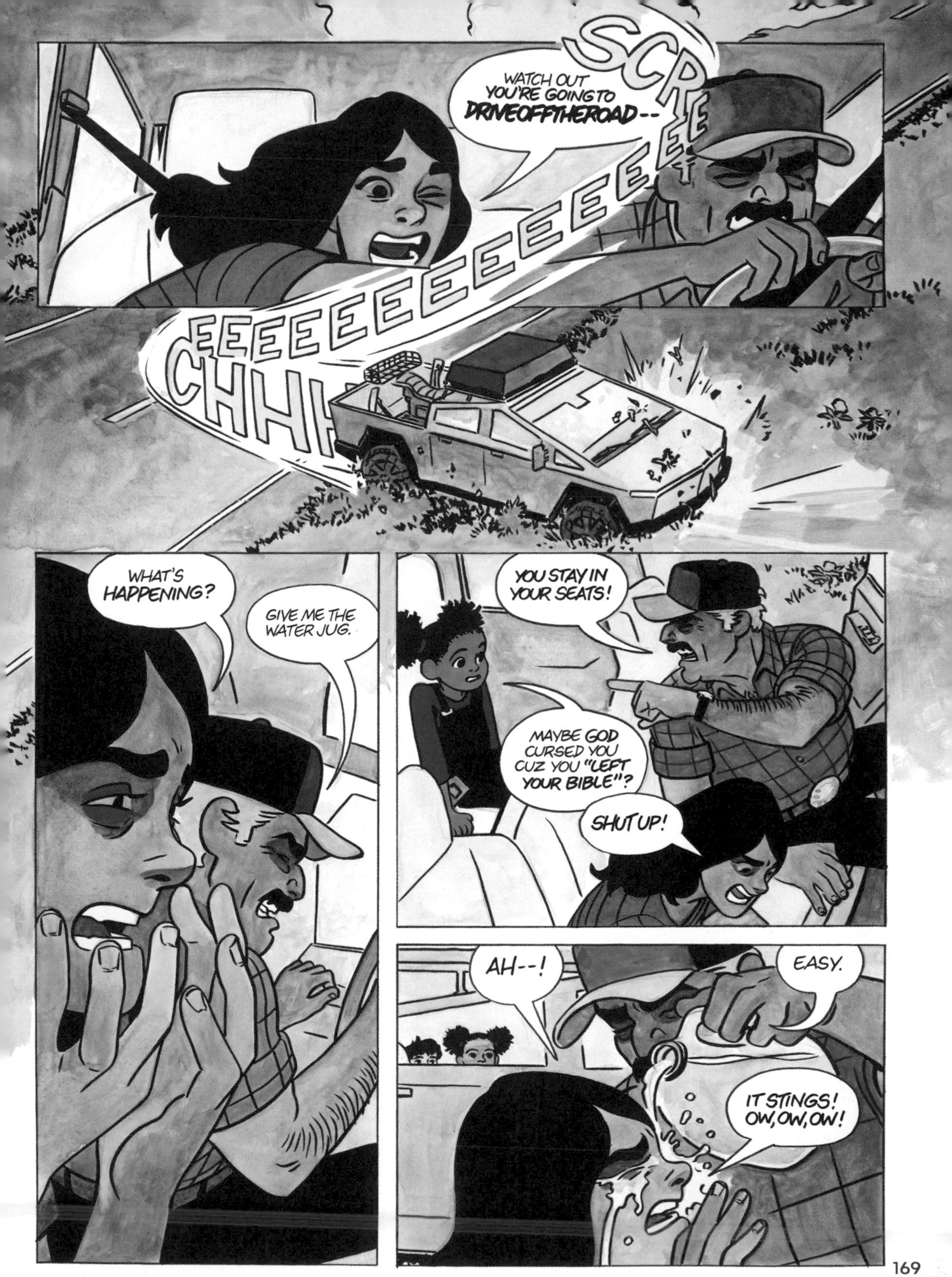

SCREEEEEEEEEEEEEEEEEEE
WATCH OUT YOU'RE GOING TO DRIVEOFFTHEROAD--
CHHH
WHAT'S HAPPENING?
GIVE ME THE WATER JUG.
YOU STAY IN YOUR SEATS!
MAYBE GOD CURSED YOU CUZ YOU "LEFT YOUR BIBLE"?
SHUT UP!
AH--!
EASY.
IT STINGS! OW, OW, OW!

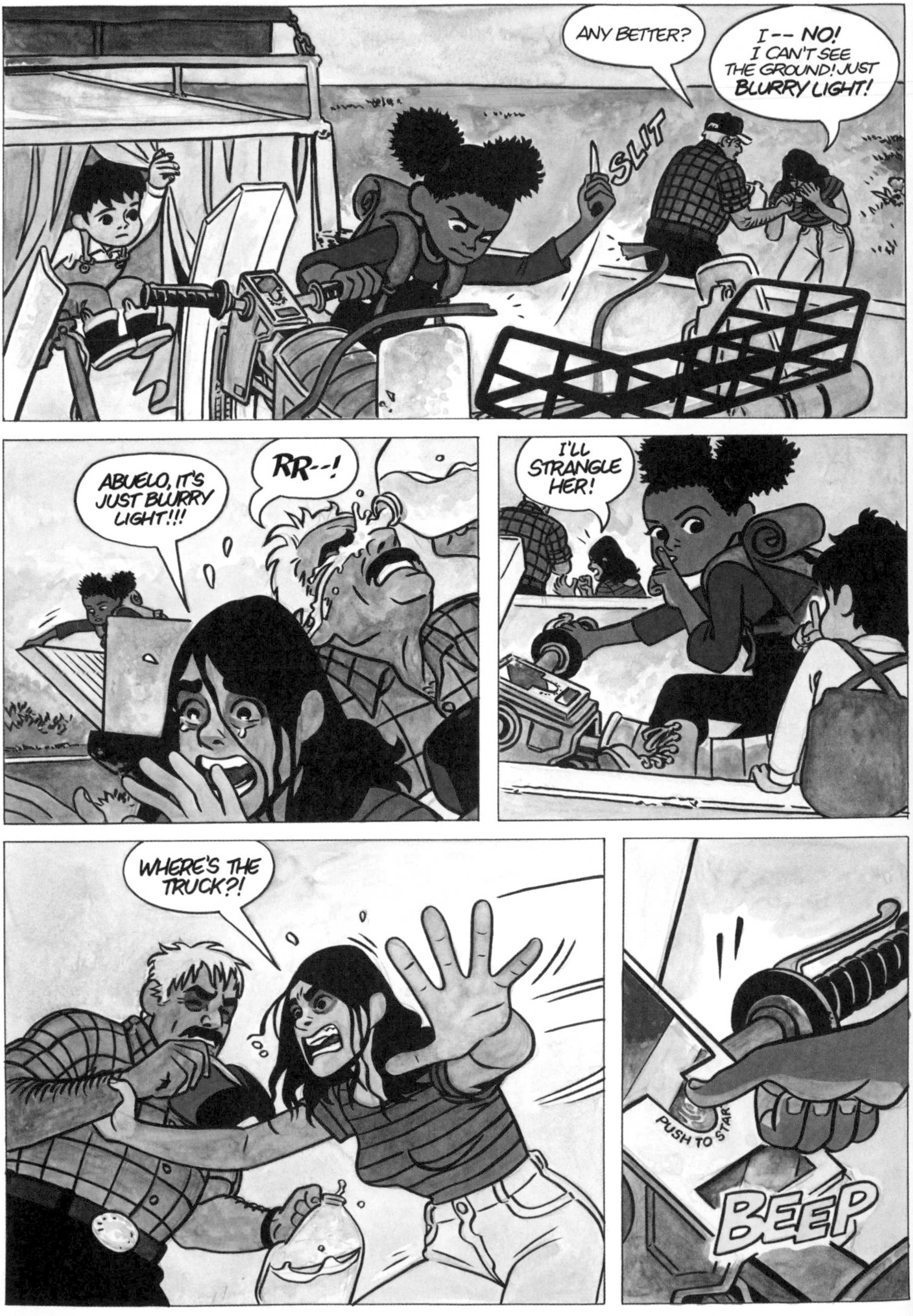
ANY BETTER?
I -- NO! I CAN'T SEE THE GROUND! JUST BLURRY LIGHT!
SLIT
ABUELO, IT'S JUST BLURRY LIGHT!!!
RR--!
I'LL STRANGLE HER!
WHERE'S THE TRUCK?!
PUSH TO STAR
BEEP

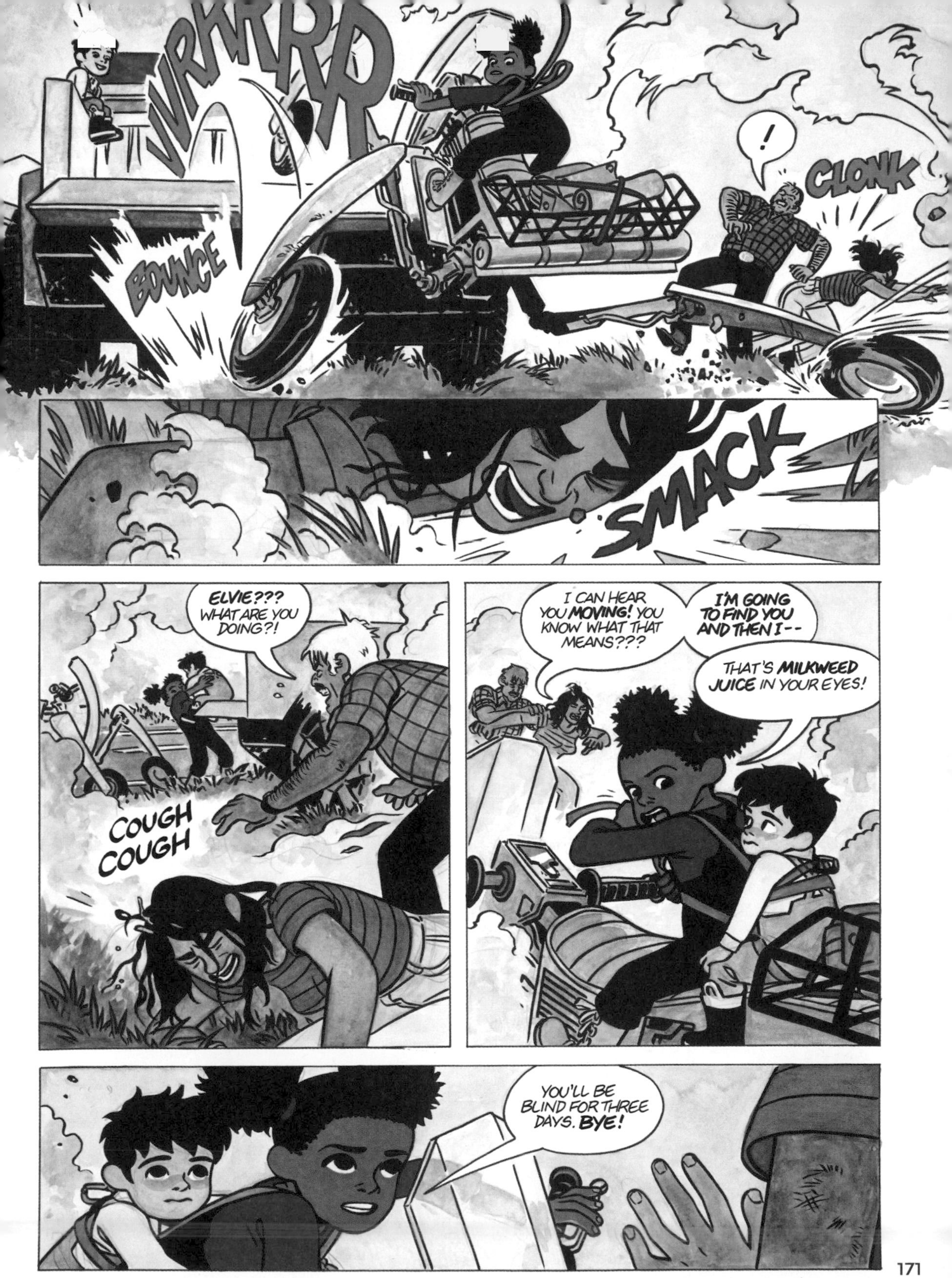
VRRRRRR
BOUNCE
!
CLONK
SMACK
ELVIE??? WHAT ARE YOU DOING?!
COUGH COUGH
I CAN HEAR YOU MOVING! YOU KNOW WHAT THAT MEANS???
I'M GOING TO FIND YOU AND THEN I--
THAT'S MILKWEED JUICE IN YOUR EYES!
YOU'LL BE BLIND FOR THREE DAYS. BYE!

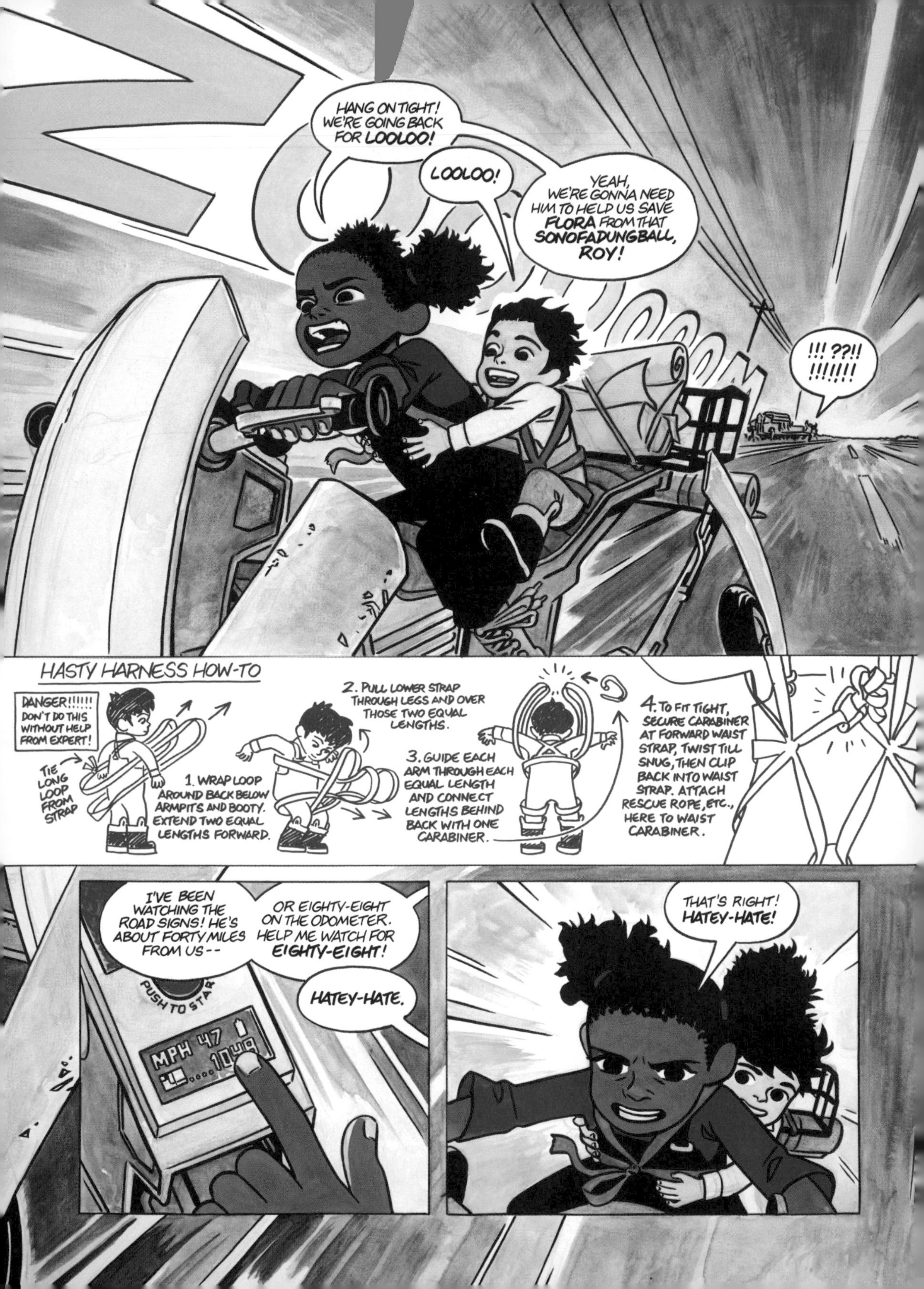

HANG ON TIGHT! WE'RE GOING BACK FOR LOOLOO!
LOOLOO!
YEAH, WE'RE GONNA NEED HIM TO HELP US SAVE FLORA FROM THAT SONOFADUNGBALL, ROY!
VROOOOM
!!! ??!! !!!!!!!
HASTY HARNESS HOW-TO
DANGER!!!!!! DON'T DO THIS WITHOUT HELP FROM EXPERT!
TIE LONG LOOP FROM STRAP
1. WRAP LOOP AROUND BACK BELOW ARMPITS AND BOOTY. EXTEND TWO EQUAL LENGTHS FORWARD.
2. PULL LOWER STRAP THROUGH LEGS AND OVER THOSE TWO EQUAL LENGTHS.
3. GUIDE EACH ARM THROUGH EACH EQUAL LENGTH AND CONNECT LENGTHS BEHIND BACK WITH ONE CARABINER.
4. TO FIT TIGHT, SECURE CARABINER AT FORWARD WAIST STRAP, TWIST TILL SNUG, THEN CLIP BACK INTO WAIST STRAP. ATTACH RESCUE ROPE, ETC., HERE TO WAIST CARABINER.
I'VE BEEN WATCHING THE ROAD SIGNS! HE'S ABOUT FORTY MILES FROM US--
OR EIGHTY-EIGHT ON THE ODOMETER. HELP ME WATCH FOR EIGHTY-EIGHT!
HATEY-HATE.
PUSH TO STAR
MPH 47
1049
THAT'S RIGHT! HATEY-HATE!

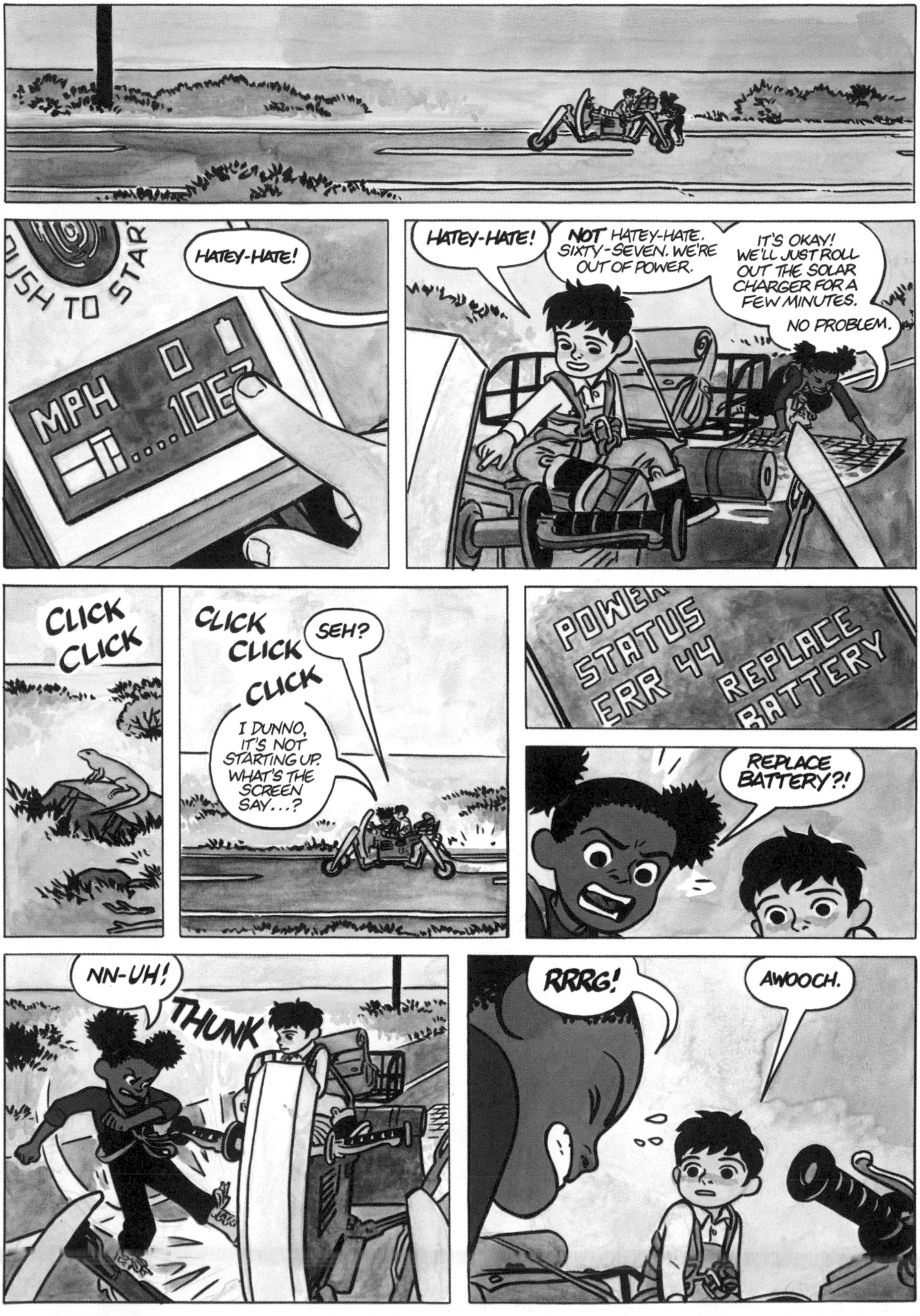
PUSH TO START
HATEY-HATE!
MPH 0
1067
HATEY-HATE!
NOT HATEY-HATE. SIXTY-SEVEN. WE'RE OUT OF POWER.
IT'S OKAY! WE'LL JUST ROLL OUT THE SOLAR CHARGER FOR A FEW MINUTES.
NO PROBLEM.
CLICK CLICK
CLICK CLICK CLICK
SEH?
I DUNNO, IT'S NOT STARTING UP. WHAT'S THE SCREEN SAY...?
POWER STATUS ERR 44 REPLACE BATTERY
REPLACE BATTERY?!
NN-UH!
THUNK
RRRG!
AWOOCH.

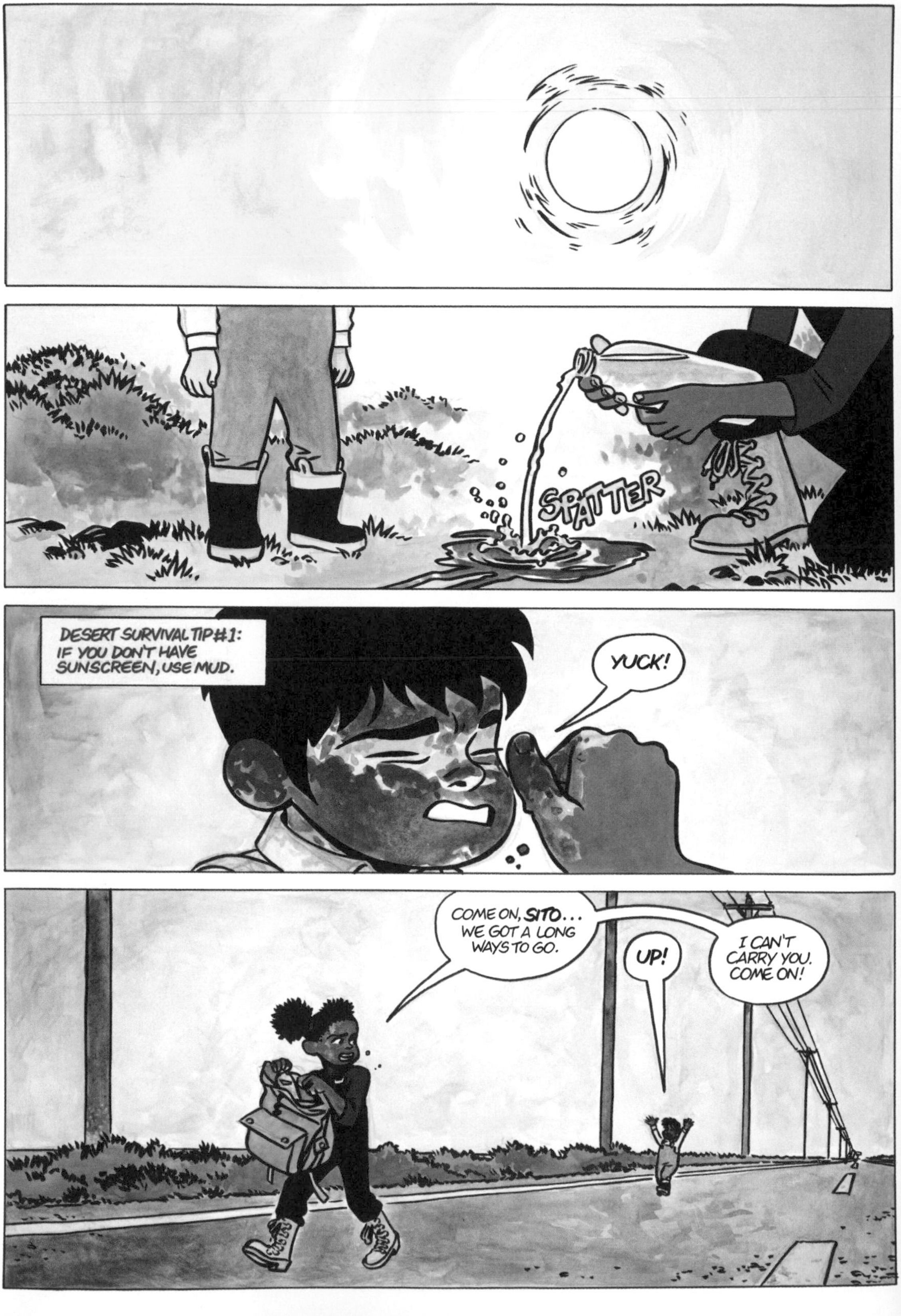
SPATTER
DESERT SURVIVAL TIP #1: IF YOU DON'T HAVE SUNSCREEN, USE MUD.
YUCK!
COME ON, **SITO**... WE GOT A LONG WAYS TO GO.
UP!
I CAN'T CARRY YOU. COME ON!

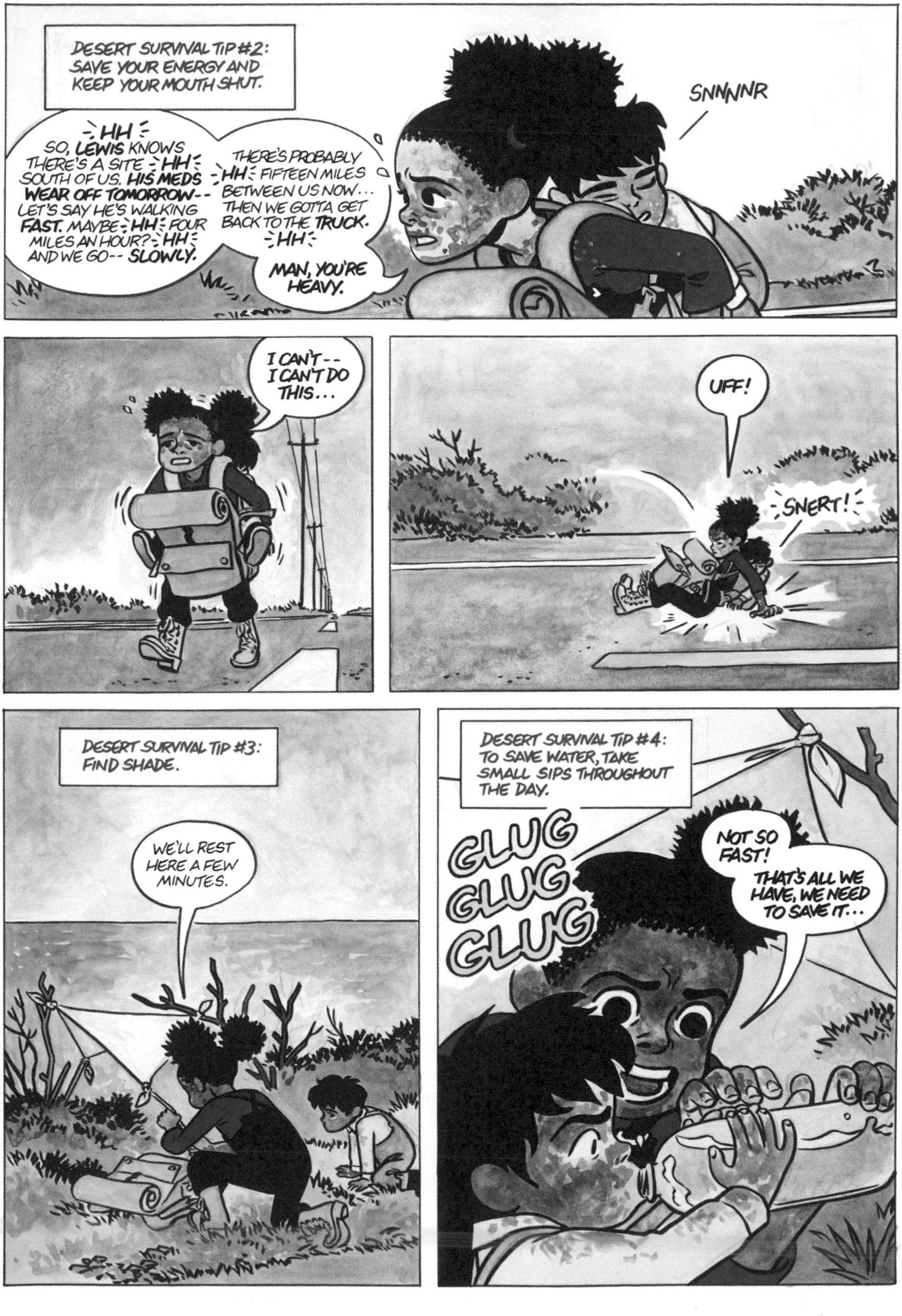

DESERT SURVIVAL TIP #2: SAVE YOUR ENERGY AND KEEP YOUR MOUTH SHUT.
-HH- SO, LEWIS KNOWS THERE'S A SITE -HH- SOUTH OF US. HIS MEDS WEAR OFF TOMORROW-- LET'S SAY HE'S WALKING FAST. MAYBE -HH- FOUR MILES AN HOUR? -HH- AND WE GO-- SLOWLY.
THERE'S PROBABLY -HH- FIFTEEN MILES BETWEEN US NOW... THEN WE GOTTA GET BACK TO THE TRUCK. -HH-
MAN, YOU'RE HEAVY.
SNNNNR
I CAN'T-- I CAN'T DO THIS...
UFF!
SNERT!
DESERT SURVIVAL TIP #3: FIND SHADE.
WE'LL REST HERE A FEW MINUTES.
DESERT SURVIVAL TIP #4: TO SAVE WATER, TAKE SMALL SIPS THROUGHOUT THE DAY.
GLUG GLUG GLUG
NOT SO FAST!
THAT'S ALL WE HAVE, WE NEED TO SAVE IT...

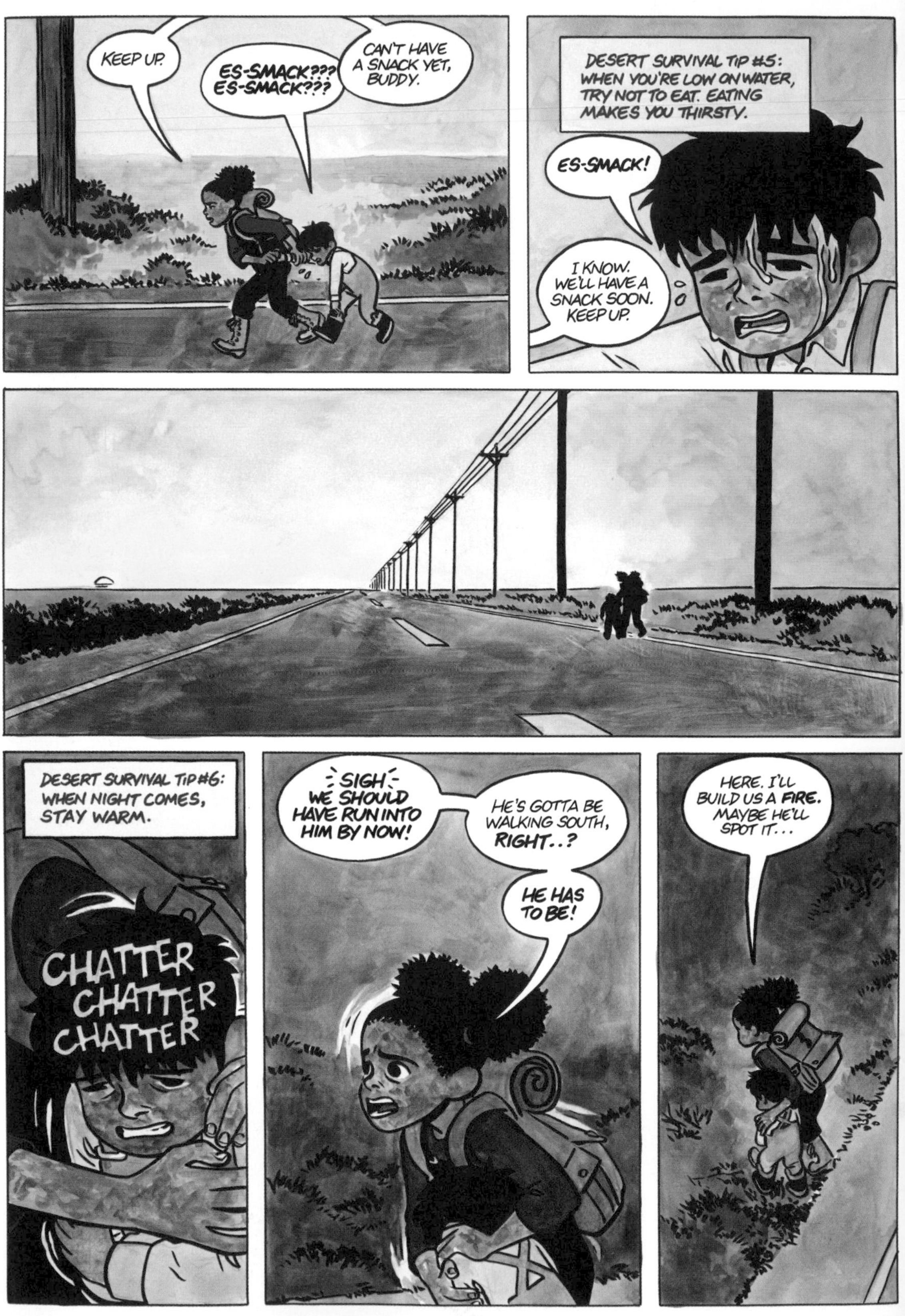
KEEP UP.
ES-SMACK??? ES-SMACK???
CAN'T HAVE A SNACK YET, BUDDY.
DESERT SURVIVAL TIP #5: WHEN YOU'RE LOW ON WATER, TRY NOT TO EAT. EATING MAKES YOU THIRSTY.
ES-SMACK!
I KNOW. WE'LL HAVE A SNACK SOON. KEEP UP.
DESERT SURVIVAL TIP #6: WHEN NIGHT COMES, STAY WARM.
CHATTER CHATTER CHATTER
SIGH
WE SHOULD HAVE RUN INTO HIM BY NOW!
HE'S GOTTA BE WALKING SOUTH, RIGHT..?
HE HAS TO BE!
HERE. I'LL BUILD US A FIRE. MAYBE HE'LL SPOT IT...

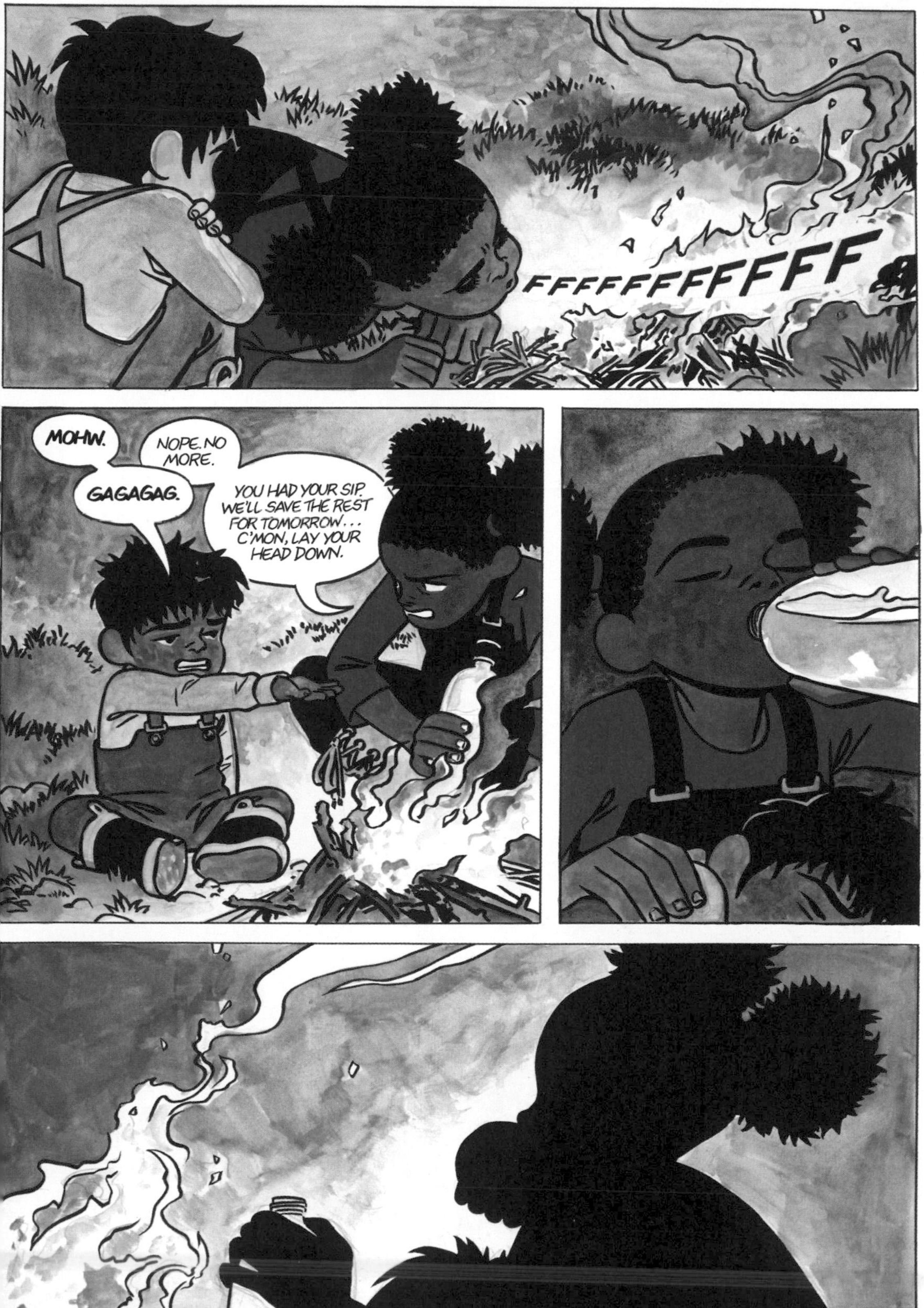
FFFFFFFFFFFFF
MOHW.
NOPE. NO MORE.
GAGAGAG.
YOU HAD YOUR SIP. WE'LL SAVE THE REST FOR TOMORROW... C'MON, LAY YOUR HEAD DOWN.

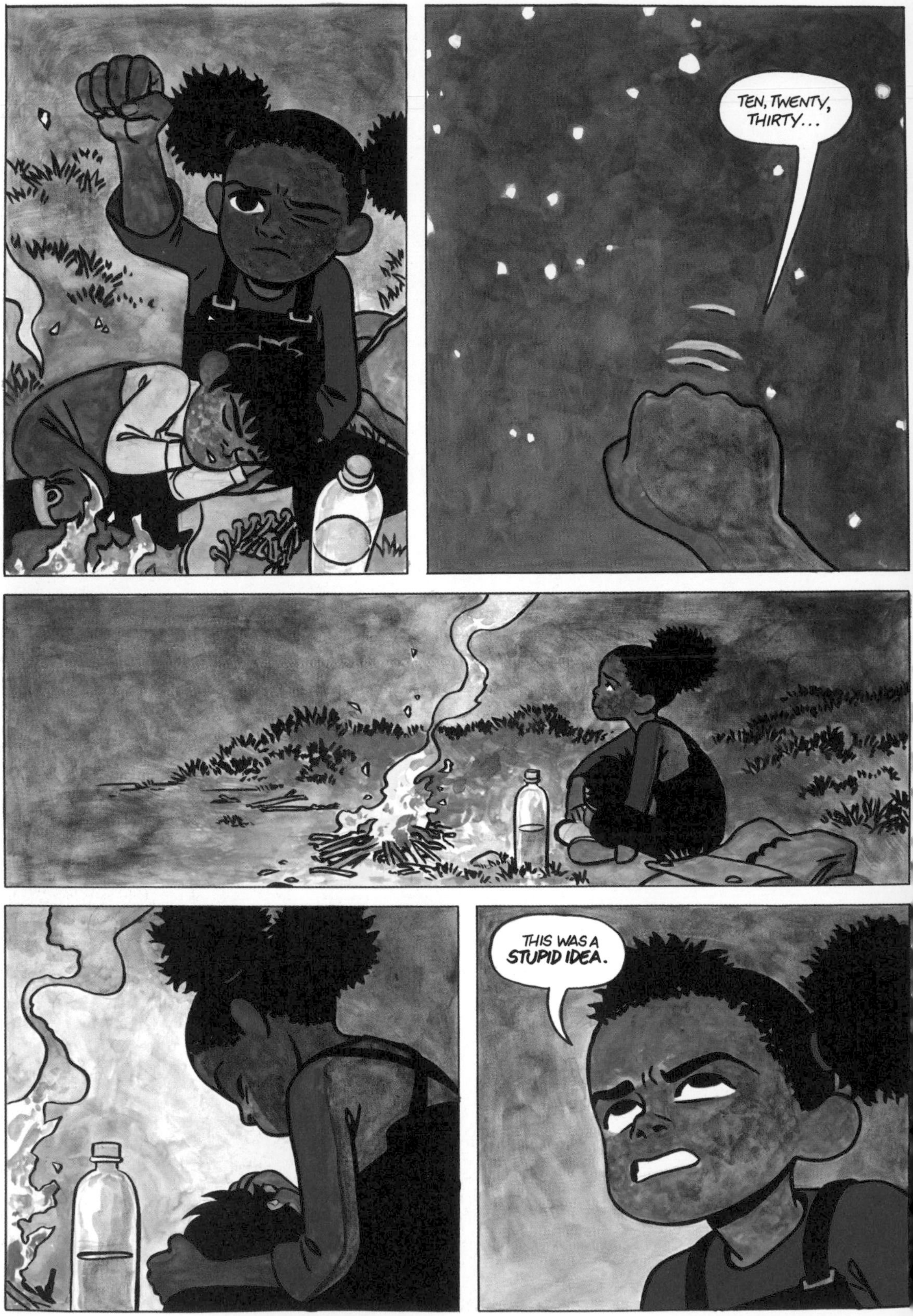
TEN, TWENTY, THIRTY...
THIS WAS A STUPID IDEA.

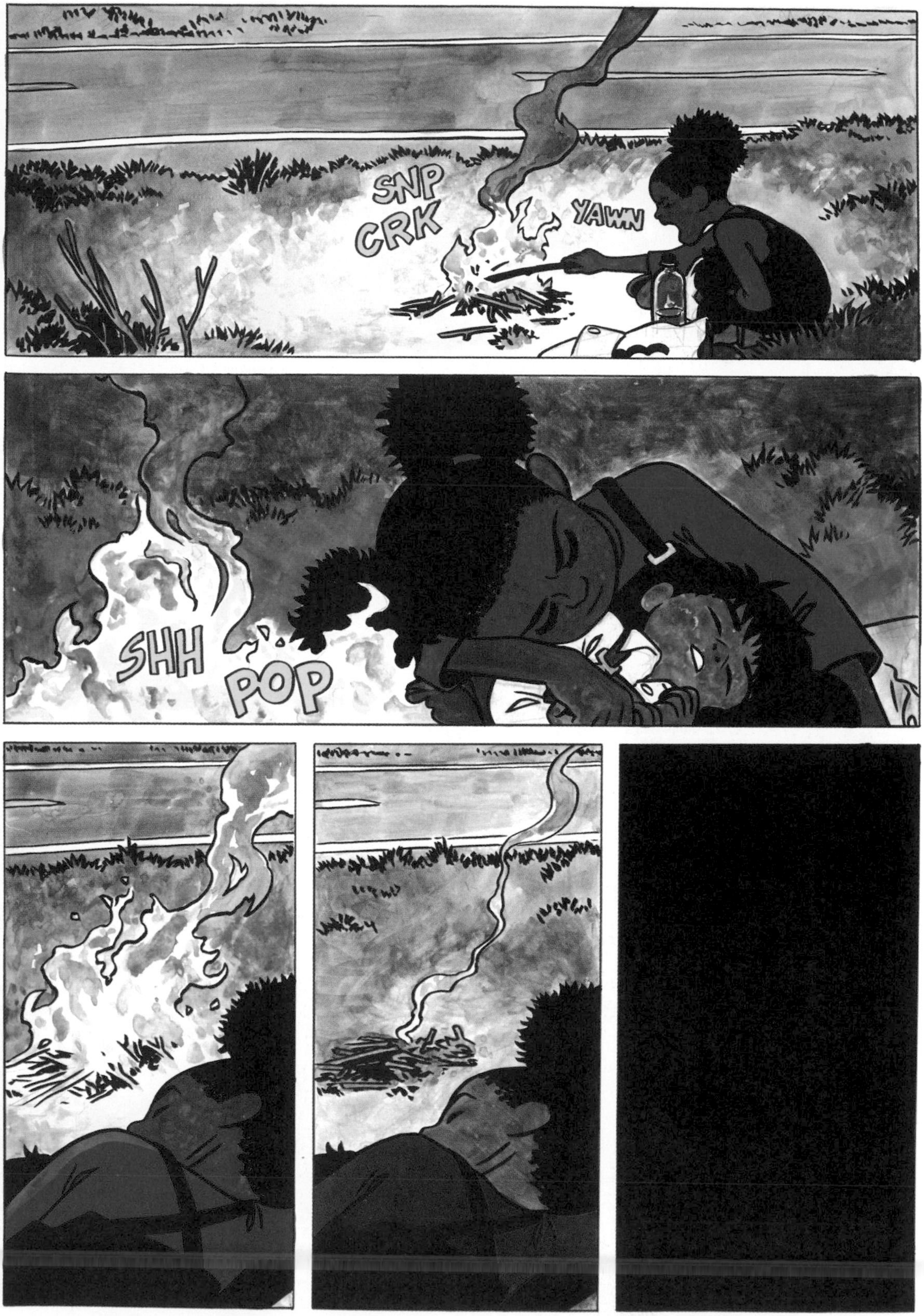
SNP
CRK
YAWN
SHH
POP

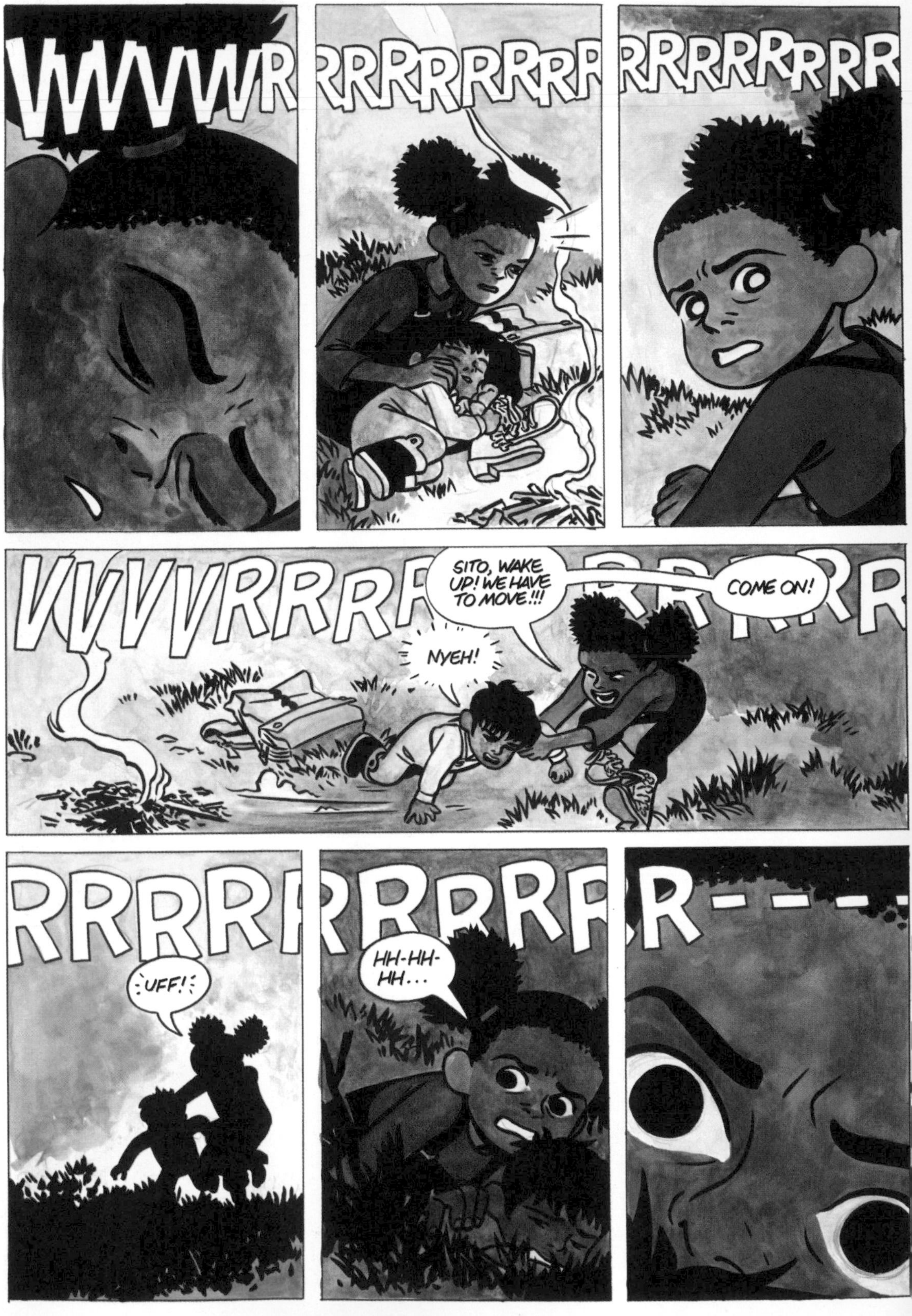
VVVVVVR
RRRRRRRR
RRRRRRRR
VVVVRRRR
SITO, WAKE UP! WE HAVE TO MOVE!!!
RRRRR
COME ON!
NYEH!
RRRRR
UFF!
RRRRR
HH-HH-HH...
R----

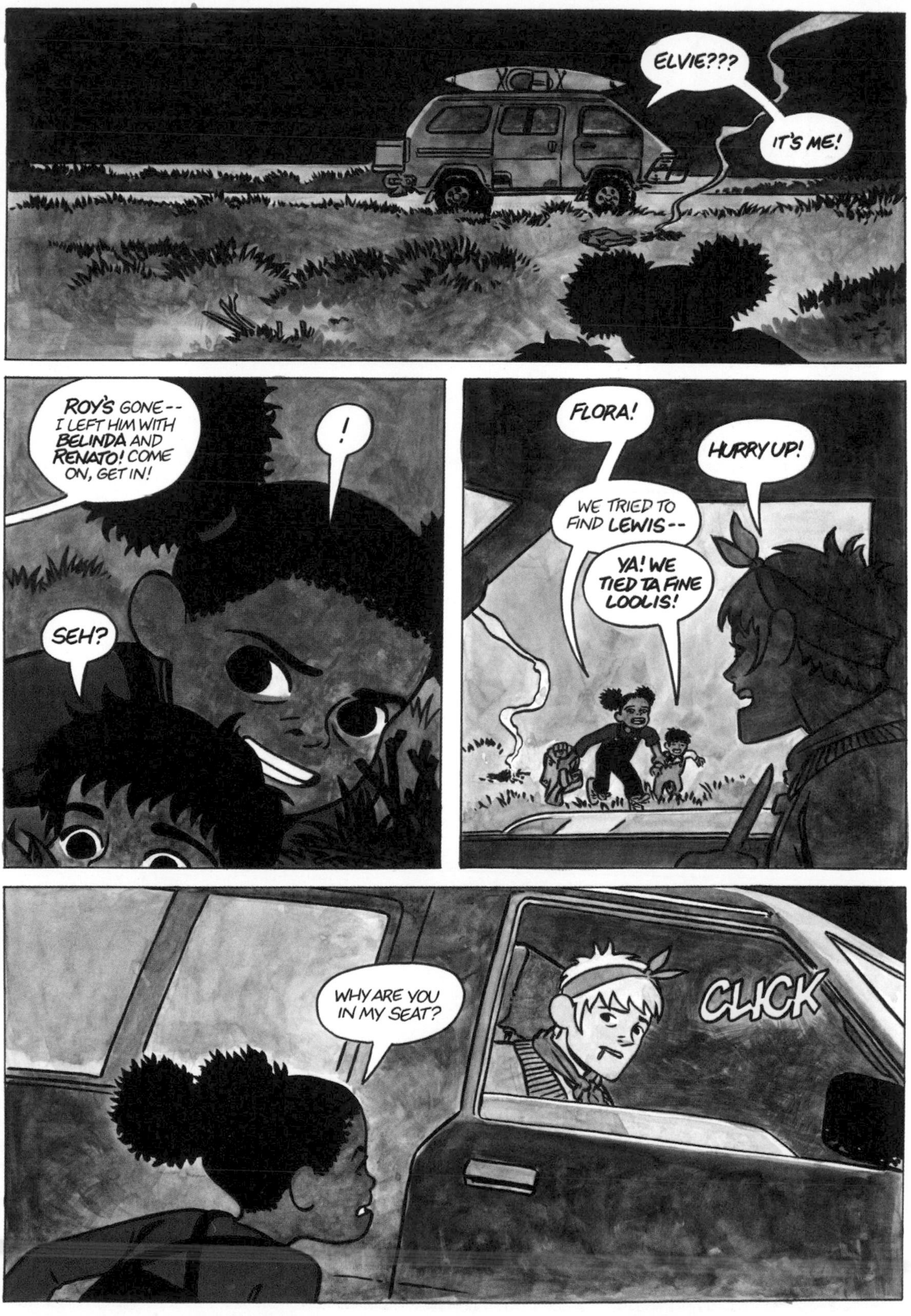
ELVIE???
IT'S ME!
ROY'S GONE-- I LEFT HIM WITH BELINDA AND RENATO! COME ON, GET IN!
!
SEH?
FLORA!
HURRY UP!
WE TRIED TO FIND LEWIS--
YA! WE TIED TA FINE LOOLIS!
WHY ARE YOU IN MY SEAT?
CLICK

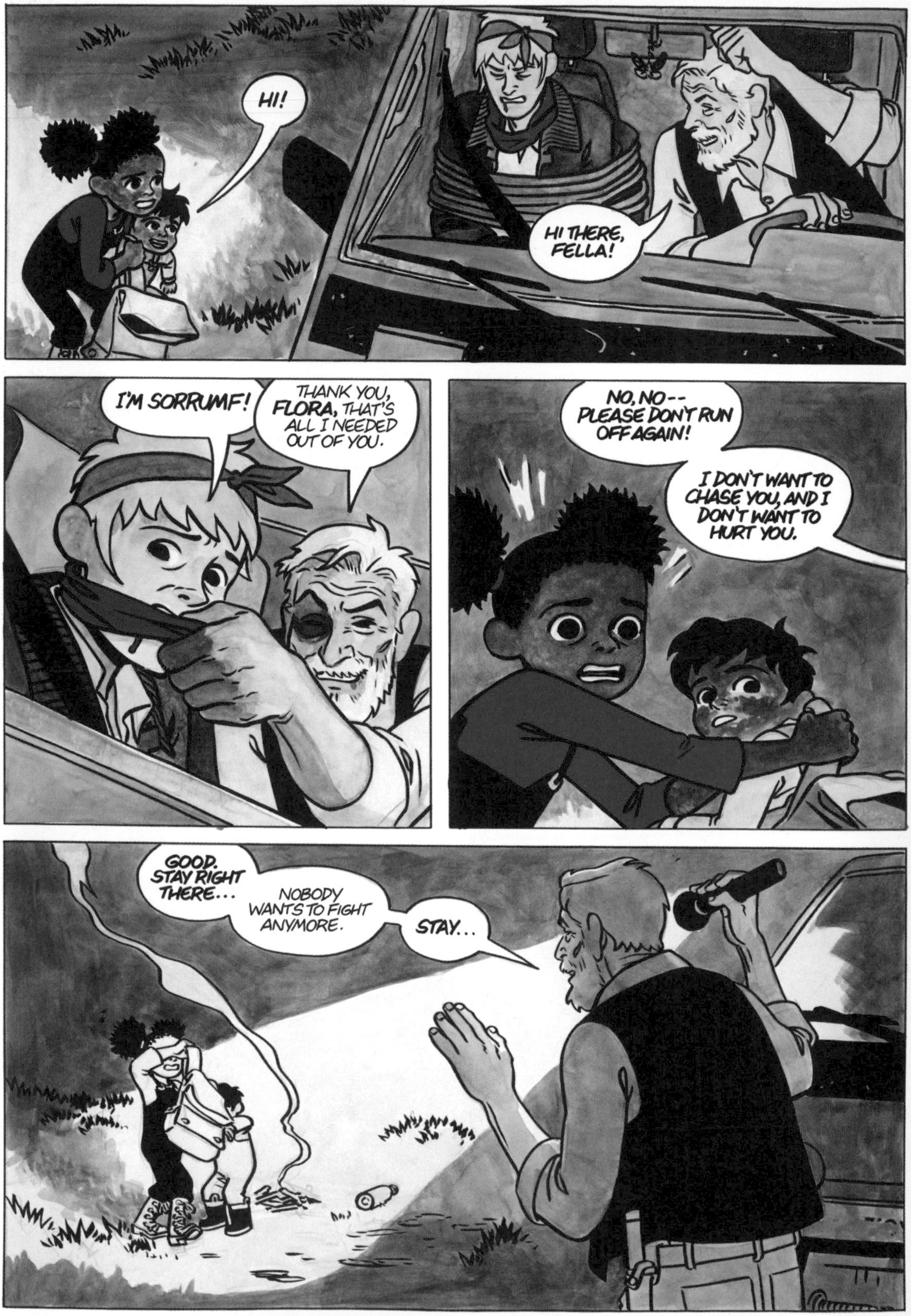
HI!
HI THERE, FELLA!
I'M SORRUMF!
THANK YOU, FLORA, THAT'S ALL I NEEDED OUT OF YOU.
NO, NO-- PLEASE DON'T RUN OFF AGAIN!
I DON'T WANT TO CHASE YOU, AND I DON'T WANT TO HURT YOU.
GOOD. STAY RIGHT THERE...
NOBODY WANTS TO FIGHT ANYMORE.
STAY...

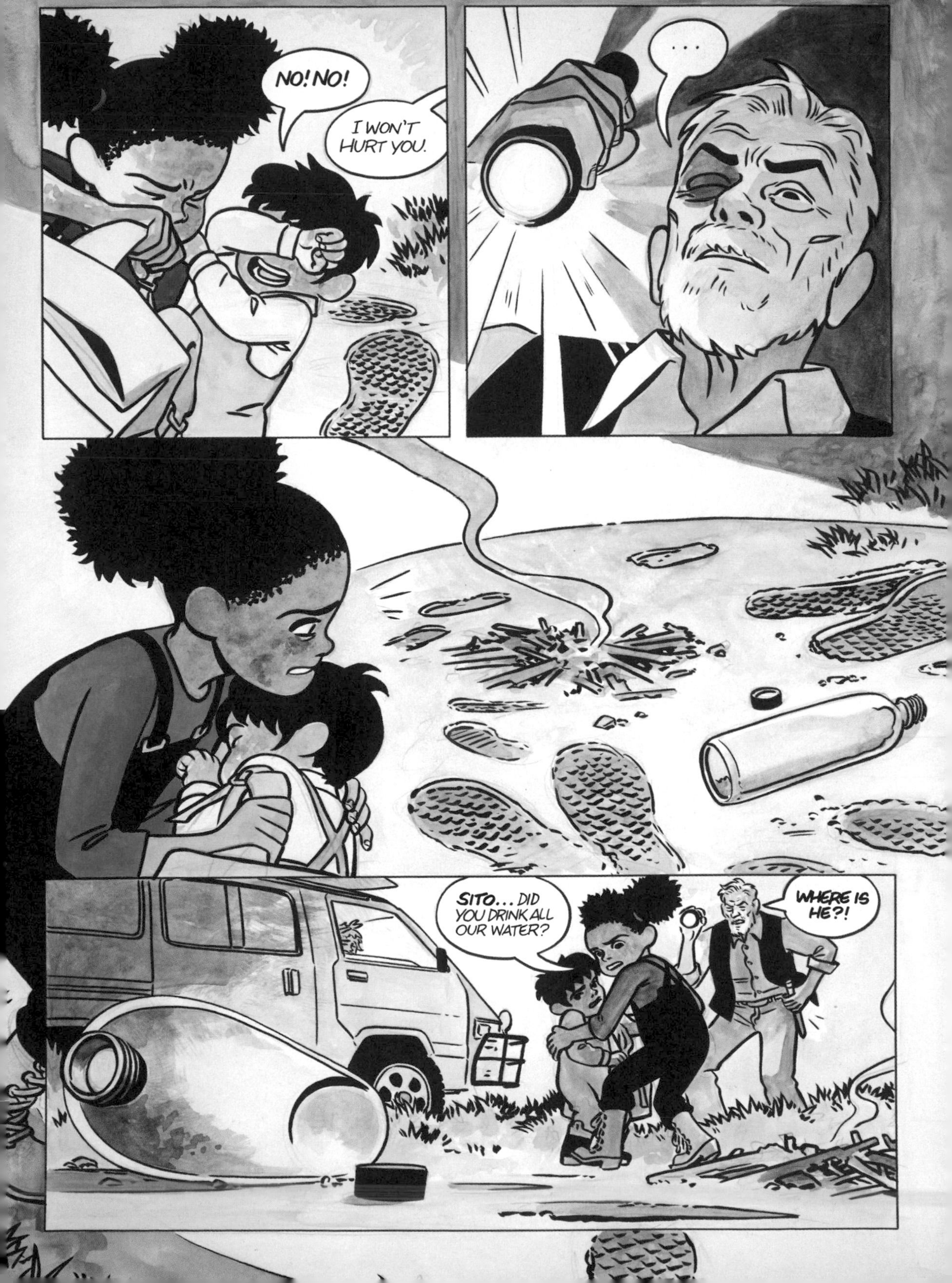
NO! NO!
I WON'T HURT YOU.
. . .
SITO... DID YOU DRINK ALL OUR WATER?
WHERE IS HE?!

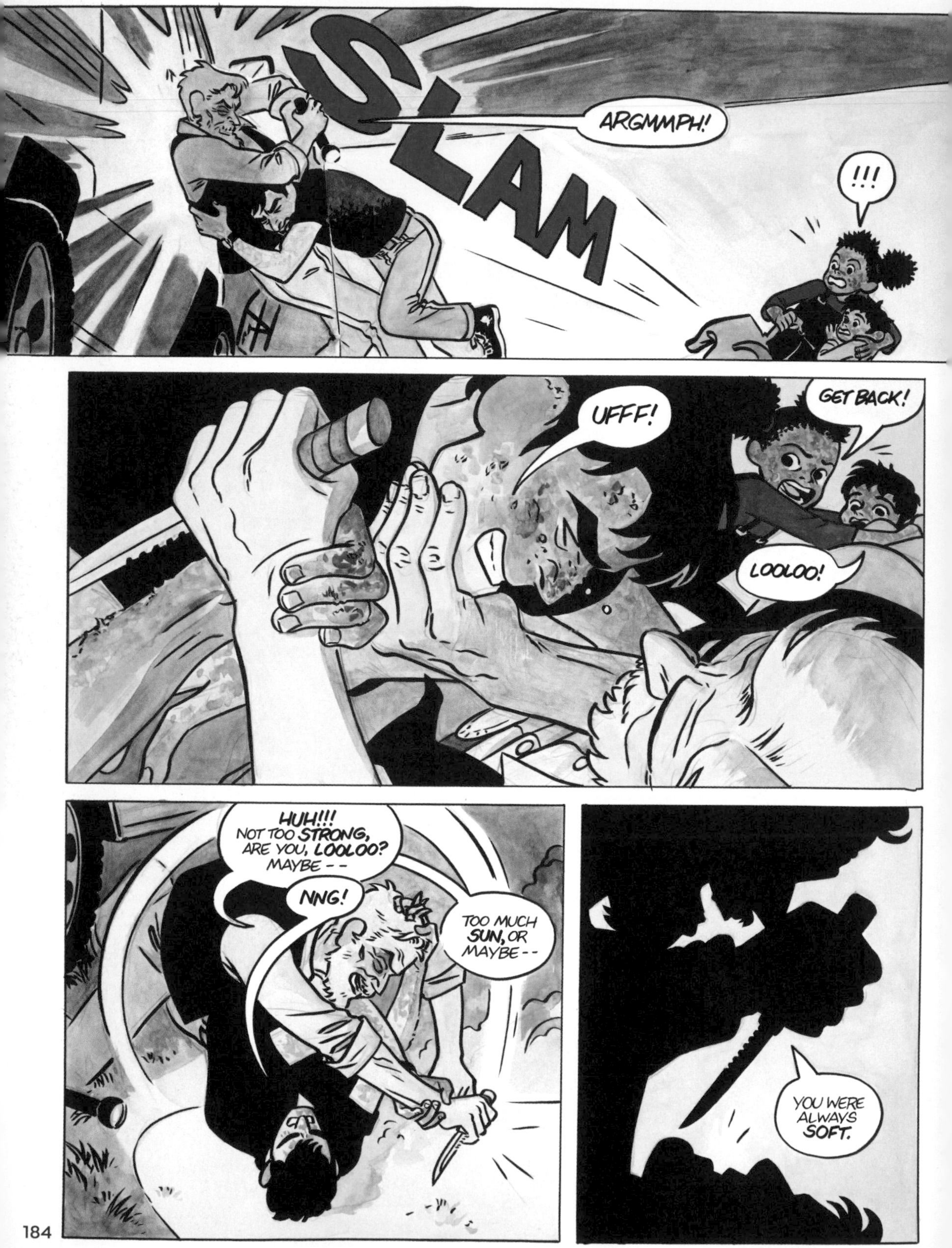
SLAM
ARGMMPH!
!!!
UFFF!
GET BACK!
LOOLOO!
HUH!!! NOT TOO STRONG, ARE YOU, LOOLOO? MAYBE --
NNG!
TOO MUCH SUN, OR MAYBE --
YOU WERE ALWAYS SOFT.

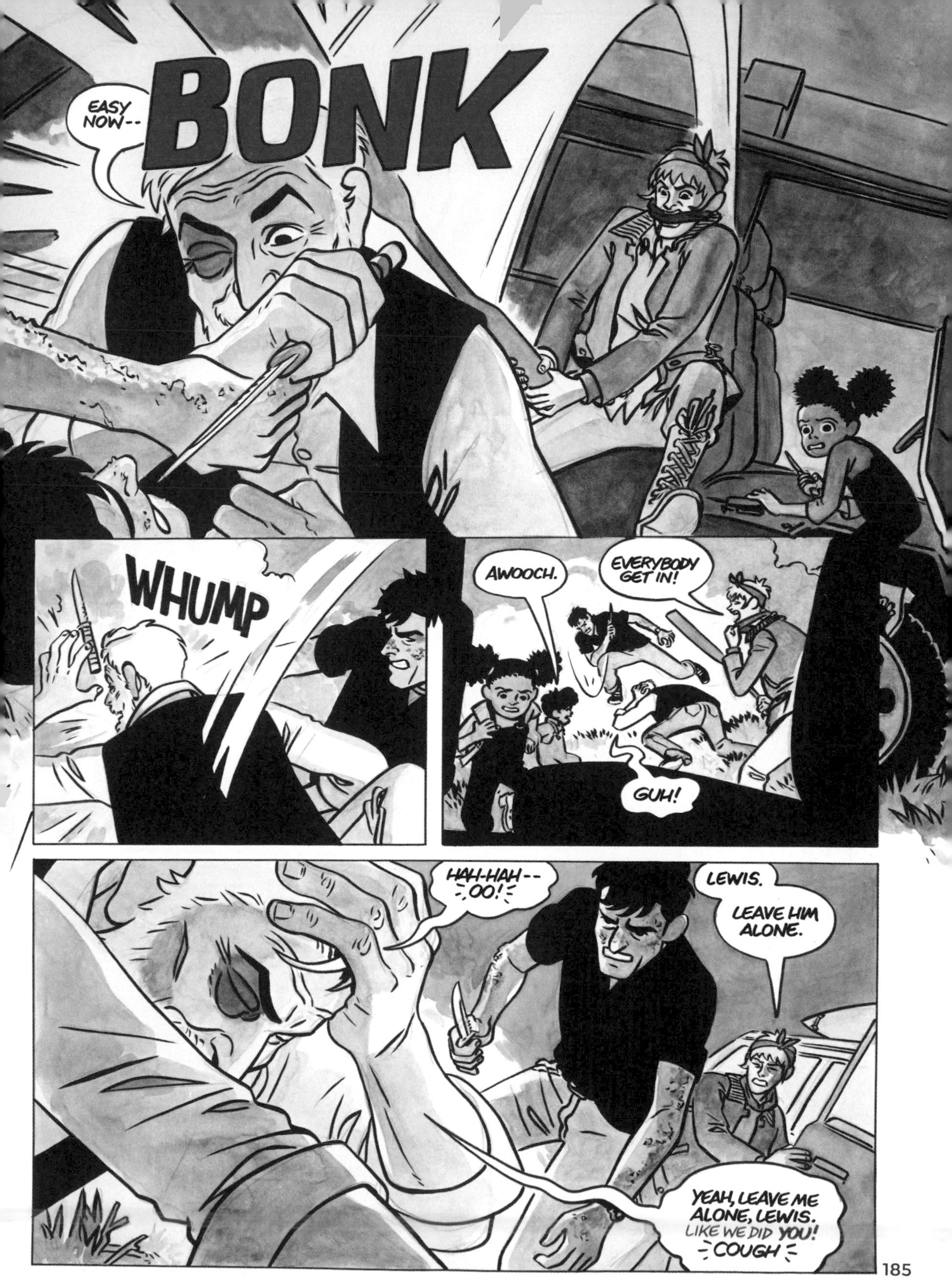
EASY NOW--
BONK
WHUMP
AWOOCH.
EVERYBODY GET IN!
GUH!
HAH-HAH--OO!
LEWIS.
LEAVE HIM ALONE.
YEAH, LEAVE ME ALONE, LEWIS. LIKE WE DID YOU! COUGH

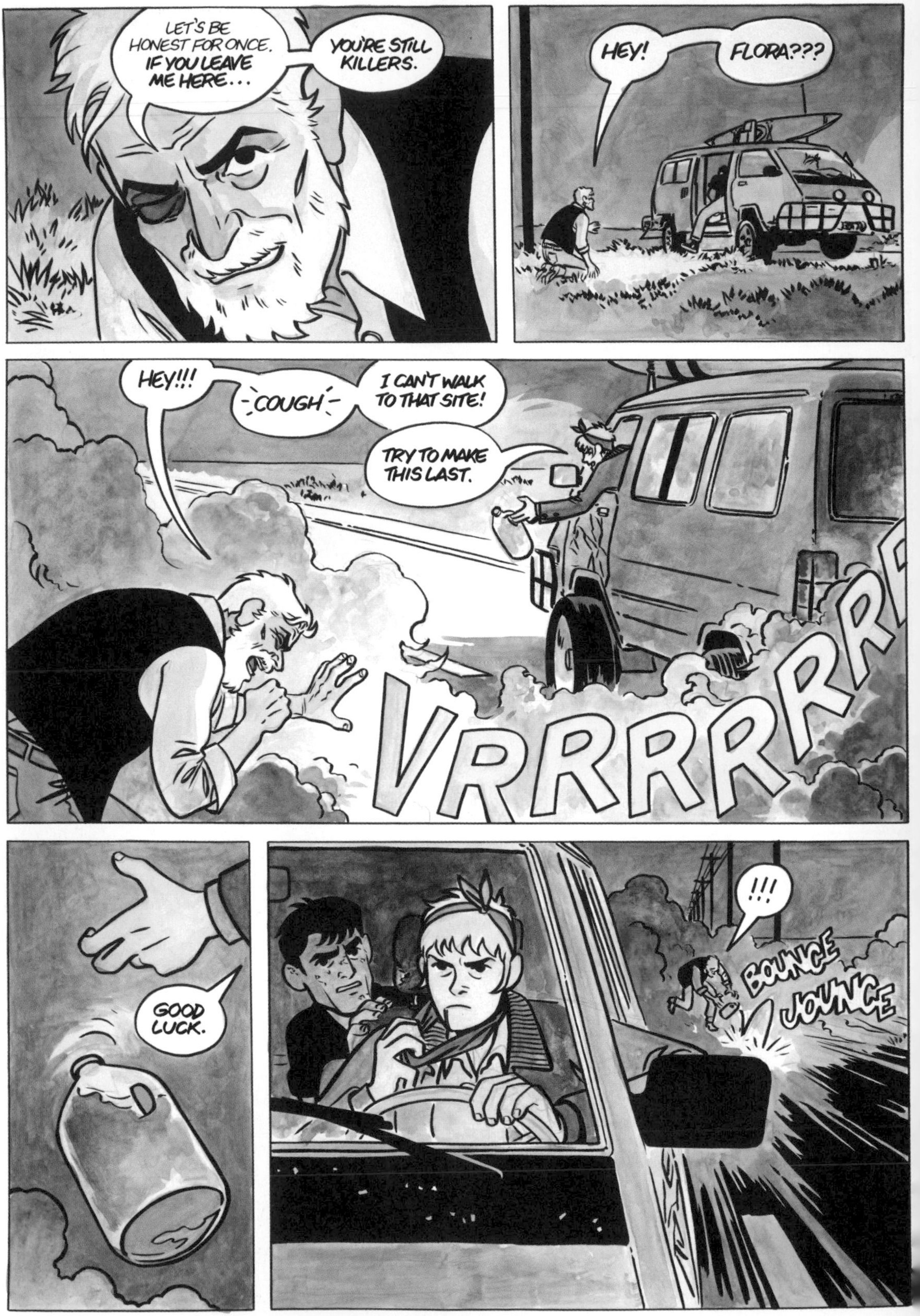
LET'S BE HONEST FOR ONCE. IF YOU LEAVE ME HERE...
YOU'RE STILL KILLERS.
HEY!
FLORA???
HEY!!!
-COUGH-
I CAN'T WALK TO THAT SITE!
TRY TO MAKE THIS LAST.
VRRRRRRRR
GOOD LUCK.
!!!
BOUNCE
JOUNCE

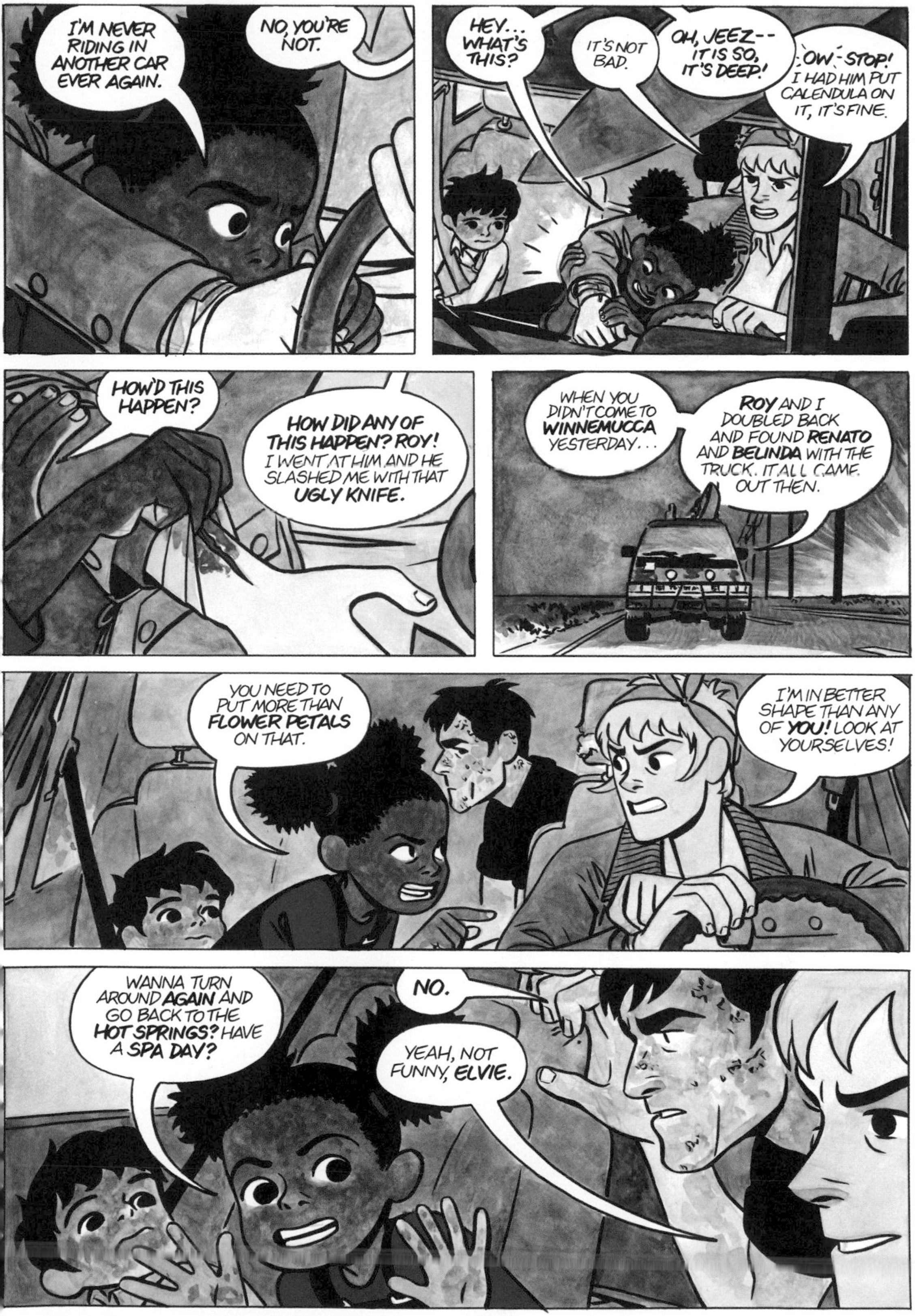
I'M NEVER RIDING IN ANOTHER CAR EVER AGAIN.
NO, YOU'RE NOT.
HEY... WHAT'S THIS?
IT'S NOT BAD.
OH, JEEZ-- IT IS SO, IT'S DEEP!
OW-STOP! I HAD HIM PUT CALENDULA ON IT, IT'S FINE.
HOW'D THIS HAPPEN?
HOW DID ANY OF THIS HAPPEN? ROY! I WENT AT HIM AND HE SLASHED ME WITH THAT UGLY KNIFE.
WHEN YOU DIDN'T COME TO WINNEMUCCA YESTERDAY...
ROY AND I DOUBLED BACK AND FOUND RENATO AND BELINDA WITH THE TRUCK. IT ALL CAME OUT THEN.
YOU NEED TO PUT MORE THAN FLOWER PETALS ON THAT.
I'M IN BETTER SHAPE THAN ANY OF YOU! LOOK AT YOURSELVES!
WANNA TURN AROUND AGAIN AND GO BACK TO THE HOT SPRINGS? HAVE A SPA DAY?
NO.
YEAH, NOT FUNNY, ELVIE.

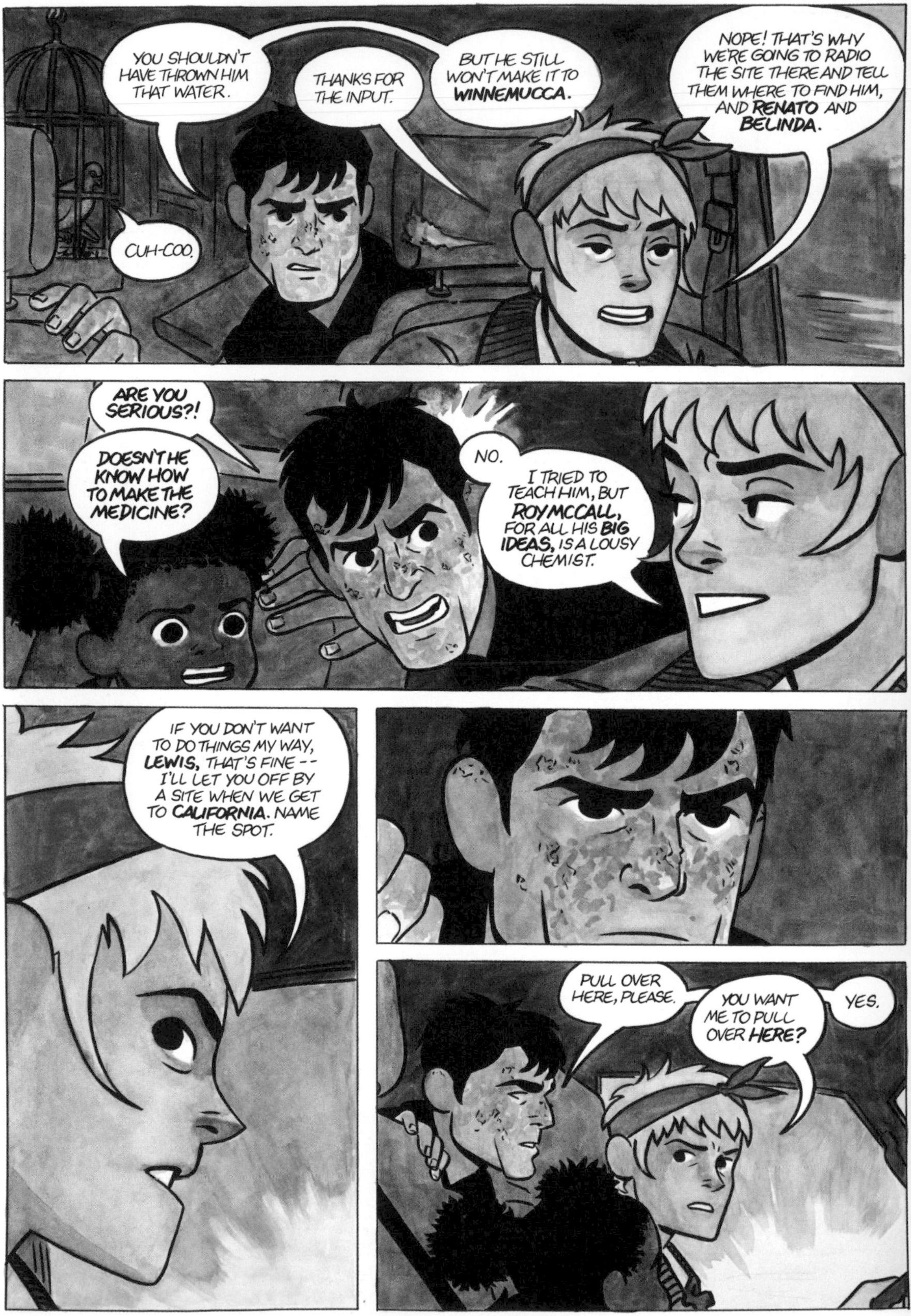
YOU SHOULDN'T HAVE THROWN HIM THAT WATER.
THANKS FOR THE INPUT.
BUT HE STILL WON'T MAKE IT TO WINNEMUCCA.
NOPE! THAT'S WHY WE'RE GOING TO RADIO THE SITE THERE AND TELL THEM WHERE TO FIND HIM, AND RENATO AND BELINDA.
CUH-COO.
ARE YOU SERIOUS?!
DOESN'T HE KNOW HOW TO MAKE THE MEDICINE?
NO.
I TRIED TO TEACH HIM, BUT ROY MCCALL, FOR ALL HIS BIG IDEAS, IS A LOUSY CHEMIST.
IF YOU DON'T WANT TO DO THINGS MY WAY, LEWIS, THAT'S FINE -- I'LL LET YOU OFF BY A SITE WHEN WE GET TO CALIFORNIA. NAME THE SPOT.
PULL OVER HERE, PLEASE.
YOU WANT ME TO PULL OVER HERE?
YES.

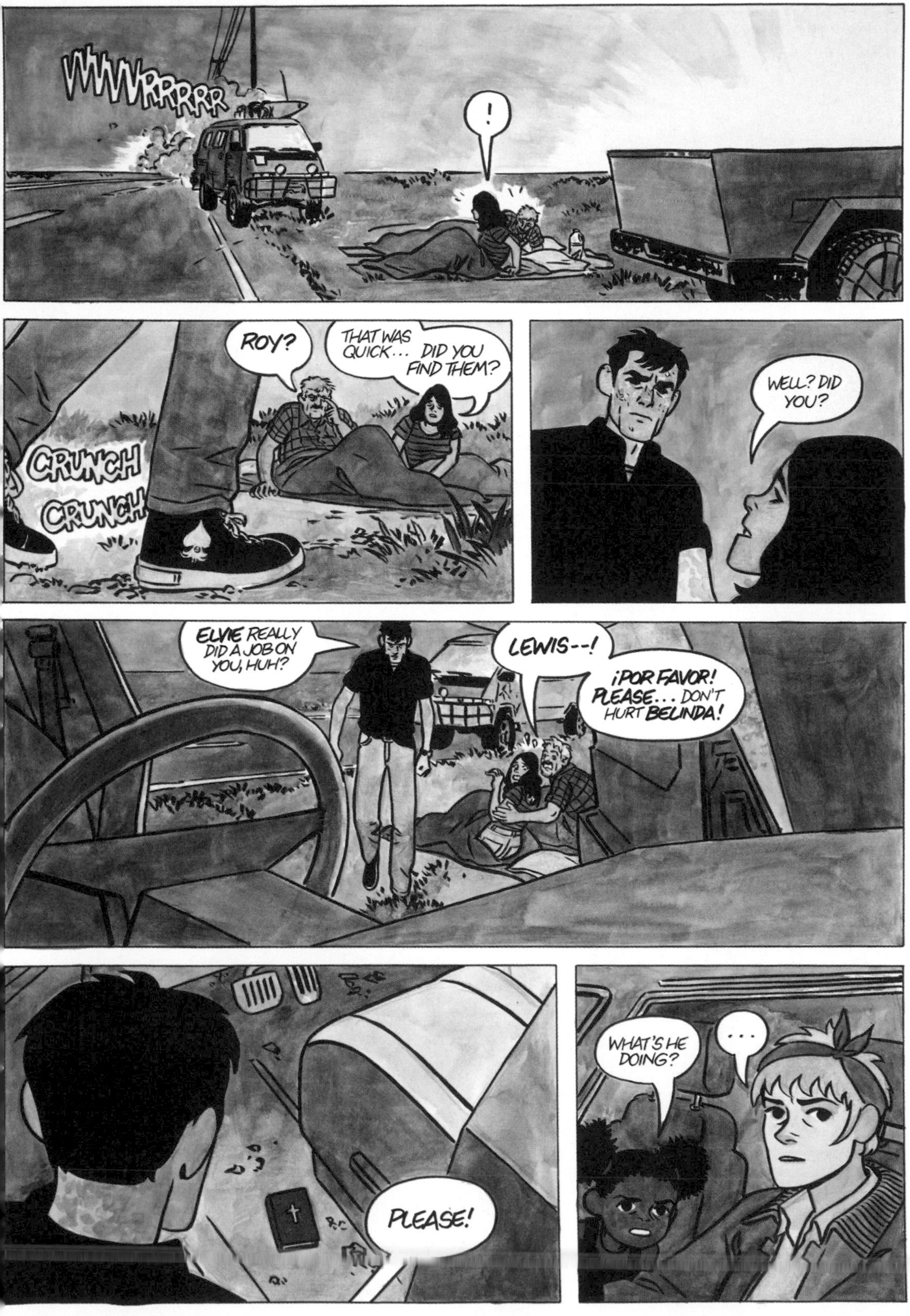
VVVVRRRRR
!
ROY?
THAT WAS QUICK... DID YOU FIND THEM?
CRUNCH
CRUNCH
WELL? DID YOU?
ELVIE REALLY DID A JOB ON YOU, HUH?
LEWIS--!
¡POR FAVOR! PLEASE... DON'T HURT BELINDA!
PLEASE!
WHAT'S HE DOING?
...

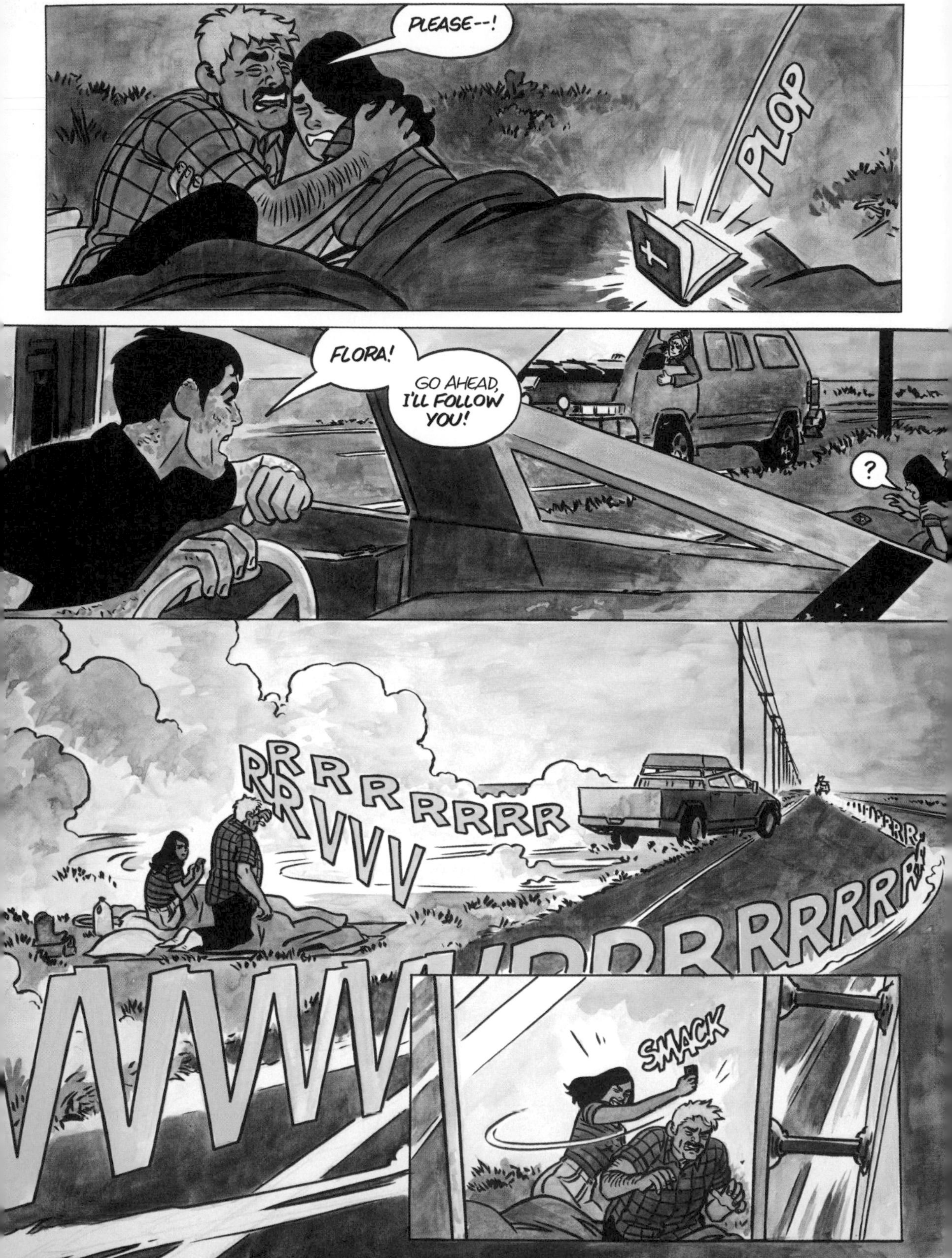
PLEASE--!
PLOP
FLORA!
GO AHEAD, I'LL FOLLOW YOU!
?
SMACK

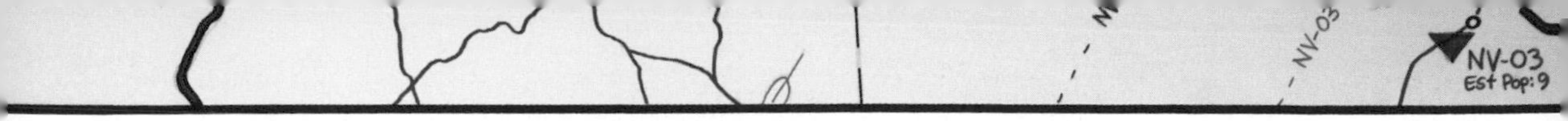
NV-03
Est Pop: 9

CHAPTER TEN
YOU'RE SICK

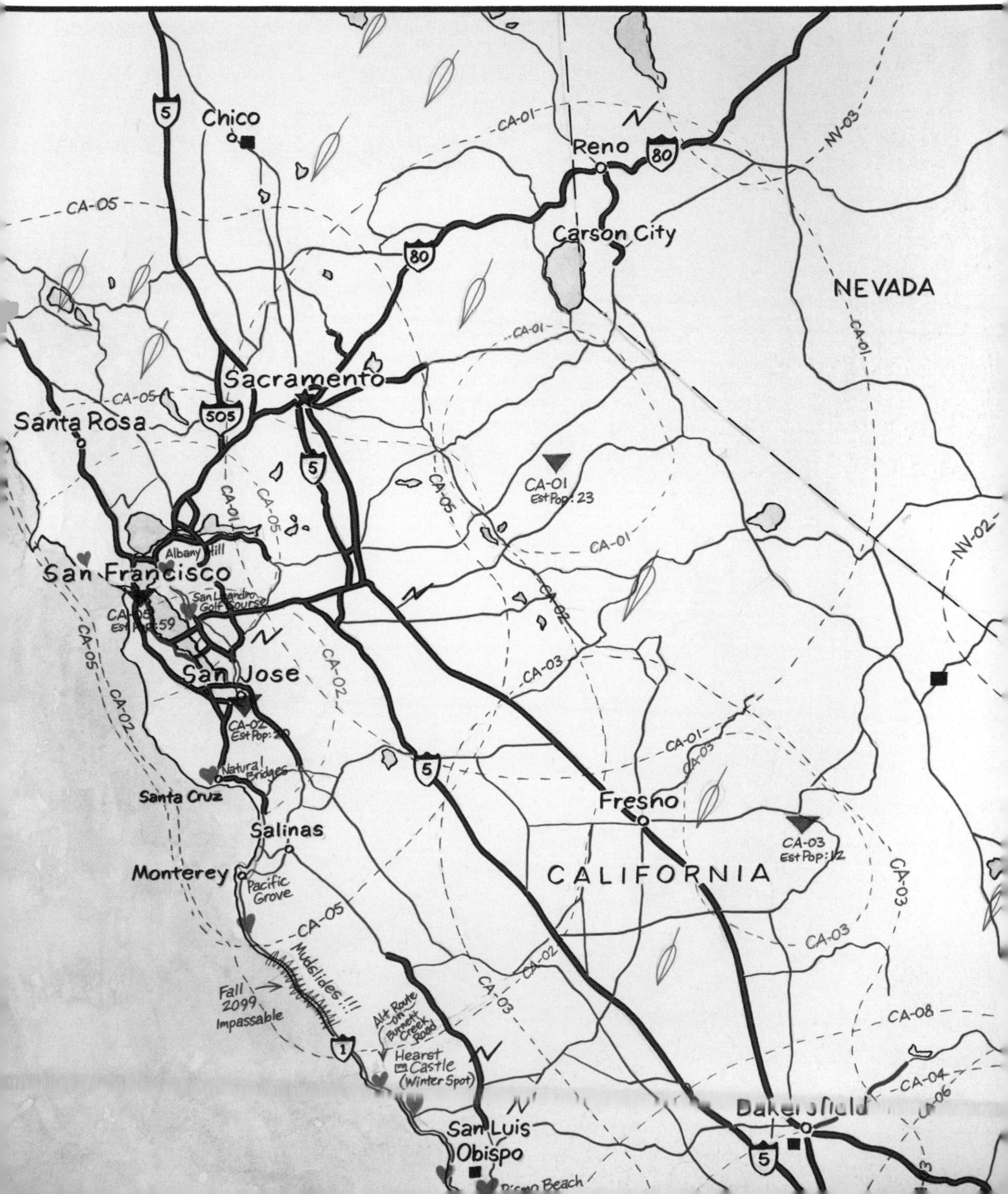
Chico
Reno
80
Carson City
NEVADA
CA-01
CA-05
Sacramento
505
Santa Rosa
5
CA-01
Est Pop: 23
Albany Hill
San Francisco
San Leandro Golf Course
San Jose
CA-02
Est Pop: 20
CA-02
CA-03
NV-02
NV-03
Natural Bridges
Santa Cruz
Salinas
Monterey
Pacific Grove
Fresno
CALIFORNIA
CA-03
Est Pop: 12
Mudslides!!!
Fall 2099
Impassable
Alt Route on Burnett Creek Road
Hearst Castle
(Winter Spot)
1
CA-08
CA-04
San Luis
Obispo
Pismo Beach

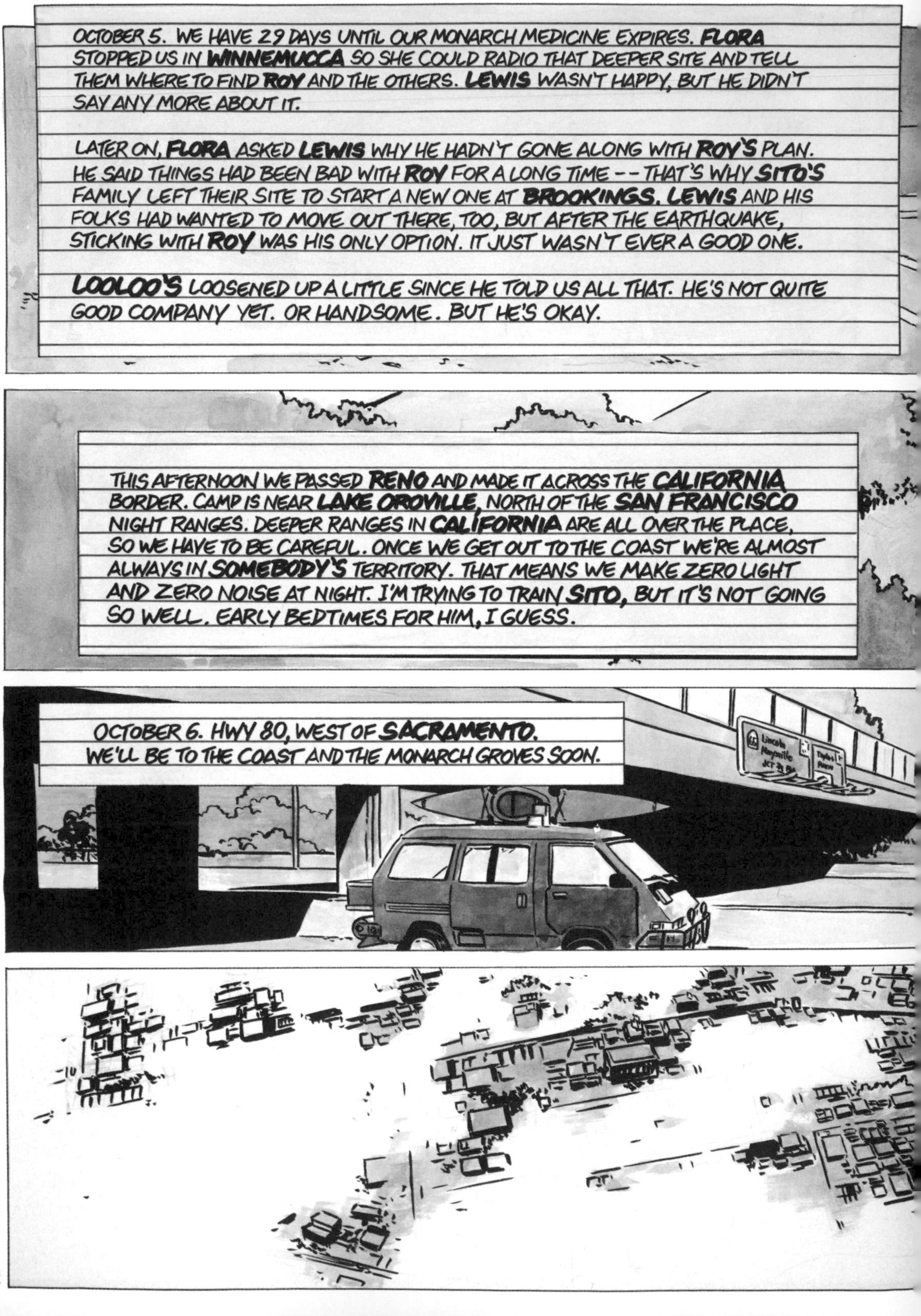
OCTOBER 5. WE HAVE 29 DAYS UNTIL OUR MONARCH MEDICINE EXPIRES. FLORA STOPPED US IN WINNEMUCCA SO SHE COULD RADIO THAT DEEPER SITE AND TELL THEM WHERE TO FIND ROY AND THE OTHERS. LEWIS WASN'T HAPPY, BUT HE DIDN'T SAY ANY MORE ABOUT IT.
LATER ON, FLORA ASKED LEWIS WHY HE HADN'T GONE ALONG WITH ROY'S PLAN. HE SAID THINGS HAD BEEN BAD WITH ROY FOR A LONG TIME -- THAT'S WHY SITO'S FAMILY LEFT THEIR SITE TO START A NEW ONE AT BROOKINGS. LEWIS AND HIS FOLKS HAD WANTED TO MOVE OUT THERE, TOO, BUT AFTER THE EARTHQUAKE, STICKING WITH ROY WAS HIS ONLY OPTION. IT JUST WASN'T EVER A GOOD ONE.
LOOLOO'S LOOSENED UP A LITTLE SINCE HE TOLD US ALL THAT. HE'S NOT QUITE GOOD COMPANY YET. OR HANDSOME. BUT HE'S OKAY.
THIS AFTERNOON WE PASSED RENO AND MADE IT ACROSS THE CALIFORNIA BORDER. CAMP IS NEAR LAKE OROVILLE, NORTH OF THE SAN FRANCISCO NIGHT RANGES. DEEPER RANGES IN CALIFORNIA ARE ALL OVER THE PLACE, SO WE HAVE TO BE CAREFUL. ONCE WE GET OUT TO THE COAST WE'RE ALMOST ALWAYS IN SOMEBODY'S TERRITORY. THAT MEANS WE MAKE ZERO LIGHT AND ZERO NOISE AT NIGHT. I'M TRYING TO TRAIN SITO, BUT IT'S NOT GOING SO WELL. EARLY BEDTIMES FOR HIM, I GUESS.
OCTOBER 6. HWY 80, WEST OF SACRAMENTO. WE'LL BE TO THE COAST AND THE MONARCH GROVES SOON.

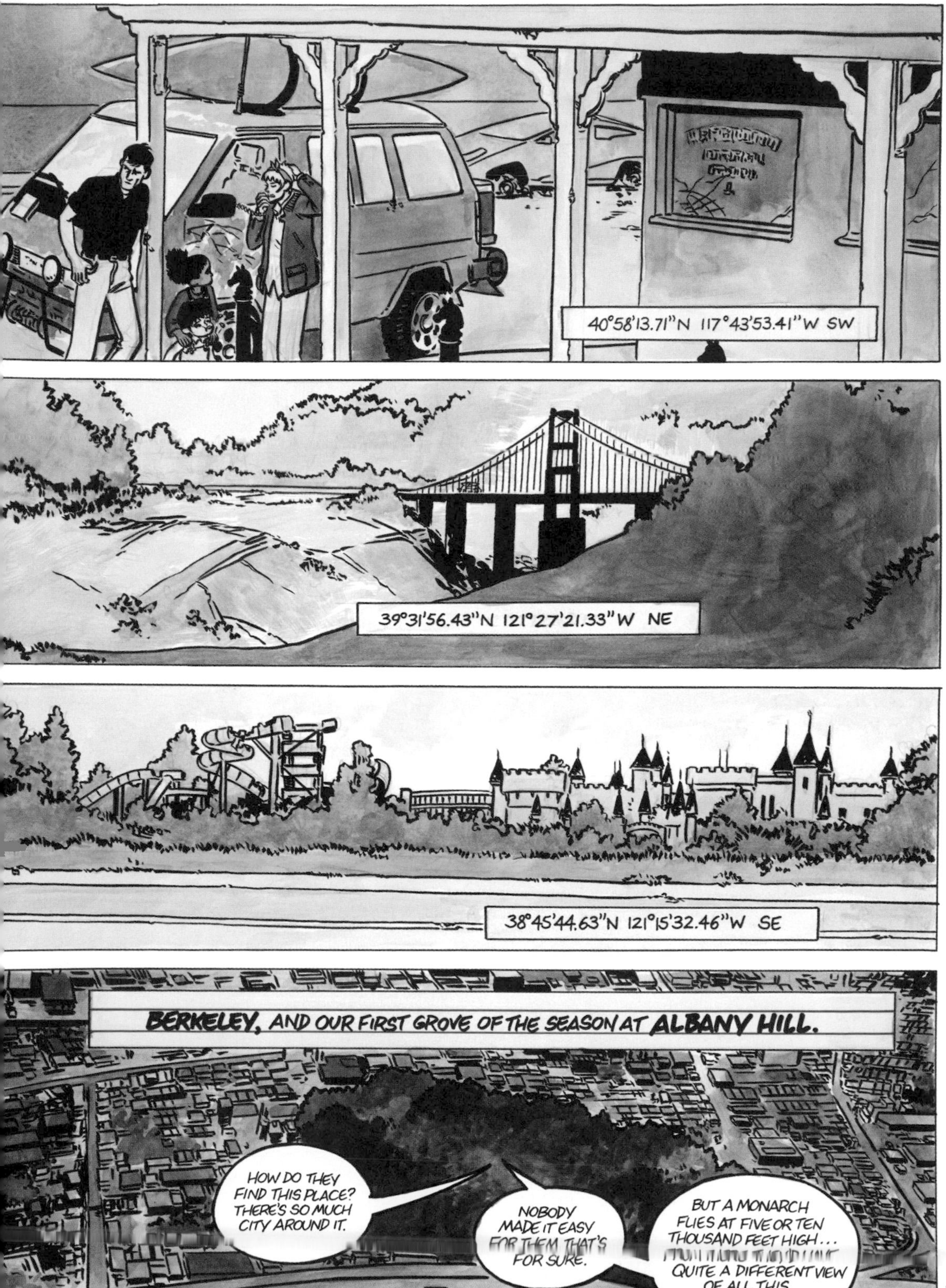
40°58'13.71"N 117°43'53.41"W SW
39°31'56.43"N 121°27'21.33"W NE
38°45'44.63"N 121°15'32.46"W SE
BERKELEY, AND OUR FIRST GROVE OF THE SEASON AT ALBANY HILL.
HOW DO THEY FIND THIS PLACE? THERE'S SO MUCH CITY AROUND IT.
NOBODY MADE IT EASY FOR THEM THAT'S FOR SURE.
BUT A MONARCH FLIES AT FIVE OR TEN THOUSAND FEET HIGH...
QUITE A DIFFERENT VIEW OF ALL THIS.

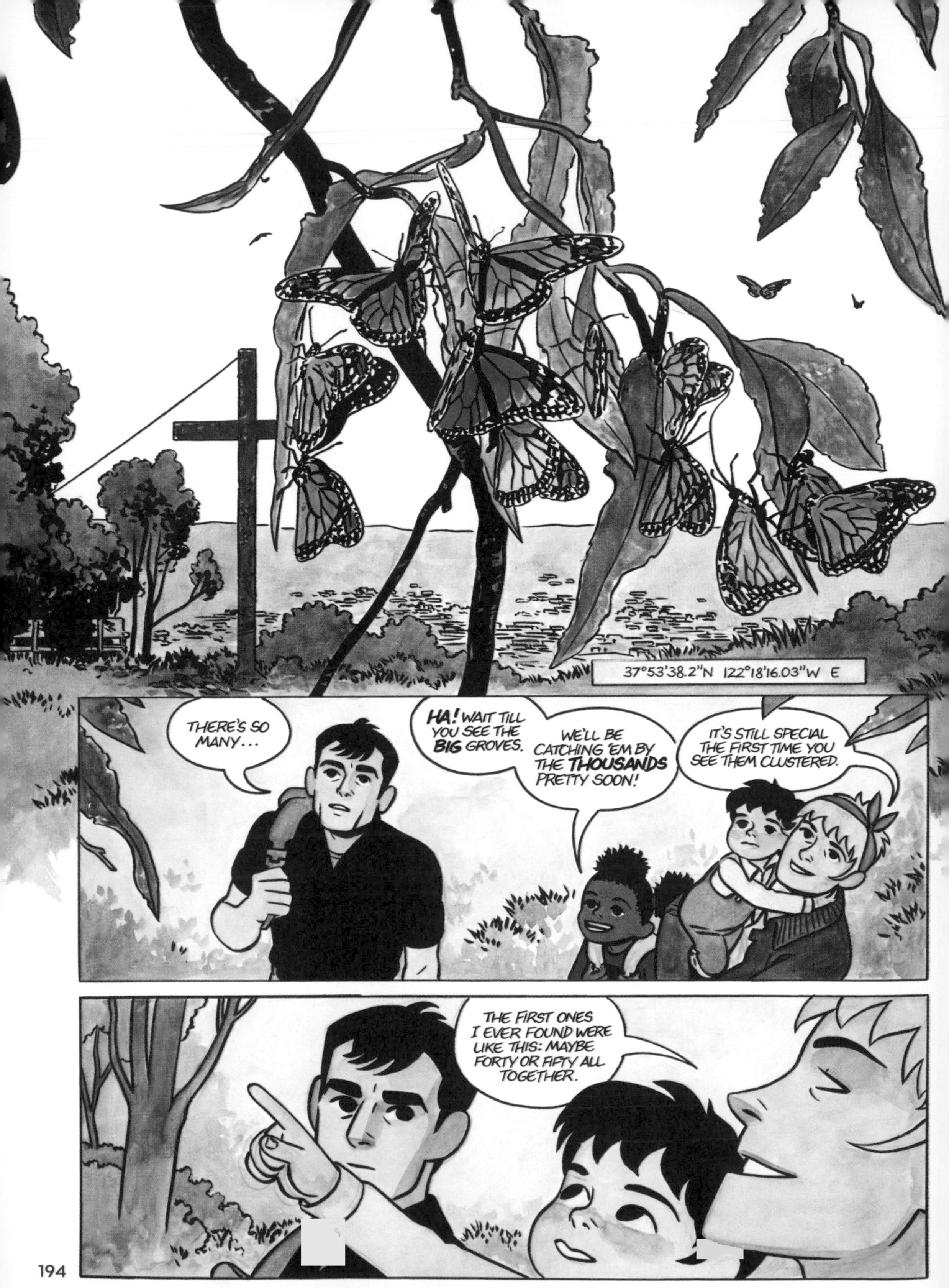
37°53'38.2"N 122°18'16.03"W E
THERE'S SO MANY...
HA! WAIT TILL YOU SEE THE BIG GROVES.
WE'LL BE CATCHING 'EM BY THE THOUSANDS PRETTY SOON!
IT'S STILL SPECIAL THE FIRST TIME YOU SEE THEM CLUSTERED.
THE FIRST ONES I EVER FOUND WERE LIKE THIS: MAYBE FORTY OR FIFTY ALL TOGETHER.

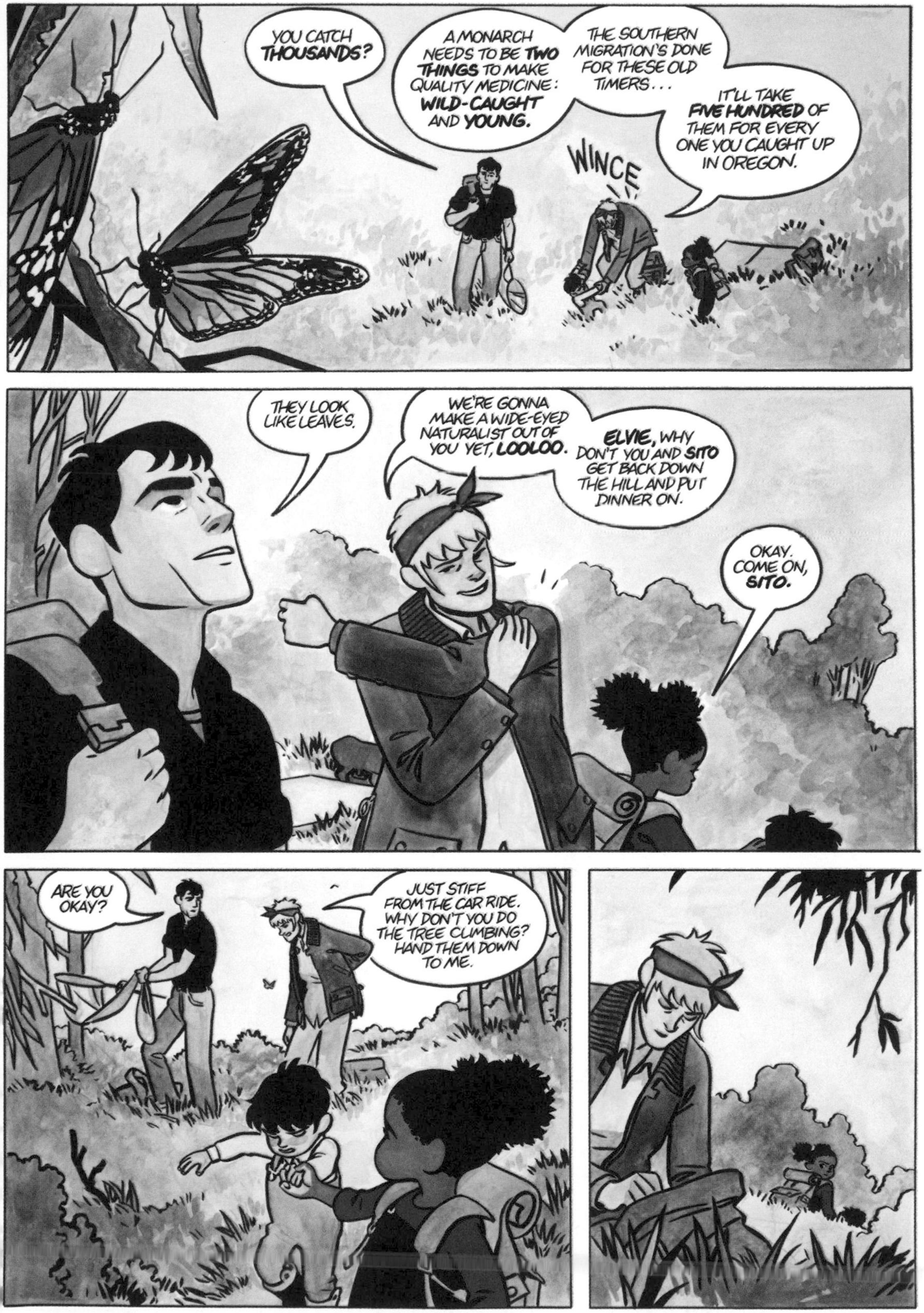
YOU CATCH THOUSANDS?
A MONARCH NEEDS TO BE TWO THINGS TO MAKE QUALITY MEDICINE: WILD-CAUGHT AND YOUNG.
THE SOUTHERN MIGRATION'S DONE FOR THESE OLD TIMERS...
IT'LL TAKE FIVE HUNDRED OF THEM FOR EVERY ONE YOU CAUGHT UP IN OREGON.
WINCE
THEY LOOK LIKE LEAVES.
WE'RE GONNA MAKE A WIDE-EYED NATURALIST OUT OF YOU YET, LOOLOO.
ELVIE, WHY DON'T YOU AND SITO GET BACK DOWN THE HILL AND PUT DINNER ON.
OKAY. COME ON, SITO.
ARE YOU OKAY?
JUST STIFF FROM THE CAR RIDE. WHY DON'T YOU DO THE TREE CLIMBING? HAND THEM DOWN TO ME.

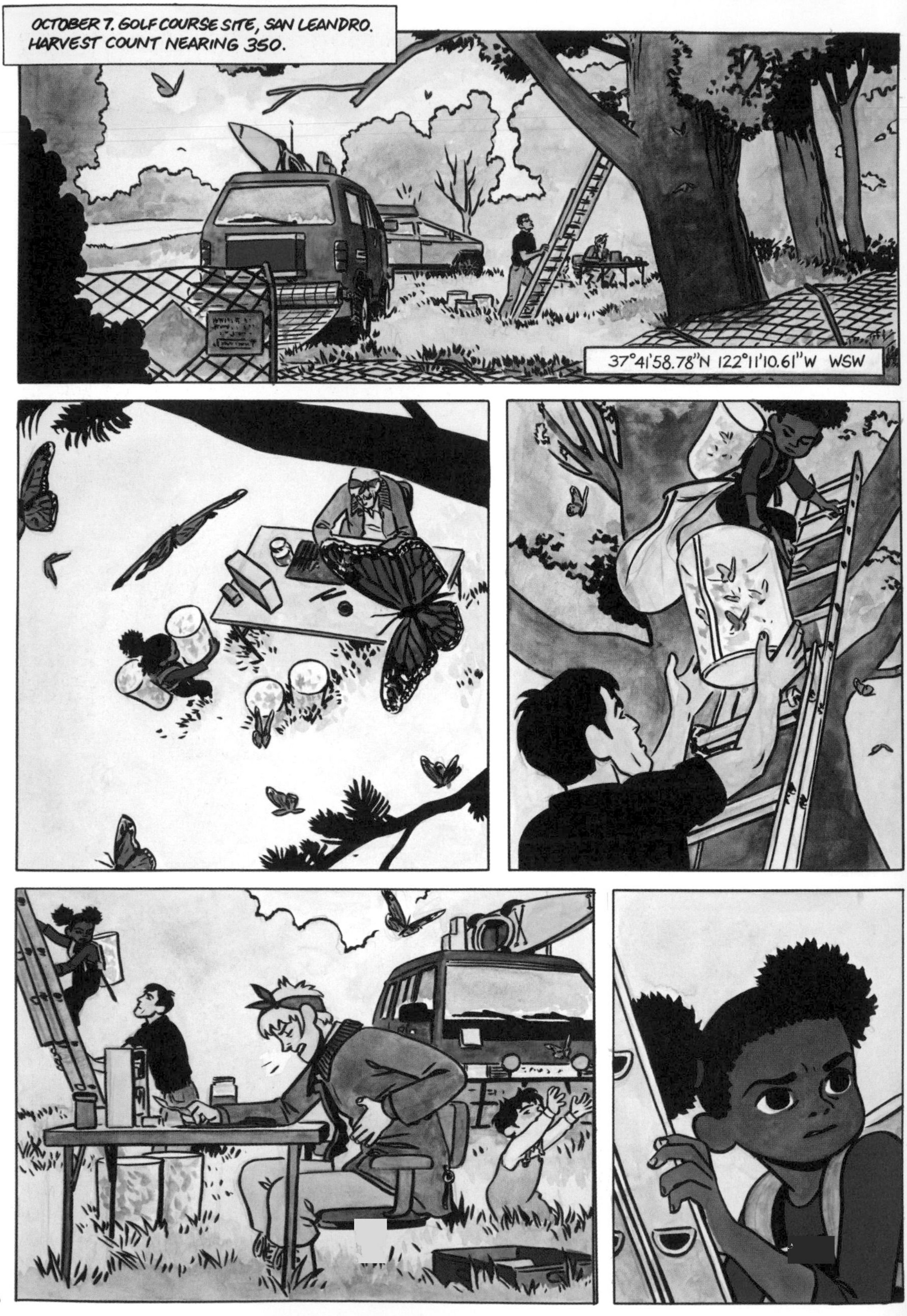
OCTOBER 7. GOLF COURSE SITE, SAN LEANDRO.
HARVEST COUNT NEARING 350.
37°41'58.78"N 122°11'10.61"W WSW

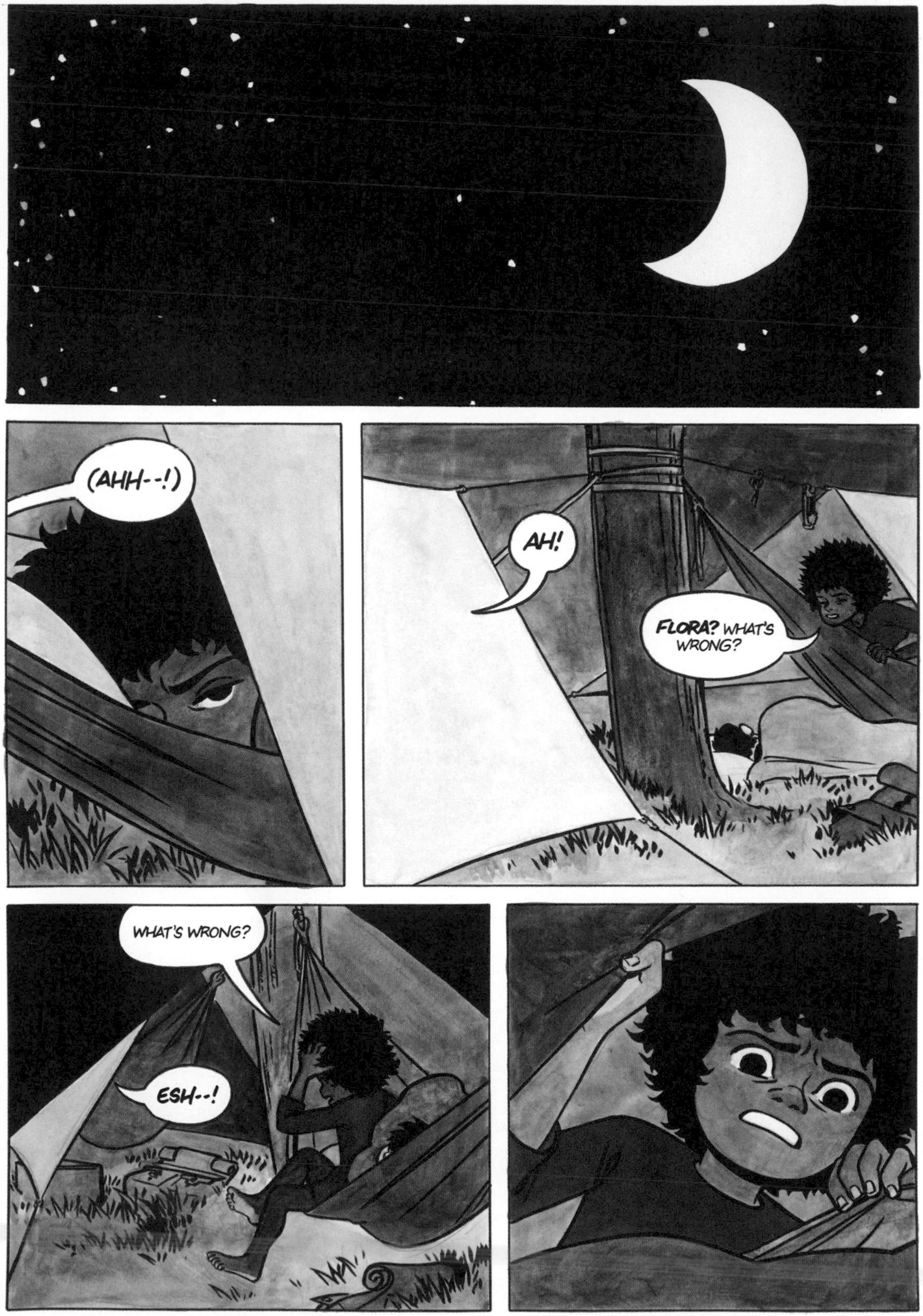
(AHH--!)
AH!
FLORA? WHAT'S WRONG?
WHAT'S WRONG?
ESH--!

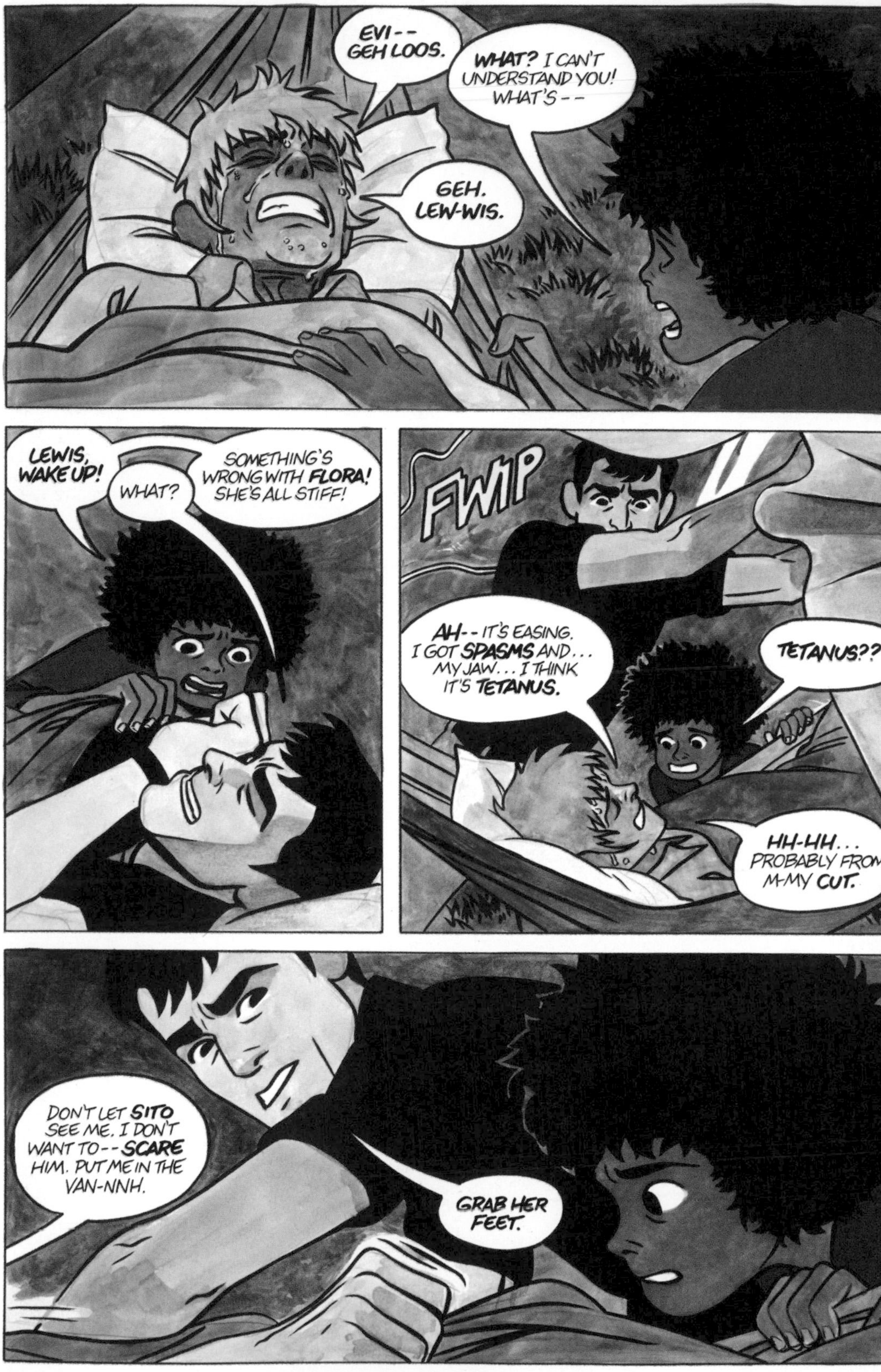
EVI--
GEH LOOS.
WHAT? I CAN'T UNDERSTAND YOU! WHAT'S--
GEH. LEW-WIS.
LEWIS, WAKE UP!
WHAT?
SOMETHING'S WRONG WITH FLORA! SHE'S ALL STIFF!
FWIP
AH-- IT'S EASING. I GOT SPASMS AND... MY JAW... I THINK IT'S TETANUS.
TETANUS???
HH-HH... PROBABLY FROM M-MY CUT.
DON'T LET SITO SEE ME. I DON'T WANT TO--SCARE HIM. PUT ME IN THE VAN-NNH.
GRAB HER FEET.

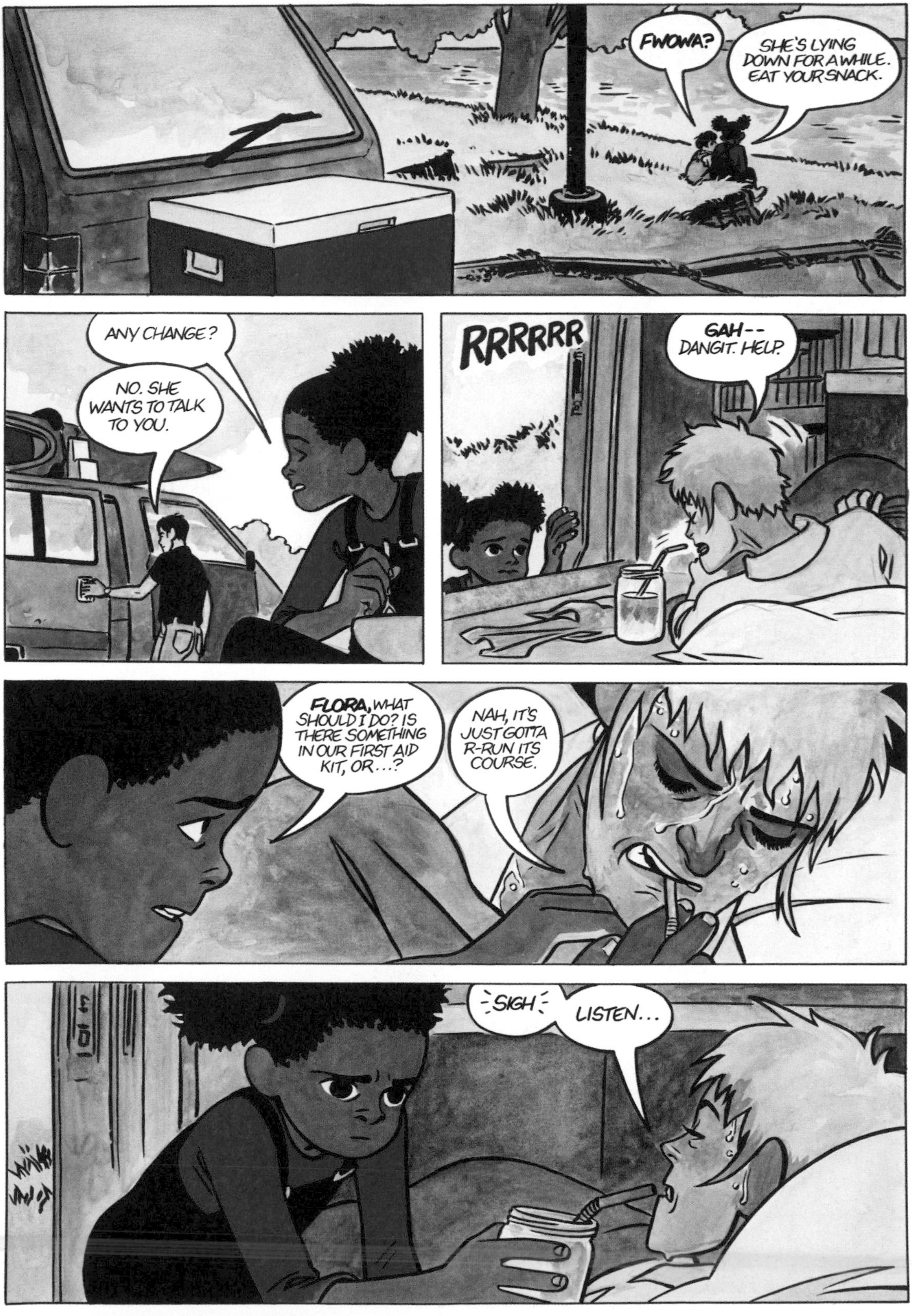
FWOWA?
SHE'S LYING DOWN FOR A WHILE. EAT YOUR SNACK.
ANY CHANGE?
NO. SHE WANTS TO TALK TO YOU.
RRRRRR
GAH-- DANGIT. HELP.
FLORA, WHAT SHOULD I DO? IS THERE SOMETHING IN OUR FIRST AID KIT, OR...?
NAH, IT'S JUST GOTTA R-RUN ITS COURSE.
SIGH
LISTEN...

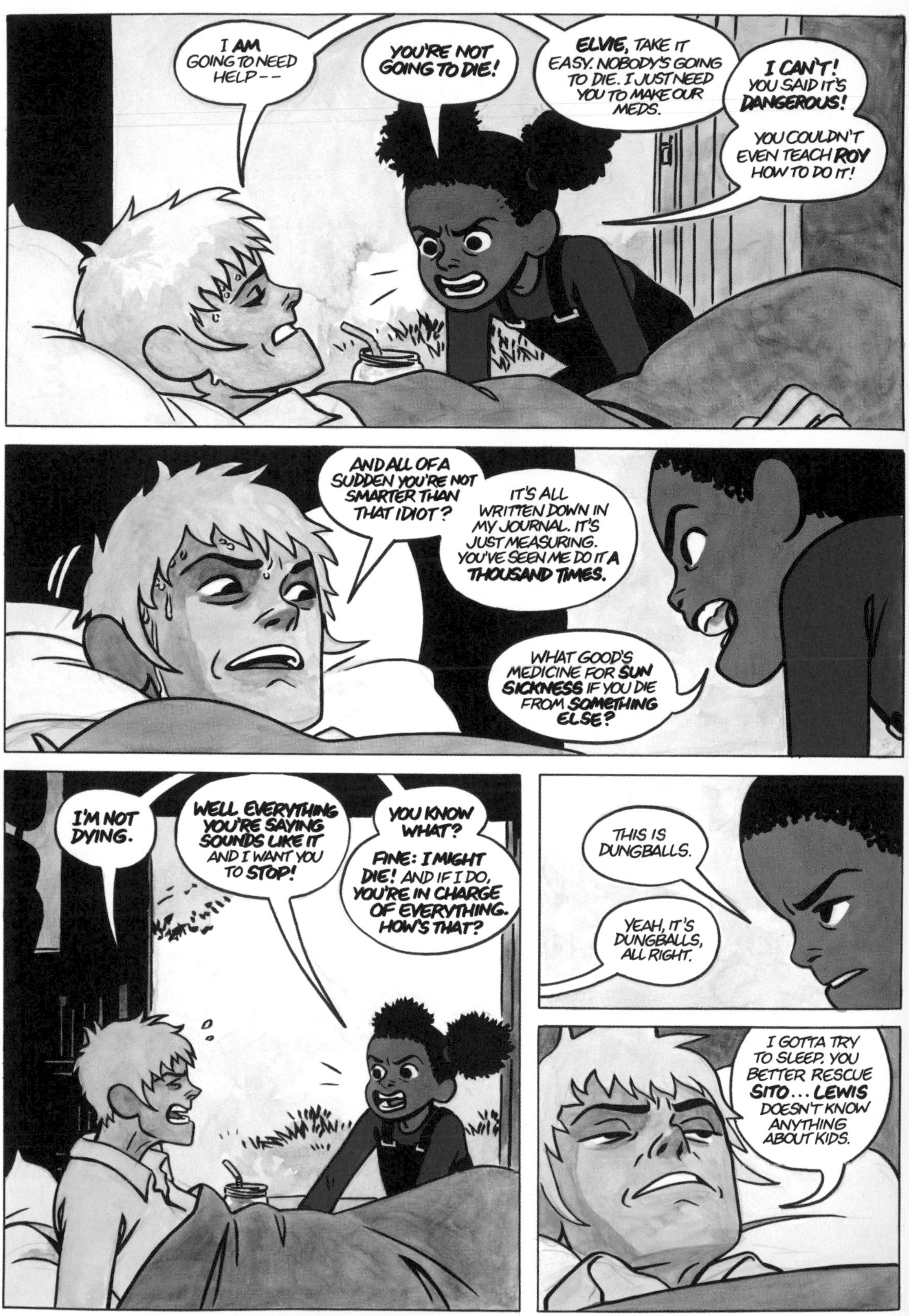
I AM GOING TO NEED HELP--
YOU'RE NOT GOING TO DIE!
ELVIE, TAKE IT EASY. NOBODY'S GOING TO DIE. I JUST NEED YOU TO MAKE OUR MEDS.
I CAN'T! YOU SAID IT'S DANGEROUS!
YOU COULDN'T EVEN TEACH ROY HOW TO DO IT!
AND ALL OF A SUDDEN YOU'RE NOT SMARTER THAN THAT IDIOT?
IT'S ALL WRITTEN DOWN IN MY JOURNAL. IT'S JUST MEASURING. YOU'VE SEEN ME DO IT A THOUSAND TIMES.
WHAT GOOD'S MEDICINE FOR SUN SICKNESS IF YOU DIE FROM SOMETHING ELSE?
I'M NOT DYING.
WELL EVERYTHING YOU'RE SAYING SOUNDS LIKE IT AND I WANT YOU TO STOP!
YOU KNOW WHAT?
FINE: I MIGHT DIE! AND IF I DO, YOU'RE IN CHARGE OF EVERYTHING. HOW'S THAT?
THIS IS DUNGBALLS.
YEAH, IT'S DUNGBALLS, ALL RIGHT.
I GOTTA TRY TO SLEEP. YOU BETTER RESCUE SITO... LEWIS DOESN'T KNOW ANYTHING ABOUT KIDS.

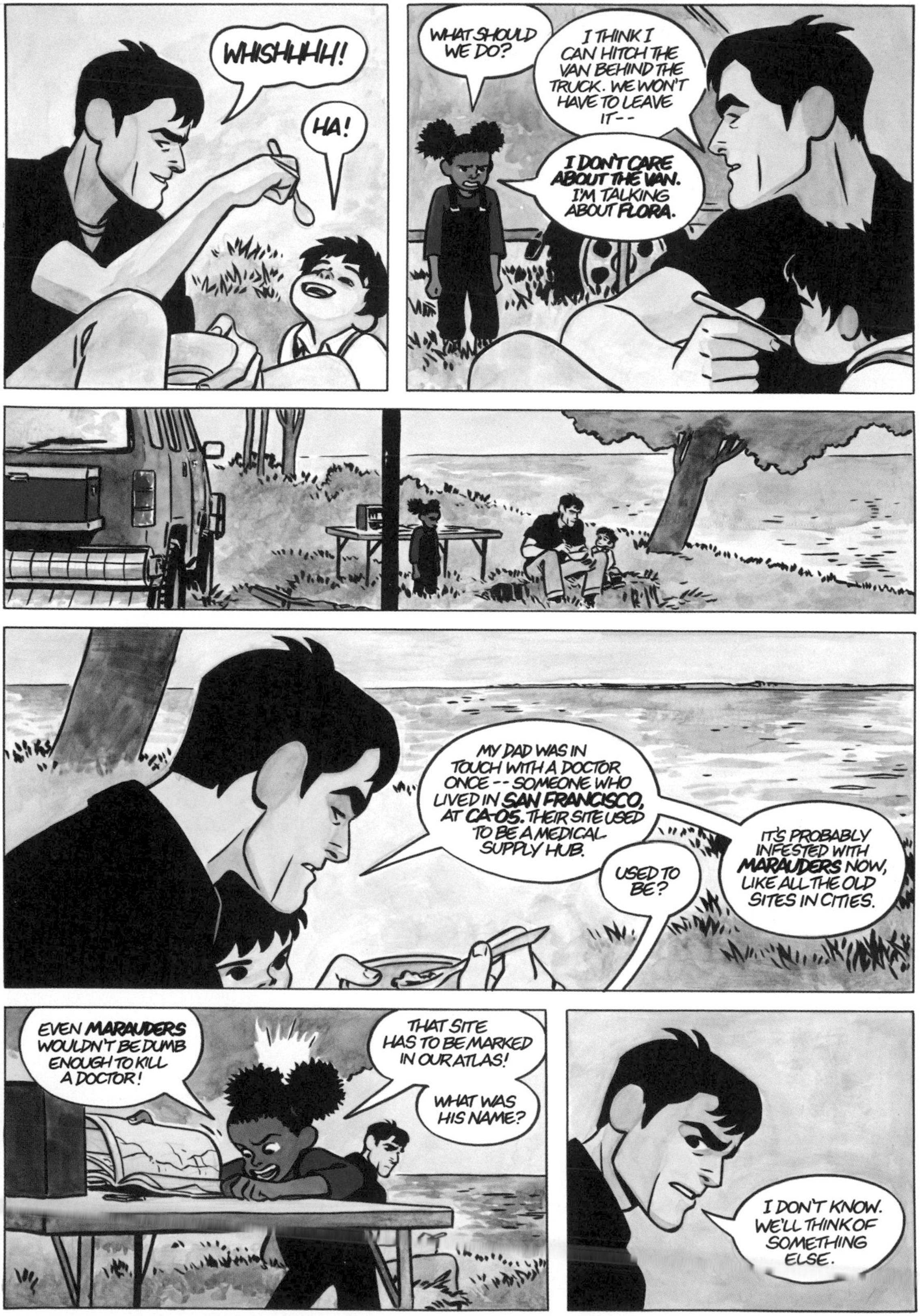
WHISHHHH!
HA!
WHAT SHOULD WE DO?
I THINK I CAN HITCH THE VAN BEHIND THE TRUCK. WE WON'T HAVE TO LEAVE IT--
I DON'T CARE ABOUT THE VAN. I'M TALKING ABOUT FLORA.
MY DAD WAS IN TOUCH WITH A DOCTOR ONCE -- SOMEONE WHO LIVED IN SAN FRANCISCO, AT CA-05. THEIR SITE USED TO BE A MEDICAL SUPPLY HUB.
USED TO BE?
IT'S PROBABLY INFESTED WITH MARAUDERS NOW, LIKE ALL THE OLD SITES IN CITIES.
EVEN MARAUDERS WOULDN'T BE DUMB ENOUGH TO KILL A DOCTOR!
THAT SITE HAS TO BE MARKED IN OUR ATLAS!
WHAT WAS HIS NAME?
I DON'T KNOW. WE'LL THINK OF SOMETHING ELSE.

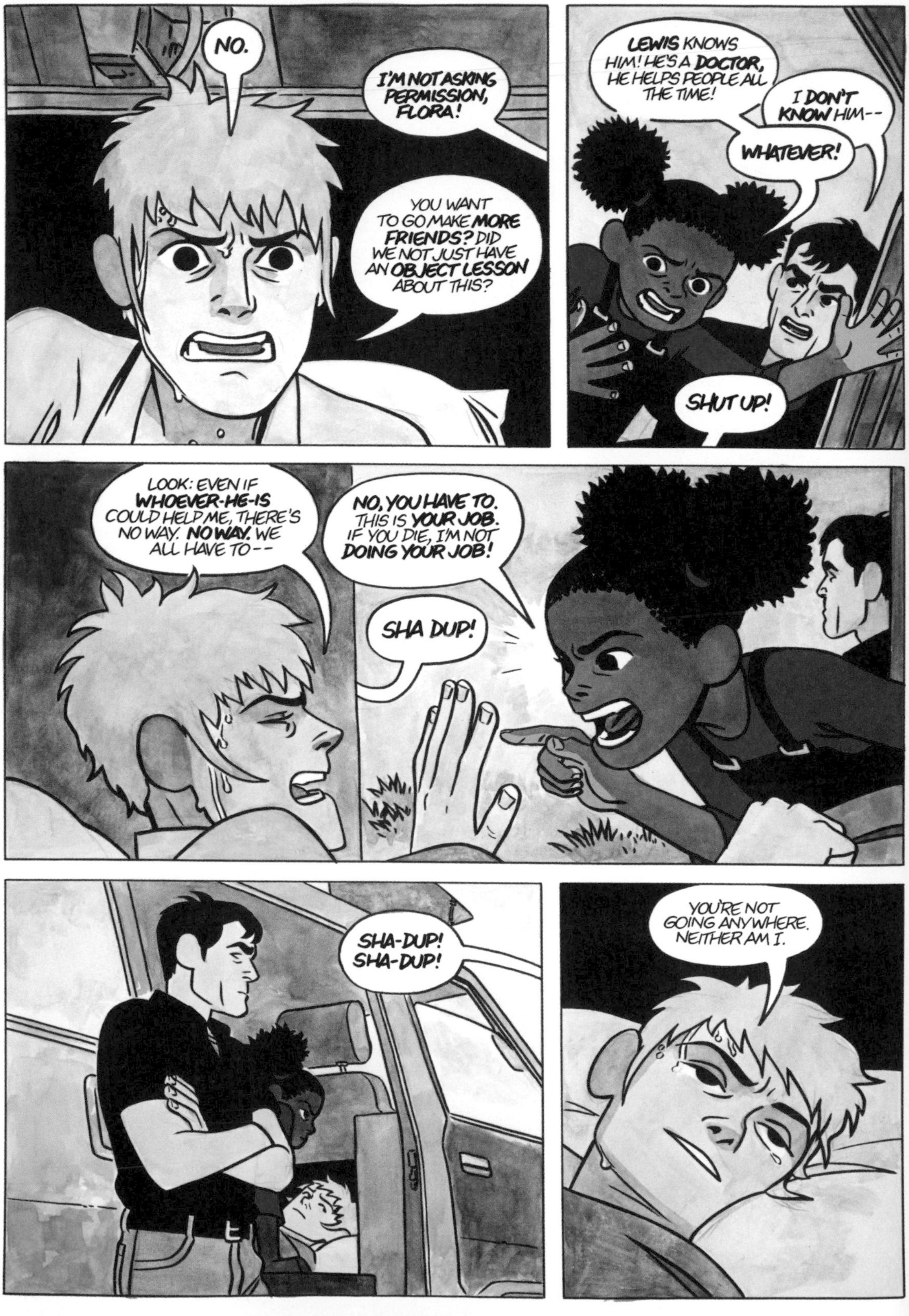
NO.
I'M NOT ASKING PERMISSION, FLORA!
YOU WANT TO GO MAKE MORE FRIENDS? DID WE NOT JUST HAVE AN OBJECT LESSON ABOUT THIS?
LEWIS KNOWS HIM! HE'S A DOCTOR, HE HELPS PEOPLE ALL THE TIME!
I DON'T KNOW HIM--
WHATEVER!
SHUT UP!
LOOK: EVEN IF WHOEVER-HE-IS COULD HELP ME, THERE'S NO WAY. NO WAY. WE ALL HAVE TO--
NO, YOU HAVE TO. THIS IS YOUR JOB. IF YOU DIE, I'M NOT DOING YOUR JOB!
SHA DUP!
SHA-DUP! SHA-DUP!
YOU'RE NOT GOING ANYWHERE. NEITHER AM I.

OCTOBER I DON'T CARE. IF THE PEOPLE IN **SAN FRANCISCO** END UP BEING MARAUDERS LIKE **LEWIS** SAID AND THEY EAT THE FLESH OFF MY BONES, HERE'S MY LAST WILL AND BLAH-BLAH-BLAH.

TO **LOOLOO** I LEAVE MY HAMMOCK, SO YOU DON'T HAVE TO SLEEP ON THE GROUND LIKE A TROGLODYTE. ALSO MY **OLD GOSPEL** RECORD, SO IT'LL SEEM LIKE YOU HAVE A PERSONALITY.

TO **SITO** I LEAVE PRETTY MUCH EVERYTHING ELSE: MY BACKPACK, MY KNIFE, MY PETRIFIED CANDY COLLECTION, **SOPHIE TURTLE**, AND MY **AUDUBON** BOOKS. LEARN TO TALK, **SITO**. LEARN TO READ, TOO. **FLORA** CAN TEACH YOU SWEAR WORDS —— JUST BREAK SOMETHING IN HER LAB AND YOU'LL HEAR PLENTY.

TO **FLORA** I LEAVE MY PORTION OF THE WHEAT BERRIES WE HARVESTED, THRESHED, AND WINNOWED LAST YEAR. I EXPECT YOU TO REALLY APPRECIATE IT BECAUSE YOU KNOW HOW LONG THAT CRAP TOOK AND HOW MUCH I HATED DOING IT. FROM THOSE WHEAT BERRIES, I HOPE YOU'LL ENJOY MANY UN-BURNED, LESS OLD, AND PREFERABLY **NOT MOLDY** BISCUITS. I ALSO LEAVE YOU MY JOURNALS.

FLORA, IF YOU END UP SURVIVING TETANUS AND DO FIND YOUR VACCINE AND GET FAMOUS, YOU BETTER NOT TAKE ALL THE CREDIT.

Elvire Jones

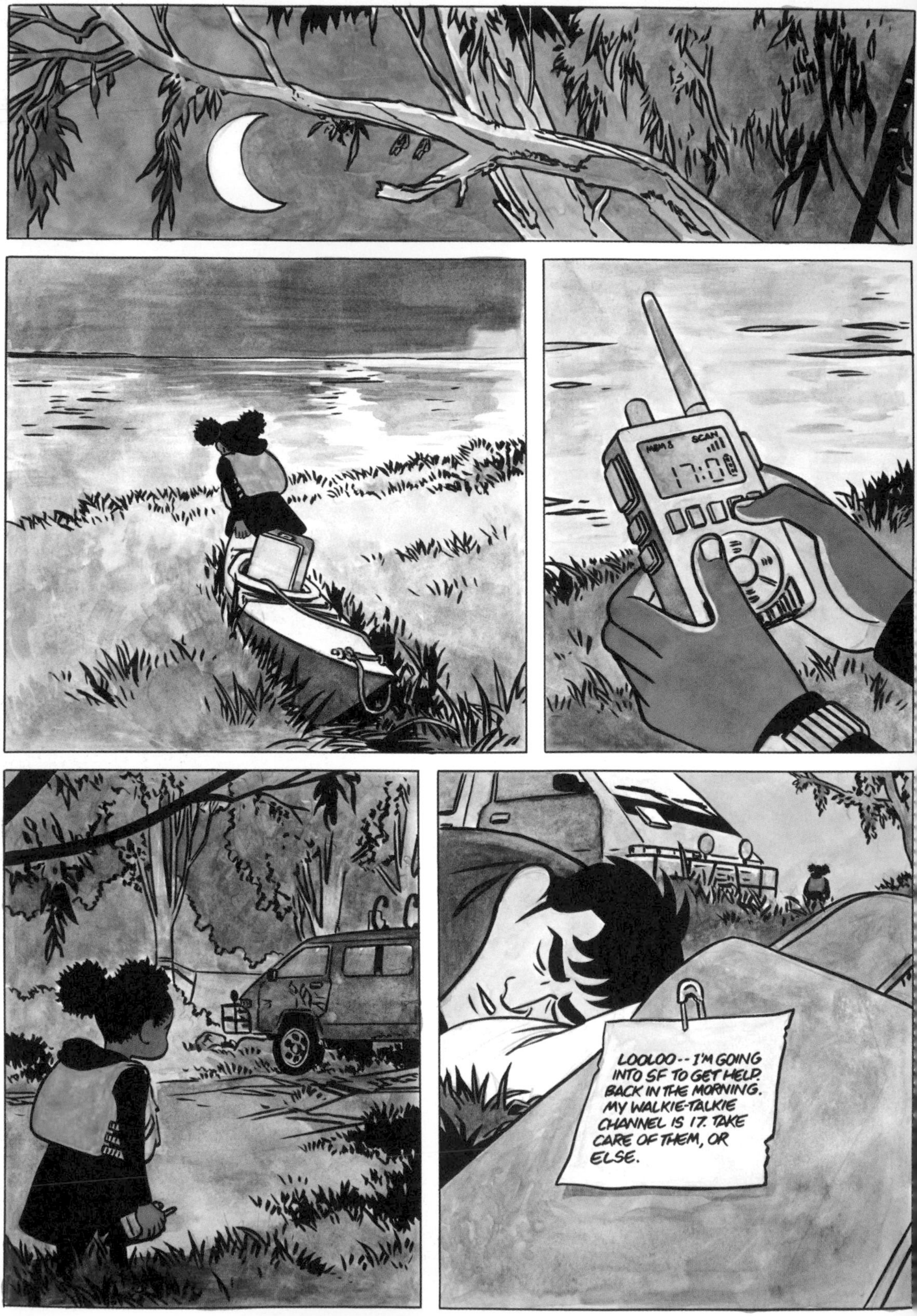
LOOLOO -- I'M GOING INTO SF TO GET HELP. BACK IN THE MORNING. MY WALKIE-TALKIE CHANNEL IS 17. TAKE CARE OF THEM, OR ELSE.

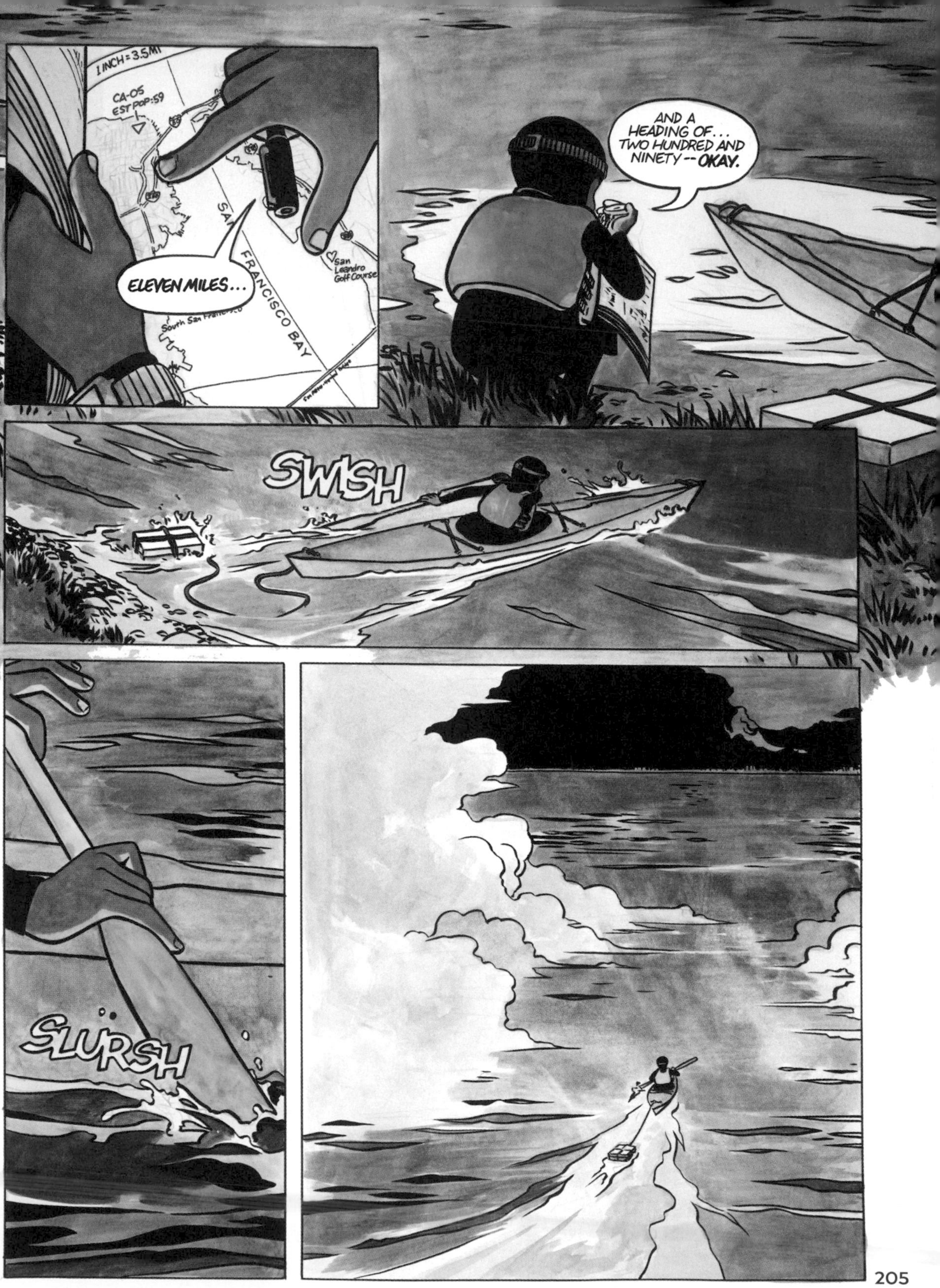

1 INCH=3.5MI
CA-05
EST POP:59
SAN FRANCISCO BAY
San Leandro Golf Course
South San Francisco
ELEVEN MILES...
AND A HEADING OF... TWO HUNDRED AND NINETY -- OKAY.
SWISH
SLURSH

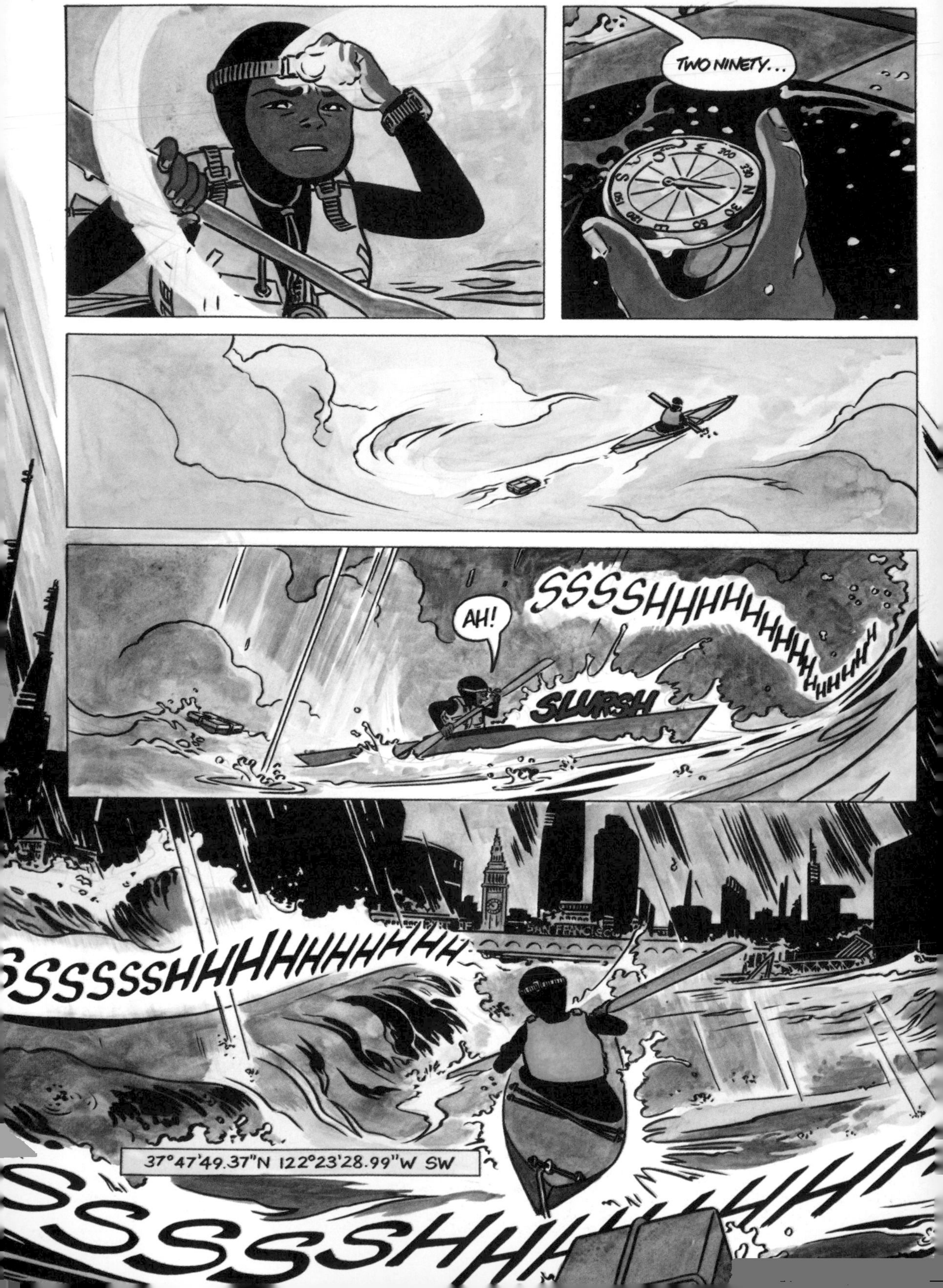

TWO NINETY...
AH!
SSSSHHHHHHHHHHHHHHHH
SLURSH
SSSSSSHHHHHHHHHHHH
37°47'49.37"N 122°23'28.99"W SW
SSSSSHHHHHHH

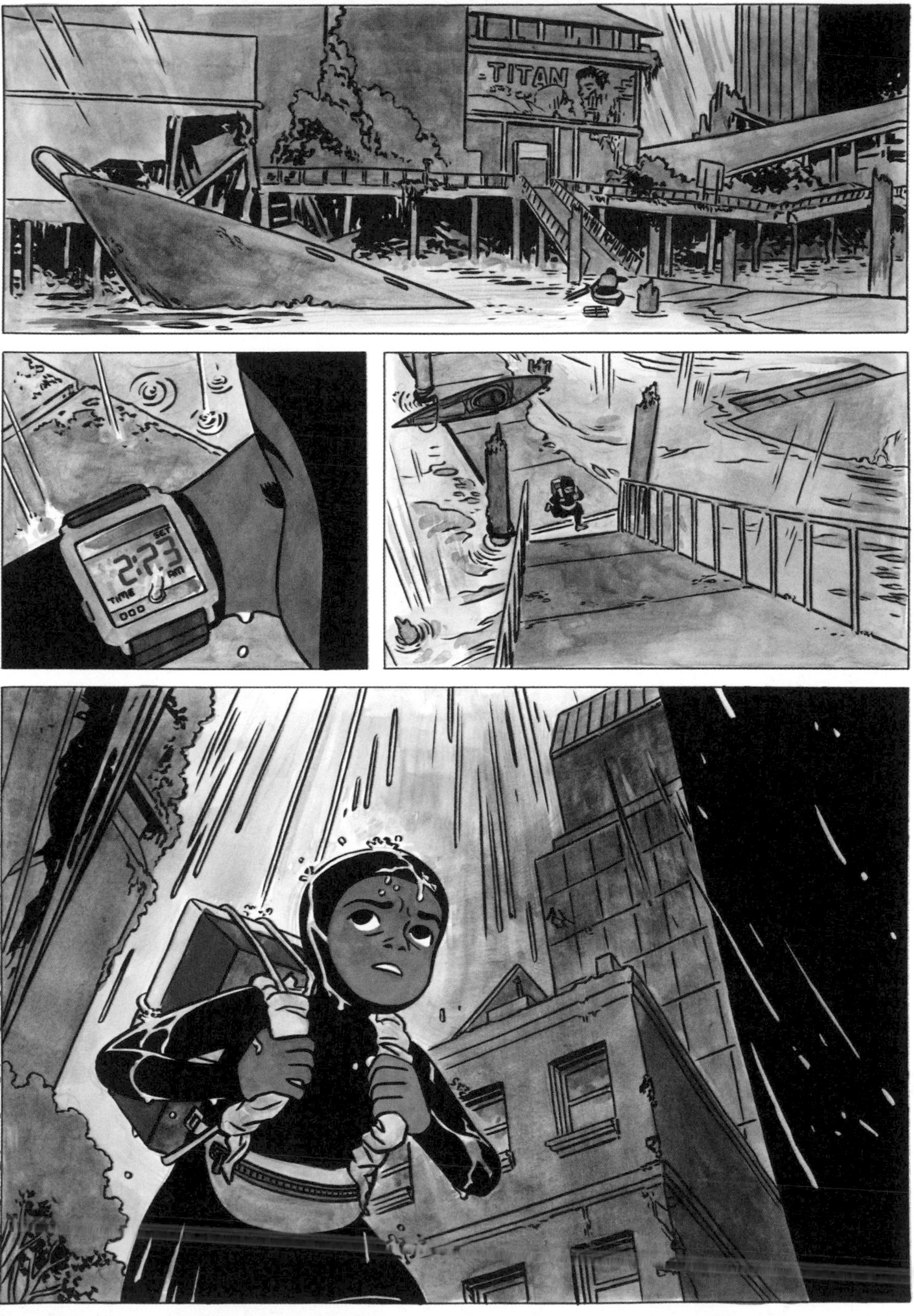
TITAN
SET
2:23
AM
TIME

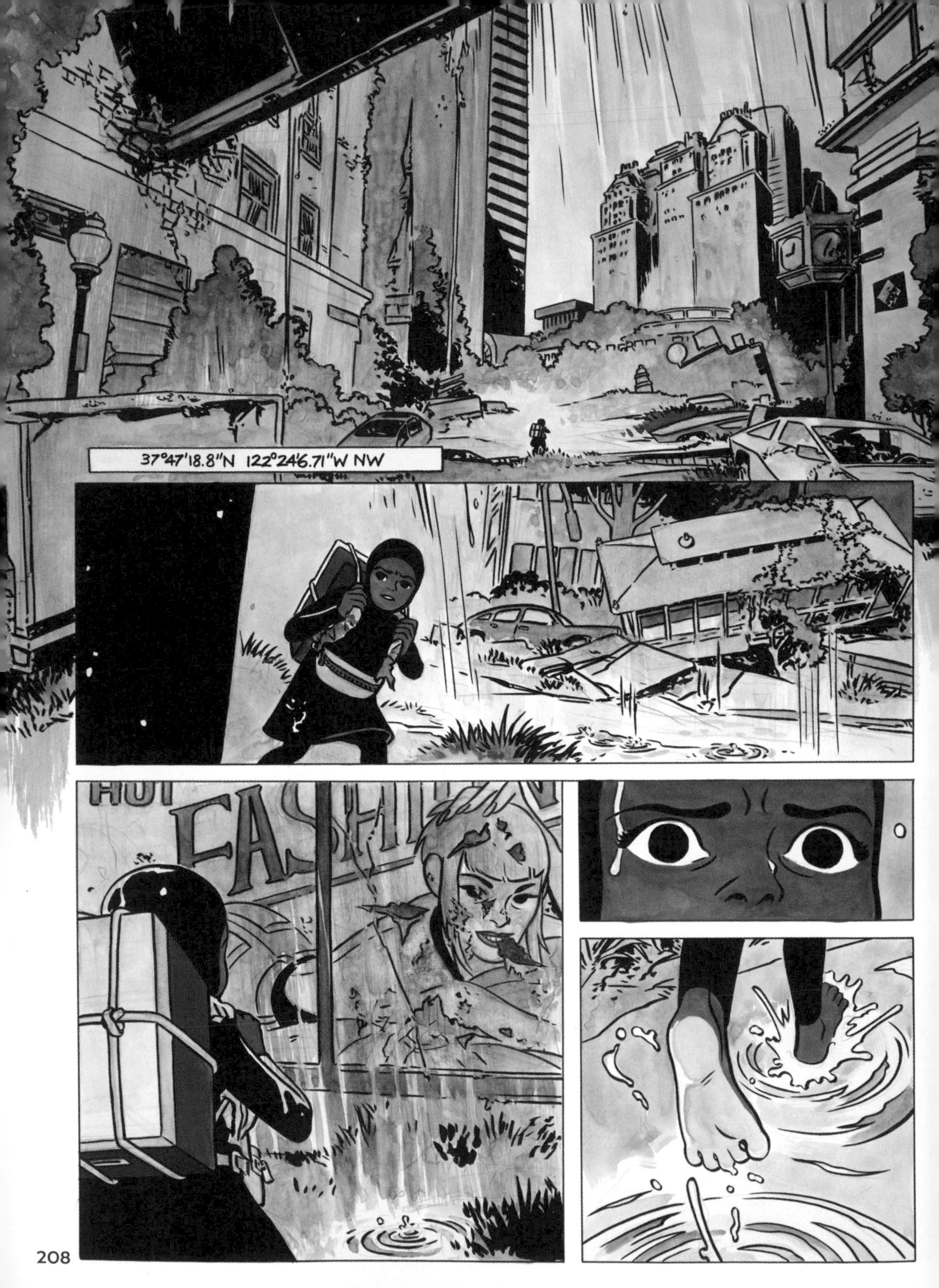
37°47'18.8"N 122°24'6.71"W NW
HOT
FASHI

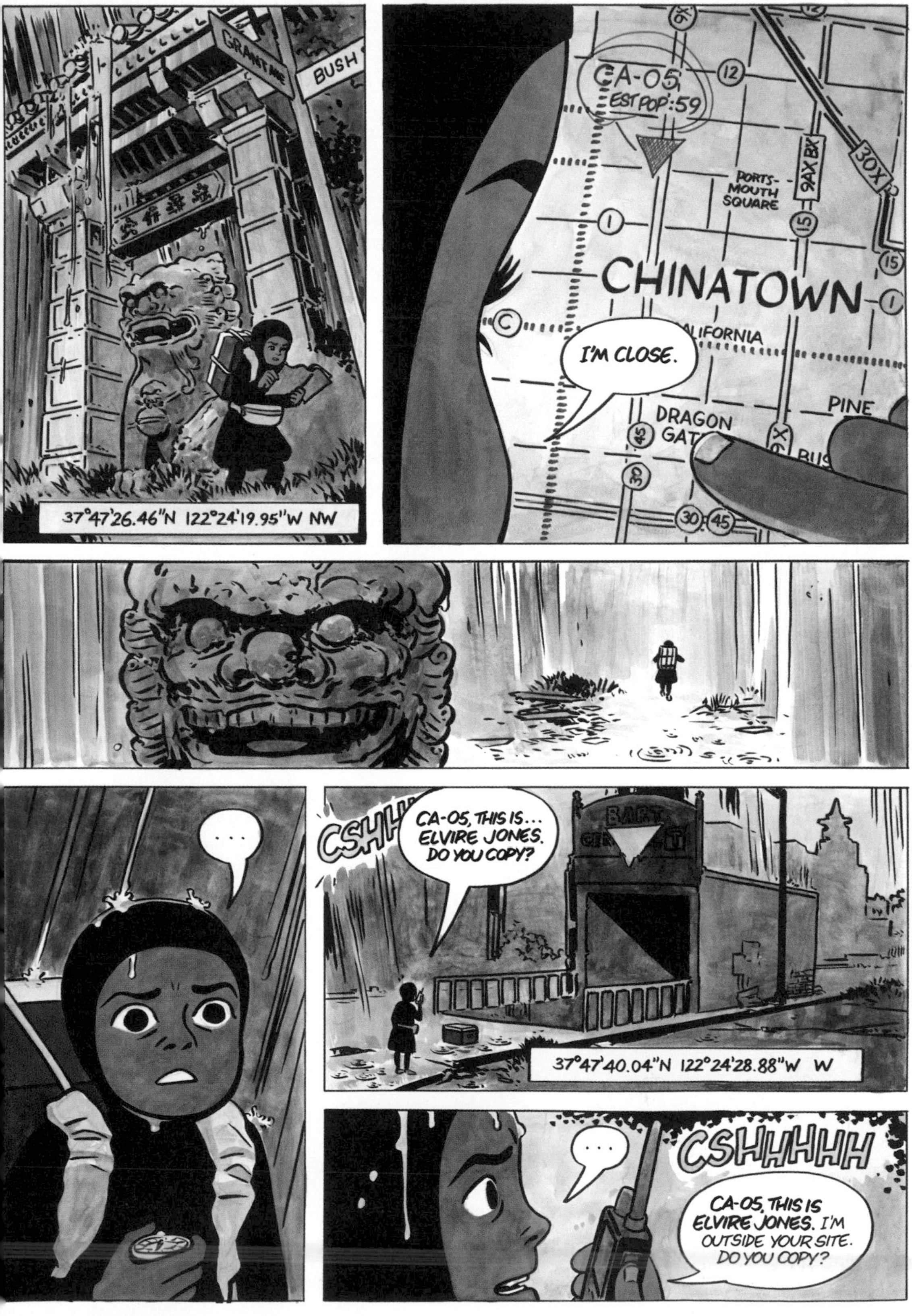

GRANT AVE
BUSH
37°47'26.46"N 122°24'19.95"W NW
CA-05
EST POP: 59
PORTS-MOUTH SQUARE
CHINATOWN
I'M CLOSE.
PINE
DRAGON GAT
CSHH
CA-05, THIS IS... ELVIRE JONES. DO YOU COPY?
BART
37°47'40.04"N 122°24'28.88"W W
CSHHHHH
CA-05, THIS IS ELVIRE JONES. I'M OUTSIDE YOUR SITE. DO YOU COPY?

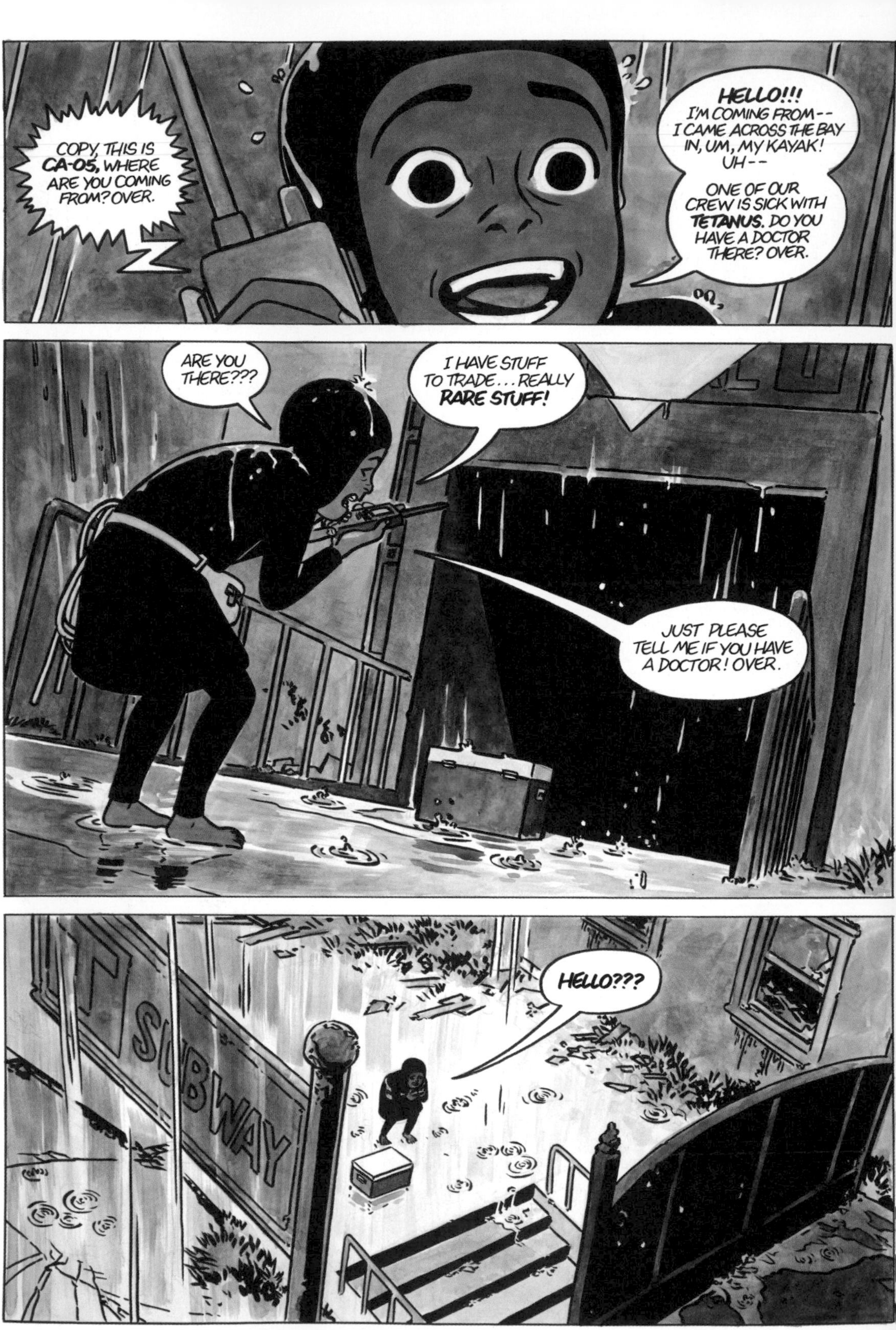

COPY, THIS IS CA-05, WHERE ARE YOU COMING FROM? OVER.
HELLO!!! I'M COMING FROM-- I CAME ACROSS THE BAY IN, UM, MY KAYAK! UH--
ONE OF OUR CREW IS SICK WITH TETANUS. DO YOU HAVE A DOCTOR THERE? OVER.
ARE YOU THERE???
I HAVE STUFF TO TRADE... REALLY RARE STUFF!
JUST PLEASE TELL ME IF YOU HAVE A DOCTOR! OVER.
HELLO???
SUBWAY

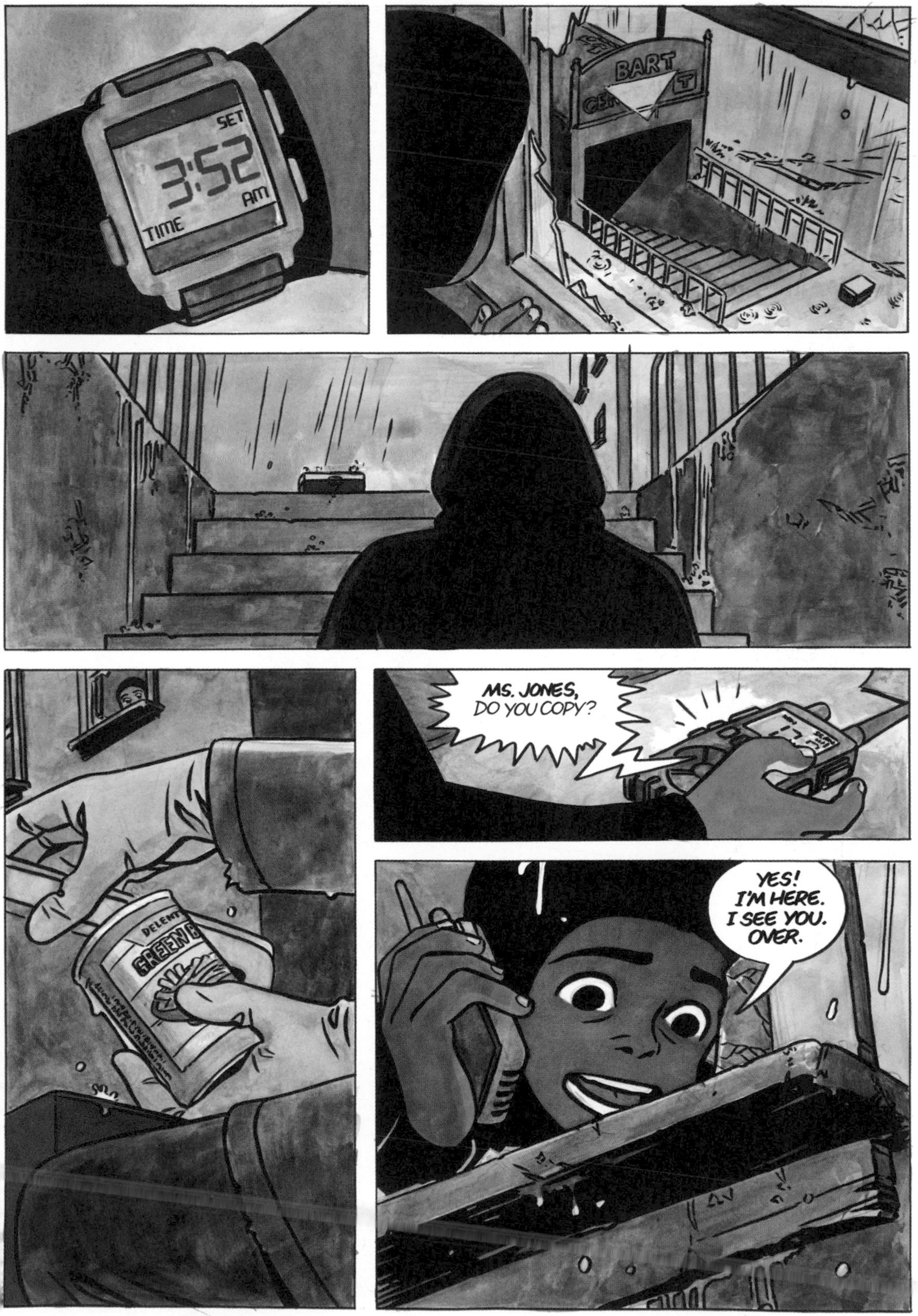
SET
3:52
AM
TIME
BART
MS. JONES, DO YOU COPY?
YES! I'M HERE. I SEE YOU. OVER.

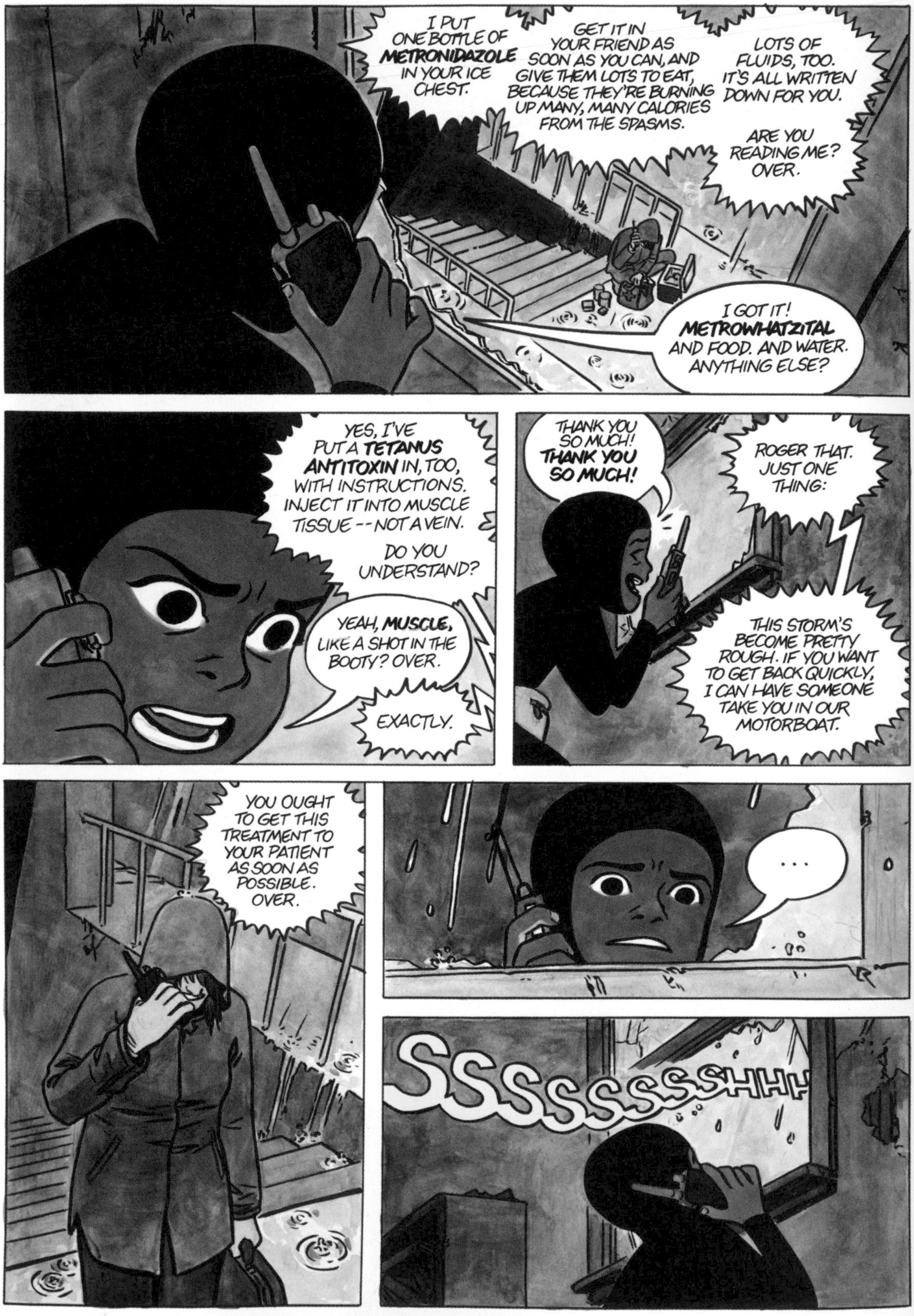
I PUT ONE BOTTLE OF **METRONIDAZOLE** IN YOUR ICE CHEST.
GET IT IN YOUR FRIEND AS SOON AS YOU CAN, AND GIVE THEM LOTS TO EAT, BECAUSE THEY'RE BURNING UP MANY, MANY CALORIES FROM THE SPASMS.
LOTS OF FLUIDS, TOO. IT'S ALL WRITTEN DOWN FOR YOU.
ARE YOU READING ME? OVER.
I GOT IT! **METROWHATZITAL** AND FOOD. AND WATER. ANYTHING ELSE?
YES, I'VE PUT A **TETANUS ANTITOXIN** IN, TOO, WITH INSTRUCTIONS. INJECT IT INTO MUSCLE TISSUE -- NOT A VEIN.
DO YOU UNDERSTAND?
YEAH, **MUSCLE,** LIKE A SHOT IN THE BOOTY? OVER.
EXACTLY.
THANK YOU SO MUCH! **THANK YOU SO MUCH!**
ROGER THAT. JUST ONE THING:
THIS STORM'S BECOME PRETTY ROUGH. IF YOU WANT TO GET BACK QUICKLY, I CAN HAVE SOMEONE TAKE YOU IN OUR MOTORBOAT.
YOU OUGHT TO GET THIS TREATMENT TO YOUR PATIENT AS SOON AS POSSIBLE. OVER.
...
SSSSSSSSSHHH

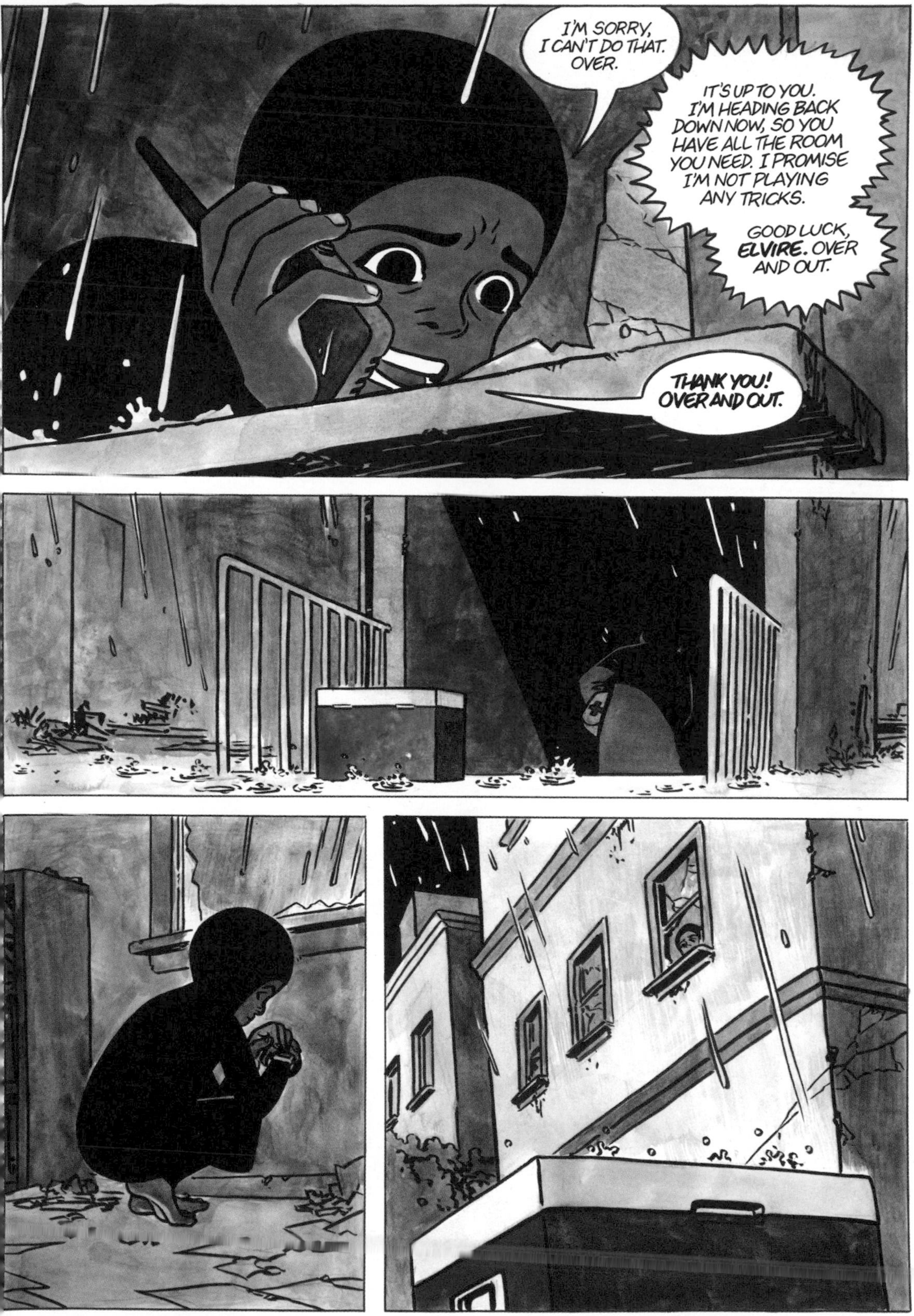
I'M SORRY, I CAN'T DO THAT. OVER.
IT'S UP TO YOU. I'M HEADING BACK DOWN NOW, SO YOU HAVE ALL THE ROOM YOU NEED. I PROMISE I'M NOT PLAYING ANY TRICKS.
GOOD LUCK, ELVIRE. OVER AND OUT.
THANK YOU! OVER AND OUT.

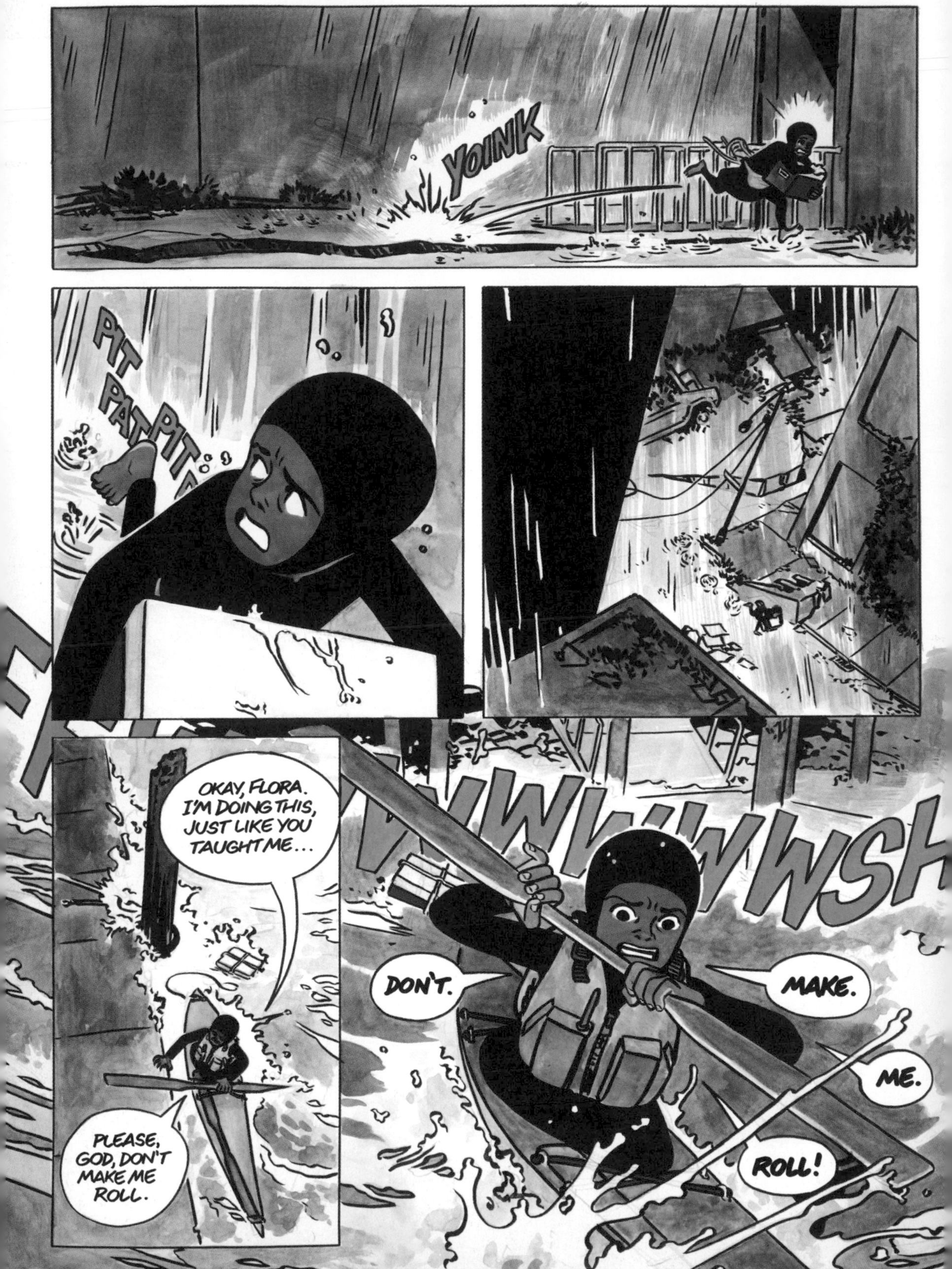
YOINK
PIT PAT PIT PAT
OKAY, FLORA. I'M DOING THIS, JUST LIKE YOU TAUGHT ME...
PLEASE, GOD, DON'T MAKE ME ROLL.
WWWWSH
DON'T.
MAKE.
ME.
ROLL!

CHAPTER ELEVEN
THE CASTLE

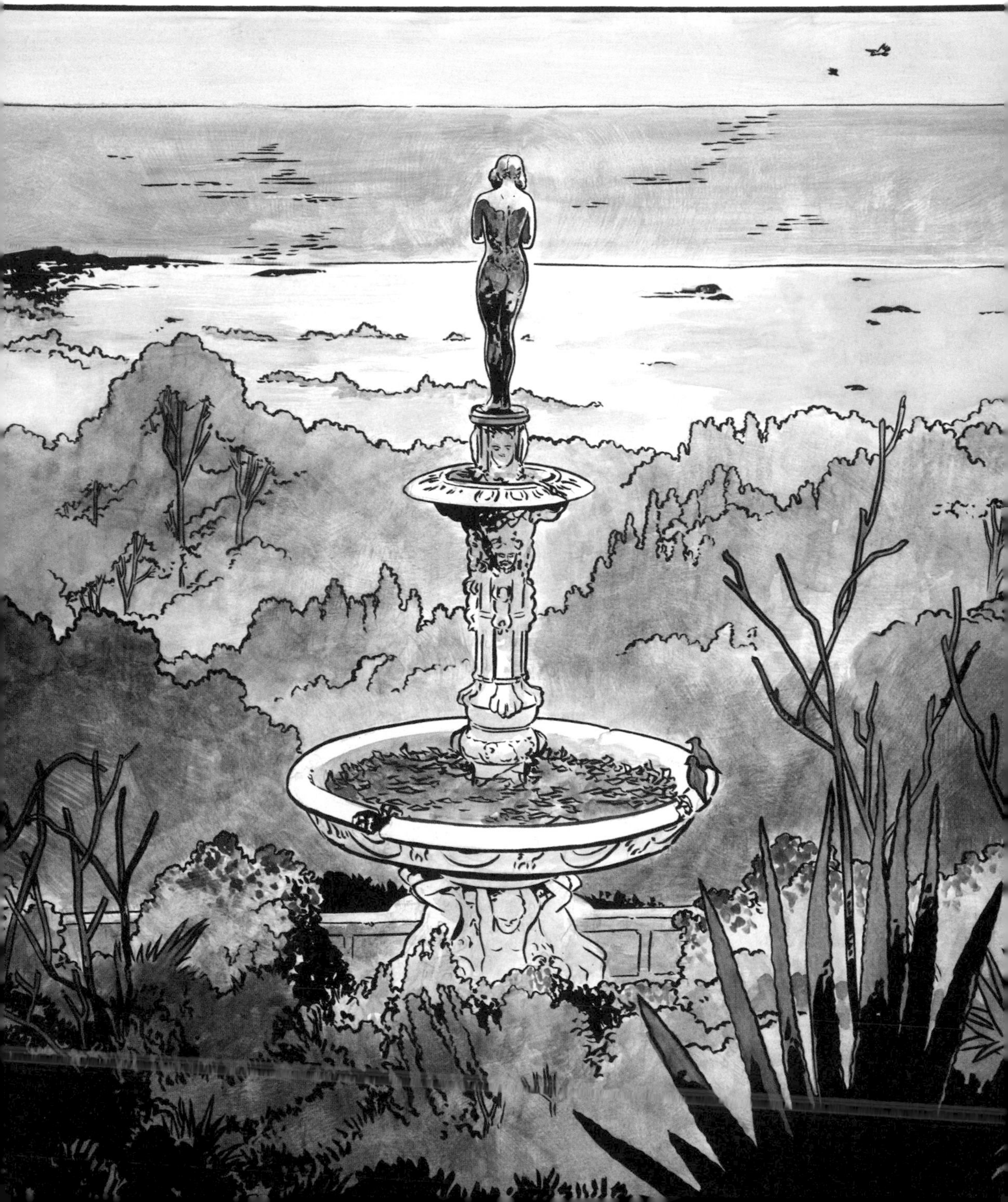

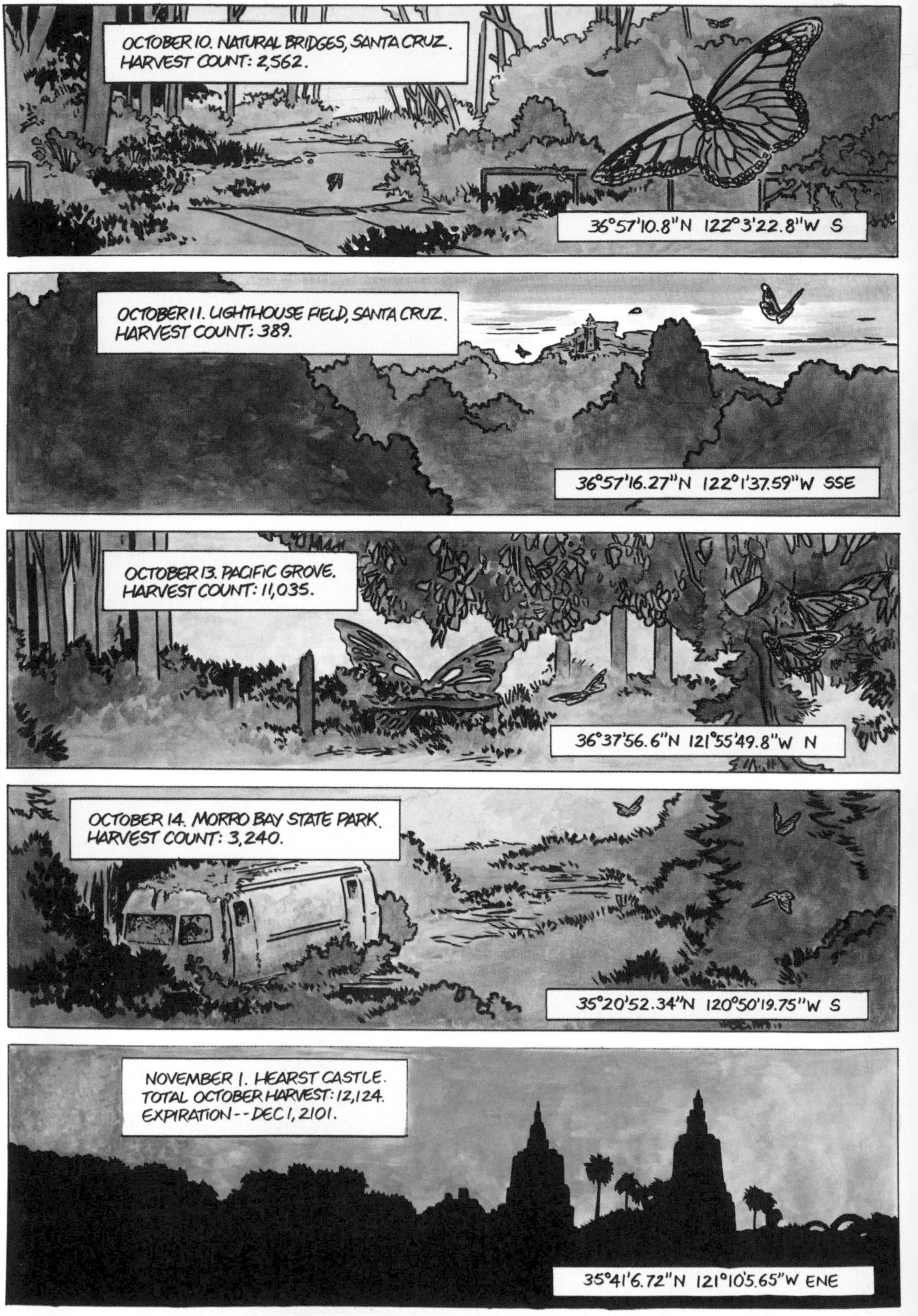
OCTOBER 10. NATURAL BRIDGES, SANTA CRUZ.
HARVEST COUNT: 2,562.
36°57'10.8"N 122°3'22.8"W S
OCTOBER 11. LIGHTHOUSE FIELD, SANTA CRUZ.
HARVEST COUNT: 389.
36°57'16.27"N 122°1'37.59"W SSE
OCTOBER 13. PACIFIC GROVE.
HARVEST COUNT: 11,035.
36°37'56.6"N 121°55'49.8"W N
OCTOBER 14. MORRO BAY STATE PARK.
HARVEST COUNT: 3,240.
35°20'52.34"N 120°50'19.75"W S
NOVEMBER 1. HEARST CASTLE.
TOTAL OCTOBER HARVEST: 12,124.
EXPIRATION--DEC 1, 2101.
35°41'6.72"N 121°10'5.65"W ENE

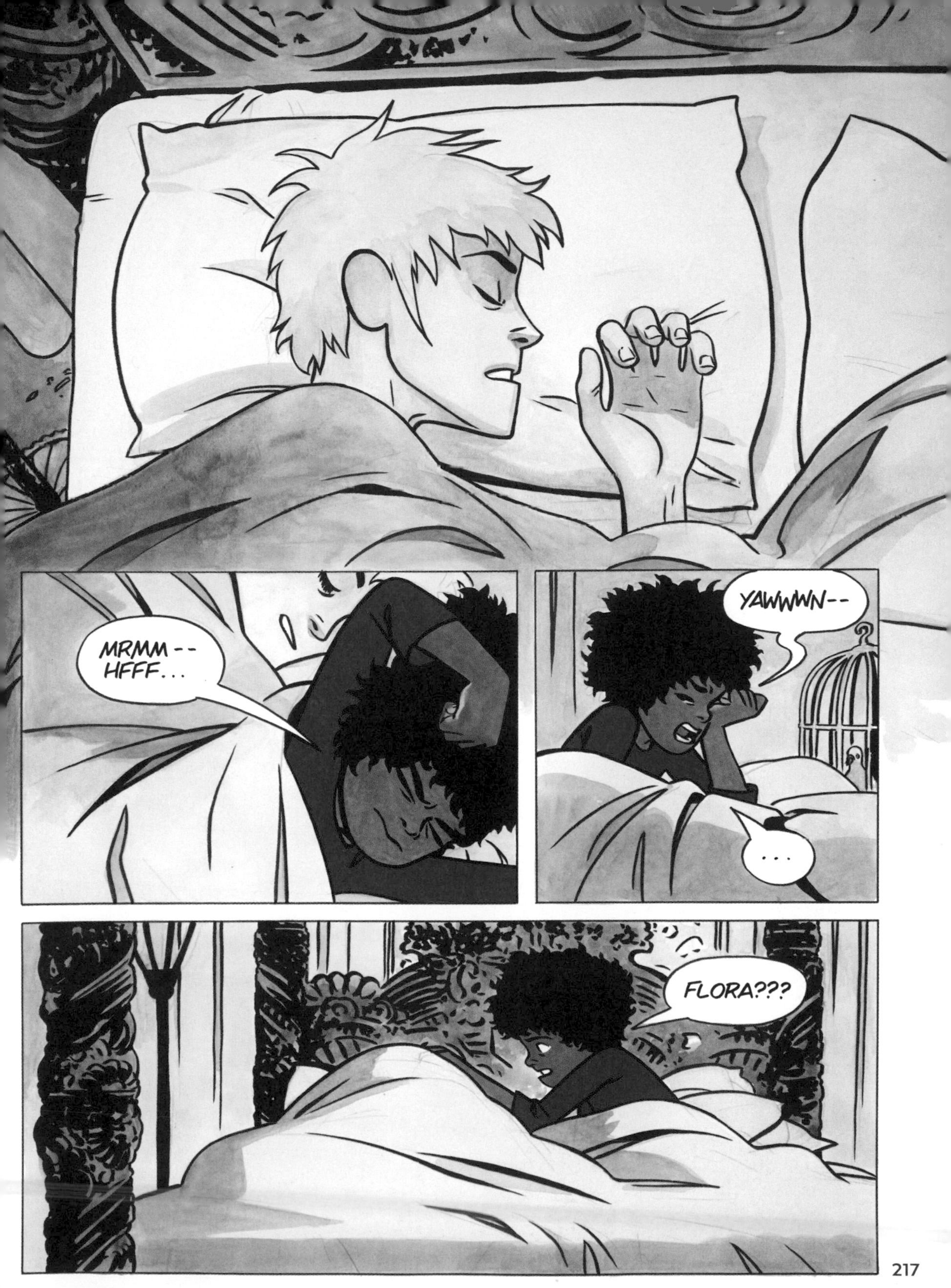
MRMM--
HFFF...
YAWWWN--
...
FLORA???

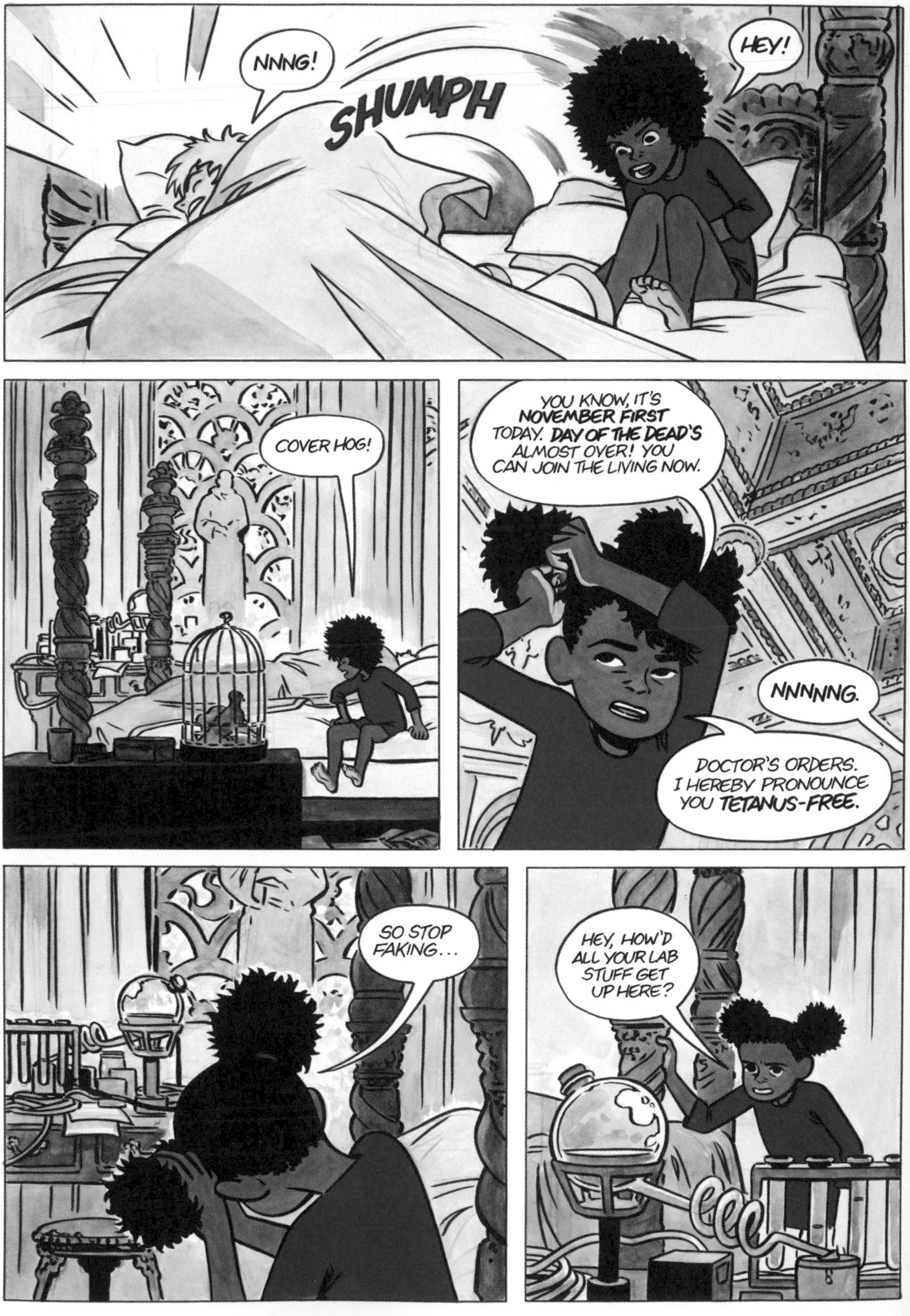
NNNG!
SHUMPH
HEY!
COVER HOG!
YOU KNOW, IT'S **NOVEMBER FIRST** TODAY. **DAY OF THE DEAD'S** ALMOST OVER! YOU CAN JOIN THE LIVING NOW.
NNNNNG.
DOCTOR'S ORDERS. I HEREBY PRONOUNCE YOU **TETANUS-FREE.**
SO STOP FAKING...
HEY, HOW'D ALL YOUR LAB STUFF GET UP HERE?

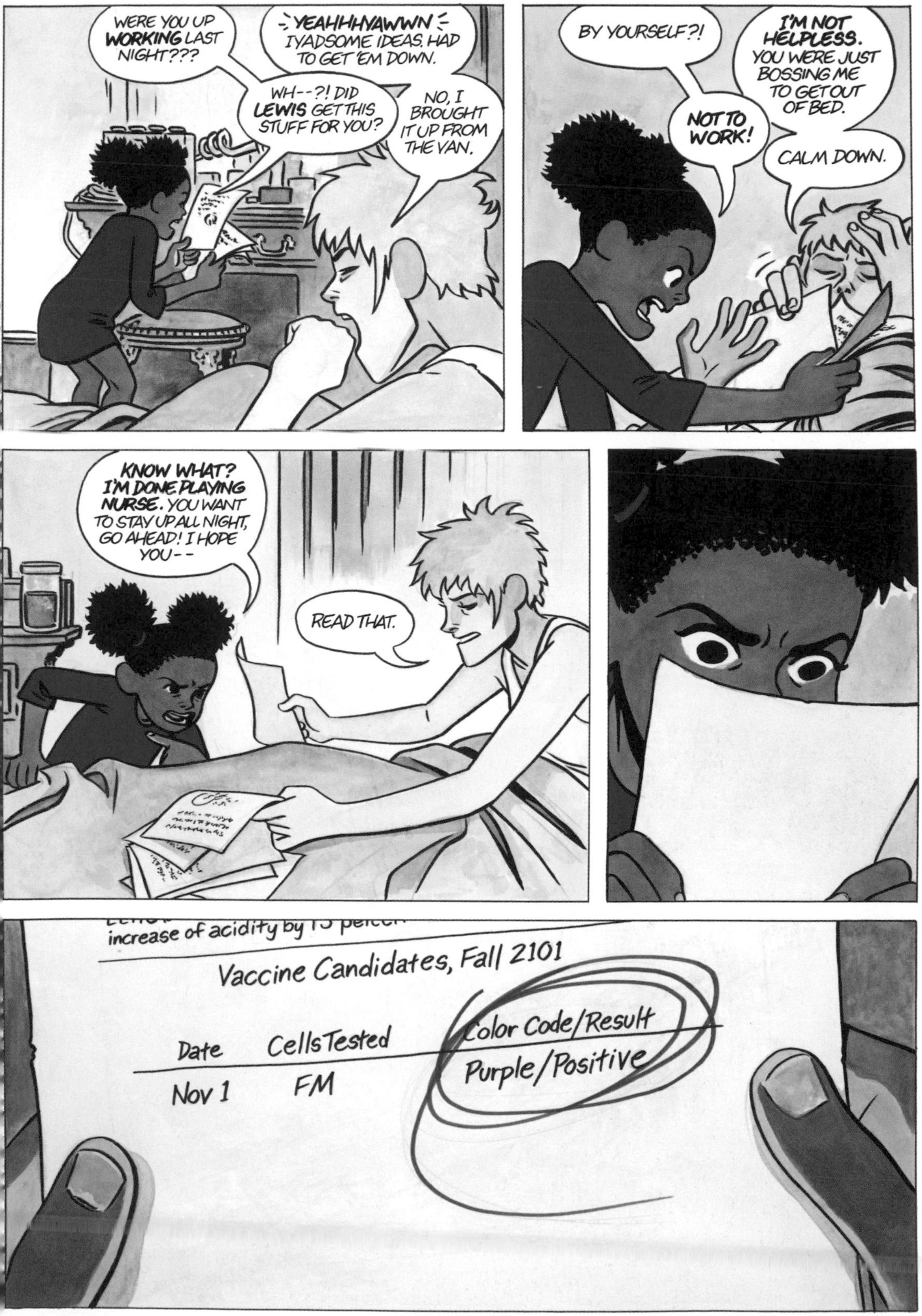
WERE YOU UP WORKING LAST NIGHT???
YEAHHHYAWWN IYADSOME IDEAS. HAD TO GET 'EM DOWN.
WH--?! DID LEWIS GET THIS STUFF FOR YOU?
NO, I BROUGHT IT UP FROM THE VAN.
BY YOURSELF?!
NOT TO WORK!
I'M NOT HELPLESS. YOU WERE JUST BOSSING ME TO GET OUT OF BED.
CALM DOWN.
KNOW WHAT? I'M DONE PLAYING NURSE. YOU WANT TO STAY UP ALL NIGHT, GO AHEAD! I HOPE YOU--
READ THAT.
increase of acidity by 15 percen
Vaccine Candidates, Fall 2101
Date
Cells Tested
Color Code/Result
Nov 1
FM
Purple/Positive

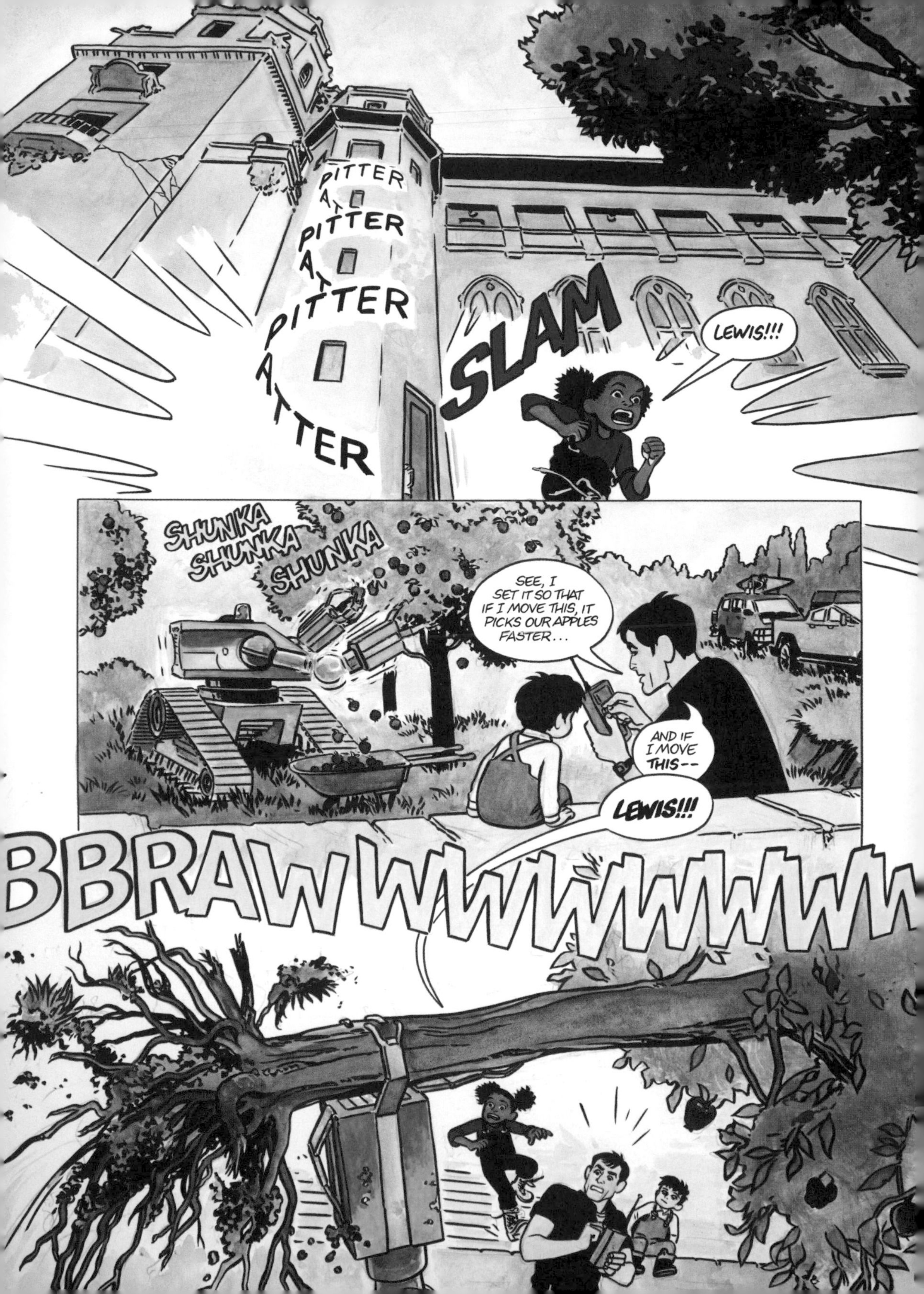
PITTER PAT PITTER PAT PITTER PATTER
SLAM
LEWIS!!!
SHUNKA SHUNKA SHUNKA
SEE, I SET IT SO THAT IF I MOVE THIS, IT PICKS OUR APPLES FASTER...
AND IF I MOVE THIS--
LEWIS!!!
BBRAWWWWWWWW

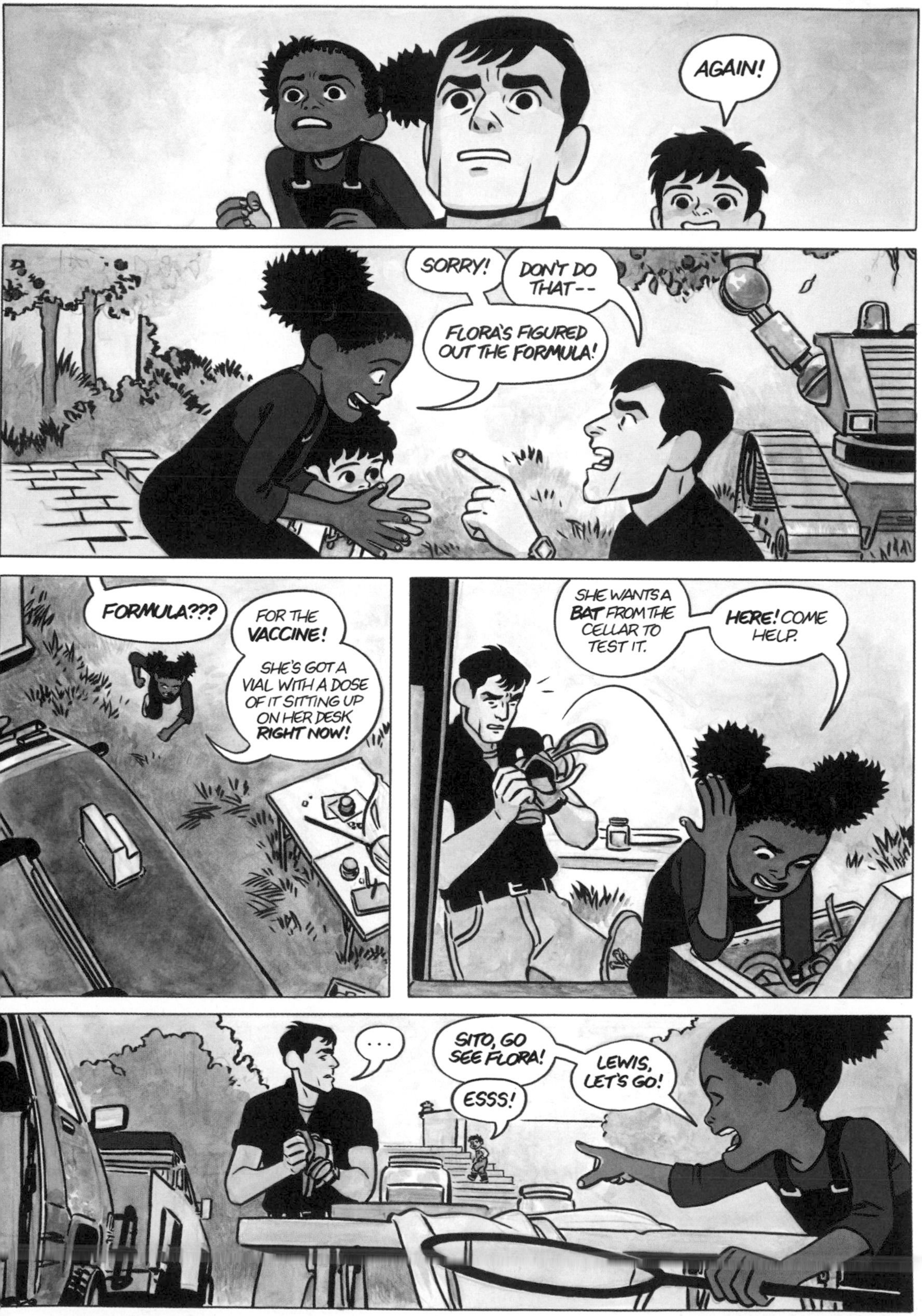
AGAIN!
SORRY!
DON'T DO THAT--
FLORA'S FIGURED OUT THE FORMULA!
FORMULA???
FOR THE VACCINE!
SHE'S GOT A VIAL WITH A DOSE OF IT SITTING UP ON HER DESK RIGHT NOW!
SHE WANTS A BAT FROM THE CELLAR TO TEST IT.
HERE! COME HELP.
...
SITO, GO SEE FLORA!
ESSS!
LEWIS, LET'S GO!

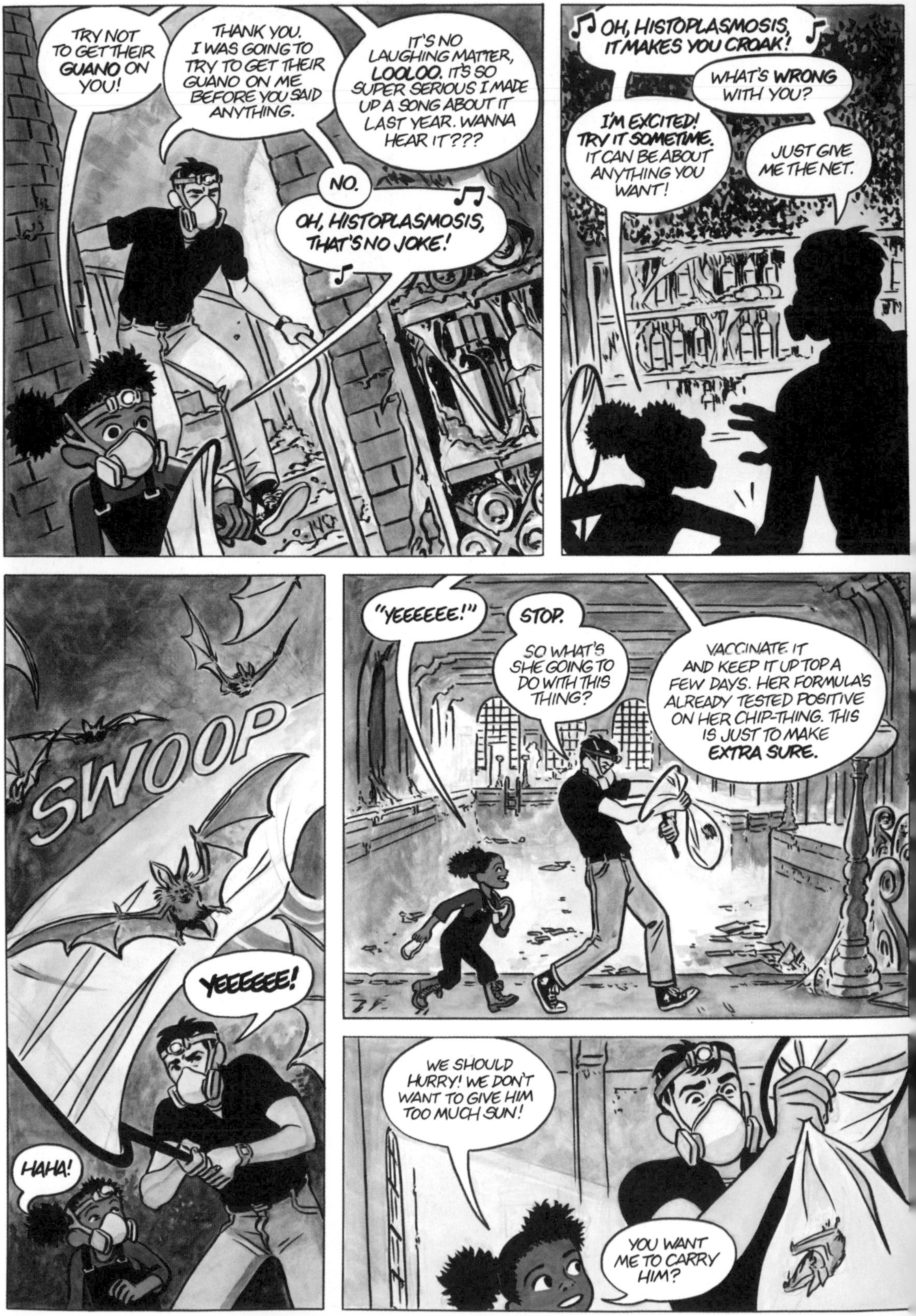

TRY NOT TO GET THEIR **GUANO** ON YOU!
THANK YOU. I WAS GOING TO TRY TO GET THEIR GUANO ON ME BEFORE YOU SAID ANYTHING.
IT'S NO LAUGHING MATTER, **LOOLOO.** IT'S SO SUPER SERIOUS I MADE UP A SONG ABOUT IT LAST YEAR. WANNA HEAR IT???
NO.
OH, HISTOPLASMOSIS, THAT'S NO JOKE!
OH, HISTOPLASMOSIS, IT MAKES YOU CROAK!
WHAT'S **WRONG** WITH YOU?
I'M EXCITED! TRY IT SOMETIME. IT CAN BE ABOUT ANYTHING YOU WANT!
JUST GIVE ME THE NET.
SWOOP
YEEEEEE!
HAHA!
"YEEEEEE!"
STOP.
SO WHAT'S SHE GOING TO DO WITH THIS THING?
VACCINATE IT AND KEEP IT UP TOP A FEW DAYS. HER FORMULA'S ALREADY TESTED POSITIVE ON HER CHIP-THING. THIS IS JUST TO MAKE **EXTRA SURE.**
WE SHOULD HURRY! WE DON'T WANT TO GIVE HIM TOO MUCH SUN!
YOU WANT ME TO CARRY HIM?

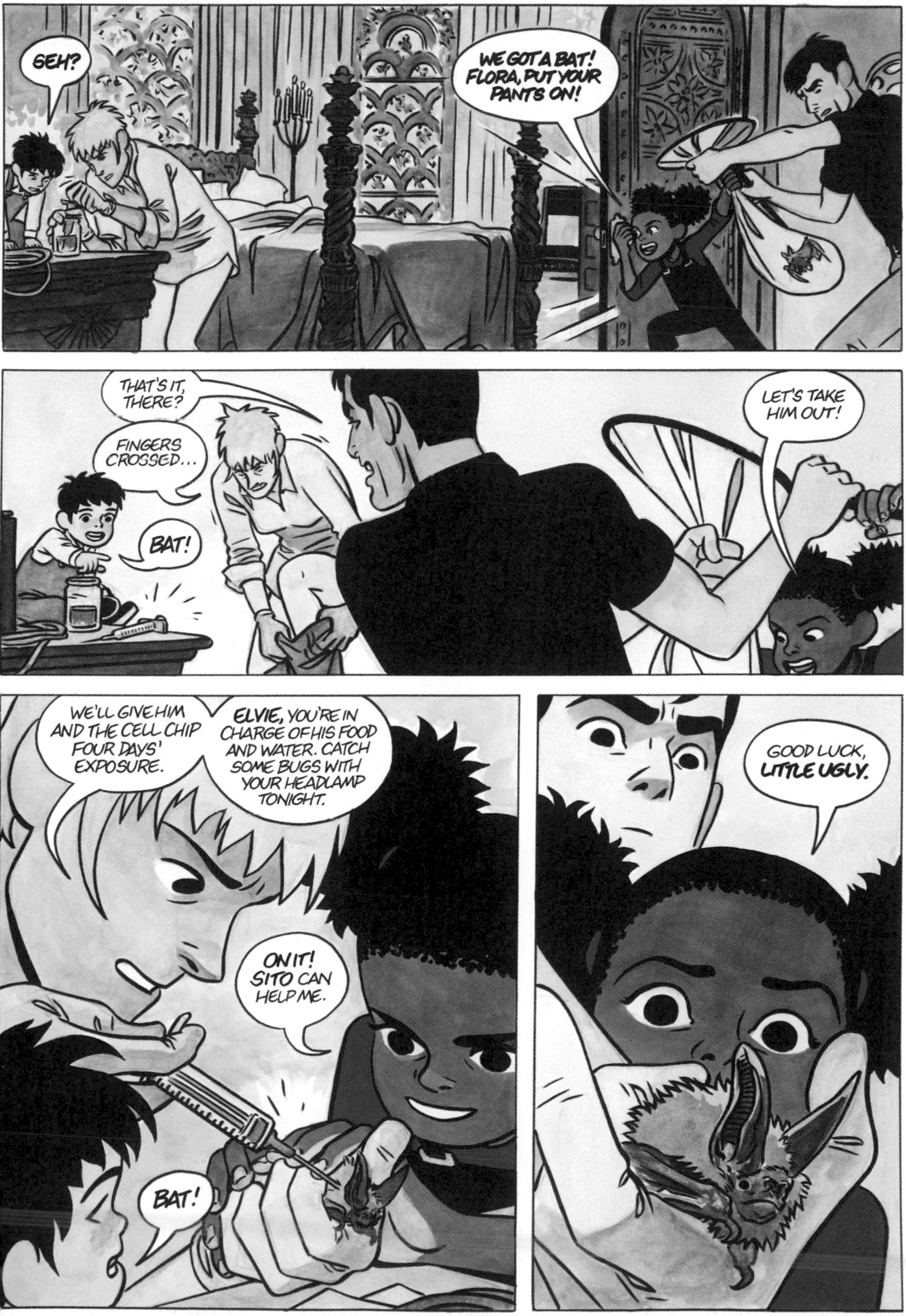

SEH?
WE GOT A BAT! FLORA, PUT YOUR PANTS ON!
THAT'S IT, THERE?
FINGERS CROSSED...
BAT!
LET'S TAKE HIM OUT!
WE'LL GIVE HIM AND THE CELL CHIP FOUR DAYS' EXPOSURE.
ELVIE, YOU'RE IN CHARGE OF HIS FOOD AND WATER. CATCH SOME BUGS WITH YOUR HEADLAMP TONIGHT.
ON IT! SITO CAN HELP ME.
BAT!
GOOD LUCK, LITTLE UGLY.

FLORA'S TONGUE | TONGUE CELLS GO ONTO CHIP

VACCINE = POSITIVE, CHIP COLOR CODE TURNS **PURPLE**— NOW AND FOREVER MY FAVORITE COLOR!

HEARST CASTLE, CALIFORNIA, NOVEMBER 2. 29 DAYS UNTIL OUR MONARCH MEDICINE EXPIRES. DAY 2 OF OUR VACCINE TRIAL WITH THE BAT. SO FAR, SO GOOD. FLORA IS CLEARLY TIRED OF ME ASKING HOW MUCH LONGER WE HAVE TO WAIT, BECAUSE SHE JUST ASSIGNED NEW SCHOOLWORK. I KNOW HER WAYS.

— BIO PAPER, WEEK 1, NOV. 2101

ABOUT BATS: BATS DO FINE WITH LIMITED SUN EXPOSURE, I.E. **TWILIGHT.** LIKE MONARCHS, THEY ACTUALLY NEED THE SUN TO CALIBRATE THEIR INTERNAL COMPASSES. WE DON'T KNOW WHY THEY TOLERATE LIMITED SUNLIGHT SO WELL, BUT IT COULD BE BECAUSE THEIR HEARTS ARE SO DIFFERENT FROM HUMANS'... THEY BEAT FIVE TIMES AS FAST, UP TO ONE THOUSAND BEATS PER MINUTE, WHILE THEY FLY! STILL, UNDER FULL SUN, IF THEY DON'T HAVE MEDS, THEY'LL DIE, JUST LIKE US.

Corynorhinus townsendii (Townsend's Big-eared Bat)

THE NEXT TEST WE'LL DO, ASSUMING THIS ONE'S A SUCCESS, IS A LONG-TERM STUDY ON WHETHER THE VACCINE CAN PASS FROM A MAMA BAT TO HER **BABIES**— EVEN IF SHE'S VACCINATED **BEFORE BECOMING PREGNANT.**

THE BIG-EARED BATS HERE AT THE CASTLE ARE PERFECT FOR THIS TEST. THEIR MATING SEASON HAS ALREADY BEGUN, BUT FEMALES ACTUALLY STORE SPERM UNTIL **AFTER** WINTER HIBERNATION. IT'S NOT UNTIL SPRING THAT THEY OVULATE AND BECOME PREGNANT. THAT WAY THEIR BABIES ARE BORN WHEN IT'S WARM AND EASY TO FIND FOOD (PRETTY AMAZING). SO, WE'LL COLLECT A FEW SOON-TO-BE-MAMAS, GIVE THEM THE VACCINE NOW, AND IF NEXT YEAR'S BABIES **ALSO** SURVIVE SUN EXPOSURE, WE'LL KNOW THAT IMMUNITY CAN PASS FROM THE MAMA'S CELLS TO HER BABY!

THAT'D BE A BIG DEAL. IT'D MEAN THAT FUTURE GENERATIONS OF PEOPLE MIGHT NOT EVEN **NEED** THE VACCINE. THEY'D BE **CURED.**

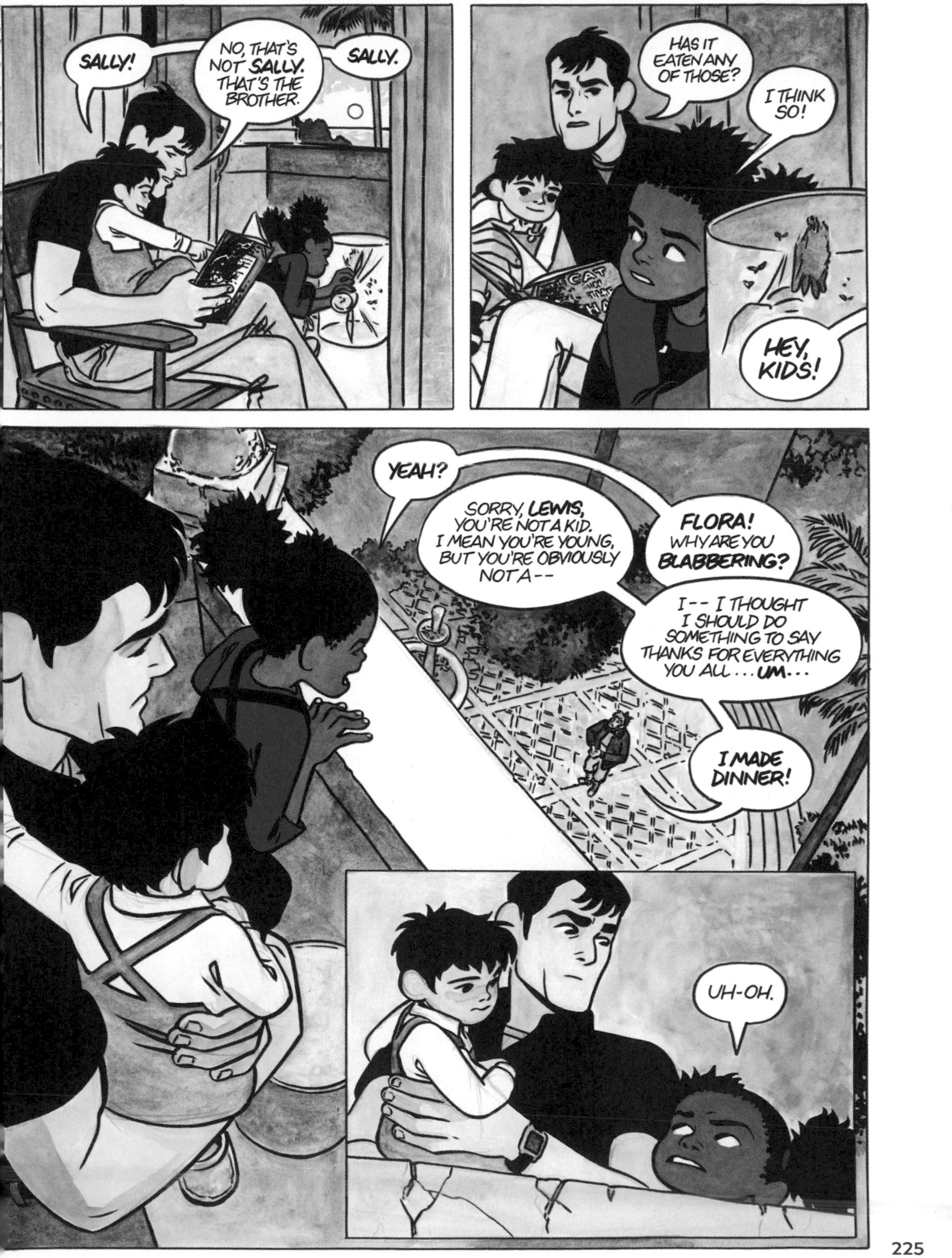
SALLY!
NO, THAT'S NOT SALLY. THAT'S THE BROTHER.
SALLY.
HAS IT EATEN ANY OF THOSE?
I THINK SO!
HEY, KIDS!
YEAH?
SORRY, LEWIS, YOU'RE NOT A KID. I MEAN YOU'RE YOUNG, BUT YOU'RE OBVIOUSLY NOT A--
FLORA! WHY ARE YOU BLABBERING?
I-- I THOUGHT I SHOULD DO SOMETHING TO SAY THANKS FOR EVERYTHING YOU ALL . . . UM . . .
I MADE DINNER!
UH-OH.

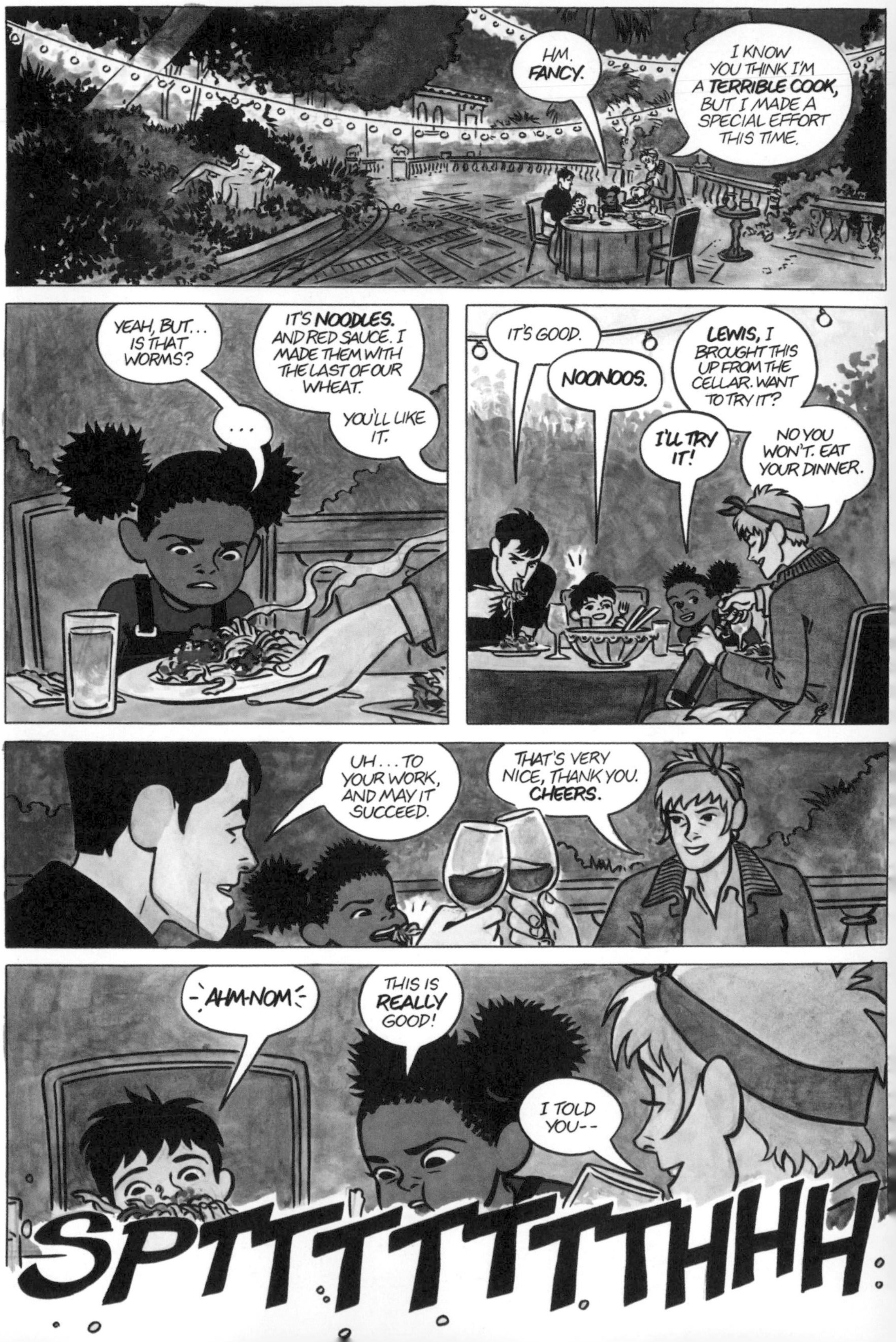
HM. FANCY.
I KNOW YOU THINK I'M A TERRIBLE COOK, BUT I MADE A SPECIAL EFFORT THIS TIME.
YEAH, BUT... IS THAT WORMS?
IT'S NOODLES. AND RED SAUCE. I MADE THEM WITH THE LAST OF OUR WHEAT.
YOU'LL LIKE IT.
...
IT'S GOOD.
NOONOOS.
LEWIS, I BROUGHT THIS UP FROM THE CELLAR. WANT TO TRY IT?
I'LL TRY IT!
NO YOU WON'T. EAT YOUR DINNER.
UH... TO YOUR WORK, AND MAY IT SUCCEED.
THAT'S VERY NICE, THANK YOU. CHEERS.
AHM-NOM
THIS IS REALLY GOOD!
I TOLD YOU--
SPTTTTTTTHH

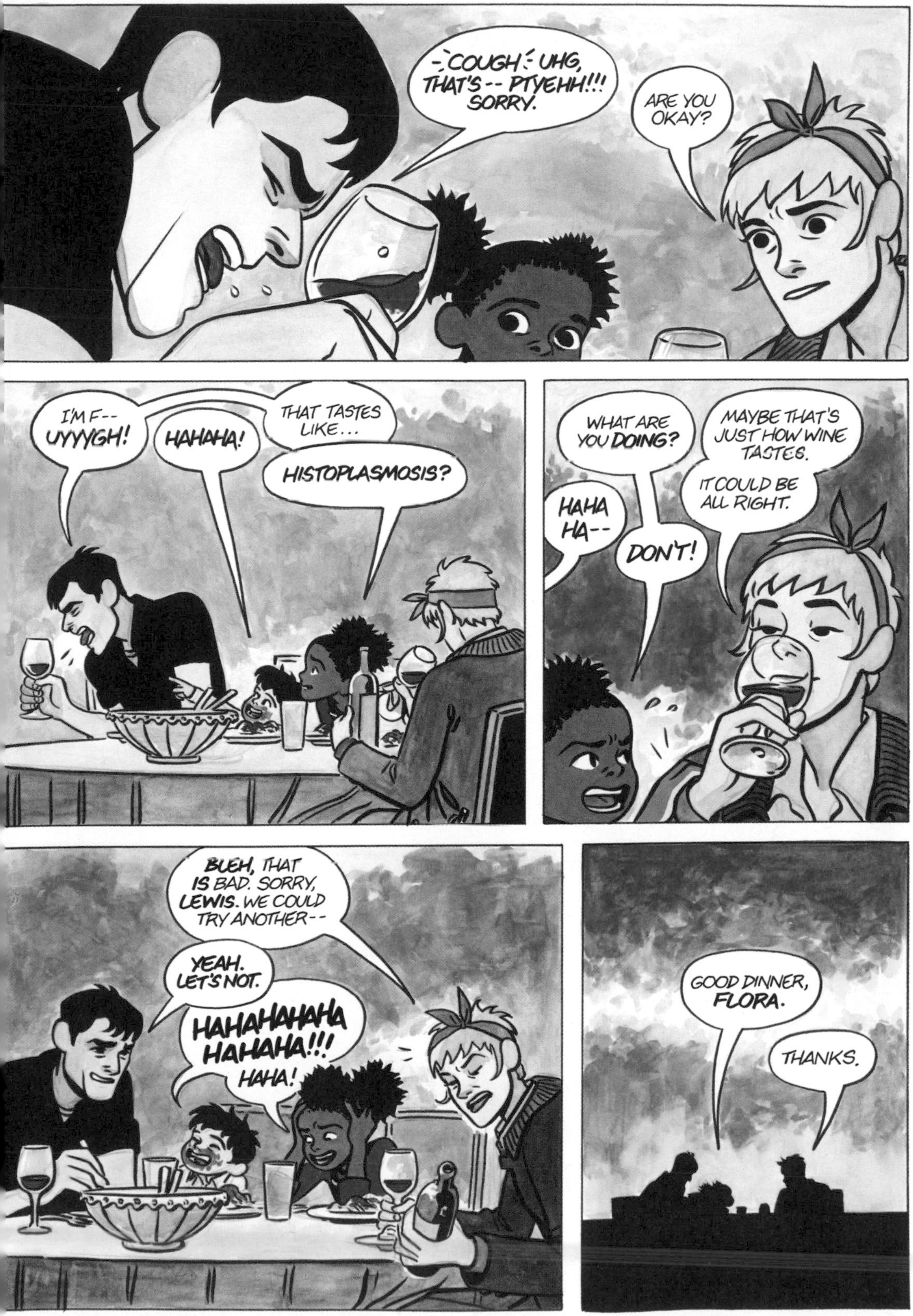
-COUGH- UHG, THAT'S-- PTYEHH!!! SORRY.
ARE YOU OKAY?
I'M F-- UYYYGH!
HAHAHA!
THAT TASTES LIKE...
HISTOPLASMOSIS?
WHAT ARE YOU DOING?
MAYBE THAT'S JUST HOW WINE TASTES.
IT COULD BE ALL RIGHT.
HAHA HA--
DON'T!
BLEH, THAT IS BAD. SORRY, LEWIS. WE COULD TRY ANOTHER--
YEAH. LET'S NOT.
HAHAHAHAHA HAHAHA!!!
HAHA!
GOOD DINNER, FLORA.
THANKS.

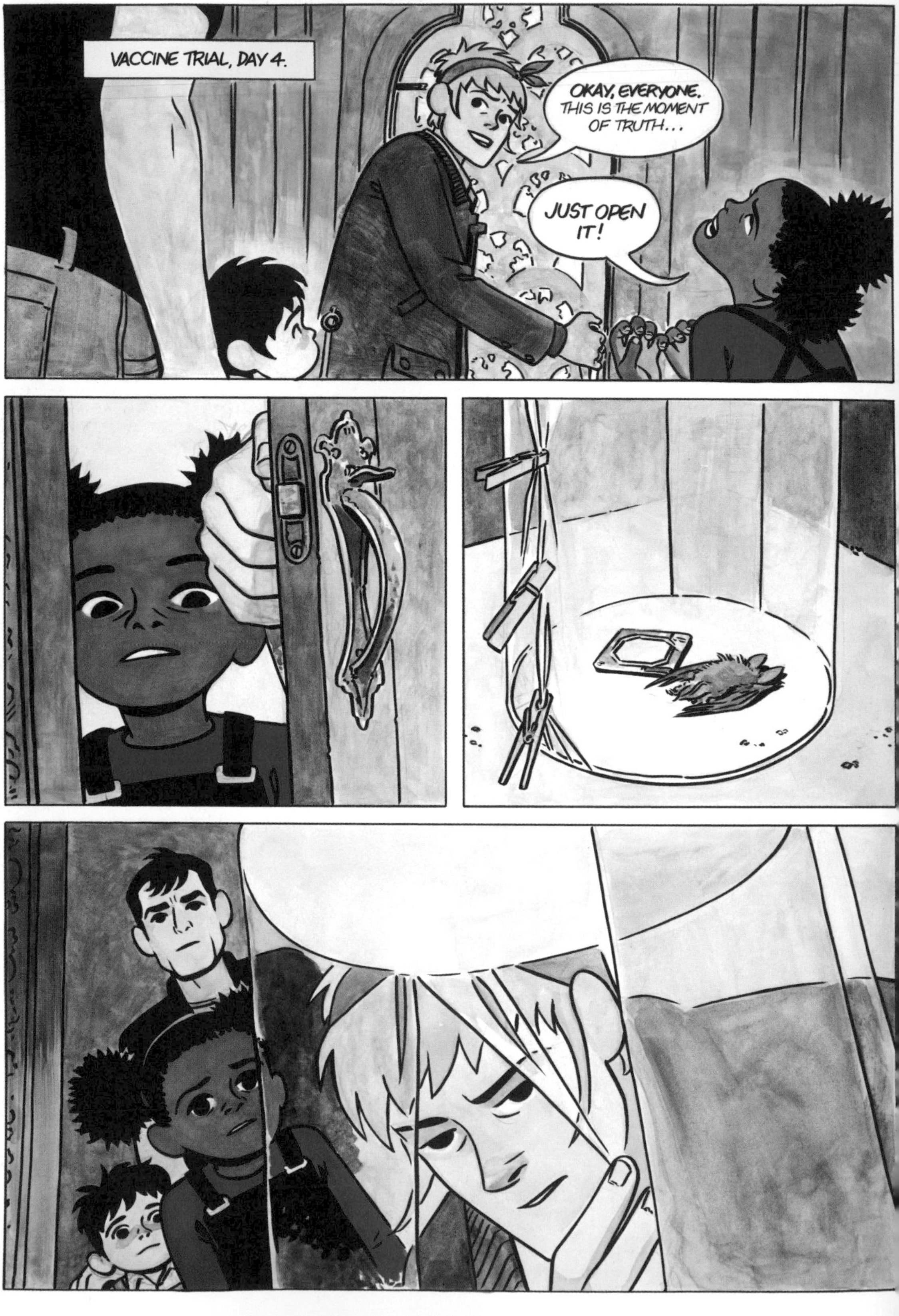
VACCINE TRIAL, DAY 4.
OKAY, EVERYONE. THIS IS THE MOMENT OF TRUTH...
JUST OPEN IT!

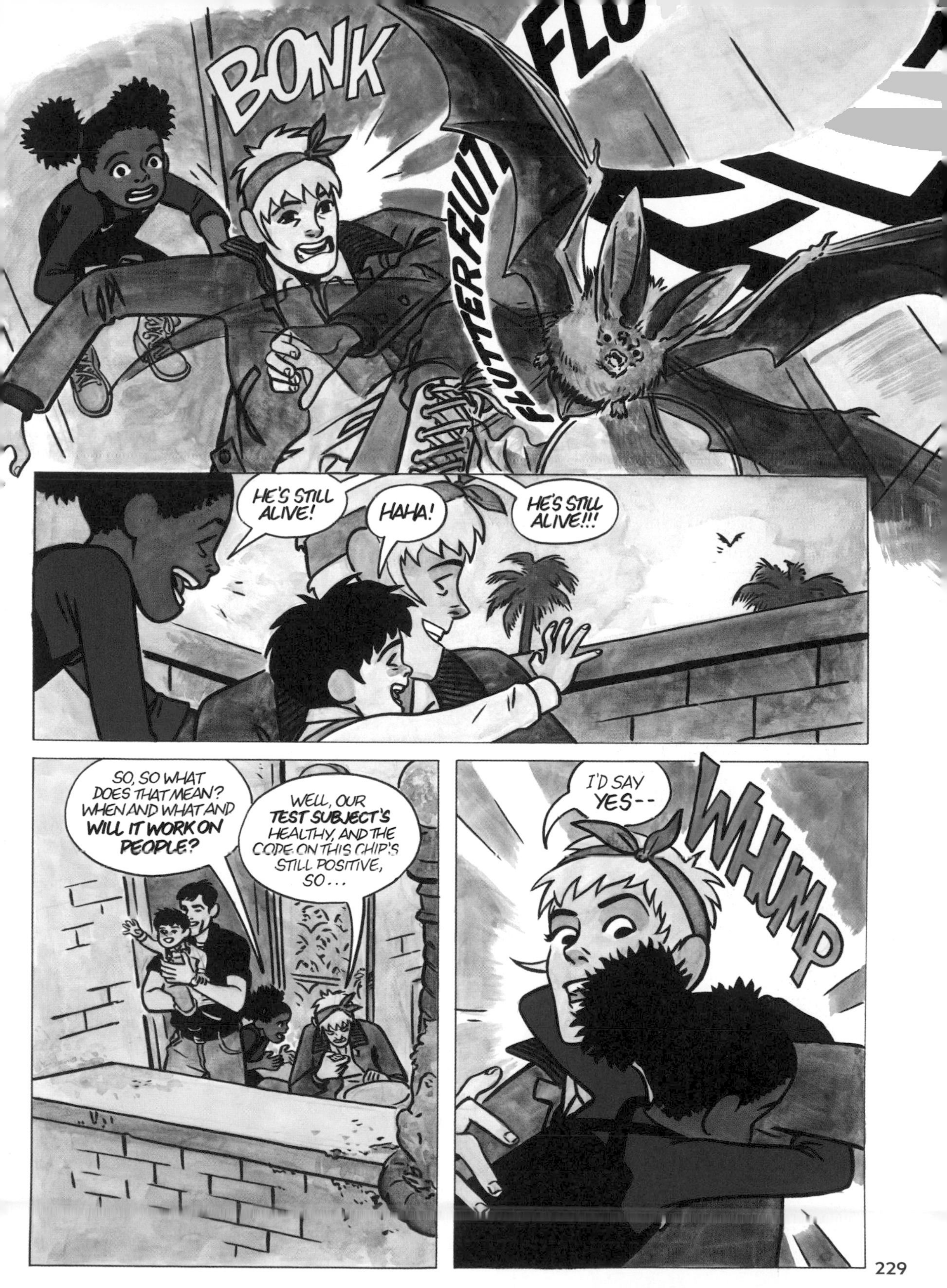
BONK
FLUTTERFLUTT
FLU
HE'S STILL ALIVE!
HAHA!
HE'S STILL ALIVE!!!
SO, SO WHAT DOES THAT MEAN? WHEN AND WHAT AND **WILL IT WORK ON PEOPLE?**
WELL, OUR **TEST SUBJECT'S** HEALTHY, AND THE CODE ON THIS CHIP'S STILL POSITIVE, SO . . .
I'D SAY **YES- -**
WHUMP

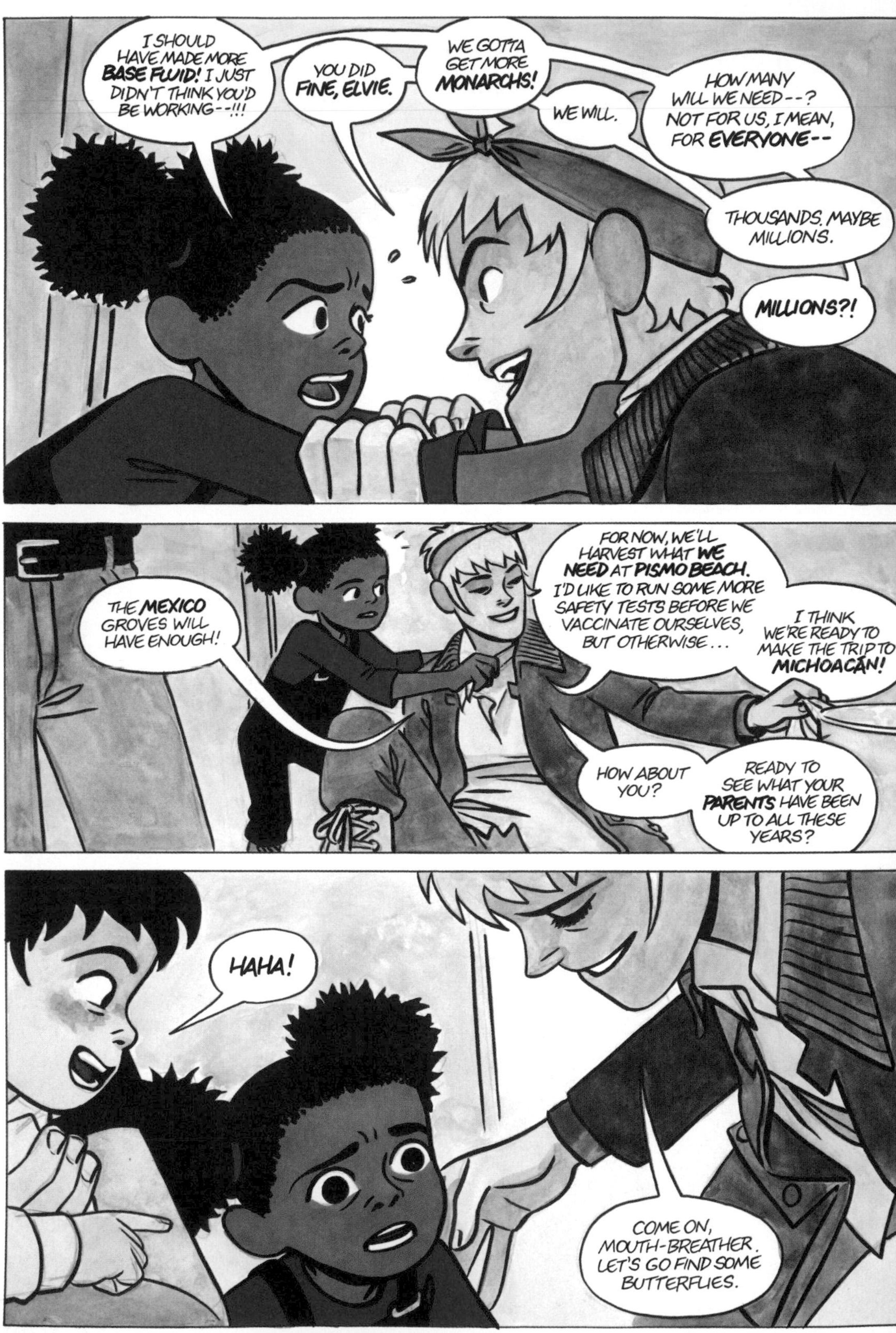

I SHOULD HAVE MADE MORE **BASE FLUID!** I JUST DIDN'T THINK YOU'D BE WORKING--!!!
YOU DID **FINE, ELVIE.**
WE GOTTA GET MORE **MONARCHS!**
WE WILL.
HOW MANY WILL WE NEED--? NOT FOR US, I MEAN, FOR **EVERYONE--**
THOUSANDS. MAYBE MILLIONS.
MILLIONS?!
THE **MEXICO** GROVES WILL HAVE ENOUGH!
FOR NOW, WE'LL HARVEST WHAT **WE NEED** AT **PISMO BEACH.** I'D LIKE TO RUN SOME MORE SAFETY TESTS BEFORE WE VACCINATE OURSELVES, BUT OTHERWISE...
I THINK WE'RE READY TO MAKE THE TRIP TO **MICHOACÁN!**
HOW ABOUT YOU?
READY TO SEE WHAT YOUR **PARENTS** HAVE BEEN UP TO ALL THESE YEARS?
HAHA!
COME ON, MOUTH-BREATHER. LET'S GO FIND SOME BUTTERFLIES.

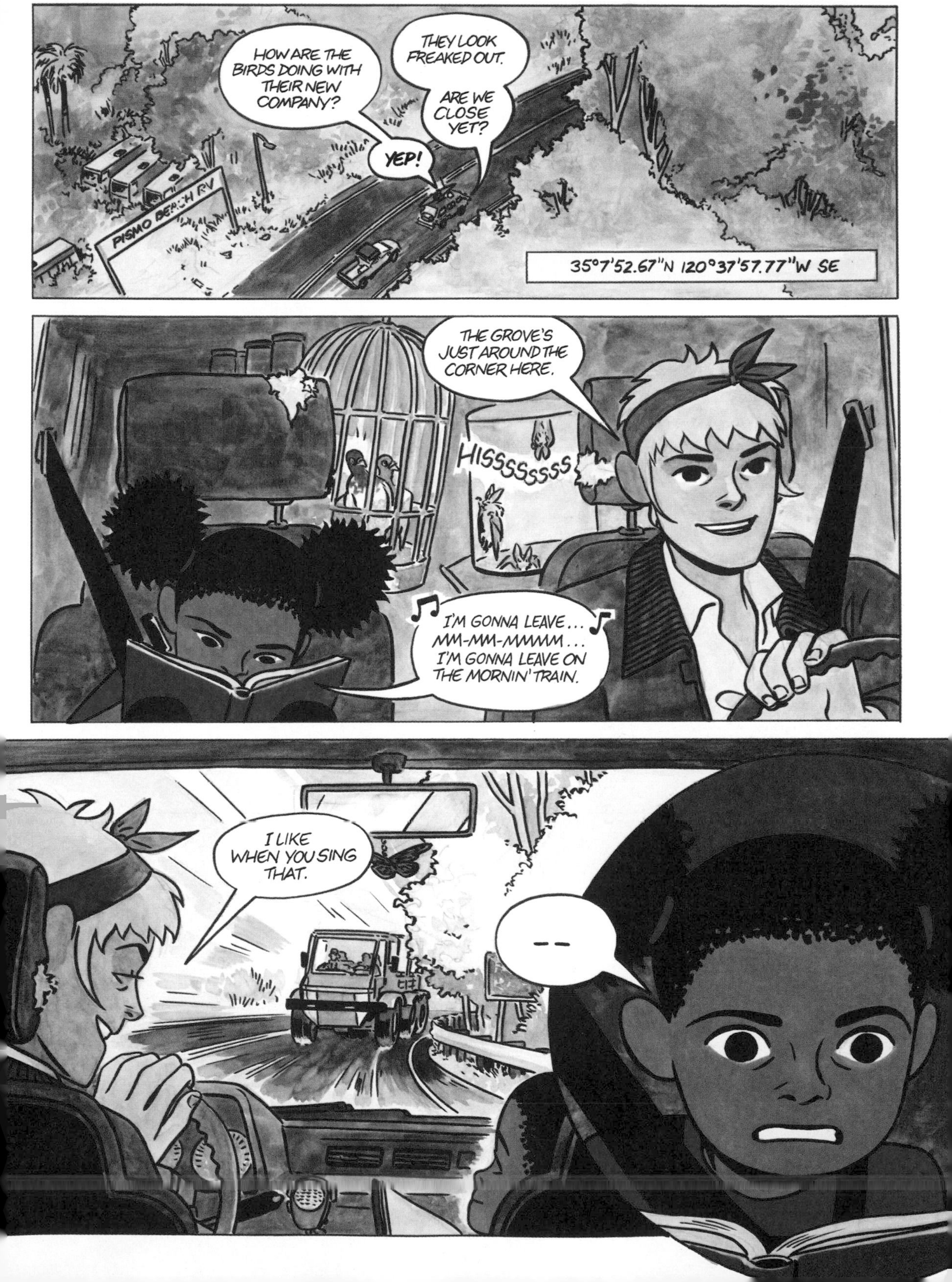
HOW ARE THE BIRDS DOING WITH THEIR NEW COMPANY?
THEY LOOK FREAKED OUT.
ARE WE CLOSE YET?
YEP!
PISMO BEACH RV
35°7'52.67"N 120°37'57.77"W SE
THE GROVE'S JUST AROUND THE CORNER HERE.
HISSSSSSSS
I'M GONNA LEAVE... MM-MM-MMMM... I'M GONNA LEAVE ON THE MORNIN' TRAIN.
I LIKE WHEN YOU SING THAT.
--

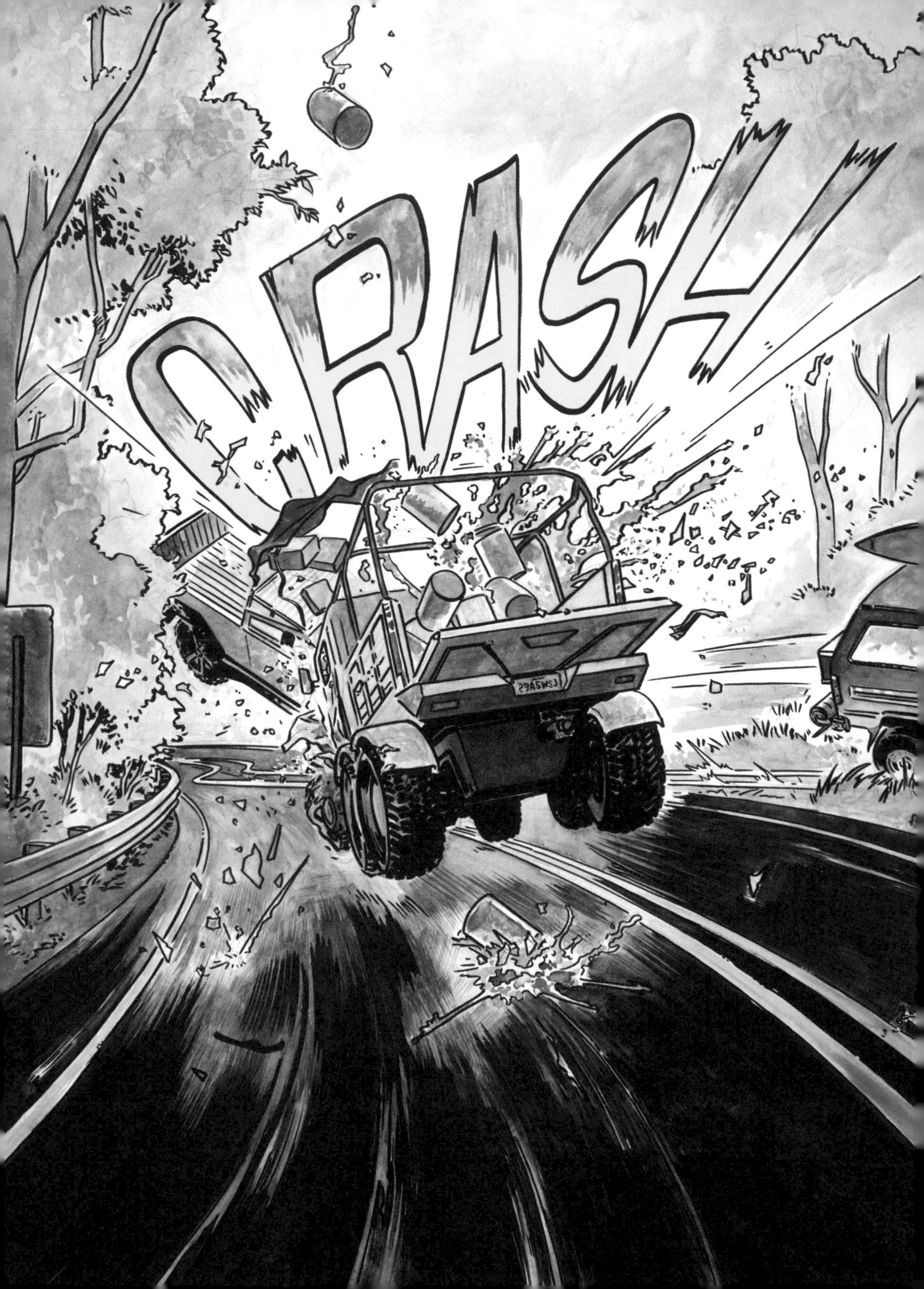
CRASH

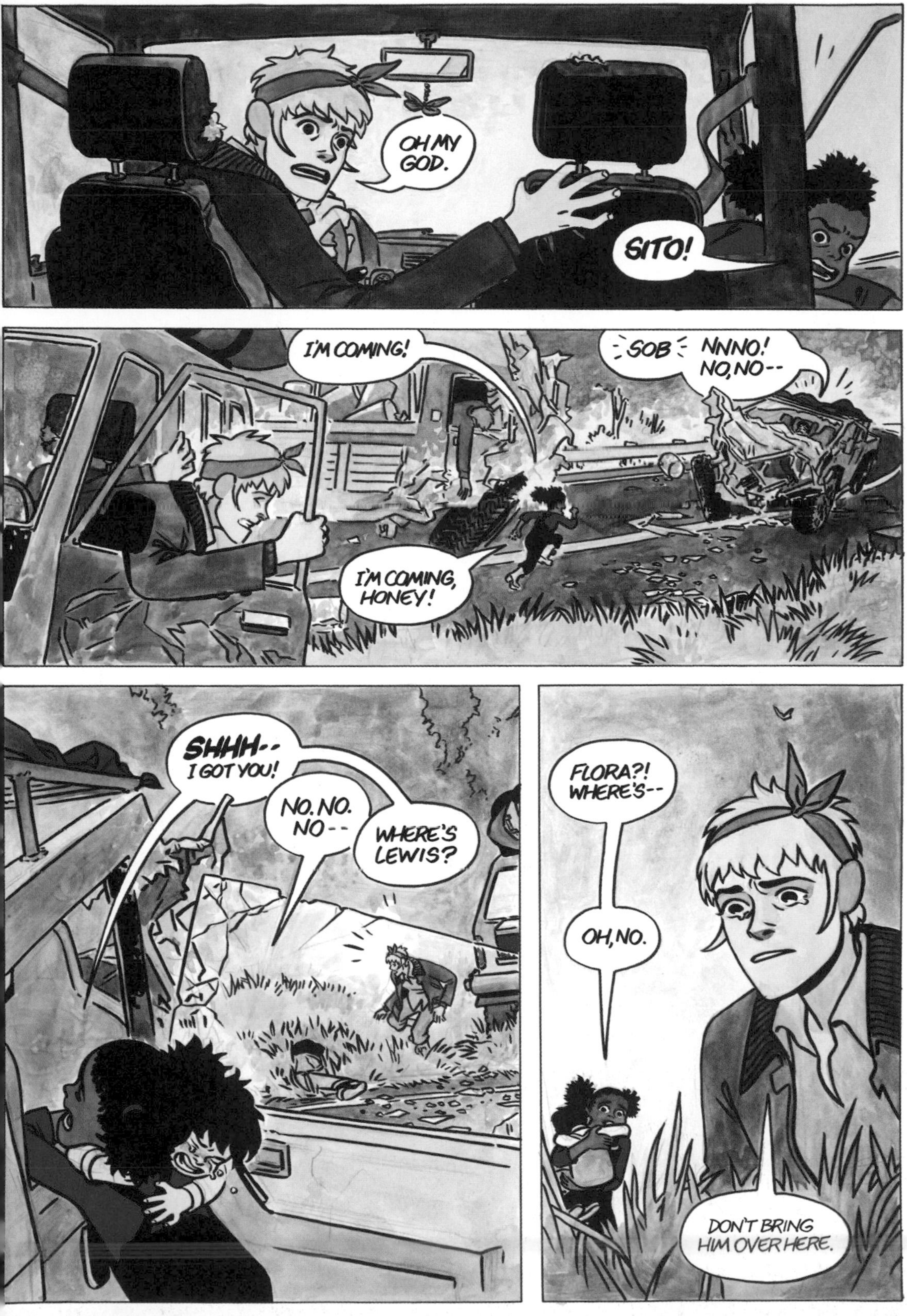
OH MY GOD.
SITO!
I'M COMING!
SOB
NNNO! NO, NO--
I'M COMING, HONEY!
SHHH-- I GOT YOU!
NO. NO. NO--
WHERE'S LEWIS?
FLORA?! WHERE'S--
OH, NO.
DON'T BRING HIM OVER HERE.

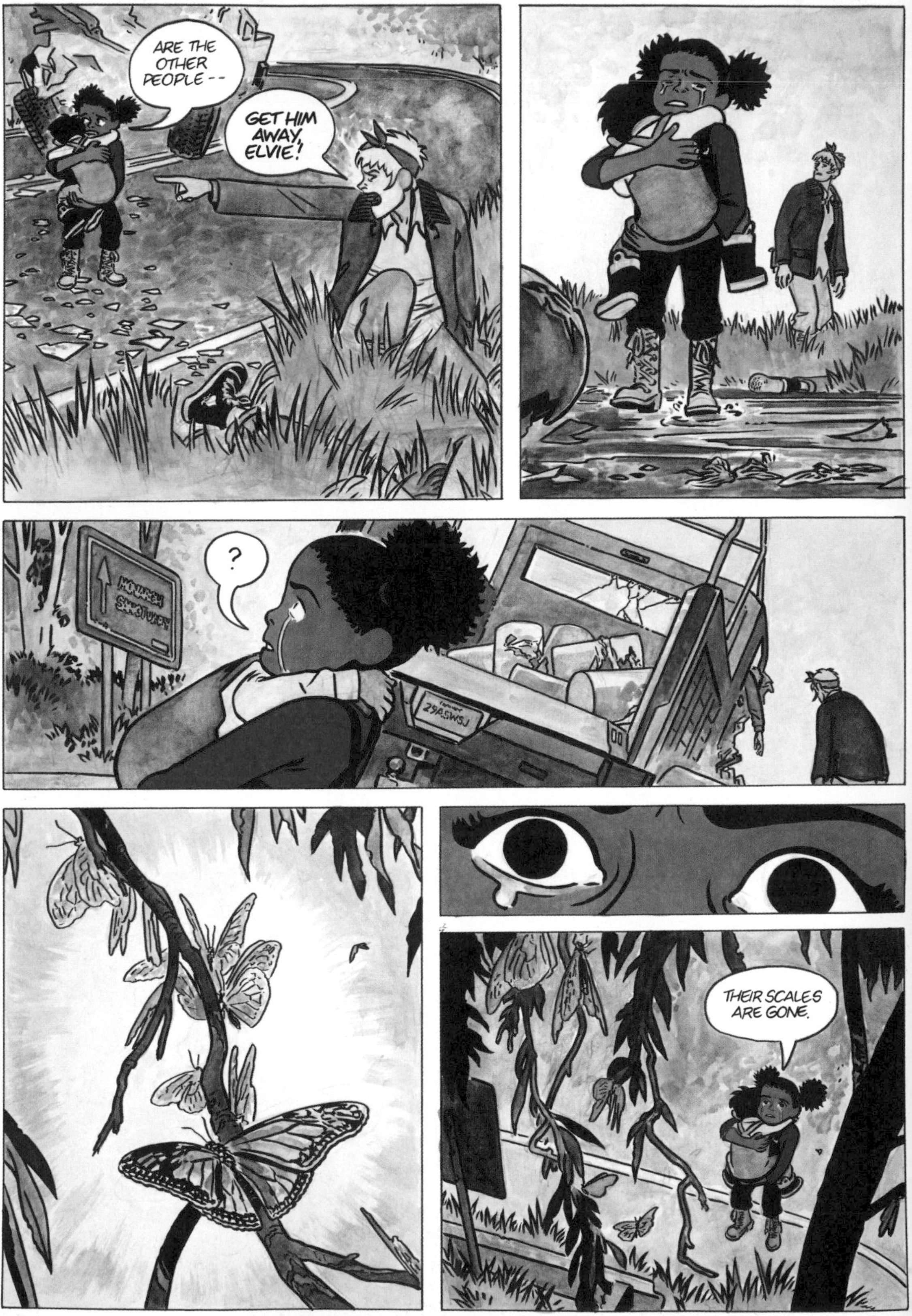
ARE THE OTHER PEOPLE --
GET HIM AWAY, ELVIE!
?
THEIR SCALES ARE GONE.

CHAPTER TWELVE
THE SONG

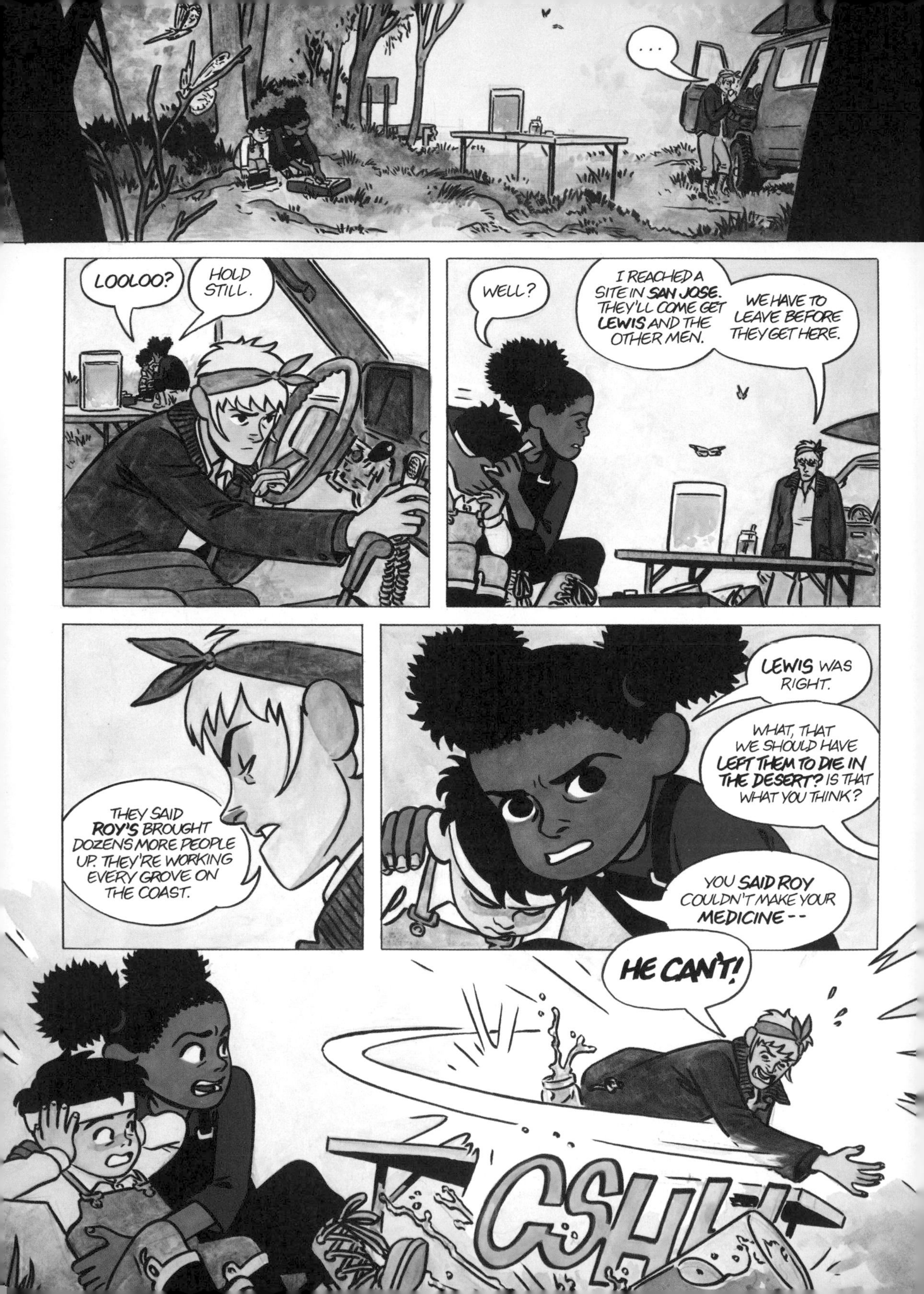
...
LOOLOO?
HOLD STILL.
WELL?
I REACHED A SITE IN SAN JOSE. THEY'LL COME GET LEWIS AND THE OTHER MEN.
WE HAVE TO LEAVE BEFORE THEY GET HERE.
THEY SAID ROY'S BROUGHT DOZENS MORE PEOPLE UP. THEY'RE WORKING EVERY GROVE ON THE COAST.
LEWIS WAS RIGHT.
WHAT, THAT WE SHOULD HAVE LEFT THEM TO DIE IN THE DESERT? IS THAT WHAT YOU THINK?
YOU SAID ROY COULDN'T MAKE YOUR MEDICINE--
HE CAN'T!
CSH

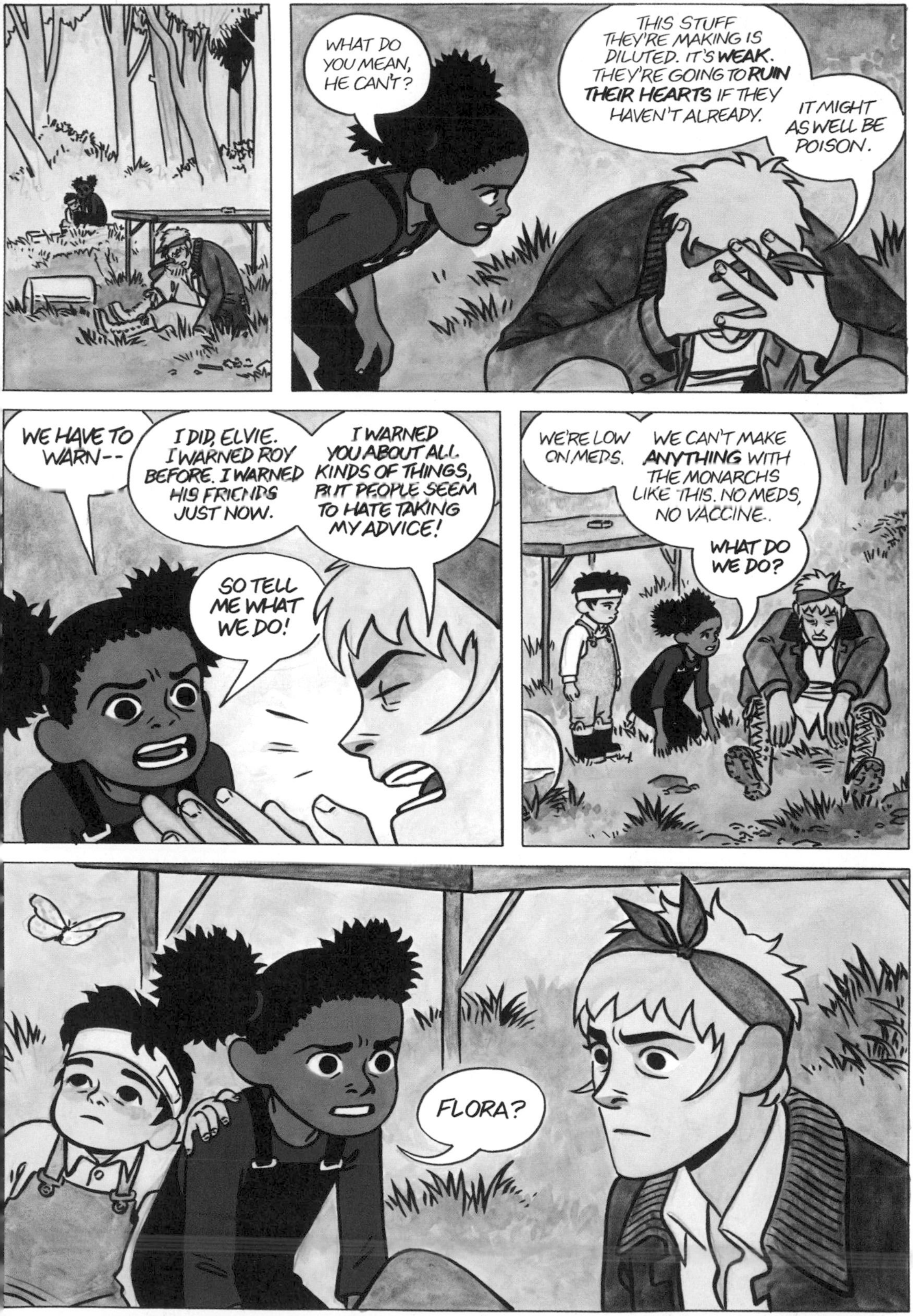
WHAT DO YOU MEAN, HE CAN'T?
THIS STUFF THEY'RE MAKING IS DILUTED. IT'S **WEAK**. THEY'RE GOING TO **RUIN THEIR HEARTS** IF THEY HAVEN'T ALREADY.
IT MIGHT AS WELL BE POISON.
WE HAVE TO WARN--
I DID, ELVIE. I WARNED ROY BEFORE. I WARNED HIS FRIENDS JUST NOW.
I WARNED YOU ABOUT ALL KINDS OF THINGS, BUT PEOPLE SEEM TO HATE TAKING MY ADVICE!
SO TELL ME WHAT WE DO!
WE'RE LOW ON MEDS.
WE CAN'T MAKE **ANYTHING** WITH THE MONARCHS LIKE THIS. NO MEDS, NO VACCINE.
WHAT DO WE DO?
FLORA?

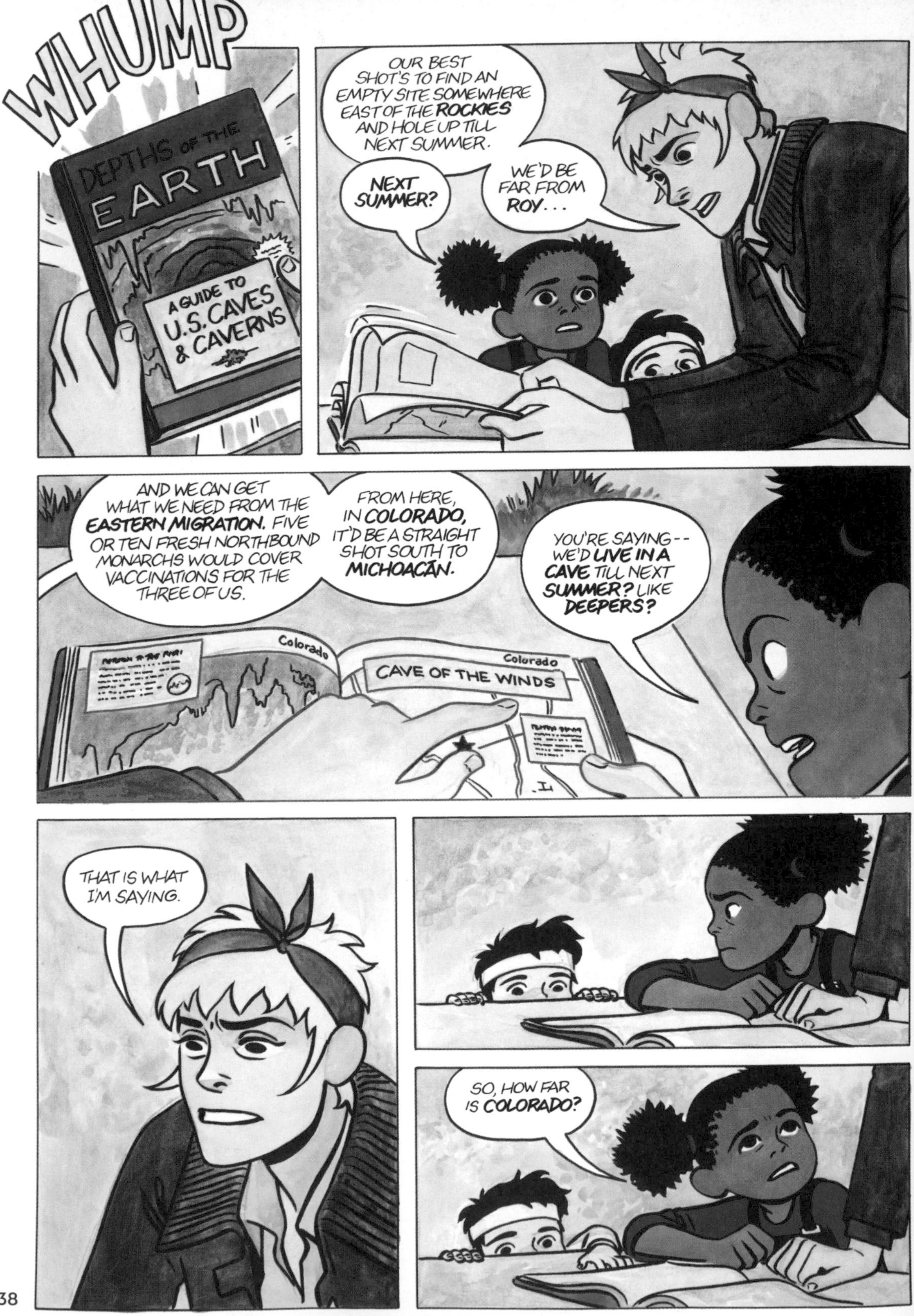
WHUMP
DEPTHS OF THE EARTH
A GUIDE TO U.S. CAVES & CAVERNS
OUR BEST SHOT'S TO FIND AN EMPTY SITE SOMEWHERE EAST OF THE ROCKIES AND HOLE UP TILL NEXT SUMMER.
NEXT SUMMER?
WE'D BE FAR FROM ROY...
AND WE CAN GET WHAT WE NEED FROM THE EASTERN MIGRATION. FIVE OR TEN FRESH NORTHBOUND MONARCHS WOULD COVER VACCINATIONS FOR THE THREE OF US.
FROM HERE, IN COLORADO, IT'D BE A STRAIGHT SHOT SOUTH TO MICHOACÁN.
YOU'RE SAYING-- WE'D LIVE IN A CAVE TILL NEXT SUMMER? LIKE DEEPERS?
Colorado
Colorado
CAVE OF THE WINDS
THAT IS WHAT I'M SAYING.
SO, HOW FAR IS COLORADO?

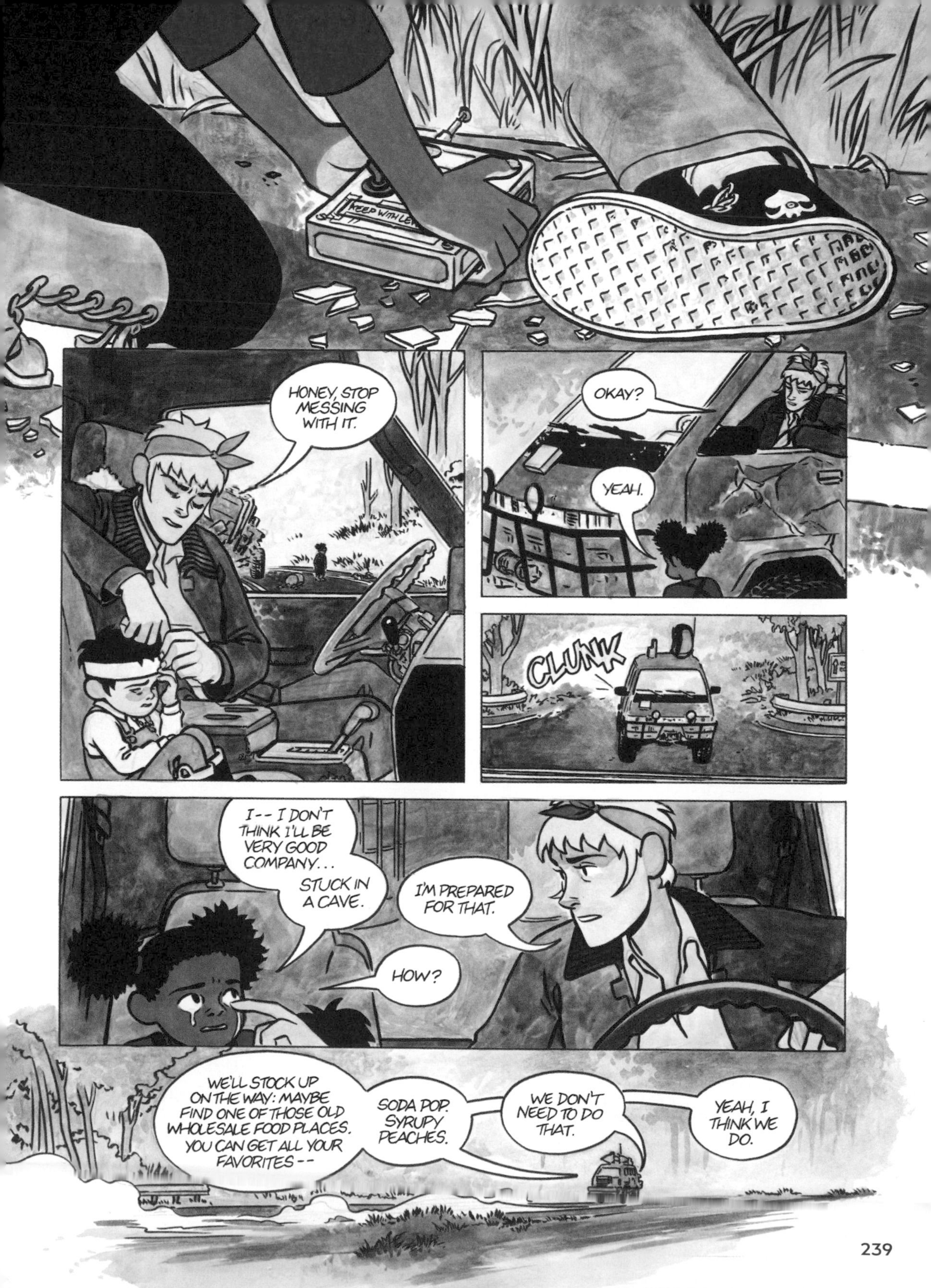
HONEY, STOP MESSING WITH IT.
OKAY?
YEAH.
CLUNK
I-- I DON'T THINK I'LL BE VERY GOOD COMPANY...
STUCK IN A CAVE.
I'M PREPARED FOR THAT.
HOW?
WE'LL STOCK UP ON THE WAY: MAYBE FIND ONE OF THOSE OLD WHOLESALE FOOD PLACES. YOU CAN GET ALL YOUR FAVORITES--
SODA POP. SYRUPY PEACHES.
WE DON'T NEED TO DO THAT.
YEAH, I THINK WE DO.

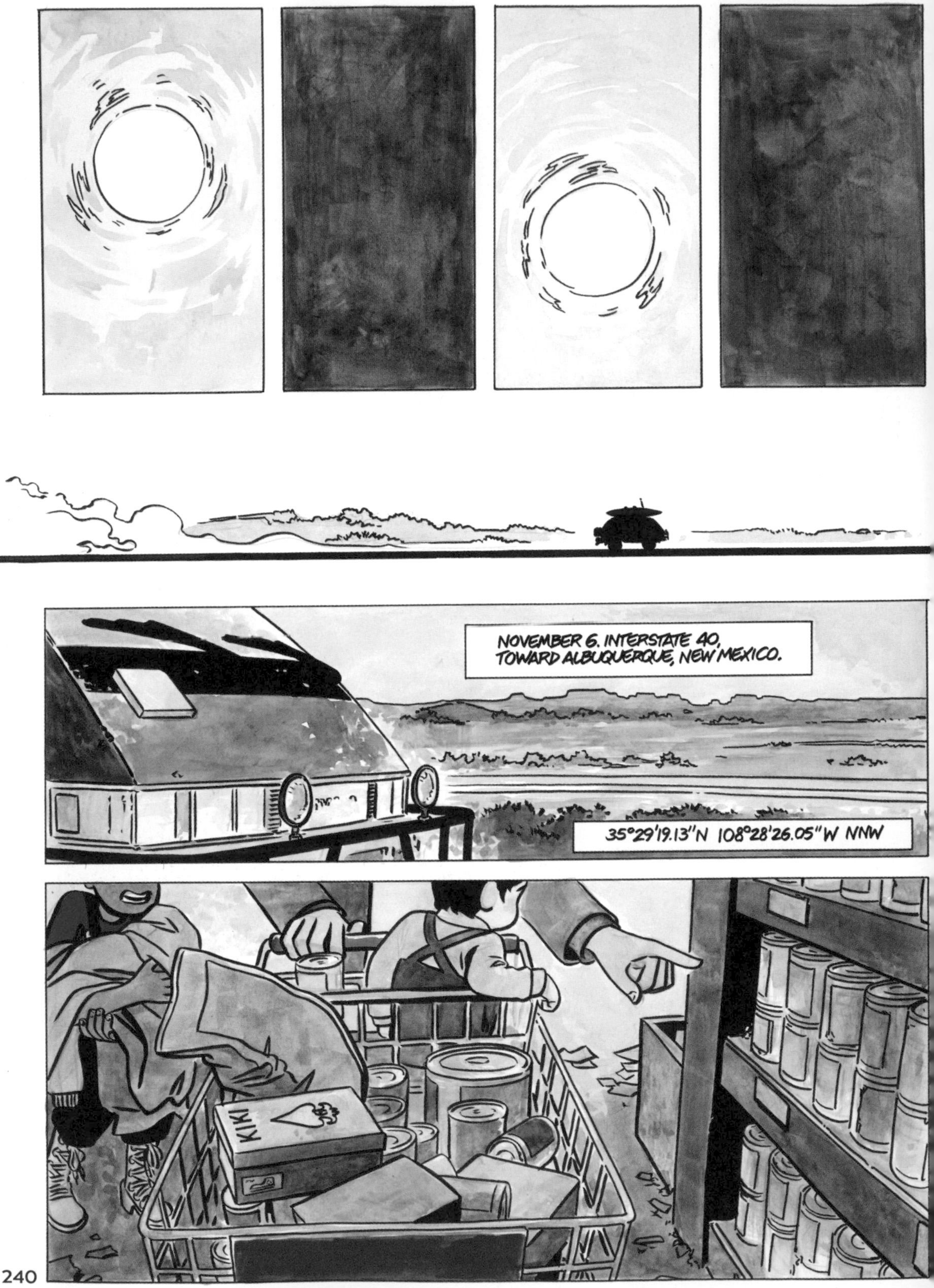
NOVEMBER 6. INTERSTATE 40,
TOWARD ALBUQUERQUE, NEW MEXICO.
35°29'19.13"N 108°28'26.05"W NNW
KIKI

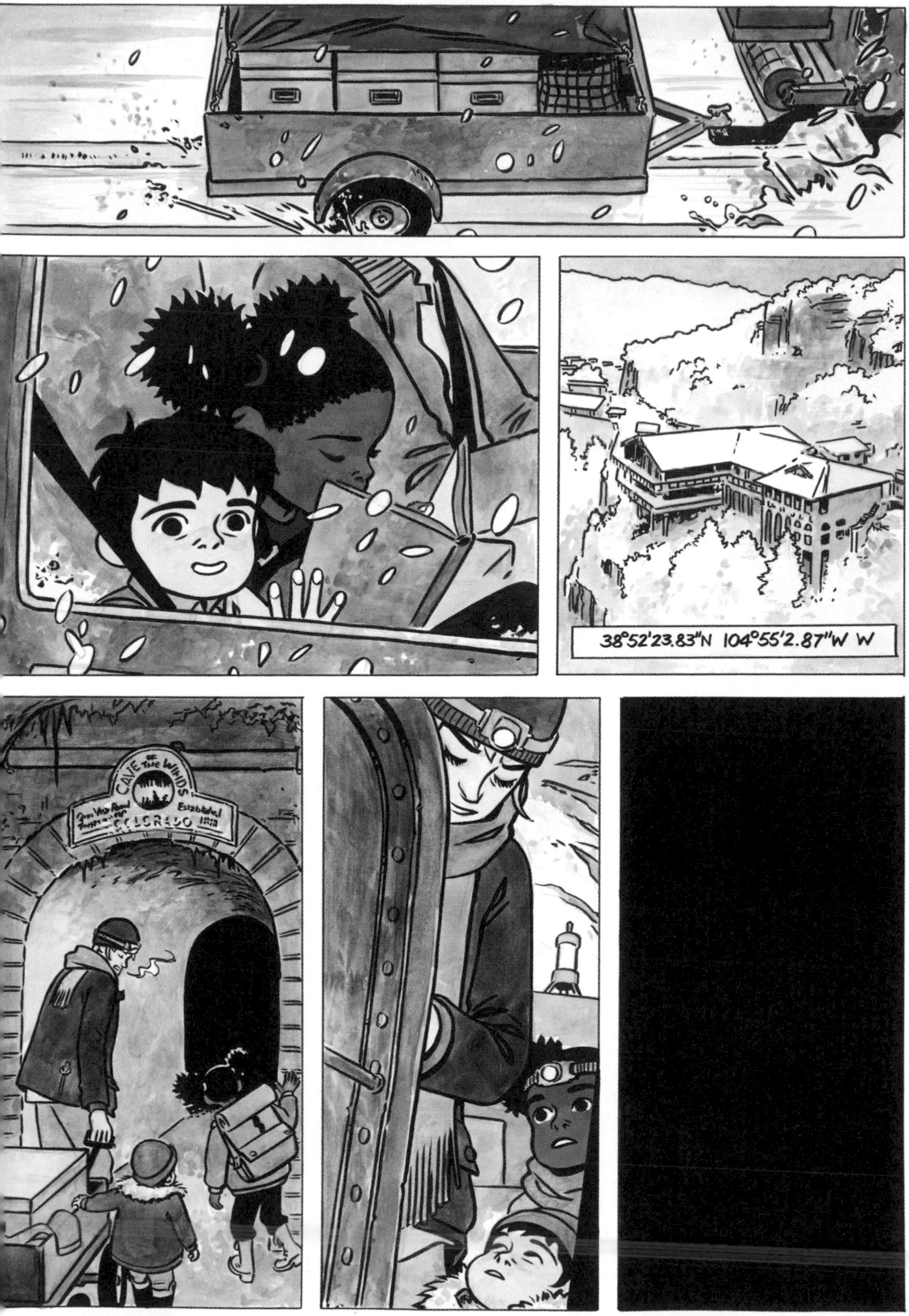
38°52'23.83"N 104°55'2.87"W W
CAVE OF THE WINDS
Established
COLORADO

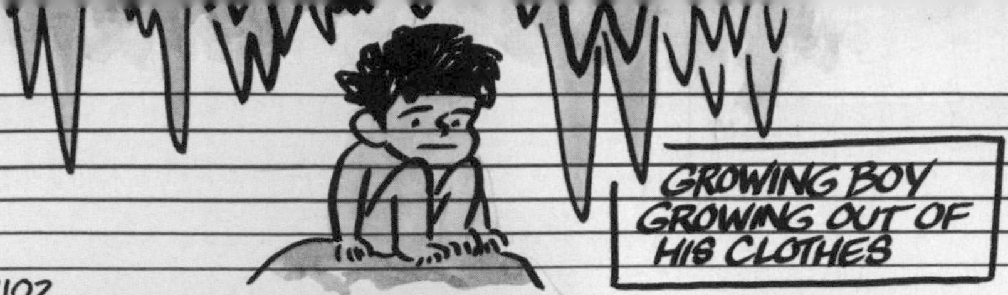
GROWING BOY GROWING OUT OF HIS CLOTHES

JANUARY 12, ~~2102~~ 2102. CAVE OF THE WINDS, COLORADO (NO MONARCH MEDICINE LEFT).

I'M DONE WITH THIS JOURNAL. THERE'S A FEW PAGES LEFT, BUT IT'S A NEW YEAR AND I NEED A FRESH START. IT'S BEEN TWO MONTHS SINCE I SAW DAYLIGHT, AND I'M **GRUMPY.** I WISH WE COULD HIBERNATE AND JUST WAKE UP IN THE SPRING, OR WHENEVER THE MONARCHS COME NORTH.

I HAVEN'T BEEN ABLE TO CRY ABOUT **LEWIS** SINCE WE LEFT **PISMO. FLORA** SAYS THAT DOESN'T MEAN I'M BROKEN OR THAT I DON'T CARE -- IT'S JUST HOW SOME PEOPLE ARE WITH A LOSS. I DON'T KNOW. IT SURE FEELS WRONG TO **WANT TO CRY** AND NOT BE ABLE TO CRY. I WORRY I WON'T REMEMBER HIM. SHE SAYS I SHOULD WRITE ABOUT **LEWIS.** I MIGHT.

FLORA OVERHEARD A RADIO EXCHANGE WHILE SHE WAS NIGHT RANGING LAST WEEK. WORD'S GOING AROUND THAT DEEPERS OUT WEST TRIED TO COME OUT IN THE DAYTIME AND SOME OF THEM DIED. I GUESS SHE WAS RIGHT ABOUT **ROY'S** CHEMISTRY. HOPEFULLY SOME MADE IT BACK UNDERGROUND SAFELY. WHAT AN IDIOT.

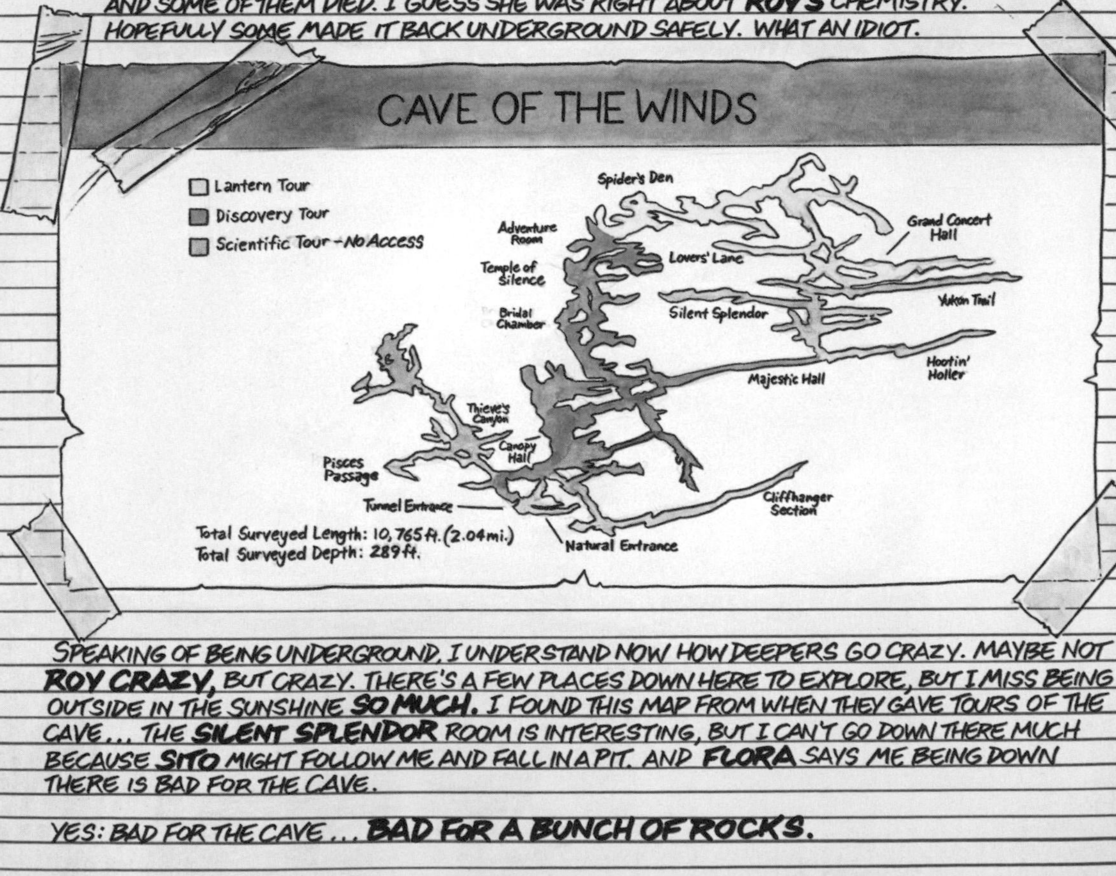
CAVE OF THE WINDS
Lantern Tour
Discovery Tour
Scientific Tour - No Access
Spider's Den
Adventure Room
Temple of Silence
Bridal Chamber
Lovers' Lane
Grand Concert Hall
Silent Splendor
Yukon Trail
Hootin' Holler
Majestic Hall
Thieve's Canyon
Canopy Hall
Pisces Passage
Tunnel Entrance
Cliffhanger Section
Natural Entrance
Total Surveyed Length: 10,765 ft. (2.04 mi.)
Total Surveyed Depth: 289 ft.

SPEAKING OF BEING UNDERGROUND, I UNDERSTAND NOW HOW DEEPERS GO CRAZY. MAYBE NOT **ROY CRAZY,** BUT CRAZY. THERE'S A FEW PLACES DOWN HERE TO EXPLORE, BUT I MISS BEING OUTSIDE IN THE SUNSHINE **SO MUCH.** I FOUND THIS MAP FROM WHEN THEY GAVE TOURS OF THE CAVE... THE **SILENT SPLENDOR** ROOM IS INTERESTING, BUT I CAN'T GO DOWN THERE MUCH BECAUSE **SITO** MIGHT FOLLOW ME AND FALL IN A PIT. AND **FLORA** SAYS ME BEING DOWN THERE IS BAD FOR THE CAVE.

YES: BAD FOR THE CAVE... **BAD FOR A BUNCH OF ROCKS.**

THE CAVE CERTAINLY DOESN'T TREAT **US** GENTLY. IT'S ACTUALLY TRYING TO SMOTHER US. WHENEVER WE BREATHE OUT CARBON DIOXIDE IT GETS TRAPPED IN HERE AND THE ONLY WAY TO SOLVE THAT IS TO OPEN THE ENTRANCE DOOR IN THE DEAD OF NIGHT TO CYCLE FRESH AIR INSIDE (AND EMPTY OUR TOILET BOWL). THIS IS THE **WORST JOB**, NOT JUST BECAUSE OF POOP, BUT BECAUSE IT'S COLDER OUTSIDE THAN AN EXTINCT POLAR BEAR'S TOENAILS. ACCORDING TO **FLORA, COLORADO** GETS HOT IN THE SUMMER, BUT I'LL BELIEVE THAT WHEN I SEE IT.

SUMMER WILL BRING MONARCHS, AND HOPEFULLY, **FINALLY**, VACCINATIONS. SO FAR THE MAMA BATS WE BROUGHT ALONG ARE DOING WELL, SO **FLORA'S** MORE AND MORE CONFIDENT ABOUT HER FORMULA. EVEN AT THAT, WE WON'T TRY GOING TO **MEXICO** UNTIL MID-FALL AT THE EARLIEST. **FLORA** THINKS MAKING THE TRIP TO **MICHOACÁN** IN THE MIDDLE OF SUMMER WOULD BE NEAR-SUICIDE BECAUSE OF THE HEAT, AND WE SHOULD GO SOUTH ALONG WITH THE MONARCHS WHEN THEY GO. I'LL BELIEVE THAT WHEN I SEE IT, TOO.

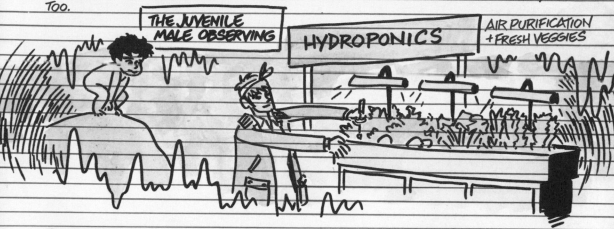

THE JUVENILE MALE OBSERVING

HYDROPONICS

AIR PURIFICATION + FRESH VEGGIES

BELIEVING, IT TURNS OUT, IS PROBABLY EVEN HARDER THAN REMEMBERING.

FOR EXAMPLE: I WONDER HOW LIKELY IT IS THAT I HAVE A **SINGLE** REAL MEMORY OF MY PARENTS? ~~EVERY STORY~~ EVERY STORY **FLORA** TOLD ME COULD BE MADE UP. I DON'T REALLY THINK SHE'S EVER **LIED** TO ME, BUT I WILL SAY THIS: SHE DOESN'T **BELIEVE** WE'LL FIND MY FOLKS IN **MICHOACÁN**. SHE'LL NEVER ADMIT THAT TO ME, BUT I CAN READ HER FACE WHEN SHE TALKS ABOUT THE TRIP -- LIKE SHE'S TRYING TO COME UP WITH WHAT SHE'LL SAY IF WE EVER **DO** GET THERE.

"OH, SORRY, **ELVIE!** MUST HAVE JUST MISSED THEM. **RATS.** WELL, BACK TO WORK!"

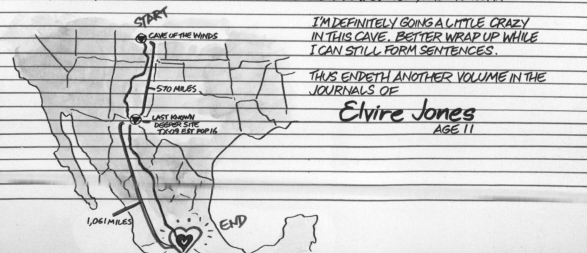

START

CAVE OF THE WINDS

~570 MILES

LAST KNOWN DEEPER SITE TX-09 EST POP 16

1,061 MILES

END

I'M DEFINITELY GOING A LITTLE CRAZY IN THIS CAVE. BETTER WRAP UP WHILE I CAN STILL FORM SENTENCES.

THUS ENDETH ANOTHER VOLUME IN THE JOURNALS OF

Elvire Jones
AGE 11

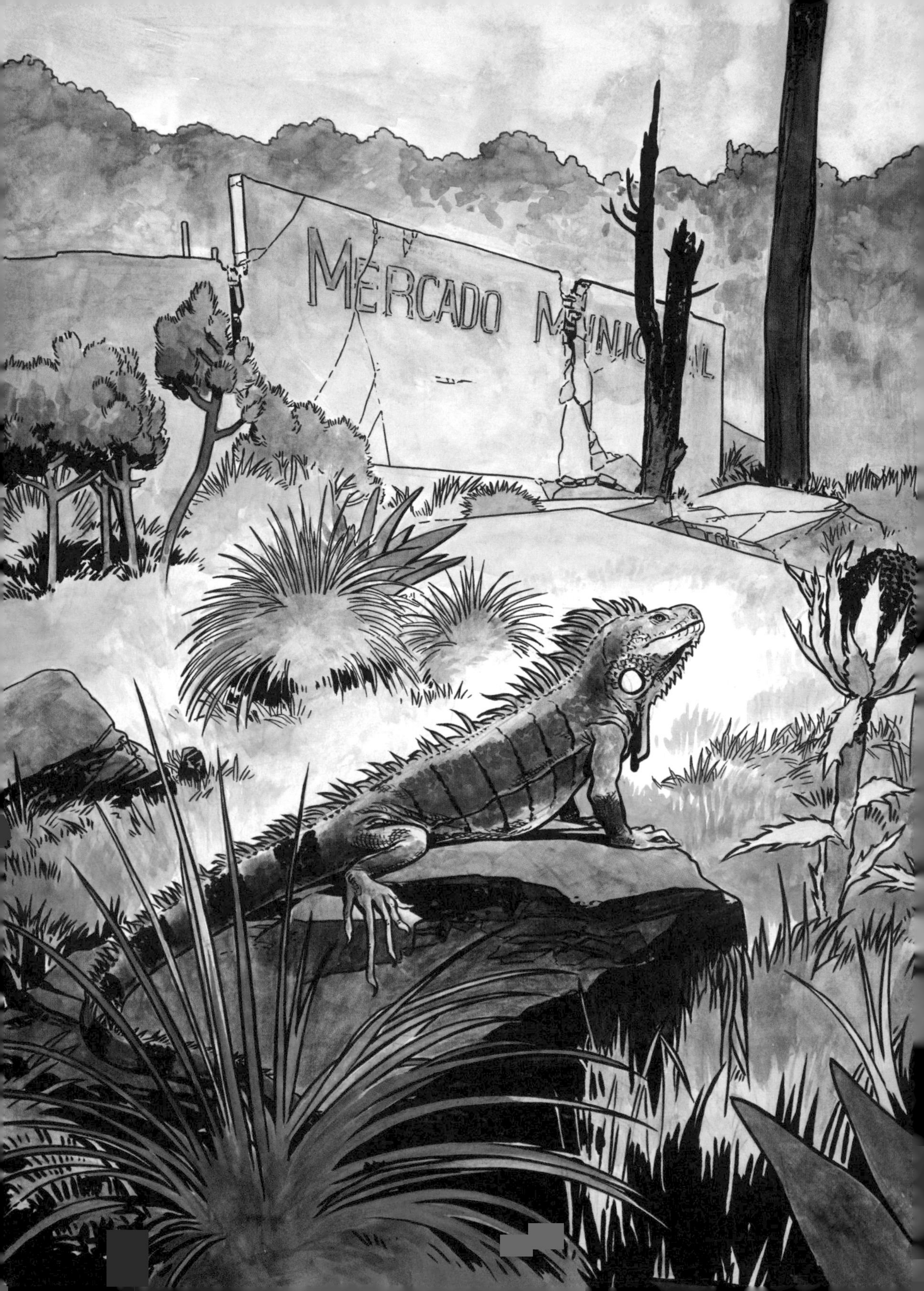
MERCADO

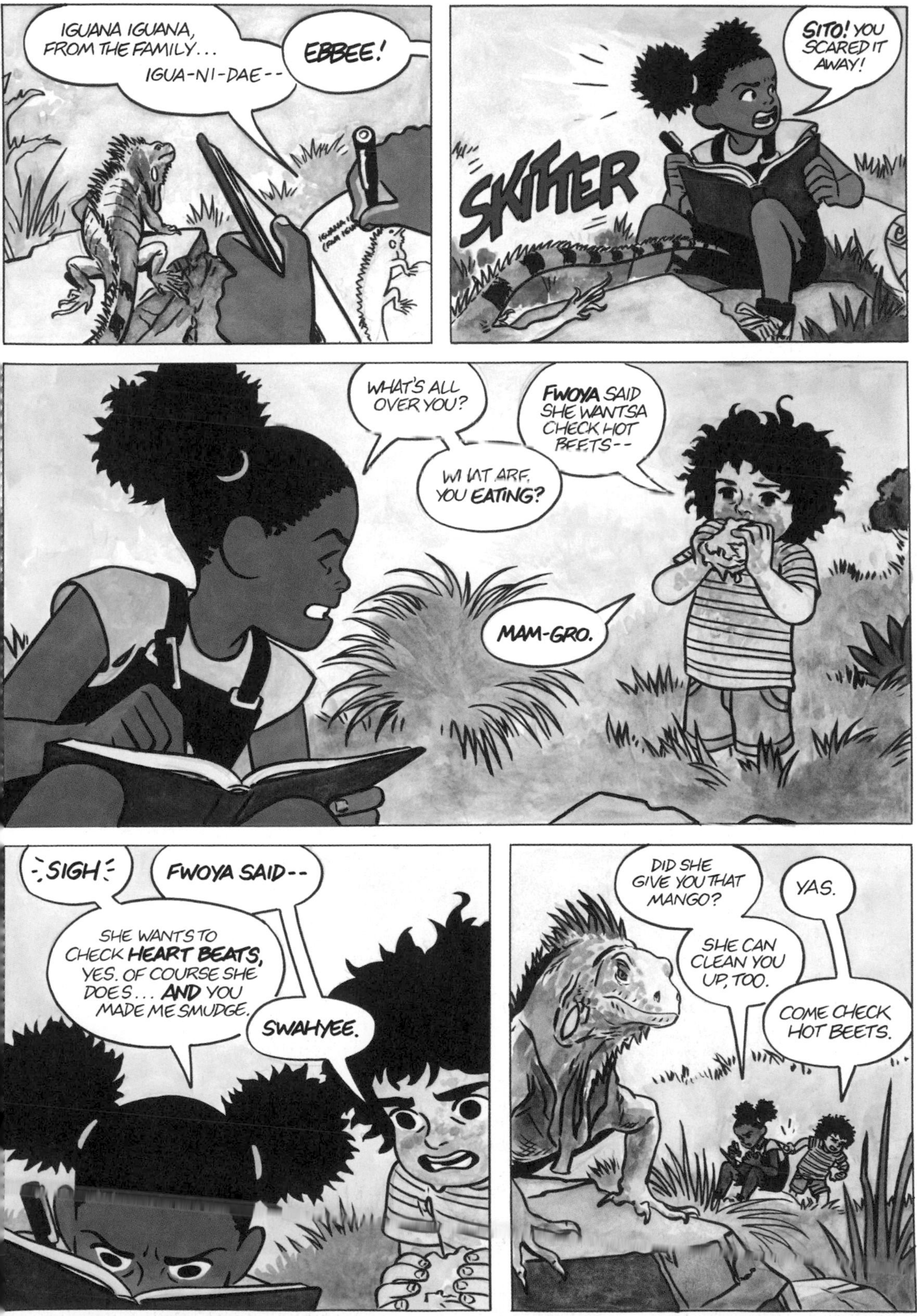
IGUANA IGUANA, FROM THE FAMILY... IGUA-NI-DAE--
EBBEE!
SKITTER
SITO! YOU SCARED IT AWAY!
WHAT'S ALL OVER YOU?
WHAT ARE YOU EATING?
FWOYA SAID SHE WANTSA CHECK HOT BEETS--
MAM-GRO.
SIGH
FWOYA SAID--
SHE WANTS TO CHECK HEART BEATS, YES. OF COURSE SHE DOES... AND YOU MADE ME SMUDGE.
SWAHYEE.
DID SHE GIVE YOU THAT MANGO?
YAS.
SHE CAN CLEAN YOU UP, TOO.
COME CHECK HOT BEETS.

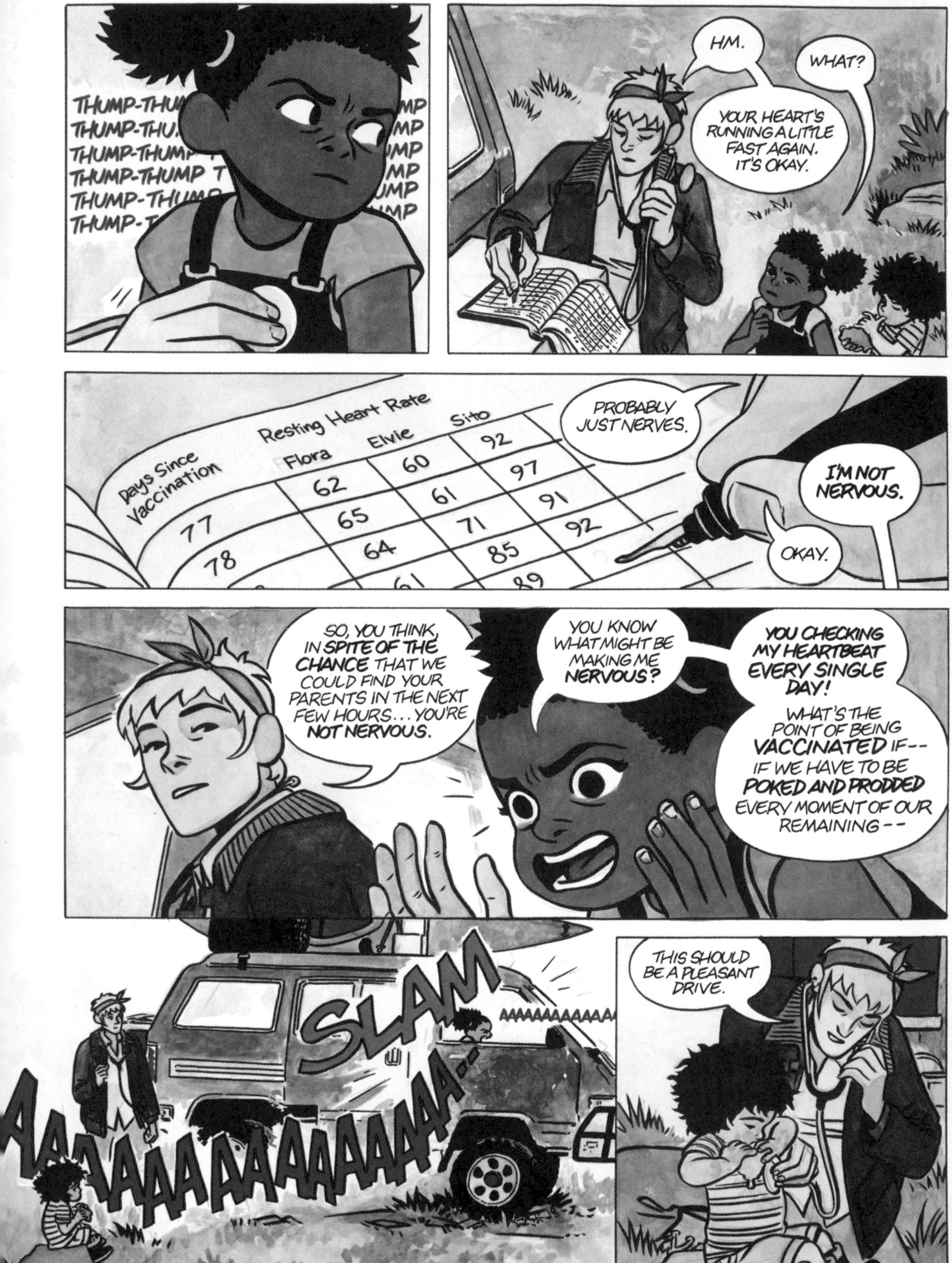
THUMP-THUMP
THUMP-THU
THUMP-THUMP
THUMP-THUMP T
THUMP-THUMP
THUMP-T
HM.
YOUR HEART'S RUNNING A LITTLE FAST AGAIN. IT'S OKAY.
WHAT?
Resting Heart Rate
Days Since Vaccination
Flora
Elvie
Sito
77 62 60 92
78 65 61 97
64 71 91
85 92
89
PROBABLY JUST NERVES.
I'M NOT NERVOUS.
OKAY.
SO, YOU THINK, IN SPITE OF THE CHANCE THAT WE COULD FIND YOUR PARENTS IN THE NEXT FEW HOURS... YOU'RE NOT NERVOUS.
YOU KNOW WHAT MIGHT BE MAKING ME NERVOUS?
YOU CHECKING MY HEARTBEAT EVERY SINGLE DAY!
WHAT'S THE POINT OF BEING VACCINATED IF-- IF WE HAVE TO BE POKED AND PRODDED EVERY MOMENT OF OUR REMAINING--
SLAM
AAAAAAAAAAAA
AAAAAAAAAAAAA--
THIS SHOULD BE A PLEASANT DRIVE.

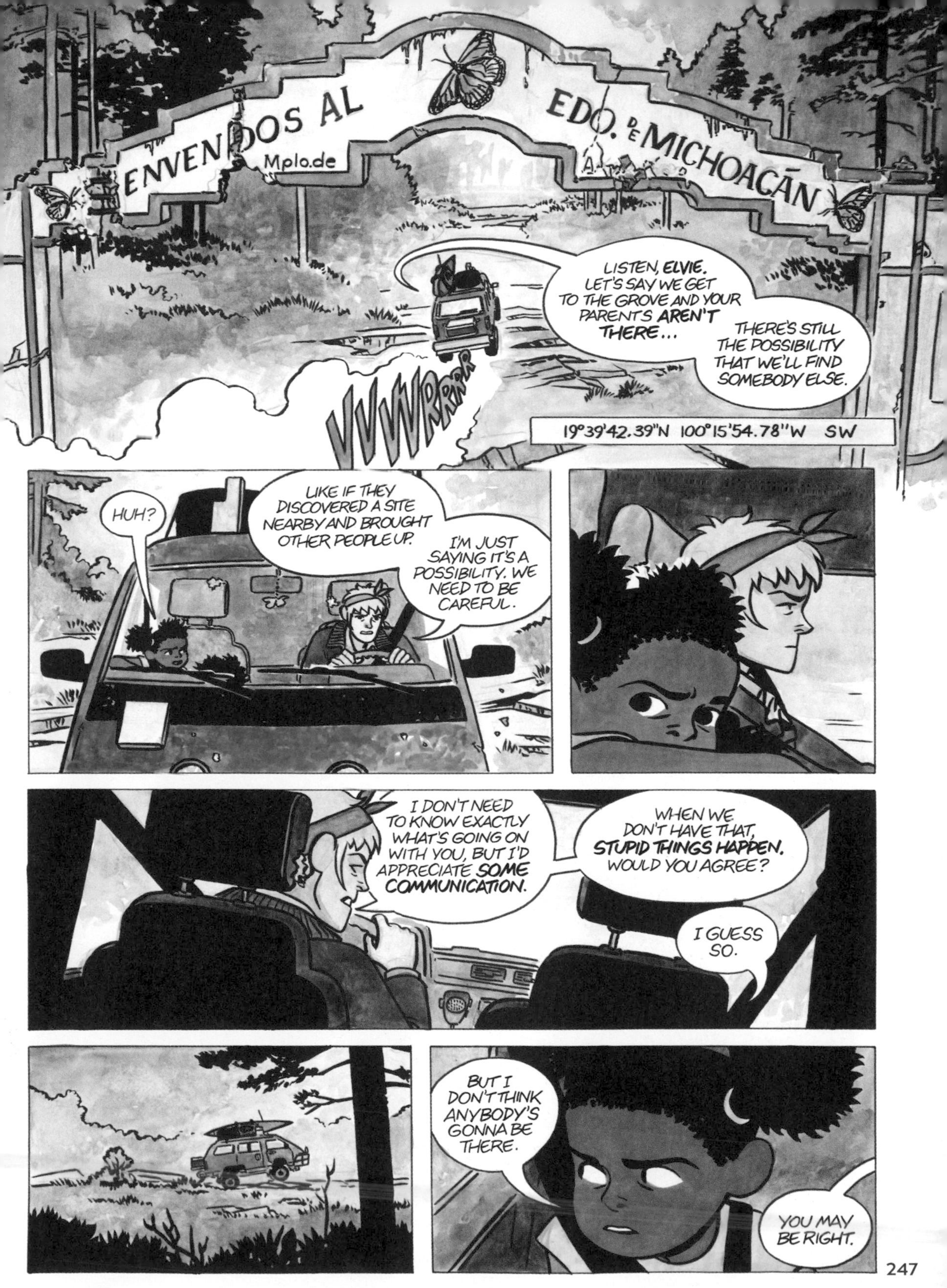
ENVENIDOS AL EDO. DE MICHOACÁN
Mplo.de
LISTEN, ELVIE. LET'S SAY WE GET TO THE GROVE AND YOUR PARENTS AREN'T THERE...
THERE'S STILL THE POSSIBILITY THAT WE'LL FIND SOMEBODY ELSE.
VVWRRRRR
19°39'42.39"N 100°15'54.78"W SW
HUH?
LIKE IF THEY DISCOVERED A SITE NEARBY AND BROUGHT OTHER PEOPLE UP.
I'M JUST SAYING IT'S A POSSIBILITY. WE NEED TO BE CAREFUL.
I DON'T NEED TO KNOW EXACTLY WHAT'S GOING ON WITH YOU, BUT I'D APPRECIATE SOME COMMUNICATION.
WHEN WE DON'T HAVE THAT, STUPID THINGS HAPPEN. WOULD YOU AGREE?
I GUESS SO.
BUT I DON'T THINK ANYBODY'S GONNA BE THERE.
YOU MAY BE RIGHT.

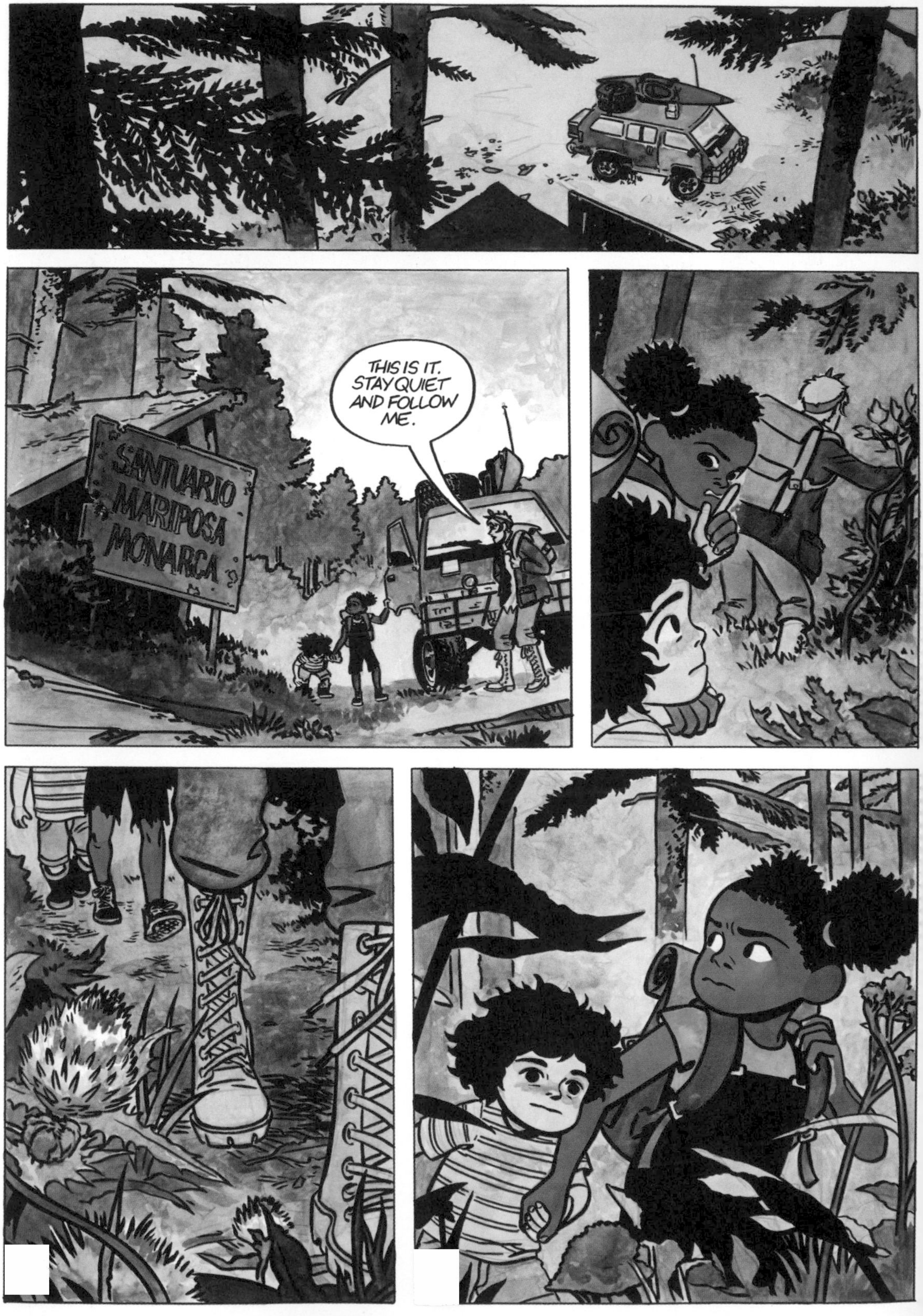
SANTUARIO MARIPOSA MONARCA
THIS IS IT. STAY QUIET AND FOLLOW ME.

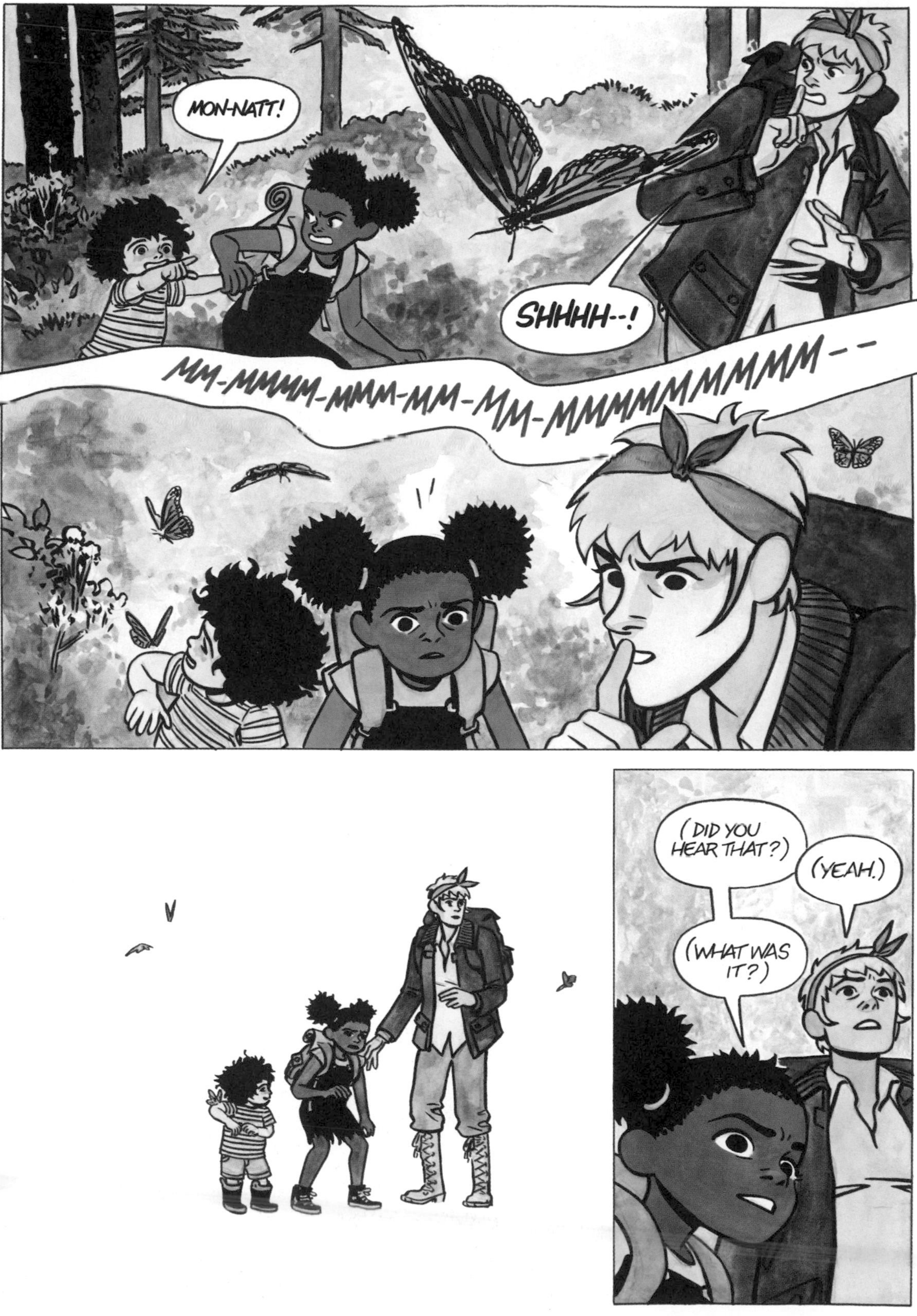
MON-NATT!
SHHHH--!
MM-MMMM-MMM-MM-MM-MMMMMMMMM--
(DID YOU HEAR THAT?)
(YEAH.)
(WHAT WAS IT?)

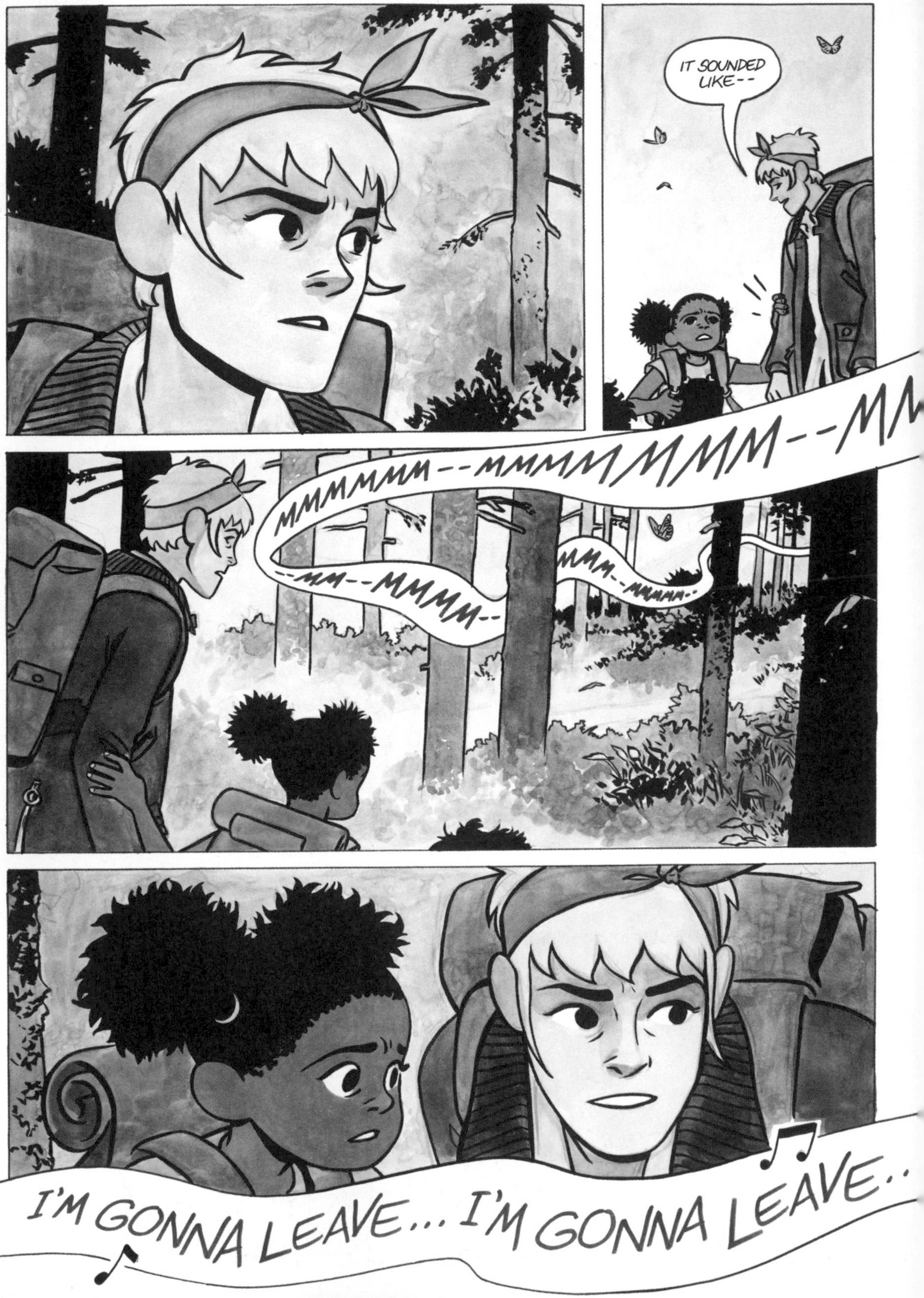
IT SOUNDED LIKE--
MMMMMMM--MMMMMMMMM--MM
--MM--MMMMM--
MMM--MMMMM--
I'M GONNA LEAVE... I'M GONNA LEAVE...

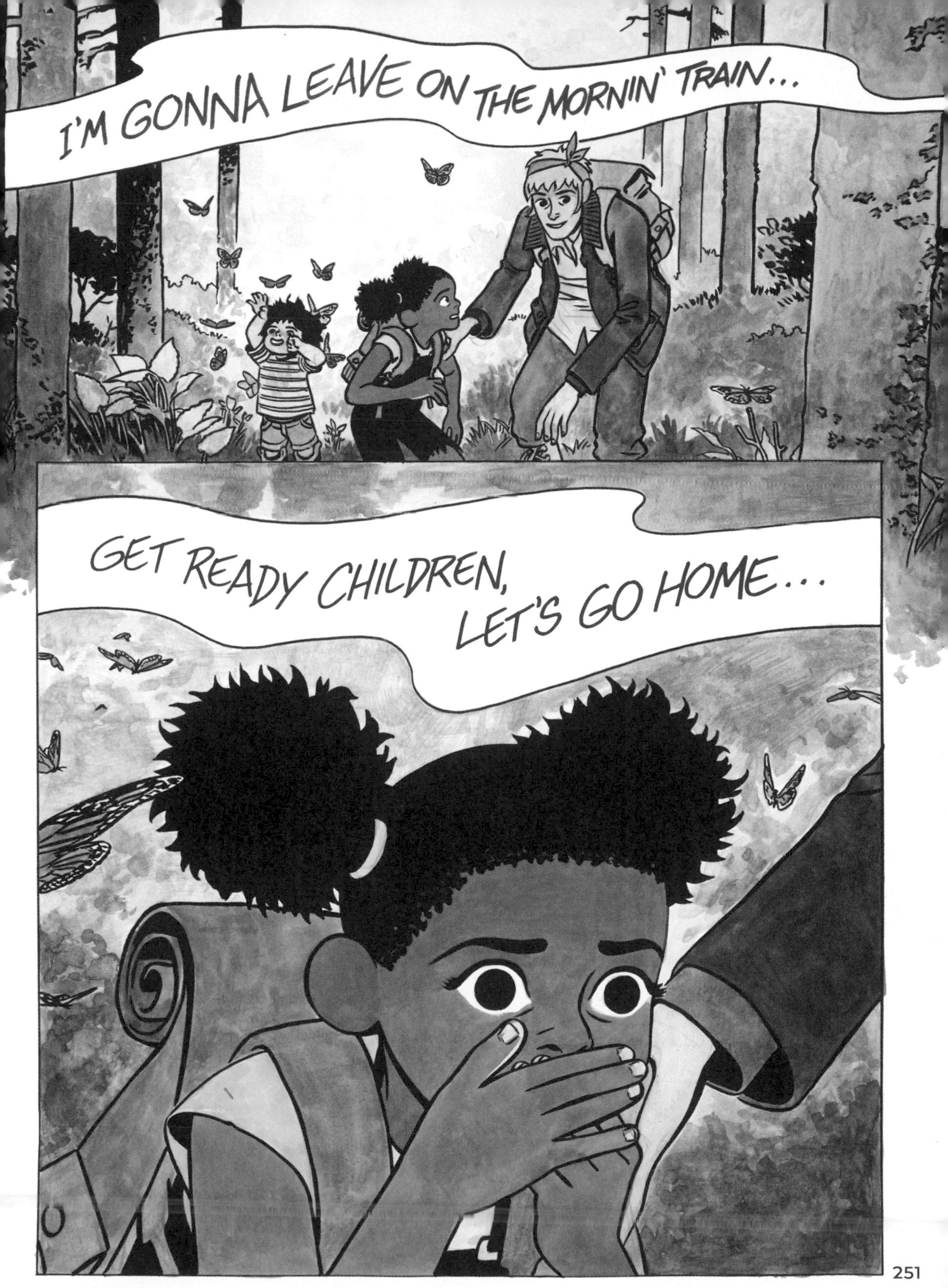
I'M GONNA LEAVE ON THE MORNIN' TRAIN...
GET READY CHILDREN, LET'S GO HOME...

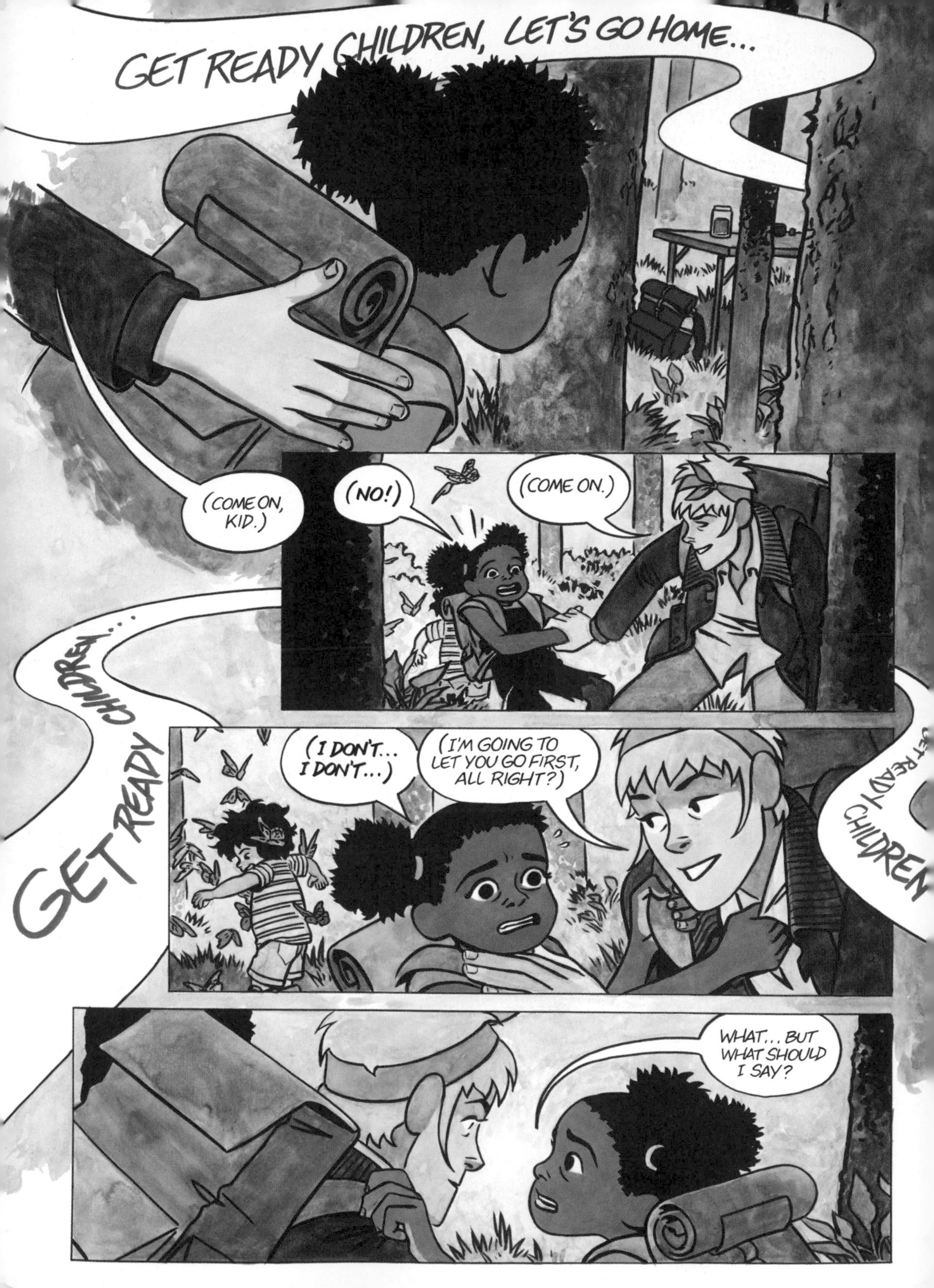
GET READY CHILDREN, LET'S GO HOME...
(COME ON, KID.)
(NO!)
(COME ON.)
GET READY CHILDREN...
(I DON'T... I DON'T...)
(I'M GOING TO LET YOU GO FIRST, ALL RIGHT?)
GET READY CHILDREN
WHAT... BUT WHAT SHOULD I SAY?

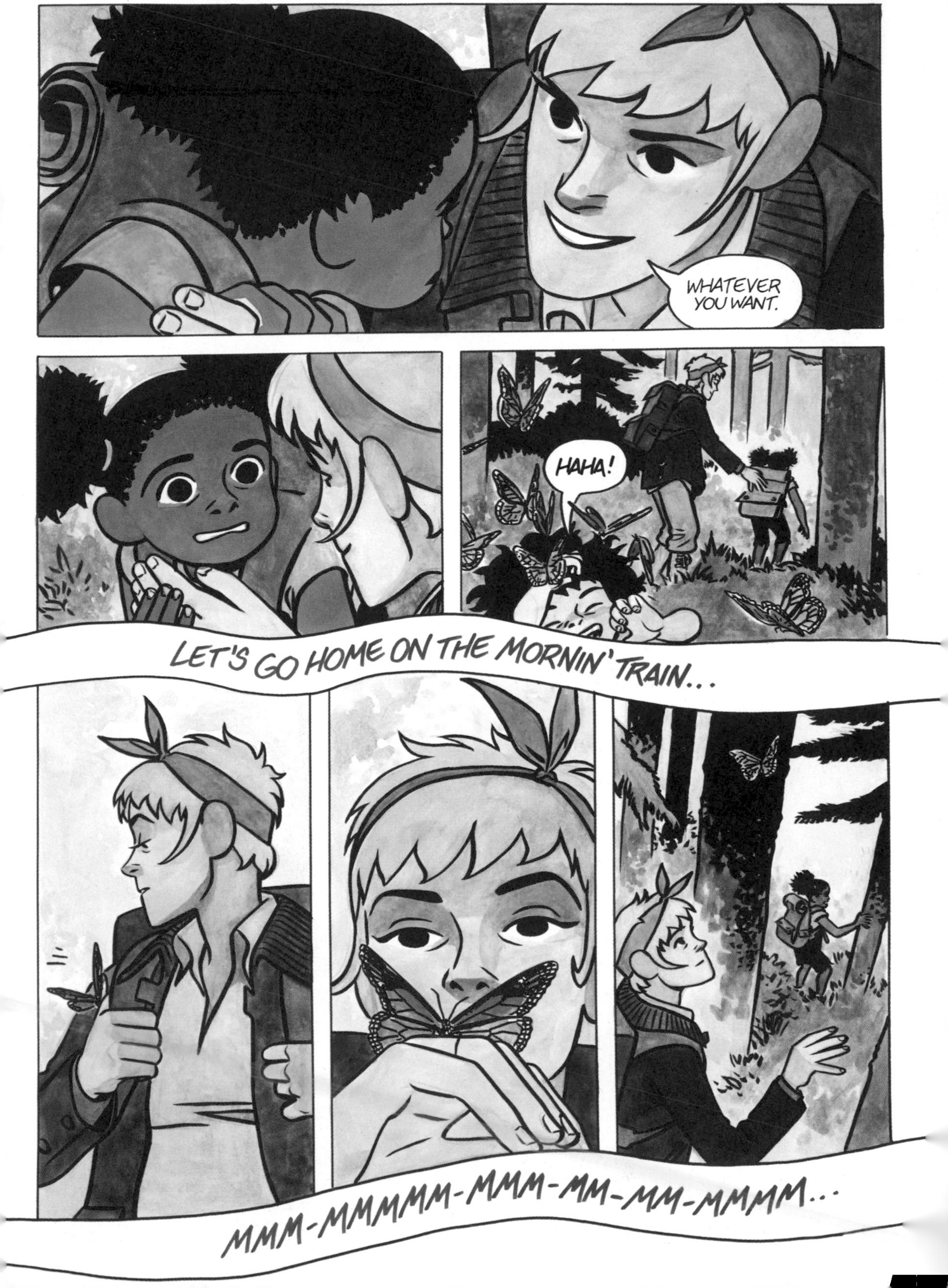
WHATEVER YOU WANT.
HAHA!
LET'S GO HOME ON THE MORNIN' TRAIN...
MMM-MMMMM-MMM-MM-MM-MMMM...

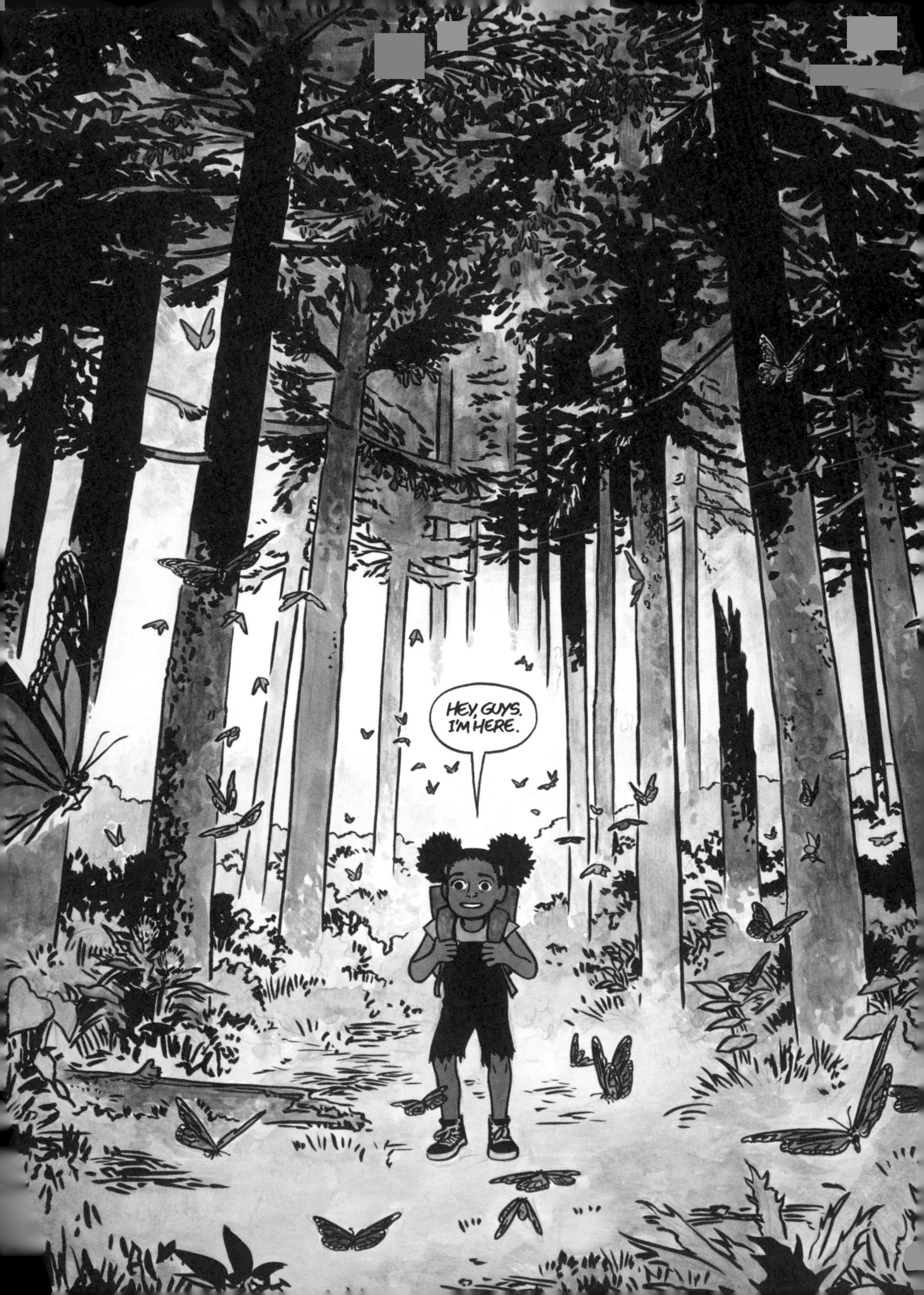
HEY, GUYS. I'M HERE.

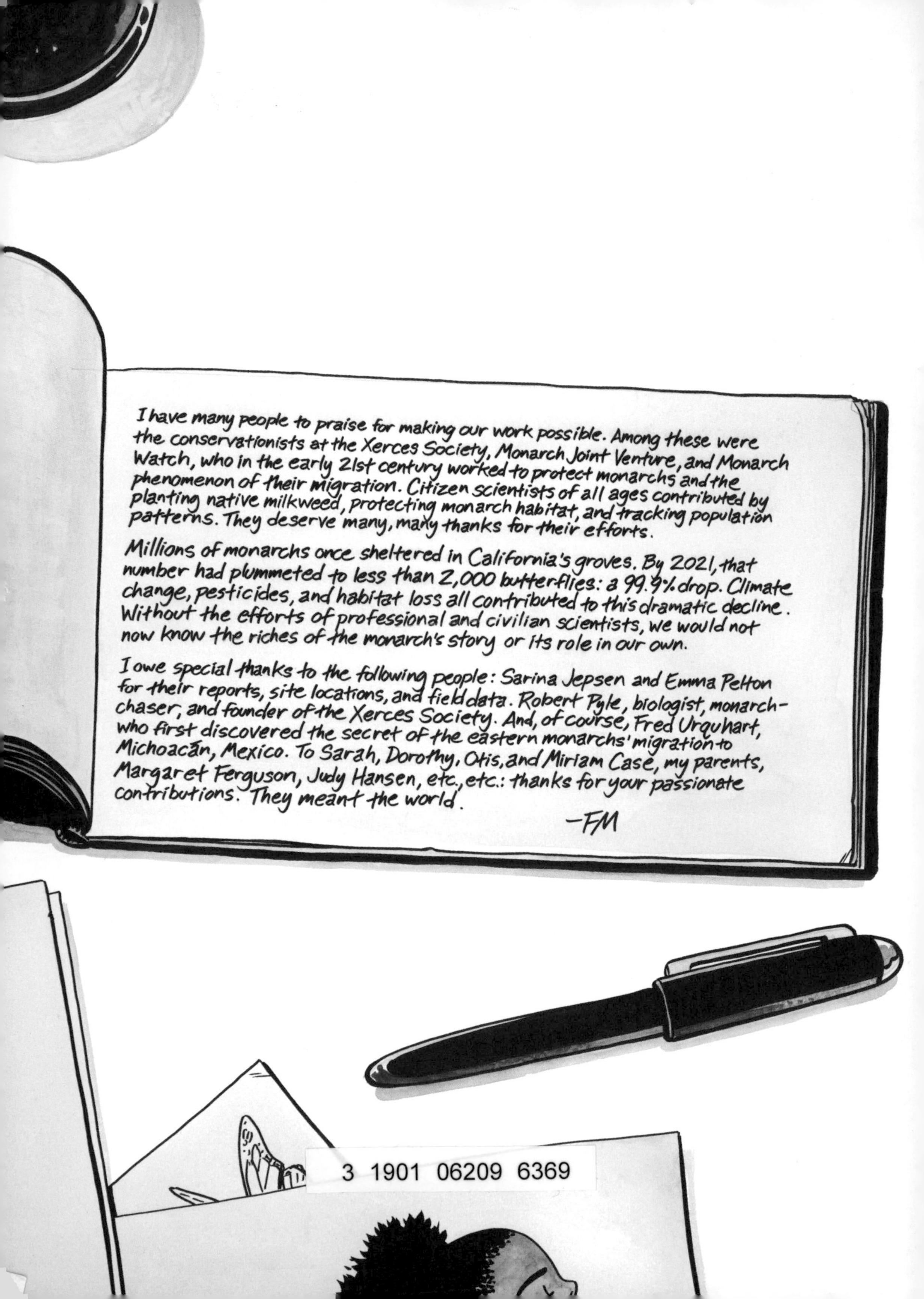
I have many people to praise for making our work possible. Among these were the conservationists at the Xerces Society, Monarch Joint Venture, and Monarch Watch, who in the early 21st century worked to protect monarchs and the phenomenon of their migration. Citizen scientists of all ages contributed by planting native milkweed, protecting monarch habitat, and tracking population patterns. They deserve many, many thanks for their efforts.
Millions of monarchs once sheltered in California's groves. By 2021, that number had plummeted to less than 2,000 butterflies: a 99.9% drop. Climate change, pesticides, and habitat loss all contributed to this dramatic decline. Without the efforts of professional and civilian scientists, we would not now know the riches of the monarch's story or its role in our own.
I owe special thanks to the following people: Sarina Jepsen and Emma Pelton for their reports, site locations, and field data. Robert Pyle, biologist, monarch-chaser, and founder of the Xerces Society. And, of course, Fred Urquhart, who first discovered the secret of the eastern monarchs' migration to Michoacán, Mexico. To Sarah, Dorothy, Otis, and Miriam Case, my parents, Margaret Ferguson, Judy Hansen, etc., etc.: thanks for your passionate contributions. They meant the world.
—FM